D0860036

The Stonewycke Trilogy

The Stonewycke Trilogy

by

Michael Phillips
&
Judith Pella

Inspirational Press
New York

First Inspirational Press edition published in 1996.
Inspirational Press
A division of BBS Publishing Corporation
386 Park Avenue South
New York, NY 10016

Inspirational Press is a registered trademark of BBS Publishing Corporation.

Published by arrangement with Bethany House Publishers.

Library of Congress Catalog Card Number: to follow
ISBN: 0-88486-133-3
Text designed by Hannah Lerner

Printed in the United States of America

CONTENTS

THE HEATHER HILLS OF STONEWYCKE

To Brenda Scott,
for her friendship,
help, and encouragement.

CONTENTS

Prologue

❈

LIKE VANISHING SMOKE, generations fade and life passes into life. Dreams are born, hopes kindled, families and tribes and nations rise and fall. But men and women return to the earth as they came. All that remains is the land—one enduring reality under heaven's eternal gaze. The land *remains*, while over it the inexorable march of history passes—man to man, woman to woman, child to child.

In its early days the Isle of Britain remained unmolested by the warring hordes that swept through the rest of Asia and Europe. But progress brought larger ships and broader horizons; eventually the slender estuary separating Britain from the European mainland no longer proved an obstacle to those desiring to cross and invade. The land was verdant and fertile. The climate, though not temperate, was equable and healthy. In the first century B.C. the Romans, under Gaius Julius Caesar, vanquished their natural fear and hatred of the sea, sailed across the channel, and within a century had subjugated the scattered groups of Britons into Roman Brittania.

Seeking refuge from the Romans in Gaul and South Britain, various tribes migrated north into the Scottish highlands and lowlands. Protected as these northernmost reaches were by rugged terrain and severe weather, these tribes, the Picts, settled the land. Uniting gradually under one king after another, by the sixth century they controlled the greater part of the territory north of the line between the Firth of Forth and Loch Linnhe.

The Picts were first to discover the massive heap of granite some four miles inland from the shore—five huge boulders piled on and about one another in apparently random fashion, thrown into their positions by the convulsive prehistoric quakings of the earth. In the early days of the settlement, the great stones provided a reference point of the ridge bordering the fertile valley. A youngster at play might have been the first to notice the narrow passage through two of the rocks and under a third which led to a secluded little dell, invisible from any point on the high moorland which surrounded it. The *wicket*, or little door (*through the stones* it came to be called), many a Pict child scampered through to elude his friends.

In the course of time, the Britons, the Angles, and the Celtic Scots established themselves firmly, along with the resident Picts, in northern Britain above Solway Firth and the Cheviot Hills. All four peoples possessed individual backgrounds and histories, and there formed no obvious natural alliance between them. Inevitably, the Picts found themselves in perpetual conflict with the other three as each gradually encroached northwards on the kingdom the Picts had established.

A perilous balance thus continued in Scotland until the ninth century. The most powerful of the kings of the Picts, Oengus, had conquered the Scottish kingdom of Dalriada, and the kingdom of the Picts seemed well on its way to establishing a permanent united rule over the northern third of the British Isles.

But then from over the seas came the invading wave of Nordic pirates— ruthless, driven not by necessity or circumstances or cramped homelands but by the sheer appetite for pillage and conquest. If the soul of the Vikings lay in their thirst for adventure, the symbols of that quest were their sleek, long, fast ships—wicked and bright, finely carved with dragon-shaped prows and high, curving sterns. Along the sides sat the brutal Scandinavian rovers of the sea, with oars poised, swords ready, long rows of shields ranged along the sides.

The Viking storm broke in fury in 835. Huge fleets of three or four hundred vessels began plundering shore towns and villages, rowing up the rivers of England. Pict blood spilled freely in a desperate attempt to hold off the invaders from the north. The great granite heaps were stained with the blood of violent death; even a child could find no refuge behind the stone wicket. But if the Viking warriors came seeking the treasure about which they had heard, they found only the spoils of living victims.

As the Norse invasion disturbed the political balance of the north, the kingdom of the Picts gradually collapsed. Preoccupied with defending themselves against the Vikings from the sea, the Picts failed to recognize the growing menace of the Scots on their southern flank. By the time a Scottish party of settlers arrived at what had been the Pict village of *Steenbuaic*, all that remained was a ruinous reminder of the bloody annihilation of an unsuspecting village at the hands of the marauding Vikings. It now remained for the Scot children to discover anew the door under the mighty granite sentinel whose mute power had proved useless to stem the Nordic assault. From etchings on the rocks the ancient name was discovered and saxonized to *Stanweoc* and thereafter used to denote that heathland south of the new Scot village of Straithland on the coast where the Picts had once thrived.

The ancient kingdom of the Picts was thus lost in the warring wreckage of the ninth century, and within a hundred more years the Picts had been entirely supplanted by the Scots, who claimed this land as their right of conquest. Whatever influence and native individuality the Picts had once possessed was muted as the two cultures intermingled and the Picts were amalgamated into the whole.

Meanwhile, the Danish and Norwegian raiders stayed longer every year. In the summer, the fleets would sail from their homelands to plunder and destroy. But each year the tendency was to linger longer in the more genial southern climates. Eventually the warriors began to bring their wives and families; some intermarried with the natives of the lands they had pillaged. The familiar terrain and climate of sparsely populated Scotland especially suited them. As the Scots had assimilated the Picts, the colonizing Vikings mingled and were absorbed, becoming, like the Basques, the Celts, the Picts, the Angles, and the Britons before them, the ancestors of future Scottish generations.

The Viking domination of the island lasted less than a hundred years; in 1066 the Normans from the coast of France, themselves descended from the Vikings, invaded England under William the Conqueror. To the north, the Scots maintained a unity in spite of the individuality of their many distinct family clans. The Anglo-Norman clan Ramsaidh achieved prominence in the thirteenth century when King David I granted lands in Lithian near Glasgow to Simon de Ramsay. Simultaneously, the chief of the northern branch of the clan, Adam de Ramsay, was made baron of Banff while others of his family, bearing his crest, were settling in Strathy, the valley town just to the east.

Throughout the following centuries the Ramsays were conspicuously engaged in the border wars with England; for his great valor in the services of King James V of Scotland, Andrew Ramsay was given the marquisate of Stonewycke in 1539. The Stonewycke estate overlooked the rich valley of Strathy east of Banff. The granite sentinels lay within the estate some three miles to the south in the midst of a heath ridge which had centuries before been known as Branuaic. But no eyes turned toward those barren moors during the time of Andrew; all attention focused instead on the grand castle he had set out to build. Sir James Hamilton, the king's own architect, lent his talents to the raising of the magnificent structure, nearly seven years in the building. When completed it became known as the jewel of the northern coast, established on a lovely green hill; when lighted at night with candles and lanterns, it bedazzled many a fisherman who gazed in awe at the sight.

But the jewel dimmed some hundred and fifty years later when Iver Ramsay invested heavily in the ill-fated Darien Company. Losing his fortune, Iver only barely managed to hang onto the estate. The grandeur of the castle declined, and eventually Iver left Strathy altogether and was reported to have taken up residence in a simple Edinburgh townhouse. For the next twenty years the grand house of the Ramsay lineage fell to the mercies of mice, spiders, and decay. The empty rooms, stripped of their furnishings by the desperate lord, only whispered of past life; dust and cobwebs clung ghostlike to the gilt-edged mantels and ornate balustrades.

While Stonewycke slept, political upheaval and military conflict pitted Scottish against English in the battle for supremacy, possession, and ultimate rule of the wild and beautiful Scottish lands. Thomas Ramsay, son of Iver, fell in with the Jacobites, blaming, as he did, his father's financial demise on the English. Changing the spelling of his name to Ramsey as an act of individualism, Thomas determined to restore his ancestral home of Stonewycke to its former position of glory, prestige and influence. Life returned again to the turrets and towers, the ballrooms and corridors, the stables and grounds. But Thomas Ramsey died six years before his dream of a Jacobite rebellion against the English could be realized. But he passed on to his son Colin a passion for his homeland and its cause. Colin was among the first to join Bonnie Prince Charlie in his idealistic grasp for the throne in 1745, and was struck down to his death at Culloden in a desperate attempt to shield the Prince from a dreadful blow.

In honor of her husband's loyalty, Christina Ramsey harbored the fugitive Young Pretender and would-be king for a time. And it was at Stonewycke where Prince Charles Edward came distressingly close to discovery. A troop of English militia, acting on the word of an informer, stormed the castle, but a thorough search revealed no fugitive. Little Bobby Ramsey had taken the prince to a spot where the offspring of ancient Pict children still hid from one another in their play. And for the space of a few days, the sombre mounds surrounding the sunken dell and watched over by the granite peaks became an unlikely palace for the man who dreamed of being king.

Finally, forty years after the humiliation of Scottish insurrectionists at Culloden Moor, King George III reinstated the heirs of the Scottish clan leaders to their former landowning positions as a gesture of unity and goodwill.

Robert Ramsey, son of Colin Ramsey and descended from Baron Adam de Ramsay and Andrew Ramsay, was endowed in 1784 with the estate of Stonewycke which had been his father's at the time of the uprising. He lived another twenty years, after which his son Anson became laird of the expansive and prosperous valley of Strathy on the northern coast. Greatly beloved by the people under him, Anson governed only another twelve years, when his life was suddenly cut short. His two sons had not been cast in his mold; their lusting hearts were set on riches rather than service to their people. The legend of the wealth of the ancient Picts still circulating, these ambitious sons, fearing disinheritment and loss of their chance at the treasure, grew increasingly estranged from their father until a mysterious hunting accident ended Anson's life. Measures to ensure the protection of the land he loved had been undertaken, but remained unfulfilled at his death. His unscrupulous son Talmud succeeded him.

Still the land remained, as generations of occupants rose and fell with the winds of history. Still the people tilled the soil and built their homes upon its hills. Rarely, however, did their eyes now turn toward that barren heath where this valley's first inhabitants had overturned the rocks to begin working the stubborn earth. But recognized or not, there still stood the immovable garrison of granite with its narrow wicket of stone, standing as a mute reminder of the ancient peoples who first populated this rugged northern land.

Ramsey Family Tree

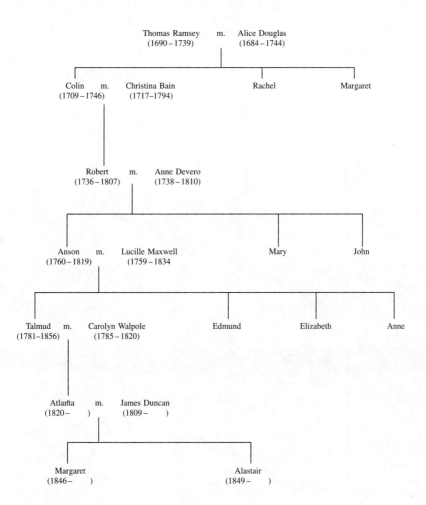

Thomas Ramsey   m.   Alice Douglas
(1690 – 1739)   (1684 – 1744)

Colin   m.   Christina Bain   Rachel   Margaret
(1709 – 1746)   (1717 – 1794)

Robert   m.   Anne Devero
(1736 – 1807)   (1738 – 1810)

Anson   m.   Lucille Maxwell   Mary   John
(1760 – 1819)   (1759 – 1834

Talmud   m.   Carolyn Walpole   Edmund   Elizabeth   Anne
(1781 – 1856)   (1785 – 1820)

Atlanta   m.   James Duncan
(1820 –   )   (1809 –   )

Margaret   Alastair
(1846 –   )   (1849 –   )

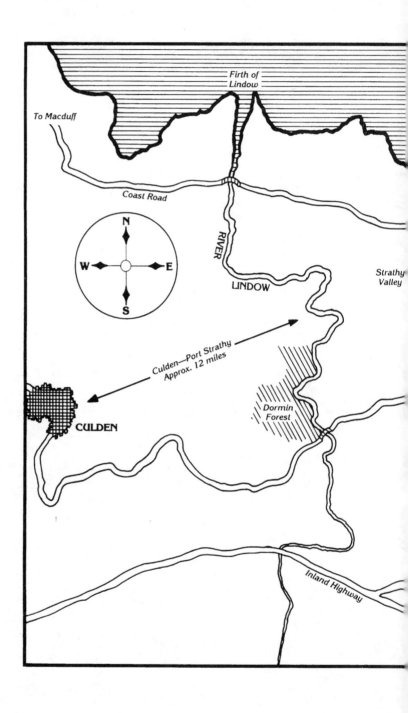

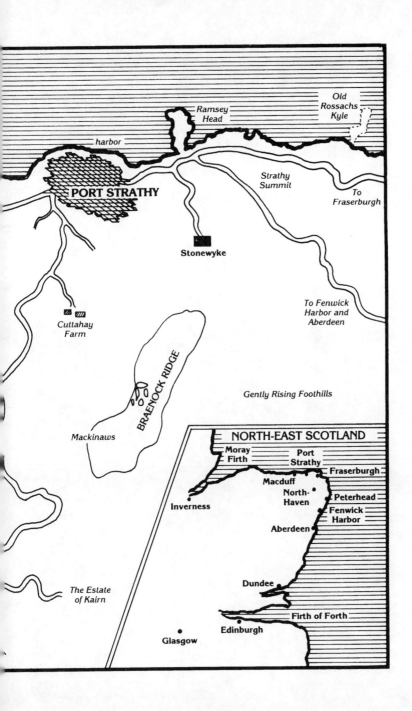

Ramsey
Head

Old
Rossachs
Kyle

harbor

PORT STRATHY

Strathy
Summit

To
Fraserburgh

Stonewyke

To Fenwick
Harbor and
Aberdeen

Cuttahay
Farm

BRAENOCK RIDGE

Gently Rising Foothills

Mackinaws

NORTH-EAST SCOTLAND

Moray
Firth

Port
Strathy

Fraserburgh

Macduff

North-
Haven

Peterhead

Inverness

Fenwick
Harbor

Aberdeen

The Estate
of Kairn

Dundee

Firth of Forth

Edinburgh

Glasgow

1

Root of Contention

❧

THE WARM AFTERNOON sun had passed its zenith and begun its slow descent west. Maggie had not been out of doors today—unusual for the thirteen-year-old girl who so loved the Scottish countryside of her upbringing. Today's mood had been thoughtful and melancholy, and the ordinarily vibrant youngster had instead spent most of the day haunting the solitary corridors and empty rooms of the great mansion.

In mid-afternoon she wandered into the library, not particularly enthusiastic about reading but having exhausted her other possibilities for amusement. She looked around at the endless stacks of books, took one down, sat on the sofa, and thumbed through it casually as her eyelids began to grow heavy.

Suddenly Maggie started awake.

How long she'd dozed off she had no idea, but there were voices close by, raised in heated debate.

"How dare you attempt such a thing!"

"I assure you, nothing was further from my mind. I only—"

"And behind my back!" interrupted a woman's voice which Maggie knew to be her mother's. Hearing the tone she could almost see the dark eyes flashing like flint.

"I didn't want to trouble you with—" Maggie's father began, for the other disputant was indeed the girl's father. But once again he was cut short.

"Ah, of course. You didn't want to worry my feminine head about such an uninteresting business transaction, is that it?"

"Of course, my dear," replied James. He had been unprepared for his wife's hostile outburst and now hoped to soothe her with conciliatory tones.

"Ha!" flared Atlanta, her voice revealing bitter sarcasm. "You would dare sell off Braenock Ridge without my consent?"

"You know as well as I that we need the money it will bring. And I've been pledged a handsome amount."

"*You* need the money you mean! You are determined to buy that brewery whatever it costs the estate."

"I've negotiated a shrewd deal," replied James confidently.

"You would sell off the land bit by bit for the sake of a profit." Atlanta's voice shook with emotion. "But," she went on, "I will not allow you to sell off generations of the Ramsey's lifeblood . . ." Her voice caught on tears she would not let rise to the surface.

Now James's own anger vent itself upon his wife.

"Not allow!" he fumed, spinning around to face her. "*Not allow!* You would dare challenge me in affairs of business?"

"You forget, dear husband," answered Atlanta, her tones cooling with her effort at self-control, "that this land is mine, not yours. Everything that goes on is my affair. You can do nothing without my approval."

"And you never allow me to forget it, do you, Atlanta?"

She said nothing.

Young Maggie crouched low behind the back of the sofa, stiff with terror lest she be discovered as a common eavesdropper. She had never intended to fall asleep. Yet once her parents entered and began their heated discussion, she desperately wished she could escape undetected. Now she remained motionless.

Her parents argued often. Maggie was well aware of the tense distance between them, even when their words were civil. This particular dispute seemed more dreadful than usual, the conflict perhaps heightened by the knowledge that she was a secretive listener to their private words.

The grim iciness of her father's tone, as he resumed the conversation, sent a chill through Maggie's body.

"We shall see," he said. "My solicitor is drawing up papers regarding Braenock. It's all legal, I assure you. My name is on the documents of this estate as well as yours."

Atlanta stared at her husband for a moment, her vacant gaze scarcely revealing a hint of the enmity churning within. Whatever love that may have existed between the two of them was far from visible at this moment. Both were strong and determined, and, during the past several years, their clashes over the future of the estate had grown more frequent as James's ambitions had widened.

"I warn you, James," she said at length, in deliberate and measured tones, "do not misjudge me. I still have more control than you may think."

"We shall see."

"James, don't push me too far. I will not be moved. You shall not sell Braenock."

"If you think to intimidate me, Atlanta, save your strength. I will do what I am compelled to do—for the good of the estate."

"Dispossessing our tenants is for no one's good," Atlanta replied. "And what of our children? If we followed your suggestion, they would end up with nothing. The land would all be gone!"

"They will applaud the wealth and prestige I will bring them."

"Not Margaret. Your money will mean nothing to her. She would applaud nothing that would destroy—"

"I can handle Margaret. And don't try to interfere with me. She is my daughter as well."

"And one with a mind of her own."

"A mind of her own, precisely," he shot back, "unless you try to fill her head with lies about me! But I am her father and she loves me. She will do what I say."

Atlanta did not reply.

Maggie, shielded behind the sofa and several towering bookcases, heard her father's footsteps retreat from the room followed by the final slam of the door. She felt, rather than saw, her mother's tall, proud form standing motionless, staring after her husband, observed only by a thousand dusty, leatherbound witnesses of ages past. Maggie remained still, and after another few moments heard the click of the door as it opened and closed. She had not even heard her mother's soft retreating footsteps.

Finally young Margaret stirred, rising slowly to peer over the edge of the sofa, still not sure she was truly alone. Trembling, she slid from the sofa and stood. A tear trickled down her cheek, and she bit her lower lip to still the quivering. What could it all mean?

How could her father speak so harshly to her mother? Maggie had always thought of him as such a loving and unselfish man. He loved her, didn't he, as only a daughter can feel loved by a father she adores and looks up to with pride and an almost reverent regard?

Was this the same man whose voice she had just heard? There had been arguments before, but none quite like this. And what had he meant when he'd said he could *handle* her?

Confusion surged through her. Her face was hot; her tears were rising again. She had to get out of the house—to ride, to forget. Maybe all would be different when she returned.

Maggie crept softly toward the stair, began her descent quietly; then halfway down she gave way to the pounding in her chest and broke into a run all the way to the stables.

2

Cinder

FROM THE HOUSE Maggie led her charcoal-gray mare north toward the road and then down the hill into Port Strathy. She had to find a place to run, and the beach west of town was one of her favorites.

Arguments between her parents may have grown more frequent lately, though she chanced to hear them only rarely. But when she did they were never pleasant. Her impulse was always to flee, especially when she sensed that she herself was somehow bound up in the conflicts which erupted over the land.

Though she and her mother were close, her father had always held a special place in her heart. His words of affection during her early years had struck deep root and she had grown up adoring him. And he had never given her any reason to suspect that the feeling wasn't mutual. True, they spent little time together; she often begged him to go riding with her, but he was usually too busy. Nevertheless, the carefree child rarely paused to think that the relationship might be one-sided, that while she had given all of her trusting and vulnerable young heart to him, her father might have larger matters to occupy his mind. She took for granted that the love in his heart matched the wellsprings from her own, and never dreamed of questioning his feelings for her. Indeed, at her tender age, how could she begin to fathom the grip of the world of Mammon upon such a man as her father?

Braenock Ridge, Maggie thought to herself. *What could be so special about that particular corner of the land?* The grand estate called Stonewycke had been Atlanta's inheritance. Located in the north of Scotland, it occupied miles of rich pasture and farming land and accessible coastline, unusual in the northern Scottish highlands. In 1860 it was, indeed, a marquisate of no small repute in Britain. James Duncan had married into the fortune, and on an estate containing such a rich heritage, he had never ceased feeling the outsider. Whether the disputes between Mother and Father stemmed from this fact would be hard to say.

But somehow their daughter found herself increasingly caught in the middle.

Avoiding the small fishing village of Port Strathy, Maggie at length arrived at the beach to the west of the harbor. The low tide offered a long, flat expanse of sand, hard and wide—just right for the gallop she needed. Maggie dug her heels into Cinder's flanks and swung the mare westward.

After a high, plunging kick, the horse tore into the wet sand and flew away into the afternoon sun. Within a few moments horse and rider dwindled to a mere speck on the distant coastline; no observer at the pier of the harbor would have been able to make them out. But at last, near the rocky shoal bordering the expanse of sand to the west, the speck swerved a little and grew steadily larger until once more horse and rider could be distinctly seen. Still Maggie urged the mare on as if her own emotions could be spent through the exhaustion of the powerful beast. The horse galloped along the water's edge, sending lumps of wet sand flying from its hooves like a random storm of loose-caked clods. In front its hooves scattered dainty wisps of foam, left behind by the ebb and flow of the incoming tide.

Halfway down the beach, Maggie suddenly wheeled the mare around and dashed headlong into the sea. At first the horse struggled, but her load was light, and when they reached the deep water she swam strongly with her head high out of the water. Nothing could have quieted the raging of Maggie's spirit more than the chill of sea water. Although the mare seemed laboring for her very life, Maggie knew her animal well enough to recognize that nothing could have pleased the mare more after such an energetic gallop.

When Maggie judged her mount had had enough, she turned back toward the shore. Out of the water they came, still at a run—the unusually colored gray mare and her small but confident mistress perched atop her soaking back—with a great splashing of foamy sea water and high-kicking hooves, much to the delight of the young rider, whose deep red curls flew out in the wind behind her.

Straight on Maggie drove Cinder, over the wide expanse of packed sand, and straight up the grassy dune which bordered the beach. Up the loose sand they charged, the sun-bathed dance of splashing water now followed by a stormy cloud of gray dust flying upward before the churning hooves.

At last, as they gained the small seashore summit, Maggie reined the mare in. Cinder stood, sides heaving as her great lungs gasped for air, the wide distended nostrils shooting out steamy breaths.

Maggie sat still, also exhausted from the effort. At last the array of confusing thoughts had subsided and her mind was clear. To be out with Cinder, astride the spirited animal, was what she always needed when life at home grew too overwhelming. She drew in a deep sigh, patted the horse gently on her black head, bent forward, and mumbled some soft words of affection. Then easing her gently forward, she descended the other side of the sandy slope.

"Let's ride out to Braenock, shall we, Cinder?" she said.

The summer afternoon was warm and Maggie steered a course directly away from the sea. Though she was still a child in many ways, she knew the countryside as well as any farmer several times her age. She and Cinder had ridden and explored everything between Rossachs Kyle and the Dormin Forest together. Riding through the fields and meadows, splashing through the streams, climbing the rugged hills, and exploring the coastline of her native home of northern Scotland, provided Maggie's one great pleasure of life. Notwithstanding that she was a Duncan who lived in the imposing mansion of Stonewycke, the farmers and fishermen loved young Margaret, for she seemed to feel about their beloved homeland much as they themselves did—a bond they were not accustomed to sharing with the titled landowners.

Leaving behind two or three ridges of dunes covered with pale seagrasses, horse and girl came upon a stretch of rolling meadowland which lengthened out in the distance before them. This wide and fertile valley, for which Port Strathy had been named, was dotted here and there with small cottages of the farmers—the crofters, who worked the land on behalf of the Duncan estate, of which Maggie was the eldest offspring. To her right as she rode, some two or three miles distant, could be seen clumps of thick pines and fir which bordered the Lindow River as it wound its way leisurely from the mountainous south toward the North Sea. On her left, composing the opposite boundary of the valley, the terrain rose steadily into a range of high hills, of which Strathy Summit was the closest. She could make out her own house with its straggling stone walls and ancient turrets nestled among the firs about a third of the way up the summit. In the distance ahead of her to the south, the mountains rose gradually to peaks which had only recently doffed their white winter's cap.

The way Maggie now pursued lay straight up the valley, past numerous farms, none too prosperous, yet each with a certain charming flavor of its own. Usually there was a vegetable garden, half planted with potatoes, a few dozen chickens scratching about the grounds, and a cow or two. Without fresh milk furnished by the family cow, and the abundant supply of potatoes, many of the families would not have been able to make it through the long northern winters. *How much improved some of the dreary-looking cottages would look*, thought Maggie, *with a few flowers planted here and there about the yards.*

Maggie leaned low over Cinder's damp neck and spoke to her again in unintelligible tones, then veered toward the road which connected Port Strathy with its nearest neighbor, the inland village of Culden, some twelve miles southwest across the Lindow. Reaching the road, Maggie followed it for about a mile, then diverged to the left, while the road continued its course westward toward Culden.

Maggie had learned to ride almost by the time she could walk, but only in the past four years or so had she taken to such extensive wanderings throughout the countryside. Cinder had been given to her—a foal barely three weeks old—by her father's groom Digory. He had been called from the estate to attend the mare's birth at the farm of one of the poorest, though most respected, families in the valley. The delivery grew complicated, lasted well into the night, and without Digory's assistance it is doubtful that either foal or mother would have survived. In gratitude the old farmer had presented Digory with the newborn animal. The filly was not a thoroughbred, to be sure, the old man had said, but her line had been part of Strathy's equine heritage for more than ten generations. The charcoal body and jet black head certainly presented such a striking picture that the horse could stand proud, unique among the most lettered of purebreds.

Digory accepted the gift thankfully and offered the foal to the ten-year-old young lady of the house he served. Maggie had instantly fallen in love with the filly, and the two had become inseparable.

On Maggie and Cinder walked, the shrubbery growing gradually thicker and the terrain more steep and rocky. On her right Maggie could make out the peak of Marbrae, with the sun descending behind it, standing as if to guard the peaceful Strathy valley to the north. Veering to the east Maggie eased Cinder carefully down the side of a steep, dry gorge, then re-ascended the opposite bank until she stood at last, nearly three miles south of the mansion, on the high moorland known as Braenock Ridge.

Three or four cottages were scattered over the surrounding plateau, but this land was clearly poorer than the lush, green valley and was used mostly for grazing. There were, of course, a number of families for whom this was home. The struggling flocks of sheep and free-grazing goats had been a traditional part of the land for as far back as anyone could remember.

It was neither the most beautiful nor the most prosperous section of the estate. Why would her mother object so adamantly to its being sold? On the other hand, why would anyone want to buy it? As long as Stonewycke's borders east of Rossachs Kyle and west of the Lindow were preserved, what could this remote southern parcel of arid, shrub-filled heath matter?

Sunk in her reverie, Maggie had not heard young Mackinaw come over the rise behind her. The ringing tinkle of the sheep's bells reached her ears just as the voice spoke.

"Aft'noon t' ye, Miss Duncan."

Maggie spun around in the saddle.

"Why, Stevie! I thought I was alone," she said. "You're out herding the sheep by yourself today?"

The boy appeared about Maggie's age, but was in reality two years younger. His lanky frame was lean and awkward, vacillating between boyhood and adolescence. In his face appeared already the hint of lines that would etch themselves deeper through years of looking at the sun and facing the harsh northern elements. His brown leathery skin gave the appearance of age beyond his years. The only assertively boyish feature was the massive crop of wiry red hair which shot out in all directions from his head.

"I have since the weather's turned fair," he replied. "My daddy's gettin' some too lame t' trample o'er these parts lookin' fer grass t' graze the sheep, ye know."

"I'm sorry to hear that, Stevie. Is your mother well? I haven't been out here for some time."

"Fair t' middlin', miss. Only this past winter was a rough one fer her. The wind's cold as ice sometimes."

"But surely you keep a fire going?"

"Yes'm," he replied. "But ye know, the peat be none too o'er warm when a body's sick. But noo that the sun's oot, we're feelin' right well, miss."

As the two spoke, the sheep following their master had edged their way over the rise and had begun to crowd about them. Cinder stamped nervously, but Maggie held her firm.

"Well, tell your mother and father I'll be by for a visit one of these days."

"They'll like that real good, miss," he said, looking away shyly as he pretended to tend the sheep. "An' thank ye, miss," he added. "An' good day t' ye!"

Maggie waved as she maneuvered Cinder through the herd. Then she urged the mare into a slow gallop and headed north, back toward the house along the ridge.

3

Digory

BRILLIANT HUES OF pink and orange marked the early summer sunset as Maggie neared home. She loved the summer gloamin'. Darkness fell but for a few hours on those near-arctic reaches, and her freedom to roam about the countryside was greatly extended. Approaching the stables from the south, Maggie rode up without being seen. She dismounted and led the mare inside.

"Weel, lassie," came an ancient voice from the dimness of the interior. "I was beginnin' t' wonder when we'd see ye again."

Startled, Maggie peered inside as her eyes adjusted to the darkness. At length she spied the old groom perched on a three-legged creepie stool. "Digory," she replied, "what do you mean?"

"They was frettin' aboot ye in the hoose."

"I was only out for a ride."

"Aye, an' a long one! But they haven't grown so accustomed t' yer ways as I have."

"Have I caused a stir?"

"Only a wee one, lass. They went me oot t' look fer ye. But soon's I saw Cinder's empty stall I knew the two o' ye were oot together an' there'd be no use my traipsin' about lookin' fer ye."

"I hope I didn't cause you trouble," said Maggie.

"Ah, lass," he replied with a laugh that resembled a cackle, "ye'll hae t' be gone longer than that t' cause me trouble. Though ye be but a yoong lassie, ye been comin' an' goin' mostly as ye please fer long enough that I'm confident ye ken what ye're aboot."

"I wasn't planning to be gone so long. It was just that I . . . had to go, and—"

She looked up, her sincere eyes struggling to fight back tears at the remembrance of what had driven her from the house.

Digory stood, straightening his body by slow degrees. He reached out and placed his bony hand on her shoulder. "I'm sure ye meant no harm," he said. Then he approached the horse and reached gently for the reins. "Ye've had yersel' quite a ride, I can see."

He led Cinder toward her stall, began to unhitch the saddle, and whispered softly to her while stroking her back with his free hand. Maggie could never understand his words at such times. But she had long since grown accustomed to his gaelic utterances to the animals he loved.

She watched in silence as Digory performed his ministrations to the horse. Normally she liked to rub the mare down herself, a routine contemplated with quiet pride by the groom, for he had taught her everything she knew about caring for a horse. But today Maggie was content to observe. Digory's actions were as natural to him as eating or laughing or breathing. Though his shoulders were bent with the unmistakable signs of age, he moved with a certain loving grace. His arthritic hands made up in tenderness what they lacked in dexterity as they curried the rich gray coat. At times, especially in mid-winter when drifts of wind-tossed snow piled higher against the north wall of the stable than the roofline, his hands became too painful to maintain their grip on the brush. Still, he bore his sinewy frame as a statement of his hardy Scottish endurance—a far more eloquent presentation of his character than his simple speech could attempt. His jagged facial features had frightened Maggie as a youngster, but as she had grown and begun to spend more time around the horses he tended for her father, the intimidation dissolved. The soft drawl of his deeply accented voice became to the growing girl a source of warmth and pleasure. Though her first introduction to prayer had been with James and Atlanta around the dinner table, such blessings had remained a formal affair. From the gentle voice of the groom Maggie had first heard of God as a tender and compassionate Father.

"Digory," Maggie began after some moments of silence, "you've been here a long time . . ." Her voice trailed off as if she were uncertain of what she was attempting to say.

"Aye, that I hae," he replied. "Yer grandaddy an' I used t' romp t'gether on the great lawns when we were jist wee bairns."

"You were born on the estate?"

"Aye. My own daddy served yer great-grandpa Anson. A great laird that man was—not that yer own daddy is na a fine laird too . . . if ye take my meanin'."

"I don't know much about him."

"Laird Anson Ramsey were special, least so my daddy always said. 'Tis a long time ago, t' be sure. Stayed his whole life at Stonewycke. Didna even keep a home in the city as most do. Cared fer the people o' the land, even the poor fishers an' crofters. Always was oot among them. The people, they loved him. 'Tis a shame he died so yoong an' his son had t' become laird at such a yoong age. I never thought I'd outlive yer grandaddy. He was a tough one, not at all like his father."

"Who was that?"

"Talmud . . . Talmud Ramsey. A hard man."

"Digory," said Maggie. "What's so different about Braenock Ridge?"

"Braenock . . ." Digory reflected and was silent a moment, then went on slowly. "There couldna be a more desolate piece o' land. How anythin' can live oot there, none can tell. But live they do—the goats, the sheep, an' the folks. An' they all be the hardier fer it. Maybe that's what makes it special. I've heard some call it godforsaken. But I'll not be believin' that. The Lord doesna forsake any o' His creation. Remember that, child, when ye're older an' ye think God's left ye alone. He's always there. An' maybe a place like Braenock Ridge holds a tender place in His heart jist because it never gives up. The wind sweeps icy o'er the moor. An' yet ye can still find a primrose or a tiny daisy peekin' oot from 'atween the rocks."

"My father wants to sell Braenock," Maggie said.

"'Tis it so?" replied Digory, shaking his head slowly and thoughtfully. "Weel, he be the laird. He knows what's best. Still," he went on, his tone indicating the doubt he felt was not new to him, "'tis a sad thing t' see him sellin' parcels here an' there on the corners o' the estate. But 'tis na my place t' be speakin' aboot it."

"I rode out there today," Maggie said. "I saw Stevie Mackinaw with his herd of sheep."

"There be several families that live oot there. Canna do much wi' it. But 'tis aboot the only place some o' them can afford t' live."

"What would happen to them . . . if Papa sold the land?"

"Who could tell?" replied the groom. "The Mackinaws an' the others there are like the land—they are the enduring ones . . . the survivors."

"Mrs. Mackinaw is sickly," said Maggie. "I hope Papa doesn't sell it."

Digory said nothing, but looked down and smiled at the young girl he loved as much as the daughter he'd never had. *She's a Ramsey, t' be sure,* he thought to himself. *She'll be a lady someday. Lovin' this estate as she does, Anson—an' who knows, maybe even hard-bitten o' Talmud too—would be proud.*

"'Tis good that ye care fer the folks, lass," he said at length. "'Tis what holds Stonewycke an' all the people that make it t'gether."

4

Mother and Daughter

THE SUN HAD nearly set now, and as Maggie walked slowly back to the house, the great stone walls of the ancient mansion rose up like ghostly shadows before her. The gray walls, covered intermittently with climbing ivy, presented a stark and chilling contrast with the congeniality of the stables she had just left. Austere as its name implied, Stonewycke was not the most inviting of places. But it was home, and one grows accustomed to one's surroundings, and usually even learns to love them.

Maggie was too young to care about, or even notice, the many outward adornments that accompanied her family's position of wealth and influence. Stonewycke was awe-inspiring to her for other reasons. Many were the times she had thought of all those who had lived within its walls before her. For long hours she had daydreamed about them, trying to imagine what her ancestors were like. What did they do as children? Did they ride, burrow through the straw in the hayloft, climb trees? Or were they kept inside by strict nannies and somber tutors? Did they wander through the endless maze of rooms, like her, looking for something interesting to do—but usually finding it out in the barn or stables instead?

Maggie turned the latch on the massive oak door and it swung open noiselessly. Every detail of the house, down to the monthly oiling of the door's hinges, was always kept in perfect order.

Inside she stopped, bracing herself to face her mother and father. They could not guess what prompted her evening's ride, yet she felt guilty knowing about their argument. As she glanced up her eyes fell on the grand stairway which swept from the ground floor toward the upper reaches of the house. Its rich walnut banister and rails curved gracefully up to the second floor—perfect for an exhilarating ride down—when no grown-ups were looking, of course. To the left of the stairs the entryway opened toward several large doors which led to drawing rooms, a banquet hall, and a smaller dining room for the family. Farther toward the rear of the house, and through two or three more corridors, lay the kitchen, the servants' quarters, and many additional rooms and passageways—each with its own nooks and crannies which Maggie had still not yet fully explored.

To the right of the stairs lay the grand ballroom. For the most part, she would always have chosen to be out of doors with Cinder rather than in just about any room in the house—with the possible exception of the library. But this one room always gave the young girl a thrill. The walls were decked with pale lavender gilt-edged flowers and walnut paneling, and splendid purple velvet curtains were pulled back from the tall windows with golden rope-ties. The floors, always polished to a high gloss, reflected like mirrors. But most striking of all was the crystal chandelier. When the sunlight came through the windows just so, striking hundreds of leaded prisms, thin shafts of color cascaded like gentle fairies all about the room.

Maggie could remember but one party in the ballroom, given about five years ago, before her grandfather had died. Maggie had been too young to appreciate it fully. All she could remember of that evening, besides the beautiful dresses of the ladies, was being scurried off to bed while the guests were still arriving.

Tonight she opened the door a crack and peeked into the ballroom for a moment. It was one of the few places she was not allowed to enter without permission. Turning away and easing the door closed, she heard her mother's step descending the stair.

"There you are, Maggie," Atlanta said, with the sharpness that often accompanies concern.

"Hello, Mother," she replied somewhat nervously. "I was out riding. I . . . I forgot the time."

"I was worried, my dear. I sent Digory off to find you. You must leave some report of your whereabouts if you are to continue these long rides."

"I'm sorry, Mother."

"Well, you are here now—and safe. Come along and have your supper. I had the kitchen keep it warm for you."

Atlanta led the way to the dining room where, at her bidding, the remnants of the recently completed light supper were brought to the table. With an inner sigh of relief Maggie cast her eyes quickly around and noticed her father was not present. For the moment, she was glad she didn't have to face them together. She didn't want anyone wondering where she had been and asking what had put Braenock into her head all of a sudden. Her younger brother, Alastair, was still seated at the table dawdling over a dish of butterscotch pudding. He barely seemed to notice as his mother and sister entered, but did manage to shoot Maggie as much of a smirk as he dared. Young Alastair always took special delight in his sister's misfortune, and on this occasion—having witnessed the growing cloud of worry as Maggie's absence had extended longer and longer into the evening—he had anticipated some disciplinary action. Though barely ten, he had learned an infinite number of cunning methods to manipulate his parents far more expertly than his older sister, and was adept at presenting himself as a model child—well-mannered and thoughtful in every way. His deception was bolstered by the fact that, through the years, it was usually Maggie who walked onto the carpet with muddy shoes, knocked over a prized piece of china, or appeared at the dinner table with smudged face. On the rare instances when little Alastair's misdeeds caught up with him, he was able to put on such an angelic and repentant face that he usually escaped punishment.

Maggie ate in silence. Afterward Atlanta announced that there was a nice fire burning in the hearth upstairs. As soon as he was excused, however, Alastair bounded away to his own room. Maggie followed Atlanta up the stairs to the cozy parlor where the family gathered on most evenings. The fire was blazing and sent waves of warmth out into the room. Maggie curled up on one of the low sofas while Atlanta sat down in a chair opposite and picked up a piece of needlework from her basket. With precise and deliberate motions she began to work the needle in and out of the cloth.

She was not a beautiful woman. Her features were too severe for beauty. But a stately, almost swan-like gracefulness caught the attention of any observer in an instant, and her surface plainness quickly receded into memory. In youth, Atlanta's hair had been golden, a reminder of her Saxon heritage. But now, at forty, it had begun to dim with encroaching strands of gray. She wore it pulled tightly back into a bun at the nape of her neck, and she often wore black taffeta as if in perpetual mourning. The rustle of the fabric as Atlanta moved about was to Maggie a soothing substitute to the gentle words her mother was unable to vocalize.

Maggie stole a glance at her mother. She loved to watch her while she sewed and stitched intricate designs with her nimble fingers. Atlanta sat straight and tall—her statuesque dignity reminiscent of the Normans, and the Vikings before them, who had inhabited the land from which she had sprung—in the high-backed mahogany chair, not once relaxing her disciplined frame. But her hands moved effortlessly at her work, never slowing, never erring.

"*The Lord is my shepherd, I shall not want,*" Atlanta murmured, then looked toward her daughter. "This is how I learned the scriptures as a child, Maggie, stitching them into cloth. My father always thought religion frivolous—best left to the women. I suppose one proof he was wrong was that he died an unhappy man. Yet on the other hand," she sighed, turning her eyes again to the work before her, "perhaps in one way we are all doomed to the same fate. I wish I had something more lasting to pass on to you than Bible verses sewn into linen."

"You've taught me many good things, Mother," Maggie offered, not quite certain how to respond to her mother's unusually candid thoughts.

"Not near enough, I'm afraid."

"Digory says the best teacher of religion is God himself," said Maggie.

"Good heavens. I hope you are not getting your religious education from our groom," replied Atlanta, more amused than alarmed, and leaving once more the realm of her pensive feelings. "We are paying Graham good money to fulfill the position of tutor. I had hoped he would include religion in his program."

She had *hoped* it, Atlanta thought to herself, even more strongly than she would admit to her daughter—or anyone else. For of late she had grown more aware of her own inadequacies in the area of faith, while at the same time the clashes with James—which revealed conflicts within herself—were convincing her more and more of its importance. But she forced her attention back upon her daughter who was speaking.

"Mr. Graham knows history and mathematics," said Maggie. "But it's different when I'm helping Digory clean out the stables, or when he's helping me groom Cinder. He knows so much about . . . well, everyday things. Today he was saying—"

She stopped short, suddenly realizing she had nearly breached treacherous ground.

"Saying what?" queried Atlanta, cocking her left eyebrow inquisitively.

"Oh, nothing important," returned Maggie with a momentary tremor in her voice.

"It must have been important for you to mention it," pressed Atlanta.

"No . . . not really." Maggie could feel the red rising to her neck and cheeks.

"Maggie," said Atlanta, growing impatient. "I would like to know what our groom has been telling you."

Maggie remained silent.

"He . . . he said," she finally began, unable to endure her mother's insistent gaze, "he said Braenock Ridge was not godforsaken as some call it."

Maggie swallowed slowly.

"And?" said her mother. "Is that all?"

"He said he thought such places held a special place in God's heart because they are so strong and hardy and never give up. He almost made it sound more beautiful than the valley."

"Why was he talking about Braenock?" Atlanta asked, forcing her words slightly, as if she also knew they had intruded upon delicate ground.

"I—I asked him about it," Maggie replied.

What had sparked Maggie's interest in Braenock Ridge Atlanta could not even guess. To be sure, there was a hesitation in the child's voice which hadn't been there earlier. Yet Atlanta could not bring herself to probe further. Was it her own vulnerability she feared? She would not have wanted to admit it. But forces were at work threatening to upset the balance in her life. She feared for the estate and what James might do to it. But even more she worried about her daughter who was fast growing up, and whom she feared she might lose in the feud with her husband. But she had learned early in life that a lady never caused a scene, never allowed tears to flow in public, never exposed her unguarded inner feelings. So Atlanta pulled her well-composed facade about her like the walls of a crypt, and said no more.

Watching her mother, Maggie saw only her dignified grace and, she thought, noble bearing. Little could her young mind begin to comprehend the inner struggles tugging at the heart of her proud Scottish mother. She saw but the shell of surface fortitude, interpreted it as a sign that all was well, and concluded that she had become upset for nothing by the words in the library.

"It's getting late," Atlanta said after a lengthy silence. "You had a long day, my dear. It's time you were in bed."

"Yes, Mother."

Maggie left the drawing room and made her way down the corridor, now dimly lit and cool as the evening advanced. When she reached the stairs she remembered she had failed to ask about her father.

5

Stonewycke

THE NEEDLE SANK into Maggie's flesh. Quickly she thrust the finger into her mouth—the last thing she needed was to stain this pure white linen with a spot of blood.

"This is impossible!" she grumbled.

Maggie sat alone in the dayroom on the third floor of the great house. It was one of her favorite retreats in the early hours of the morning because its windows, facing east, caught the full glory of the rising sun. But even more importantly, it was seldom frequented by any of the household, and she knew she would not likely be disturbed.

Normally she would retreat here with one of the Waverly novels—or perhaps Shakespeare if she was trying to impress Mr. Graham. But today she had taken her sewing instead. She'd begun this embroidery project so many weeks ago that by now she had grown impatient with it. With summer bursting out all around her, bringing with it such glorious days for riding, she could barely manage to squeeze in a spare moment for anything else.

She looked down at how her work had progressed thus far. The colorful border of primroses and forget-me-nots was completed, and she openly admired how well it had turned out.

But now the tedious remainder, the seemingly endless names which had sparked her interest when she had begun, blurred together on the small piece of cloth. Atlanta had warned that she might have chosen something too difficult. But Maggie had resolved in her determined young mind to copy the large tapestry of her family tree which hung in her childhood nursery. Atlanta had helped her simplify the design, but there was little to be done to simplify the generations of names and dates which now had to be carefully outlined.

Maggie withdrew her finger from her mouth and, making sure there was no telltale blood to mar the cloth, began once more. An exacting girl, she wanted every letter to turn out precise and uniform—all the more so because Atlanta had stitched the original tapestry. Though her mother had been nineteen at the time, Maggie nevertheless hoped the finished product of what now lay in her young hands would be nearly as lovely as the original.

R-o-b-e-r-t R-a-m-s-e-y . . .

The *y* was causing her particular annoyance at the moment.

Her mind wandered back to the day several years earlier when she had first really taken notice of the tapestry. The brilliant colors had caught her attention before anything else. Then slowly other details came into focus.

"Mother," she had asked, "who are all those names?"

"They are your family, Margaret," had been Atlanta's answer. And though she could not have been more than seven or eight at the time, the note of pride in her mother's voice was by no means lost on the child.

"Do they live in London? I don't remember anyone by those names."

"They are all dead," replied Atlanta. "Except your father and me. These are your ancestors—all the lairds and ladies of Stonewycke. Not all, of course. I only began the family tree with Robert Ramsey."

"Why him?"

"It was to him that the land was reinstated after the Jacobite Rebellion," Atlanta replied. "So that was a significant time for us Scots, when King George III returned our land to us in the 1780s."*

---

*After the death of Charles II, King of England, in 1685, James II became king of a precariously united England and Scotland. Demonstrating bad judgment, he became increasingly unpopular. Thus in 1688 certain English parliamentary leaders invited William of Orange in the Netherlands to assume the English and Scottish crowns. James abdicated and took up refuge in France.

However, William was not as popular in Scotland as he was in England. The Scottish dissenters who still backed the displaced Stuart monarchy of James came to be known as Jacobites. In 1715 they followed the Earl of Mar in a hapless attempt to restore James's son, or "the Pretender," to the throne.

The Jacobites were still active a generation later when Prince Charles Edward Stuart, son of "the Pretender" and grandson of James II, came to the Highlands in 1745 to rally support for his claim to the throne. Having sailed from France with only seven friends, Bonnie Prince Charlie was a brave and hopeful leader. Soon the majority of Scotland's clan leaders were on his side.

The Highlanders marched to Edinburgh and there the Prince proclaimed himself King of Scotland. Then they blazed their way into England with an army of 6,000 men. But when the English army advanced north to meet them, the Highlanders were forced to retreat. Back in Scotland support for the Prince was eroding. The retreat continued through Glasgow and north toward Inverness. The English army pursued Bonnie Prince Charlie and met the insurrectionary forces at Culloden Moor east of Inverness on April 16, 1746.

"Did Robert Ramsey know the king?" asked Maggie with wide eyes.

"I don't know, child," laughed her mother.

"Oh, I'd like to know!" said Maggie excitedly.

"He was my great-grandfather," said Atlanta, then paused, reflecting. "This family tree marks but a hundred years of our existence," she went on at length. "But the Ramseys had been at Stonewycke for almost two hundred years before that."

"Oh, I'd like to find out all about it!" exclaimed Maggie. "What about the Duncans, Mother?"

"That is your father's family," Atlanta returned rather crisply. She hesitated, and then softened almost imperceptibly. "They live mostly in London and have their own side of the family tree. Perhaps you should ask your father about that side of your family."

"Will there be no more Ramseys at Stonewycke?" asked Maggie innocently.

Atlanta winced but regained her composure before her daughter noticed.

"*You* are a Ramsey," Atlanta finally replied. "My father had but one child, a daughter instead of the son he would have preferred. But Stonewycke will not suffer because my name was changed to Duncan. Ramsey blood will never grow thin here—not as long as you love Stonewycke with your very soul, as I do."

"I do love it, Mother," young Margaret had replied, hardly aware of what she was saying, but moved by her mother's passionate eloquence.

"Always remember, my daughter, that it is more than the land you are loving. The lifeblood of the land comes from the people—not only these names you see before you, but also all those who live under our care and who work the land of the estate. As long as you love them, Stonewycke will be whole . . . whatever your name may one day become."

Maggie's thoughts drifted slowly back to the present as her eyes focused once again on the names in front of her. She wished her mother would fall into such reflective moods more often. But never again since that day had she heard her talk about her family or the love she obviously held deep in her heart for Stonewycke.

With a sigh Maggie turned her attention again to the *y* of Ramsey on the linen before her. Just then there was a sharp rap at the door.

The rebel army of some 5,000 men was crushed and scattered in a final and decisive defeat. Miraculously the Prince escaped and wandered for months, a fugitive with an English bounty on his head.

King George II of England took the uprising of 1745 as an opportunity to humble Scotland for its insubordination and took their lands away from the Jacobite clan leaders. However, some forty years later, when the tide of anger had abated against the Jacobites, George III reinstated the heirs of the clans to their former landowning positions.

6

Father and Daughter

❖

MAGGIE HADN'T REALIZED how quickly the time had slipped by, but glancing up she could see that the sun was now high in the sky. She was also puzzled to think who could have found her this far into the upper reaches of Stonewycke.

The door opened and James walked in. "There you are, Margaret," he said. "I hope you don't mind my disturbing you."

"Of course not, Father," she replied. Notwithstanding a certain awe she felt in his presence, Maggie was always glad to see her father. Like most impressionable young daughters, she adored him and lived for the moment when she might bask in the fleeting glow of one of his smiles or a tender word of praise. To please him was the one ambition in life; to be loved by him—for him to return but a glimmer of the exuberant and trusting childlike affection which beat in her heart for him—that was *everything*! But at almost fourteen Maggie was shy of disclosing herself, for James had not cultivated intimacy with his daughter. He rarely came near just to visit; there was always something specific on his mind.

James entered and closed the door behind him. He stood in the middle of the room for a moment with his hands clasped awkwardly behind him. Maggie put down her sewing and sat with hands folded in her lap and eyes focused on the pattern of the Persian rug on the floor. James cleared his throat.

"I'm surprised you are not out riding today," he said at length.

"Cinder threw a shoe and Digory is repairing it," Maggie answered, glancing up briefly, then back at the floor.

James formed his lips into a smile as if he were trying it on for size. He walked over to the window, feeling the awkwardness of the moment and not wanting to make it worse by sitting down. *She's grown up too deuced fast*, he thought to himself. Now she was at such an uncertain age. One moment he'd look at her and see his little baby; the next, he'd hardly recognize the changes taking place. It was no wonder he always felt a bit clumsy trying to make conversation. Even though she was his daughter, sometimes he scarcely knew her.

James was not an imposing man. At five-foot-eight he stood shorter than his wife, but he bore his small frame like a military officer—shoulders square, back straight as an iron rod. His dark, unwavering eyes penetrated their object, and he had always taken a special pride in being able to look another man in the eye and cause him to glance away first. Unfortunately this ability was equally as effective on his daughter as it was on business associates. By now she had learned to avoid rather than seek his face. It did not make for easy conversation.

"I hear you are becoming quite the little horsewoman," he said, gazing out the window. "It's been some time since we rode together. We shall have to go out again soon."

"That would be nice, Father," Maggie said.

"Where do you take your rides?" he asked.

"Different places. I like riding on the beach or in the valley."

"Do you?" he asked thoughtfully. "Well then, we shall have to go there one of these days."

"Perhaps we could—" began Maggie with uncertainty, then hesitated, suddenly losing her courage.

"Perhaps what, Margaret?"

"I was just thinking . . . I mean, I was going to ride out to visit the Mackinaws . . ."

"Whatever for?" asked her father, turning away from the window to face her. His voice contained a slight edge.

"I saw Stevie the other day. His mother's been sick. He said it had been a rough winter."

"My dear," replied James with an amused laugh, "you have much to learn about dealing with crofters. These tenants will do anything to gain our sympathies, even stoop to sending their children to appeal to the delicate sensitivities of the laird's daughter. You must learn to take a hard line or they'll walk all over you."

"They didn't send him," protested Maggie, confused.

"Of course it would never appear that way, but you must not allow yourself to be so easily fooled. My dear little Margaret," James went on, assuming a fatherly tone, "one day you may be mistress of the estate. It would be your duty to rule with wisdom. These rustic poor folk will lose respect for you if you are not firm. And, Margaret, you must always keep their respect."

"Yes, but—"

"No buts, Margaret. Giving in when they complain is a sure sign of weakness, and they will look down on you for it."

"Yes, sir," Maggie replied with a sigh which went unnoticed by her father as she cast her gaze back down at the carpet.

"Now, as to why I sought you out in the first place," James began in a new vein; "tomorrow we shall have a special guest visiting Stonewycke. I want you to be on your best behavior—no running about the house, that sort of thing. Lord Browhurst is a very important friend of your father's. He and I have some serious business to discuss, and I want him to have a good impression of Scotland, and of my family."

"I'll do my best, Father," Maggie replied, eager for a chance to please him after his marked disapproval of her interest in the Mackinaws. Yet she couldn't help feeling disheartened at his tone. He still addressed her as if she were a little girl, just as he spoke to Alastair. She longed for him to notice that she was growing into an attractive young woman.

"Fine . . . fine," James went on, oblivious to the conflicting struggles in the heart of his young daughter—the gleam of hope in her eyes at the thought of gaining his favor, and the disillusionment at his condescending tone. Maggie's tender emotions and her need for approbation were as foreign to James Duncan as the motives and pressures driving him were to young Margaret. He turned and made his departure without another word. Maggie's eyes followed him from the room, and her face slowly fell. How she longed for him to put aside the hasty pace of his schedule! She thought wistfully back to the simpler days of childhood. Part of her still longed to climb up on his lap, to snuggle in his arms at the end of the day. Oh, just to have a *papa*, she thought! But she had never, even then—though her heart had been full of him—had that kind of a *papa*. She had had instead a father who was away from home a good deal and was more interested in his business pursuits than he was in his growing daughter.

When the sound of his footsteps had died away, Maggie rose and quietly left the house by another route. On such occasions Cinder was always ready to yield a corner of her living quarters as a refuge for the lonely child. Avoiding Digory, Maggie crept in the rear entrance to the stables, sought out Cinder's stall, flipped up the rusty latch, walked in, and closed the door behind her. The manger was full of fresh-cut grass and Cinder was presently occupied at the far end, her long black head buried in a trough of oats and fresh hay. She turned to see who this visitor might be and gave an amiable snort of recognition as Maggie came nearer and stroked her head and nose.

"Ah, you're a fine horse, my Cinder," she said softly.

She slipped her arms around the mare's neck and squeezed her tightly, then stepped back. It was so cool and dark, and Cinder was such pleasant company, that Maggie often sought seclusion here with the horse she considered her closest friend in the world.

Maggie sat down near Cinder's head in a pile of clean straw; Digory had no doubt refurbished the stall only moments before. Gradually the fountain of tears which she usually managed to hold in check began to overflow their gates. And when their supply had been exhausted a few moments later, Maggie was sound asleep.

By instinct sensing the troubled spirit of her young mistress, Cinder bent toward Maggie and gave the peaceful face three moist licks with her long wet tongue. Then she turned back to the oats.

7

James Duncan

❧

HAVING LEFT MARGARET in the dayroom, James strode briskly down the hall. By the time he reached the stairs he was humming a little tune. He may not have Braenock, he thought—Atlanta had seen to that—but he *could* manage his children. Things would go his way in the end. It was especially important to maintain their loyalty, even more so since this cool distance between him and Atlanta had grown so pronounced. Margaret was a vital link in his future if he was to maintain control of Stonewycke.

She was not the only link, to be sure. He smiled smugly. *Let Atlanta have Braenock*, he mused. *It's nothing but wasteland anyway*. He would still obtain the brewery. That's why Browhurst was coming, after all. He determined to make sure everything was just right.

James carried himself with confidence and self-assurance. But to be practical, he had to admit that there were times when it would certainly have proved profitable had he been titled in his own right. It was only natural, then, that to make up for his provincial background, he occasionally had to find just the right way to impress a business associate. "Greasing the wheels of commerce," as he said, had long been his unspoken creed. James prided himself at having learned to disguise his art skillfully. Rarely did one of his colleagues know he was being manipulated, so adeptly did James ingratiate himself with favors and promises and indulgences.

Browhurst was, he thought, already in the palm of his hand. But if he could find one more weak spot in his character, one flaw he could exploit, one unfulfilled desire of Browhurst's that he could satisfy, then he would feel sure of the deal. He would have to keep his eyes opened once the old man arrived.

James reached the foot of the stairs, continued past the dining room, down several corridors, and finally arrived at the east wing of the house. In this little-used portion of the sprawling castle-like mansion, he maintained a private and secluded office. The rooms were small and plain and not kept up regularly like the rest of the house. In times past they had been used as a billet for soldiers. A persistent rumor in the family maintained that Bonny Prince Charles had spent several weeks here during the months following his rout at Culloden Moor. But some treachery on the part of one of the servants alerted the Earl of Cumberland to the Prince's place of hiding and the Young Pretender had had to flee for the Continent. Whether there was any truth to such reports, James had never bothered to consider. He hated superstition and old wives' fables in any form, and considered the Prince Charlie story as a hybrid of genuine legend and pure poppycock. Whatever their history, the rooms were now mostly empty except for a few used for storage.

James opened a door, ascended a narrow staircase, then paused before another door. The room he entered was little more than a cubicle, not more than twelve feet by fifteen feet with a single window looking out onto the rear portion of the grounds. Against one wall several shelves contained stacks of books, rarely used—mostly technical volumes, legal and surveying reports, and one set of ancient law whose backings of leather were badly cracked and chipped away, so brittle had they become with age. Most had come here during Anson Ramsey's time, and James had never so much as looked at them. On the wall opposite hung a variety of ancient weapons: several ornate swords, one encased in a leather sheath in no better condition than the law buildings; a dagger with jeweled handle; two pistols; and one round shield with curiously carved figures on it. Each obviously had its own silent history and many stories to tell.

James's attention for the moment, however, centered on a roll-top desk shoved against the wall underneath the window. The top was up; such was the clutter upon the desk itself that it would have been impossible to roll the top down. A multitude of papers and dusty old journals and ledgers lay in seeming disarray. A worn leather-covered oaken chair, the leather broken in half-a-dozen spots revealing the horsehair innards of the cushion, sat in front of the desk. At first glance the room seemed a most inappropriate setting for an office for such a one as James, with his lofty plans and high ambitions. But it suited James's needs perfectly.

Of course he maintained a finely appointed study upstairs, with a rich oak sideboard and handsome secretary, where he took brandy with friends and associates. But this cubicle was where he retreated to plan and plot out his major business dealings. Atlanta was, no doubt, aware of the existence of the room. She had, after all, grown up here. But she had never ventured to invade her husband's private domain. Even *she* knew that certain limits existed. Both strong in their own way, James and Atlanta had over the years established their distinctive battle lines beyond which the other dared not cross.

James moved aside a ledger on the desk, nearly overturning a bottle of ink. Sorting through a sheaf of papers, he at length found the one he had been seeking, pulled it out, and gazed at it with apparent satisfaction.

"Yes," he murmured to himself, "yes . . . this is just fine. Everything is in order."

James Duncan had known what he wanted early in life. He longed for the power and prestige his father's mismanagement had deprived him of. The family had owned a large estate in the central lowlands of East Lothian, but gambling and poor investments had finally forced Lawrence Duncan to sell the estate to pay his debts. In the end the family was left with only a tenuous hold on the privileges of the lordly circles they had once been so proudly a part of. Even Lawrence's own brother, the wealthy Earl of Landsbury, would have little to do with him and refused him so much as a shilling in assistance.

Lawrence Duncan aged more rapidly than his years accounted for and became a sickly recluse. Young James was forced to work in order to maintain for the family what little they had managed to keep. Having a temperament for the aristocratic life and a taste for life's finer pleasures, James bitterly resented his father's placing him in the position of a common laborer. With only two years at the university in Edinburgh, he could find little employment suitable for a gentleman, as he styled himself. But he possessed a quick mind, was adept at figures, and eventually secured a post in one of the city's mid-sized banks.

As demeaning as he considered the position, a bank did afford him the opportunity to rub shoulders with people of importance, and, more significantly, people of wealth. It did not take long for James to curry the bank president's favor. Though lowly situated in the company's hierarchy, aggressive young James Duncan grew to become the president's personal lackey and with the important man's eye upon him, he began to advance more rapidly than would have been appropriate under any other circumstances.

James met Talmud Ramsey, the eleventh marquis of Stonewycke, while the latter was in Edinburgh on bank business. The older man was so taken with young James that his good word further heightened the president's view of him; before long James Duncan, barely thirty-four, had been promoted into the office management of the bank, causing no little stir among his fellow employees of more advanced experience and greater tenure.

More important than occupational progress to James, however, were the fringe advantages accompanying his widening association with the Ramsey family. Invited by the marquis to visit their London home whenever bank business drew him to the south, James was drawn back into the coveted circles of English wealth and influence his father had relinquished.

The Marquis' only daughter rarely left the Ramsey estate in northern Scotland, though her father traveled to London six or eight times yearly and maintained a fully-staffed home there. But on one such excursion in 1843, twenty-three-year-old Atlanta decided to accompany her father. James Duncan chanced to be in London simultaneously, and the two met for the first time.

James immediately perceived that Atlanta was no beauty. But neither was she unsightly, and he had only a passing interest in beauty. His views on relationships were far too pragmatic for that. Atlanta was the daughter of the Marquis of Stonewycke, and what was more, heiress of the estate. She was certainly well mannered and refined—striking, he would say. He found no difficulty in persuading himself that he loved her—not that love was a necessary prerequisite to their union, but it did cast a sheltering veneer over his other, more utilitarian, motives.

Atlanta, on her part, found James perfectly suited to the ideal marriage she had already been forced to consider. Having no living brothers or uncles, she had long known the estate would pass to her. Though eleven years her senior, James was untitled; thus in marrying him she would be able to maintain control of Stonewycke, and thereby prevent its being swallowed up in the holdings of a suitor more affluent and powerful than James. If he could provide her with an offspring into whom she could pour herself and to whom she could in turn pass on the legacy, she would be satisfied. Love and romance were of equally little concern to Atlanta alongside the possibility of losing Stonewycke. She could endure any marriage, she thought, if it meant keeping control of her father's land and the heritage of the Ramsey name. And she had to admit, James *was* handsome. He was a magnetizing man whose blandishments were not lost on the young heiress. The marriage, of course, could not have been more to old Talmud's liking.

So in their union, James and Atlanta each found something they wanted, had hoped for more, and had undoubtedly been disappointed in the years since. But neither had been deluded, for happiness was not a commodity they sought, even now. If they harbored any silent regrets, they were too stubborn to admit they had grasped for the wrong things fifteen years earlier.

The birth of their first child brought a certain joyful optimism to the household. In those early days there even began to develop a degree of tenderness between Atlanta and James as husband and wife. But they were never to know if it could have matured into a greater bond of love, for it was all too suddenly shattered by the death of Atlanta's father. As the estate passed to Atlanta, James felt his dispossession more severely than ever. Of course, the husband held certain legal rights by virtue of his position, but he could not help feeling like an adopted orphan.

Perhaps even then the marriage would have held together if his subconscious resentment over what his father had done to him—aggravated by Talmud's death—had not led James into his terrible indiscretion. How he could have been so foolish he never knew. His anger at himself was worsened in that Atlanta had been almost gracious about it. A child by an ill-advised affair was bad enough, but he could easily have swept the situation under the carpet. When the child's mother died, however, James was presented with a regrettable responsibility. The fact that the child was a son made him all the more loathe to give him up, for he knew there would be no more children by Atlanta. He still wondered how he was able to convince Atlanta to take the infant in and, for the sake of propriety, claim him as her own. She claimed the child, but forever after rejected the father.

Atlanta had not set out intentionally to make James resent her dominant position. At first she was hardly aware that his apparent jealousy over her power was in fact a misplaced malice still seething in his heart against all those of rank and wealth and privilege—commodities which he felt by right should have been his but which had been torn from him. But as she saw more and more deeply into his soul, Atlanta realized she had no intention of allowing an outsider (which she considered him, husband or not) to become master of the estate. Stonewycke was her heart and life, and she could barely hide the disdain she felt each time James was referred to as the *laird* in her hearing.

But James did not sit back and accept the second post easily. He refused to allow a woman eleven years his junior to dominate him, no matter what her maiden name. He adopted the mantle of laird with sober determination. Thus the ensuing conflict was inevitable, for each met the other with stout resolve.

The recent dispute over Braenock Ridge was merely one brief skirmish in the ongoing war, a battle in which James grudgingly had to admit defeat. He would perhaps not have yielded quite so readily had he not seen another means to achieve his goal.

The paper he now held in his hands was precisely that means. And it needed only Lord Browhurst's signature to render it legal.

A mere name on the line . . . James thought confidently, running his finger along his short-cropped moustache. *That's shouldn't be too difficult.*

8

A Bargain Is Struck

LORD BROWHURST DUCKED low to avoid cracking his head against the lintel of the carriage. A tall man, he had often remarked that carriage-makers must bear some special malice toward persons of full stature. His head cleared without mishap, and he stepped out to his first view of the manor known as Stonewycke.

These Scottish castles are always so dreary, he thought to himself.

Further speculation was cut short as his host stepped forward to greet him.

"How good of you to come!" said James with enthusiasm and an outstretched hand.

"I wouldn't think of refusing your kind invitation," Browhurst replied in a detached tone, "especially since Port Strathy offered such a convenient layover for my yacht."

"I trust you have enjoyed a pleasant sail?"

"Ah, yes. Fair winds and clear skies—couldn't have asked for better," he replied in a deep, resonant voice. At fifty-nine, Browhurst was a handsome man with gray eyes, ruddy complexion, and silver hair. His normally large frame, however, had taken on a few extra pounds of late, especially in his midriff and in a slightly doubled chin.

James presented his family, and Lord Browhurst extended his hand toward Atlanta, greeting her with a politeness that bordered on indifference. Atlanta's smile was strained, but she offered her hand to their guest. She was certain this visit was not purely social but had been unsuccessful in her attempt to discover what scheme James was concocting.

Browhurst cast but a passing glance toward the two children standing silently beside their mother.

After Browhurst had refreshed himself in his room, he and James took a leisurely stroll about the grounds. James was proud of Stonewycke, even if he was but a graft into the long line of generations which had built it. He took a great satisfaction in its grandeur, in the vast wild beauty of the lands. He was, after all, the laird of this mighty estate, and it necessarily reflected well on him.

"I hear you are something of a celebrated horseman," James ventured as they neared the stables.

"I gained a bit of renown in my youth for my equestrian pursuits," Browhurst replied, exhibiting a thin attempt at modesty.

"Then you shall definitely want to have a ride on our highland paths—an experience you won't soon forget."

"I bow to your discretion in the matter," said Browhurst with a good-natured laugh.

They reached the stables and found Digory puttering about with his routine chores. The guest sauntered down the row of stalls, admiring each animal in its turn.

"I must admit, Duncan, you have an impressive stock here."

"I have made horseflesh something of an avocation," said James modestly, knowing full well the other's consuming passion for a fine steed.

"Well, my friend, you have succeeded most admirably."

"Digory," James called. "Saddle up the bay and the gelding. We'll be taking them out right away."

Digory set down a pail and shuffled toward one of the stalls. He lifted the saddle and was about to heave it into the bay when Browhurst's voice boomed through the quiet stable:

"Is there any reason I shouldn't take out this gray?"

He had come upon Cinder's stall and was gazing at the horse with admiration as if to suggest that perhaps Scotland was good for something after all.

"She were a wee bit lame yesterday, my lord," Digory answered. "She might be wantin' a rest today."

"Nonsense!" interposed James, approaching the stall. "You gave her a new shoe, didn't you? She should be perfectly fine. Saddle her up."

"But, my lord," Digory persisted, "I would not like t' see her—"

James turned on Digory, his black eyes glaring at the old groom. "Enough of your insolence! Do as I say or you'll feel the lash of my whip." Then turning to Browhurst, he added, "You have a fine taste in horseflesh. This one's from a long line of Scottish thoroughbreds. Not only is she unique in appearance, but she is as stout and surefooted as any I've seen."

"I shall be the judge of that," returned Browhurst.

"A favorite of my daughter's."

"Most unusual coloring. I don't know when I've seen such an extraordinary combination of black and gray. It's positively stunning."

Digory had sucked in a deep breath to calm himself and had then turned obediently to the task of saddling Maggie's mare. When finished he took one final look at the right front hoof which had caused the problem yesterday. He lifted the foot gently; even to his cautious eye it appeared perfectly sound. However, he still didn't like the idea of this Englishman riding the little lady's horse.

When the two men returned from their ride later in the afternoon, Browhurst was flushed both from exertion and pleasure. He had given Cinder several vigorous runs and found that James had not been idly boasting about her.

"Splendid creature!" he exclaimed. "Perfectly splendid!"

"Did I not tell you?" James replied with pride.

They dismounted and, leaving the horse in the care of Digory, who hovered protectively about Cinder, made their way back to the house.

"She would make a fine show in London," Browhurst continued, almost to himself. "I cannot get over the remarkable shades of her coat . . . never seen anything to match it."

"I have given that some thought," said James slowly. "But London is such a trip for a horse, and she is still young."

"I say, Duncan!" exclaimed Browhurst in a sudden burst of resolve, "what would you take for her?"

"Take?" responded James quizzically. "I don't quite follow you."

In reality, however, James understood all too well.

"Yes . . . how much? Every man has his price."

"Well, I don't know. You mean you—"

"Come, come, man!" Browhurst went on with rising impatience. "I want to buy the animal!"

"I've never given a thought to selling her," said James slowly.

"I don't want to haggle over the price. I'll give you whatever you ask."

"Indeed, I doubt I could put a price on such a grand animal—"

"Don't be coy, Duncan!" Browhurst snapped.

"As I was saying," James continued, apparently heedless of the interruption, "I could never put a price on her. But . . ."

He paused, drawing out his words for maximum effect.

" . . . but," he went on, "I would happily present her to you as a gift, a token of Scottish hospitality."

Browhurst had hardly been prepared for this. The insistent words that had already begun to form on his lips fell immediately into silence as he fumbled for an appropriate response.

"I must say, Duncan," he began, recovering from his momentary shock, "I . . . ah . . . I hardly know how to respond. This is indeed a most unexpected gesture. I . . . I will certainly be forever in your debt."

James accepted the words of gratitude with due modesty, but inwardly could not help feeling extremely pleased with himself. Every man did have his price, as his guest had indicated, and James congratulated himself that he had apparently found Browhurst's.

Later that evening, following dinner, James was able to bring his plan to completion. He and Browhurst had returned to the formal setting of James's sitting den, where they sipped an expensive brandy together and relaxed as the conversation drifted to business. James found no difficulty in bringing the brewery to the forefront of the discussion. From reliable sources he had learned that Browhurst was exploring options of expanding his financial base. He had, in fact, been making informal verbal forays among his associates whom he thought he might interest in investing in future breweries and distilleries to add to the four he presently owned in England.

In his most skillful manner, avoiding all hint of coercion, James laid out the details of his plans to produce a fine Scottish ale which would eventually become one of the best known in England as well. He made such a strong case that Browhurst might well have decided to throw in with him regardless of the gift of the horse. But James had no regrets, for there was little doubt that the mare had sealed the deal. When Lord Browhurst signed his name on the document James had drawn up in advance, James had difficulty containing his delight.

Browhurst was no less pleased with the arrangement. He had fully realized that the gift would not be without strings; that was in the very nature of such affiliations. He also had done his checking on James. He knew him to be a calculating and opportunistic businessman and was aware from the outset that the invitation from the Scottish laird undoubtedly contained ulterior motives. But the contract between them was satisfactory, whatever the other man's designs. Now he not only had a bloody fine horse, but also a reasonable investment in what he deemed would become a highly lucrative venture.

9

Loss

JAMES HAD BEEN absent the whole morning making preparations for shipping the horse to London. Browhurst's yacht, one of the largest vessels to sail into Strathy harbor in recent memory, was scheduled to continue its southerly voyage with the evening tide, and a suitable berth for Cinder had to be fashioned before that time. James had employed two local carpenters and Browhurst had overseen the operation, unable to contain the glow of satisfaction he felt in anticipating the envy his London associates would show upon his arrival.

James had not yet seen Maggie, and thus the dreadful news was all the more awful when the first hint of it came in sing-song jeers from Alastair's taunting voice, "Papa gave your horse away. Papa gave your horse away. . . ."

Not believing her brother, yet alarmed by his words, Maggie said nothing but ran immediately to the stables to check Cinder's stall. To her great relief Cinder stood inside calmly munching away at her supply of hay. But whatever relief she may have felt was short-lived, for Digory was there also, making what appeared to be ominous arrangements with a feedbag and a special harness Maggie knew was used only when one of the horses was to be transported.

"Digory," she asked in alarm, "is father taking a trip?"

"No, child," he answered in a voice which sounded peculiarly weak, "I dinna believe he is."

"Then why are you getting one of the horses ready to travel?"

He went on with his work, saying nothing. It was not like Digory to remain so subdued. A lump of fear began inching its way up into Maggie's throat from the pit of her stomach.

She turned and fled. Digory looked up only in time to see her heels vanish through the open doorway.

"Child . . ." he called after her, but she did not turn back.

He continued his gaze until a silent tear blurred his vision in one eye. He swept over it with the back of his rough hand, then bent himself once more to the loathesome task he had been given an hour earlier. No one but he could have grasped what damage the loss of this horse would inflict within the heart of the wide-eyed and sensitive child. He wept not only for her, but also for his master. For he doubted that James Duncan would ever after this day know his daughter again. And he ached with the anguish of realizing how the father's separation from the daughter would sharply wound the young girl he loved with all his heart.

"Oh, God," he prayed quietly, "protect the wee bairn from the bitterness o' this loss. Dinna let this break her heart, O Lord. Wrap yer great arms o' love aroun' her!"

Still disbelieving what her heart told her was true, Maggie ran straight to the house in search of Atlanta. The look of suffering on her face spurred Alastair's demon of cruelty on to greater heights and he took up his jibes once more.

"You were always jealous of Cinder!" Maggie screamed at him, then ran upstairs to Atlanta.

"Mother . . . Mother . . ." she began before the sobs overcame her.

Atlanta said nothing, but approached her forlorn daughter with open arms. Her fists had been clenched, but she relaxed the anger she harbored toward James long enough to offer comfort to Maggie who alone had to bear the most painful brunt of his selfish act. She held her daughter close to her breast and stroked her hair while Maggie went on crying. After a few moments she relaxed her hold and entreated the girl to lie down.

"You'll feel better after a rest," she said, feeling helpless.

But Maggie could not rest. Nothing could still the wracking throb in her chest. All she wanted was to be with the only friend she had—the friend who was being taken from her. At length she ran down the stairs, out the door, across the yard, and again to the stables. This time Digory was not present. Carefully she entered Cinder's stall. Oblivious to the machinations about her, Cinder gave a short neigh of pleasure to see her young mistress. Maggie moved forward, folding her arms about the long, gray, horsey neck, and lay against the hairy mane. After standing thus for some time, she sank to the floor and began crying again.

When her tears were spent she looked up at the horse, feeding away as if food were everything and a new master and a trip to London were nothing at all.

But a moment that is far off comes as inevitably as if it were the next instant, and Maggie's temporary feeling of peace in the stall beside Cinder did not stop the reality from approaching at the appointed time. The moment came shortly before noon when the horse was scheduled to be taken to its new temporary quarters. Still sitting on the floor of Cinder's stall, Maggie heard footsteps approaching. Then the latch was lifted and, to her dismay, two men she did not know came in, and, heedless of her presence, untied Cinder and began to lead the mare away before her very eyes.

Maggie jumped to her feet and threw herself at the bewildered pair, pounding at them with her small fists.

"Thieves!" she shouted.

Treating her gently, but with firm hands, one of the men restrained her, trying to soothe her with kindly words. In the end, realizing she was powerless to stop them, Maggie abandoned her struggle. Staring after them with tearful eyes, she stood alone, forsaken in the stall which had been Cinder's.

When Maggie finally came to her senses, she rushed from the stable back across the yard into the dark house which no longer held any promise of comfort for her. Dashing up the stairs to her own room, she threw herself onto the bed, buried her face in the pillow, and overcome with grief, wept herself to sleep.

She had not moved when James found her about four o'clock that afternoon. He knocked softly on the door, and when no answer came he turned away, resolved to try again later. But a sensation he couldn't readily identify—being none too acquainted with the pangs of conscience—compelled him to enter the room.

He turned back toward the door, tested the handle, eased the door open, and walked in.

Afternoon shadows lay across the room.

"Maggie, dear," he whispered.

She made no response from the bed.

He cleared his throat and searched his mind for what to say next. "Your mother tells me you are upset about the horse," he began feebly. "I can't understand . . . that is, I had no idea it meant so much to you."

Maggie rolled over and faced him, shot through with a sudden ray of hope. It had been a mistake after all!

"You—you will get Cinder back?" she said with rising expectation.

"I'm afraid that is impossible," her father answered. "The yacht has already sailed."

"Sailed!" shrieked Maggie with a wail of agony. "Father, how could you!"

She threw herself back on the bed sobbing uncontrollably.

"You must understand, dear," he said, trying out his businessman's logic on her, remaining erect where he stood. "Losing a horse is but a small sacrifice for the good of our family and our financial future."

"What could possibly be worth losing Cinder?" cried Maggie through fresh choking sobs.

"It's only a horse, child," James began again. "You shall have another. The last time I was in London a fine thoroughbred mare had given birth to a grand chestnut—the owner knew I was interested and I'm sure the foal is still available." He forced cheer into his voice, attempting to portray as much optimism as possible. "In fact, I'll write this very afternoon. It shall be your very own horse . . . and a thoroughbred to boot!"

"I don't want your old London horse!" Maggie shouted, spitting out the words. "I don't care about a thoroughbred. Cinder is the only horse I could ever care about!"

"Margaret, be reasonable," James began. His tone revealed his growing frustration. He was trying to make up for her loss. He knew she liked the horse. But she was carrying her affection for the beast beyond the limits of his tolerance.

"Cinder was the only friend I had!"

"Nonsense!" said James, his impatience bursting through the restraints of his self-control. "You have your mother and me. And of course Alastair."

Maggie's only reply was a new outburst of sobs, partially stifled in her pillow.

"Well, well," he added checking himself and trying to lighten the tension in the room with a slight chuckle, "you shall feel differently once you see the new animal. Why before you know it, you will forget the other horse ever existed!"

"I'll *never* forget Cinder," came Maggie's reply, taut with emotion.

"You will see," he said " . . . you will see."

Maggie did not respond.

James turned to leave the room. Just before the door closed behind him he heard his daughter speak again. But this time her words were cold and impersonal, sounding more like a solemn vow than an outburst of childish anger:

"And I'll never forget what you did to me today."

He hesitated briefly but did not turn around again. Then, deciding he had done all he could to rectify the situation, he closed the door behind him and continued on down the hall.

After all, he reasoned as he descended the stairs, he was master of his home and laird of the Duncan estate. What kind of man would he be if he allowed the females, not to say his very children, lord it over him? He had to do what was best for business, best for the estate, and best for him. These confounded vixens! Now Margaret was beginning to act just like Atlanta, taking it into their heads they could dictate what he should do. He had done the right thing, James was sure of that. Browhurst was no small man to have given such a magnificent favor. He wouldn't forget. Yes . . . they would all thank him one day for his shrewd foresight.

Maggie did not leave the room for the rest of the afternoon or evening. Atlanta had some food sent up, but it remained untouched on the bureau.

10

The Passing of Childhood

❈

DIGORY STRETCHED TALL and rubbed the soreness from his lower back. He was glad for the onset of warm weather, but even the long sunny days would not keep away advancing age.

"Weel, the Lord be praised," he rasped as he hoisted the saddle to the workbench in front of him. "I'll soon be wi' Ye, I reckon."

He stooped down, picked up a dirty rag, scooped a handful of a brown, oily substance from a tin, and began to rub it into the leather. Others used what they called saddle soap, but Digory swore by the concoction handed down to him by his father. The smell was strong, and it browned the hands that used it for at least three days. But the half dozen or so native Scottish ingredients moistened even the toughest leather and preserved it as nothing else could. Digory had done it so many times he scarcely gave the oily rubbing down of one more saddle a second thought—especially today, when his mind was occupied with his young mistress. He had laid eyes on her only once or twice in the three weeks since Cinder's departure, and then only at a distance. She had not ventured near him or the stable in all that time. The somber atmosphere throughout the estate made clear to everyone, servants and family alike, that something had snapped inside the once cheerful girl—everyone, that is, with the possible exception of her father. Digory had not seen her speak to anyone in all that time, but had only seen her walking slowly about, without apparent purpose, with a glazed expression of empty distance in her eyes. The redness from her tears was gone; replaced by a steely resolve never to let herself be hurt like that again. Digory prayed for her morning and night, fearful that James's selfishness might scar his own relationship with Maggie and cause her to shut him out as she had everyone else.

So engrossed was the groom in his mingled thoughts and prayers for his near fourteen-year-old friend that Maggie entered the stable unnoticed. The soft dirt floor sprinkled with sawdust muted her footfalls, and she approached without being heard. An aromatic blend of hay and feed, with an occasional whiff of manure from the pit in back, added to the special atmosphere of the place. On this particular morning the streams of sunlight pierced the cracks in the eastern wall of the barn, and millions of brilliant motes danced in the narrow shafts of sun. Here and there the snort of a horse could be heard, but most were still busily engaged with the breakfast Digory had given them earlier.

"Hello, Digory," said Maggie quietly as she approached.

He looked up from his work, and the trace of a smile parted his lips. If he was startled by her sudden appearance, he gave no sign of it.

"Mornin', to ye, lassie," he said. His voice sounded as normal as he could make it and did not betray the surge of joy he felt in seeing the girl once more in the stable. "Can I be saddlin' up a horse fer ye?"

"No, not today. Thank you."

She hadn't intended to ride. Even the thought of sitting astride a horse again evoked memories too painful to be exhumed. She just wanted to be in the stable again, to breathe in the sweet fragrances and hear the gentle stomping and scuffling and snorting of the horses in their stalls. Even the steady drone of flies somehow soothed her spirit. And to be near Digory again. She knew—whether they spoke openly of it or not—that he understood what the past weeks had been like for her.

Maggie wandered slowly from one end of the stable to the other, rekindling her fondness for the place she had always loved so dearly, reaching in occasionally to pat one of the horses that glanced up toward her. Digory went on with his work, saying nothing. She was quiet, even detached and withdrawn. Her voice rang with—he couldn't be sure exactly—a new degree of independence. Or was it a form of maturity? Had these past three weeks aged her beyond a mere twenty days? Indeed, Digory could see hiding beneath her eyes a new appearance—was it the look of dawning womanhood? But as quickly as the change appeared and the old man thought he had grasped hold of it, suddenly it was gone, retreating once more below the surface features of childhood, awaiting its time. Still her face wore the pained expression of undeserved hurt; for had she not been betrayed by one she had trusted and to whom she had given all?

He watched her noiselessly as she explored again all the old familiar crannies of the stable, fiddling with the equipment, kicking against the burlap bags of feed, as if she were discovering new relationships with the stuff with which horses were cared for all over again. One moment he was observing his youthful friend Maggie as he had so many times in the past, the next he was watching a stranger he had just met for the first time. Her face and body seemed to hover awkwardly between childhood and womanly adolescence.

Digory sensed that the events of the past three weeks had in some deep way stricken the innocence of Maggie the child, out of whose death was even now beginning to emerge Margaret, the future lady of Stonewycke.

The groom's reverie was broken as out of the corner of his eye he saw Maggie pause for a long moment in front of the black mare's stall. The horse was snorting steadily and pounding its hoof against the hay-strewn floor. A length of rope was twisting back and forth in the hay. Noticing it, Maggie realized the mare's back hoof had become tangled in the loose cord.

She opened the door and stepped in. "Take it easy," she said softly, rubbing the horse's white face. "What have you got yourself into here?" She continued murmuring gently while edging her way to the mare's hindquarters. She knew full well what a restive animal could do if approached carelessly from behind. Slowly she knelt down to loosen the rope which had by now become snarled between both hind feet.

"There, Raven . . . that's better, isn't it?" she said, running her hand along the shiny black flank. It was the first time she had been in the horse's stall, although her father had owned the mare for more than a year. Still, she knew the name of every horse on the estate.

"She's a braw one, she is," came Digory's voice behind her.

"I suppose so," Maggie replied.

"'Cept I been so busy here o' late," he continued, "that her coat's gone a bit scraggly. She could use a good currin'."

Maggie said nothing.

She had always felt so close to Digory, even wanted to be like him. She had envied the peace she had sensed within him, had hungered to feel the same way toward God as he felt. But now, everything seemed changed—even Digory. Or was she just imagining it? Withdrawing to protect her own feelings from further hurt at the hands of those she loved, she hardly realized that she had pulled back from him, too.

"Ye wouldn't be wantin' to give an old man a wee hand, would ye, lass?"

"Digory," answered Maggie flatly, "I'll never forget Cinder." Her voice quavered slightly as she spoke the name.

"An' I'll not be wantin' ye t'."

"You weren't trying to trick me into—" began Maggie with a note of mistrust clinging to her voice.

"Ye remember 'twas me that brought Cinder into the world. She was some special horse t' me too, lass, an' I'll be missin' her sore mysel'."

"I'm sorry," replied Maggie, her old tenderness toward the groom reviving momentarily. "I thought you were trying to make me forget with another horse."

"Oh, lassie, my poor lassie," he said, placing a bent and workworn hand on her shoulder. "I wouldn't be wantin' ye to forget her. She was a fine . . . such a fine horse—"

"I hate him for selling her!" interrupted Maggie, the cold, distant *woman* taking charge of her personality again.

The words stung the old man almost as if they had been directed at him. What he feared most was that bitterness would take root in her tender young heart. And clearly the shoots had already reached down to lodge deep in her memory. How could she, at her impressionable age and with feelings so delicate, understand that only forgiveness could provide the healing balm—not only to rectify her relationship with her father, but also to cleanse that agony of loss within her own heart?

"Lassie," Digory began slowly, realizing his mere words could never bring healing in themselves, "when ye try t' punish others when they wrong ye, weel . . . ye're more than likely the only one who'll be hurt."

"But I've already been hurt," she said cynically.

"Ay, but not so much as ye will be when ye strike back wi' hatred."

"He deserves it!"

"Maybe 'tis so. Only the Lord knows. An' 'tis true that ye didna deserve what he did t' ye. But t' hate him only heaps wrong upon wrong."

"It's all I've got left," she replied bitterly.

"'Tis only one way t' heal the hurts ye don't deserve, child, an' it comes from yer own heart, an' God in it. To begin wi', it has almost nothin' t' do with yer father an' what he's done t' ye."

"I don't understand you, Digory."

"Forgiveness is a sorely complex thing," said Digory as a perplexed wrinkle added itself to his already creased brow. "I don't understan' all aboot it mysel'. But I do know it begins when ye open yer heart first t' God's love."

"How could I ever forgive him?" said Maggie, growing hostile once more. "He's off in London—he probably doesn't care at all, doesn't even remember."

"I doobt that's true, lassie. Ye never ken what kind o' pain people are carryin' aroun'—even men like yer father. Seein' them wi' God's eyes, that's the beginnin' o' true forgiveness. But time will tell," Digory replied.

"You may be right," Maggie said. "But right now I can't forgive him . . . I won't!" She spoke the words through clenched teeth as if to give even more force to her resolve.

Time will tell many things, Digory thought mournfully, as he uttered a silent prayer that it would also help mend Maggie's wounded and resentful heart.

"Now, Maggie," he went on, trying with a positive voice to divert her attention, "this poor horse hae been sorely neglected. An' I'm too old t' gi' her the workout she needs. She'll gi' ye a good ride."

"Perhaps . . . well, maybe I could," replied Maggie slowly. "After being all tangled in that rope, it would probably help her to feel better."

"I'm sure o' that, lass!"

Together Digory and Maggie saddled the mare known as Raven. She did seem anxious to get out of the confinement of her stall, and Maggie's anticipation rose at the prospect of being out in the countryside once again. She was soon astride the silky black mare, and in her blue frock with her red curls falling about her shoulders, she looked, Digory thought, just like a figure from a picture book.

With a crisp click of her tongue, Maggie urged the horse forward in a slow, uncertain canter. But within a few strides the enthusiasm she had been suppressing gained the upper hand and she dug her heels into the animal's flanks, and Raven glided quickly into a full gallop. She barely slowed as they passed through the great iron gates leading away from the grounds.

Digory's brown face broke into a grin. It not only pleased him to see horse and rider enjoying themselves, but he knew that a victory—however small—had just been won. The bitterness toward her father might take some time to mend: she had been devastated by his action and the results would not quickly or easily disappear. But at least one obstacle had been overcome on the road toward healing—she had turned her eyes away from herself long enough to once again enjoy God's creation. It was a small, but necessary, beginning.

"She'll be doin' fine," he murmured. "May take some time, but He'll see her o'er this thing."

The bairn is growin' up, he thought. *Why, t' see her from this distance, one might already mistake her for a grown woman, the grand lady of Stonewycke she is destined t' become.*

11

The Birthday Celebration

❋

A WARM BREEZE swept over Stonewycke from the south. Perhaps it portended rain, but for the moment it resulted in an invigorating late-summer's evening.

The light wind carried the full fragrance of the foothills, where the heather had only recently exploded into brilliant purple bloom. The spring of 1863 had been unusually wet, bringing rains well into the summer months, and the trees and fields were still green and luscious.

Some of the guests, having traveled great distances, had already been on the estate one or two days. Those just arriving by carriage and coach from Inverness, Fraserburgh, Aberdeen, and even Dundee took full, sweet draughts of the pure northern air before entering the great house where the rugged highland landscape gave way to the influences of London.

Inside, Atlanta's efforts at adornment were evident. The ballroom floor shone as it had never shone before, and the grand crystal chandelier sparkled. The servants had worked for days preparing the mansion for this particular day; now they scurried about, carrying away hats and coats, serving beverages and hors d'oeuvres and caring for the other hundred details that inevitably were part of such a gathering.

Atlanta stood at the foot of the stairs in an elegant brown velvet-and-taffeta gown, greeting the new arrivals. Though her hand was cool, her smile was pleasant and she spoke a personal word of welcome to each who passed her stately and gracious form—every inch the marchioness she was.

But this was not her evening; it was Maggie's. This was the long-awaited day to celebrate the coming out of the young lady who would one day assume her mother's mantle and carry the Ramsey blood and the Duncan name into the future. That Alastair also bore the name, she hardly considered. The line of the blood was what mattered most to Atlanta.

She had to remind herself again that Maggie was now seventeen years old—a woman, almost. How difficult it was to concede entirely to her daughter's maturity. The guests, when they saw her, would no doubt exclaim that young Margaret was truly a woman. But Atlanta could still make out the faint shadow of the little girl about her. Something in her mothering instinct clung to that part of Maggie which receded further into the distance with each passing day. Atlanta knew how difficult womanhood could be, and she desperately wanted to protect Maggie from the heartache she herself had known. She had hoped to celebrate

Maggie's seventeenth birthday with only a quiet family gathering. But Maggie had insisted on the party.

"In the ballroom." Her words had been emphatic. "And I will stay up until the very last guest leaves!"

Therewith Atlanta proceeded to plan for her daughter a festive event that would not soon be forgotten by any who attended. She invited barons and earls, lords and ladies, from throughout Scotland and several from as far away as London. If her only daughter must become a woman, then let all of British society behold what a grand lady she was.

"Sorry to have deserted you like that, my dear," James's voice broke into Atlanta's reverie. But she only barely heard it above the din of the guests and the orchestra. "Byron Falkirk cornered me," James went on to explain, "and I only this moment got away."

"I would have thought you could refrain from business—on this day, at least," Atlanta replied. Her words were terse, and for a brief second her smile faltered.

"I intended to," he began coolly, but before he could say anything further he was interrupted by a new arrival. "Ah, Lord Cultain. How very good to see you! And Lady Cultain, you do look lovely this evening."

James lifted the woman's plump hand to his lips and kissed it lightly.

A casual observer would scarcely have detected the tension between host and hostess, so cleverly did they masquerade their feelings, so skillfully did they play their respective roles, greeting the guests warmly and graciously.

"Where is Margaret?" James asked when there was a lull.

"She'll be down soon," Atlanta answered.

"Planning to make a grand entrance, is she?" said James with a chuckle.

Before Atlanta could answer, another arrival diverted James's attention. A solitary young man approached them; he was tall and angular, and to all appearances between twenty and twenty-five. He carried himself well, moving through the crowd as if he were accustomed to commanding respect. When he reached his hostess, he took her hand and kissed it with a grace far exceeding his years. He gave a slight bow to James and asked after his health.

"Never better, George," James answered. Then turning to Atlanta, he added, "Atlanta, you remember Falkirk's son, don't you?"

"Of course," Atlanta replied, her smile firmly in place. Had she been totally truthful, she would have had to beg his indulgence for a slight lapse in her memory, for he had been a mere child when she saw him last, and she would never have recognized him. She had to admit that he had grown into quite a dashing figure of a man. "But you were away in London for some time, were you not?"

"Yes, I was, my lady," he replied with a gleam in his eye Atlanta could not quite identify. "But I am residing once again at Kairn, reacquainting myself with the workings of the estate."

"The high-society life of the south too much for you, eh, George?" burst in James with an attempt at wit.

"I wouldn't say that, Mr. Duncan. The fashionable London season is not without its allure, I must say. I still visit the south from time to time."

"To see the young women there, no doubt," added James with a sly grin. Young Falkirk rejoined with a laugh but said nothing.

"Then you are planning to remain in Scotland?" asked Atlanta.

"Yes, my lady. How could one stay away from our bonny homeland for long?"

"And we hope," James added, patting the young man on the back, "that we shall be seeing more of you, George."

"I will look forward to that," he answered.

Before the words were fully out of his mouth, a hush descended over the crowd and all eyes instinctively turned to the top of the stairway. The face of the young gentleman from the neighboring estate of Kairn looked upward as well; first astonishment, then a broad smile broke out across his countenance when his eyes reached their object.

Maggie had been waiting days . . . weeks, for this moment.

Now as she stood on the landing, every eye riveted to where she stood, her stomach quivered and her lips suddenly felt very dry. She tried to smile, then took a tentative step forward and began her descent.

The guests were evidently stunned by the young heiress of Stonewycke. Her shimmering silk gown reflected the pink of the heather in full bloom. The fitted bodice, studded with pearls, outlined every curve of her small but shapely figure. Around her neck hung a single strand of pearls, creamy and lustrous like her skin. Her auburn tresses fell to the middle of her back, adorned with sprigs of heather and baby's breath.

Ignoring the trembling of her knees beneath her, she made her way slowly down the stairs. Halfway down a voice called, "Bravo!" Then followed a chorus of encouraging words and praises which at length erupted into a round of applause. By the time she reached the last step, Maggie's faintheartedness had vanished. She glanced toward her mother, who returned her smile and reached out to give her hand a heartening squeeze. This was her day, and she now had no reason to believe it would not be everything she had hoped.

From his vantagepoint near the foot of the stair, George Falkirk had already begun to reconsider his earlier estimation of the evening's entertainment. He had come to Stonewycke principally as a courtesy to his father, and because he needed a base from which to reestablish his own position and reputation with respect to acquaintances in the area. True, he was not lord of Kairn yet. But it certainly never hurt to plan early with an eye toward such eventualities. He knew his father had been shrewdly courting the Laird of Stonewycke. Though the older Falkirk had been subtle about it, George was no fool. His father had designs of his own, and he was well aware that a marriage uniting the two estates had been discussed by the two older men.

George was sufficiently a traditionalist to recognize his duty. He would accede willingly to whatever his father arranged for him—even if he never laid eyes on Margaret Duncan ahead of time. He would do it, for the estate, for his own claim on the future. Whatever his commitments in Scotland, he always had a bonny lass or two awaiting him in London. But now, as he looked upon the lovely figure descending the stairway, he had to admit to himself that duty need not always prove odious.

Moving past her mother and father, Maggie's face was drawn to his, for it was not a countenance a young girl could easily miss. Falkirk smiled and offered a suave bow. Maggie returned his smile, then swept past him into the ballroom.

George Falkirk, however, was not one to stand back waiting for an engraved invitation. In two quick strides he was at her side.

My lady," he said, stopping her with a hand on her arm, then bowing deeply, "I would count myself the most fortunate of men if you would honor me with the first dance."

"But I don't even know you!" Maggie protested, the hint of a coy smile playing at the corners of her lips.

"I am George Falkirk, son of the Lord of Kairn. You are a picture of loveliness this evening, my lady. And if you will but grant my request, I will be the most blessed of men."

"Then how can I possibly refuse you?" Maggie replied, extending her hand with another smile and a curtsey. He took her offering gently, and led her to the middle of the dance floor.

The orchestra, as if awaiting their cue from the handsome couple, immediately struck up a rousing Strauss ländler. George reached firmly around Maggie's waist with his right hand, took her right in his left, and led forward, much to the delight of the onlookers. His sure steps and authoritative lead relaxed Maggie as she followed his experienced motion, and she smiled up at him. Together they flowed with the music as if they had been dancing with one another for years.

Before long other couples joined in and the ballroom soon became a swirling palette of shimmering color, music, and movement. A waltz followed, again by the Viennese Strauss, and again Maggie found herself in the arms of George Falkirk. Not to be outdone, a number of other eligible young bachelors made their way forward to contest for her attentions. Waltz followed waltz, with now and then another ländler or a polka, and Maggie whirled back and forth between Falkirk and several other handsome gentlemen in turn. She had dreamed of this day since the day she was nine and had only been able to glimpse the grand ball from afar.

"A toast to our guest of honor!" cried a voice as the last notes of a waltz faded to an echo in the great hall.

Glasses were lifted toward Maggie amid scattered toasts and cheers.

"Good show, Duncan!" said someone in James's direction.

"Lord Duncan," cried out another, "a dance with your daughter!"

"Splendid idea!" James laughed. "Though I've scarcely been able to get near her all night with all these young bucks vying for her."

"Come on, James," urged another. "Let us see the turn of your feet!"

Enjoying the limelight and smiling broadly, James set down his drink, sought his daughter, took her hand, and led her to the middle of the dance floor.

Maggie complied, and not even the most trained observer could have detected the sudden coolness of her demeanor or the stiffness in her bearing as she followed her father through the strains of the perfunctory waltz. Even James himself, hardly adept at reading his daughter's innermost feelings, never knew that the smile which she forced to remain on her lips could never substitute for the smile that had drained out of her eyes.

When the dance was over James released her to revel in the congratulatory praises of his friends while Maggie, the color of her cheeks and the sparkle in her eyes returning, was swept in another direction by a troop of waiting admirers.

An hour later, out of breath and a little dizzy, she came to stop near the refreshment table. Three young men scurried off to fetch her a glass of punch at once, but it was Atlanta's hand instead that held out a glass to her.

"Mother," Maggie laughed, "isn't it grand!"

"I'm glad you are enjoying yourself," Atlanta replied. She was truly proud of her daughter. Not only was she lovely, she also carried herself as her station demanded. She walked, spoke, even danced with growing confidence. Atlanta had to remind herself that only three years earlier Maggie had cared for little but horses.

"I'll never forget this, Mother," Maggie was saying. "Thank you for making it happen!" Impulsively she kissed her mother on the cheek.

"You're welcome, dear," replied Atlanta. Her voice was soft, and in the excitement of her surroundings Maggie did not detect the slight quiver in her words. Atlanta was struggling to check the tears which had risen dangerously near the surface.

Just then one of the young men returned with a glass of punch which he eagerly shoved in front of her.

She held up the glass Atlanta had given her and smiled as if to say, "Sorry . . . I already have one."

The boy glanced around sheepishly, feeling more embarrassment than the slight awkwardness would account for, until Maggie laughed good-naturedly. She grabbed the glass from his hand, turned and handed both glasses to her mother, took his hand, and led him out to the dance floor once again.

12

Harsh Words

※

FOR TWO DAYS it rained. But Maggie's lingering exhilaration following the party in her honor could hardly be dampened by a few thundershowers.

And neither could her father's. James glanced out the library window into the gloomy mass of gray, but the sullen atmosphere outside did not for a moment quence his spirits. He re-read the letter in his hand, and smiled again. Then he laughed outright.

Even in his most wildly optimistic moments he could not have foretold that in a mere two years' time the brewery would have created such a substantial revenue. Yet the figures before him did not lie. Nor did the cheque which had been tucked in with the letter. Though the sum represented but a pittance to a man like Lord Browhurst, James knew he would be well pleased. It would add a stamp of credibility to this venture. The other investors, including Byron Falkirk, would now look upon James in an elevated light and view his future proposals with greater respect.

Not that Falkirk's respect mattered that greatly to James, but he had placed his family's future on the line to persuade his neighbor from Kairn to throw in the final sum needed to turn the brewery into a reality. At the time the elder Falkirk was still reeling from the loss of Braenock Ridge, the purchase of which—for reasons James could never quite grasp—he had set his heart upon. Why Falkirk had been so determined to obtain that barren stretch of moor, seemingly at any price, Duncan couldn't guess.

In any case, once Atlanta stepped in to kill all further negotiations between them, James had found it necessary to do some hasty talking before Falkirk would concede to part with his money. How James despised having to curry the favor of the old buffoon! But sometimes such condescension was necessary in the world of business and finance. *And Falkirk will whistle another tune now*, James thought with smug satisfaction. "He'll be crawling to me," he said to himself, "begging to be let in on my next deal."

The door opened and Atlanta walked into the room. "Excuse me," she said, stopping abruptly. "I didn't mean to disturb you," she added, preparing to retreat.

"No, I was hoping to see you anyway," he replied quickly. "Do come in."

Atlanta walked forward to the desk where James sat and stood stiffly with her hands folded in front of her.

"I wanted to share with you my good fortune," James continued, making only a modest attempt to hide his arrogance. "I have just received the annual report from the brewery, and I'm happy to say it has produced a tidy little sum."

"Is that so?" said Atlanta, preparing to leave again.

"Will you never be able to admit that I made the right move?" he asked with a mocking conceit in his voice.

Atlanta remained motionless.

"But the real problem," James went on, "is that I did it without a single farthing of yours, without so much as one pound from the estate. That's it, isn't it? You know your power over me is slipping. Yet in the end it will be *my* brewery and *my* other ventures which will keep Stonewycke intact!"

"Stonewycke will stand without the assistance of your enterprises and speculations!"

"Open your eyes, Atlanta," James returned. "Can't you see what is happening to landowners these days? They are no longer able to hide behind the sanctity of their vast acreage or their titles or their ancestral birthrights."

"Hiding! Is that what you call it?"

"That's exactly what you would choose to do. We would have sold Braenock for a handsome profit. But no. You place more value on your own sentimentalities than on the course of the future."

"It's more than sentimentality. You know what this land means to me."

"I know that judicious investments would be a wiser way to put our resources to work than for them to just sit idle while the heather grows and our debts pile up."

"The land means more than your financial undertakings."

"But it's accomplishing nothing!" retorted James, his blood now running hot. Why couldn't she see the benefits of progress and shrewd investments?

"Will you never understand, James? The land, and the people who work it—*they* are the resources of Stonewycke. Do you actually think selling parcels here and there, or building a profitable brewery, is going to replace all that?"

"It has already generated a considerable income, that much is clear to anyone with eyes to see," he returned, waving the cheque he still held in front of her face. "*This*," he went on with considerable weight to his tone, "is far more dependable than a scraggly assortment of dirt crofters and poor sheepherders."

"It's not the money, is it?" Atlanta said with derision in her voice. "It's England, it's rubbing shoulders with that Duke of wherever-he's-from. It's powerful men like Browhurst whose egos you massage to get at their purse-strings. It's Parliament . . . making a name for yourself in the south. That's what it's really all about, isn't it?"

"Oh, Atlanta, you are so naive! Look around. Those who fail to broaden their base are certain to go bankrupt. If you want to keep Stonewycke in one piece, you must make concessions. That's how the game is played."

"But that has little to do with it, keeping Stonewycke in one piece. Whom do you think you're fooling?"

"I'm trying to fool no one. I'm simply taking the measures of a prudent businessman."

"You would parcel off Stonewycke and sell the fragments to the highest bidder if it would advance your career!"

"I care about this estate too, my dear."

"Ha! It's all for yourself—your own success! That's all you care about!" Atlanta accused.

"My political aspirations are none of your affair!" James shot back angrily. "If you were half the wife you ought to have been, you would try to support me rather than destroy me!"

Atlanta sucked in a sharp breath. As much as she despised James in this moment, perhaps the words were too close to the truth for her to respond with anything but contrition. Yet that was a step she was unprepared to take.

Without another word, she turned on her heel and left the room.

13
The Estate of Kairn

TWO HOURS LATER James Duncan stood in the center of the study at the house of Kairn. The estate, not nearly so sizable but more sprawling, bordered Stonewycke to the south.

The room was one of the most masculine James had ever seen. Swords and paintings of battles and various war mementos made up the greater part of the room's decor. The study seemed especially out of place when contrasted with the rest of the house, which was garishly decorated in spindly French Provincial and delicate lace.

Byron Falkirk had done a fifteen-year military stint in India before malaria forced him home. As officer in charge of a military hospital, Falkirk had been sent to India in 1850, stationed at Delhi. Four years later, when the War of the Crimea broke out and England was drawn into the conflict, he had initially been disappointed to have been removed so far from the center of action. When reports reached him of the terrible sufferings of the English army, however, he began to congratulate himself on his good fortune.

The Crimean War was hardly over when England had to face another conflict, this time closer to Falkirk's post. Without warning in 1857 the sepoy mutiny broke out. But Byron Falkirk's blessed life had continued, for only a year before he had been reassigned to the newly annexed district of the Punjab to oversee a new medical facility. When the rebellion broke out, the first march of the natives was to Delhi where many English soldiers and their families were massacred. But the uprising did not spread so far west as the Punjab, and by the end of the following year it had been completely stamped out.

Though he had seen no action, Falkirk managed to puff up his importance somewhat by encouraging those to whom he related his heroic exploits "on the front" to think of him as occupying a position closer to the smell of gunpowder than had actually been the case. He did little to discourage the conclusions they might draw from his suggestive comments, enjoying, perhaps, the sense of heroism—realities clouded by the passage of time—when returning to his native land from a war-torn battle across the sea. How he longed to have been sent home with a live battle wound (a small one, granted) rather than suffering from the indignity of a vile eastern malady.

Upon his return to Scotland, Falkirk brought with him a ten-year accumulation of Indian culture and "war mementos," as he called them—everything in the room chosen to further the impression that Byron Falkirk had indeed been one of the realm's finest military men. All his paraphernalia had to be crowded into this single room, for Lady Falkirk would have none of it in any other part of her home. She despised India, and perhaps for good reason. It had not been a pleasant experience for her. In the beginning she had tried to endure it for her husband's sake. But after two years she simply could take no more and returned home. If Falkirk could have obtained a transfer back to the Isles, he never tried. As hard-pressed for medical help as the army in Turkey was, he feared they might send him there instead. Better let well enough alone.

By the time hostilities were over in Turkey, the sepoy uprising was about to begin, and a transfer at that time would have been out of the question. Finally, in 1858, malaria forced him to accept early retirement and make the voyage home. James could not help wondering, however, if even India—with malaria—might not be preferable to the overbearing Lady Falkirk. But now that the man was here, his only retreat into the world he had once loved was this single room where, alone, he could bask in past glories, envisioning himself a valiant leader of men.

James stood in front of the flagstone hearth admiring the magnificent tiger skin which hung above it; Falkirk returned to his guest, carrying a tray laden with a decanter of brandy and matching glasses.

"Ah, India!" the host remarked dreamily. "A dirty, uncivilized land—how I loved it!" Here he paused to enjoy his wit. "Rotten malaria! Still get bouts of it now and then—bloody business."

James shook his head in appropriate gesture.

"Did I ever tell you how I managed to get out of Delhi just before the insurgents from Meerut arrived? Was lucky to escape with my life! They were hell-bent to put one of their old Mongo descendants on the throne and kill every bloody one of us. Right over there," he went on, gesturing to a sideboard where a number of knives and daggers lay, "is the dirk I was wearing when—"

He stopped abruptly.

"—but I'm certain you didn't come all this way to hear of my exploits during the war years."

Byron Falkirk stood some six inches taller than James, but he was thin to the point of being gaunt. In his earlier years he had been muscular and even a bit handsome, though timid. One of his favorite stories, considerably embellished and in which actual truth did not seem to be a necessary ingredient to his enjoyment of the telling, involved two Indian sisters—daughters of a Marharish—who nearly killed each other over him. But malaria and inactivity since returning home had quickly reduced him to a shadow of his former self.

"Well, perhaps another time," James replied, sipping his brandy. It was the worst brandy he had ever tasted and he could not help but pity Falkirk who, despite their wealth—inherited, not saved from officer's salary—could not persuade his wife to buy better.

"Yes," said Falkirk, swallowing the unfinished portion of his tale. He glanced up at the tiger on the wall and remembered the moment he had shot it. "Now *that* is a grand story to tell!" he said aloud, almost in spite of himself. "Out in the jungle stalking the big game, what a time to remember! The animal charged toward us in full flight. I raised my rifle to my shoulder just in time to get off two shots . . ."

His voice trailed off as the memory of the incident grew clearer. *Wasn't it the native guide who brought down the animal?* he recalled. *Yes, that was it. He had been the one to put a bullet through his head from about ten paces. Cagy fellow, that guide. Wouldn't take anything less than two pounds to keep quiet and tell the story my way. Yes,* he thought, *quite a story!*

Jarring himself loose from his reverie, he turned to James and said, "You were saying you had good news?"

James pulled the envelope from his breast-pocket. "This may interest you," he said with a broad smile.

Falkirk slowly opened the envelope. He gazed at it a moment, obviously baffled by the contents. What did this have to do with the Punjab? He seemed momentarily bewildered, lost between past and present. Faint recognition began slowly to spread across his face, a glimmer of mild interest.

"Our brewery," James prompted.

"Ah yes . . . of course! The brewery," said Falkirk, his face lighting. "I'm afraid I'd forgotten. It seems to have done well."

James held his tongue and clasped his hands behind him so tightly that the nails dug into his skin. *The man is exasperating!* he thought. *Perhaps the malaria has advanced the onset of senility.*

"Lord Duncan," said a feminine voice, entering the room behind him. "I had heard you were visiting. How good to see you!" She extended her hand, which James took politely.

"Lady Falkirk," he replied, "you look well, as always."

Agnes Falkirk was as short, round, and robust as her husband was the complete opposite. Her gray hair was mounded atop her head in a futile attempt to convey the impression of height. Even with her upright carriage and hair piled high, she only reached her husband's shoulder. But she more than accommodated for her diminutive stature with her irrepressible vitality.

Her small black eyes immediately caught sight of the envelope in her husband's hand and squinted imperceptibly. Falkirk handed her the envelope.

"James rode over to bring us this," he said.

Lady Falkirk scrutinized the contents and the cheque with a far keener display of interest than her husband had shown.

"This is indeed a pleasant surprise," she remarked. "Yes, this is very impressive. It's doing well, then?"

"Of course," James answered, eager at last for the opportunity to boast of his business acumen. "After a mere two years of operation, I would say extremely well. That is why I decided to deliver this cheque in person—I thought our joint venture deserved a bit of a toast."

"It is apparent you possess keen business sense, Lord Duncan," the lady said in measured tones. It was just the sort of thing James wanted to hear. "Now, let me refill your glass."

"I still have plenty," replied James. "Don't trouble yourself."

"No trouble," she insisted, taking the crystal decanter from its tray and pouring another ounce of brandy into his glass, then her husband's. She took none herself. Smiling, James lifted his glass toward Falkirk, then raised the glass to his lips once more.

"It occurs to me," his hostess went on, "that we have another happy event to toast as well."

James lowered his glass slightly and replied with a puzzled expression.

"Certainly you haven't forgotten the little compact we made on the day we agreed to invest in your brewery? A *bargain* I believe is what we called it at the time . . . concerning your daughter."

"Oh, that," replied James. "Certainly not. I haven't forgotten."

"I presume we may still anticipate . . ." Her voice trailed off in unspoken implication. Though polite and steady, a hard glint could be detected deep in her eyes which said far more than her words could convey.

"In fact, I saw your son the other night," James went on.

"And . . . ?"

"I gave my word," James replied tersely.

"Yes, of course," the lady said. "And I would never disparage the integrity of a promise from the lips of one so highly respected as yourself. But I have been thinking it might be well for us to think in terms of a more tangible evidence of our mutual accord. A public betrothal, perhaps—"

"The girl is a mere child!"

"The young lady that graced the ballroom of Stonewycke two nights past is certainly no child," Agnes Falkirk returned with a cunning laugh. "One look at her will tell you that."

"Neither a book nor a child may be judged by its cover," James answered. "She is but seventeen—your son would be more content if we waited two or three years."

"I was barely sixteen when I married," the lady replied, as if sealing the argument against further rebuttal.

James was tempted to inquire how that fact had affected the Falkirks' marriage, but he checked the remark. He had to control himself. He needed the Falkirks' money more than they needed the prestige an alliance with his daughter would bring. He had to refrain from alienating this lady. Soothing words of conciliation were needed. He could manage Agnes Falkirk if only he didn't cause her to lose her temper.

"Come now, Agnes," Falkirk interceded. "These things do take time. Young George has been home only a short while. Waiting can never hurt a marriage."

"Waiting has its limits," she replied. "And I have mine. Just make sure, Lord Duncan, that you don't protract this so-called period of waiting too long and force me to take action on my own. I would greatly prefer, for the sake of appearances, that the announcement came from you two men. But I will not be put off forever."

James said nothing, but nodded as if to give an affirmation to her words, and she turned and left the room.

Returning to Stonewycke later in the afternoon, James wondered if he did not feel greater apprehension concerning Atlanta than Lady Falkirk. Of course, she need never know the full details. If she ever so much as suspected that he had traded away the hand of their daughter in exchange for his brewery, he had little doubt that she would resort to murder. But he feared she would guess it one day. And while he could manage her for the most part, if she ever bent the full power of her position against him, he knew she could make life unendurable for him. He had little fear of standing up to her. He had done so before, and would do so again. But he knew what he had conceived that day in the secretive study at Kairn with the man and woman he had just left was a despicable act in her eyes, well deserving of Atlanta's most violent wrath.

To his advantage, at least George Falkirk was a handsome young man, desired by a good many women. He stood to gain a fine inheritance from his father, appeared to have a good turn for business, and would no doubt double his wealth before he was forty. There was also an uncle somewhere in the family, childless and an earl, who could one day further his wealth and even bring him a title to accompany the vast holdings in and about Strathy which would be his. Surely Margaret would have no complaints. The girl would have to be promised eventually. At least he had chosen for her a respectable match.

If only he could fare so well for Alastair. But that would be a trifle more tricky, with the complications of the estate and the inheritance. It would be he, after all, who would carry on the Duncan name, if nothing else. Atlanta and all her talk of the Ramsey clan could not change the fact that the Ramsey name was gone forever from Stonewycke, however much of its precious blood flowed through the veins of their high-strung daughter. It was his now. The north of Scotland would one day look to the Duncan name for its future—and to him, James Duncan, to lead the way.

Let Atlanta rave. What he had done was not so sinister. Didn't they seem made for one another on the dance floor the other night? If the brewery hadn't been involved, Maggie might easily have chosen young Falkirk herself.

14

Request from the South

✦

HAD THE LETTER not first fallen into Atlanta's hands, James would have torn it up, and that would have been the end of it.

But even though she had seen it and appeared favorably disposed to the idea, he could hardly have been less concerned himself. The boy's problems were none of his worry, and he wasn't about to begin charity work at this stage of life.

His uncle's family had shunned him in the years since his father's death—never a word, never an invitation. Not that he would have lowered himself to pay his high-browed London relatives a visit—but how ironic it was that now, in their time of need, they would turn to him! The presumption of requesting a month's respite for their wayward son in *his* home! Anger burned red behind James's eyes. How could Atlanta understand the humiliation he had suffered at their hands, or the despair of his father when his own brother had turned his back at his hour of need?

"I'll not hear another word about it!" James said with finality. Though dinner had barely begun, the mood around the table had already grown tense.

"But, James," Atlanta continued in a tone more appealing than was her custom, "the lad has nothing to do with what his grandfather may have done. I'm sure he bears no animosity toward you."

"It is enough that he is Landsbury's grandson!"

"The poor child has problems."

"And when were you struck with this sudden round of compassion?" asked James caustically.

Atlanta winced, but held her composure. "I only thought we might be able to help him," she said.

"He can burn in hell for all I care!"

"James—the children!"

Alastair stabbed diligently at his potato, pretending not to hear but, in fact, hanging on every word. Maggie squirmed uncomfortably in her seat, quickly losing whatever appetite she may have had.

"It is well the children know about the Earl of Landsbury." He spoke the words as if about to proceed with a dissertation on the evils of sin. "It is well they know that though the Earl and his descendants bear the name of Duncan, they shall never have any part with us."

"But the boy—"

"A common troublemaker!" James resounded. "Just what I would expect such a family to produce. His parents would have us believe a visit to the country would have a calming effect on him."

"Scotland is more peaceful than London."

"Rubbish! They only want to burden us with him, to get him out of their way. *You* read it," he said, waving the letter toward his wife in a mocking gesture. "Surely you can see the fine hand of deceit between the lines. And what do you care, anyway? You've always despised my side of the family."

Atlanta shrugged. "I don't know," she said with a sigh. "I suppose I thought a change of pace might do us all some good."

"A change of pace! The boy's been an embarrassment to them. I've heard of Theodore Duncan's escapades. Believe me, we don't want his sort upsetting our sleepy little village of Port Strathy."

"Of course, that is a good point," Atlanta replied, conceding at last to her husband's point of view. "I can see what you mean."

"Well," said James, his ruffled feathers settling back into place.

"You are certainly within your rights to turn the lad away. Your cousin no doubt expects that very thing. And I would guess he might even be somewhat relieved not to find himself beholden to you."

James stared at her with a puzzled expression.

Pretending to take no notice, Atlanta continued, "I expect it would gall him to have to thank you for your help."

The light gradually dawned in James's countenance and a cunning smile spread over his lips. *Atlanta and I may have our differences*, he thought to himself, *but I have to admire the woman*. She could be every bit as crafty as any man he had known. And he had to admit—he hadn't considered that particular aspect of the earl's request. It would be a sweet revenge, indeed, to see him grovel in appreciation. Not to mention the glowing reports of the wealth and prestige of Stonewycke and its laird that the lad would undoubtedly send back to the Earl of Landsbury.

What could have sparked Atlanta's sudden wave of charity he had no idea. Some scheme of her own, no doubt. But aside from that, her words rang with good sense.

"Ah, Atlanta, my dear, you are a clever one," he replied with a smug grin. "I don't know what possible interest you could have in our acceptance of cousin Roderick's request. But you are absolutely right. I would, of course, be loathe to put Roderick in the position of being indebted to me." He paused for a moment, then went on with a wily twinkle in his eye, "Still, how can I turn away the young man when we may be his only hope for redemption. Send a reply off immediately to Landsbury telling him his son is more than welcome for a visit here. Yes, more than welcome."

Later that evening, alone in his cluttered cubicle, James pondered further the merits of allowing the visit of his cousin's son. What would a month or two hurt? With Alastair going off to school in a few weeks, Atlanta's hours were bound to become idle. She would have all the more time to meddle in his affairs, a prospect she would undoubtedly greet with relish. And she should be kept occupied as he orchestrated the union of their daughter with Falkirk's son. He had to devise a plan to marshall events to bring the two young people together without any suspicion of design.

Atlanta had to be kept out of the way—and young Theodore Duncan would provide the perfect and fortuitous solution to that problem. If all reports were true about the boy, Atlanta would indeed have her hands full. The second son of the Earl of Landsbury was rumored to be a reckless gambler, and reports charged him with heavy drinking as well. With a chuckle James recalled one story he had heard about a brawl in a certain disreputable public house which had supposedly left the young rogue with a nasty scar across his forehead. He had been hauled before the magistrate several times, but his father's name and reputation had preceded him, and justice was not to be had in the court. At twenty years of age, Theodore Ian Duncan had certainly made his mark in the world, albeit a notorious one.

Despite the unsettled feeling of discomfort in the pit of his stomach, James considered this a most providential turn of events after all. Young Duncan would stir things up enough to make a marriage proposal seem the blessed event he intended it to be. *It couldn't be more perfect*, he resolved.

His chair creaked as James leaned back and began to consider how he should go about arranging a second meeting between Margaret and young Falkirk.

15
The House on Braenock Ridge

SHE FEARED SHE had not made this ride often enough, and now that she was returning to Braenock Ridge, she hoped she wasn't too late. Prompting Maggie's decision was a chance rumor that Mrs. Mackinaw's health was failing quickly. The very next day she rode out to Braenock Ridge.

There were no trees about the place, only some scraggly shrubs, rocks and stones, and a brawling stream some fifty feet behind the house, tumbling on its way from the mountains to the south into the valley, and on into the Lindow.

The small cottage stood in the middle of the barren moorland, built with an outside wall of rough stone and lime, with another wall of turf within, lined here and there with fir planks. The roof was thatched and a huge pile of cut peat stood against one wall as fuel for the fire which burned constantly inside. On two sides of the cottage stood a half-cultivated area where a small field of oats, a large square of potatoes, and several stocks of cabbage and kale struggled to survive under the harsh conditions. Mrs. Mackinaw had tended the garden until a few weeks ago, while her husband and Stevie had charge of the sheep in the fields. Now the sheep would have to rely solely on the boy for shepherding, and the father would have to coax what food he could for them from the obstinate soil. He was growing old too, but had not yet begun to feel the burden of age as had his wife.

When she had taken to bed, her husband and Stevie had set themselves to pull what quantities of heather they could from the surrounding hills. Binding the heather into tight bunches they squeezed them close together and boxed them in the board frames of a bed. The top made a dense surface, which, when covered with two or three blankets, made a far more luxurious bed for prolonged use than the usual ones of oat chaff. Upon this handmade bed of love Maggie found the old woman, lying against the southern wall of the cottage, which was always the warmest. Her nearly transparent skin stretched thinly over her high cheekbones and large eye sockets. She had been rather a large woman at one time, and the thickness of her bones accentuated her present frailty all the more. The once bright and lovely eyes, now covered with sagging lids, were a rheumy brown.

Maggie knelt down on the earthen floor beside her and grasped one of the woman's thin hands. The bones seemed to groan silently at the very touch, but she managed a tremulous smile as she gazed up into her visitor's face.

"Weel, my leddy," she said, her voice straining over the words, "what brings ye t' oor humble cottage?"

"I heard you were ill, Mrs. Mackinaw," Maggie replied.

"Nothin' fer ye t' be concerned aboot, jist a bit o' trouble that comes wi' age, ye know." Even as she said the words, however, a spasm of pain assailed her which Maggie could see reflected in her eyes.

"I've brought you a few things," Maggie said, trying to make her voice sound cheerful. "There's some chamomile—it'll help you rest. And Nellie was baking fresh bread as I was about to leave, so she made me wait long enough to bring you a loaf."

"'Tis kind an' neighborly o' ye, an' Nellie too—she's a sweet girl," Mrs. Mackinaw replied. "But I'm feared I'll na be much company fer ye, lass."

"Don't worry. You just rest while I brew you a nice pot of chamomile tea."

The woman nodded wordlessly and closed her eyes. Maggie rose and walked to the hearth—little more than a hole in the middle of the earthen kitchen floor surrounded by a ring of flat stones. A peat fire burned in the hole. There was no chimney, only a small hole at the peak of the roof. The smoke rose into the thatch, keeping the cottage very warm and dry, but also very sooty. Finding the shortest route to the outer air, the smoke filtered through the many cracks and fissures in the walls and roof. Over the fire a pot hung on a heavy iron tripod, along with hooks to hold various other implements for the fire. The peat had burned low and Maggie set to work with the poker and a small handbellows which hung nearby. Within a few minutes a satisfactory blaze appeared. She filled the kettle from a bucket of what appeared to be clean water and then hung it from one of the hooks over the fire.

As she waited for the water to boil, Maggie took stock of the cottage. It was hardly a wonder that Bess Mackinaw was so ill and appeared twenty years older than her fifty-three years. The cottage was composed of a single large room and, though stout, its walls could hardly insulate against the severities of the weather of the place. The floor was hard and cold, and the single window emitted little light. Maggie knew what the icy winter wind was like as it blew down from the snow-covered slopes of Kincairnmor over the foothills now covered with heather, and across the moor that had come to be known as Braenock. This tiny hovel could hardly keep out the chill of a summer evening, much less provide substantial shelter from that frozen blast. Yet the Mackinaws had lived in this very house for years beyond Maggie's time.

She sat down on a stool near the fire. What kind of a world was it where such poverty could exist within sight of the grandeur of the Castle Stonewycke? Was there nothing that could be done . . . should be done? If she were ever in the position to exercise control over the affairs of the estate, she would certainly have some decent homes built for these people. Were they not the charge of her family? Did they not work the land and pay their due to the estate from the proceeds? Why should they have to feel the bite of the cold without even the small comfort of a rug at their feet?

The face of her father rose before her mind's eye, and her cheeks grew red as a judgment against him. For the past three years, since the day she sat weeping in the empty stall over the loss of Cinder, Maggie's bitterness toward him had mounted. He was a wealthy man, growing wealthier by the day with his brewery and other "investments," as he called them. Why hadn't some of his good fortune gone toward improving the lot of his tenants?

Unaware that the ills of the land existed long before James Duncan's time, she considered him a villain, blaming her father for every grievance she could heap upon him. *He could change all this*, she thought angrily, *but he cares about no one but himself.* He had demonstrated that again and again. He had given away her horse, and now he cared nothing that one of his own people lay in poverty, sick and dying.

All at once this surge of enmity was interrupted by the sound of boiling water. She rose quickly and looked around for a thick rag with which to grasp the iron handle of the kettle. When she had removed it from the fire she scooped two large spoonfuls of the dried chamomile leaves into the water. It steeped a few minutes, then she poured the steaming tea into a coarse wooden mug.

As Maggie finished the process she was suddenly struck by the ludicrousness of waking the poor woman to give her a tea designed to help her rest. But Bess Mackinaw's feeble voice drew Maggie immediately to the bedside.

"Ye're still here, are ye, lass?" she said. "Ye are a patient child."

"I made some tea."

"I been a-watchin' ye. Ye're at home in a poor woman's cottage, though ye come from a great mansion. 'Tis t' yer credit, child."

Maggie smiled in gratitude at the words. "Won't you have some tea?" she offered.

"'Tis somethin' o' a difficulty t' take anythin' by mouth . . ."

"I'll help." Maggie knelt on the floor and gently eased her hand under the woman's frail gray head and lifted it slightly. She raised the cup to her lips and the woman took a sip or two. Then she motioned for Maggie to lay her back down.

"I'm reminded o' somethin' I read jist the other day in my Book," she said. Maggie fancied that her voice sounded a little stronger already. "'Fer I was an hungred, an' ye gave me meat,'" she continued. "'I was thirsty, an' ye gave me drink. Naked, an' ye clothed me, sick, an' ye visited me. Fer inasmuch as ye hae done it unto one o' the least o' these my brethren, ye hae done it unto me.' Sweet words, don't ye think, my leddy? An' true. An' ye hae been wonderful t' me an' I'll never ferget it. An' neither will oor Lord—ye are truly His servant, my leddy."

She stopped and sighed deeply. "Oh, my! My auld husban' says I shouldna talk so much—it wears a body oot." She smiled at Maggie and gave a weak chuckle.

Uncomfortable at her words, Maggie turned away for a moment. She felt compassion for Bess Mackinaw, but she could hardly admit to being the Lord's servant when she knew so little about Him. Her former friendship with Digory, who had so openly talked to her about God and His ways, now seemed far in the past and remote. Then, quickly, she looked back and returned Bess's smile.

Recalling the incident in later years, the mere memory of poor Mrs. Mackinaw would bring tears to Maggie's eyes. Her brave attempt at laughter amidst the hopelessness of her life, and the woman's kindly words toward her when her own father could have eliminated their poverty, or certainly, at the very least made it easier to bear, revealed to her the fibre from which Bess Mackinaw was made. A quality of spirit was demonstrated to the young girl that she had seen in only one other, her old friend, Digory.

"You deserve far more than I could ever hope to give," Maggie murmured, wondering if Mrs. Mackinaw had fallen asleep again.

"I only wish—" the woman began again. ". . . but I reckon I'll ken soon enough. My reward be na too far away, I think."

"You mustn't say such a thing," Maggie answered, suddenly afraid of the death which the old woman so took for granted. "A good rest and a proper diet will see you as good as new. I'll see that some food is brought out."

"Save yer strength, lass. I'll ne'er be good as new." Again she attempted a laugh. "Not till I see my Lord face t' face . . ."

For a brief moment her mottled countenance shone. "Dyin' be na such a bad thing when there's the hope o' a better life on the other side. An' when folks get t' a certain age, lass, they begin t' sense when their time is comin'."

A better life . . .

Maggie pondered the words. Was that what this woman's faith was all about? And yet here was she, Maggie Duncan, an heiress, who had a *better life* by all appearances, yet she still felt a deep emptiness within. What gave Bess

Mackinaw her strength, her hope, her *better life* in the midst of this destitution all around her? Was Digory's God her God? Was their faith in Him what set her apart from them?

But she could no longer continue to fill her mind with such questions. How could she admit that alongside Digory and Bess, she was empty of life's greater meaning? Having made the initial admission, she might further have to ask *why*, to wrench open a part of her heart that even after three years she kept tightly shut against all intruders—including herself.

"I hope the Lord'll fergive me fer sayin'," Bess went on, unaware of Maggie's thoughts, "but I'll sorely miss auld Hector, an' little Stevie too. Although he's na so little anymore. He'll be a help t' his daddy. I only wish his brothers hadna had t' go—but it couldna be helped . . ."

There had been two older Mackinaw sons, but they had migrated years ago, one to London and the other to America. A sister had died during an outbreak of cholera and another girl, the youngest, had died in childbirth. Drummond had returned to visit twice from London. But Mrs. Mackinaw had not seen her eldest son Drew since he sailed from Port Strathy to Aberdeen, thence to London and finally New York, over twelve years earlier. Eking out a scant farmer's living with his family in America, Drew Mackinaw had improved his lot over what it would have been in Scotland, but saving money for a visit to his homeland was out of the question.

Bess Mackinaw endured a multitude of sufferings before this present illness had come upon her, yet she never appeared disheartened. Notwithstanding that she had lived most of her days in a ramshackle hovel on the bare edge of existence, she always had a cheerful word to offer. "Weel, lass," Maggie remembered hearing her say once long ago, "it may be a desolate moor, cold in the winter an' dry in the summer, but leastways ye always know what t' be expectin'." As a youngster Maggie had laughed; almost a joke it had seemed at the time, followed as it was by Bess's hearty and infectious laughter. *But it is hardly humorous now*, Maggie thought, tears welling up in her eyes. Quickly she brushed them away, but not before the older woman had noticed.

"Dinna be pityin' me, lass," she said. "I hae no pity on mysel'—I hae had a good life wi' a fine man who couldna hae loved me more, an' fine sons fer me t' love t' carry on after me. A woman couldna ask fer one thing more . . ."

Love, Maggie reflected. Was that it? Was that the well from which Bess drew her hope, her meaning in life?

The ancient voice began to weaken toward the end of the touching speech and finally disintegrated into a paroxysm of coughing. Flecks of dark blood appeared at the corners of Bess's mouth.

"An' now, lass, if ye dinna mind," she went on, when the coughing had subsided, "I'd like t' see my menfolk, if ye could find them fer me."

"Of course," said Maggie, "and then I'd best be going."

"Oh no, lass, ye mustn't leave jist yet," interposed Bess. "Much as I hate t' impose on the laird's daughter t' run erran's fer me, 'tis so nice t' hae another one o' oor kind arou', ye know, what wi' my own daughters gone. God's been good t' me, lass, an' given me what strength I need, but it's still a sore trial t' lose two daughters."

"I'm sorry."

"Na, na, we'll hae no sorriness aboot here. We're told t' be thankful in all things, an' mostly I am. 'Tis jist nice t' hae ye here, that's all. Especially that I hae not been able t' get t' town or t' the kirk on Sundays fer some months now. Sometimes it jist gets lonely oot here. Now, if ye'll get my man fer me, I'd be obliged even more t' ye."

Maggie found Hector Mackinaw shambling about the byre, a make-shift affair attached to the west wall of the cottage to house the family's single cow and what few chickens they managed to keep. The dejection on the man's face could find no relief even in the many tasks to which he was attending about the croft. As Maggie approached, the color drained from his ruddy cheeks, making him appear all the more wretched.

"She wants to see you, Mr. Mackinaw," said Maggie.

He dropped the pail in his hand and hurried out of the byre with scarcely a word. He stopped abruptly in the doorway and glanced back. "Would ye mind fetchin' Stevie?" he asked. "He's oot in the pasture."

Maggie found Stevie climbing among the rocky ledges of Braenock Ridge, so named for its position between the valley and the rising hills to the east. She called his name, but he did not heed her. A large granite boulder spanned a small cleft in the earth, and Stevie was struggling to lower himself down. Drawing closer, Maggie saw that the boulder was supported by two even larger stones, creating a rude bridge over the narrow opening between the two upright ones. Then she realized why he had ignored her. A lamb was tangled in a patch of thistles growing between the two large rocks. Stevie climbed down from the top one, smashed away the brush as best he could in the narrow opening, and at last retrieved the lamb. Seeing Maggie watching him from above, he called out.

"Take the lamb, will ye, my leddy?" He held it up with his arms outstretched.

Maggie knelt down, and reaching as far as she was able, barely managed to lay hold of the tiny animal.

"Grab a handful o' its wool an' hold on tight," Stevie called.

Maggie obeyed.

"Okay, my leddy, now pull it up t' ye."

Maggie did so, and in a second or two the lamb was returned to the safety of the tableland.

Stevie scrambled up the huge rocks the way he had come and was soon at Maggie's side. "Thank ye," he said. "This be some fearsome trap fer the sheep when they wander too close. Kind o' a little ravine here an' they hae not the sense t' stay back from the edge. There's lots o' other rocks close by all aboot an' it attracts them t' the place. I used t' play here, hidin' in amongst the huge rocks an' that little door between them. But 'tis all growed o'er wi' brambles now."

He was still the same Stevie Maggie had always known, only taller and more gangly as manhood tugged more firmly at his body with each passing year. The effusion of red hair remained the same. His friendly grin revealed two chipped front teeth.

"Weel," he said, "ye be some far from home, an' wi' no horse aboot either."

"I came to visit your mother," Maggie replied. "She's not doing well, is she?"

Stevie only nodded.

"She sent me out here to get you—"

The broad grin on the boy's face had suddenly disappeared.

"Then the time has come," he said numbly.

"No," replied Maggie abruptly, searching for some word of comfort and refusing to believe the look on his face. "She . . . she only wanted to see you. She—"

Yet suddenly, in the very poverty of her words, Maggie sensed that perhaps Stevie knew better than she why his mother had summoned him.

Stevie ran toward the cottage and Maggie followed as quickly as she could. She was not as accustomed to the exertion as he, nor was she used to the feelings roused within her by this family crisis into which she had inadvertently stumbled. Somehow she sensed that, because of her place, her station, she should *do* something to help ease their pain. Yet events were moving beyond her control, and she was powerless to stay forces that only the heavens truly understood.

Stevie well outdistanced Maggie to the cottage. When she arrived some moments later, out of breath, she entered quietly. Father and son were kneeling by the bed of heather. Hector's frame was rigid, his stone face revealing little of the emotions raging inside. But tears streamed down fourteen-year-old Stevie's smudged and dirty cheeks.

"Ye'll get along jist fine." The feeble voice sounded distant, as if it had already been enveloped in mists from the other side. "I love the two o' ye, my two *men,* w' all my heart."

"Oh, Lord!" burst out Hector, "strengthen my woman!"

"Strengthen me t' die wi' yer grace, Lord," prayed his wife.

"Amen," whispered Hector in a faint voice, seeming for the first time to accept the reality of what was taking place.

"I'm countin' on ye, Stevie," she went on, stretching out a frail hand and placing it on top of the weeping boy's head, "t' help yer daddy. An' the both o' ye keep the hope in yer heart. An' give my love t' Drummond an' t' Drew when ye write them next. We'll be together one day . . . one day soon. An' know when ye dream aboot me, I'm that very moment thinkin' aboot ye wi' all the love in my heart from somewhere above."

Then noticing Maggie standing just inside the door, the aged face brightened. She extended her hand and motioned Maggie forward.

". . . an' ye too, lass. Keep the hope o' the Lord in yer heart . . . always—"

Her head fell back on the pillow.

Stevie burst into a sobbing wail. Hector rose up on his knees and stretched his great arms around the withered body.

"I'm . . . I'm goin'—" Maggie could barely make out the scarcely audible words, "—goin' where there's no more—Hector . . . Stevie—"

The final word remained unfinished as her final breath slowly departed from her body in one long sigh. As the earthly light faded away, the look of troubled suffering on her face gradually gave way to an expression of radiant contentment, and Bess Mackinaw was gone, folded in the loving arms of husband and son.

16

The Heather Hills

MAGGIE HAD NEVER seen death before.

She had always pictured it as a frightful, hideous thing. Yet Bess Mackinaw seemed but to slip into sleep—the most peaceful sleep she had ever known. As she rode away from the ridge, Maggie could not erase from her mind the faint smile on the thin, blue, wrinkled lips.

Man and boy had both wept openly. Even stoic Hector Mackinaw could not contain his grief, though he made scarcely a sound as his tears flowed and his broad shoulders shook with convulsive agony. Maggie felt like an intruder, her presence shattering the intense exclusiveness of the awful moment. Without a word she slipped from the cottage and within moments was astride Raven, charging over the moor at a full gallop. She had no destination, she only had to ride.

By now she had crossed the wide moor and was racing up the expansive hills of heather that rose higher and higher toward the south and east. Where the estate of Stonewycke ended and that of Kairn began, Maggie neither knew nor cared. Tears streamed down her face, and on she sped.

These were new emotions erupting within her, and she did not know how to respond to them. Her mind reeled with conflicting thoughts and unanswered questions. She barely knew the woman; why was she suddenly flung into such depths of despair by her death? Was it because of the two men Bess was leaving behind? Was it because her life had been so hard and her death seemingly so friendless and forlorn?

A new sensation welled up in Maggie—*anger*. Anger that people should have to live like the Mackinaws. No one at Stonewycke had caught the cholera. No one in the castle was exposed to the harsh winter weather. They were not forced from their homes because of a scanty harvest when there was not sufficient food to go around. Where was the justice in the world? Why did some have so much and others have so little? How could the woman have received her so graciously when the Mackinaws had every right to be bitter over their treatment by the laird of Stonewycke, the laird of their little plot of ground on the most desolate corner of the magnificent estate? Why didn't they hate their masters? How could they open their hearts with such love toward her? Was she not a Duncan as well?

Digory had spoken of God's love. Even old Bess Mackinaw had talked about the Lord as if He were her friend. But where was that love? What had He done for her?

Maggie slowed Raven to a walk, her tears spent for the moment. She stopped, dismounted, and sat down on the ground. This had always been one of her favorite rides. Behind her Braenock Ridge spread out on each side and the valley opened up in the distance, stretching to the sea. She looked around from her high vantage point halfway up the steadily steepening foothills. It was a good land, a rich land despite the many areas too stony and arid to grow anything. When the hills burst into their brilliant shades of pink and purple late in the summer, as they were now, she wished the whole earth was covered with heather. Carefully Maggie plucked a sprig of the wiry plant and held it up to the sunlight.

Scottish heather . . . the distinctive feature of her beloved homeland.

Yet, she thought, the melancholy of her former mood returning, *what do purple hillsides of heather and lush green rolling valleys really mean when old women can die in such poverty? The heather is beautiful,* she mused, *but the life of the poor is often ugly.*

How can they occupy the same land? Why does God allow it? How can God allow a man like my father to control it?

The instant her father's face came to mind, all Maggie's confusion and frustration came into focus as an indictment against him.

I hate him! she thought. *He killed her. Not the cold winters, not the sickness—he killed her, just like he did Cinder! God . . . I hate him!*

She threw the heather from her hand, but even as she did so, Digory's words of so long ago rushed back into her memory. She had tried to block them out, but they had remained: "When ye try to punish others when they wrong ye, ye're the only one who'll be hurt. To hate him only heaps wrong upon wrong. Forgiveness begins when ye open yer head first to God's love."

"I won't forgive him!" she stormed aloud. "I won't! Not for Cinder, not for Bess Mackinaw!"

She jumped on Raven's back, turned, and headed back, down the hill toward the cottage. In the midst of her irrational thinking she realized that if her father had been responsible for the old woman's death, she must do what she could for the husband and son.

Back at the cottage Maggie rode up slowly, dismounted, and quietly went inside. Stevie was not there: Hector still knelt at the beside.

"Is there anything I can do?" Maggie asked softly.

Slowly the stricken man rose and turned. "There's naught that any can be doin' now," he said.

"If I could . . . well, perhaps I should send someone out—to help," said Maggie in a faltering voice, struggling in her youthful way to atone for the loss.

"That's kind o' ye, miss."

The door opened and Stevie reentered the house, his red eyes swollen but temporarily dry. He walked to his father, and the large man enfolded him in his arms and pressed the boy tightly to his chest. Once again Stevie burst into a torrent of fresh tears.

Embarrassed at the touching scene, again Maggie turned to go.

"Thank ye, mem," said Hector. "Thank ye fer yer visit—an' fer stayin' here wi' us fer a spell."

"I wish I could do more," replied Maggie.

"Maybe ye could jist tell the beadle aboot poor Bess so he can make the arrangements. We'll be wantin' a proper funeral, ye know—she deserved that."

"Don't worry. I'll take care of it."

"Thank ye kindly, mem," Hector returned. "We'd be honored fer ye t' attend, if ye are o' mind t'."

"Of course," Maggie said. "I will be there."

She turned, left the humble cottage, and began the ride home to Stonewycke.

17

The Funeral

THE DAY OF the funeral the sky hung low, gray and overcast.

A fine mist drizzled down as Maggie walked to the stable to saddle Raven. She had told no one in the house where she was bound.

As the Mackinaws' cottage was several miles from the village and unsuitable for such an occasion, the mourners gathered at the church for the service instead. Tying her horse, Maggie walked in and sat down, hoping to avoid any undue attention. Every eye, however, turned toward her for an uncomfortable instant. The fact that a member of the laird's family was in attendance at a crofter's funeral could hardly go unnoticed. No doubt it would be talked about for days.

A moment later a man in shirtsleeves, dressed—like all those present—in black, appeared at the door of a side room to the main hall.

"If any o' ye wants t' see the corpse, now's the time," he said to the company, "afore I fasten down the lid."

No one responded to his offer and the carpenter turned and reentered the room. A few moments later the solitary sound of a hammer could be heard, driving home the last few nails into the covering of the coffin. Throughout the proceedings all present sat in utter silence. Hector Mackinaw and Stevie occupied the front row, composed and still.

Most of the parish seemed to be in attendance, for though the Mackinaws were likely the poorest members, they were nonetheless loved. Bess was always ready to help a neighbor in need, and she was not forgotten on this, the final day of her earthly pilgrimage. As Maggie sat awkwardly in the midst of so many unfamiliar faces, she knew the tears being shed around her were genuine, the grief deeply felt.

At length Hugh Downly, the parish minister, arrived, walked to the front of the church with somber gait, opened his Bible, and began the service. He read Isaiah 55 and the second chapter of 1 John, reminding his listeners that they were Bess Mackinaw's favorite passages. As Maggie listened to the scriptures, the words seemed descriptive of the saintly woman and of the love for the Lord which was in her heart. They sounded warm and inviting, and Maggie found herself wishing that she understood them better:

Incline your ear and come unto me: hear, and your soul shall live. . . . Seek ye the Lord while he may be found, call ye upon him while he is near. . . . For as the heavens are higher than the earth, so are my ways higher than your ways, and my thoughts than your thoughts. For as the rain cometh down, and the snow from heaven, and returneth not thither, but watereth the earth, and maketh it bring forth and bud, that it may give seed to the sower, and bread to the eater: so shall my words be that goeth forth out of my mouth: it shall not return unto me void, but it shall accomplish that which I please, and it shall prosper in the thing whereto I sent it. For ye shall go out with joy, and be led forth with peace: the mountains and the hills shall break forth before you into singing, and all the trees of the field shall clap their hands. Instead of the thorn shall come up the fir tree, and instead of the brier shall come up the myrtle tree. . . .

As the reading of the Word ended and the traditional prayers of the Scottish funeral ceremony began, Maggie could not help thinking that the mountains and the hills of the scriptures were the mountains of snow and hills of heather upon which Bess Mackinaw had lived her life. Were those same hills and mountains, at this very moment, rejoicing in song at the triumphant entering into life of Bess Mackinaw?

Hardly had the prayer drawn to a close before the sound of trampling feet in the adjoining room bore witness that one Simon Cready, the undertaker, and his assistants had already hoisted the coffin from the table and were trooping out to the horse-drawn hearse which stood waiting. The company gradually rose from their seats, withdrew from the room, watched in silence as the box was loaded, and then fell in behind it and began to move in an irregular procession toward the graveyard, some three hundred yards distant. Maggie followed on foot at the back of the column.

The sonorous tone of the beadle's bell deepened the hush of the crowd as they walked along, the nodding plumes atop the hearse silently waving in the gentle breeze. On the way they were joined by several who had not been in attendance inside, until at last they arrived at the final resting place of the dead. Just before they reached their destination, a few patches of blue peeked out from behind the clouds, and through one shot a beam of sunlight, as if to proclaim: "She for whom you grieve is not dead but alive! Cast off your burdensome cloaks of mourning, for behold the light of her *morning* has come!"

But few of the dour faces took notice, and within moments the patch of light was clouded over again.

The beadle opened the gate to the cemetery and the procession filed in, finally coming to a stop beside the freshly dug grave. The graveside ceremony was brief. With hats clutched in hand, all heads bent downward in one final parting look as the humble box was lowered into the earth. Tears streamed down Maggie's face as the first spadeful of dirt slammed against the lid of the pine coffin with an echoless thud. She wiped her eyes, bit her lip firmly, and remained stoically in place. And though the wind blew and the drizzle grew steadily heavier, not a soul moved from the spot until the hands of Bess Mackinaw's friends and neighbors, assisting with spade and shovel, heaped the sheltering earth high over the grave.

As soon as the labor was ended, the gathering began to retreat from the graveside, not in formal recessional as they had come, but randomly, each in his own direction.

At the gate Maggie heard one of the farmers remark, "Weel, auld Jake MacKale'll be free t' go t' his reward noo."

"Aye," replied another. "An' let's hope poor Bess has a good long watch."

"My Bess'll na be waitin' by no gate," interposed Hector Mackinaw's trembling voice. "She's sittin' this very minute with her Lord an' she'll hae no part in yer superstitions o' one deceased keepin' watch o'er the yard till the next burial!"

"We meant no harm, Hector," returned the first. "We was only sayin' we hope there na be another death in oor parts anytime soon."

"Let none deny that she's sittin' there this very minute," went on Mackinaw, heedless of the apology. "The Book says so plainly. 'Tisn't that so, Mr. Downly?"

"Why—ah—yes," replied the Reverend who, walking behind the others, had been paying little attention to the gist of their conversation. His was a quiet nature who could speak easily in front of his Sunday morning congregation with the sure aid of a sheaf of notes. But in the more intimate relations of man to man, his was not a nature that found ease expressing itself. "Let me see," he went on, "the exact passage is—"

"Today shalt thou be with me in paradise," interrupted Stevie's voice, sounding almost manly in its tone, as if he meant to verify that his mother's deathbed faith in him was well placed. "I was readin' it this very mornin'."

"Yes—ah—that is . . . of course," said Downly, plainly relieved. "Our Lord himself said those words to the thief who—ah—asked for mercy." Inside he was comforted to know that he had, at least, found the text for his sermon the following Sunday when he would be much better equipped to expound on this important truth to his congregation.

Returning toward the church, Maggie politely declined an invitation to attend the gathering following the funeral, and instead mounted Raven and slowly made her way home.

The images of the faces she had seen remained vivid in her mind. Even in the midst of the inevitable pain of such an occasion, she could sense a staunch strength and pride within these people: a pride in their land, in their humble dwellings, in the hard-won victories they gained over the land and the severity of the northern elements. She sensed the caring bonds of relationship which bound them together in intimate community with one another. At a birth they gathered to celebrate each the other's joy; through life they lifted strong arms and caring hands to bear one another's burdens; and now, at death, they gathered once more, this time quietly and reverently to share another's painful loss. Maggie found herself regretting her position, supposedly so far above these peasant people. Did they not, in fact, possess a quality of life which she and her family had never known?

But what would happen to Hector and Stevie now that Bess was gone? Surely they were indeed part of the community of caring; somehow they would get by. Their friends and neighbors would see to that. Yet it would not be easy for them. Bess Mackinaw was one of those persons who lent strength and support to those around her, even though it was scarcely noticed at the time. She would be greatly missed; such a void is never easy to fill. Already the haggard look in Hector Mackinaw's countenance was clearly visible. And Maggie wondered if she would ever be able to push from her mind the bitter tears Stevie had shed on the day of his mother's death. If only the two older brothers, and their families, were not so far away!

Maggie turned into the entry of Stonewycke, hardly noticing that the great iron gates stood wide open. Though preoccupied as she was, she could not help but see the unfamiliar black coach sitting in front of the stables. The horses had been unharnessed and were apparently now inside. There was not a soul to be seen about the place.

She had been so absorbed in the events surrounding Bess Mackinaw's death and the funeral that the impending arrival of her father's cousin had completely slipped her mind.

But even had she remembered, the sight of the coach would have remained a mystery. For Theodore Ian Duncan had made his appearance a week ahead of time.

18

The Guest from London

AS MAGGIE ENTERED, the house seemed inordinately quiet.

She closed the solid oak door slowly, but as it thudded shut, the echo reverberated through the hall. Certainly she had been alone in the solitary mansion on previous occasions. But with Alastair now off to school at Eton, the absence of his high-pitched voice left a strange—though welcome—emptiness. Coming from the gloomy atmosphere of the graveyard into the deserted house deepened Maggie's pensive mood.

Wondering where everyone had gone, Maggie walked to her room. All was equally cheerless there. She wandered aimlessly toward the library. Perhaps now was the time to seek out a friendly book to divert her mind from the grief of Hector and Stevie Mackinaw.

She reached the library, opened the door, and walked in. Less than five feet in front of her stood a young man before a shelf of books.

"Oh, dear!" she gasped at the sight of the stranger, stopping in mid-step. "I . . . I didn't expect anyone—you startled me!"

He glanced up, revealing little surprise. If he was in any way caught off guard at being burst in upon suddenly by such an exquisite specimen of youthful womanhood, the only hint was a slight rising of his eyebrows.

"It seems I find myself in just the opposite position," he replied in a slightly mocking tone. "I came expecting someone, but found no one."

His impertinence caught Maggie by surprise. Unsure what answer to give, whether to excuse herself or demand what he was doing in their house, she stood silently for a moment. Suddenly she became aware that his eyes reflected amusement at her discomfiture.

"I beg your pardon," Maggie sputtered, annoyed, "but what are you doing here?"

"Doing here? Why I am a guest, of course," he replied with more presumption than Maggie could well tolerate.

"I'm afraid you will have to leave until my father—"

He interrupted her with a laugh. "Of course," he said, "you have no idea who I am." He offered a graceful, if exaggerated, bow toward Maggie. "I am Ian Duncan. And I have no doubt you are Lady Margaret Duncan."

Embarrassed by her outburst, Maggie struggled to regain her composure. "You must be my father's cousin," she surmised, "but I thought your name was Theodore."

"True, but I am generally known as Ian. And I am your father's *second* cousin," he corrected pointedly.

He continued to stare toward Maggie in a most disquieting way. Although provoked by his intrusive manner, she could not help noticing that the eyes which returned her gaze were attractive, brown as chestnuts. Though of medium height, his erect posture gave the semblance of greater stature, and the cut of his tweed jerkin emphasized straight, assertively broad shoulders. He was but twenty, and his tanned face contrasted richly with the golden coloring of his hair.

"Well, Mr. Duncan," said Maggie rather formally, "perhaps I should apologize that no one was here to greet you upon your arrival."

"No need," he replied. "I am quite adept at entertaining myself."

"So I have heard," replied Maggie with a hint of sarcasm in her voice.

This time he threw his head back in a merry laugh.

"I see my reputation precedes me," he said at length. "But surely it can't be that bad?"

Her initial testiness thawing in the presence of his infectious geniality, Maggie tried to make up for her caustic remark. "Oh, no . . . not really. It's just that my father said—"

She stopped abruptly, realizing she was only making it worse.

"Oh?" he asked, the amusement never leaving his countenance. "What did your father say?"

"Nothing . . . much," Maggie replied, wishing she had never spoken.

"Please, you mustn't spare me."

"Well, if you must know," she replied finally, giving way to his cheerful insistence, "he said you were a common troublemaker."

"Oh, did he!" replied Ian with another great laugh. But as the laughter faded, something akin to a cynicism crept into the corners of his mouth. This was clearly not the first time he had been confronted with such an accusation. Just as quickly the caustic expression dissolved into another laugh. "Well, I must heartily disagree!" he went on buoyantly. "I am the second son of the Earl of Landsbury. Therefore, I am in no way *common!*"

He laughed again, and this time Maggie laughed with him.

"When did you arrive?" Maggie asked.

"Only long ago enough to unhitch my horses, find them some oats in the stable, knock on the door of the house, admit myself, look around for a soul to welcome me, and stumble through various corridors until I came upon the library, where I had been about ten minutes before you came to rescue me in my wandering."

"You drove alone?"

"My father never would, of course. But then he considers his second son a ne'er-do-well in need of the proper barnyard skills and all that. Besides, he doesn't provide me with a servant or groom of my own."

"It's too bad your arrival had to be like this."

"Never fear, my lady. I'm used to fending for myself . . . as you've no doubt also heard, eh?" he added, with eyebrow cocked.

"I'll say nothing further this time," returned Maggie with a timid smile. "I can't imagine where the servants are. Mother must have given them the afternoon off."

"No matter," said Ian.

"But you must get settled in and be shown about your new quarters."

"And I can't think of a better guide than yourself, my young cousin," said Ian with a jovial grin. "Even if you are several years my inferior, you seem equal to the task of taking care of your wild and roguish cousin from the south. Lead on!"

Not quite sure how to take his words, Maggie hesitated, then turned and led the way out of the library with Ian, smiling broadly, delighted at the prospects for amusement this young demoiselle would no doubt afford him.

Later in the evening, dinner was at best an uncomfortable affair.

James occupied the head of the table, stiff and silent. He had offered little more than the most perfunctory welcome to his guest when he and Atlanta had returned from Kairn, apparently forgetful of his earlier enthusiasm over the idea. Once he had given his approval to the visit by the boy, he considered his obligation fulfilled. He cared not whether the young malcontent carried reports back to Landsbury of his kindness and generosity—only of his wealth and power.

Atlanta made several weak attempts at conversation, mostly in the way of inquiring innocuously about Ian's life in London. But it was clear either the afternoon's ride or her visit to the neighboring estate had been unsettling, and when Ian's answers to her questions proved disconcerting, she also fell silent.

For the first time in her life Maggie found herself actually wishing Alastair was present, if for no other reason than at least to keep a chattering conversation going. The only one enjoying himself was Ian. Observant enough to note the uneasiness Maggie felt at the silence of her parents, he was yet blithe enough to relish the awkward turn of affairs. He found the entire inter-family feud senseless. He knew he could never curry James's favor, nor did he desire it. He therefore saw no reason to feel injured over his cool reception.

The moment dinner was completed, James rose and left the room without a word. Atlanta delayed long enough to appear civil and then followed, murmuring a hurried apology. Maggie and Ian sat at the table for a few moments in silence. Searching her mind for the best inroad toward conversation, Maggie was relieved when Ian at last spoke.

"Your father is quite a conversationalist, isn't he?" he said with a smile.

"I don't think he means to be rude," replied Maggie, trying to put Ian at his ease. "But he's . . ."

"Less than cordial on occasion?"

"That would not be an untrue way to phrase it," replied Maggie, recalling her own hurt at the man's words.

"I can't help but wonder why he sent me an invitation. It begins to appear he disdains me as much as he does my father."

"I think my mother may have had more of a hand in it than you realize."

"Oh?" replied Ian with a drawn-out, half-inquisitive tone.

They were interrupted that moment by Alice, the serving girl, who appeared at the door to the dining room.

"Mr. Duncan, sir," she said somewhat sheepishly. "Beggin' yer pardon, but his lairdship has requested the honor o' yer presence in the east parlor fer an after-dinner brandy—if ye would care t' join him."

"Please thank the laird for his kindness, miss," Ian replied graciously. "Tell him I will be happy to join him."

Alice turned and darted from the room. Ian rose to leave.

"I'd best not keep the man waiting," he said by way of parting remark. "Perhaps I misjudged his coolness at dinner."

"Such invitations are few and far between," said Maggie.

"Especially to kin of the Earl of Landsbury, no doubt," Ian replied.

"The family tensions. It seems they never go away."

"One could hardly be a Duncan without coming under the influence of this ridiculous feud. Rather droll, if you ask me. But then I suppose every family must have its black sheep."

"And who might *that* be?" Maggie asked, stiffening at the apparent affrontery, but more for the sake of pride in her particular branch of the family tree than for any concern about her father's reputation.

"That's a good question," Ian replied with a laugh. "I can certainly tell you who the black sheep is in *my* part of the family. As for your father's role in the larger question, I would not care to venture a guess."

"Does everything always entertain you so?" asked Maggie, not knowing how to characterize this London cousin of hers.

"Life, *my lady*," he said, stretching out the words in a facetious manner for maximum effect, "would be sheer hell if one were not able to laugh at it."

Hardly realizing he was poking fun at her with the feigned use of her title, she replied, "I've never thought of life as *that* bad."

"Ah, of course," he said, assuming even more of the merry tongue-in-cheek, "but you see, Miss Duncan, when you have lived as long as I have, and have gained the benefits of my worldly experience and wisdom, then things will take on more of their true perspective."

"I doubt I'll share your cynicism, even when I'm—"

"Twenty," he answered for her.

"Even when I'm twenty." Why Maggie was taking the side of optimism she couldn't have said, for before this day she would have considered herself as skeptical as anyone regarding the possibilities for happiness in life. Perhaps she was just making conversation. Or perhaps something in her wanted to take the opposite point of view, merely as a way to test the doubts she was afraid to voice herself.

"You'll never convince me," he replied. Briefly the edge of his voice sharpened. But just as quickly the flash of a smile supplanted the momentary peculiar look. "Good evening, *my lady*," he said, again emphasizing the title whimsically, then turned and walked toward the door.

Maggie watched him for a moment, then suddenly opened her mouth before she had a chance to think about the words. "Do . . . do you ride, Mr. Duncan?" she blurted out impulsively after him.

"I've been known to," he replied with a sly grin as he stopped. "A bit too recklessly for some."

"Stonewycke is reputed for its fine stable."

"Will I find you there?" he asked.

"On most days," Maggie replied.

"Then I shall most assuredly find my way there in the morning," he said, and closed the door behind him.

19

Ian Duncan

IAN DUNCAN HAD not wanted to come to Scotland. He had grown comfortable with his somewhat rowdy London lifestyle. Perhaps something within him needed to play the knave, although he had never considered the question. He only knew it afforded him an identity, a sense of recognition and esteem. Women smiled at him, his drinking cronies laughed at his escapades, and he was able to glean a certain satisfaction from their approval. Barely past adolescence, he never stopped to reflect on what his habits signified. Beyond an undefined sense of occasional disquiet it never dawned on him that his happy-go-lucky roguery was in reality a mask to cover the anger hidden deep within, never entered his mind that he was a youth on the run, hiding from the one person he feared most to look straight in the eye—himself. Taking refuge behind his affected rough exterior and ever-present—and occasionally chafing—sense of humor, Ian laughed his way recklessly through life, giving the impression that to him the world was a stage and he was the principal actor in its comedy of chance.

The constant activity functioned like a stimulant to an addict—the frenzied pace sustained him. Or rather, it served to prevent his having to face what he dreaded most. He would have been unable to name his fears, would have readily denied any apprehensions in life whatsoever. But in the furthest corner of his soul, where the unrecognized angst of misgiving resided, he nevertheless felt the sting of the reality upon which those fears were grounded—the rejection he had received at the hand of his father.

For Ian was, after all, only the *second* son.

Roderick Clyde Duncan, the Earl of Landsbury, was the kind of man who could focus his attentions only on one thing at a time, to the exclusion of all else. Unfortunately for Ian, the whole of his time, energy, and devotion had been lavished on his firstborn. When a second son came along, five years younger than his brother, there was little left in the way of fatherly devotion for him. By then the Earl's affections were well entrenched. A second baby boy failed to move him as his first—*his heir*—had done.

Early in life young Ian had learned that misdeeds were the only sure way to earn attention from his father. So unconsciously his actions directed themselves along an increasingly frenetic path to garner that attention any way he could. However, while certainly gaining the attention he desired, the boy found himself criticized and rejected all the more. He and his father drifted further and further apart, and by the time Ian was fourteen no mending of ways could have healed the wound on either part. Ian grew to hate his life at home and turned to the streets, where, in his laughter and toughness, he discovered an identity—albeit a disreputable one. The more he laughed, the more he drank, the more he played the part of the genial ruffian, the more he found himself accepted by those around him. True, his revelry often landed him squarely in the midst of trouble. But it was rarely serious enough to worry about. Besides, he could laugh or talk his way through most anything. And his father's wealth and position were pledges sufficient to insure him few serious difficulties with the law.

When his mother had suggested Scotland, he had laughed outright. *A change, a diversion*, she had called it. *A diversion from what?* he had asked. He needed no change.

But it did not take long before he learned he had little choice. Only a few days before, he had once again fallen into the hands of the magistrate. But this time the charges had been more serious—assaulting an officer of the Crown. He had been hauled away and locked up without so much as a routine questioning. Ian was furious. He had been driven to the act, he insisted, only when the man, himself having had one toddy too many, persisted in his coarse treatment of one of the barmaids in Ian's favorite pub. All that mattered to the authorities to whom the case was turned over, however, was that Ian had a previous history of causing trouble and that the woman was a known prostitute.

At first the earl refused to ransom his second son.

"He can sit there and rot for all I care!" he had raged to his wife. "That boy is a blot on my name. What he needs is a good stint behind bars!"

She attempted to pacify him with reason. "But what will people say?"

"The people can say what they bloody well please!"

"But it will reflect on you, dear," she went on, in a softer tone. "What will they think of you when they learn that your son is sitting in the tollbooth?"

The earl paused in his outrage and thought for a moment.

"Let me send him away for a while, out of London," she went on.

"Hmmm . . . perhaps you're right," replied the earl slowly, considering the stake of his own reputation in the decision.

"I can arrange everything," she said, her hope rising that she had at last discovered a way to mediate between father and son.

"Yes—yes," the earl continued, "that's a possibility . . . a bloody good idea, actually. Get the boy out of London, away from his carousing friends. Yes, do it. A clever idea."

"And you'll talk to the authorities?"

"Yes, of course. I'll talk to them immediately. Just get the blackguard out of town, and out of my sight, for a while. A good long while!"

The Earl had not known until it was too late that his wife intended to send the lad north to Stonewycke. When he discovered that the would-be benefactor of his renegade son was none other than his cousin James, old Landsbury was so enraged that Ian began to look more favorably on the prospect. If his father were so dead set against it, he reasoned, it must have promising possibilities. The mother had managed to keep the boy out of further difficulty until plans for the journey were set, and now here he was in the wild north—with no bright and inviting London streets beckoning to him with their evening life, no pubs, no women, no friends, no tables strewn with cards and money and ale, no sounds of laughter—no sounds *at all* after nine o'clock except that infernal chirping of crickets, the faint sound of running water from a stream outside his window, and an occasional snort from the stables. But he had always prided himself in making the best of it in any situation, and one way or another he would survive this rustic prison as he had London's worst.

His drink with James was brief, and, though cordial enough, did not altogether dispel Ian's earlier reservations concerning the man about whom he had heard all his life. Climbing the stairs to the room he had been given earlier in the day, Ian entered, walked toward the window, opened it, and peered out. All was blackness . . . and quiet. Deathly quiet!

He reassured himself that he missed the streets of the city. But a disquiet had been stealing over him; it had begun during dinner. He couldn't identify it, but whatever it was he would brush it aside with a laugh. He would never let this sort of life *get to him*. He couldn't. He wouldn't permit it.

He rose again and paced about the room. He opened the window again and listened. The faint rustle of the trees could be heard gently moving in the breeze. The stream below sang its way toward the sea. He sucked in a deep draught of the night air, and swore under his breath.

He threw the window shut with a crash—angered at the peacefulness of the still night air, angered at the crickets, angered at that tomfool horse who couldn't sleep and insisted on keeping the stable awake—and returned to his bed where he threw himself down.

A diversion . . . *a change*—his mother's words came back to him. He hadn't wanted to come in the first place. He had been coerced into it by circumstances. Why the very thought of this place *moving* him was . . . well, it was downright preposterous!

20

A Country Ride

❊

A GOOD NIGHT'S sleep banished for the time Ian's discomfort with his new surroundings. The up-and-down nature of his emotional constitution always enabled him to bounce back from any difficulty with a smile and a cheery face. His optimistic personality managed to find possibilities in whatever circumstances it found itself. Thus the damp chill of the following dawn found him in the stable outfitted in leather jerkin and breeches, along with fine black riding boots.

The place seemed deserted. The only sounds present were the horsey noises coming from behind the walls of the stalls. In the light of morning the stomping and snorting and munching wasn't nearly so upsetting. Actually, they were nice sounds, with a hint of the musical in them. Looking about, Ian realized the girl had certainly not been exaggerating about the fine stock. He drew a deep breath, sucking in the fresh, crisp, hearty air, blended in sweet and fragrant mixture with the odors of hay, oats, straw, manure, and horseflesh.

Ian couldn't remember the last time he had been up so early. But he had to admit, it felt positively refreshing. All that worry last night was over nothing. *Yes,* he thought, *a fine collection of thoroughbreds. Perhaps this out-of-the-way little Scottish burgh has possibilities after all.*

Just then he heard the shuffling of feet, turned, and beheld the ancient visage of Digory.

"Ye must be none other than the laird's cousin," the old man said, studying the youth as best he could in one hasty glance.

"At your service," Ian replied with a friendly extension of his hand.

A good handshake, Digory thought. *Firm and confident.* But he'd heard too much about this youngster not to remain a little on his guard.

"I was told I would be welcome to a ride," Ian said.

"If the weather holds up," replied Digory noncommittally. He then turned and began to busy himself with the feeding of the horses. In the midst of what had always been his domain, his natural caution asserted itself in the presence of a stranger.

Ian walked slowly along the rows of stalls and finally came to a halt in front of Raven's quarters. As he stretched out his hand to rub the animal's silky white muzzle, Digory's voice interrupted him—

"That'll be Lady Margaret's horse."

"Oh," said Ian, aware that Digory had been keeping a watchful eye on his movements. He found the old groom's apparent protectiveness of the girl humorous. "Can you recommend another for me, then?" he added with the trace of a smile.

Realizing his comment had been construed as impertinence, Digory returned the smile, and softening said, "Hoots! Dinna mind me. I'm only the auld groom. 'Tis hardly my place t' tell ye what horse t' ride. But I wouldna want ye t' try this one; that is, except ye'd talked t' Lady Margaret hersel', fer she's partial t' Raven here."

"Raven, eh?" replied Ian, then backed away and continued down the row of stalls. He stopped and eyed the groom curiously for a moment as Digory entered Raven's cell with a bucket of feed. He had known household servants like this. They'd been around so long and outlived so many different masters that many times they wielded more power than the masters themselves. He knew it was not wise to cross their paths. He had no idea if such was the case with this guardian of the stables of Stonewycke. But he was a man worth watching, nonetheless.

Yes, Ian thought, *this might be an interesting place after all.*

"How about this chestnut?" he asked at length. He had progressed down three or four bays until his eye had caught the chestnut whose mane and tail were ebony black.

"'Tis a fine horse," Digory replied, proud of the selection of animals and well-pleased that the lad could pick out a mount equal to Raven. "Ye've made yersel' a braw choice. Let me saddle her up fer ye!"

"Thank you kindly," said Ian, caught off his guard by the warming charm of this unique old groom. "What's her name?"

"Maukin," Digory answered as he found the saddle.

"An odd name," Ian remarked, "if I comprehend my Scottish aright."

Another voice answered his remark.

"You'll see when you ride her, Mr. Duncan," said Maggie, entering the stables behind him, "why we named her a *hare*. For she is fast. If you are in the least rusty, you might consider another mount."

Ian noted the twinkle in her eye and the coquettish set of her lips. Not a trace of the previous afternoon's occasional antagonism was left in her voice. A night's sleep had apparently put to rest some of her doubts, as well as his own. A second look revealed that Maggie had donned a fine riding habit in the anticipation of an outing with their houseguest. Her woolen skirt was the red and black Ramsey tartan, the black leather jacket fit her delicate waist snugly, and a black silk bonnet, tied about her neck with a ribbon of black velvet, stood out in rich contrast to her auburn tresses and creamy skin. Ian could hardly help but take a second look. *Indeed*, he thought again, *an interesting place after all.*

"I've never been known to back away from a challenge," he laughed merrily. He chose to ignore the fact that he was indeed a trifle rusty, for carriage and cab had been his usual mode of transportation of late in the city, though he tended to drive his carriage as fast as safety permitted, and often faster.

"A ride suits my mood today," said Maggie. "I could show you our lovely countryside."

"Thank you, my lady," Ian returned with a twinkle in his own eye, and casting a playful wink in Digory's direction. "I should be honored. Once again . . . lead on, fair maiden!"

They rode west and south as a gentle breeze played at their backs off the sea and a sky dotted with only a few patches of blue hung overhead. But the gloomy late-summer day could not diminish the brilliance of the blooming heather on the rolling hills nor the gay spirits of the youth who had never seen the likes of such rustic landscape in his life.

Still carrying the trace of a self-satisfied grin on his face, Ian followed Maggie along, smug in the thought that he was humoring this inexperienced country miss with his presence. But he was quite unprepared for the gradual changes which crept over him as he rode. Slowly the same thoughts which had so disturbed him the night before returned. But today they were not nearly so fearsome. The true face of Nature rarely made an appearance on London's streets and was never noticed by Ian Duncan when it did. But as they rode, the heady fragrances of heather, earth, wild grasses, trees, with just a hint of salt spray from the sea, mingled together, filling him with an intoxication of a sort with which he was quite unfamiliar. A lark winged overhead and his ears caught the sound of its silvery voice. *Was this the first time he had ever in his twenty years heard a bird sing?* How could it be? At least it was the first time he remembered the striking and simple beauty of the sound. He glanced around himself with pleasure. As far as his eye could see in all directions there was not another human being to be found. The two of them rode in a solitude he had never experienced, always shied away from. Today, however, the earth, the sky—it all seemed so big . . . so overwhelming . . . so majestic!

What was happening to him? The countryside of peasant farmers had always been something he had scorned. The bustle of the city was his lifeblood. What, then, was this strange feeling welling up from the depths, the sense of joyful lightheartedness, of jubilant exhilaration in the midst of this remote wilderness? What was this strange tingling within, almost like a memory of a memory, of something that had never been, rising out of the distance, not of years but of centuries; an intense longing of unfulfilled desire containing yet a feeling of great bliss? He was lifted into huge clean regions of vacant northern sky, feeling both the intense pleasure, and the piercing stab of pain which accompanies the longing for the unknown.

Ian threw his head back and laughed.

"What is it?" asked Maggie, joining in the laughter with him.

"It's . . . it's *wonderful!*"

"What?"

"Everything! Don't you see? It's all so . . . huge—so empty—so pure!"

Maggie said nothing and they rode on in silence for a few moments. Turning reflective, Ian at length stopped his horse, dismounted, and bent down over a small lonely flower which had struggled to the surface in the midst of weeds and taller field grasses.

"Look at it. It's so small, so delicate. Yet its leaves are rough and thick and hearty. And it's so alone!"

"They usually bloom in the early spring. I suppose it took this one all this time to push out of the undergrowth."

"What's it called?" Ian's voice was barely more than a whisper.

"Why, it's a primrose," answered Maggie. "I thought you knew. They grow like weeds here."

Ian tenderly plucked the thick stalk, eyed it intently for a moment, then handed it to Maggie. "Well, Margaret Duncan," he said with a voice full of energetic urgency, "thank you for introducing me to this tiny wonder. And however many there may be, there aren't enough! Why, I don't ever remember seeing such a lovely face in all of London. The gardens should be full of them! Every house—in London . . . in Scotland . . . *everywhere*! Every house should be surrounded with primroses, I tell you!"

He stretched out his arm in a sweeping circular motion. "You should all be growing primroses!" he shouted to the empty hills of purple and green. "Do you hear me? Primroses!"

Now it was Maggie's turn. She laughed enthusiastically.

"I must say," she said finally, "I didn't quite expect this. You seem altogether overcome with the exuberance of our countryside."

"I didn't expect it myself," returned Ian, settling into a quieter, more thoughtful tone.

He mounted his horse and they continued along their ride. "In fact," he went on, "I don't know what got into me."

"Scotland is like that," said Maggie. "So are these heather hills in the late summer and autumn. They get into you. They draw you, they lure you, and before you know it—"

She left the sentence uncompleted.

"Before you know it . . . what?" asked Ian.

"I was going to say that before you know it the land has become part of you. And you're in love with it."

Neither spoke for a moment. All at once, without warning Maggie urged Raven to a gallop. For a few seconds Ian forgot to follow as he watched her glide away, her hair streaming out behind her. She was like a goddess astride a cloud of black velvet. Suddenly he came to himself, shook off the reverie, mounted and spurred his own horse after her.

"Come on, Maukin!" he yelled.

Sitting rather precariously in the saddle, Ian felt as if he were riding a lumbering elephant in contrast to Maggie's graceful figure receding in the distance. He did not reach her until after she had come to a stop atop a small knoll about three furlongs away.

Maggie dismounted and stood watching his cumbersome gallop. Unwilling to slow the animal for fear Maggie's lead would increase all the more, he had given her full rein and Maukin had risen to a pace that gave her name credit. As they drew closer, the horse slowed not a whit, only pulling up at the final moment in reluctant obedience to her rider's urgent commands and frantic yanks on the reins.

When Ian caught his breath and regained his composure, he managed a sheepish grin. It was the first Maggie had seen of the lingering boy in him, previously hidden behind the facade of feigned manhood.

"Perhaps I overstimulated my riding ability," he said.

Suppressing a giggle, Maggie replied. "You held your seat well, Mr. Duncan. Not many can on Maukin. She is truly a hare, always in search of a good scamper."

"Well, I intend to improve," he replied earnestly. "That will be a good occupation for me during my stay at Stonewycke."

"To keep you out of mischief?" suggested Maggie playfully.

"Touché!"

Ian dismounted and looked about him. "It's an absolute sea of heather!" he exclaimed. "Truly worth nearly breaking my neck over."

"Our Scottish poets are always extolling the virtues of the heather. Everyone becomes a poet in August."

"I can see why. Only a cold heart indeed would not be moved by such a scene as this."

"But besides being pretty," said Maggie, "it's just a wiry little shrub, not good for anything."

"Except decorating the hills in August," replied Ian. "Might not that be reason enough to justify the Maker's creation?"

"Perhaps."

"It's opening my eyes," said Ian pensively. "At least it's starting to."

"Opening your eyes?" said Maggie. "To what?"

Ian looked away, scanning the distant hills, then sweeping his gaze around northward toward the sea.

"To myself, I suppose," he replied at length. "But," he went on, seeking to divert the gist of the conversation from himself, "recite me a poem about the heather."

"Oh, I couldn't," said Maggie. "I don't know any."

"I bet you know a dozen. All I'm asking for is one. Come now, for your cousin from the city who's never seen or heard the likes of all this."

"Oh, all right," said Maggie. "Since you put it like that, how can I refuse?" She sat down on the grass, looked away, tried to imagine herself alone as she so often had been here, and in a soft dreamy voice, began:

Fair wast the heather, 'pon hill and muir,
    Fair wast my luve's smile in that sweet place.
So fair the heather 'neath leafy birk,
    An' still fairer the one wha's joy did melt my hert.
But winter steals 'way heather an' birk,
    An' 'way my luve must gang frae me,
      A fechtin' Highlan' wars.
To come again 'pon hills o' heather sweet,
    Like autumn in its verdant grace.

Her voice fell still and for a moment Maggie remained silently enfolded in the mood of the old poem. Suddenly she remembered her companion, and a blush stole into her cheeks.

"That was lovely," Ian said. "Is it your own?"

"Oh no," she laughed. "I discovered it in an old worn book of my mother's. I bring it out this time every year and reread it again and again."

"The poet of those words must truly love Scotland."

"Yes," Maggie agreed. "I suppose that's why I like the verse so. I can feel her love for the land and its people and its history."

"What did the poet mean, 'A fechtin' Highlan' wars,' if I remember the words."

"The poet was a woman. She said her 'love must go from me, afighting Highland wars.'"

"When were the *Highland wars?*"

"There were no specific wars by that name. But the inhabitants of the north of Scotland, the highlands, have always been a fighting people. We fought the Vikings when they first began to invade, and all throughout our history there has been fighting, until more recently when we fought the English at Culloden Moor west of here. That's probably the most famous battle."

"What happened?" asked Ian, growing more and more intrigued, both by this maiden cousin and the land from which she had sprung.

"There was a huge massacre. The English troops had marched into Scotland after our Bonnie Prince Charlie who tried to establish himself as King of Scotland. Your King George II didn't like that at all. Many Scotsmen died. But there have been battles and clan feuds and border skirmishes against the English down through the centuries, always taking young men away from their ladies."

The two continued to gaze out over the purple expanse of the hillside. "But despite our colorful past, Mr. Duncan, you will probably find the Scotland of the present rather dreary after London."

"So I thought myself," he replied. "But I surprise even myself. I am discovering that it, too, may have its merits."

"I agree."

"It may even turn out that I will grow fond of it. Perhaps my mother was right after all."

"In what way?"

"Saying I was ready for a change."

"What made you choose to come to Scotland?"

Ian laughed dryly. "Believe me, it was hardly by choice that I came. But it was preferable to the other alternatives facing me. I must remind you that you have welcomed a completely unsavory fellow into your home."

"So my father says," replied Maggie turning toward him. "But I find that hard to believe. How much harm could you have done?"

Ian grinned, wondering if he should tell her the truth of his latest caper. Part of the rowdy city-Ian slowly began to surface, relishing the lark of shocking the innocent girl with tales of being thrown into prison after a drunken brawl over a low-bred prostitute.

"I was exiled from my home as an alternative to a lengthy stay in Newgate," he said.

"Why? Whatever did you do?" asked Maggie with alarm.

"I doubled up my fist and applied it with great speed against the nose on one of the Crown's officers," replied Ian, attempting to add a touch of levity to an incident which had been no laughing matter once the dust settled.

"Well, then," Maggie replied, neither laughing nor showing signs of the shock Ian had halfway anticipated, "Scotland must indeed look rather good to you."

A shadow of self-reproach crossed Ian's face, and another part of him struggled to free itself from the unseen perils and fears of the past. Even as he found the old half wanting to boast in its villainy, the unfamiliar new half wished himself free to take advantage of the opportunity to start fresh presented in this new environment.

He threw his head back and laughed, but there was a quality of defeat in the tone that drained it of its mirth. To lay down his past would never be accomplished without an equal—and painful—laying down of pride.

"Truly spoken, indeed, my lady," he replied, saying the words of titular respect for the first time sincerely. Perhaps it was time to begin acting the part of the gentleman he was supposed to be.

Ian was the first to remount, and he kept a healthy pace all the way back to Stonewycke. Suddenly he had become afraid of those heather-covered hillsides. He rode hard to escape the tiny purple eyes which seemed bent on penetrating the depths of his soul, forcing him to face truths about himself he had managed to keep hidden—until now. His youthful mind was filled with possibilities that had assaulted him unbidden and which he had never considered before.

Maggie did not see her cousin for the rest of the day.

21

A Dinner Invitation

JAMES MADE NO mention of the fact that he had orchestrated the invitation from the Falkirks. It had arrived the previous day and even Atlanta seemed remotely pleased with the idea.

Plans were progressing well. Their visit to Kairn last week was cordial enough despite Atlanta's annoyance over Lady Falkirk's brusqueness, and would pave the way for her later acquiescence to the notion of George as a suitable son-in-law. And today's visit, when George himself would be present, fairly teamed with opportunity, if only he could keep his impetuous daughter in tow. The only flaw was the presence of that boy—Theodore, or Ian, or whatever his name was. He couldn't very well leave their houseguest behind with no explanation. But he wasn't about to drag him along, either.

Shortly before eleven he sought the boy out in his room. Ian had risen only a short while earlier. He had not been up with the cocks again since the morning of his ride with Maggie two days earlier.

"Well, my boy," James began, "what do you think of our northland so far?"

"A far cry from the streets of London, that much is certain," replied Ian, wondering to what he owed this sudden overflow of friendly hospitality.

"Not to your father's liking, of that I am sure," said James. "But how about you?"

"I'm growing more accustomed to it every day."

"Ah, good for you. I have some business at a neighboring estate this afternoon. You don't mind more-or-less fending for yourself for the rest of the day, do you?"

"Not at all," answered Ian, more than a trifle confused. Not having seen James more than two or three times since his arrival, Ian could not help feeling a natural curiosity about the laird's sudden concern for his welfare.

"Fine, fine! By the way," James continued, as an apparent after-thought, "my wife and daughter will be accompanying me to Kairn, sort of a family matter, you understand. I'll have the cook set something out for you this evening."

He turned and left the room.

Ian smiled to himself. *Why all the deceit?* he wondered. *Why didn't he simply tell me I'd be dining alone this evening?*

He shook his head, walked to the window, and looked out. The sun was already high in the sky. "I really should try to get up earlier," he said to himself. "That morning of the ride was positively glorious."

Several hours later Maggie, along with her father and mother, rode up to the house on the estate of Kairn. When the young groom reined in the two horses and brought the carriage to a stop, the three stepped down and walked to the door. The driver took charge of the horses and carriage, and a servant showed them in through a spacious hallway and into the drawing room where Lady Falkirk awaited them.

"I'm so happy you could come," she said warmly, "and especially you, my dear," she added, turning toward Maggie. "I haven't seen you since your birthday last month."

Before Maggie could respond a door at the opposite end of the room opened and Lord Falkirk, followed by his son, walked in. Falkirk extended his hand toward James while George, bowing politely but hastily in Atlanta's general direction, walked straight toward Maggie.

"Welcome to Kairn, Lady Margaret," he said, taking her hand and raising it gently to his lips. "I must say, you look nearly as lovely today as you did in your pink silk the night of the ball."

"Thank you," replied Maggie, feeling the heat rising in her neck. "How could you possibly remember what I was wearing? I thought men paid no notice of such frivolity."

"I make it a point of remembering beautiful things," he answered with an arresting smile.

His eyes lingered on her face momentarily. Then he turned to greet James. "Good day, Lord Duncan," he said. "It's an honor to have you visit our home."

"The honor is mine, George," said James, pleased with the strong grip of the young man's handshake. "This is quite a son you've got here, Byron," he said, still holding onto George's right hand. "He'll make some young lassie in these parts a manly husband." He shot a quick wink at the young man and then released his hand.

"And an ambitious one," replied Falkirk.

"No doubt—no doubt!" laughed James.

As Lady Falkirk led the way into the dining room, George offered Maggie his arm. She placed her hand lightly in the crook of his elbow and they followed, while the two fathers brought up the rear. The two elder men sat at opposite heads of the table and, after seating her most graciously, George took his place next to Maggie.

As they were being served, George remarked, "I see you so rarely, Lady Margaret. Now that you have come of age, it would be proper of you to be out among the local gentry more frequently. Would you consider allowing me to call, and perhaps take you to visit some of the neighboring estates?"

"Yes . . . of course, certainly," replied Maggie.

"May I also call, just to visit *you*, Lady Margaret?"

"I suppose there would be no harm in that," said Maggie, glancing uncertainly toward her mother.

Atlanta smiled and gave a slight nod.

"I would consider that a pleasure," George went on. "Ever since that night when we first danced together, I've found myself—hullo! what's this?" he exclaimed as a servant placed directly in front of him a platter displaying a large roasted pheasant.

"You said you wanted to carve it, Master George," the man said.

"Oh, yes, so I did," said George. "Shot it myself only this morning," he remarked to no one in particular. "Thought I'd complete the sport by turning my hand to the knife. May I slice you a nice thick wedge of breast, Lord Duncan?" he asked.

"Thank you, George. That will be perfect," replied Maggie's father, fully delighted with the course of events.

As the dinner progressed it was some time before George spoke again to Maggie directly.

"I would like to call on you, Lady Margaret," he said at length. "I would be privileged to take you for a ride in my gig."

Maggie glanced away bashfully, then back. "That sounds like fun. But we do have a guest—"

"Nonsense!" interrupted James. "Come right over, George, at your convenience. The girl will be only too pleased to go with you."

"I don't want to interfere," replied George, displaying genuine concern.

"Rubbish!" said James. "The boy's a no-account cousin of mine from London. Nothing but a troublemaker. His mother sent him to me to see if I couldn't make a man of him, but it's useless. Got too much of his father's blood in him for his own good."

"He's not quite the rogue James makes him out to be," said Atlanta. "But the boy's been in some trouble, and we agreed to offer him a change of environment."

"Perhaps I ought to call on *him*," said George with a laugh. "Sounds like he needs to be taught some old-fashioned Scottish manners."

"Capital idea, George!" roared James, "positively splendid! We'd have the young blackguard straightened out in no time."

Reveling in the merriment of the idea, George went on, "I'd be happy to show the lad around, Lord Duncan, that is if I could be of some help to you. I imagine I could hold my own, even when pitted against a knave from London."

"No fear of his getting the best of you, George," said James, wiping his eyes from the laughter. He couldn't remember when he'd had such a good time. "The lad's three inches shorter and at least four years younger than you. A mere boy alongside a strapping man like yourself."

George brushed off the compliment with a laugh, but could hardly help the pleasure he felt at James's words, glancing out of the corner of his eye to see whether Margaret had taken notice.

"So, it's all settled, then," said James, heartily anticipating the potential diversion such a visit by young Falkirk would provide. Landsbury's son would discover soon that the men of Scotland were no country bumpkins to be toyed with. "We'll look for your visit with eagerness—won't we, my dear?" he added turning toward his daughter.

Maggie smiled sweetly, but said nothing.

Driving back to Stonewycke early in the evening, James was in obvious good spirits, and even Atlanta seemed considerably warmed to the notion of a closer bond of relationship with the family of Falkirk. George had not spent the entire force of his blandishments on Maggie, but had reserved a good share for her mother as well. And his engaging and likable manner had not gone unnoticed. Atlanta had gone to Kairn on her guard, but had come away positively aglow. Witnessing this proceeding, James noted with satisfaction that Lady Falkirk had apparently communicated his scheme most adroitly to her son, and he had carried out his part with all the sophistication of a gentleman far more advanced in the ways of the world than his years would indicate.

"Why so silent, Margaret?" asked James, detecting, in an uncharacteristic moment of sensitivity, his daughter's somber countenance.

"No particular reason, Father," she replied. In truth, she had been considerably rankled by the sport James had made over Ian at the dinner table, and now driving home she was reminded again of how she despised the way he treated people to serve his own ends. Her smoldering anger at her father, however, had not diminished the attraction she had felt for George Falkirk. He was, indeed, a captivating and dashing man. And notwithstanding the embarrassment of his obvious and forward attentions, she had to admit that his words had warmed her within.

"Come, come! Are you not thinking of young Falkirk?" her father insisted. "The young man was clearly taken with you. How could you not have noticed?"

"Of course I noticed," she snapped, with a trace more emotion in her voice than she had intended. "But the way you were all eyeing us, what could I do? It was awkward to say the least."

"Nonsense!" replied James, not the least pleased with his daughter's tone. "The man was simply paying you the courtesies of a gentleman."

"It's not hard to see that George likes you, dear," said Atlanta in a moderated, motherly tone. "We only want you to be happy, and George certainly is charming."

"I know, Mother," replied Maggie blushing. "Of course I find him attractive. Naturally—it's . . . but he's so much older than I am—so traveled—educated. I'm only seventeen."

"But a beautiful seventeen, darling," added Atlanta. "You're a woman, dear, not a girl. Many young ladies are married at your age. And men stand up and take notice of a face like yours."

"Especially when you have the figure to match!" said James, still feeling jovial from the four glasses of wine he had consumed after dinner.

"Father!" said Maggie. "If you don't mind, I would appreciate your keeping your opinions of my body to yourself!"

Shocked at such a rebuff from his daughter, James held his peace. But it would not take many more such outbursts before he would respond in kind. He couldn't allow a daughter of his to talk with such affrontery. He would let it pass this time, just this once. Perhaps he had spoken out of turn, anyway. If so, it was the fault of that cheap wine of Falkirk's!

"But if he does call, dear," went on Atlanta, "we'll try not to interfere. You never know, you might grow rather fond of him."

"Mother," said Maggie, "I *have* been fond of him, as you put it, ever since he asked me to dance at my party. I just don't want Father hovering around trying to push me into the man's arms!"

James remained silent. Just as long as Falkirk married the ill-tempered vixen, he could hold his tongue. But, by Jove, she'd better watch herself! As long as she was under his roof, his daughter would keep a civil tongue in her mouth!

Meanwhile, he sat back and tried to enjoy the ride, at least to the extent that the pitted and rocky road would allow. Maggie lapsed again into the silence of her own thoughts, determined to stand up to her father if he ever again made an attempt to draw her into his personal schemes. She sensed more behind his good spirits leaving Kairn than a fine meal with neighbors. If he was up to something, she would have no part of it.

I couldn't prevent his taking Cinder, she remembered bitterly. *Next time he will not so easily have his own way.*

Meanwhile, she smiled at the memory of the meeting just past. George Falkirk *was* an appealing man. And handsome!

22

Lucy Krueger's Daughter

SINCE BESS MACKINAW'S death a gradual desire had stolen upon Maggie to be closer to the people of Strathy valley. No longer, she felt, could she take such a vague and detached interest in their lives and well-being. Though she never dreamed of having much influence where her father was concerned, she felt compelled to become more involved in their affairs. She sensed her union with them in a common birthright, jointly linked by blood and by history to the land and the Scottish heritage they shared—by virtue of their ancient ancestors rather than by accidents of pedigree and breeding.

She resolved, therefore, to continue making calls on Hector and Stevie. At the same time Maggie found herself increasing the frequency of her visits to the town and the church, and thus progressively widening her circle of humble acquaintances in the tiny village. When her father learned she had visited the Gillies family and offered to teach their crippled daughter to read, he flew into a rage.

"As if you were a common domestic!" he exclaimed.

"She wants to read," Maggie argued, "but she can't get to the school."

"She can be taught by others!"

"There is no one else," Maggie insisted. Why couldn't her father accept her growing maturity and independence? Why did he insist on rejecting all the things she held dear, forcing the rising woman within her to rebel all the more strenuously against him?

"No daughter of mine will be tutor to a crofter's child!"

"But—"

"Remember your place, Margaret," said her father.

"My place is as one of these people!" she snapped.

"You are a *lady*," he returned. "*That* is your place!"

"Then isn't it my responsibility," asked Maggie, making one last attempt to reason with him, "to show kindness to our people?"

"Your responsibility," he answered with cold finality, "is to do as I say! *And nothing else!*"

Maggie turned and left the room, seething with bitterness. When she learned soon afterward that Lucy Krueger had just given premature birth to her firstborn child—who was not expected to live—she began immediate preparations to visit the girl. Her father could upbraid and denounce and punish her all he wanted—she was going to see Lucy!

The two girls, while not friends in the strictest sense of the word, had for years been as fond of one another as the distance between their respective stations would conveniently allow. Lucy could never have hoped to be on intimate terms with someone like Maggie, of course, but she had instinctively been drawn to the laird's daughter. They were separated by two years—Maggie the younger of the pair—and had from time to time seen one another on certain festival days when the laird's family had joined in with the crofters. Once, when they were mere children, Maggie had impulsively given the girl one of her favorite dolls, and Lucy had been thoroughly devoted to her since that day. The previous Christmas, Lucy and Maggie had visited at length. Lucy had only recently married, and Maggie was genuinely interested in her new life as Charlie Krueger's wife.

Maggie was saddling Raven to ride out to the Krueger farm when Ian ambled into the stable.

"How about a ride?" he asked.

"I'm sorry," she explained, "I'm on my way to visit a girl whose baby is about to die—they think so, at least."

Ian's disappointment was obvious, but a spark of human concern flickered near the regions of his heart at the same time. "Perhaps when you return," he said.

"I may be gone most of the day," said Maggie.

Unable to bear the prospect of another boring day alone, Ian suggested, "Might I join you?"

Hesitating a moment, Maggie answered, "Of course . . . if you can be ready in five minutes."

"I'll only take me three. I won't be in the way?"

"I don't think so. But not a word to my father of this!"

Relishing a mystery, Ian flashed a grin and ran off to find a saddle for Maukin. He could saddle her himself in a fraction of the time it would take to find Digory and explain the situation to him.

True to his word, in three minutes he exited the stable into the bright sunshine, leading Maukin on foot.

The morning was clear and warm, one of the last such they could expect as summer ebbed into fall. Again Ian took great pleasure in the splendid country-side. They made their way west until they struck the road which joined Port Strathy with Culden some twelve miles southwest. This road they followed for perhaps a mile before veering off south. In the craggy foothills between the valley and Braenock Ridge, the Krueger place was situated on the last tolerably tillable patch of rising land before the desolation of the moor began. Even at that it was considerably more rugged than the grassy farmland of the main expanse of the fertile valley. Sheep could be seen grazing among the rocky crags, and in the small plot of soil stalks of wheat and oats struggled to grow.

The cottage was built after the fashion of the Mackinaws', only larger and more protected from the harsh blasts of the elements. The one notable distinction, however, lay in a small plot of ground directly in front of the house which had been lovingly worked by Lucy until she had been able to produce a bright bed of nasturtiums and begonias. The dirt path to the front door divided this colorful little garden with flowers growing abundantly on either side. Approaching the cottage, Ian was filled with pity at the hopeless attempt to cover the wretchedness of the hovel with the contrasting cheeriness of the flowers. *How can anyone call such a place home?* he wondered. London had been rife with poverty, yet it had never touched him personally. Now, face to face with actual men and women and children struggling to survive, he found the sight all the more poignant.

Charlie Krueger strode out of the byre to meet them. He was tall and muscular, but his round, homely face was gaunt with anxiety and his eyes revealed sleepless nights. Shading his eyes from the sun with his left hand, he smiled a wan welcome to his esteemed visitors and extended his right hand to Ian. Then he turned to Maggie.

"Weel, my leddy," he said, his voice thick with self-conscious reserve, "what can I be doin' fer ye? Though I'm doubtin' there's aught a poor crofter can do fer the likes o' yer leddyship."

"I heard about Lucy, Mr. Krueger," Maggie replied. "I thought I might pay her a visit. I thought—"

She hesitated, searching for the right words so as not to seem condescending to the poor, proud farmer. Perhaps her father had been right—it wasn't her place to interfere. But before her thoughts went any further, a gentle voice from the doorway of the cottage put her questions to rest.

"Why, ye didna need t' do that, my leddy," said Lucy, "but it's so nice t' hear yer sweet voice again."

Maggie turned toward the cottage where Lucy, looking pale, stood leaning against the doorjamb. The moment she had heard Maggie's voice outside, she had hastily wrapped a blanket about her shoulders and come to the door. "Oh, Lucy, my dear!" said Maggie, turning toward her haggard friend. "You look so tired!"

Lucy smiled and opened her arms to the young heiress of Stonewycke. "Never too tired fer a visit from ye," she said.

"I brought some bread and cheese," said Maggie.

"That's kind o' ye," said Lucy. Then in a different tone she turned to her husband. "Weel, Charlie, show the leddy an' gentleman in, an' gi' Leddy Margaret a han' w' her bag." Charlie obeyed somewhat sheepishly, took the parcel from Maggie's arm, and led the way clumsily into the cottage.

"We'd be proud fer ye t' bide a wee wi' us," Lucy continued. "Ye can see oor little bairn."

"We'd love to," Maggie replied.

Maggie followed Lucy into the cottage. Ian stood for a moment hesitating, then followed the others inside. He blinked in the darkness and when his eyes finally adjusted to the dim light, he saw a peat fire in the center of the room with its trail of smoke lazily drifting upward through the ceiling. A kettle bubbled over the fire, indicating that Lucy had been busy despite her weakness.

Maggie and Lucy were already huddled over the coarse wooden cradle.

"Come, sir," Lucy invited Ian proudly. "Have a wee peer at oor sweet bairn."

"She's beautiful!" exclaimed Maggie. "What's her name, Lucy?"

"Weel, since she was christened last night, we named her Letty."

"Christened last night!" said Maggie. "You mean you've had her out already?"

"Hoots! no, my leddy. She was born but three days ago. Na, na. Mr. Downly came oot himsel', seein' that she weren't expected t' live. But just look at her!" Lucy beamed. "She'll hae a proper church christenin' yet!"

The infant was tiny, utterly helpless, neither knowing nor caring that its very life hung on a slender thread. *But why should she struggle so to live?* thought Ian as he glanced around. *What does she have to look forward to? Nothing but a life of poverty and deprivation.*

"She has your eyes, Lucy," said Margaret.

Awkwardly searching for something to say as he stood over the cradle, Ian was suddenly horrified to see a large kitchen knife tucked in beside the child in the mattress.

"I say!" he exclaimed. "I think you've misplaced something."

He reached in to removed the knife, but Lucy placed a restraining hand on his arm.

"Oh no, sir," she said. "Leave the knife be, though 'tis there mainly fer Charlie's daddy's sake."

"What in heaven's name for?"

"'Tis t' keep the fairies from stealin' away oor wee Letty an' replacin' her wi' a changelin'," she answered. "I told Fergus Krueger that God'll be watchin' o'er oor Letty an' we needed no such auld superstitious aroun' here. But he said a person couldna be too careful an' he is the child's gran'father an' has a certain right t' speak his mind. But 'twas the Lord that brought the child safe through that first night, an' the nights since, an He'll keep her safe from any ol' fairies."

"She's a strong child, then," said Maggie. "She truly is."

"'Tis kind o' ye t' say," replied Lucy.

"A braw one, 'tis what we would say," interposed Krueger, finally breaking the silence from the uncertainty he felt at having such guests in his poor home.

"Aye, the Lord's given us such joy o'er oor little one," said Lucy. "'Tis why we named her Letty."

"I don't understand," said Maggie.

"Letty . . . 'tis from the name *Letitia*; it means *happiness*."

"How wonderful!" exclaimed Maggie in delight.

"An' we are happy, my leddy, aren't we, Charlie?"

Blushing imperceptibly, Charlie nodded his head.

"Aye," Lucy went on, "the Lord's promised us the wee one will live t' be strong an' healthy an' will someday make her mark fer the good o' this land we all love. 'Deed, my leddy, the Lord has blessed us more than we can deserve!"

A brief silence descended, which was broken after a moment by the sound of Maggie's laughter. "Well, I'm so happy for you, Lucy . . . and you too, Charlie," she added turning to face him. "A braw wee bairn indeed!"

"Ye do right well wi' the sound o' yer native land on yer lips, my leddy!" said Lucy with delight.

Lucy rose, walked toward the hearth, and began to fix her guests some tea. But Maggie could see that she had already been on her feet too long.

"You lie back down, Lucy," she said. "I can warm water and stir up a pot of tea."

"I couldn't have a leddy like yersel' waitin' on *me!*" expostulated Lucy.

"Nonsense!" returned Maggie. "Besides, I insist. I'm giving you no choice in the matter."

Uncomfortable with the reversal of roles, yet glowing from the combined radiance produced by motherhood and having the lady of the estate take such a personal interest, Lucy yielded and sought out the bed upon which she had been lying before her guests arrived.

"I was jist tendin' my animals when ye came," said Krueger. "If ye'd like t' see the byre, sir, ye can follow me while I finish my chores."

"Certainly, my good man," replied Ian, enthusiastic about any prospect other than baby-watching with two women.

He followed the lumbering farmer out of the cottage and into the barn, which was attached to one wall of the house in the rear.

"Here's the byre," he said, "where we keep the livestock."

Entering the darkened structure, which was in reality little more than a huge shed, Ian was struck by the destitution of the place. *If this is what the man considers livestock*, he thought, *there isn't much here.* Two cows shuffled impatiently at the far end. Krueger walked straight toward them, unlatched the stall, and proceeded to lead them out of the building.

"I was jist readyin' t' let the nowt oot t' pasture," he said. "The field's not far. They're mighty hungry by now, I reckon."

Ian followed Krueger through the byre and walked alongside—the gentleman from London in clean, pressed clothes; and the humble farmer in dirt-smeared dungarees—as they accompanied the two lean black-and-white cows toward a fenced area about two hundred yards from the house. He could not think the little available grass afforded them much to look forward to in the way of breakfast.

"Don't you also feed them oats or hay?" he asked, making conversation.

"Hay, when'er I'm able," answered Krueger. "But na oats. They're too precious fer oursel's, ye know. But the beasts get by."

Returning to the barn, Krueger grabbed two handfuls of some kind of seed and scattered it over the fence of a small coop where some dozen or so chickens immediately flurried about pecking at the ground for every morsel of grain each could hoard to itself.

Back into the barn Ian noticed for the first time two lethargic pigs lying in a filthy and odiferous mixture of mud and manure. Into the feeding trough Krueger scooped a measure of some horrible concoction. At the sound of its splat onto the wooden slats at the bottom, the two pigs leaped to their feet snorting furiously, then plunged their snouts into the mass in a frenzied attempt to consume as much as possible in the shortest amount of time.

To Ian the whole ritual appeared pathetic, eking a bare substance from what the rocky ground and scraggly farm animals could produce. How could this man and his wife actually claim to be *happy*? Was there a wholesome purity that filled Charlie Krueger with a sense of life's fulfillment as he struggled—just he and his family and his plot of ground—against the elements of nature? Was it the challenge of the hard life that imbued this man and this woman with their happiness? What else could it be?

It was certainly a challenge he had never known . . . would never know. Life—if by life one meant food, clothing, shelter, money, and possessions—had always come easy for him. He'd never had to work a day in his life. Krueger's arms, on the other hand, were rough and brown, his hands cracked and tough from daily contact with the earth and its demands. Those hands, and what he managed to do with them, put oatmeal on their table and kept potatoes boiling in the kettle—hands that were not afraid to work the stubborn ground until they were black, hands that were not afraid of the stinging winter's cold.

Ian glanced down at his own hands—soft and white, the hands of a gentleman, the son of an earl, not the hands of a man who had to use them vigorously in order to eat dinner that same day.

Ian could not help but envy Krueger in a way; the farmer at least had something truly to call his own. It wasn't much—hardly more than twenty acres with little to show for it. But as humble as his cottage was, and as few and gaunt his animals, at least it was by his own labor that they were sustained. And now he had a wife and a child to care for, to provide for, to protect, and to love. What more could any man desire? *Yes*, he thought, *maybe there is happiness here.* Perhaps the little baby's name signified more than simply a momentary joy that God had chosen to deliver her from her danger and give her into their hands to love and nurture. Perhaps the child was somehow symbolic of the life marked out for its parents to live.

There *was* something here. Maggie was right. The people and their love for the earth beneath them could not help but affect any observer. Something was tugging at him, pulling at a deep longing in his heart to experience this elusive, intangible dream called *happiness* which Lucy and Charlie Krueger shared.

Leaving Krueger to complete his chores himself, Ian turned from the barn. He had come here intending simply to idle away a few pleasant weeks and then return to London as if nothing had happened. But something *was* happening inside him which he couldn't explain, for which he had been totally unprepared. Everything had changed since that first ride in the country. The place and its people were touching him, moving him. He was struck by the impression that the real significance of life was to be found—of all places!—*right here*, and not in London at all!

And then there was the girl Margaret, tantalizing wisp of maturing femininity, he had to admit, but so full of contrast! Silent one moment, angered over some verbal injury the next, and then bold and vivacious. Tender and open to Lucy Krueger; heartless and cold toward her father. Was her initial reticence toward him born out of a fear of letting anyone draw too close? He had observed that often in James's presence, she stiffened into a frigid statue of marble.

What could he do, he wondered, to thaw her heart? Not that he was *interested* in her, he would have hastily added. After all, had he not been seen with some of London's finest on his arm? This young Margaret was but a country cousin— attractive, to be sure, but a tad young. She was an intriguing case, certainly full of powerful emotions—some of which surfaced; others, he concluded, which she kept locked away for no eyes but her own.

With such thoughts swirling in confusion through his brain, Ian began the ride home with Maggie an hour later. She too had been profoundly moved by the visit, for the tears were rising and only her tough Ramsey heritage kept them firmly in check.

Neither spoke, and they were some way down the rocky path when a breathless voice shouted after them from behind. "My leddy . . . my leddy, hold!" It was Krueger.

The two reined in their mounts and turned to look back. He had been running to catch them, and when he stopped it took a moment for him to catch his breath before he could deliver the message. Finally he said: "My wife, she wanted ye t' hae this as thanks fer all yer kindness." He held up a handkerchief of bright white linen trimmed in tatted lace. Two bright pink primroses decorated one corner. "She made it hersel'," he added proudly, little realizing how infinitely more precious this made the simple gift.

Deeply moved, Maggie reached down for it, hardly daring to speak lest she be overcome. With a husky and tremulous voice, she managed a soft, "Thank you."

The she turned Raven toward home and, with Ian following a few lengths behind, she trotted off. The urge to be alone had come upon her and she pressed the pace. But Ian spurred Maukin and managed to pull up even with Raven in time to see the unguarded tears streaming down Maggie's pale cheeks.

"Miss Duncan?" he said, for he knew of no other words to offer.

"Forgive me, Mr. Duncan," she replied, brushing away the tears and holding her trembling lips tight, swallowing hard. "This is deplorable!"

"No . . . no, it's not," he answered, and for one of the few times since his arrival his voice contained not a trace of sarcasm. "It's completely understandable. I would be a willing listener if you need one."

"Thank you, Mr. Duncan," she replied, gathering her reserve around her once again. "I am fine." She was not quite ready to offer him that much trust just yet.

Maggie tucked the handkerchief into her pocket and offered not another word until they parted at the door of the stables.

Perhaps I do need a listener, Maggie thought. *But not someone in any way reminiscent of my father.* She had trusted him as a child; she had loved him. And worse, she thought he loved her! Until the incident with Cinder she had never realized how little he cared for her feelings, or cared what was important to her. She had never recovered from the shock of what he had done, and had vowed that very day never to trust him again. Never again would she allow herself to be hurt like that—by him, by any man! She wasn't about to risk cracking the shell of self-protection she had been able to build by now opening her soul and confiding in this cousin of her father's. He would probably find an equally suitable opportunity to laugh in the face of something which was important to her—like this beautiful little handkerchief. He had already shown a great fondness for poking fun at life wherever he could. But it would not be at her expense!

Perhaps such hidden motivations lay at root in Maggie's vigorous pursuit of the friendship of the crofters. Not only did she love the land and the people who worked it, something in the subconscious well of her soul no doubt realized that, since by rank and position they were separated beyond reach from her, she would never have to encounter with them the potential pain of intimacy . . . the heartache of not being loved in return. Or worse—as had been the case with her father—of losing a love she thought she had by discovering it had never existed in the first place.

Yes, Mr. Duncan, perhaps I do need a listener. But the price is far too high.

23

The Bluster 'N Blow

THE NEXT DAY might have ended on a better note if Maggie had been about. But no sooner had they returned from Lucy Krueger's than she disappeared. After a token appearance for dinner, she retired immediately for the night.

The visit to the Kruegers' had left Ian's emotions in disarray, and when he arose the following morning nothing had been resolved. Not knowing why, he sought out Maggie, if for no other reason than to be around someone to take his mind off his thoughts. Another ride, perhaps—this time just to ride, not visit.

He searched the stable, wandered through the house, poked his head into the library, then back to the stable. Digory had seen nothing of her, and Raven had not left her stall.

Reentering the house he encountered Atlanta. She stopped and made an attempt to engage him in friendly conversation. But his mood was not one that lent itself to small talk, the interview grew awkward, and Atlanta—either remembering or inventing an urgent errand—quickly excused herself.

Ian was thoroughly disgusted with the turn of the day. Coming here was a gigantic mistake. Where in blazes was Lady Margaret?

The flighty thing has probably had her fill of me, he thought, *and is now off amusing herself in the company of those pathetic crofters! It's no wonder she enjoys their company more than mine. She's cut of the same cloth. All the people up here are a hundred years behind the times! Dirty, miserable creatures! Bloody crime to bring a child into the world under such circumstances!*

But just then the angel clothed in Scottish tartan rose to put the demon of his past life to sleep momentarily. In his mind's eye Ian again saw the picture of Lucy Krueger beaming down with radiant face at her newborn child, her eyes filled with something Ian had witnessed too little of in his life—simple, honest, pure, and total *love.* Did the child, in fact, have more to look forward to in life than he himself?

Ian laughed. But the sound which came from his throat had little of its usual enthusiasm and more resembled a dry groan. *What would that pathetic baby—what was its name? Letty, that's it. Happiness!*

He laughed again. *No doubt! no doubt! What would she think of having more to look forward to in life than the son of an earl!*

What was it about these people? At first he had pitied them. Was he actually now—unbelievably!—*envying* Charlie Krueger? A sensation he had not experienced since childhood suddenly took him by surprise: a warm, moist tear rose in his eye and without warning flowed down his cheek. Quickly the back of his hand obliterated the evidence of his momentary tenderness, and he turned and began pacing nervously.

Alas! The angel's stay was but a brief one and the demons once more asserted themselves.

I must be going mad! The thought of envying a wretched farmer like Krueger! Why, the thing is unthinkable!

Blast that Margaret! he thought. *Where could she be?*

Well, there must be something to do in this ridiculous place without her.

In the purposelessness of his turmoil, he left the house and hastened to the stable, asking Digory gruffly to saddle Maukin.

"And make it lively!" he said. "I'm in a hurry."

He remembered passing through a little village on the way to Stonewycke. Strath—Port something or other! Surely there must be something there. He leapt on Maukin's back and tore off almost too fast to control the galloping hare.

Reaching Port Strathy it was not difficult to locate the place he sought, the only establishment of its kind for miles. The local inn stood on a promontory overlooking the shore, only a few long strides along the path down the embankment to wet sand. Its stone walls were perhaps the newest in the village, and the carved wooden sign bearing the name *Bluster 'N Blow* was freshly painted.

Tying his horse in front, Ian caught a fragrant whiff of tangy salt spray and the crusty odor of herring. The oaken door of the inn swung open before him with a creak. The interior of the premises would have been dim had it not been for the early afternoon sun streaming through skyline windows, located toward the tops of all but the wall where the door was located.

"Guid afternoon t' ye, yer lairdship," called a woman from across the room. She was the only one inside.

"I trust you are open," Ian said as he strode toward a table.

"Would ye be wantin' a room?" she asked, eyeing him almost greedily. She was a tall, large woman with muscular arms showing out below the short sleeves of her drab gray frock. She was clearly no stranger to hard work; the inn sparkled from her efforts. Her small black eyes were sharp and truly bespoke her shrewd character. For in addition to working hard, she was a cagey businesswoman. Her thick hair, about the color of her dress, was cut rather short. She hated any encumbrance that interfered with the handling of her duties.

"No," replied Ian, "but I am thirsty."

"Weel, yer lairdship. I'm none too accustomed t' servin' the barley bree fer another hour or so."

"Surely you would stretch your regulations for a guest of the Lord of Stonewycke."

"Ow, ye must be the nephew visitin' from London, yer lairdship?"

"Cousin," Ian corrected. "Second cousin to be exact. A distant relation, I assure you."

"Any relation o' the laird's be a gentleman in these parts," the lady said.

"And furthermore," Ian went on. "I'm not 'yer lairdship'—I am lord of nothing. Mr. Duncan will suffice."

"As you wish."

"Now, how about that drink?"

"Right ye are, yer—er, Mr. Duncan. I suppose I can allow one or twa fer ye, special guest that ye are."

In reality she allowed nearer to three or four tumblers before the regular evening guests began to arrive a few hours later. Ian chatted easily with the buxom woman, laughed heartily at her stories concerning a few of the more notable locals, and found himself far more at home than he had felt since leaving London.

"You have a fine place here, Mistress—" Ian said after his first glass of whiskey.

"Mistress Rankin," she replied as she filed his glass again. "But everyone round here calls me Queenie."

"Well, it's a fine pub," said Ian again. "And I should know. I am well acquainted with every such establishment to be found in London."

"Thank ye fer speakin' well o' the Bluster 'N Blow. My husban' an' mysel' began buildin' it na twa years ago. The other inn was brought right doon in the muckle storm that year. 'Course it was near ready t' fall doon anyway."

Ian drained his glass and extended it toward her for another refill.

"That Scotch whiskey's mighty powerful stuff, Mr. Duncan. Would ye like t' try a glass o' oor finest ale? Brewed down by Glasgow, it is. Fine ale!"

"Pour me a round!" replied Ian with a hearty laugh. "I'll drink your ale and your whiskey and whatever else you have!"

She complied.

"Well," said Ian lifting his glass high. "Here's to you and your inn, Mistress Rankin. May no storms ever dampen your door again. Here's to stout walls and fair weather from here on out!"

When the first of the locals began to trickle in some time later, they were at first cautious and soft-spoken around the youthful stranger. But Ian was a master of the trade and had soon livened up the crew with his infectious laughter—aided not a little by the whiskey that had by then reached his blood, and the blood his brain—his stories of derring-do in the south, and most importantly, by the round of drinks he ordered for the whole lot. By the time the sun had been down an hour, the sounds of raucous laughter and merry singing could be heard from outside the Bluster 'N Blow.

Queenie had by now lost count of the number of drinks her young guest had taken, but she had begun to eye him with concern. His fine English accent was slurred almost beyond recognition, and with each new toast he offered he managed to spill nearly as great a quantity as passed between his lips.

Finally, lifting one final glass toward the red-faced and tipsy gathering, he rose to his feet on shaky legs and attempted to climb on top of the bench on which he had been sitting. He quickly recognized the impossibility of such a proceeding, however, and thus contented himself with merely remaining on the floor and—for the moment—on his feet.

"*Here's ta the heath, the hill, an' the heather,*" he began with his tongue so thick he could scarcely pronounce the words, " . . . *the bonnet, the—the—*"

One of his companions stood up at his lapse of memory, threw his arm around him, and supplied the missing line—

"*—the plaidie, the kilt, an' the feather!*"

"That's it!" exclaimed Ian with exuberance. "*Here's ta the song—that auld Scotland can boast. May her name never die! Tha's a Highlandman's toast!*"

On the last line everyone joined in so boisterously that the sound no doubt reverberated throughout a good portion of the village. Much laughter and applause followed, and Ian's comrades, themselves inebriated far beyond their normal limits, hardly noticed that their new young friend had slumped back onto the bench, nearly unconscious.

No one noticed but Queenie, who was always alert to the state of her guests. She made her way toward him, and as gently as her fat and calloused hand could manage, patted his cheek.

"Mr. Duncan," she said. "Mr. Duncan. I'm thinkin' 'tis time ye were on yer way."

Ian pulled his wobbly head away from the back of the bench. "Lemme shee, ye're Queenie, arn' you?"

"Aye, yer lairdship—"

"Mussen call me tha, Queenie, my frien'."

"'Tis gettin' late. Hae ye a way home? I can hitch up the wagon—"

"No, no, my dear Queenie," he replied, pulling himself halfway toward a sitting position. "I'm fine . . . fine—never needed anyone to take me home yet."

He rose to a wobbly stand, unable to discern whether he or the room was spinning in a slow circular motion. "Where's the door?" he asked.

Queenie took his arm and led him outside. The crisp night air should have helped the young rouster's condition. Instead, Ian grasped for Queenie's arm.

"I'm gon'ta be sick, Queenie," he moaned.

"Jist suck in a breath o' that clean air," she replied.

"'Tis the air that's makin' me sick."

He clutched her arm and tried to focus on his horse.

"Are ye sure ye can make it, Mr. Duncan?"

"I'll be home an' a'tween my covers afore y're rid o' the rest o' those wastrels in there," he said, attempting a laugh which was merely an echo of his already-spent mirth.

At last the night air began to clear a few of the cobwebs away and he was able to climb, awkwardly to be sure, onto Maukin. The horse, perhaps sensing his master's unsteady seat, took a slow and gentle gait back to Stonewycke. Queenie watched with some trepidation for several moments, then returned to her guests in the inn.

Had Ian been more sober, he would have been surprised to have made it back at all. He hardly knew the road, the night was dark, and his senses were blurred. As it was, he barely noticed the great iron gates as he passed. He left Maukin to her own devices, staggered toward the door of the great house, pondering whether to go in at all. What if the spectre of his host stood waiting on the other side, ready to storm at his insolence and seize this opportunity to throw him out for good?

Closing the door carefully behind him, Ian found to his great relief all was dark and quiet. Fumbling through the entryway, he kicked against a pedestal, heard a rattle, and his hands just laid hold of the vase sitting on top of it in time to prevent its falling to destruction on the floor. As gently as possible, he replaced it, then crept by inches through the hallway, and eventually found the stairs. Clutching the rail he began his ascent. He turned to the left, took two steps, then suddenly heard a suppressed gasp.

"Mr. Duncan!"

"Oh, my lady," he replied, realizing he'd nearly collided with the one whose absence had sent him on this binge in the first place. He attempted a bow, but wavering, he steadied himself against the wall instead. "Wha'a surprise t' fin' you here."

"I couldn't sleep. I thought a glass of milk—" She stopped abruptly.

"I don't have to explain myself," she stated flatly. "What are *you* doing here?"

"Milk! Ah, yes," said Ian, ignoring her question. "I remember such a drink—helps you sleep, but not forget. Have no use for it mysel'."

"Mr. Duncan, you're quite drunk!"

He threw his hand to his mouth in mock dismay and shock. "So that's what it is! Thank God! I thought I was dying."

He laughed at his own feeble joke.

"Hush! You'll wake the whole household!"

"Heaven forbid! We mussen disturb anyone's time in slummerlan', must we?"

"Mr. Duncan," Maggie returned, "You are rude and disgusting."

"*My lady*," he said, assuming a grave and serious tone, "I told you that your father had welcomed an unsavory reprobate into his home." He was unable to hold back his laughter any longer. "Now you know I never lie," he said, letting it loose.

"Go to your room! And for goodness sake, hush, or my father will hear you!"

"You're a sassy wench, my lady," he said with a drunken grin.

"Don't call me that!" she snapped with a flash of hot temper. "My name is Margaret Duncan—*Miss* Duncan to you!"

"Forgive me," he said, with somber expression; but he could hardly hold it, and dissolved into another outburst of laughter.

Maggie turned on her heel and went back to her bedroom, forgetting the milk.

She never noticed that Ian turned also, descended the stairs the way he had come, an went back out the front door.

24
Digory and Ian

D IGORY AROSE WHILE it was still dark, as that was his custom. He lit a lamp; that, too, was his custom, the only time he ever lit a lamp except once more at night before he retired. Both times the lamp only remained lit for a short while as he read. All other tasks he could perform in the dark if there was no sunlight.

He occupied two small rooms over the stable. They formed, in actuality, little more than a loft with a straw mattress, a rough wooden table and chair, and a small cast iron stove—and, of course, the lamp, and a small bookcase. They were humble lodgings. But to Digory it was home. As a trusted servant, indeed almost as a family member, he could have had any quarters he chose. He could have taken up residence in the great house, and Atlanta upon several occasions had tried to persuade him to do so. But he neither needed nor desired more. His tastes were simple, and year after year he remained where he was. All his needs were met—he took meals with the other servants, but found great satisfaction in the solitude of the life he lived.

Stonewycke had been Digory's home these many years since he had become groom in charge of the laird's stables. His father, who had occupied the position before him, had possessed a cottage on the property. But Robert Macnab had had a brood of six children, and even the roomy cottage had been a tight squeeze for the large family.

Now Digory was the only one left in the vicinity. His parents had gone years ago; the cottage had long since been rented out to others; two older brothers had died; another brother and two sisters had migrated to other parts of Scotland.

Digory Macnab followed his father into the service of the laird. He had never married and thus had no family. As a boy he had been something of a loner and as he grew, though personable and friendly, he remained meek and introverted. Casual acquaintances considered him a recluse. But those who were in closer contact with him soon came to realize that his retiring nature was simply a personality trait that in no way precluded a great love for the people around him. He was devoted to those he served, tried not to speak or think ill of his superiors, and loved young Maggie perhaps more profoundly than anyone at the estate realized, caring for her like the daughter he had never had. A new servant in the house from time to time would consider him stand-offish. But such thoughts rarely lasted more than a month or two. Among the permanent staff he was liked and enormously respected. The soft-spoken, almost mystical presence which haunted the barn and stable was a source of pride to the servants, for he was one of their own.

Digory found his Bible on the table and opened the well-worn leather cover. The pages had been turned so often that they practically opened on command. He read his customary Psalm—that was how he always began his morning, saving a corresponding chapter of the Gospels or Epistles for the evening. Then he bowed his head and murmured the Lord's Prayer in the old tongue, as he had learned it so long ago from his father:

Uor fader quhilk beest in Hevin, Hallowit weird thyne nam. Cum thyne kinrik. Be dune thyne wull as is in Hevin, sya po yerd. Uor dailie breid gif us thilk day. And forleit us uor skaiths, as we forleit them quha skaith us. And leed us na intil temptatioun. Butan fre us fra evil. Amen.

His head remained silently bowed for some moments afterward; then he slowly inched his way out of the chair. The arthritis was always worse in the chill of the morning, but he did not bother stoking up the fire, for soon he would be down in the stable. The hot breath and close bodies of the horses, along with the renewed activity of work, would soon warm and lubricate his stiff joints and sleepy limbs.

He closed the book and set it tenderly on the table. Then, seemingly as an afterthought, he bowed his aging head once more and, remaining standing, said, "An', Lord, I near fergot t' mention oor houseguest—that is t' say, the laird's houseguest. I dinna ken the lad, nor ken what t' pray, but ye do, Lord, an' 'tis enough. Amen."

Pulling on his wool cap, he made the slow descent from his quarters down creaky steps to the stable below. He began with his rounds to each compartment, giving a word and pat on the nose to each of the occupants. "Ye'll be wantin' fresh hay an' summat t' eat," he muttered. His charges were always fed before he had his own breakfast. He ran his stable like a fine boarding inn, and considered the animals under his care with as much respect as a thoughtful innkeeper. His morning began so early that breakfast at the house would not be for several hours.

Digory shuffled to a great haystack where he began to fill a rusty-wheeled wooden cart. It took several trips before the stalls were properly supplied. As his pitchfork was sifting through the hay for his third load, he heard a muffled inhuman groan and perceived a remote portion of the stack beginning to move. The ancient groom was hardly flustered, but curious to know the source of the sound. He ceased his labor and immediately walked around the huge pile to find what the mystery could be.

As he parted the hay with his hand, a light dawned upon his countenance.

"Mornin' t' ye, Mr. Duncan!" he said calmly, as if discovering a gentleman asleep in the midst of the horses' breakfast were nothing out of the ordinary.

Ian cracked open one bloodshot eye and squinted painfully up at the old groom. He tried to speak but found his mouth so dry he could not force a single intelligible sound from it.

"Weel, sir," Digory went on, "ye're a lucky man that ye chose a place no nearer my fork fer yer bed. In this hazy dawn I might never hae seen ye."

Ian stirred and tried to sit up. But his head was throbbing so severely that he fell back again into the soft pile with a groan.

"God have mercy!" he swore thickly.

"That He will, lad," Digory replied. "That He will."

Ian looked at him dumbly.

"I ken jist what ye'll be needin', lad," Digory said brightly. "Now, hide right where ye are. I'll be back 'fore ye ken."

Ian could hardly have moved if he had wanted to. The best he could hope for was to lie in the hay with the rich horsey smells floating through the still morning air about him. He fell back into a partial doze and by the time Digory returned, Ian had nearly forgotten him.

"Now, drink this, lad," the groom entreated.

Painfully Ian shook his head, "I—I couldn' . . . my head—"

"Come now, laddie."

"I don't think I can drink anything."

"'Tis Nellie's special brew," Digory persisted. "It'll cure all that ails ye."

"I'm not sick. I was only—"

He paused, trying to remember how he had come to fall asleep in the stable.

"—I am sick, but only because I am drunk—or was last night."

He wondered if the words were coming out right from his jumbled brain. "I hardly know what I am. Maybe I am sick. Rude and disgusting, that's no doubt what I am," he added as memory began to creep over him. He had engaged in worse pub-crawls dozens of times in London. Why, now, did the thought of what he had done the previous night ache worse than his hangover?

Digory could detect hints of shame in the lad's disheveled countenance. He recalled his prayer of the morning and realized that now he had something more specific to talk to his God about when he next offered up a prayer for the laird's young cousin.

"There, laddie, ye drink this—ye'll be good as new in no time." Despite his arthritic knees, Digory knelt down and tried to prop up Ian's head with his hand to enable him to sip the potent compound.

Ian raised the cup to his lips absently. His mind reeled with cloudy images and bare fragments of thought. What did it matter if he was ever good as new? Everything here had turned upside-down. Wouldn't his father relish a glimpse of him now? It would prove once and for all that his second son was indeed a good-for-nothing derelict!

"Worthless," he mumbled, hardly realizing he had spoken.

"Jist give the brew a chance t' work—"

"I'm a contemptible fool," he said, with as much anger as repentance, wincing at the reverberation of his own voice in the early quiet of the stable. "And why are you helping me unless you're as much of a fool as I am?"

"Ye've had a bad night, son."

"Why don't you kick the hay over me and get the laird? Let him mete out my punishment. No doubt he would enjoy it tremendously!"

"Nobody's wantin' t' punish ye, laddie. Punishment's an ill way o' settin' things right."

"Ha!" laughed Ian contemptuously. "Tell that to my father and to the judges who would like to lock me away. Isn't that what life's all about—God judging the wicked, like me? Hell—the great tollbooth to come—is where sinners like me wind up, haven't you heard!"

"Oh, laddie," sighed Digory with a pained tenderness in his voice, "'tisn't like that at all. We ken nothin' o' the Lord's punishment. We only ken what the Word's told us, that the Lord disciplines the ones He loves. He disciplines—not punishes, laddie—t' make us able t' bear more o' His love."

"He may discipline those He loves," said Ian, "but for those reprobates like me—"

"Son," interrupted Digory, "there is *no one* ootside the fold o' God's love. It says He loves the whole world. He jist wants t' love ye, laddie. 'Tis all the Lord wants."

"The *Lord*, maybe," consented Ian, tired of disputing the point, "but I wager it would be another reaction altogether from the *laird*."

"I'm sure if the laird knew—"

"What does it matter anyway," said Ian, half to himself. "How can I face *her* again?"

"If ye're meanin' Lady Margaret," said Digory, "she wouldna hold sich a thing against ye."

"She would have every right," Ian replied. "If only I could slip away from this place unseen."

"Ye wouldna be fair na t' give the lass a chance," Digory said, "an' the rest o' the family too. Ye mustn't be too hard on yersel', lad."

Ian glanced up at the persistent groom. *What does he care anyway?* he wondered.

As if divining his thoughts, Digory added, "If ye'd jist give yersel' a second chance, lad, I think ye might find ye'd like it here. And t'would warm my heart t' see ye fergive yersel' fer this one mishap. Fer, ye see, I've already begun t' grow a little fond o' ye."

Ian stared at him a moment longer, wondering what was behind that peculiar look in his eyes. Then he turned away, swallowed the remainder of the mysterious potion, and lay back in the hay. The churning in his stomach began to calm almost immediately, but it took five or ten minutes for the throbbing in his head to begin to subside.

Deciding he was best left alone, Digory returned to his morning chores. He had no intention of referring to the incident in the laird's presence. He shrank from any form of deceit. But equally foreign to him would have been the bringing of trouble down upon another without some specific motive toward good. In Ian's case, he did not judge that a disclosure would accomplish anything but further alienation.

Feeling gradually better, Ian lay on the haystack silently watching the old groom in the increasing light of day. He always felt this way after a drunken spree—the physical distress was nothing alongside the emotional turmoil which assailed him. Before the end of the morning he had usually come to the point of laughing it off, and by the following night had all but forgotten the mental confusion such incidents caused him.

The corner of his mouth turned up into a crooked grin. At least the night had been good for one thing—he had been able to get a rise out of Margaret. Why, she had been utterly scandalized at the whole interview. That *was* something to laugh about.

But try as he might, he could find no well of resident laughter within him. This bloody place! He would have been better off in Newgate. At least there he would have had the ever-present hope of escape, and the camaraderie of those of his kind.

But how could he escape *this* asylum, where he himself was the jailor, and his mind was the prison?

He remembered telling his mother he would use the time in the country to sort out his life.

Of course he had been patronizing her, saying the words she wanted to hear. He never took himself seriously. Introspection had been unknown in London. Day followed night . . . night followed day. Life went on, and he bounced through it. *Sort out his life*—he didn't even know what the words meant.

But the mental torment of this hangover was new to him. This time the torrent of embittered thoughts was not directed toward his father or his family or the bobby who had hauled him off to prison, but instead inward, at himself. And through his groggy brain tumbled a menacing array of confusing thoughts. He had always been proud that the tough exterior he'd managed to convey made people stand up and take notice. Suddenly he looked upon himself with disgust.

He pulled himself slowly to a sitting position.

Clutching the wall for support, he gained his feet. The room spun a little and his knees remained weak. He engineered a few tentative steps. Perhaps there was something to the groom's brew after all, for all at once he didn't feel nearly so bad.

25

Breaking the Ice

ATLANTA KNEW MAGGIE was in the dayroom.

She'd wanted to speak with her daughter, but was nevertheless reluctant to seek her out. She longed once in a while just to put her arms tenderly around her as she had when Maggie was a child. But Margaret was a little girl no longer. *It is harder now*, Atlanta thought. Harder to overcome her own natural reserve. *And besides*, Atlanta rationalized, *the dayroom is where Maggie goes to be alone*. But she had waited too long. Something was troubling Maggie; and as much as she didn't want to intrude, she could not put it off any longer.

Maggie could be so distant at times, so withdrawn into the solitude of her private thoughts. Atlanta had hoped the arrival of their young relative might draw her out. At first Maggie had seemed more cheerful. She and Ian had seemed to enjoy several rides together. But then suddenly the walls of silence around her had returned. Had the young man done something to offend her? Was it James again? He always seemed at root one way or another, ever since Maggie's remoteness toward them had begun two or three years earlier.

She had to know. She turned and mounted the steps to the dayroom.

Reluctantly Maggie put down her sewing and rose to answer the soft knock on the door. Still trying to come to grips with her own feelings, she couldn't possibly make her mother understand. She hardly understood herself. Why had Ian's visit and a simple gift from a poor farmer's wife pulled so at her heart? Suddenly her resolve not to open her heart again was giving way in the immediacy of relationships she was coming to value. It was already too late. Her heart was already open. And from within it, love was beginning to flow. But she didn't want to love again! Loving meant being hurt. She didn't want to love—not her mother, not Lucy, not George Falkirk, not anybody!

"I—I missed you at breakfast," Atlanta began nervously.

"I'm sorry," Maggie replied.

"It's only that I'm concerned—for your health." Why couldn't the love in her mother's heart find words better than this? "You hardly touched your dinner last night."

"I guess I wasn't very hungry."

"That doesn't sound like my little Maggie," said Atlanta, forcing a laugh.

"That's just it, don't you see?" Maggie burst out, not intending to lash out at her mother but having no one else present. "I'm not *little Maggie* anymore."

"I didn't mean anything by it."

"Oh, I know, Mother," said Maggie sincerely. "It's not you, it's—"

"It's what, dear?"

"I don't know. It's . . . everything! Lucy Krueger gave me this little handkerchief," she went on, handing the small piece of linen to her mother. "Something about it just—"

She stopped and looked away.

"What is it, Maggie?"

"I'm just confused. About Lucy and her baby, about what to say if George Falkirk does come to call, about the estate, about who I'm supposed to be anyway. Father shouts at me for visiting people I care for and want to see. George Falkirk pays me compliments for my face and my dress. But I don't think he cares about *me*, the real *me*." She paused, then continued in a different tone. "Mother," she said, "have you ever wished you could be someone other than who you are?"

Atlanta tried to conceal her surprise. "I suppose everyone has at some time or another."

"I mean really wished it," said Maggie. "Sometimes I think Lucy Krueger is happier in her life than I ever will be. Sometimes I wonder if all this, being part of an important family, if it isn't all worthless. Sometimes I just wish I could be a farmer's wife."

Misunderstanding her daughter, Atlanta's heart sank within her. So that was what had been on Maggie's mind; she wanted no part of her heritage—of Stonewycke, of carrying on the Ramsey line, of all that Atlanta held dear. Misinterpreting Maggie's struggle to face the crisis within herself, Atlanta swallowed to conceal her own hurt and disappointment.

"Do you know what I mean, Mother?"

"I have never wanted to be anyone but who I am—the marchioness of Stonewycke," she answered boldly, the compassionate mother in her submerging below the surface once more. "The Ramsey heritage is all I desire. Of course I care for the people, but not so much that I would become one of them. And this is always what I have desired for you too, my child, that you should follow me as governess of this great estate."

Maggie was silent and Atlanta remained still after her empassioned speech.

"Yes, Mother, you're right," answered Maggie at length, but her voice lacked conviction. "I know the heritage of the land and our place in it is more important than anything. You've always told me so. But . . . somehow I have to find what it means on my own."

She turned and looked out the window for several moments. "I hadn't noticed that the sun was already so high. I'd better go look in on Raven."

She turned back into the room and made her exit as quickly as possible.

Atlanta remained motionless in the middle of the room.

Maggie hurried through the house and out the door, crossed the lawn, and walked briskly toward the stables. She knew well enough that Raven would be well provided for without her. In addition, she was reluctant to run into Ian after last night's awkward encounter on the darkened landing when she had spoken so harshly to him. Of course he deserved it; yet still, she was timid about seeing him again.

But she couldn't face another moment with her mother just then. How could she convey to her what was on her own heart when she herself didn't even know? She loved Stonewycke. Why else would she have refused her father's many urgings that she attend school in Edinburgh or London? Yet despite that love for her family's estate, right now she might be far happier had she been born Digory's daughter, or if her last name had been Mackinaw or Krueger or Pike or MacDonald or . . . anything but Duncan. Her mind's eye caught a picture of herself running barefoot over Braenock Ridge, herding the sheep. Wasn't there something more than being a *lady* . . . a *marchioness*?

Maybe she was afraid of George Falkirk, afraid of his drawing her steadily away from the simple peasant folk she had come to know. He wanted to escort her into society, a gentleman with his lady friend from Stonewycke. But in her heart of hearts, she wanted opportunities to visit Lucy Krueger, and others like her, not the upper crust of the neighboring estates. *Ha!* thought Maggie. *Imagine what it would be like to take George Falkirk to the Kruegers' for a visit!*

Ian had known he must see Margaret again. Returning to his room, he cleaned up and remained there until the greatest part of his physical distress had subsided. He had just left the house through the scullery door when he spied her, apparently hastily on her way to the stables. He took a breath for courage, and called: "Lady Margaret."

Maggie stopped and turned. Ian could not at first glance tell whether she was annoyed or simply surprised. He hastened toward her as quickly as his aching head would allow.

"I've been hoping to find you," he began, ". . . to say I am sorry. I behaved despicably."

Interrupted in the midst of her own thoughts—which at that moment had been flitting to and fro about the person of George Falkirk—Maggie's sole response was a dumb stare.

"I would understand," Ian went on, "if you didn't wish to see me again. But I had to at least make my apologies before I left."

"Before you left!" exclaimed Maggie, coming to herself. "You're leaving Stonewycke?"

"Under the circumstances I think that would prove the best course—I don't want to cause any further trouble or embarrassment here."

"But where would you go?" asked Maggie, thinking he sounded more sober and sincere than she had yet seen him. "You can't return to London."

"I've thought about that. Perhaps my father was right, and it would be best for me to—"

"You don't mean prison! That would be dreadful!"

"It would be different for me," Ian replied objectively. "I have money. I would be able to buy certain privileges." Suddenly he stopped short and laughed. "Listen to me! I'm making it sound like Buckingham Palace."

Then just as quickly the laughter left his voice and his face grew solemn. "But to tell you the truth, I'm not quite ready to leave this place."

"Then why insist on it?" asked Maggie.

"I don't know. Actually, I don't know what I ought to do. You don't know how I feared coming here. And still do! Before I came I was afraid simply of the boredom. I was so used to London. But now . . . now I fear more what it's doing to me—making me see parts of myself I've tried to hide from."

Maggie eyed his face intently. What a new side of her cousin this was! She had thought his attitude toward life was restricted to laughing and poking fun at those around him. But he was just as confused, just as uncertain as anyone—as she herself.

"How I'd love to run away!" he went on. "A part of me yearns to get back on the London streets. That's my home! But then another part of me—a part of me I didn't know existed—whispers that there is something here for me, something I can't run from, something I can't afford to lose, as if a destiny of some kind is calling out to me. But the other part of me—the London part—doesn't want to listen."

"Don't listen to the London part. Stay!" said Maggie emphatically, hardly knowing why. Just moments ago she was angry with him.

"After last night, I just don't—"

"No one knows about last night."

"You know. Your groom knows."

"I will say nothing. And I assure you, Digory is as good as gold."

"I didn't exactly drink alone either."

"Oh—the villagers," Maggie said with an unconcerned wave of her hand. "They won't care. If anything it'll raise your estimation in their eyes. Especially with the harvest just beginning. They'll have plenty of things to occupy their minds besides you."

Relieved, Ian stood still, saying nothing for a moment, apparently thinking.

"Come . . . walk with me," said Maggie. "I want to show you a little garden nearby."

He nodded his assent and followed.

"It's one of my favorite spots. The way you were taken with the beauty of the fields the other day, I thought you'd enjoy it."

At the back of the house stood a small iron gate. A cursory glance might easily fail to reveal it altogether. And if one did chance to see it and became curious, he would undoubtedly find it locked. Maggie led Ian straight toward it, reached up to a broken piece of rock in the top of the stone hedge above her head, and brought down a key, large and rusty, apparently very old. This she inserted into the keyhole in the gate and with some effort the lock finally yielded and the two cousins entered.

No larger than a good-sized parlor, the garden was surrounded by a stone wall overgrown with hedge shrubbery and ivy. At either end sat two stone benches. A large leafy birch in the center had already begun shedding some of its leaves, a reminder that fall was near. In general it was an unkempt place with overgrown rhododendrons and azalias, and other folliage in sore need of trimming. But something about its wildness lent a mystic air of solitude to the place, and Ian could quickly see why Maggie said she loved it.

"I think I'm the only one who comes here," Maggie said as they seated themselves on the far bench. "I'm glad, though. If it were more used my mother would decide to fix it up. But I like it just the way it is." She stopped and thought for a long moment. All was silent about them. A light breeze rustled through the birch and several more golden leaves floated to the ground.

"Tell me, Mr. Duncan," Maggie went on at length, "would your father really prefer to see you in the hands of the magistrate?"

"My father . . ." Ian mused thoughtfully. Then he continued as if he had forgotten her question. "Do you know why there is a rift between our two families?"

"Only bits and pieces," Maggie replied.

"My grandfather was your grandfather's brother. When your grandfather lost his fortune, my grandfather turned away from him. They were brothers, but he wouldn't give him a farthing. My grandfather had everything—the money, the title, the estate—and yet he refused his own brother even enough to sustain his family. I understand your father's hatred. It always seemed to me that Lawrence Duncan hardly needed to be punished further. Even his self-respect was shattered. All he needed was some simple compassion, and no more money than my grandfather would have thoughtlessly spent on a new filly. But Grandfather would have called it pampering, and he steadfastly refused to give in to the pressure coming from other members of the family."

Ian stopped and exhaled a long sigh. Maggie stole a glance at his face. She could see his turbulent emotions reflected in his features.

"So when you ask about my father," he went on, "all that immediately comes into my mind. I suppose my own father comes from the same school. He learned compassion at the hands of his father—who had none."

"He's like your grandfather."

"Like father, like son," said Ian. "No pampering—especially in the case of an outcast second son."

"Outcast? You?"

"You should see my older brother, a perfect cast from the family mold. He'll make my father proud, carry on the family tradition, and all that. And maybe my father is right. Maybe I am no good. Only it would still—"

"You wish he cared about you anyway?" said Maggie, completing the thought for him.

He looked at her for a long moment. How could she see so deeply something he'd only just realized himself? "How could a father not love his own flesh and blood?" he pleaded, not so much for Maggie as to himself, and to anyone greater who might be listening.

"I've asked myself that very question," said Maggie quietly.

"You have?"

"Many, many times."

"But why? Your parents love you?"

"It's a long story."

"Would you tell me about it?"

"Not now," Maggie replied. "But sometime, if you stay long enough. Let's just say that my father, like yours, has peculiar notions about how he demonstrates familial affections. It's strange. In many ways my father has grown into a type of the very man he has always hated, your grandfather."

"The Duncan blood is common to them both. Perhaps that is why I'm so wayward—the demon blood of the Duncans!"

They both laughed. Then silence once more enfolded the small garden until Ian finally broke it.

"I'm not accustomed to talking like that. To another person, you know. I usually make it a point of keeping my feelings inside."

"It's not an easy thing to do. I'm not very used to it myself."

"But it felt good. Thank you for listening . . . Maggie."

Maggie stood and walked over to the great birch, the remainder of its yellow and green leaves rustling gently in the breeze.

"It sounds nice for you to call me by name."

"You're not offended?"

"I don't like to be called *my lady*. I want to be Maggie. I don't want to be a *lady* to people like Lucy. I want to be a friend."

"I understand."

Breaking out in a merry laugh to escape the reflexive mood, Maggie said, "The day is still fresh, Mr. Duncan. Shall we take the horses out for a ride?"

"Only if you promise to call me Ian," he replied.

She smiled and nodded. He rose from the stone bench and followed her back out through the gate and toward the stables.

26

The Race

❈

GEORGE FALKIRK SMILED a broad smile of satisfaction.

This was good land, he thought. *So much better than Father's.* Of course, land was land and he in no way despised the 640 acres he would someday inherit. But his father had not made the most discriminating purchases through the years. And he had done little to develop his holdings. He had contented himself instead with letting his stockpile of wealth simply accumulate in the bank. Thus, as he surveyed his prospects for the future, young George realized he would one day be very rich, but with little else to show for his name—no estate of renown to enhance the prestige of his reputation.

Thus, long before his recent return to Scotland, George had determined to make the most of what opportunities presented themselves. Not only was he the only son of a wealthy earl, he was skilled, educated, and—he had been told—a better-than-average looking man. He would keep his eyes and ears open and eventually, he was confident, something would turn up.

Thus the fortuitous discussion with his parents had coincided nicely with his personal ambitions. The laird of the neighboring estate, they told him, had a daughter. A trifle young, perhaps, but growing quickly into womanhood, and reported to be pretty. In ten years' time she would no doubt be a beautiful lady of some renown. Best of all, they said, complexities in the future of the estate—there was a younger brother—rendered the possibility quite likely that she would inherit a good portion of the land, possibly the estate in its entirety. And a fine estate it was, bordering Kairn along the ridge they called Braenock, and thence extending east and west and all the way to the sea, encompassing all of the fertile Strathy valley.

Indeed, his mother had said, if the two young people could come to the point in a relationship—which she was certain could be discreetly arranged—where a union of the two estates seemed likely, it would certainly enhance young George's position as a landowner in the area and propel him into prominence. George said little, keeping his opinions to himself. But ever since the girl's birthday party he had increasingly found his thoughts turning northward over the hills toward Stonewycke. This could indeed be just the opportunity he had been looking for. He would simply have to bide his time, see how things developed with the girl, gain the influence of the father, and then wait for the proper moment to make his move. Along with his recent discovery concerning Braenock, having the girl at his side would indeed represent quite a coup. After all, waiting for his father's inheritance could entail another twenty years. There was no reason not to begin flexing the muscle of his position immediately, if he could just lay his hands on that money.

But he would worry about that later. Right now he was on his way to accompany a young lady on a ride, and his anticipation mounted each mile as he neared her home.

Ian and Maggie first saw George Falkirk riding around the corner of the house as they were making their way toward the stables.

"Good morning, Lady Margaret," he said, stopping to dismount and walking toward them. "I was hoping I might persuade you to take a ride with me," he went on, ignoring Ian.

"What a coincidence," Maggie replied. "We were just about to do that very thing. Mr. Falkirk, this is my father's cousin from London, Ian Duncan."

"Ah, yes . . . Mr. Duncan," said Falkirk as the two shook hands rather stiffly. "Reports of your visit have already spread to Kairn. I had hoped I might meet you while you were here."

Ian said nothing.

"Perhaps you could join us, Mr. Falkirk," said Maggie.

Falkirk's displeasure at Ian's unfortunate presence was only barely noticeable as a faint contortion played momentarily around the edges of his mouth. But there was no apparent way to get rid of the fellow, so he might as well make the best of it.

He waited while the two saddled their mounts, wondering if there might be some way to lose the city boy in the country. Then the three rode at a brisk trot out the gates and cantered away toward the south.

Maggie had intended to ride once again to the hillsides where she and Ian had gone their first day out together, but Falkirk edged his golden stallion to the front and led instead across the gentle hills toward the rockier and steeper fells. He kept a healthy pace, and the terrain gave the more inexperienced Ian all he could manage.

At length she drew Raven to a stop and said breathlessly, "I had hoped we could go at a slower pace and take a moment to admire the scenery, since Mr. Duncan is so new to Scotland."

"I am sorry, Lady Margaret," Falkirk replied, turning his mount and drawing up next to her. "It was most inconsiderate of me to set such a pace for your guest."

"Don't worry about me," said Ian gaily. In truth he was relieved they had stopped, for he had never before ridden in such rough country.

"It helps to have such a worthy mount as that chestnut," Falkirk said smugly. It was the first time he had addressed Ian.

"I suppose if yours was as good," replied Ian somewhat carelessly, "you'd probably be up on that far ridge by now."

A smile crept slowly across Falkirk's face. "Do I detect a challenge in your words?" he asked with a glint in his eye.

A challenge could not have been further from Ian's mind. But he rather enjoyed toying with the pomposity of this debonair gentleman. "You may take whatever meaning you wish from my words," he replied with a good-natured grin and an nonchalant wave of his hand.

"It sounded as though you meant to imply that your horse was faster than mine."

Ian merely shrugged, in baiting good humor.

"I must warn you that this stallion is northern champion in both cross country and steeplechase," Falkirk boasted.

"Well, Mr. Falkirk," Maggie put in, "I know something of Maukin's bloodline. And though she has never competed, if I were a man I'd wager my last guinea on her."

"It seems we have not only a challenge, but a wager as well!" exclaimed Ian, greatly enjoying the spirit of the moment. "There is but one missing element, Mr. Falkirk."

"To the top of that ridge and back," Falkirk enjoined.

Without another word the two riders were off. Falkirk made it a point to hold back for the first several strides, thus giving Ian the advantage of starting with a brief lead. He would not have it said when he won the race that he had enjoyed an edge at the starting gate.

Within a hundred yards he had taken the lead from Ian and maintained it thereafter. Watching from Raven's back, Maggie could see that Falkirk's form was flawless—he appeared one with his steed, flowing in perfect unison with the stallion's every motion.

Ian, however, now several lengths behind, seemed to hold little, if any, control over Maukin, who refused to restrain her great power now that the word had been given. Yet Ian seemed unconcerned with the clumsy picture he presented. If his horse was to have control, then he was willing to concede as long as he was carried along in her glory.

The golden stallion flew across a gully. Maukin followed easily. Ian swayed in the saddle, looked about to fall, but managed to right himself again. Shouting commands, Falkirk dug his heels unmercifully into his stallion's flanks, clutching the horse tightly with his knees as they scrambled up a rocky ascent where the footing was less sure, gained the ridge, and turned for home.

He masked the surprise on his face when, on wheeling around, he discovered that Ian was a mere four lengths behind him.

"Keep your horse clear, Falkirk!" shouted Ian with a broad grin on his face. "I'm about to let Maukin loose!"

Falkirk's only reply was a series of unintelligible words into the stallion's ear followed with a fresh round of lashings on his hindquarters with the crop he held in his hand.

Ian laughed, made the turn, bent low as Maukin eased down the rocky slope, then gave her the rein. "Now, Maukin," he urged, "go after that stallion."

Shading her eyes against the sun, Maggie could hardly distinguish the two riders, but it appeared they had drawn closer together as the tiny specks they had become now gradually grew in size once more.

Suddenly a chill ran through her body. *Could it be?* she thought. *Are these two men competing because of me?* A smile played on her lips, and she could not avoid the momentary ripple of pleasure that shot through her. Two handsome men—fighting over her?

But her girlish reverie was suddenly broken by the sounds of approaching shouts and thundering hooves. The terrain had leveled and the sheer test of speed was on. Maukin had narrowed the gap to less than two lengths and the expressions of both riders were more determined than ever. Without knowing what had come over her, Maggie found herself yelling wildly at the riders, hardly caring whether they heard her or not.

Falkirk's face displayed genuine concern. Riding hard, yet conscious of the pounding hooves gaining beside him, he could take the pressure of the unknown no longer. Suddenly he committed what was taboo for any rider in a race: he turned back and looked over his shoulder. Maukin was so wild with speed by now that all it took was that one lapse in concentration, that one fatal error in judgment. The next instant she had pulled even.

Falkirk watched his rival with desperation. Maukin's ears lay flat against her head and her reddened nostrils were flared. Ian was no master of her speed now, and only clung on for his life, exhilarated with fear and joy together.

In one final lunging effort, Falkirk flailed the stallion with his whip and pumped the heels of his boots into its sides, and as the two riders shot past Maggie in full reckless gallop, it was the stallion's head that sped by first. Maggie continued to cheer wildly. Maukin slowed of her own accord. Falkirk tugged at his rein and swung the stallion around so as to be first to arrive back at Maggie's side.

Maggie turned to reward the victor with a flushed smile. "Well, Mr. Falkirk," she said, "it seems you and your stallion are as good as your word."

Before he could reply, an exuberant Ian trotted up and dismounted, panting as hard as his sweating horse. "Wonderful race, Mr. Falkirk!" he said, extending his hand to the other, still mounted. "What a ride!"

Falkirk dismounted, smiling but stiff. The victory had apparently not contained the satisfaction he had anticipated. He lifted his stallion's left hind foot and examined the shoe.

"Is something wrong?" Maggie asked.

"I think my horse took a stone on the ridge," he replied.

To Maggie's eyes the hoof looked fine.

"I can see why the stallion is a champion," said Ian. "You gave me more than I bargained for."

"As did you, Duncan," replied Falkirk. "Well run, indeed. You gave me quite a scare. But glory in your near-win while you can. I'll not allow you so close next time."

As he spoke his final words, his eyes turned toward Maggie and an involuntary chill crept up her back.

Ian brushed back a tousled lock of hair, threw his head back, and laughed without restraint.

27

An Afternoon Conspiracy

GEORGE FALKIRK SEETHED with anger.

He had had different intentions for his day at Stonewycke. How could the miserable blighter have made him look like such a buffoon? Riding home, Margaret had been full of praise for Duncan's loss of the race with hardly so much as a mention of his own victory.

So the trouble-making young Duncan would vie for the favor of Lady Margaret, would he? His laughing good nature fooled no one. *Well, let him try*, thought Falkirk coolly. He was a practical man, and he realized that anger would not best serve the achieving of his goal. Duncan's momentary advantage of being in closer proximity to the little prize would gain him nothing. Hardly one to be influenced by modesty, Falkirk remained confident that he could sweep the young mistress of Stonewycke off her feet at will. He had only to contrive to see her more often, and her father would help in that, he was sure.

But he could take no chances. With young Duncan roaming about, anything might happen. And he was not about to let the *real* prize slip through his fingers—it was too close. And with that safely in his grasp, he wouldn't need Margaret or Stonewycke at all, if worse came to worst. But with all three in his possession, everything he had dreamed about would be his. He knew his desire for the lady and control of Stonewycke went beyond a mere quest for wealth and worldly position. But with the lady and with her estate and with the wealth he was soon to lay his hands upon, the ultimate power he sought would all be his.

He directed the golden stallion not south toward Kairn, but rather into the village of Port Strathy. When he reached the village he, like his competitor of two hours earlier, sought out the new stone inn, the Bluster 'N Blow.

It was late afternoon and the streets were quiet. The fisherfolk were readying themselves for the evening out on the sea in search of the herring. The farmers were busy gathering their crops, for the harvest season was upon them. Only a few women and children walked along the dirt street that led past the dry-goods store, a chandlery, and one or two other shops, toward the inn. Falkirk rode past them with hardly a notice. His eyes remained fixed straight ahead, although some of the passers-by hazarded a curious look or two at the fine steed and its lordly rider.

Falkirk dismounted at the inn and strode inside, finding it dark and empty. But Queenie, hearing the creak of the door, hurried out from her kitchen in an instant. A smile stole onto her lips. *Two gentlemen in one week!* she thought.

"What can I do fer ye, yer lairdship?" she said with as welcome a tone as her gruff voice would allow.

"I'll have a pint of ale, if it's fit to drink," he replied. Without waiting for her answer, he found a place at one of the eight or ten tables which were spaced around the room. He brushed the table off with a handkerchief and waited.

He did not have to wait long. For though Queenie went to the cellar to break open a small cask of her best ale, she did not take her time about it. Perhaps word about her inn was spreading to some of the area's regal circles, and she intended to impress this lord with her finest brew.

Falkirk lifted his glass and took a leisurely swallow. *It's a good thing I didn't come here for the ale*, he thought, pursing his lips. Queenie stood by, awaiting his approval. Falkirk merely nodded, offered no word, and took another long draught.

In a few moments the door opened, emitting a bright stream of afternoon light. Falkirk continued to sip from his glass, not even casually acknowledging the new arrival.

A tall man, stocky and unkempt, shuffled up to the oaken counter. He rapped on the wood surface with the knuckles of a grubby hand. Queenie, who had reentered the kitchen for a moment, hurried back out, thinking her distinguished guest was beckoning her. But when her eyes fell on the man at the counter, no words of welcome rose to her lips.

"Oh, 'tis you, is it, Martin Forbes," she said. "What'll ye be wantin'?"

"What do ye think I came here fer, woman!" he snarled. "Certainly it'll na be yer fine cookin'."

"Weel, 'tis too early," she replied flatly.

Forbes shot a glance at Falkirk who remained totally disinterested.

"Ye're a hard woman, Queenie," Forbes said at length, then turned and left.

A moment later Falkirk drained his glass and rose to leave, first tossing a coin on the table. It rolled to the floor, but there he left it, as if intending the proprietress to retrieve her earnings from the floor.

Queenie waited until the lord was out the door, then she scooped up the coin, tucked it into her dress, and swore softly to herself. Her distinguished visitor the previous night might have been a bit on the drunk side, but she decided he was the better-mannered of the two. Had he not only this morning sent her money well and above the cost of his uproarious evening with a kindly note of thanks and apology?

As Queenie reflected on these things, Falkirk ambled around toward the back of the inn and took the steep path down to the water's edge. From out of the tall grass emerged a figure which approached him.

"I dinna ken what all the secrecy be aboot, yer lairdship," said the man.

"Don't worry about it, Forbes," said Falkirk with a tone of superiority. "As long as you do as I say."

"Aye, my lord," Forbes replied. "Didna I follow yer orders? Ye said t' look fer yer horse an' when I saw it t' come int' the inn but pretend I didn't ken ye. That's what ye said. I'll do right by ye, yer lairdship—ye can be sure o' that."

"I'll have to," Falkirk replied. "Now listen carefully. You know the place we spoke of the other night? I want you to go there tonight—there's a full moon so you shouldn't need any other light. Look for the opening we spoke of. There should be a little hollow, almost like a small valley. If you don't find it tonight, keep at it for as many nights as it takes. If you find it, touch nothing! Come immediately for me, do you understand?"

Forbes nodded.

"I'll know if anything has been tampered with. If you cross me you'll be sorry you ever sucked a stinking breath."

"Did I ever give yer lairdship reason na t' trust me?" exclaimed Forbes. "I'm na a greedy man."

"Yes, yes," replied Falkirk dubiously. "I'll trust you when hell freezes over. But until then, you just do exactly as I say. You stand to gain quite a tidy sum yourself—but if you try anything I don't like, there won't be a hole you can find to hide where I won't find you." He glared at the man, then added, "Do you have any questions?"

"Nay, my lord—I'll poke aroun', then report back t' ye."

"Can you write?" Falkirk asked.

"Not o'er much."

"Can you write *yea* or *nay*?"

Forbes nodded.

"Then," Falkirk continued, "if you find the opening, come to Kairn at night and leave a note saying *yea* with the stableboy. I'll meet you the following night at the place. Start tonight."

With these words Falkirk spun around and stalked up the hill to his horse.

28

The Maiden

MAGGIE ROSE FROM her bed with a tingle of excitement.

She sprang to the window, looked out, and smiled. The sun would grace the land at least once more with its vibrant warmth. *It's a perfect day!* she thought. She dressed quickly and skipped down the stairs.

"Oh, Mother," she said, "it's lovely out!"

"Yes. I can tell you are excited," said Atlanta, showing more than usual good cheer herself. She was relieved that the awkwardness of her previous talk with Maggie seemed, for the moment at least, to be forgotten.

Ian walked into the dining room where the preparations were nearly complete for breakfast.

"Won't you come with us, Ian?" Maggie asked.

"Of course," he replied breezily. "I'm always ready for an adventure. Come where?"

Maggie laughed. "Of course, how could you know?" she said. "Today is the *Maiden*—the day when the last sheaf of the harvest is reaped. The crofters celebrate with a huge feast."

"One of our Scottish traditions," added Atlanta.

"I never miss it!" said Maggie.

"Well, then," said Ian, "how could I think of remaining behind? Will your friend Falkirk be there?"

"My friend?" said Maggie, casting her mother a quick glance. If Atlanta had a reaction to Ian's question, she did not show it. "He's no more my friend than yours."

"Ha!" laughed Ian good-naturedly. "I doubt he was calling on me last week! And after that horse race I don't think he considers me on the friendliest of terms."

"Well, I seriously doubt we'll see the Falkirks today," said Atlanta. "The neighboring lords and ladies don't usually make it much of a habit to mix with the people of the land."

"Too bad," said Ian. "I was just beginning to like the chap!"

Ian finished his breakfast while Maggie chatted gaily with Atlanta about preparations for the day. It being the crofters' holiday, Atlanta tried not to make an ostentatious show of the participation of the Duncan family. But the feast was a community ritual of brotherhood among all classes, everyone bringing what he was able; she always added several dishes to the large tables of food. James usually managed to be away at such times, and on this occasion had conveniently been forced to Edinburgh on business. His sentiments did not generally lie with those who worked his land, and he found their observances tedious indeed. Though she could appear aloof at times, Atlanta, on the other hand, missed no opportunity to mingle with the people of the land. She, too, had her friends such as Maggie's Lucy among them, and stole out not infrequently to take a basket of fruit or a loaf of fresh bread to a fisher wife or farmer's daughter.

By mid-afternoon the company from Stonewycke was ready to depart. Sam, the servant boy who helped Digory in the stables from time to time, brought out the open wagon which would not only provide a bumpy ride to the celebration but also a platform from which to observe the proceedings. Ian jumped aboard and lifted up the three large baskets of food as Atlanta handed them to him. He extended his hand and helped Atlanta up to her seat next to Sam, then he assisted Maggie, who joined him on the large, flat, wooden-planked bed behind them.

The celebration was to take place about a mile southwest of Port Strathy in a large grassy meadow lined with resplendent birch and oak trees, turning brilliant shades of yellow and red as autumn approached. When the wagon from Stonewycke castle arrived, over a hundred of the locals were already on hand, an assemblage which would swell to twice that size within the hour. Men were busily setting out boards to make tables to hold the food and drink. In the center Charlie Krueger was engaged in the important task of getting the huge bonfire underway, while instructing Stevie Mackinaw and a dozen other eager youngsters concerning the procurement of additional firewood.

Atlanta and Maggie took their baskets to the tables while Ian strolled over to the bonfire, greeted Krueger, and mingled with the other men gathered around, two or three of whom he hazily recognized from his ill-fated night at the Bluster 'N Blow.

As the hour drew near, the guests came trooping in from all directions, some from as far as Culden. From the direction of Port Strathy came mostly the fishermen and their wives. From the valley to the south came the crofters who worked the fertile, and the infertile, soil. It was their celebration, those by whose labor and sweat the wheat and oats and barely had at last been cut and stored away in great barns for the winter. But for longer than anyone could remember, the farmers had welcomed those others of their rank and class who similarly earned their living from the sea, and the *Maiden*, at least in the environs of Port Strathy, had indeed become a community gathering of shared good will and thankfulness.

It had long been customary for the Ramseys to attend the *Maiden* celebration, and the peasants accepted their presence gladly. Atlanta walked about among the people—much more easily than she would have been able to had James been present—talking to the wives, smiling at the children, and generally living out the love she harbored in her heart with a genuine courtesy which fostered deep admiration in the minds of all those present. Maggie, likewise, joined her, flitting about on her own from time to time, and soon won all the hearts of the people. She was indeed becoming a lady, many commented, and a handsome one who did Stonewycke proud.

Lucy Krueger shyly sought out the Lady Margaret to show her the little baby girl who was nearly two weeks old.

"Oh, Lucy!" Maggie exclaimed in the merry spirit of the day. "Your little Letty is so pink and healthy."

"Didna I say the Lord would be watchin' oot for her?" Lucy replied.

"You look as happy as your name," Maggie cooed to the child.

"I'd be honored if ye'd hold her."

"I've never held a baby before, Lucy," said Maggie.

"'Tis the most natural thing in life fer womenfolk," said Lucy, "be ye high or low bred. Here, my leddy, 'tis the easiest thing in the world." She thrust the baby toward Maggie and helped her to arrange her arms properly. "'Tis jist important that ye hold the wee head, fer it still be weak."

"Oh, my," Maggie breathed. But after only a few moments her arms relaxed and the baby fit perfectly in the crook of her arm.

Atlanta watched the scene and a great warmth welled up within her. For so long Atlanta had clung to her daughter's childhood that she had never so much as imagined the thought of grandchildren. Suddenly a vision formed in her mind of Maggie someday—a day perhaps not far away—cradling her own little one. The thought was precious to Atlanta; her own little baby was practically a woman.

"Oh, Mother," said Maggie, "look . . . look at Lucy's darling little baby girl."

Atlanta smiled. "She's beautiful, Lucy."

"Thank ye, my leddy," replied Lucy with timid pride.

"You and your husband Charlie can be very proud," Atlanta continued.

"Her name means *happiness*," said Maggie to her mother.

"And a fitting name it is," said Atlanta to Lucy. "I can see it on your face. The name, as well as your daughter, is no doubt a gift from the Lord."

Beaming, Lucy reached out her arms, and Maggie tenderly handed the small Letty back to her.

All at once the distant wail of bagpipes could be heard. Everyone put down his preparations in various stages of completion, and clustered in small bunches to watch the approaching procession.

Two pipers in kilt and tam led the way, rejoicing the watchers with a rousing and glorious pilbroch of the Highland hills. Behind them creaked an old wagon filled with hay and drawn by a single, slow-stepping Clydesdale. Atop the hay sat Alie Macondy, daughter of a crofter, the proclaimed Queen of the Festival. She held the honored last sheaf in her arms as tenderly as if it had been a bouquet of long-stemmed roses from a London flower shop. But in this northern province of Scotland, in the autumn of a successful harvest, no rose could smell so sweet to the people of the land as the final sheaf of grain. Behind the wagon, completing the processional, walked a parade of crofters, marching and dancing to the skirl and drone of the pipes.

From the surrounding meadow now poured forth all those who had already arrived, to join and further swell the ranks of the merry-makers. Songs and cheers rose higher until the procession finally reached the bonfire. There they all spread in a wide circle, several persons deep, and joining hands sang several choruses and folk songs extolling the blessings of their beloved homeland. With a final shout, as caps and bonnets were thrown high into the air, the company at last disbanded.

Then began the joyous task of consuming all the food which had so lovingly been prepared. Indeed, the feast would continue on and off throughout the remainder of the evening, interspersed with numerous other activities, for as long as food and drink held out.

Gradually the sun sank into the mountains of the west and the rosy glow of the bonfire became the center of the celebration. Blankets were produced and spread on the grass to sit upon. Others leaned against, and some of the more energetic boys scampered up into, the birches and oaks. When the bags of the pipes and lips of the pipers had given their all and finally grown silent as darkness descended,

Clare Brown caught up his fiddle and struck up a merry melody. The time for ballads and stories had come.

Atlanta found Maggie and Ian close to the fire and sat down beside her daughter. None of them noticed that young Sam had taken up with the group of older youths standing around the keg of ale.

As Clare Brown began to sing, the music washed over Maggie's senses and she realized she had not felt so contented at any time she could remember. For this present moment the turmoils of her life had receded out of sight in the peaceful and dreamy atmosphere of the evening.

"Why don't ye sing the ballard o' the Douglas?" someone called out to Clare.

"Surely na such a sad song on such a gay night as this," he replied.

"Aye, 'tis sad," came the answer, "but ye sing it so well!"

"Aye. Ye'll have yer way wi' me, will ye!" said Clare with a laugh. "So here 'tis then":

"Rise up, rise up, now, Lord Douglas," she says,
   An' put on yer armour so bright;
Let it never be said, that a daughter o' thine
   Was married to a lord under night."

Rise up, rise up, my seven bold sons,
   An' put on yer armour so bright,
An' take better care o' yer youngest sister,
   For yer eldest's awa the last night.

He's mounted her on a milk-white steed,
   An' himsel' on a dapple grey,
With a bugelet horn hung doon by his side,
   An' lightly they rode away.

Lord William lookit o'er his left shoulder,
   To see what he could see,
An' there he spy'd her seven brethren bold,
   Come ridin' o'er the lea.

"Light down, light down, Lady Marg'ret," he said,
   "An' hold my steed in your hand,
Until that against yer seven brothers bold,
   An' yer father, I mak a stand."

She held his steed in her milk-white hand,
   An' never shed one tear,
Until that she saw her seven brethren fall,
   An' her father hard fighting, who lov'd her so dear.

"O hold yer hand, Lord William!" she said,
   "For yer strokes they are wond'rous sair;

True lovers I can get many a ane,
    But a father I can never get mair."

O she's ta'en out her handkerchief,
    It was o' the holland sae fine,
And aye she dighted her father's bloody wounds,
    That were redder than the wine.

"O choose, O choose, Lady Marg'ret," he said,
    "O whether will ye gang or bide?"
"I'll gang, I'll gang, Lord William," she said,
    "For ye hae left me no other guide."

He's lifted her on a milk-white steed,
    An' lifted himsel' on a dapple grey,
With a bugelet horn hung down by his side,
    An' slowly they baith rade away.

O they rade on, an' on they rade,
    An' a' by the light o' the moon,
Until they came to yon wan water,
    An' there they lighted doon.

They lighted doon to tak a drink
    O' the spring that ran sae clear;
An' doon the stream ran his gude heart's blood,
    An' sair she 'gan to fear.

"Hold up, hold up, Lord William," she said,
    "For I fear that ye are slain!"
"'Tis nothin' but the shadow of my scarlet cloak,
    That shines in the water sae plain."

O they rade on, an' on they rade,
    An' a' by the light o' the moon,
Until they cam to his mother's ha' door,
    An' there they lighted doon.

"Get up, get up, Lady Mother," he says,
    "Get up, an' let me in!—
Get up, get up, Lady Mother," he says,
    "For this night my fair lady I've win."

"O make my bed, Lady Mother," he says,
    "O make it braid and deep!
An' lay Lady Marg'ret close at my back,
    An' the sounder I will sleep."

Lord William was dead lang ere midnight,
    Lady Marg'ret lang ere day—

An' all true lovers that go t'gither,
  May they hae mair luck than they!

Lord William was buried in St. Marie's kirk,
  Lady Marg'ret in Marie's quire;
Out o' the lady's grave grew a bonny red rose,
  An' out o' the knight's a brier.

An' they twa met, an' they twa plat,
  An' fain they would be near;
An' al' the world might ken right weel,
  They were twa lovers dear.

But by an' rade the Black Douglas,
  An' wow but he was rough!
For he pull'd up the bonny brier,
  An' flang't in St. Mary's loch.

Maggie was only vaguely conscious of the melancholy words. She turned to look at Ian. As the fire reflected on his face, she saw deeper thought there than she had yet noticed. When Clare began a gayer tune, the pensive look remained momentarily, then gradually subsided. He turned, aware that she had been gazing at him, and smiled. No words seemed appropriate, or necessary.

As Clare began his final song, the great fire had burned down to bright orange embers. As the last notes died away into the still night air, as if waking from a peaceful slumber that it might go home to bed, the crowd slowly began to stir. The men stretched their tired legs, the women gathered children and baskets, and reluctantly the families of the Strathy valley began to make their way home.

Ian forced himself to a standing position, took Maggie's hand and lifted her to her feet, and went off in search of Sam. It took several minutes to discover him, nestled against the trunk of a tree, sound asleep with a smile on his face. Ian hoisted him into the back of the wagon where he sprawled out and quickly fell asleep once more.

Ian helped Maggie and Atlanta up, then jumped up himself, and, taking the reins, urged the horses forward with a click of his tongue and a flip of the reins in his wrists.

Little was said on the way back to Stonewycke, as if by common consent each wished the evening could have gone on and on.

29

The Young Master of Kairn

※

THE EVENING COULDN'T go on forever, of course. James returned late the following afternoon and with him returned the tensions he had taken with him. But James's first stop before riding back through the gates of Stonewycke had been Kairn. The visit had been a brief one, but long enough for George Falkirk to indicate subtly the difficulty he had found in getting near Lady Margaret. James extended to his neighbor's son an invitation to Stonewycke for the next day, assuring him the matter would be taken care of.

The day could not have been more ill-chosen for courting had it been contrived as a plot against the suave young Falkirk. The morning dawned cloudy, and as the hours wore on, the deep mass of gray gave way to thick menacing clumps of black storm clouds blowing down from the mountains in the south. By noon the rain had begun in earnest and by the time Falkirk arrived an hour later, all the inhabitants of Stonewycke were shut in together and the mood had grown gloomy.

Delighted with Falkirk's appearance, James put on a great show of friendliness before awkwardly beginning the task of contriving some distraction for Ian. Unsuccessful, at length he fabricated a story of a business associate he wanted his cousin to meet, passing—as chance would have it—through Port Strathy that very day. Duncan, unconvincing, deceived none of those present; and his case was hardly strengthened by the fact that he had previously made such a concerted effort to ignore Ian altogether.

Under the circumstances, however, Ian was hardly able to refuse; he consented to the ride despite the nasty weather, and went to his room for cloak and hat. Leaving Maggie in Falkirk's presence disturbed him more than he would have thought possible, even yesterday. But after the night of the *Maiden*, she had been on his mind almost constantly. All morning he had been making efforts to find a way to speak to her himself. Falkirk's inopportune arrival and James's clear ploy to thrust the two young estate neighbors together plunged him into a vortex of mixed emotions.

He had come north for reasons undefined, with expectations obscure. Now suddenly rising within him were feelings he hadn't expected, in the center of which swirled the face of his seventeen-year-old cousin Margaret. As he sat beside James in the covered gig and pulled his hat down tightly against the wind, he found his heart fairly pounding in his chest at the prospect of leaving his adversary alone with her.

As for the young master of Kairn, he had stepped unknowingly into what was for him an awkward encounter. Maggie was detached, at times downright rude to him, then suddenly turned to baiting him with coy glances of encouragement. He had only to surmise that her disagreeable nature stemmed in one way or another from the presence in the house of that wretched cousin of hers. *Not that her affections really matter in the end*, he told himself. It was all being arranged. Once she came to see him in a different light, she would come round to her senses, of that he was sure—even if it took some time.

In the meantime, he had to get her alone. When Atlanta was called away to attend to some difficulty in the kitchen, Falkirk breathed an inner sigh of relief.

When he had arrived, he had been shown into the east parlor. Atlanta and Maggie had been sitting on the setee, where they had remained for the duration of his visit thus far. Falkirk had taken a wing-backed chair adjacent to them. The moment Atlanta had left the room with the servant, he rose and strolled casually to the huge carved mantle over the fireplace.

"You don't know, Lady Margaret," he began, "how pleasant it has been to have this opportunity to visit you."

Maggie relaxed slightly, thinking he was about to take his leave.

"From the moment I met you," he continued, "I knew I must become more closely acquainted with you."

He paused for effect. Maggie squirmed slightly.

"Do you remember the day?"

Maggie nodded.

"Your party," he went on. He turned and began to move toward her. "The coming-out celebration for a young lady who is a girl no longer . . . but a woman."

He dropped down next to her on the setee.

"How grand you were that night!" he continued. "The most beautiful person there."

"Please, Mr. Falkirk," said Maggie, "you are making me uncomfortable."

"Your beauty has grown even greater to me since that day," he went on, ignoring her.

The words should have pleased Maggie, but instead she felt suddenly stifled and hot, as if she needed a window opened. The feeling intensified as Falkirk drew nearer. She found herself inching away from him.

"Margaret, my heart pounds when I think of you, and nearly stops now that we are together."

He grasped her hands. They were cold and trembling. Perceiving that she was nervous, he moderated his advance.

"You must think me terribly forward, even impetuous. Forgive me."

Maggie forced a smile and nodded her concurrence.

"But the throbbing of my heart compels me to speak thus. Please grant me permission to see more of you."

Maggie tensed again.

It was all too clear what George Falkirk wanted. He was a forceful man, with sophisticated manners and a fine inheritance to press his claim. Why wasn't she flattered by his attentions?

Wavering between outrage at his presumption and pleasure at his flatteries, Maggie floundered for an answer.

"Why, Mr. Falkirk," she began, "I . . . I don't know what to say. There are so few people in the neighborhood of my age—of course, it would be nice to share your company—"

"That's not exactly what I had in mind," he cut in sharply; then the edge in his voice immediately softened. "That is to say, I had hoped you might allow me, as I mentioned before, to act as your escort to some of the neighboring estates, and perhaps to some social functions."

"I'm not ready to make that kind of decision, Mr. Falkirk," said Maggie.

"What's to decide? I am a young man with experience. You are a beautiful young woman. Why shouldn't we be seen together? I see no reason—"

"I'm still very young," said Maggie feebly.

"The time must come, Lady Margaret, when you enter into your calling as the future mistress of the estate."

"What do you know about the future of Stonewycke?" asked Maggie pointedly.

Realizing he had revealed too much about what he knew, Falkirk attempted gracefully to soothe her.

"I only meant," he said, "that *should* you ever become the mistress of the estate—should your brother choose to advance his career in London, for instance—then it would behoove you to give thought to your calling."

She seemed temporarily mollified by his explanation. As he spoke he eased closer to her and slipped his arm around her onto the back of the setee. "Before long you will have suitors lined up at your door. And—sooner than you might think—the time will come when you must think of marriage."

"My marriage plans are my own concern," replied Maggie, on her guard again. "Marriage is too far in the future for me to think about. Besides, as I said before, I am still young. I have much to learn."

"Then let me be your teacher," he said, drawing so near that Maggie felt the heat of his breath on her face. "It's time you learned what life has to give you. Let me be the one to water the lovely bud of Stonewycke, the Lady Margaret Duncan."

He had pressed so close that his lips brushed her cheek. A fleeting pulse quickened her heartbeat. She wanted to yield to his words of affection, but suddenly she felt hot and trapped. She could feel the red rising up the back of her neck and into her cheeks.

"I . . . I just—" she began, then as if by impulse she jumped up from the setee and moved quickly to open the large window. She drew a deep breath of air and immediately felt her flushed face cool.

But the next instant Falkirk's unsolicited hands slipped around her waist. "I must tell you," he whispered in her ear, "that I cannot so easily distract my mind from its infatuation with you, and I intend—"

At that moment Atlanta's step could be heard on the landing outside the door. Falkirk immediately pulled away with a silent curse as she entered the room. Maggie's hands rose to her reddened cheeks while she continued to gaze out the window, saying nothing. Surveying the scene, Atlanta discerned that she had returned none too soon. More perturbed than flustered, Falkirk smiled and began an immediate conversation with Atlanta about nothing of particular consequence.

Later in the day James returned with Ian, having been unable to locate his friend, but taking advantage of the time for several minor items of business he had been putting off. Falkirk returned to Kairn, somewhat disconcerted at the effort it was apparently going to take to further his advance toward the headstrong little heiress. But he was pleased with himself nonetheless. The little lady would capitulate in time; especially with the father advancing his cause, there was little need for concern. The veneer of her reluctance was all too transparent. His words of love would win her over. They had worked for him before, and she was no different than all the rest.

The rain had ceased but the sky remained black as he rode through the gates of Kairn. He was softly whistling a tune, feeling in good spirits, and relishing the thought of a tall mug of cold stout after his long ride. The stableboy took the horse, relieved that the young lord, who could be a hard master when things were not to his liking, was in an agreeable mood.

The boy led the horse to a stall, then stopped abruptly.

"My Lord!" he called out, hoping not to get his ears boxed for nearly forgetting.

"What is it?" demanded Falkirk, turning.

"A man brought ye this earlier. Tole me t' give it t' ye."

He handed the dirty, crumpled paper to Falkirk, who would have indeed boxed the boy's ears had he not been absorbed in the message.

It simply read *yea*.

30
The Dormin

THE ANCIENT FOREST called Dormin stood on the west bank of the River Lindow which ran through the western portion of the Stonewycke estate. It stood in solemn splendor just as it had stood perhaps a thousand years ago—nearly untouched by man because some good king ages ago had laid eyes on it, and had loved it so that he passed laws against killing its animals or felling its trees or harming so much as a petal of the tiniest flower. Disobedience had been punishable by death.

In later years, of course, the severity of the punishment had been moderated, but the Dormin still remained under royal protection. Every so often a poacher would be found and arrested, but usually he faced only a stiff fine, and was not imprisoned unless the penalty went unpaid.

Yet few were bold enough to tread the tangled paths of the forest. Its treasures, therefore, remained all the more preserved for the infrequent beholder. Dozens of mosses clung to the trees, some so rare and exquisitely delicate that even botanical experts had not seen the like. The Dormin's trees—massive and ancient—appeared rather like living sentinals—old Scots fir, birch, aspen, alder, rowan, and oak—custodians of the past, guarding against intruders of the present. Interspersed between them were thick growths of high heather and other wet and woodsy shrubbery, pervaded by the ever-present hint of decay—rotting logs, fallen leaves and needles, and the continually dying, cyclically renewing dense underbrush. Even flowers could be found in their season, wherever they could push their lovely faces out of the tangled mass—crocuses, primroses, daffodils. Watching over them, from atop their higher perch, as king of the Dormin's flowering shrubbery, were the many-colored blossoms of wild rhododendron, ready to bestow the sweet pleasure of their faces to the more adventurous forest wanderer.

Maggie always experienced a shiver of apprehension as she approached the forest. Here her great-grandfather Anson Ramsey had been mysteriously killed one gray autumn day. She remembered well the story of his final days at Stonewycke. *A hunting party had driven three stags from the forest near the castle. Two were killed almost immediately, but the third, a magnificent pale animal, received only a superficial wound. The party tracked it for the remainder of that day, certain it could not get far.*

But at dusk the white stag still ran free, and the party was ready to concede defeat and turn for home. All, that is, except for Anson, who convinced his two sons, Talmud and Edmond, to keep up the hunt with him. They continued to trail the blood track and prints on the ground all night and into the next morning. Though they wandered in great circles, never heading for the high mountains, they were still unable to approach the mighty animal but could only make out the silhouette of its great antlered head over the next brae. During the afternoon of the second day, Anson tracked it across the Lindow only to watch his prey disappear into the depths of the Dormin. The great stag paused as he gained the opposite bank of the river, turned toward Anson as if to remind him that the last man to kill his prey in the forest behind him had been hanged, then bounded over a log and quickly disappeared from sight.

Anson knew the stag would easily elude them in the dense forest within moments, but too much time had been invested by now; he could not simply stand by helplessly, allowing the animal its victory without one final attempt.

Shouting for his sons to follow, he charged across the river and into the

Dormin with renewed vigor and speed. Edmond and Talmud followed not far behind.

But Anson returned home that day with no prize.

He was draped over his horse, dead of a broken neck. His sons recounted that they had found him in the forest sprawled on the ground. They could only speculate that his steed had stumbled on a fallen branch and thrown the lord; in death, his disappointed gaze was still focused in the direction of the lost stag.

But family history was far from Maggie's mind today.

Raven and Maukin splashed across the shallow ford of the Lindow. Ian whistled gaily as they clambered up the opposite bank and beheld the seemingly impenetrable wood immediately before them. He stopped and gazed with wonder, sensing the mystery of the place. It seemed to emanate forgotten secrets and undiscovered histories. Maggie plunged Raven ahead into the labyrinth of vines and bushes and ferns, and Ian cautiously urged Maukin to follow. *It is almost a challenge,* he thought, *merely to cross the invisible threshold of this wood's border.* He wondered if that soft rustling sound was not some murmur of the trees, for there was no wind that fine September morning. But whether their leafy voice spoke welcome or boded ill, he could not tell.

After riding a few minutes, they stopped and dismounted, speaking in hushed tones. They stepped lightly on the carpet of fallen leaves and moss which graced the small clearing where they stood. Around them the few shafts of sunlight which were able to penetrate the foliage shone on a resplendent array of autumn reds and golds and yellows and browns, spread like fairy dust over the greenery beneath. Ian's eyes looked upward as he walked about; suddenly Maggie's soft but urgent voice warned him of a huge root protruding dangerously from the ground in front of his foot.

He avoided stumbling over it, thanked her, and bent his gaze toward the forest floor.

"Not only am I ungraceful in the saddle," he said, "it seems I need a guide for my feet, too!"

Maggie laughed softly.

"This is marvelous!" he exclaimed. "You could truly forget yourself here."

"If you wanted to forget," said Maggie. "I think it's the kind of place that would allow you to be whatever you needed to be."

"You've been here before, I can tell," said Ian.

"Many times."

"You make it sound almost reverent."

"I suppose I do reverence this place," she replied, "almost like a garden of Eden. It's so . . . so ancient."

"And that's what makes it holy?" asked Ian seriously.

"I don't know. It makes it awesome, that much is certain. But then I think Digory would say it isn't age that makes a thing holy, but . . ."

"But what?"

"I don't know what I was going to say exactly."

"Purity," said Ian, hardly realizing such an answer was in him.

"Purity . . . innocence? Then the more pure a thing is, the closer to holiness it comes. Is purity the same as godliness, do you suppose?"

"Well," said Ian briskly, trying to shake the spell of the place, "that's a question I will never have to worry about."

"Why?"

"I'm no philosopher. I'm just a fun-loving Englishman!"

"So I've discovered," replied Maggie with a laugh. "But you know people are not always what they appear on the surface," she went on with a playful gleam in her eye.

"Is that something else Digory would say?"

Maggie smiled.

"Come on," she said, "before we spend all day philosophizing when I've so much for you to see."

She grabbed his hand and would have skipped forward if the terrain had allowed it.

"Will we be able to find our way out of here?" Ian asked, though there was more laughter than anxiety in his voice.

"If we ever want to leave," she replied. "I know the way. I'm your guide, remember?"

Leaving the horses where they had tied them, Maggie led deeper into the forest. Gradually the light dimmed; only patches of sunlight and pale blue sky could occasionally be seen between the trees as they formed a lattice overhead like a fine lace mantilla.

They followed a tiny stream for a ways, stopping beside a freshet for a drink of icy mountain water. How long had it been since anyone had drunk from it? Or were they the first?

As she stood up from the stream, Maggie realized Ian was gazing at her instead of the forest, his eyes bright. *What is he thinking?* she wondered. Had she been able to see inside that head topped with tousled golden hair, she would have seen that he was chiding himself for his flippant attitude when they had first met. It seemed so long ago; in reality it had only been a matter of weeks. But that short time had added years to his life, extended his horizons of awareness—both of the world around him and of himself. Indeed, as he gazed deep into her eyes he realized that he regarded Maggie as a gift he had been given, a gift which stimulated his new discoveries and insights. But looking up to meet his gaze, Maggie knew none of this.

"Oh, look!" Maggie had spotted a tiny purple and white primrose, nestled among several dead branches; she whispered, as if her voice might somehow cause it to fold up its leaves and hide from them.

They stooped down together to observe it more closely. Ian moved back some of the leaves and branches and stretched out his hand to pluck it.

"Stop! Don't pick it," Maggie cried, placing her hand on his and drawing it away.

He turned, keeping hold of her hand. "I was going to give it to you," he said.

They drew apart, then, as if moved by the same impulse, and sat down on the ground, staring in the direction of the solitary primrose.

"Thank you," said Maggie. "I didn't mean to pounce on you so."

Ian said nothing, only glanced away, restlessly.

"Is anything wrong?" Maggie asked.

"No," he replied. "I mean . . . there's something—"

"What is it?"

Ian hesitated. "I've been . . . you know—in London. Playing the part of the carouser, the lady's gentleman. Words of love falling off my tongue more easily than the ale poured down my throat. But . . ."

Heat rose up the back of Maggie's neck. Her heart was pounding within her chest so loudly that she feared Ian must hear it, so loudly it echoed in the silence of the forest; but not loudly enough to silence the words she knew Ian was struggling to say. The fear now burning hot in her cheeks was so different from what she had felt when alone with George Falkirk. Now she was afraid of the words she *longed* to hear, longed to shout out herself!

"Maggie," Ian went on with stammering determination, "you've . . . you've given me something since I came here—different from anything I've felt with anyone before."

He stopped and breathed deeply, then jumped to his feet and paced about nervously, trying to find the right words. Then he dropped to the ground again at the foot of a rowan tree and leaned his head back against its trunk. Maggie slid to her knees next to him.

"Oh, it's no use!" he exclaimed.

Maggie turned toward him and gently placed her hand on his arm. "Try, Ian," she said. "What were you going to say?"

"I would never have noticed that insignificant flower without you," he said at last. "I might have even tried to step on it if I had seen it—unknowing, uncaring, unfeeling. Now I can never again look at the plainest of flowers, at a mountain stream, at a desolate moor, at a heather hill, without—"

Her lips were silent, but Maggie's eyes said, *Yes?*

"—without thinking of you."

Now that he had said it, Ian was finally able to turn and look Maggie in the face. She was smiling, a silent tear running down her cheek.

"I did nothing, Ian," she said softly. "You must have always had that love for God's creation within you. But you were too bound up in the distractions of your life, afraid to open yourself to that kind of beauty, afraid to let out your true feelings, afraid of being vulnerable."

"But it's more than a sensitivity to all this beauty around us," he said.

"I know," she said softly. She wanted to say, *It's more for me, too,* but she couldn't make the words come out.

"It's *you*, Maggie," he said. "The reason I can love that flower or the heather is that for the first time I really care about someone—about you."

He turned away, embarrassed at the awkwardness of his speech, and fearing her reply.

Maggie, too, remained silent. What could she say? Did she even know what she felt herself? She had been holding back for so long; now suddenly something cried out within her to open her heart again. With every ride she and Ian took, with every chance meeting of their eyes, each time she heard him laugh in such high-spirited joy, the crevice in her heart opened a bit wider. Something was driving them together, and she could no longer resist its force.

Misconstruing Maggie's silence, Ian was overcome with self-consciousness. If the forest around them remained silent one second more, he feared he would burst; to break the hush he suddenly blurted out the thoughtless remark—

"Of course, I know that you and our friend Mr. Falkirk—"

"George Falkirk!" interrupted Maggie. "What about *him*?"

"Aren't you and he . . . ?" Ian completed his sentence with a look of questioning.

"Ian," said Maggie, "George Falkirk means nothing to me."

A stab of hope shot through Ian's heart. He turned toward Maggie, eyes aglow with the laughter he was for the moment content to keep inside.

"Don't you know . . . haven't you seen, Ian?"

Only his eyes spoke, searching her face for the final words he sought.

"Don't you know that I feel the same way about you?"

At last he could contain his delight no more. Ian burst into a hearty laugh, more exuberant than Maggie had yet heard from him. She could not keep from joining him.

When the verbal expression of their shared joy was spent, Ian rose, took her hand and raised Maggie to her feet. Arm in arm they walked silently back through the forest the way they had come.

31

The Locket

IAN WANTED TO give Maggie a present. Perhaps his gift would never mean as much as Lucy Krueger's simple handkerchief, but nevertheless, he wanted her to have something from him. He had looked through the belongings he had brought from London, but nothing was suitable.

The day was drawing to a close. On a sudden impulse he decided to ride into Port Strathy. Surely he could locate something there. Maggie so loved this valley that a gift from its quaint fishing village would be the best thing, anyway.

Pat Brodie was about to hang his *Closed* sign on the door of the mercantile when Ian rode up in a gallop and quickly dismounted.

"Weel, ye're in a fine rush, ye are, lad," he said with an amiable smile.

"I've mind to buy something," Ian replied, approaching the front of the shop. "I won't keep you long."

"I've ne'er been one t' keep away a customer . . . come in." The shopkeeper opened the door and with a sweep of his hand welcomed Ian inside.

One look at the interior of the store made Ian wonder if he'd over-estimated his chances of finding something. The place was crammed with a vast array of merchandise, none of it appearing to be in any particular order. A hammer could be found with linen handkerchiefs, or a pair of shoes tucked in between sacks of chicken feed. The foodstuffs seemed generally to be along the right-hand wall, but then Ian noticed a pair of long underwear jammed between several tins of cured herring.

Ian edged his way between crates and bins and sacks, somehow hoping the right token of his feelings might miraculously jump out to greet him. He had no idea what he might be looking for; a hasty scan of the premises revealed little other than the most practical necessities of humble Scottish life, and he was about to give up. He had already overstepped the bounds of courtesy in keeping Brodie past the usual hour.

As he turned with a sigh to go, a small wooden create perched atop a bin of plowshares caught his eye. He walked toward it for a closer look, and discovered the crate to be filled with smaller, delicate boxes.

Further investigation revealed that each box contained a ring or brooch or some particular article of jewelry. So Brodie did stock a few impractical trinkets after all! Most were large gold-covered pieces with cheap, showy imitation gems. Familiar enough with quality jewel-work, Ian realized that such costume pieces might be fine for a poor fisherman's wife who had never in her life seen a real pearl—but none were suitable for Maggie. Persistently, however, he opened each box until at last his efforts were rewarded. Near the bottom of the crate he discovered a delicate heart-shaped locket, golden in color, hanging from a delicate gold chain. Ian perceived at a glance that it could not be genuine. It was clearly the sort of thing the crofters might buy for their sweethearts—Maggie's poorest gem would easily outshine this trinket. Yet for right now it was just what he wanted: a simple memento of his feelings. There would be plenty of time to purchase a fine expensive piece in London later.

He removed it from the crate and made his way to the counter, only discernible as such in that Brodie was standing patiently behind it.

Brodie's eyes twinkled as he caught sight of Ian's selection. "Ah, now I see what ye was in sich a hurry fer. 'Tis a fine locket! Will make yer lass happy fer sure. They come t' me all the way from Glasgow. An' 'tis only two shillin's."

Ian placed the money on the counter.

"Now, in the big city," Brodie continued as he carelessly dropped the coins into a tin urn, "they engrave fancy words an' such on these things—but I'm afraid I dinna hae the art."

"It'll do fine the way it is, Mr. Brodie," Ian replied. "Thank you so much for letting me in."

Leaving the shop, Ian felt great satisfaction with his purchase. He hoped this gift might, in a way mere words never could, clarify what he had been trying to express to Maggie in the Dormin. He urged the chestnut to a trot, now eager to return to Stonewycke and see the lovely face once more.

As he turned from Port Strathy's chief street toward the hill leading out of town, he spied a rider rapidly approaching down the hill. Though the features of the face were not yet visible, there could be no mistaking the golden stallion and the confident carriage of the rider. In an instant, Ian perceived that the horseman had only just come from the mansion and his spirit sank within him.

"Good evening, Mr. Falkirk," said Ian crisply as they met.

"Good, indeed," Falkirk replied sharply, the gleam in his eye revealing unspoken contempt. "Flying back to the little nest, are you?"

"What is that supposed to mean?" retorted Ian, in no mood to exchange quips with his rival.

"You think yourself pretty clever, no doubt," answered Falkirk, "getting your tentacles about the little lady of Stonewycke. But don't be too sure of yourself, Duncan. The women I have known take pleasure in a prize with more, shall we say, gratuities, than I believe you have to offer. And this wench is no different."

"Is that how you think of Maggie, as a common wench?"

"Ah, Maggie, is it?"

"I asked you a question, Falkirk!"

"Playing the shining knight—a good move. But it won't help you get your clutches around Stonewycke. That tasty morsel will be mine, along with its little lady."

"That's all you're after, isn't it, Falkirk! You care nothing for Maggie!"

Maukin moved about nervously and stamped her foot, feeling her rider's growing anger tightening in his muscles.

"Don't be plebian, Duncan."

"That's what you consider affection between a man and a woman?"

"You come from a family of breeding. You know how the game is played."

"I love her, Falkirk. That means more than your breeding!"

"Love?" sneered Falkirk. "Pshaw!"

"I'll die before I see her with you," retorted Ian angrily.

"Another challenge?" mocked Falkirk.

"Make of it what you will," replied Ian, moving his horse aside to continue along the road.

"Even if you did love the girl," Falkirk called out to him in a taunting voice, "you stand no chance with her. I have her father's approval. And I will win her in the end!"

"We shall see!" yelled Ian over his shoulder, then dug in his heels and galloped away.

The fury Ian felt for Falkirk was quickly suppressed by the impact of his own words, which now rushed back into his memory with staggering power.

I love her, he had said.

It had been an emotional outburst. Yet as his head began to clear and he slowed Maukin to a walk, he tried to recall when the exact moment of realization had come. Perhaps it had come upon him so slowly because the feeling had been there from his first day at Stonewycke.

32
Words of Truth

BY THE TIME Ian had arrived back at the mansion, he had all but forgotten his unsettling encounter with George Falkirk. His spirits were alive with thoughts of Maggie.

Digory heard him approaching, walked to the entrance to the stables, and stood in readiness to take charge of Ian's mare and lead it inside.

Whistling happily, Ian lightly swept the groom aside. "Let me take care of the horse, my good man! Have yourself a rest. Take a walk . . . it's a beautiful day!"

Thanking him, Digory noted that both the day and his years were rather far advanced for walks of any extended nature, and then went inside. Following him, Ian, still whistling, began to unsaddle Maukin.

"Ah, Digory," he said. "I'm a lucky man. While my friends are languishing away in the stone and gloom of London, I am here in the most beautiful land on earth."

"Aye, 'tis a wondrous place."

"Truly God's land, wouldn't you agree?"

"That I would, sir," Digory replied.

"Why on a day like today, I could almost believe that God does care about us. How else could it be so beautiful?"

The words took Digory by surprise, spoken as they were with unabashed cheerfulness.

"Sir?" he said, not knowing how else to respond without seeming to offend the laird's houseguest.

"Yes," Ian went on, caught up in his exuberance. "A god could have created Scotland, with all its lovely visions. Don't you think?"

"I *know* He did, sir," Digory replied. "Not jist could hae, He *did*. But I'm also knowin' He created London, too."

"Extraordinary," Ian breathed, almost in a daze, still thinking about the magnificent countryside. He turned with a start as Digory's last words seemed finally to reach him.

"You believe in God, then?"

"I do, sir," replied Digory, "wi' all my heart."

"I think I should like to believe too," Ian said.

"An' what's stoppin' ye, sir?"

"I suppose if one could just see Him, or understand Him, it would make believing in Him easier," said Ian thoughtfully.

"Did ye never love somethin' that ye couldn't fully understan'?" asked Digory. "Mysel', sometimes I canna understan' these horses, but I love them nonetheless fer it."

Ian said nothing. His thoughts turned to the primrose whose beauty he and Maggie had shared in the Dormin. Just seeing it had prompted such wellsprings of delight, such love, inside him that he had hardly been able to contain it. Yet he hardly knew a thing about the tiny plant. Then he thought of Maggie. Yes, he loved her without knowing all about her or understanding her. Perhaps the old groom was right.

"I dinna ken how or why, but I ken He gives us good gifts, like the land an' horses, an' —"

"And flowers?" suggested Ian.

"Ye're right there," said Digory. "An' flowers . . . because He loves us. An' we don't need t' understan' all aboot that love, or aboot Him, in order t' receive that love o' His."

"Perhaps you're right. But how or why He would love such as us I don't know."

"'Tis His nature t' love," said Digory. "When He made the world, 'twas because He loved. When He made man, 'twas because He loved. Whatever He does now, 'tis because He loves."

"His *nature* . . ." Ian mused. By this time he had hoisted Maukin's saddle onto its rack and was vigorously rubbing the animal down with a stiff brush. At another time, in another place he would have laughed off the groom's words, indifferent to the serious impression they made in his mind. He had never thought much about *love* before now, about its nature or its source. He had always wanted love, of course—both to give and to receive it. But he had never admitted that need, not even to himself. Now for the first time, such feelings did not frighten him. He was growing accustomed to the changes within him, even beginning to accept them.

"Does everyone know that about God?" asked Ian, stopping his work and turning to face the groom squarely.

"Ken what, lad?"

"That He loves . . . that it is His nature to love?"

"I doobt it, lad," Digory replied. "Nay, I think we'd be behavin' different if we all did. An' even those of us who *think* we ken, even we probably dinna grasp jist how deep His love fer us is."

"Yes," replied Ian absently, "yes, I suppose you're right."

"But what everyone thinks or kens dinna matter so much," Digory went on. "'Tis that ye ken *yersel'* that God loves ye—that's what matters."

Ian did not reply, but stood contemplating the words. At last he handed the brush to Digory and, without a word, turned to leave the stables.

33

The Granite Pillars of Braenock

GEORGE FALKIRK AND Martin Forbes made an unseemly pair.

Falkirk was the gentleman in every proud sinew of his body, while Forbes sat slouching in the saddle of his borrowed horse, outfitted in coarse dungarees, dreaming of the day he would be rich enough to kick dirt in the face of such as Falkirk.

Unlikely and mismatched as they were, the two now rode in common cause.

The sun had disappeared somewhere behind the Dormin, and the shadows of evening blanketed the desolate Braenock Moor. The September nights were growing longer and cooler, and without a moon the riders would have a measure of cover, at least as much as was possible until late in the winter when the sun would set by mid-afternoon.

The horses found their footing with difficulty over the rocky ledges; the fact that they had already traveled this path made little difference. Why those ancients would ever build a village out here, Falkirk could not even hazard a guess. Perhaps it was different a thousand years ago. Perhaps this unlikely location offered some advantage in case of attack—who could tell?

He recalled the gruesome tales of those days and the talebearers he had had to endure. But those visits to dark, smelly back rooms had at last paid a rich dividend. The moment of victory was almost at hand.

The first account he had heard had been at the university during a lecture on ancient history; the professor had spoken of the various ruins scattered about Britain. Falkirk's interest was mildly aroused when the professor mentioned a ruin on the Stonewycke property, only a few miles from Kairn. He would have thought little more about it except that later in the same discourse, the professor had dwelt for some time on the wealth discovered by a team of archaeologists in a dig near Craigievar Castle farther to the south, some twenty miles west of Aberdeen. The value of most of the items in such finds had, of course, been measured purely in historical terms, an issue of little interest in Falkirk. But the word *wealth* had impressed itself upon him. Further investigation stirred up shadowy stories about hastily dug vaults containing more tangible riches than mere artifacts and relics.

Whispers about the Pict ruin near Stonewycke said that over a thousand years earlier, the village had been ruthlessly attacked by marauding Viking warriors, supposedly for a few morsels of food. Though the legend was mentioned from time to time, few, if any, of the local inhabitants had ever set eyes on the place. Those who knew where it was offered differing opinions. Just a pile of rocks, some said. Boulders piled high to block the entryway to a small ravine, said others. But no one bothered to investigate further. Even young Stevie Mackinaw, who had played on the very spot, had no inkling of the history that had passed beneath his very feet.

As if fate were drawing him to the ruin, young George Falkirk's attentive ears continued to gather tidbits of information, important pieces in the puzzle.

"Who'd kill like that?" he had overheard in Culden's only public establishment, a small pub with a warm fire and cheap ale.

Falkirk glanced about him inconspicuously and eyed two farmers, apparently talking about the ruin.

". . . an' jist fer a bit t' eat?" the man continued.

"'Tis how folks was back then," replied his companion.

"But how could even the Vikings be so cruel as that?"

"I suspect 'twas more like what *I* heard aboot it," said the other.

"An' what was that, noo?"

"Jist this, that them Pict fellows had a heap o' somethin' they was hidin' that the Norsemen found oot aboot."

"An' they killed them fer it?"

"So I heard."

His companion laughed. "So why aren't ye oot lookin' fer it?" he scoffed.

"I got a croft t' run," he answered. "An' if there was somethin' there, them Vikings got it long ago, no doobt."

His curiosity kindled, Falkirk had taken a longer route home that day, riding to Braenock in search of the ruin. He found what he thought were the granite boulders and had poked around among them. But he soon realized it would take a concerted effort to delve into the secrets of the ruin if he hoped to discover anything of value. Other cares waylaid him for a time, but through research and journeys to several of Aberdeen's universities, he did eventually manage to learn something of the original structure of that ruin. He had also learned of the stone door, which he had reason to believe was an entry to the fulfillment of his plans.

He had then discussed with his father the purchase of the ridge, ostensibly for other reasons. Lord Falkirk asked few questions and made the offer; George had been hopeful. He had to keep his keen personal passion for the site quiet, for if Duncan fell privy to the information he possessed, all would be lost. But the sale had been quelled at the last moment by Duncan's wife, who determined to hang onto every inch of Stonewycke as if it were Eden itself.

George's initial rage soon quieted into controlled determination; he now had to discover some alternate means to achieve his ends. His desire to unearth the secrets of Braenock Ridge had become so single-minded, he would have spared nothing to gain his goal, an intensity stimulated by the influence of one Sallo Grist.

Grist appeared as ancient and mysterious as the Picts themselves. More than his antiquity produced the aura of reverence which seemed to cling to him: his entire person emanated an image of legend and magic, enhanced by the coarse woolen robe belted with hemp rope, and the thick white hair massed upon his head. His medicinal remedies and cures—well known in all the lower portions of London—lent further credence to his ancestry. He lived along the Thames under bridges, or in any one of several greasy taverns on the docks. One was never sure where he might be found. Some thought him a vagrant, some considered him a doctor, still others swore he was a sorcerer in the tradition of Merlin—or worse. Most simply called him mad.

An acquaintance of Falkirk's in London had told him, "If you want to know about the Picts, go to Sallo Grist—he claims to be a descendant of Oengus. Of course," he added with a laugh, "he also claims descent from Moses."

Falkirk had laughed with his friend over two more tumblers of dark stout—the best beer to be found in London. But nonetheless, the following day he sought out Grist. Sallo knew of the Stonewycke ruin, he said, and swore a treasure remained buried there to this day. Bidding Falkirk to remain where he was, he disappeared into a darkened room and reappeared a few moments later bearing a crumbled shred of paper in his hand.

"A map," he said, "o' the veery place!"

"Why haven't you gone after it, then?" asked a suspicious Falkirk. He didn't much care for the cold glint in Grist's one open eye.

"I did . . . long ago."

He drew Falkirk close across the table, moving the flickering candle aside. "Ye see this?" he said, blowing the stench of his rotten breath into Falkirk's face. He pointed to his eye, partially closed and badly scarred. "'Twas my reward fer that. Th' bloke nearly blinded me, 'e did. Them lairds trust no one—'specially strangers. Tried t' get someone else t' come wi' me, but no one'll believe me." His voice was raspy and low.

"So you've decided to give away your secret?" said Falkirk in a suspicious tone of contempt. "Just like that? What do you take me for, old man, a fool?"

"You look t' be a gent'man," went on Sallo in the harsh tone which seemed his only mode of expression. Heedless of Falkirk's accusation, he paused to scratch his partially bearded chin. "I s'pose ye'd 'ardly notice partin' wi' a few quid—this map's worth mor'n fifty . . . but I'll settle fer that."

"Fifty quid!" Falkirk exclaimed. "You must take me for an imbecile!"

He rose from his seat and moved toward the door. He was more than able to pay the fifty, and almost willing to go that high. But not if there was a chance of getting by with less. And the thought of being outwitted by this low-life Thames tramp galled him.

"All right, mate—twenty-five," conceded Sallo quickly, "but na a farthin' less."

Falkirk came away with the map, still far from convinced Sallo Grist wasn't London's foxiest and most cunning con man, but nevertheless intrigued with his prospects. When Forbes found the opening between the rocks, called a *door* on the map, George Falkirk gained a new respect for Sallo Grist. He did not, however, intend to pay Sallo the extra twenty-five quid from the proceeds of their findings. He was a shrewd one himself, and if he never saw Sallo Grist again in his life, it would not be soon enough for him.

Centuries earlier the so-called door had apparently been used as an entryway into a secluded cleft in the expansive moorland. But it had grown thick with brush; and as the surrounding rocks and pieces of ruin had fallen, some had crumbled into smaller pieces, so that upon first glance the ancient building sites, which had stood on both sides of the huge granite boulders, were barely distinguishable from the scattered rocks of the rugged heath. Only when one gazed upon the site for some time, from a distance, did a certain order begin to form among the vague shapes. And now George Falkirk knew what he was looking for, if Sallo's map was to be worth its price—a small cave-like opening in the side of the hill just behind the door through the boulders.

So on this cool September night his treasure hunt would, he hoped, culminate at last—if the idiot Forbes had indeed found the right spot. It would have been better to have done it all himself, but he couldn't risk being seen and recognized. If Forbes were seen wandering about, who would think anything of it? Against his better judgment, Falkirk had to trust the dullard.

The huge rocks stood in black shadows, heaps of granite and stone piled in fragmentary disarray, like the ancient memories they represented. Not even the vaguest outline of habitation still remained in the thick dust. Moss and vines grew over most of the stones, and heather and bracken had infringed upon the rest.

Forbes led the young heir of Kairn around the east side of a particularly large mound of granite. They tied their horses and continued on foot, descending to the base of the largest two stones. There Falkirk could see that some of the smaller stones had been removed and the brush cleared away. Forbes pointed through the tight space between the two vertical boulders, a hole barely large enough to squeeze through.

"Ye said t' touch nothin'," said Forbes. "But I had t' get inside o' the thing. This here openin' looks like it might lead t' where ye want t' go. Ye see, if ye jist look through there—"

He pointed into the blackness. "Can ye see? Looks like there could be a cove o' some kin', there agin' the bank."

Falkirk could see that the area had not been disturbed beyond the initial removal of a few stones, and for that reason alone he believed Forbes. He didn't like the man. Nor did he trust him. But in this business he had to do what he could with the help he could find.

"Get the tools," Falkirk ordered. "Let's see what's inside there."

Forbes was the one to do the work, though grudgingly. He hammered and pried at the jagged edges of rock covering the entrance of what seemed to be a small opening, perhaps a cave, through the rocks. Peering after him from beside the granite towers, Falkirk could see nothing but blackness. At last, with the aid of a pick, the rocks were removed, an opening was discovered into the hillside large enough to accommodate a man—lying on his belly—and Forbes, after communicating this fact, was instructed to crawl into the crevice.

Falkirk stood and waited impatiently. The cold had begun to bite into his bones. After what seemed an interminable time, he heard a muffled yell from Forbes. Either the bloke had struck his head or had discovered something. When he emerged a few moments later, scooting out with feet first, the only evidence of his labor was a nasty gouge on his forehead.

"Ends in a solid wall o' granite," he said, wiping his head with a dirty hand.

"Are you sure?"

"'Course I'm sure!"

"No box . . . no chest of any kind?"

"I bang my head an' the bloody place near caves in on me, an' ye ask if I'm sure!" retorted Forbes sharply.

Again Falkirk regretted bringing the rotter into his secret plan. Yet Forbes did serve his purpose. The worst that could happen if Forbes were caught snooping around would be a short stint in jail. Falkirk himself would remain in the clear in any case.

Not having expected their initial foray to the ruins to pay off completely, Falkirk was not overly disappointed. The time would come when triumph would be his.

"Well," said Falkirk, ignoring Forbes's wound, "we're not beat yet. We've found the place, but it's too late to dig any farther tonight. Load everything up and let's get out of here."

34

Glasgow

THE CLYDE CERTAINLY wasn't the Thames. And Glasgow had nothing to compare with Piccadilly or Kensington Gardens. But Scotland's largest city fulfilled James's need to be in the hub of activity when he was unable to make the distance to London.

More importantly, the brewery was located just five miles outside the city.

Though he knew relatively little about the actual process of making dark Scottish ale, he loved the whine and thump of the steel and wooden machinery and the smells of yeast and fermentation.

Best of all, it was his! This brewery was one of the few things he could truly claim as his own, and it represented the means to further wealth and more enterprising investments in the future. He could see now that the failure of the Braenock deal had worked to his advantage. Had he acquired funding for the brewery in that manner, Atlanta would have managed to keep her hold on this, too. The arrangement as it had finally come about was far superior. He'd much rather be indebted to men like Browhurst or Byron Falkirk than to his wife. And as it turned out, he was still able to maintain a majority financial interest in the business.

At last, after three successful years, he was ready to expand his holdings. One of Scotland's largest distilleries had recently come on the market. The owner had died, and his only heir now lived in America. The man wanted no part of overseas holdings and was thus selling off the entire British portion of the inheritance. He was no amateur, that much was plain, for he was asking a pretty penny for the distillery. But it was well worth it, James thought. Its Scotch whiskey was renowned throughout Britain and found a regular market in exports as well. Last year alone its revenues were several hundred thousand pounds. If grown men could drool, the anticipation of latching onto such a vast enterprise would doubtless have had such an effect on James. Yet he again found himself faced with the dilemma of garnering the necessary funds for a beginning. Since he was not a wealthy man on his own, he still was forced to use other people's money for his schemes.

James sat in the plush restaurant slowly sipping his brandy and wondering what this meeting with Lord Browhurst would produce. He had already obtained a commitment of sorts, and the Lord had been to London attempting to tap some of his more wealthy associates.

James shifted uneasily in his seat. He was never sure just how far to trust Browhurst. His words had always been perfectly cordial, but something in the look of his eye worried James, as if the cunning Lord were only waiting for him to make a mistake so he could move in to pick up the pieces. But then, James Duncan was hardly in the habit of trusting anyone.

Soon he spotted Browhurst's imposing figure striding across the dining room floor. He showed his white teeth in a hasty grin as he spotted James.

"Ah, Duncan!" he said, seating himself at the table. "I've not yet been to this establishment—not bad for Glasgow. But I doubt the food will measure up."

"We must take what we can get," James replied amicably. "London isn't the only place on earth, though it may be the most civilized."

"You are right—there is Paris. And even New York is beginning to attract some in the influential circles. But Glasgow, I'm afraid . . ." He let a wry chuckle complete his thought.

A waiter hurried to the table, took their order, and within moments Browhurst was holding his own glass of the house's finest brandy.

"I must say, Duncan," said Browhurst with a chuckle, "how a man of the world like yourself can stand to remain where you do, with nothing but a sleepy little fishing village for miles, surrounded on all sides by that bloody, wiry shrub—what do they call it?"

"Heather? The weed the peasant girls wear in their hair?"

"Oh, yes, heather, that's it!—as I say, how you can tolerate living there is beyond me."

"It's not so bad, once you get used to it."

"If you're going to be a businessman, you really ought to live in the city."

"Perhaps you're right."

"Certainly I'm right. Business is done in the city, not out on the bloody hills."

"But you must admit, Browhurst," replied James, "that we Scots do make the world's finest whiskey."

"You'll get no argument from me there."

"Which brings us to the purpose of this little discussion. We do have something other than geography to discuss."

"Yes, *that* . . ." For the first time Browhurst's countenance clouded. "I'm afraid I was none too successful in London."

"Your investors turned you down?"

"For the moment, yes—it appears that way."

"But they would gain from the venture," James insisted.

"They feel it's a large sum of money, and too great a risk."

"You showed them last year's figures?"

"Of course I did," Browhurst answered, a trifle annoyed. "They were impressed. But one fact did not pass their scrutiny—a large percentage of the whiskey is exported to America. With the war raging there between the North and South, who can tell what will happen to the market?"

"The war didn't affect last year's profits."

"True, but perhaps it was too early for potential ill-effects to be felt in sales."

"Bah! There won't be any ill-effects on the sale of whiskey!" James said with rising irritation. "People drink whether they're at war or not."

"You know what the experts say, that if the North didn't win the war in the first year, it could drag on interminably. There are rumors of blockades—"

"They'll always want whiskey," James argued. "Especially soldiers, far from home and lonely."

"I'm not the one you have to convince," said Browhurst. "You've made a strong case with me and have won me over."

He paused and took another sip from his glass. "Although," he went on after a few moments, "it appears there may be a slight problem with my investment as well—"

"A problem!" James exploded. Several nearby patrons turned and shot glances in the direction of the two men. "What kind of problem?" he asked in a more subdued but equally intense tone.

"Nothing major," Browhurst assured in the most conciliatory of voices. "However, in reevaluating my various investments, if it turns out that I find that

I am spread a . . . ah . . . a bit too thin, so to speak—in a case such as that I would have—ah—no alternative but to, shall we say, trim back my initial commitment somewhat."

"Listen, Browhurst," said James quietly, but with a cold, determined intimidation in his voice. "if you are looking for a way to weasel out of—"

"Not in the least," Browhurst answered quickly.

James eyed the man intently. Was Browhurst toying with him for some motive of his own? What was his game?

"We both know this will be a good investment," Browhurst continued; "why else do you think I am stretching myself to the limit on this one?"

"Well, without additional funds it's a venture that may never get off the ground," James replied with a sour note of exasperation. He had already invested a great deal of time and effort to set up this deal and was none too pleased to see it starting to slip through his eager grasp. What could this latest stall of Browhurst's mean? James wondered. He didn't like the thought of being a pawn in anyone's scheme.

"I too have stretched myself to the limit," he said finally. "Yet there still remains a sizable portion to be obtained."

"What about Lord Falkirk?" asked Browhurst.

James did not reply immediately, for the answer was not a simple one. He was already in too great a debt to his neighbor. He had already promised his daughter. What more did he have to bargain with?

Falkirk *did* have the cash. It vexed James to be so close to his goal and yet be powerless to lay his hands on it. There was but one way to entice Falkirk to part with any further money.

A wedding.

On that day—and only on that day—would Anges Falkirk allow her husband to invest another pound in a business venture, no matter how lucrative it might prove. Falkirk was not ambitious. He had his own motives, as did his wife. And they involved his son's future, not the expansion of their capital holdings.

But there was little time. If he did not act with dispatch, the American owner might well find another buyer. Yet . . . weddings could be hastily arranged.

"Yes . . ." James mused after several moments of silence, "I think Byron Falkirk might come through for us."

He paused, contemplating the practicalities involved. "Yes," he added, "I think he just might at that."

He smiled at his decision, lifted his glass to Browhurst, and said—

"Meanwhile, I'm going to talk to the American's solicitor. I think the time has come to put up some earnest money to secure the deal."

35

The Tapestry

❊

OCTOBER HARSHLY SHOVED aside the tranquil days of September, leaving no doubts that it was indeed the harbinger of winter. For the first days of the month rain poured relentlessly from heavy skies. And with the rain came winds of such force that three boats in the harbor were slammed against their moorings and wrecked almost beyond repair. The fisherfolk were only thankful the herring season had ended before the storm.

That week, the Lindow reached the top of its banks. And when there was no letup in sight, the farmers began attempts to seal off as much of their property as possible. Everyone was keenly aware that if the Lindow flooded, there was little they could do to save their possessions against the deluge. Many were the stories still circulating of the flood of 1802 when every farm within ten miles of the river had been washed out to sea. Stonewycke castle had been the only refuge, and hundreds of peasants had poured up the hill, able to save only what they could carry with them.

The last fair weeks of September had been glorious. Maggie and Ian had ridden nearly every mile of the estate and ventured as far inland as Culden and as far along the coast as Gardenstown. Their deepening friendship evolved naturally, splendidly, into love of a more permanent kind. When the truth of what was happening between them dawned on Maggie, she accepted it joyfully. The walk in the Dormin had been the beginning, but she had become more sure than ever of his love when he had given her the locket. What a wonderful memory that moment was! Ian had been so shy, even blushing slightly as he pulled it from behind his back where he had been hiding it. When he had placed the locket about her neck, he kissed her lightly on the cheek. She had never thought a man could be so gentle. And as much as she loved him, she could not help a moment's surprise that such tenderness was to be found in Ian with his seemingly flippant, almost cynical personality. But the considerate care in his touch was something she would never forget. After that day she had worn the locket hidden beneath her clothing—always close to her, always a reminder of the sweet love that had finally opened her heart.

Each had wrestled through uncertainties, giving much to one another in the process; thus they came into the realization of their love stronger and more confident about one another than would have been possible before. Maggie was now ready to open her heart again, to love and be loved in return. Ian accepted the changes within himself as if his past life in London had merely been the dream of another world.

Both were in love, but with one another only. They had not yet learned to look up to the Source, to that greater Love from which all loves are born. But they were learning to love for the first time, and would look up when the time was ripe. Through their love each for the other, the Source was drawing them. And through the pain of their love, they would come to know His.

The inclement weather seemed bent on spoiling their earthly joy. On hill and moor they could be free—to laugh, to talk, to run, to jump, to delight in one another. But under the watchful eye of the household they were compelled to remain distant and aloof, still keeping their affections hidden. Though she knew the time would have to come, and soon, Maggie could not bring herself to open the subject to Atlanta. Had not James been absent from Stonewycke for two weeks, the pressure would have been unbearable.

More trying than ever were the frequent visits of George Falkirk. Far from being intimidated by the rain, he relished it, always arriving in good spirits, sweeping Atlanta off her feet with praise and shallow indulgences, and managing to isolate Maggie into some private room, there to weave his confident spells with her.

She learned to fend off his open advances with vague words, coquettish smiles, and witty words, giving in just enough to appear charmed by his adept seduction, but keeping her distance all the while. Falkirk was thus kept off his guard, hopeful of ultimate victory and unconcerned by the threats of her buffoon of a cousin. But with each succeeding visit Maggie found it more and more difficult to rebuff him. An outright denial of his attentions, she feared, would lead to great conflict with her father, ultimately threatening her love for Ian. But how long could she hold Falkirk off before he pressed his advantage too far?

Such thoughts plagued Maggie as she sat staring out the window in the little sitting room adjacent to the east parlor. A fire crackled cheerfully in the fireplace while the rain beat relentlessly against the window; the smaller confines of this familiar haunt offered warmth and coziness to Maggie.

The door opened and Atlanta peeked in. "I thought I left my sewing in here, dear," she said, explaining her presence. "Oh . . . there it is."

She picked it up and turned back toward the door. But something prompted her to linger.

Atlanta had seen a change in Maggie of late—a small corner of her taut fabric was relaxing. An undefined peaceful glow radiated from her eyes. When had her melancholy daughter last been so content as she had during the past month?

How Atlanta wanted to break through the distance which separated them! Both felt the strain. Each desired a closer approach. Love beat in each heart for the other, but neither knew how to break the bonds of silence.

Still Atlanta tarried.

"There's little else to do these days," she attempted, gesturing with the needlework in her hand.

"I know," said Maggie with a sigh.

"The rain keeps falling and falling."

"Will it never stop?" said Maggie, thinking aloud rather than addressing her mother. Her hands moved absently, sending the needle through the cloth.

"You've been outdoors so much lately," Atlanta replied, "it must be doubly difficult for you being inside all day."

Maggie glanced up from her work toward her mother with a questioning look. Had Atlanta drawn her own conclusions after seeing Ian and her together so frequently?

Maggie struggled to force her trembling fingers to continue the needlework.

"It's warm in here," Atlanta continued, groping for words. "The other rooms get so drafty. We may live in a grand house, but it has its drawbacks. There's always a chill. But that must just be my age showing. You young people probably don't even notice it."

Maggie nodded, mumbling a few words of assent, assuring Atlanta that she felt the chill also. She had hardly heard anything else her mother had said.

"Speaking of young people," Atlanta went on awkwardly, "have you been able to tolerate our houseguest adequately?"

Maggie's head bounded up again. This time Atlanta could not mistake the agitated expressions on her daughter's face.

"My dear . . . what is it?" Atlanta asked with concern. "Have you had difficulties with him?"

"No," Maggie replied quickly. "No, not at all—he's been . . . he's been a perfect—gentleman. I . . . we've . . . that is—we've had a nice time together. I mean, I've tolerated him wonderfully . . . just fine—"

She stopped short, realizing that in the confusion of her thoughts she had nearly stammered out too much. She wanted to tell her mother! But the last time they had tried to talk seriously, Atlanta hadn't understood. What if she couldn't understand about Ian? She did seem altogether taken with George Falkirk. Both she and her father seemed intent on pushing her toward him.

Yet, what if . . . perhaps—what if she *would* understand?

"If there's a problem—" Atlanta began.

"No. There's no problem," Maggie insisted. "We've become . . . friends."

There was something in Maggie's tone: an urgency, more emotion than she was allowing to show. Slowly the truth began to flash across her heart.

"Friends?" Atlanta said, the hard Ramsey crust forming again. "That's nice . . . I'm glad."

"Do you mean, Mother . . . do you really mean that? I thought you would be . . . opposed to—"

"Of course I mean it," replied Atlanta, softening as she sensed Maggie's effort to tell her something deeper. "Why would you think—?"

"There's Father. You know what he thinks of Ian."

"Your father and I do not always see eye to eye."

"I thought you might also . . ."

"I know you needed someone—"

"Oh, I do need him, Mother!" burst out Maggie before realizing what she had said.

Atlanta walked closer and sat down on the chair next to her daughter. She laid aside the sewing project she had been carrying in her hand, then thought for several long moments, carefully measuring each word before she spoke. She painfully recalled the many times she had thoughtlessly quelled such rare tender moments between them. There would be few further opportunities.

"I thought I had noticed a change in you," Atlanta said at length. "You've seemed so happy."

"I am happy," replied Maggie, looking down at the floor. "That is except for—"

"What?"

"I shouldn't have thought it."

"What doesn't make you happy?"

"I know you think he's quite the gentleman."

"Who?"

"George Falkirk."

"Me? I don't think that highly of George Falkirk."

"You don't? I thought—"

"Your father and Mr. Falkirk are great friends. And on those grounds George seems to assume he has the right to consider himself a welcome guest here at any hour he chooses."

"And you don't—?"

"I must say I don't share your father's fascination with the young man. His charming ways are more than I can tolerate."

"Oh, Mother, you don't know how glad it makes me to hear you say that!" exclaimed Maggie. "All this time I thought you wanted me to encourage him."

"I take it our friend Mr. Falkirk is not the cause of your recent radiant smiles."

"No, Mother," replied Maggie with a smile. "It's someone else."

"Am I to take it that our houseguest from London means more to you than merely a distant relative?"

Maggie looked up at Atlanta full in the face.

"I love him, Mother," she said.

The words sent an involuntary chill through Atlanta's body, much like she'd felt the night of the *Maiden* when watching Maggie hold the tiny Krueger child. Her daughter had taken another step toward maturity. In Atlanta's heart pulsed both joy and sorrow—sorrow at having to let go of her baby daughter, joy at seeing Maggie so happy for the first time.

"And Ian . . . how does he feel?"

A tentative smile tugged at Maggie's lips. She nodded, then said, "He loves me also. We have even . . . spoken of marriage."

At the word a great heaviness fell upon Atlanta's heart. "Does anyone else know of this?"

"Only you," Maggie answered. "We couldn't—well, I'm simply glad that you finally know."

Already, however, Atlanta's thoughts were on James. If he should learn of this development, there would be no telling what he might do. One thing he would *never* do was accept a marriage between his daughter and the son of the Earl of Landsbury!

Atlanta's attention gradually returned to Maggie, who had risen and stood quietly gazing out the French doors at the steady stream of rain splashing against the glass and down onto the small enclosed courtyard below. *Why must it be my duty,* Atlanta thought, *to bring my daughter back to reality?* How desperately she wanted her daughter to be able to enjoy a few moments of contentment, for she knew too well how few such moments a lifetime could contain. Yet she also knew how futile was the hope that Maggie's dream world with Ian could long remain unshattered.

"Maggie," she said gently. "Are you sure this is what you want?"

Maggie spun around, every feature of her face glowing with resplendent affirmation.

"Oh, yes, Mother!"

"You know how difficult your father can make life for you."

"I don't care about him," Maggie replied flatly. "He showed a long time ago that he didn't care about me."

Atlanta winced, feeling the pain of her daughter's silent burden.

"I asked if you were certain," Atlanta continued, "only because if it truly is what you want, you may very well have to fight for it."

"I know, Mother," said Maggie.

"You know how your father feels about Landsbury."

"Yes. But what I'm more concerned with is—how do you feel about it, Mother?"

"I want you to be happy, Maggie."

"You approve?"

"Of course."

"Oh, thank you, Mother!" exclaimed Maggie, embracing Atlanta.

Slowly Atlanta's arms reached about her daughter and held her close. She felt tears filling her own eyes, the unfamiliar response of her own deep need to love and be loved. Silently they stood for some moments, as if the walls between them had never been.

"And you won't say anything to Father?" asked Maggie softly.

"No," answered Atlanta. "But your secret won't last forever. I have seen it all over your face."

Maggie laughed. Then she pulled away from her mother's embrace suddenly and said, "I must go find Ian, to tell him."

Atlanta laid her hand on Maggie's arm. It had never been her habit to act impulsively. Yet she was not yet ready for this precious moment with her daughter to come to an end.

"Maggie," she said, "before you go, I have something to show you."

Dabbing her eyes, Atlanta led the way out of the room. They walked upstairs, Maggie assumed to Atlanta's dayroom, but instead they stopped at the door next to it. Atlanta pulled the door open, and the large windows on the opposite wall admitted what was left of the afternoon light. Immediately a faint odor of mothballs assailed them.

"My old nursery!" exclaimed Maggie. "I haven't been here in years. It has hardly changed."

"I've kept it as it was when you were a child," said Atlanta. "Those memories are dear to me."

Maggie looked up at the stately woman, and to her amazement saw the tears which her mother had been unable to control.

"Oh, Mother," she said, walking toward Atlanta and again putting her arms around her. She gently laid her head against her mother's chest as she hadn't for years.

Now at last the tears flowed unchecked down the solemn cheeks of the great mistress of Stonewycke, the last remnant of the Ramsey line. Maggie wept openly as Atlanta stroke her hair. The daughter was at last a woman, and finally in this poignant moment of sorrow and bliss the two women were able to lay aside their fears and uncertainties and embrace each other in the love they had long possessed but rarely expressed.

The two stood silently in the center of the thick rug where Maggie had spent hours playing as a toddler. To one side of the door sat a small bed, canopied in lace, and a bureau lined with dolls and stuffed toys. In another corner stood Maggie's cradle.

When the embrace and the tears had accomplished their healing work, Maggie stepped back. They laughed, squeezing hands as if to say, *It is good!*

Then Maggie began to look around as memories of the past flooded her. She could not help notice that the room was clean and dusted, although it had been twelve years since she had last used it.

Atlanta motioned her toward the bed.

Then Maggie saw it—the grand tapestry of the family tree, just where it had always been. But something was different. A fine new gilt-edged frame surrounded it, and the tapestry itself seemed brighter, fresher. She looked questioningly toward her mother.

"I've had it restored and reframed," Atlanta explained. "I had hoped to present it to you on your birthday, but it wasn't ready in time. Then I thought I'd save it for Christmas. But now . . . somehow today just seems like the right moment. I want you to have it, Maggie."

"You're giving it to me?" asked Maggie. "But, Mother . . . it's yours—it's far too precious for me to have!"

"I want you to have it."

Atlanta's words came closely, cautiously, as she continued to measure the fragile emotions which had been stirred so deeply. "There are so few things a mother can truly pass on to her daughter," she began again. "Especially things which convey the heritage she wants to transfer. This family . . . this estate—"

Atlanta stopped, unable for the moment to continue, choking back the lump which seemed so insistent on blocking the words. Now that the vault had been cracked open, the tears seemed determined to flow all the more readily.

". . . this home . . . these people," she tried to begin again in shaky tones, "it's all part of me, Maggie. It's my lifeblood. There is so much I want to give you. Let this be a start."

Sensing the tenderness of her mother's emotions, Maggie stretched out a hand and laid it on her arm.

"You will marry soon," Atlanta continued, "and become part of a new family. The Ramsey name may fade in your memory—"

"Mother," interrupted Maggie. "That will never happen! Don't you know how dear it is to me? I regret that I have never borne the name, but it is no less real to me. I shall *never* forget that half of my blood is Ramsey blood, and all I am is bound up in the ancestry of Stonewycke."

Atlanta's eyes smiled first, and then her lips.

"Then all the more reason for you to have the tapestry."

"But it means so much to you."

"That is why I want you to have it," Atlanta said. "I always intended to pass it along to my daughter, though at the time I stitched it you were only an idea in God's mind."

Maggie gazed at it for some moments, remembering her own awkward attempts to reproduce it. Then, she was a child; the years which had passed seemed a lifetime ago. Suddenly within Maggie rose the strong sense of being part of something deeper and more permanent than anything she had felt before. All those names from generation to generation belonged to her, and in some mysterious way, she belonged to them, too. Years from now her descendants would stand where she was standing now, admiring it and wondering about the person who had been called Margaret Duncan.

Examining the tapestry more closely, Maggie suddenly became aware of the new addition.

"Mother, there's my name!"

In its own special block directly under those of her parents stood the words *Margaret Isabel Duncan*. "Surely you didn't embroider that in place when you first made it? I don't recall seeing it there before."

"I added it only recently," said Atlanta with pride.

"But where is Alastair's name?" she asked.

"Come," said Atlanta quickly, apparently heedless of Maggie's question. "Let's take it down and move it to your room."

"Take it down?" Maggie questioned. "But it has always hung here. It seems like it belongs in the nursery. How could we hang it somewhere else?"

"But you won't be able to enjoy it if it hangs where you never see it," Atlanta insisted.

"It will take some getting used to," said Maggie thoughtfully. "It belongs in the nursery. But it is such a great treasure, I do want to be able to see it."

Together they lifted the large frame from its hook and Maggie carried it carefully to her room. There they hung it above her bed in similar position to its original location in the nursery. She stood back to admire it, realizing for the first time that this tapestry was far more than a simple family heirloom. Not only was it a line backwards in time, but also a line forward into the future . . . the unknown. What the years ahead would hold, she had no idea.

"Thank you, Mother," Maggie said at last. "It's beautiful. It really is a treasure."

36

Atlanta's Discovery

ATLANTA HAD ALWAYS tried to respect the sanctity of James's cubicle.

She had never once set foot inside his private retreat since their marriage, never even alluded to its existence. He had never told her about it, and she rarely so much as ventured into the corridor where it was located. She knew about it, of course, and its contents and uses occasionally played upon her curiosity. But she believed every person needed a refuge, one place to which he could retreat that was entirely his own. Perhaps it was her way of subtly admitting to the pressure he faced from her, though she would never have admitted it outright.

She loathed, therefore, what she was about to do. Her heels echoed on the bare stone floor of the hallway. Though she knew James was not expected back from Kairn for hours, impulsively she glanced back over her shoulder. But her step continued firm and determined. Since his return from Glasgow the situation had grown intolerable. George Falkirk visited nearly every day; he and James grew more familiar by the hour. Ian was rarely to be seen, and Atlanta knew Maggie was miserable.

Something had to be done.

Atlanta had never been one to allow obstacles to deter her from her goals. She had known fear from time to time, but for her it had served as a driving force, compelling her to do her part to preserve her ancestral estate intact. And she knew to achieve that end she had to maintain her power over James, who would wrest it from her if he could.

Anxiety compelled her again—this time, through concern for her daughter. Fear for Maggie's future forced her to make this furtive journey. She had to find something to bargain with, something which would constrain James to give his blessing to Maggie and Ian and their future together. Even as she thought it, Atlanta realized the impossibility of her quest. James's hatred was so concentrated that the very name of Landsbury was enough to send him into a rage. And the fascination of his hatred, his desire for revenge, precluded any possibility of a change of heart. For true hatred, as well as true love, is long-suffering and will make any sacrifice in order to expend itself upon its object.

Atlanta stood before the door as if to finalize her resolve. She placed her hand on the latch. It yielded to her pressure, but almost as quickly she drew back. *Had he trusted her so much that he did not lock this most private of rooms?*

The thought was staggering. Their relationship had endured over the years, but she would never have numbered trust among the causes. Was she now betraying the only thread of decency left to their marriage?

Seconds passed; but it could have been an hour. Did this temporary indecision spring from some dormant sense of guilt, some notion that she owed a loyalty to the man who was her husband? What did such loyalty mean at this point in their marriage? Were the inevitable lines between them at last being drawn? Was the choice no woman should have to make finally being thrust upon her—the choice between husband and child?

But why should such a moment of crisis come as any surprise? The choice had been made long ago when she had produced an heir to Stonewycke—the only heir there would ever be from her body. The battle had been enjoined when she knew she would have to fight for her daughter's place—a battle she could not now abandon for any brief moment of sentimentality.

She paused, and the door swung open.

Stepping inside, Atlanta was astonished at the sight. She had considered James a meticulous man, but this, his most private of rooms, was in complete disorder. Books, papers, maps, journals, folders, swords, guns, boxes, and other parapher- nalia were strewn about at random. Whether or not he actually worked here was doubtful. Rather than an office, it appeared to be simply a storage closet for rubbish of all kinds.

But she had work to do. Laying aside her initial shock at the disarray, Atlanta set immediately to her task, glad at least that her little foray into James's forbidden world would not be noticed. She approached the desk, looked about, and began randomly to sift through the several piles of papers scattered over the top. Then she glanced around. If she didn't discover anything here, she would have to concentrate her attention on the drawers in the bureau and cabinet, of which there were many. There might not be time to sort through every drawer, especially since she didn't know what she was looking for. This place was such a mess. It would take forever to investigate every nook and cranny.

She turned her attention back to the desktop.

Within a few moments her search was rewarded, and she need worry no longer about having to rummage through the endless drawers. The bureau could keep its secrets; this was all she needed. A small note, written on formal business paper, was nestled between a sheaf of business documents. It had clearly been thrown down on top of the desk, then inadvertently covered with other papers. As she read it, Atlanta wondered why James had not destroyed it. Perhaps it had arrived with other documents, for the two men were involved in several financial arrangements together.

As she read the words on the page, Atlanta's hand, then her entire body, shook with outrage. She had been told, of course, that the Falkirks had asked that their son be permitted to visit Maggie, even to court her. She had been upset to begin with, after their first visit to Kairn. But later visits had proved more cordial, and she had reconciled herself to the idea of his presence, though she was not particularly enamored of the conceited young man. He did have a way of flattery that could beguile even her at times. Maggie had seemed to enjoy his company at first. But then after learning her true feelings for Ian, Falkirk's very presence had become an aggravation. She never dreamed that James's duplicity could extend to such a businesslike manipulation of his daughter to gain his own financial ends.

The words of the note left little doubt. But this time James had gone too far. It was one thing to seal an agreement with a horse or some other token of friendship. But his own daughter!

In a frenzy of passion, Atlanta read the words again—

I am pleased with the progress of your ventures and I trust our bargain will further pledge our future together in ways profitable to us both. My son is taken with your daughter and has assured me that a marriage will be announced soon. From this I see my investment and my confidence in you was well placed. As I said, I will certainly be eager to consider future liaisons once the wedding has taken place. But first things first, I always say. I remain

Yours most sincerely,
Falkirk

Atlanta stuffed the paper into her pocket, slammed the door behind her, and marched down the corridor in a rage. She would never lower herself to try to win James's favor again. He had forfeited his right to bless his daughter's marriage! He had forfeited whatever rights of fatherhood he had ever possessed!

She walked straight to the sitting room, locked the door behind her, and sat down to think.

That this development changed the complexion of everything there could be no doubt. Falkirk's more frequent visits and private discussions with James, as well as James's repeated rides to Kairn, all fit into a grand and cunning scheme. When she had blocked his sale of Braenock, his twisted genius had found another opportunity, now making use of his daughter instead of her land.

But she would stop him . . . somehow!

As the heat of her anger gradually settled into cold, silent wrath, Atlanta's only alternative became clear. To thwart James's cruel design she had to move, if not quickly, certainly decisively. She contemplated the implications, settled her resolve firmly in her mind, rose, placed the letter of treachery in a drawer, and left the room with a fixed look and an unswerving gait.

She found Maggie and Ian in the dining room. She had not heard the call to dinner, and her stomach was too knotted to feel hunger.

Her face revealed her passion instantly.

"Mother . . . what is it?" asked Maggie in alarm.

Atlanta closed the door behind her, excused the maid who had been serving, then continued to pace the floor searching for the right words with which to begin. Ian glanced at Maggie with a questioning look, but said nothing.

"I don't know how to . . . the words to say what I must tell you are difficult to find—"

She paused, continued pacing, then took a deep breath and began again.

"There are some circumstances which have just come to my attention— developments . . . which affect both of you, your father, Maggie—and even the future of Stonewycke."

She stopped again for another breath, for her heart was still pounding. "Maggie," she continued, looking at her daughter, "you have told me that you and Ian are in love."

Maggie glanced down and blushed.

"Excuse me, Ian, for being so blunt. But you will soon see why events compel me to speak thus. So I must ask you too, Ian, I must ask you both. Is what Maggie told me true? Are you in love?"

Ian glanced over at Maggie beside him at the table, took her hand, then returned his eyes to Atlanta.

"Yes . . . yes, it is. Insofar as I can speak for Maggie, Lady Duncan, yes—we are in love."

"Maggie?" said Atlanta.

Maggie nodded.

"And you have spoken of marriage?"

"Yes," replied Ian.

"Then as sudden as this seems," said Atlanta, "I am now going to urge you to move with haste."

A puzzled expression came over Ian's face.

"What exactly are you saying, Lady Duncan?" he asked. "That we should make an announcement of our betrothal?"

"More than that, Ian," Atlanta replied. "I am suggesting—if you are truly serious in your intent—that you marry without delay, at the soonest moment to present itself."

The forceful words shattered Atlanta's two listeners into speechlessness.

"Mother . . ." began Maggie, too incredulous to know whether to weep or laugh.

"But there are so many considerations," faltered Ian. "Our families . . . a proper period of engagement."

"There's no time for all that," insisted Atlanta. "I told you, there have been developments. You'll just have to trust me when I say the matter is urgent."

"I don't understand—what would Father say?" asked Maggie.

"Maggie," Atlanta returned flatly, "your father has given up his right to any say in the matter."

"What do you mean?"

"Your father has deceived us and we must act without delay . . . and without his knowledge or consent."

A silence came over the room, each lost in his private thoughts. Finally Ian broke the quiet.

"I believe you, Lady Duncan," he said. "And I value the trust you place in me by desiring that your daughter be my wife. But I want to consider what is best for Maggie. I wouldn't want to act in haste if she were in any way unsure about—"

"Oh, Ian," said Maggie. "I *am* sure. I love you."

"If you wait," Atlanta broke in, "all could be lost. Believe me, it will be in Maggie's best interest for you to move without delay."

"Naturally," said Ian, "I am eager for us to be married. I love Maggie. But I do not want her pressed into it."

"The choices before my daughter are severely limited," said Atlanta. "If you wait, she may never be able to marry you at all."

The two young people were silent.

"Don't you understand?" implored Atlanta. "I didn't want to have to tell you. Oh, Maggie, I don't want you to be hurt anymore."

"Mother, Mother . . . what is it?"

"Oh, Maggie . . . your father—he has—your father has pledged you—in marriage—to George Falkirk."

Maggie looked at Ian, stunned.

"It's true," said Atlanta, then slumped to a chair where she too remained silent.

"No wonder he has been so cocky and confident," said Ian at length. "That explains everything."

Atlanta nodded.

"Then you are right," Ian went on, "we do have little choice. But how . . . what should we do?"

"James is planning another trip to Glasgow in two or three weeks," said Atlanta. "He will be away several days. That will be the best time. I will handle Falkirk and will keep you appraised of any developments. The two of you can go away—Fraserburgh would be good; there's a kindly old vicar there—and be back to Stonewycke before James returns. By then he will have a new son-in-law."

"And when he finds out?"

"We'll decide how to handle that when the time comes. For now you have my blessing . . . and that is enough."

37

An Unexpected Encounter

※

DAYS PASSED, STRETCHING into a week, then two. The visits of George Falkirk continued; gradually, Maggie became barely able to endure his presence. Fair weather held, yet Ian and Maggie—confined to brief moments when there was no danger of discovery by James—dared not go out together. Angered by Falkirk's presence, Ian nevertheless kept calm and waited patiently. Maggie wanted to tell her father everything, to have it out in the open, yet she feared for Ian's sake of the result. Likewise, Ian favored a full disclosure rather than their secretive plan. But in the end, both submitted to Atlanta's persuasion to wait until after the wedding, when James would be powerless to stop them.

Maggie dared not look her father in the eye for fear of betraying herself. James began to question Atlanta about their daughter's moodiness. Mealtimes were strained, with Maggie sitting stiff and silent. Ian's attempts at humor and conversation were rebuffed by James, whose fondness for Falkirk had grown more and more blatant. He began to question Ian as to the time of his return to London. Ian vaguely sidestepped his questions. "Isn't your month about over?" James asked. Ian laughed and commented that he hadn't anticipated enjoying the north so much. James muttered something about taking advantage of hospitality and then said no more; his face, however, revealed his keen displeasure.

Days continued to slip by. Storm clouds again rolled in, and Maggie announced she was going for a ride before the rain descended. Waiting long enough to arouse no suspicion, Ian excused himself, left the house by another door, then followed Maggie to the stables. He found her saddling Raven.

"I don't know how much longer I can take all this sneaking around," he blurted out, revealing the tension that had been building inside. "I'm not so sure we should have followed your mother's advice. We ought to just tell your father how things are between us and suffer the consequences."

"I've tried to summon the courage . . . several times," Maggie began lamely.

"We can't go on like this."

"The time hasn't seemed right."

"Don't you see? There's never going to be a *right* time! I want to tell him I love you and want you to be my wife. Then I want to tell Falkirk to stay away!"

The sharpness of his words stung, and tears began to form in Maggie's eyes. Realizing he had taken his frustrations out on her, Ian approached Maggie and gently placed a hand on her shoulder.

"I love you, Maggie," he said tenderly. "I just want him to know."

Maggie rubbed a quick hand across her face.

"I'm sorry," said Ian.

Maggie pulled the cinch tight and pulled it down through the round brass buckle, then moved to lead Raven to the door. "I have to think," she said. "I know what Mother says. But I want to tell him. Still, I need courage to face him. Maybe it takes more strength than I have."

"Oh, Maggie," said Ian. "Why won't you let me tell him? I can bear his anger. It's my place—my responsibility."

"No, Ian . . . I have to do it."

Why she insisted so strongly that she be the one to confront James, Maggie didn't know exactly. But she had to prove that she was no longer bound to her girlhood relationship with her father, that she could stand on her own feet as a woman and face him squarely.

Ian fell back and watched her swing easily up into the saddle. *Is she regretful about this hasty decision?* he wondered. As if reading his thoughts, Maggie looked down and smiled in reassurance. But she could force no words beyond the tightness in her throat. How she wanted to jump down and run into his arms and let the man she loved hold her! But for the moment, she kept that longing inside, spurred Raven around and sped down the road.

She gave no thought to where she rode. If she had stopped to choose, she would have chosen to ride on the beach, for the stormy tide was always magnificent in its frightful power. Instead, Raven carried her south. Perhaps her downcast spirit subconsciously sought the mournful comfort of the barren moor. Its harsh tenacity might give her the strength she needed. Hadn't Digory said that Braenock held a tender place in God's heart?

While the rains had held back, the winds had redoubled their mighty efforts at blowing away every frail leaf or loose twig left on the countryside. It lashed at Maggie's face like a whip of ice, but in her present mood she welcomed it as tangible proof there was strength beyond her own weakness.

"Oh, God!" she wailed. And indeed, only the Almighty could have heard her above the howling winds. "Oh, God . . . help me to do what I must do, and bear what I must bear. Help me stand up to him, though he has never loved me . . . and will now hate me for what Ian and I are going to do."

On she rode, the wind whipping against horse and rider, her hair streaming behind her violently, tears running down her cheeks as she struggled to form into definite prayers the painful, mingled memories of childhood and maturity. Then her hand found its way to her throat as it had so often of late, to seek the firm reality of Ian's love. She eased the locket from its hiding place and touched the fine chain, but it only brought new pain to her aching heart.

"Dear God . . . why must I choose between a father and a husband? All I wanted was to be loved by him . . . but now I will never know even that. He will hate me—and he will hate my husband even more. Dear God . . . how can I bear it?"

The wind lashed about her from every direction. Was it a messenger in answer to her prayers, or a cruel rebuttal? Raven continued up the ridge while Maggie closed her eyes against the sting of the wind. But the cries of her heart overshadowed the terrific power of nature.

"Dear God . . . help me!" was all she could say.

A brief lull in the blast jolted Maggie awake. She stopped Raven, opened her eyes, and listened. All was calm.

Almost as quickly as it had died down, the wind picked up again and soon resumed its efforts to unseat her. Still Maggie sat unmoving on Raven's back, wondering if the passing moment of tranquillity had not come from within her own heart. What was it that Digory had once told her about a still small voice?

Had that lull been the still small voice of God speaking His presence to her, offering the gift of His strength, assuring that her future was in His hands?

She could not question it, for she had no other way to turn. She could not refuse the gift. She could only accept that God had indeed heard her cries and had, in that brief glimpse of time, promised to help her as she had asked.

The winds continued to sweep over her with their fury, but a tiny recess of inner calm remained in a corner of her heart. Suddenly Hector and Stevie Mackinaw filled the eye of her mind. The thought of a brief respite from the icy wind, a warm fire, and perhaps a hot cup of tea was especially inviting to her and might also help crystallize her thoughts before returning to the tensions of Stonewycke.

She turned Raven immediately toward the cottage and urged her forward, judging herself about a mile away.

In the flurry of wind and in the turmoil of her thoughts, however, Maggie had lost her bearings. For all at once looming before her Maggie saw the granite heaps of the ancient Pict ruin. And there, tethered to a scraggly tree, were two horses—one of which was unmistakably George Falkirk's golden stallion.

The last thing Maggie wanted at this moment was to be seen by that man, yet curiosity compelled her forward. There was no one to be seen. Maggie judged the men—whoever they were—to be in the hollow surrounded by the rocks. If so, they would be unable to see her—or hear her approach because of the wind. What could they be doing here, alone late in the day on her father's land? She had no idea. But thoughts about James temporarily suspended, and her sense of danger and adventure aroused. Maggie tied Raven to a low shrub, and inched her way closer to the two horses.

She walked straight on until she came to within a hundred feet of the horses. She could make out figures in the small sheltering ravine below in the gathering dusk. She crept nearer, keeping behind the formations of rock as much as possible. Reaching the point where the moor began its steep descent, she stopped behind a boulder, and peered carefully down.

There were two men. One was definitely Falkirk, stooped over a mound of freshly dug earth. The other was on his knees with his back toward Maggie alternately wielding a pick and shovel, enlarging the hole they were apparently making in the opposite embankment.

The wind had subsided slightly, but it still muted their voices. Maggie dared go no nearer and strained to hear as best she could.

"There's na other way," said the other man.

". . . too noticeable . . ." came the remnant of Falkirk's words.

". . . do us na good t' steal the laird's . . ."

". . . belonged to the Picts . . . not his at all—"

"Picts or no," replied the man on his knees, whose face Maggie had still been unable to see, ". . . the laird wouldna take kindly . . . still his land."

". . . could be right," Falkirk conceded. ". . . can't risk . . . found out now . . ."

". . . need more horses . . . I'll get twa more an' . . ."

". . . tonight . . . late . . . wait no longer . . . too many delays . . ."

". . . rain's likely . . ."

"Don't argue!" snapped Falkirk. "This is the best time. You won't be seen." Raising his voice, Maggie could hear him clearly now. He stood and turned partially toward her and Maggie slipped back behind the protection of the rock. "Now let's get out of here."

Together they shoved what appeared to be a heavy chest beneath the projection of some rocks, then headed toward their mounts. Long before they had climbed back up to their horses, Maggie had run to Raven, mounted, and galloped for cover behind a low hill covered with shrubbery some two hundred yards distant. Her precaution mattered little, however, for the two conspirators did not even glance in her direction, so bent were they on getting out of the torrents of wind.

Abandoning her visit to the Mackinaws, Maggie turned and made her way homeward as soon as the two men had disappeared from sight. Falkirk was up to no good. What they had found she didn't know. And whether it, in fact, belonged to her father she didn't know either.

But one thing was certain. This land was the property of the Stonewycke estate, hers as much as her father's. She couldn't let them get away with their scheme, not until she at least knew what they had found.

She would have to decide what to do quickly. From the fragmentary conversation she had heard, she gathered that one of the men was planning a return visit to Braenock Ridge later that night.

As Maggie neared home, she recalled the reason for her ride in the first place. The immediacy of the events on Braenock suddenly faded as she remembered the awesome task that lay ahead of her. She could not wait until after they were married to tell her father. An inner resolve of her maturing womanhood compelled her to take a stand. She must tell him about Ian—tonight! She recoiled at the thought of such a confrontation. But at last she knew she had been given the strength necessary to see it through.

38

Advances

❖

A SHOCK OF panic surged through Maggie when she saw the golden stallion in front of the stables. Falkirk must have departed from his companion somewhere on the valley road and hastened directly here.

Maggie dismounted and cautiously walked Raven inside, wishing to delay the inevitable meeting as long as possible. He was probably in the house by now, sharing a glass of brandy with her father. She dropped the reins and turned to unsaddle the mare.

"Ah, back from a windy ride, eh?" came a voice from deep inside the stable. Maggie gasped. "You startled me," she said, turning. Her voice wavered.

"That was certainly not my intention, Lady Margaret," returned the smooth tones of George Falkirk. "The groom said you had gone for a ride and I decided to wait for you out here."

"I'm sure my father would have been delighted to entertain—"

"I didn't come to see your father, Margaret," replied Falkirk with an air of confidence. "This time I didn't want to go into the house and have to vie with your parents and servants, and even your houseguest, for your attentions. I thought I would have a better chance of speaking with you alone out here."

"Alone?" said Maggie.

"Oh, come now, Margaret," said Falkirk. "Surely you don't mean to suggest that you are unaware of the reason for my visits. Clearly, it isn't simply to pass the time with your father."

"I'm afraid I don't know what you mean," stalled Maggie.

"Oh, Margaret," he replied, his moderate tone thinly disguising the cocky, self-assurance he felt. His discovery on Braenock Ridge had so intoxicated him with his own importance and good fortune that he could barely keep from telling her everything. How could she waste her time with that ridiculous fellow Duncan when he—the future earl of Kairn *and* Stonewycke—was right before her eyes? In addition, he was soon to be rich in his own right. How could she act so disinterested? He knew she longed for him. He must simply help her overcome her girlish fears.

"Margaret," he said, "you are so lovely with your hair blown by the wind and your face flushed from the ride—" He moved toward her and reached out to touch her hair.

"Mr. Falkirk, please!" Maggie backed away, more irritated than afraid.

"Margaret," he said, with a hint of insistence. "I've waited long enough for you to come to your senses. It's time—"

"Come to my senses?" she interrupted. "What do you mean?"

"You know very well what I mean. You know our parents have spoken about us."

"I know of no such thing!"

"Then it's time you found out. What else do you think my visits and my words of affection mean?"

"I'm sure I have no idea."

"Margaret, don't you see? It's time we make definite plans. I want you, Margaret. I want to marry you."

"Please . . . no," Maggie said, trying to back away.

He continued to press himself toward her. "We have your father's blessing, Margaret. You need but say the word and the estates of Kairn and Stone-wycke—"

"No . . . no—I can't. I—"

"*Can't!* Come, Margaret. Don't pretend to be so naive. I know you want me also. I know you. I've seen the look of love in your eyes."

He continued the advance, backing Maggie against the rough side of Raven's stall.

"Mr. Falkirk," Maggie began again, "I . . . I don't want to marry you. I'm sorry if you inferred otherwise."

Her eyes darted about for a way to flee, but Falkirk's arms blocked her on either side.

"I tell you, I've seen it in your eyes, Margaret," he insisted, undaunted by her words. "I know what love looks like."

"If you have, Mr. Falkirk," said Maggie, breathing deeply and trying to utter calmly the words she wanted to scream at him, "I'm sorry. Perhaps you have seen love in my eyes. But it was not meant for you."

He colored slightly and his voice quavered momentarily; then he swiftly regained his composure.

"Am I not good enough for the grand lady? Are you insinuating you would rather bestow your favor on that rascal of a cousin—"

His careless words were ill-chosen if he thought to win Maggie's favor by insulting her fiancé.

"Don't you dare speak that way of him!" she cried, her fear of Falkirk at last giving way to anger.

"So that's it, is it?" he snarled as his hands inched closer and then clamped down on her two shoulders. Then he laughed, still convinced his menacing charm could overpower any impressionable young girl. "You'll change your tune after you have tasted a *real* man!"

He pulled her to him and forced her lips to his. She struggled, but his hands on her shoulders held her fast.

"Please—don't—" she managed to say before his passionate breath suffocated her.

After a moment he released her. Her hand flashed to his cheek with a resounding slap so that her palm stung; his face reddened with the force of the blow.

Falkirk staggered backward, stunned at the affrontery of her scorn. Then a grin of malicious intent crept over his face, and he rubbed his cheek ruefully.

"So that's how we would play this game, is it?" he said as the leer grew wider. "Well, my captivating little heiress, let me give you the feel of a man with power."

He pressed his body against her, his arms holding Maggie's tiny frame in a vise-like grip, his lips ardently crushing down on hers. "Don't worry," he said, "you'll enjoy it once you're taught what love is all about." He kissed her again, and again.

Terror seized Maggie. With both hands against his chest she tried to repel him, but fighting was useless against his superior strength.

"Digory!" she tried to call out. But her voice was dulled by Falkirk's nearness. "Don't worry about him . . . I sent him away."

In one final surge, Maggie shoved with all her might, wrenched herself partially free, and lurched toward the door. Falkirk grabbed at her sleeve and the leather of her jacket tore with a sickening rip. In shock she stared at the torn sleeve, then up at him, incensed at what he had done. His grip loosened, then he retreated a step.

"I'll be back," he said. "And make no mistake, Margaret. I *shall* claim you as my wife—with or without your consent!"

He spun around and was gone.

Maggie slumped to the ground and burst into tears, hardly aware of the pounding retreat of the stallion's hooves. She was still weeping several minutes later when Digory ambled into the stable.

Hearing her choking sobs, he hurried to her side. "Lady Marg'ret!" he exclaimed, kneeling down beside her. "Are ye ailin', lass?"

She shook her head, but no words would come. At last she struggled to whisper the single word, *Ian.*

Digory understood and hurried away as quickly as his arthritic bones would carry him. When he returned, Ian was at his side. He rushed to Maggie, still lying on the stable floor, and his face turned ashen. His mind reeled as he reached out his hand to her trembling body; he dropped to her side and wrapped his arms about her.

"What happened?" he asked softly.

She tried to speak, but every word caught in a sob.

Ian tried to calm her, then glanced up at Digory with a questioning look.

"Were it the gentleman, lassie?" asked Digory.

"What gentleman?" asked Ian sharply, his hot blood rising.

"Mr. Falkirk," Digory replied. "He were here jist a few moments ago—he was a-ridin' off jist before I came in."

Suddenly the scene before Ian's eyes took on deeper and more sinister meaning. He saw the torn sleeve for the first time and suddenly realized the reason for Maggie's sobs.

"Maggie . . . ?" he said. "Was it him?"

She managed a nod.

Ian leaped to his feet. "Which way did he ride, Digory?"

"I couldna tell, sir, but—"

"Ian, no!" exclaimed Maggie. "Don't go . . . please!"

"I'll kill the miserable scoundrel!" he cried.

"No, Ian!" implored Maggie, rising.

But Ian had already thrown himself on Raven's back, where she stood still saddled from Maggie's ride.

"Ian . . . Ian! This isn't the way!" Maggie screamed after him. But he was gone.

Maggie numbly fell back against the wall. Fear and darkness surrounded her, and for a moment she forgot Digory's presence altogether.

Gradually she felt Digory's loving hands reaching out and pulling her to her feet. Then she became aware, as if coming to her from a distance through a fog, of his gentle voice repeating tender words she could not understand. Her first thought was that he was attempting to console her. Then suddenly it dawned on her that he was praying, and that his mellow words of compassion and healing were not intended for her at all.

By degrees she relaxed, and the tears abated. But with the calming of her spirit came the reawakening of her thoughts.

"I have to stop him," she said.

"In time, lass," Digory soothed, ". . . in time."

"There is no time. We must stop him!" Her voice rang through the quiet that had descended on the stable.

"Noo, lass," Digory tried to calm her. "The lad will do na harm—only cause a bit o' a row, as lads'll do." Then his voice rose with the uncharacteristic outrage he had been hiding for Maggie's sake. "An it'll serve that yoong de'il right!"

Immediately he repented his words. "Dear Lord, forgi'e me—but the man deserves na better."

"But Ian could be hurt! Falkirk had rage in his eye when he left."

"I'm thinkin' yer yoong cousin can take care o' himsel'."

"He'll be back. I know he will!" said Maggie, hardly heeding Digory's attempts to calm her.

"Then the bla'gart'll hae the whole Duncan clan t' fecht!" said Digory, his highland blood rising at the thought, as if he were himself the chief member of the clan he had given his life to serve.

Maggie had now come to herself. Thoughts were finally crystallizing in her mind. If she were indeed, as people had been saying all her life, the heiress of Stonewycke, now was the time for her to step into that calling. She couldn't help Ian, not right now at least. But maybe there was something she could do—something which would thwart Falkirk's scheming designs, and possibly keep him out of their lives forever.

She sprang up, her strength reviving with renewed purpose.

"Digory," she said, "saddle us two horses. And bring out a workhorse too—and sacks. We'll need several."

"I don't think we'll be able t' get t' town in time t'—"

"We're not going into town, Digory," interrupted Maggie.

The groom stood staring at his young mistress, wondering if the stress had finally been too much for her.

"Hurry!" Maggie urged, heading for the stalls to begin preparations by herself.

Two hours later the three horses plodded heavily back past the iron gates of Stonewycke, their covert mission accomplished under the cloak of darkness. The rain still withheld its torrents, and only the wind impeded their step; their labored journey was nearly at an end. At the back of the house the horses stopped near the walled garden where Digory and Maggie unloaded from their weary backs the heavy bags they had carried all the way home. They had ridden hard to the granite mounds of Braenock Ridge, covering the distance in half the usual time. Finding it still deserted, Maggie located the spot without difficulty and flew to the task with the aid of her trusted groom. The return trip, though slower, was no easier for the faithful beasts of burden with their cumbersome cargo. When the bags were off their backs, Digory led them to the stables while Maggie—making sure they were not seen—began lugging their find into the little-used and overgrown arbor which would, until she could devise a better permanent cache, serve to conceal their find from Falkirk and her father. There was a breach in the back wall she thought would do just fine. There remained many difficulties, but she would manage them somehow, as soon as Ian returned. At least she had it out of Falkirk's scheming grasp.

As Maggie tucked the key in her pocket a plan began to form in her mind. Perhaps, had she thought it through, she would have seen its folly. But in her desperation from the heightened fervor of the evening's events, it seemed the only way. Falkirk would return to the ridge tonight with his accomplice— whoever that was—and find his treasure gone. In the morning she would send him a cryptic message: if he wanted his treasure, he would have to meet her conditions, the most important of which was never to set foot on Stonewycke again.

Perhaps it was foolish. In the light of day she might find herself unwilling to yield the long-hidden cache. But at this moment all she could think of was ridding her life of Falkirk forever. No price seemed too great to ensure her happiness with Ian.

Oh, if only he would return so she could tell him everything! He would know what was best—to expose Falkirk; or to employ any number of other possibilities.

Meanwhile, Maggie entered the house by a little-used back door and still unseen, hurried up the flights of stairs in search of a place to hide the key to the garden.

Back in her room a short while later, she paced in front of her window, her ears straining for sound of Ian's return. She tried to pray, but no prayer could find coherent expression in her harried mind. There was only confusion, fear. On Braenock Ridge hours ago she had felt so confident in her resolve—but now it was gone. The image of her father crossed her mind and unconsciously her hand crept toward her neck and to the locket.

It was gone!

Despair flooded her. Was this the final horrible answer she had dreaded to face? Once more something precious had been lost to her. And could this be anything but a sign that the giver of the beloved object would be torn from her as well?

Maggie desperately tried to focus her mind—where could she have lost it? She had had it earlier on Braenock Ridge. Had it fallen off since? Could it have been snagged on something when she and Digory were digging? If so, how could she dare return for it? *Oh, where is it?* her heart wailed.

Why had Ian not yet returned?

39
The Fight

THE SHADOWS OF dusk had given way nearly completely to night. Raven, little more than a swift black streak, raced down the valley road leading south.

In his fury Ian dug his heels in relentlessly. The miles to Kairn should have cooled his wrath, but they only served to sharpen and further define it. Unaware that she was, even now, making her way in the same direction on an altogether different mission, all Ian could see through the distorted images of his agitated brain was Maggie crumpled on the floor of the stable. Her sobs tore painfully at his memory. *I should have been there,* he thought. *I could have protected her.*

His own selfish words still vibrated in his ears. He had only been thinking of himself. He should never have let her ride off alone! In anguish and guilt, Ian drove Raven on.

Falkirk had no right! Whether he knew about the betrothal or not, he had behaved like a fiend. But the dog would pay! He would force the miscreant to his knees before this night was through. He needed no weapon. With his bare hands he would teach Falkirk to behave like a gentleman!

He had never been to Kairn. He eased into a trot when he reached the rows of trees lining either side of the road. He could barely make out their shapes in the darkness, but he knew he must be approaching the estate. Soon the silhouette of the house loomed in front, dark, too, except for two or three pale windows. Ian brought Raven up short at the doorstep of the mansion. Flying from the saddle, he ran up the few steps and pounded on the door.

The wait was long and he continued to pound. Finally the door swung open.

"Do ye want t' wake the veery dead wi' yer poundin'?" bawled a woman who appeared to be the housekeeper.

"I want Falkirk!" shouted Ian. The woman retreated a step or two, as if Ian would attack the portress herself.

"The laird be t' bed," she replied, unabashed by his insolent tone.

"The young Falkirk!"

"He's na here."

"Where then?" demanded Ian.

"How should I ken?"

"I tell you, I want him," said Ian, moving forward.

"An' I tell ye, I dinna ken his whereabouts," she said, ready to slam the door. But Ian caught it with his foot and glared at her.

"The yoong lord comes an' goes," she continued, at last feeling the intimidation of this wild stranger who would not be turned aside by her gruffness. "He went t' Port Strathy this mornin'—"

Ian waited to hear no more.

He spun on his heels, leaving the woman at the open door with her unfinished sentence in her mouth, flew back down the steps, leaped on Raven's back, spurred her on mercilessly, and tore back down the road the way he had come.

The long ride back to Port Strathy moderated Ian's initial passion, but a steely determination replaced it. What would he do if his suspicion as to Falkirk's location proved to be wrong? But he needn't have worried. The golden stallion was tied in front of the inn where Falkirk had come both to celebrate the good fortune of his find on the moor, and to deaden the humiliation of his rebuff by Maggie.

A storm of renewed violence assailed Ian. He quickly dismounted, hardly bothering to tether Raven at the hitching post outside, and strode angrily toward the door.

Inside, Falkirk had already passed the midpoint toward complete intoxication. The combined emotions of exhilaration and mortification operating upon him, he had been loud and boisterous, at one moment toasting the health of his companions with elation, the next lapsing into the despondency of solitude, ready to break out suddenly in a challenge against any and all present. He was anxious to reconcile his defeat at Stonewycke by demonstrating his virility, itching to vanquish with his fists any farmer foolish enough to stand up against him. For the young lord was no stranger to the arena, having boxed with greater than average ability in the ring at the university. To this point in the progress of the evening, however, the locals had prudently managed to sidestep his slurs against everything from their town to their wives in an attempt to incite someone to stand against him. The effect of his impotence, working in combination with Queenie's drink, had by now raised the neighboring lord to such a pitch of agitation that he was ready to find provocation to violence in the slightest pretense.

A glass of ale was raised to his lips when the door suddenly burst open with a crash.

"Falkirk!" shouted Ian, "Step outside!"

Turning toward the threat, Falkirk's lip curled into an evil sneer. He set his drink on the table.

"You must be jesting, Duncan," he drawled, rising slowly from his chair and starting toward him.

"You will pay for what you have done!"

"Playing the knight again, are you?" replied Falkirk, skillfully covering the wobbly sensation in his knees.

"If you want it here, that's fine with me!"

"So you're upset that the little flower has a crumpled petal," Falkirk went on, the alcohol working in his brain to instill a confidence where he had no reason for it. "But no, that's not it," he taunted with a sardonic grin of disdain. "You're just a poor loser!"

But the words were unwisely spoken. If there had been any restraint in Ian, it now broke before the full force of his anger. He took two strides toward his opponent, who was still not fully apprised of his danger.

Falkirk opened his mouth to speak once more as Ian approached.

"Why, you good-for-nothing b——!"

But before he had the chance to finish the word, Ian's fist smashed directly into his face. Falkirk stumbled backward, stunned, caught himself on a bench, then touched his lip and felt a slow trickle of blood.

"You scum!" he shrieked in a diabolical voice. "You will pay for this, you mangy cur!"

Sobered from the pain and the sight of his own blood, Falkirk sprang on Ian with a flurry of well-placed blows. His experience quickly regained him the upper hand and Ian found himself thrown back against the wall with a sharp stinging sensation over his right ear, from which he, too, felt a warm oozing down the side of his cheek.

But he had not come to be on the defensive, warding off Falkirk's punches. Ian had experience too, not from the university but from the streets of London. He struck back without restraint, attacking Falkirk with the fury of righteous indignation, battering his fists about the other's head and midsection. The two fell across a chair which crashed to pieces, and then to the floor.

The small gathering of men in the common room were content to stand by and observe—not often were they provided with such splendid entertainment, and they had long since tired of Falkirk's abusive behavior and coarse tongue. But Queenie was not about to stand by while her new tables and chairs were demolished by the two ruffians. She ran forward as quickly as her oversized frame would allow and frantically exhorted the onlookers to do something. Receiving no help from that quarter, she hastened into the midst of the fray herself.

"Ye bloody blokes!" she cried. "Ye can kill each other if ye want. But not in my place!"

Then turning again to her customers. "Grab 'em, will ye, afore my place is in shambles!"

The two combatants tried to push Queenie aside, but by that time several of the men had approached them where they rolled and wrestled on the floor. They pulled Ian off Falkirk, who had just received a volley of tormenting punches about his head. Seeing his quick advantage, Falkirk jumped to his feet and lunged forward, delivering a punishing blow to Ian's ribs. Ian crumpled to the floor where the men, still holding him, attempted to help him back up.

Painfully Falkirk gathered his hat and staggered toward the door, then outside. Regaining his breath, Ian shrugged off the help of his supporters and struggled toward the door.

"I'll kill you!" he yelled. "Do you hear me, Falkirk? If you ever touch her again, I'll kill you!"

The small gathering of men remained silent in the aftermath of the row, but Queenie—anxious to soothe tempers and calm the atmosphere in her respectable establishment—hastened to Ian's side.

"I dinna ken what the bloke did t' ye," she said. "But I'll warrant he ne'er does it again."

She led Ian, in a state of mental and physical exhaustion, back into the room and to a table. "An' na doobt he deserved it!" she added as if to seal the matter for all present.

"Sit ye doon," she said with a husky gentleness. "Ye'll be needin' a drink."

She brought out a bottle of her prime Scotch from behind the counter and poured him a large measure. "This'll put the starch back int' yer bones."

Slowly the others resumed their former places, one or two of the men helping Queenie straighten the furniture and pick up the broken chair, and gradually the buzz of conversation resumed. Ian sat alone in a daze. The voices around him were but a subdued blur. Even Queenie's friendly tones registered only vaguely in his consciousness. For the moment all the latent violence within him had been spent. The energy which had driven him to such convulsive hysteria only a few moments before was gone, and his body sagged in weariness.

The only action of which he seemed capable was to raise the glass in front of him to his lips and let the whiskey burn down his throat.

He signalled for Queenie, and she poured him another.

40

Discovery

✤

MAGGIE HURRIED FROM her room the moment she heard the hoofbeats.

It was very late, but sleep had been impossible. She hastened down the stairway, the long wait at last over, desperately hoping the horse she heard bore Ian and not Falkirk returning as he had threatened.

She forgot her coat, and the rush of cold wind bit through her thin frock as she stepped outside. Gingerly she crept toward the stable through the darkness of the yard. Peering inside, the blackness was deeper still.

"Ian . . . Ian . . . is that you?" she whispered.

The jingling and creaking sounds of bridle and saddle being unfastened stopped. Ian stepped out of the shadows. She could just barely see his face, but it was enough.

"Ian . . . oh, dear Lord!" Maggie cried. "You're hurt!" Carefully she reached up and touched his bruised and bloodied face.

He took her hands and wrapped them around him instead.

"Ian, I was so worried . . . so afraid—"

"You don't need to worry anymore, my love," he replied.

"Did you . . . did you find him?"

"Yes. And he will not hurt you again." The chill of his voice frightened Maggie; the words sounded so decisive and final. She could smell that he had been drinking.

"Ian, while you were gone," she began, then stopped. "Ian," she continued after a moment, "I know how we can keep him away—"

"Hush, my Maggie . . ." he interrupted in a soft, strained voice. "Just hold me. I need so much for you to hold me." He tried to focus his muddled vision on her face, barely visible in the darkness. "He won't bother us ever again."

"How can you be sure? Ian . . . what happened?"

"Not now. Maggie . . . not now."

His voice contained a cold foreboding; Maggie shuddered involuntarily.

"I've done something I want to forget," he went on. "I need you to help me forget. Just hold me."

She complied. For a few moments nothing else existed for the two lovers who were yet compelled to hide their love from view. And even before it could be made public, outside forces threatened to destroy their love and wrench them apart. But for now, in this one moment of quiet bliss, even the smells of horses and hay, the howling wind, and the gentle squeaking back and forth of the stable door all receded into the distance. All that mattered was their love, and they clung to one another, holding tight to that solid reality.

They did not hear the footsteps approaching across the cobblestone drive, and saw the light from the lantern too late.

"So!" growled the voice they knew all too well. "This is how I am repaid for my kindness!" James Duncan's voice resounded with the hatred of a lifetime against the offspring of Landsbury.

The couple fell apart and gaped with horror at the man as if they were thieves caught in the vary act of stealing his treasures. Through the unfolding of the events of this evening, James had been the furthest thought from their minds. Maggie had all but forgotten her earlier resolve to tell him everything.

"Father—" she tried to begin.

James ignored his daughter and turned instead to the cousin whose father he loathed.

"What have you to say for yourself, Duncan?" he shouted angrily.

Ian stepped forward. Despite the pain from Falkirk's blows, he stood straight and tall. He had already faced one foe tonight; he would not be easily cowed by another, even Maggie's father.

"Your daughter and I are in love," he began in a calm, unflinching voice.

"Love!" replied James with a spiteful laugh. "What do you know of love, you baseborn son of a swindler!"

"We intended to tell you—"

"You intended to tell me!" James roared. "But you knew I'd never allow it! And I won't—not for an instant!"

"We weren't intending to ask your permission," said Ian resolutely. "Your approval, or lack of it, cannot change our love for one another. We only wanted you to hear it from us first."

"You blackguard!" shouted James, seething with rage. The impudent scoundrel was challenging him to his face.

"I'm sorry, sir," began Ian again, "we had hoped—"

"You get out of here!" James ordered. "You'll never lay eyes on my daughter again."

"Father, you must listen to us!" implored Maggie.

"Quiet, Margaret!" James commanded. "You get to the house immediately. I'll deal with you later."

"Please, Father," returned Maggie, standing her ground, "please hear what we have to say."

"Why, you insolent hussy! By Jove, I tell you to get—"

"No, your lordship," said Ian, his composure at last giving way. "You'll not speak to my fiancée in such a tone. You no longer control what she may or may not do."

"What!" he shrieked. "You . . . what right have you? By heaven, if I were a younger man, I'd thrash you and throw you out myself! Now, begone, you charlatan. I command you—"

"No!" Ian resounded. "You do not command us. We are going to be married!"

The words hung in the air like a thunderhead ready to burst at any instant. In disbelief James stared at the audacious couple before him as if he recognized neither of them.

His countenance slowly turned to ice. When he spoke, his voice was low like a distant thunderclap, portending another explosion of lightning soon to follow.

"What evil hoax you are trying to deceive me with, I do not know," he said. "But this I do know—before I am finished, I will destroy you. As for you, my slut of a daughter, I will never—so long as you take up with this vile excuse for a man—look upon your face again!"

Maggie burst into tears.

"We had hoped to reason with you," Ian tried again. "We had wanted your blessing!"

"My blessing!" James spat out the words like bile. "You'll have *nothing*—do you hear me, Duncan . . . nothing! And you'll never have my daughter! She *will* marry George Falkirk. That is what she shall do. And you shall go to the devil!"

"I tell you, sir," said Ian, fighting with all his might to control his rising temper, "we *will* be married—with or without your consent."

"Do you think that matters?"

"There is nothing you can do to change it."

"How naive you are! That marriage will mean no more than an old birch shilling by the time I get through! I have influence, and I will grind you, and your so-called marriage, into the dust beneath my feet!"

Ian opened his mouth to speak again, then hesitated.

Suddenly the desperation on his face was unmasked, as exposed in stark reality as the wounds on his face. Suddenly a voice inside said that James could win after all, that his words were not mere empty threats. All at once the weight of the evening's events crashed in upon him. The throbbing in his head, the numbing effect of the alcohol in his blood, and the onslaught of James's verbal abuse pressed mercilessly against his brain.

"I warn you, Duncan, if you try to take my daughter away, any so-called *marriage"*—James spat out the word with revulsion—"you contrive to arrange will be over—ended forever—within two days! It will never have been! I will have my way. Margaret will marry George Falkirk!"

Ian heard only a few words of James's final odious speech—". . . over . . . ended . . . marry George Falkirk!"

"No!" he screamed like a madman. "She will never marry Falkirk. I won't let it happen—never!"

Ian stumbled past James out of the stable. He could barely see in front of him. He had no destination in mind, no intent. He just had to get away. His old self welled up from deep within and cried out to him—"Flee! . . . Flee from Stonewycke . . . Flee from Scotland!"

The rain, so long pent up in the swelling clouds overhead, at last poured down and enveloped Ian as he ran into its dismal darkness.

41

A Midnight Plot

❉

RAIN PELTED THE granite embankments as if after a thousand years it might finally beat the boulders back to the dust from which they had been forged.

The dark figure cursed aloud, then spat on the ground.

"Tha' dirty bla'gart!" he growled. "Thinks 'e can dooblecross me, does 'e? Cheat me oot o' my share?"

In spite of his tattered woolen overcoat he was soaked to the skin, and now he bitterly realized that all his efforts had been in vain. The empty wooden cask told him all.

"Thinks 'e can do what 'e pleases cause o' him bein' a gent'man . . . thinks I'll stan' fer't, does 'e?" he muttered with revenge in his voice. "Oh, I'll get my share, my fine earl," he snarled greedily, kicking at the ancient box and knocking the fragile wood to splinters, "or I'll get all o' it!"

He pulled a crude wooden-handled dagger from his belt. Even in the dark it flashed with evil intent. He tested the edge with a calloused finger. "Jist let him try t' cheat me! He'll pay . . . that 'e will!"

He mounted his horse and sped off, already having forgotten that his own traitorous design had brought him to the ruin well over an hour ahead of the appointed rendezvous. He had forgotten that he, too, had planned to fleece his partner by making off with the loot himself. But even had his own felonious motives crossed his mind, he would not have been hard-pressed to convince his feeble conscience that he somehow possessed a greater right to the treasure. The fine-talking lord had more than enough wealth for one lifetime and certainly had no need for more. Besides, he reasoned, he had himself been kicked around for years by such noblemen with nothing to show for it. "Highborn rascals!" he mumbled.

Hatred and indignation rose within him, and mounted with every hoofbeat.

He flogged his horse pitilessly down the ridge, across the darkened fields, and to the valley road. Reaching it he spun toward the left, dug in his heels, urged his steed on at still a more furious gallop, and was soon out of sight, lost to view in the gathering hills to the south.

The storm-blackened sky grew only vaguely lighter as dawn approached. The angry clouds permitted the vaguest intimation of light—enough to show that, though unwelcome, morning would eventually come.

Leaning heavily on the door of the Bluster 'N Blow, Ian pounded his fist on the hard oak. Rain-soaked, mud-splattered, with dried blood on his face, he gave the appearance of a London street vagabond. His fine clothes drooped on his beaten frame, evidence of a lost battle. When a surly and sleepy-eyed Queenie Rankin opened the door some moments later, he lifted a bloodied hand to her but could only mumble incoherently.

"I . . . I need—"

"Good Gaud!" Queenie exclaimed, her perturbation at being roused at such an untimely hour dissolving in the shock of his appearance. More disturbing than the tattered look of his clothes was the vacant stare in his eyes which seemed to say that life no longer meant anything because he had done the unthinkable.

"Look at ye!" she cried. "Ye'll catch yer death in them wet clothes!"

She led him to the hearth and gently pressed him into a chair. "Ye sit doon here by the fire."

She stooped down, poked and blew at the dying embers from the previous evening's blaze, added a few sticks of dried oak, and coaxed the coals once more to give off their warmth. When the crackle of flames had resurrected to her satisfaction, she rose, and saying, "I'll be right back," hurried off toward the kitchen. She returned with a basin of water to which she had added several drops from a vial in her cupboard, and laid Ian's hand in it. He winced sharply and withdrew the hand, but she guided it back into the stinging potion of water.

"'Tis a fine gash ye got there," she said. "Ye must soak it or 'twill fester sure as ye blink."

Ian said nothing, only closed his eyes and took a deep breath. The pain awoke him gradually to reality. "I knew a young bloke once," Queenie went on, trying to ease Ian's mind with random conversation, "got jist a wee cut in his hand. He didna clean it proper, an' afore ye know it, he lost his whole hand. Had t' cut it clean off, they did. Wears a hook now—an' that's God's trowth! Ever seen a man wi' a hook fer a hand? 'Tis a gruesome sight—and these eyes o' mine hae seen jist aboot everythin' there is t' see."

Ian allowed Queenie to nurse his wound, thinking she came as close to a compassionate mother and ministering angel as could be found under the circumstances.

How a gentleman like this could get into such scrapes, thought Queenie, she couldn't guess. He had everthing he could want. Why did he go out and get himself into such trouble?

Yet she was drawn to this poor lad. He had shown her a courtesy all too rare among those of his breed, and taking him in now was a thing hardly to be questioned.

"Whate'er brings ye oot on such a foul mornin'?" she asked.

"I don't know." His voice had no tone. "I was out."

"Weel, ye should be at Stonewycke where ye can get proper fixin'."

"No!" said Ian with some alarm. "Not Stonewycke . . . I can't."

"Weel, a han'some lad like yersel' dinna want t' be goin' round wearin' no hook!"

"I didn't know where else to go."

"Dinna ye worry. I'll take care o' ye the best I can. Don't hae no clothes fer ye, though. My husband was a small man—dropped dead a week after this place was built. Still canna believe it mysel'. His clothes would ne'er fit the likes o' yersel'. Weel," she added, "maybe the fire'll do the job."

When his hand was clean and a warm cup of tea had passed his lips, she led Ian upstairs. She stripped him of his outer garments and eased him into bed, pulling a thick layer of blankets over him.

"A guid night's sleep's what he'll be needin'," she murmured, softly closing the door.

Ian slept. Perhaps that was what his body needed. But his soul could not rest. When he awoke several hours later, fatigue still wracked his aching frame and a vague apprehension had settled on his heart.

Dreams had disturbed the refuge of his sleep, dreams that were in a tangled mass of disarray—filled with a terror of the unknown, with a premonition he couldn't quite lay hold of. He rode, like the wind but he was not on Raven's back, nor on Maukin's, but on a mighty steed of great power and fierce, red eyes. Its coat was black as death and its long tail flew in the wind as he bolted across the moor with a speed no animal of equine origins could match. Now he was surrounded by heather, the very heather that had filled his heart with such joy when he had first seen it with Maggie. But now there was no joy—only desolation and loneliness. Suddenly a figure on the ground before him arrested the mad flight of his courser. Ian was on the ground walking toward the heap before him. He stooped down amidst the full blooming heather. Suddenly, to his horror, he realized the lovely blossoms of purple had altered their hue and had changed to the color of blood. In terror he jumped to his feet and tried to scream. But no voice would come . . .

Ian pulled himself up in bed, dripping with cold sweat. *Thank God!* he thought, easing back onto the bed, still breathing deeply from the panic of the nightmare.

All at once words came into his mind. Were they from his dream or were they words he had heard somewhere before? " *'O choose, O choose, Lady Marg'ret'* he said, *'O whether will ye gang or bide?'* "

What choice? he asked himself, as wakefulness gradually returned. *What Margaret? Was his own dear Maggie wrestling with a choice?*

He tried to shake the jumble of questions from his mind. Where had he heard those verses?

Then the old ballad he had heard that peaceful night around the huge fire so many weeks ago flooded back upon his memory.

No! he wanted to shout. *This can't be!*

He clasped his hands to his ears, as if to keep out the thoughts and accusations, the threats and fears.

But he could not escape them. If Maggie were struggling with a choice between himself and her father, even as the maiden in the Douglas ballad, then at least he had to know. He had to face it. Then, if her choice was against him, he could run once more. But he would have to return in order to discover what his future held.

42

Constable Duff

※

AMID THE FURY, pain, and stupor of the previous night, Ian had no recollection of retrieving the chestnut mare. But when he stumbled out of the inn about an hour before noon, Queenie brought Maukin around to him. The horse had been tied out in front, she said, and while he slept, she had fed and cared for the animal.

He looked at the woman for a long moment, incredulous that he could remember nothing of returning to Stonewycke for the horse following his altercation with James. Then, coming to his senses and realizing all the rough old woman had done to befriend such a vagrant as he, Ian swallowed hard, wondering how to thank her.

A woman not given to shows of emotion, Queenie laid a pudgy hand on his sleeve.

"Noo, where might ye be off to, if ye canna gang t' Stonewycke, as ye said last night?" Her tone was full of concern, for she could still see in his eyes the look of fatal hopelessness.

"I must go back," Ian replied flatly.

She scrutinized him carefully. He looked a bit better than he had several hours earlier. And his clothes, while still untidy, were at least dry. His hands no longer trembled, but that wound on his left hand required attention, as did the nasty cut above his ear. She wondered if he would get it at Stonewycke.

Ian mounted Maukin. Queenie was glad she had had sense enough to tend to the poor animal during the night, for it had been in nearly as bad shape as its master. Wherever the lad had ridden the mare during the night, it must have been long and hard.

Ian threw her one more glance, nodded in thankful salute, and spun around toward Stonewycke.

During the night the storm had blown out its fury, leaving the land washed with gloom. Little evidence of the summer just past remained. Ian recalled riding in the valley with Maggie—how lovely the heather hills had been beneath their feet, with the deep blue of the sky overhead! Gentle breezes had carried the odors of warmth and freshness on their wings. All had been so new, so delicious. Maggie's laughter, her smiling face rose into Ian's mind. It had been such a short time ago, yet it seemed another lifetime, a time when their budding love was joyous in its innocence. Hardly had they had the chance to realize they were in love before the blossom of that love seemed to be crushed, snatched from them. He could not believe summer would ever come again for him. Here, in these fields and hills, he had found his greatest joy. Would his greatest agony be here as well?

"Oh, God!" he cried. "Why do you allow a man to possess a tiny moment of ecstasy only to tear it from him? Do you delight in breaking our hearts?"

On he slowly rode. All the pleasures of the times so soon past soured within him. The treasured memories became instead knives of pain.

I would rather never to have lived than face this! he cried within himself. *God, I curse you for giving me breath!*

His hopelessness had turned to complete despondency by the time he approached the manor gate. Even if Maggie still wanted him, what could she do against her father's threats? If only they could go away . . . far away . . . to America! But she could never leave Stonewycke. What could he do? The man had threatened him. Just to show his face again could jeopardize Maggie's safety and happiness.

The gate stood open. Two strange horses grazed on the front lawn. Another impulse to turn back, to run, to flee, swept over him. Still he forced himself forward, approaching the house with trepidation. He dismounted, tied Maukin, walked to the door, and raised his hand to knock. Almost immediately the sound of approaching feet could be heard from within as though they had been waiting for him.

The door opened, and beyond the silent figure of the answering butler stood James with two men Ian had never seen before. The confrontation was more sudden than he expected.

"You have your impudence!" James said, spitting the words at him, "showing your face around here! But I'm glad you did."

Then turning to one of the men, "Constable, I believe this is the man you are seeking."

One of the strangers stepped forward toward Ian. He was shorter than Ian, somewhat stocky, and dressed in a coarse but respectable tweed coat and woolen trousers. His round face sported a thick moustache. His sharp black eyes left no doubt that he was wise as any serpent, but they also held an affability—as anyone viewing him with his granddaughter in his lap would have discerned in less than a moment.

"Mr. Duncan?" the man said.

Ian nodded.

"I'm Angus Duff, the constable from Culden."

"Culden?" said Ian, perplexed.

"Yes. But my duties extend to Strathy."

Ian did not reply, still unable to tell what the unusual scene portended.

"I've come to ask you some questions," Duff went on. The constable had never been a man to judge another by his appearance. But this young Duncan definately looked as if trouble were no stranger to him.

"What questions?" asked Ian flatly.

"About the gentleman who was killed," Duff answered, carefully making note of Ian's reaction. "Seems you two had words last night—"

"Killed?" Ian said in a hoarse voice, barely able to get the words past his dry throat. "Who?"

"Come now, Duncan," James cut in with derision in his tone. "We can all see well enough past your attempted ignorance. I told the constable how you left here last night with blood in your eyes."

"Who?" asked Ian again, hardly aware of anything but the pounding in his skull.

"The young master of Kairn," the constable answered. "Mr. George Falkirk. Stabbed to death in the middle of the night, as far as we can tell."

Ian's face turned ashen.

"The folks in town said your words at the inn last evening came to blows. It would be good to know where you were for the rest of the night?"

Ian did not respond. For an instant the thought crossed his mind to turn and run back through the door through which he had just come. But his legs had suddenly been drained of their strength. My God, he thought, *the night was so hazy. Could it be possible . . . what if . . .*

His thoughts were suspended as something all at once drew his eyes to the stairway above him. There stood Maggie on the landing, her eyes red-rimmed, her skin pale. She started to descend the stairs but James's voice shot out at her.

"Margaret! Remain where you are!"

She froze.

It is a choice, Ian thought. *Between her father and myself. O choose, O choose, Lady Margaret . . . whether you will go or stay.*

With eyes riveted upon the young woman he loved, Ian's heart sank as she paused in fearful obedience to her father. He could not sustain his gaze, and looked away.

But then hope rose again at the sound of her footstep continuing on down the stairs. With each step she seemed to say to her father that he would not—could not—vanquish the love she bore in her heart for Ian. Reaching the floor, Maggie walked straight to Ian's side, ignoring the astonished look of supreme offense on her father's face at her flagrant disobedience of his command. *I have made my choice, Father,* she seemed to say, *and I make it with the man I love!*

"Mr. Duncan," said the constable patiently, "you still have not answered my question."

Ian looked toward Maggie; hers was the only trust he had needed.

"I was out," he said, ". . . thinking."

"By yourself?" the constable pressed.

Ian nodded.

"Could you tell me," Duff asked, "where you went?"

"Places. I was just . . . out—I don't remember . . ."

Ian's head was hot. He had no idea where he'd been. He could not stand up under many more of Duff's unrelenting questions, for he had no defense. But suddenly the constable said—

"Well, Mr. Duncan, I won't be troubling you any further right now. But I will be talking to you later."

It was James who spoke now. "What! Is that all you're going to do?"

"I'm sorry, your Lordship. We have more investigating to do. We mustn't act too hastily."

"You'd let him go free because he's the son of the Earl of Landsbury!"

"Your Lordship," rejoined Duff, miffed at Lord Duncan's interference, "the boy's father has nothing whatever to do with this. When the time is right and the facts are straight, justice will be done. For now, I thank you for receiving us into your home."

Then turning to Ian, he added, "You are planning to remain in the area for some time yet, I presume?" But he did not await Ian's reply, for his words—though framed as a question—carried the ring of an order. He and his associate turned and strode from the room. Just as they reached the door, Duff paused as if the question had only just occurred to him, and once again addressed Ian:

"Oh . . . one more thing, Duncan," he said. "That's a nasty cut you've picked up there on your hand . . . mind telling me how you got it?"

Ian shot a quick glance at Maggie, then back at the constable. "I'm afraid I don't know, sir," he said. "It must have happened sometime during the night. Maybe in the fight with Falkirk. I don't remember."

Duff nodded with knowing expression, then turned and disappeared out of the house.

As the door closed behind the two men, James flung a hostile and menacing glance toward Ian and his daughter.

"I tried to tell you what kind of man this was!" he said to Maggie scornfully. "Now, you would marry a murderer!"

"He is no criminal," answered Maggie quietly.

But James Duncan cared little for any defense; he had already convicted the man who stood before him. Whether or not he was guilty of murdering Falkirk hardly affected his opinion of Ian. It simply provided a convenient way of allowing the law to do his work for him. But if that fool of a constable did nothing, he would see to it himself. One way or another he *would* destroy this imposter, the so-called betrothed of his moonstruck daughter. No matter that Falkirk was now gone, and with him his father's money; he would repay these two idiots for what they had done to him!

"Mr. Duncan," James continued as if Maggie had never spoken, "you will leave these premises immediately. You will not return! If you ever set foot on Stonewycke again, I shall consider you an intruder and will be justified in whatever I may do. Is that understood?"

But it was Maggie, not Ian, who answered him: "We will leave right away, Father."

"You, Margaret, are going nowhere." James replied dispassionately, as one who knows his victory is assured.

"No!" she screamed.

"Don't force me to carry out my threat here and now," said James, leveling his icy stare at his daughter as if she were the enemy.

Suddenly from over James's shoulder came Atlanta's voice, quiet and controlled:

"Maggie, let Ian go for now," she said. "We will work this out. You will be with him soon."

Maggie shook her head in agony, desperately afraid that once he was gone, in some hideous way her father would keep her from Ian forever.

"This is best," Atlanta said. "By tomorrow you will be together again. Ian . . . will you go peaceably?"

Ian stared blankly at Atlanta. Could he believe that in one more day it would all be over? Yet even as he doubted, something in her resolute, unflinching tone spoke assurance to him, communicating more than her mere words that she would be able to deliver what she promised.

Ian looked at Maggie, his heart crying out to hold her one more time. Slowly he walked toward the door, He turned his eyes away, afraid to look at her again for fear of losing his resolve.

"Ian!" Maggie cried out after him. "Ian . . . I love you!"

He turned, cast her one quick glance, blinked back the rising tears, then hastened through the door. On he walked through the great iron gates of Stonewycke, leading Maukin, down the road, and on.

As the west wind stung his face, even as a few rays of sunlight beat down trying to warm the chilly earth, Ian looked toward the sky in anticipation of tomorrow.

Perhaps in another time, summer will come again after all. He could only hope . . . and wait.

43

An Unknown Assailant

STONEWYCKE BECAME A prison to Maggie.

All that was dear in life now stood outside those somber stone walls. She could think of nothing but Ian—out there somewhere.

Even Raven remained out of reach. For Maggie knew that if she once drew near to the horse, she would inevitably be drawn directly to him. Only one thing kept her from seeking out her love: the glare of hatred in her father's eyes. She had little doubt of the lengths he was prepared to go against Ian.

Thus she wandered about the solitary house; each hour seemed an eternity as she waited for her mother to fulfill her promises. On the second day she overheard two servants speaking with concern about Digory. He had risen as usual in the morning and had begun his regular tasks. But around midday, Sam had unexpectedly found him sitting in his chair in the loft, staring straight ahead with fixed gaze, shaking with chills and a low fever.

Without considering the consequences, Maggie rushed from the house and toward the stables. Sam had helped Digory to his bed, and there Maggie found him, apparently asleep. As Maggie stood silently over him, her mind was filled with fearful visions of Bess Mackinaw, helpless and dying.

Oh, God, she thought, *don't take him now!*

After a brief moment an eye cocked open and a gentle smile formed on the lips of the old man.

"Weel, lassie," he said in a cheerful, but noticeably weak voice, "I canna gi' ye a proper welcome today."

"Oh, Digory," she said, "is there anything I can do?"

He chuckled. "'Tis na so bad, lass. Jist a touch o' ague. I'll be na up t' give the lads an lassies below their evenin' feedin'."

"You most certainly will not! I'll feed them myself if I have to. But you must stay right where you are."

"Ye hae enough on yer mind, lassie," Digory replied, "wi'out tyrin' t' do my chores, too."

"Oh, Digory," Maggie sighed, a flood of childhood memories flowing into her confused mind. The long past days of her childhood may have contained hurts of their own, but they now seemed sweet and carefree in comparison to the present. Would she trade Ian for a return to those days of innocence? Her sigh caught in a sob, and before she could stop them, tears rose in her eyes and spilled down her cheeks.

"Dear child," Digory whispered, "dinna ye forget that our God will turn everythin' t' good in the end. I ken 'tis hard t' believe when ye're in the midst o' yer trial. But if ye can hold on t' that truth, it'll help ye through the pains o' life."

Digory always spoke as if God were so kind, Maggie thought: He spoke of God as his loving Father. But the only father she had ever known was cold, selfish, and vengeful. She wanted to believe that God was a *good* Father like Digory said. How delightful it would be to have such a Father whose loving arms were warm and inviting and full of tenderness and forgiveness!

"Jist remember," the groom had gone on, "God'll never forsake ye. He loves ye an' will make everythin' come t' good when ye trust Him."

"I'll try," Maggie replied, forcing as much conviction into the words as she could. As much as she envied the simplicity of Digory's trusting faith, at this moment God seemed too distant to help.

Yet Digory knew Maggie even better than she knew herself. He formed a silent prayer in his heart. "Oh, Lord, keep yer hand on this dear child. Dinna let her from yer care, whate'er comes her way."

To Maggie he then said, "Child, could ye read me a bit from the Book? It would help me t' rest."

She glanced around, found the worn leather Bible on Digory's table, and took it to him. He pointed out several Psalms, and she read them aloud to him. But the words came out toneless and Maggie could scarcely hear her own voice. The words which Digory hoped would speak life into her troubled spirit would have to wait to do their work. But as the rector had read at the funeral of Bess Mackinaw, that time would come as surely as the rain came down from heaven to nourish the plants of the earth. At this moment, however, Maggie was no more aware of the work of heavenly rain from this old man and his oft-read Bible than she was of the surgery of God's scalpel deep within her heart in the midst of her tribulation.

Digory was soon asleep and Maggie gently closed the book, sighed deeply, and rose to go.

As she stepped from the stable after descending from Digory's room, the shadows of evening lay across the grounds. Hoping to avoid a confrontation with her father, yet not ready to return to the house, she turned toward the left and walked along the outer hedge which led around to the courtyard at the front of the mansion. She had just passed the rusty iron gate of the forsaken little garden, thinking of the first time she had shown it to Ian, when suddenly a hand shot out from the shadows and clamped down roughly on her.

"Dinna say a word!" threatened a deep voice in little more than an evil whisper.

Maggie tried to force a scream but her sounds were cut off by the harsh pinching of fingers against her lips. Terrified, she felt herself being dragged into the cover of the shrubbery where her assailant had been hiding.

"I'm na goin' t' hurt ye, ye little jade!" the unfamiliar voice grated.

Maggie twisted and struggled, but the cruel hands held her tight. The stale smell of ale and the stench from his unwashed body sickened her. Maggie gagged, then wrestled again to free herself.

"I'll not hurt ye," the voice went on, "long as ye cooperate. Now I got my knife here an' if ye scream oot, I'll use it." He poked the blade into her back until she winced.

"Now," he went on with rasping voice, "I'm goin' t' take my hand from yer mouth. If ye try t' yell . . . weel, blue blood'll flow as easily as any. Am I makin' my meanin' clear t' ye?"

Maggie stiffly nodded her head.

By slow degrees he loosened his grip on Maggie's mouth. But he only lowered his arm enough to keep a tight grip on her shoulders. His foul breath was overpowering, but Maggie did not struggle further, for the steely reminder of his purpose remained pressed against her back.

"I been hearin' ye was pretty friendly wi' Master Falkirk," he said, settling into the business for which he had come, for his prey was now safely in the spider's power.

"I—I don't know what you mean . . ." Maggie replied, her feeble voice quivering in fear.

"Ye're in on this wi' him! I ken it!"

"No!"

He loosened his grip for an instant and fumbled in his pocket. The knife continued to press against her. "Deny that this is yers then, leddy!" he said, shoving a shining object into her face.

She gasped. "Where did you get that!" she cried, not realizing how dangerous her impulsive words could be. "Give it to me!" she gasped out, grabbing for the locket. She could not bear to see the gift from Ian in that vile hand. She watched it drop into the dirt and the man's hands closed more tightly around her.

"Ha, ha!" he snarled. "What better place fer the laird t' hide his booty than wi' his sweetheart!" A villainous laugh followed, which gave way to a low, hacking cough.

"I hardly knew Mr. Falkirk."

"Come, lassie," the man replied, growing angry, "ye wouldna be so foolish as t' be thinkin' t' keep it all yersel', would ye?" He purposely jabbed her with the tip of his blade, still poised in readiness in the event she should scream. "Weel, ye can ferget that, ye trollop! I earned my share, an' I mean t' get it . . . one way or the other. Now talk!"

"I don't know what you mean," said Maggie, her voice trembling as she realized, indeed, *exactly* what he meant. Could she make him believe her lie?

"Ha! I dinna believe that any more than ye believe I'll let ye go alive if ye dinna tell me!"

His grip tightened and she felt the knife tearing through her clothes.

"*You* killed him, didn't you!" she accused, hardly realizing what she was saying until it was too late.

The muscles of his arm tensed in momentary anger, then relaxed. "Ne'er bite the hand that feeds ye, I al'ays say," he replied. "The way I hear it, that fancy gent'man fr' Lonnon killed the laird. They're sayin' he swore t' kill him that very night."

"It was you I—"

She stopped short, realizing anything she said about the murder would reveal her knowledge of the treasure, thus endangering her all the more.

"No more o' yer accusations, ye hear? Me an' the laird hardly laid eyes on each other. Now . . . where's the loot!"

"I . . . I don't know."

"'Tis a good week fer the spillin' o' blue blood," he sneered. "I suppose ye'll be joinin' yer lover."

Suddenly the reflection from an approaching lantern illuminated the darkness where they stood, and the assailant's grip slackened for an instant. Maggie thrust her elbow into his ribs with all her might and struggled to free herself. A sting of pain shot through her back, and she screamed in terror.

She heard footsteps running toward her, saw the lantern swinging in the darkness, and could make out vague yells. The foul grip loosened, and she fell to the ground in a swoon.

"What is't, my leddy?" asked Sam as he knelt at her side.

The sound of his voice brought Maggie's mind back into focus, but when she opened her mouth she found herself unable to speak. She shook her head, reached for his hand, and pulled herself partly up, still trembling. Then she felt again the sharp throbbing in her back.

"Is he gone?" she gasped.

"Who, mem?" he asked. "I thought I heard voices. Were it an intruder, meme? I'll gang after him."

"No, Sam!" Maggie replied, grabbing his arm. "It's too late. I'm sure he's gone by now."

Sam helped Maggie to her feet, then caught up something from the ground.

"Look, my leddy," he said. "This be yers?"

She snatched the locket from his hand as if he were the thief. Clutching it tightly in her trembling hand, she sped to the house. She managed to make it to her room without being seen, and lay facedown on the bed. She had to think.

Surely a report of what had just happened would lift suspicion from Ian. Yet her father might well twist her report around somehow to suit his own designs. Constable Duff had appeared sympathetic. But if she tried to get a message to him, James might well intercept it.

She had to see Ian!

She rose from the bed, changed the blood-splotched dress and tended the wound in her back as best she was able. The cut was merely superficial and, though painful, would not be serious. Then she sat down once more to sort out her jumbled thoughts. But before she came close to arriving at a course of action, she fell into an exhausted sleep.

44

Preparations

BECAUSE MAGGIE HAD not rested well in days, she slept till almost noon. When she finally awoke she jerked up with a start, and cried out sharply as the pain cut through her back. She reached behind her, still forgetful of the events of the previous night. Gradually her numbed mind began to clear. She had to see Ian, that much was certain.

Outside the sky was blue and thin rays of sunlight beat against the windowpane. It was turning into a fine day, one the harried land well deserved. *But what is one more day of sunshine?* Maggie thought. *Only a cruel reminder of the joys that may never again come.* Would even Atlanta be able to bring her and Ian together again? Was the hope of marriage but a fading dream?

As if in answer to her silent question, a soft knock came to the door.

"Maggie," came Atlanta's welcome voice.

Atlanta entered bearing a tray with breakfast for her daughter. But Maggie set it aside and urgently faced her mother.

"I must see Ian," she said.

"The time will come, Maggie," replied Atlanta. "But we have to be patient. Your father has postponed his trip to Glasgow. We must simply wait until—"

"It can't wait!" interrupted Maggie with urgency in her voice. "There is someone who may have had reason to kill George Falkirk."

"Who?" asked Atlanta. Though she would have supported Ian for the sake of her daughter, she yet believed him guilty of the crime.

"I don't know."

Atlanta eyed her daughter inquisitively, as if to say, "Is that all?"

"I don't know what he looks like," Maggie went on, "but . . ."

All at once it dawned on Maggie how sketchy her notions about the mysterious attacker really were. Unable to identify him, even if she told everything she had seen and heard that night on Braenock Ridge, it would still not remove the guilt from Ian's head. He *had* threatened Falkirk. And to divulge what she knew would only increase the danger to herself. With a stab of dismay, Maggie suddenly realized the treasure would implicate her and Ian all the more.

"I have to see Ian," she repeated lamely.

"It's too dangerous," Atlanta replied. "Your father is watching me. He is doubly on his guard after what I said the other day."

"But surely you see that Ian is innocent!"

"He can't account for his whereabouts," said Atlanta, voicing her doubts.

"Even if he *did* kill Falkirk," said Maggie in despair, "that would change nothing for me."

"You are still determined to marry him, even though that could make you the wife of a murderer?"

"Oh, Mother, I love him. There is nothing that could change that."

Atlanta needed no further inducements. She knew it would be foolhardy to oppose them once their minds were made up. And she knew arranging a marriage now would be dangerous with James on the prowl. But she doubted whether any more suitable opportunity would present itself in the near future. Better she have a hand in it than to force the two lovers into some reckless course of action. A meeting between Ian and her daughter was ill-advised; the preparations must be made under the cloak of secrecy. Then they could flee Stonewycke cleanly and safely and remain away for as long as necessary. She could no longer stand against the despairing tone in her daughter's voice. Whatever James's threats, she could not refuse her daughter the happiness she so desperately wanted.

"I will return soon," Atlanta said, turning to leave the room. "All will be arranged."

Atlanta did return to Maggie that afternoon with news. From that moment on the choices made themselves.

Before two more days had ended, in response to a brief letter Atlanta had smuggled into town, a visitor appeared at the great door of Stonewycke mansion. The maid opened to a stout, rough-hewn creature, only a vague semblance of a woman, who spoke in hard, masculine tones.

"What do ye want?" asked the maid, filled with suspicion. There had been such strange goings-on lately, she wasn't about to offer any extra hospitality to such a creature as this.

"The name's Queenie," the woman answered, undaunted. "I'm bearin' a message fer the mistress o' the house."

"I'll take it t' her," said the maid.

"I'm t' give it int' her hand my own sel'," said Queenie firmly.

The maid stood indecisive for a moment, then decided to find Lady Atlanta. But before she turned to leave she said, "Ye wait here . . . dinna move!"

Moments later Atlanta appeared with the dutiful maid scurrying along behind her. Atlanta also eyed Queenie cautiously.

"Yes," she inquired, "what is it?"

Queenie stepped forward and, for one of the few times in her life, felt intimidated. Atlanta was perhaps the grandest lady she had ever seen; so close to the regal presence, Queenie suddenly felt her own roughness more acutely than ever before.

"Weel, my leddy," she began. "I got a message here." She handed it to Atlanta and prepared to make a quick retreat.

"Wait," said Atlanta. "A reply may be necessary." Atlanta scanned the paper, then returned her attention to Queenie. She handed the innkeeper a sovereign and said a brief, "Thank you."

"No. Thank ye, my leddy," Queenie protested. "I dinna do this fer the money." She began to back toward the door. "I jist hope ye can help the lad." Then she turned and exited quickly, if not gracefully.

Atlanta stood motionless for some time. When she finally did move, it was toward the stairs.

She did not go directly to Maggie's room. She walked straight to her own sitting room, quickly sat at her elegant French desk and began to sort through several sheaves of papers. She had already been through them several times in anticipation of this moment, though she had all the while prayed that circumstances would never come to this extreme. Even now as she placed two of the papers into a thick brown envelope, she tried to convince herself that her precaution would not be needed. Even if it were, there remained one more document which she kept from the others. Maggie would be back, of that she was sure, and she would carry on the fight for the land. But just in case something happened, she wanted to be doubly certain James could never have the power to do the unthinkable.

Yes, it was best she keep this one paper secret.

She tucked it into a drawer and locked it securely. She would have to find a better hiding place for it later. But there was no time now. She hoped she would be able to forget about it altogether, just as it had lain forgotten for nearly half a century.

Now she must think of Maggie. James was nearly mad; Ian's life was in danger, and—whether guilty or innocent—he was soon to be the husband of her daughter. Banishing her last-minute hesitations, Atlanta reminded herself that she had to help them in every way she could, for the sake of her daughter's happiness, and for the sake of Stonewycke. She rose and made her way to Maggie's room.

She walked in without knocking. The drapes were drawn against the afternoon sun, giving the room a dim, deathlike appearance.

"Maggie," Atlanta said with an urgent tone. "I've a reply from Ian."

Maggie jumped up and faced her mother with a look of radiant expectation.

"He wants me to get you out of the house tonight. He says he has made all the arrangements."

"Oh, Mother!"

Up until that moment Atlanta had spoken with a calm urgency. But with the words of excitement from her daughter, her lip began to quiver and a tear brimmed over, tracing a path down her cheek.

"Oh, my baby!" she cried, embracing Maggie.

The two women stood thus, bound in the mutual embrace they had known all too seldom, until the tears of their varied emotions were exhausted.

At last they separated.

"I have given your father a sedative," said Atlanta. "He is asleep now and will remain so until morning. But you must waste no time. He will not know where you have gone, but he is bound to search until he learns the truth. So do not stay more than two or three days in one place. Go to Aberdeen or Edinburgh if you can. In his present temper, if James finds you I do not doubt he would kill Ian. So the two of you must stay away for at least a month. Get word to me of your whereabouts through the woman at the inn in Port Strathy. Then I will advise you as to developments here and when you may safely return."

"Yes, Mother."

"Your father is mad with rage. He blames Ian for Falkirk's death and the failure of his latest schemes. Who is to tell what he may do? He may seek his revenge on me, Maggie; I do not know what evil lurks in that man's heart. So you must plan for the possibility of being away for a very long time. Whatever is very dear to you, take with you. I will hope to see you within a month, my daughter. But if it should not be, we must be prudent. Do you understand me?"

Maggie nodded.

"I'll be back soon," said Atlanta, leaving the room. "And quickly, dear. Ian will be waiting for you within the hour."

Maggie began to sort through her things, and one by one filled a single carpetbag with the most important. The essentials left little room for even the smallest keepsakes of the home and land she loved. She glanced up at the grand tapestry her mother had made and regretted she couldn't take it with her. There was a place in the bag, however, for her own smaller reproduction—paltry by comparison, she thought, but at least a reminder of the mother she loved so dearly. This was a thrilling moment of anticipation, and a painful moment of separation.

Sorting through her bureau, Maggie unexpectedly discovered a small music box hidden deep in the back of one of the drawers. Tears fell afresh as she picked up the delicate instrument. She wound the key and lifted the lid, and once again the sweet strains of Brahms' lullaby filled the room as they hadn't for years. As the nostalgic tune played on, sobs shook her body and she snapped the lid shut. Her father had presented the gift to her on her fifth birthday. The memory rose in her mind, as clear as an image in a polished mirror. He had chosen it himself, he had said, in one of London's finest shops. All she remembered was that it was the only gift he had ever given her. *Yes,* she thought bitterly, *the memory is clear. But like the reflection in the mirror, it is not real.*

Maggie's immediate impulse was to smash the box against the wall, but she found herself dropping it into the carpetbag along with her other possessions. Why, she could not tell. Neither did she ask.

Atlanta returned some moments later.

"Your father is sleeping soundly," she said. "You and Ian will be safe for the rest of today and tonight."

Then she held the envelope she had prepared out to her daughter. "Maggie, I want you to take this with you. You need not open it; you may scarcely even grasp its significance. But I want you to have it, in the event that something should happen to me, or in case you are gone longer than we anticipate. It is yours. It is the promise not only for your return but for the safety of this land we love. I love you, my dear! God forbid that I will not see you again! This will always be your home, whatever happens. Do you understand me? *It is yours!* When all this is settled, you must come back. I will be waiting for you!"

"Mother, I love you!" said Maggie, embracing her again. Fresh tears streamed down both faces.

Maggie's mind was racing too fast to try to grasp the meaning behind all of Atlanta's words. She could not think of such things now. All she knew was that Ian was waiting for her, and that she was going to marry the man she loved! She tucked the envelope into the pocket of her coat. Then she wrapped her heavy woolen cloak about her as an added protection against the cold of the fast-approaching winter.

Atlanta placed a strong, motherly arm about her daughter, and together they walked downstairs to the stables. There, Maggie realized, a different farewell faced her. Raven was waiting saddled, and by her side stood Digory, looking as though he had never been ill.

"You look better," said Maggie huskily, her voice betraying the emotion she felt inside.

"Didna I tell ye?" Digory replied. His voice, too, was strained and taut with tenderness for the girl he had seen grow from a baby into a young woman.

"Oh, Digory!" cried Maggie, flinging her arms around the groom's bony shoulders. "I shall miss you so!"

"An' I will miss ye too, lass."

"How will I ever get along without you?"

"Oh, ye will, lass," he replied, the tears streaming down his wrinkled cheeks glistening in the failing sunlight. "The Lord'll be goin' wi' ye, an' so will my prayers. Ye dinna need an auld groom when ye hae all that."

Maggie's heart found little comfort in his words, though she treasured them because they were Digory's. She tried to impress his voice on her memory so she would never forget.

She walked again to where Atlanta stood, weeping openly, and gave her a final squeeze.

"I shall miss you, Mother."

"And I you. But we will pray it will not be longer than a month!"

"Thank you for everything!"

"I wish you happiness, Maggie! How I would like to share this time of joy with you!"

"We will think of you when we say our vows, Mother. You have made it possible. Thank you. I love you."

Maggie mounted Raven, thankful that at least she did not have to give up *this* friend.

She cast one more wistful glance toward Digory and her mother as they stood side by side in the yard. Then Maggie turned and urged her horse forward. She sucked in a deep breath of the late afternoon air, wiped her eyes, and tried to think of the joyous hope within her. Sad as these good-byes were, her future did not lay here, but with the man she loved and to whom she had pledged herself. Whatever happiness her life would hold lay in that future, and not in her past.

She walked Raven from the stables around the house, then urged her forward at a trot out the gate and along the road.

The sun was just beginning to set when she reached the main road leading down the hill into Strathy. Her heartbeat increased at the sight of Maukin standing alongside the road. The chestnut mare stood quietly grazing by a clump of trees with a small field of clover at her feet. Maggie jumped from Raven's back and ran forward, her chest heaving not from the exertion of her short ride, but from the thought of at last seeing Ian.

He was seated on an incline with his back to her, as if fearing to believe he would actually see her face. She ran up behind him shouting his name. He turned and beheld her, and his radiant face told her that she was the fulfillment of every dream of his heart.

He jumped to his feet and embraced her. They clung to one another for a long while, neither willing to add the dimension of speech to that glorious moment of reunion.

At last Ian broke the silence.

"Don't you know it's bad luck to see your future husband before the wedding?"

Maggie laughed. "I love you!" she said.

"And I love you," he replied. "And now, my bonny lassie," he went on, "what would you say to us going and getting married?"

They turned, hand in hand, ran back to where Raven and Maukin were patiently waiting, leapt on the horses' backs, dug in their heels, and galloped up the hill along the eastern road toward Fraserburgh.

45

A Decision

THE SUN HAD long since set on the two riders. The winding dirt road spread out before them like a silver thread, illuminated by the half-moon caught in the treetops. With the anxieties of the past days behind them, it was a peaceful ride. Ian and Maggie almost felt as if they were again riding upon the heather-covered hills, laughing and sharing and growing in their love. For the moment, neither wanted to admit that the wondrous purple blossoms were now gone and the barren brown of dormant life signified that winter was quickly approaching. In their hearts it was summer again, and all was fresh and bursting with possibilities.

Maggie glanced over at Ian. His gaze was straight ahead as he concentrated on the darkened road. How she loved him! It hardly seemed possible after all that had happened that they were actually going to be married. But Fraserburgh was less than an hour away!

Ian reined Maukin to a stop.

"Let's take a rest," he said.

"I don't need a rest!" exclaimed Maggie exuberantly.

"Well, the horses do, at least," he laughed. It felt good to laugh again. "And Queenie insisted on packing us some food. We'd best fortify ourselves for what lies ahead."

"You sound as if we're on our way to a funeral," said Maggie with a playful scowl.

"Isn't that how most men look upon their wedding day—the death of their freedom?" He laughed again. Then with a more serious tone, he added, "But I am not among them, Maggie! Today is the true beginning of life for me." He leaned over and kissed her lightly on the cheek.

"It will be a beginning for both of us, Ian," Maggie replied.

Then they dismounted and Ian began to rummage through his saddle pouch. He withdrew the packet of food prepared by Queenie.

"That's odd," he murmured.

"What is it?"

"My dirk—it's gone. I last remember putting it here . . ." But his voice trailed away as the feared images of forgotten horrors began to creep into his mind. When had he put the dirk there? A week, two weeks ago? Three days ago . . . ? The night hid the cold pallor on his face.

Maggie caught the faltering in his voice and cheerfully broke into his thoughts. "We don't need it," she said. "Let's eat like the country folk!"

She led him to a dry patch of ground thickly covered with pine needles and drew him down next to her. She opened the packet and found bannocks and cheese and dried herring.

They ate in silence for a while, then Maggie said, "Shall we go to London after Fraserburgh?"

"London?" Ian asked in the detached tone of one whose mind is elsewhere. "London was another lifetime ago for me," he said. "I could never go back. My father would make life unbearable for us. My future is here . . . with you."

"My father will not make life easy for us, either. We may not be able to return to Stonewycke for some time."

"We will have to come back eventually. I won't have us trying to start our marriage on the run, always looking over our shoulder for your father. I'll stand up to him."

"Ian," Maggie interposed, "as long as I'm with you, I'll be happy. I don't care if we never go back. I don't want you in any danger."

"But, Maggie, if we go away it will look as if I'm truly guilty of murdering Falkirk. I have to clear myself."

"You are innocent," said Maggie firmly. "You could never have done something so horrible."

A cloud came over Ian's face as self-doubts overwhelmed him.

"Maggie," he began in a disconsolate tone, "what if . . . *could* I have—is it possible?"

"No . . . no, my dear Ian!" persisted Maggie.

"I had been drinking, and was so filled with rage."

"Please, Ian, don't talk like this!"

"You don't know what it's been like," Ian said. "I've relived that night in my mind a hundred times . . . *but I still can't remember!*"

"It will come back," Maggie said, trying to soothe him. "Then it will all be made right."

"But it may be too late. By then they'll have hanged me."

"Ian! don't say that . . . it frightens me."

"I'm sorry . . . I didn't mean to—"

"Ian, let's just go away—as far away as we can! They'll find the real killer eventually. Then it will be safe to return. But not now, not anytime soon."

"I can't run. Don't you see? I have my pride, my honor to think of. I have to face your father like a man. And I have to face the charges, too."

"My father is wild," Maggie implored. "Your guilt or innocence in Falkirk's death has nothing to do with it anymore. If we stay here, I'm sure he'd try to kill you. Maybe even me. I'm afraid for you. I want you as far away from him as we can get. We can start over, at least for a while, somewhere far away."

"Maybe you're right," sighed Ian. "And unless I can remember what happened, there is no way to prove I'm not a murderer."

"There might be a way to prove it—" Maggie said suddenly.

"What do you mean?" interrupted Ian. "Is there something I don't know?"

"I wanted to tell you before," Maggie answered, "but so much has happened—it almost seemed unimportant. The other night I was walking on the grounds and a man accosted me—"

The sudden look of anxiety on Ian's face stopped her short.

"Sam frightened the man off," she assured him. "He and Falkirk were conspiring to steal a cache of gold. He thought I had it and threatened me."

"My God!"

"But don't you see? He must have been the one to kill—"

"Did he hurt you?" asked Ian with panic in his voice, not even stopping to wonder why Maggie knew of Falkirk's plot.

"No . . . a small cut—Ian, don't you see? He must have killed Falkirk over the gold. If we can only persuade the constable to listen."

"Who was the man?"

Maggie shook her head dismally. "I don't know. I never saw his face."

Any hope this development may have sparked in Ian immediately died. Who would believe a story of a faceless, nameless murderer? Especially coming from the prime suspect's own wife! And if this man were the murderer, he would roam free, free to . . .

Suddenly Ian said, "You're right. We have to get away! You're in danger, too. That changes everything. I don't care if I'm branded a murderer for running. I don't care if they follow; I have to get you away from here!"

They both fell silent for a few moments. At length Maggie spoke in a soft voice. The time for decision had come, and each seemed to sense it.

"I'll go with you wherever you want, Ian," she said. "Just as long as it's far enough from here that my father can't follow. I love you. We'll do whatever you think is best."

Ian stood up as if he would take flight right then, then paced about.

Every thought in his confused brain pointed toward the same conclusion. But it was such a far-fetched notion! Maggie had said *far away*. But neither of them had meant *that* far. Yet James Duncan was an influential, compelling man. He wielded great power. Where could they hope to go to avoid his reach? Wherever they went in Scotland, even in England, he could find them and ultimately engineer an indictment for Falkirk's death. Could even his own daughter stand against him? And how could he—miserable, confused, hapless Ian Duncan— hope to keep the daughter of such a man? But the idea was too daring, too wild.

Would Maggie willingly oppose such a father and thus relinquish her ties to her beloved Stonewycke? The roots of her heritage which bound her to this land extended generations into her past. Would she give all that up for him?

The conclusion remained the same. There was no alternative if this love was to endure. Could he ask it of her, knowing of her love for this land? Yet he had to ask, for he could not face the thought of what might happen otherwise.

Ian looked deep into Maggie's face. "If our marriage is to last," he said intently, "we must do as you say; we must go *far* away."

He paused, summoning the courage to say it all.

"We must, Maggie," he went on at length, "*go to America.*"

Maggie returned his gaze with eyes of love. Even as he said the words, the resolve seemed already settling upon her that this was indeed the only way left to them. "Where you go, Ian, I will follow."

Ian breathed a sigh, hardly realizing he had been holding his breath, bracing himself for the most dreaded of answers. "Could you . . . Stonewycke, everything here you love?"

"I love *you*, Ian. That's all that matters to me now."

"Oh, think of it, Maggie! It's always been a dream of mine. I've read books about it. Didn't you tell me the Mackinaws had a son who migrated there?"

"Yes, their older son, Drew."

"We could be so happy away from here."

"It's so far, Ian. But I want nothing more than to be with you . . . for us to be happy together."

"Maggie," Ian said with a laugh as he sat down beside her, "just think of it—freedom from all this . . . we'd be free!"

He wrapped his arms tightly around her, kissed her, then cradled her head against his shoulder and stroked her hair.

"I love you," he said.

Maggie looked up into his face, the moonlight filling her eyes with the words of love her voice could not speak.

By common consent, they rose hand in hand, put away their provisions, mounted Raven and Maukin, and rode off on the final leg of their journey.

46

The Groom and His Master

WHEN JAMES AWOKE late the following morning, it was too late to overturn the deception that had been worked on him. Pulling himself out of bed, he sensed immediately that his sleep had not been natural. He threw on his clothes and set out on a rampaging search, first for Atlanta and then for his daughter. He could find neither, though had his search been more thorough he would have discovered his wife weeping in Maggie's favorite haunt, the dayroom.

The servants cowed into the security of their tasks. What could be happening in this family they served? Certainly the master of the house had always been a hard man, given occasionally to harsh words. But they had never seen him like this.

Unsuccessful in his inspection of the house, James stormed out toward the stables. Maggie always retreated there with her four-footed friends and that old lout of a groom. Why he had kept him around all these years he didn't know.

A downcast Digory was going about his tasks in an aimless manner. Already he missed his young mistress; without the vibrancy of her life at Stonewycke, all had turned pale. But he forced himself to do what must be done. There was still a Master to serve.

James found Digory bent over a workbench, mending a broken harness.

"Were are they!" he bellowed.

Digory looked up from his work and could hardly believe what he saw. Standing before him James appeared as a wild man, his clothes hanging haphazardly on his body, his rumpled shirt uncharacteristically open at the neck. Never one to be coy, Digory answered the laird's question with silence, only because the scene before him filled his heart with such sadness that he could find no words.

"Answer me, you miserable cuddy!" James shouted.

Digory fastened his eyes on James and quietly stood his ground. "I dinna ken where the lass has gone," he replied, hoping no more would be asked of him. But in truth, he knew no more than he had told.

"You dirty traitor!" James screeched. "After all this family has done for you, you betray me in the end. Well, I'll teach you some respect!"

James caught up a riding crop and stalked angrily toward the groom. "You'll soon learn where to place your loyalties after this, you lying cur!"

Before the sound of the words had parted his lips, a painful crack of the hardened leather lashed across Digory's head. A thin red line under his ear and across the back of his neck began to ooze with blood as James whipped the tip back and sent it snapping at his shoulders and midrift. The groom stood silent with head bowed, uttering no word of defense through the agony of his pain.

"What do you have to say now?" asked James, interrupting his torture. "Where has she gone? Tell me what you know!"

"I will that, laird," answered Digory in a barely audible anguished voice. "All I ken is this, that yer daughter didna want t' go. All she wanted was yer love—"

"Why you insolent . . . how dare you!"

But James was too caught up in the renewed frenzy which Digory's words brought on to complete his cursing denouncements. His whip spoke instead.

Digory crumpled to his knees under the onslaught, nearly senseless from pain, blistering welts already rising on his skin under his shirt and breeches. Head bowed, he said no more. Instead, he did the only thing he could. He quietly prayed. But this time it was not for the two young people he loved, nor for the family whose distress made his heart ache.

Instead, he prayed for James alone, for the master of the house who knew not what he did, who was too blind to see what was happening before his very eyes. Then Digory knew no more. He did not awake until the following day when he opened his eyes to see Atlanta's compassionate face looking down on him. He was in his own loft, in his bed. A fresh cup of tea stood on the stand next to him. Atlanta clearly had been tending him for some time, for her eyes appeared weary.

She had, in fact, been at his bedside the entire night.

Later that same day James was seen in Port Strathy riding in a frenzy. He made two or three stops, after each of which he galloped off in a greater passion of rage than before. He was last seen with two other riders, both of questionable character. The three whipped their mounts up the hill, but they did not turn off the road when they reached the entrance to Stonewycke. Instead, they tore along the coast road toward the east.

47
Ian and Maggie

THE SUN PIERCED the window with splintered shafts of cold light.

Maggie turned her head toward its rays, wondering why she felt so odd. Then she remembered—the rainclouds had gathered the night before, and she hadn't anticipated seeing the sun again for days.

Next she became aware of the sleeping figure next to her. The shining of the sun was not, after all, the only change this morning held. Would she ever again waken after a night's slumber without a thrill at seeing Ian by her side?

She lay back and exhaled a long sigh of contentment. He would always be there, of that she was confident. Nothing else mattered. How she longed to reach out and touch his shoulder! But she did not want to risk waking him; the look of peaceful repose on his face was too beautiful to disturb. Maggie wondered if he were dreaming. *If so,* she hoped, *may they be good dreams.* Even in sleep the muscles of his arms and chest rippled with vitality. She murmured a prayer for him, for them both, that they would have only good dreams from this moment on.

Slowly she took in their surroundings. It had been dark as they had entered the previous night, but even then she had realized that they could hardly have chosen a more perfect setting for their first night together. Now, in the daylight, she was sure of it.

They had not arrived in Fraserburgh until the evening was well advanced. When the vicar had answered their knock on the parsonage door, his puzzled expression and his nightclothes both testified to the unusual circumstances of their visit. Explaining themselves, the light finally began to break over his countenance as he recalled Ian's letter of several days earlier. He admitted the two unlikely aristocrats, simply clad in traveling clothes, then disappeared for what seemed ages before he and his wife returned fully dressed. The ceremony had been awkward, brief, scarcely mirroring the depth of love the young bride and improbable groom felt in their hearts for one another.

When it was done they shared a cup of tea with the older couple. Then they bid them good night, but not before receiving directions to the cottage where they now lay, a place which would always harbor fond memories of their first moments as husband and wife.

They had planned to stay in the inn, but arriving late and unaware of a local late-autumn festival, they had found it full to overflowing without a single room to spare. Explaining their difficulty to the vicar, he directed them to an empty dwelling some four miles from town. The tenants had been forced to leave for an undetermined period of time a month earlier. The wife had come down with a severe case of pneumonia; the doctor said he would treat it as best he could, but that in the wet climate of the north it would probably recur, and he therefore recommended their spending the winter as far to the south as possible. Poor though they were, the wife had a sister in Liverpool, and with the help and generosity of the parish they had been able to make the journey. The vicar had been asked to keep watch over their cottage until their anticipated return in the spring, and to the young bride and groom he now offered their simple abode as honeymoon cottage.

Entering in the dark, Ian managed to build a fire. The place was humble indeed, reminiscent of the Krueger cottage, but missing Lucy's homey touch. But that night, with the rain pouring down on the thick thatch roof overhead, they had noticed little of it other than the welcome fact that it was dry. Maggie was glad Atlanta had insisted they take along an extra blanket. "Those inns are never warm enough," she had said. Maggie smiled as she thought of her mother, thankful for the recent healing and strengthening of the bonds between them.

The warm fire and blanket, along with the few other provisions which had been left behind, could hardly have been sufficient to keep out the blasts of cold penetrating the cracked walls of the cottage. But the newlyweds, discovering the wonders of each other, were oblivious to the cold. Maggie had always dreamed as a child of being a simple crofter, with no pressures and anxieties other than to raise her children and serve her husband. Now she could almost lay her head back and dream it had come true.

Her husband . . .

She could barely comprehend the truth that she and Ian were married! How good God was to provide her with this one most important wish. Digory had told her many times there was always hope. She would never again give up hope, not as long as there was a God who cared.

Had it all been worth it? The bitterness of her father's rebuff? All her life it seemed she had only been able to see people grasping for what they could get themselves. She had closed herself off, never considering anyone worthy of her trust again. Repelling her father, she had unknowingly shut out Atlanta's reluctant but tender heart as well. Both mother and daughter had suffered in silence as a result.

But when Ian had stumbled into her life, laughing and gay, a crack began to open in that wall of self-protection. Slowly it widened. Before long she and Ian were sharing open expressions of love, and she and her mother were reaching out to one another in ways she had never thought possible.

Maggie glanced over at him.

Yes, she thought, *he has made me believe for the first time that relationships do not have to be founded on isolation and resentment. He has made me believe that trust is possible, that I can truly give myself to another without the danger of being hurt.* He had shown her what love could be like.

Part of her had resisted, still afraid of the risk of being hurt again by someone she loved. But Ian loved her in return. He would never do anything to hurt her. Only hours ago, as he had pledged his love, he had said, "I will never leave you or forsake you."

Maggie believed him. As impossible as it would have seemed to her a year earlier that she would ever believe such words from anyone, she was confident of Ian's love. His simple, honest, trusting manner had dissolved her doubts. His gentle voice reverberated with understanding, compassion, and caring. Though his own past remained unknown to her, he had changed just as she had. He, too, had learned to rise out of past hurts into present love. Together they had struggled to overcome their painful histories and together were now ready to face the future—whatever obstacles were thrown against them.

Ian rolled sleepily over and she watched him stir into gradual wakefulness. A smile came to his lips as he beheld her watching eyes.

"Good morning!" he said. "You were right. There is no finer bed than the straw mattresses of these northern peasants!"

"What a sleepy sluggard you are," she replied playfully. "I've been waiting for hours."

"Then why isn't my breakfast prepared?" he asked with a mock frown.

She laughed. "Ah, yes . . . breakfast," she said. "One detail I overlooked. Now we're simple rustics . . . no pantry . . . no servants."

"And I am the simple farmer," laughed Ian, "who has not even provided my wife the food for our sustenance. "Come on!" he said, jumping out of bed. "Let's see what we can find in this *wee but an' ben*."

"*Your wife* . . ." repeated Maggie reflectively. "I like the sound of it."

Ian turned, then eased himself back down onto the bed beside her and pulled her close to him. "Oh, Maggie, is it right to be so happy?"

"Yes," she breathed as he kissed her. Then after a moment, she said reluctantly. "We're not finding our breakfast this way."

"Who needs breakfast? Besides, we brought no food." He kissed her again.

"That's your London upbringing showing through," she said. "Now if you were a true Scotsman, you'd know that food abounds all around us. All you have to do is know where to look."

He leaned back on his elbows and grinned. "Weel, my wee highland lassie, then ge' yer guidman sommat t' eat."

She laughed. "You're a Scotsman at heart at least, *aren't ye noo, my guidman?*" she replied, imitating his brogue accent. "Wherever did you pick up our native tongue?"

"Here and there. You forget—you married a man of diverse and hidden talents."

They did not have far to search for food. The garden at the back of the cottage contained unharvested potatoes, carrots, and turnips. Weeds had overgrown portions of it, but they easily found sufficient for their present needs. Within an hour a large iron pot boiled over the fire with a frothy mixture of potatoes, carrots, turnips, and salt bubbling cheerily away.

Later, as they partook of their simple breakfast of boiled vegetables, they found themselves savoring every moment, knowing they were storing away each one as a precious memory of their first day together—memories which would never grow dim. For that morning, their lives started and stopped in that rough-hewn hut. There had never been a past, and the future would continue on and on as a joyous extension of the blessed present.

"Ian, this is how I always dreamed it would be," Maggie sighed with deep contentment. "And when we get to America, we could have a cottage just like this."

"In America they call them log cabins," said Ian. "That's how people live out in the American west. There's so much land that everybody can have as much as he wants. And it's good land, Maggie." His eyes brightened in anticipation. "We'll start over . . . build a new life together!"

48

A New Beginning

❧

ONCE THE DECISION had been made, Maggie and Ian's enthusiasm mounted by the moment.

"How will we arrange it, Ian?" asked Maggie.

"Ships leave from Aberdeen every week. Passage to London will be easy enough to arrange. Then we can transfer to one bound for New York. I tell you, Maggie, we can do it!"

"The thought of freedom sounds so wonderful. But I'll miss Stonewycke and my mother."

"You'll be able to see them before we leave. We'll go back to say good-bye."

"But my father?"

"He can't do anything to us now. We're married, Maggie!"

"Oh, yes!" Maggie exclaimed. "How could I forget?"

"I've always thought of sailing to America, but just as a lark. Now we can leave our past completely behind us."

"We'll have our own little house—or log cabin, or whatever you call it. I'll plant flowers and put up curtains."

"Just like two peasant newlyweds?"

"Such a life sounds so peaceful."

"But honestly," replied Ian, "I don't know what I could actually *do*. I have enough money to get us there. But I'm hardly wealthy. My father has seen to that. I'm afraid you have married quite a good-for-nothing—"

She raised her finger to his lips and shook her head. "You won't have to do anything but be there with me," she said, her earnest tone communicating far more than her words. "Whatever we do, wherever we go, whether we come back to Scotland or stay in America, whether we live as royalty or as crofters on the land, I will still need you. I will go anywhere with you. I love you far more than I do any country or home."

"I suppose I could try my hand at farming. The Mackinaw fellow in New York would surely help a fellow countryman make a beginning. But I doubt I'm cut out for it."

"It sounds wonderful to me," Maggie replied dreamily. "I have confidence that you can do anything. And when Stonewycke becomes mine we can return here."

"We may prefer our little log cabin by that time and not want to leave," he said. "And besides, won't Alastair inherit Stonewycke?"

"Alastair will inherit the title and be the marquis, I suppose. But I'm to get Stonewycke, I think. It's all so confusing. I think Father has some other property that's tied up in it too. But I've never tried to understand it." Then she threw back her head and laughed and sighed all at once. "Who cares! As long as we're together, I don't care if it's in Hector Makinaw's old place."

"I wonder if we might not be happier there anyway . . ." Ian mused, but he let his words trail away unfinished.

What will we find when and if we ever do return to Stonewycke? Ian wondered. *Will James ever moderate his hatred of me? Could he ever accept me as a son-in-law?* Only the future could answer such questions. At present, that gnawing feeling of apprehension was a reality Ian did not want to admit existed. Now was not the time for any thoughts but those of joy.

At last they were one—now and forever. Nothing else mattered. Ian remembered when he had been a boy, so alone, so empty of anything that deeply mattered to him. But Maggie had changed that. He would never lose the sense of belonging Maggie had given him.

He reached for her hand and brought it gently to his lips.

"Thank you, my Maggie," he whispered.

"For what?"

"For loving me," he answered. "For giving yourself to me."

"I have given you no more than you have given me," Maggie replied. "And is that not what makes our love so right? We have grown in a way we never could have apart."

Neither spoke again. Ian knew she was right. That love would continue to sustain them whatever the future held, for it was a love that would never die. All that mattered at this moment was the glow in the eyes of his bride as they anticipated their new beginning in America together.

FLIGHT FROM STONEWYCKE

To five special boys:
Michael
Jonathan
Gregory
Robin
Patrick

CONTENTS

Introduction

TO AMERICA THEY came!

From every background, every economic status, every corner of the world. America was the land of hope and promise, opportunity and new beginnings. They assaulted its shores, blending and mixing into one, until a mighty nation was formed.

The reasons for migrating were as countless as the 35 million daring souls who left their homelands in the 19th century to make for themselves new lives in the melting pot over the Atlantic to the west. America offered a haven from troubles left behind, an unexplored corner of the world in which the bold adventurer could strike out and seek his fortune. Each voyager had his own private story to tell. Some fled poverty, others the inevitable shrinking of the family plot of land in the old country, still others were lured by tales of wealth. But all had visions of better times ahead and hoped in the prosperous new world to find them come true.

More often than not, however, reality dimmed the dream.

The journey by sea took most of the capital a willing immigrant could raise, usually his whole life's savings. Those who had no savings had to sell what they possessed, even themselves, if there were nothing else left. But the lure of "the dream" was great and they did what they had to do. The fortunate and enterprising ones among them found the resources.

Boarding a clipper, however, was only the beginning of a new life. The weeks which followed were enough to daunt the hopes of even the strongest and most optimistic. The majority found they had only sufficient funds to travel steerage; scores of immigrants were crammed into the hulls of a ship; food was in short supply, sanitation almost nil, and disease ran rampant. Many died en route, and their dreams with them.

Yet the financial cost and physical suffering often did not represent the greatest sacrifice to this budding new generation of Americans. Most painful of all for many was the emotional sacrifice of being uprooted from all that had been dear—the country of their birth, the villages where generations of ancestors had been born and raised and died. They said good-bye to familiar homes and loved ones with scant hope of ever seeing them again. A one-way ticket had taxed their meager resources to the limit; there would likely be no return voyages. Parents, grandparents, brothers, sisters, homes, inheritances—all had to be left behind. Such was the price of new life in a new land.

Such sacrifice was indeed great among the Scots who left their beloved and enchanting homeland. For those who left the Highland fields—the primrose, the heather hills—for them the land had always held special significance, for nobleman and peasant farmer alike. The land was everything. The land had bound their ancient clans together and had torn them apart. They were a proud people, these Celts who settled the land more than 25 centuries earlier. And now as they left it for new frontiers, the parting could never be without sorrow. The earth gave meaning. Only one's land offered a permanence to the heritage which could be passed on to one's offspring. The land held the community together as a whole, as it had for centuries.

No one left such a heritage without personal and inward sacrifice. Even as they left, full of hope, what they left behind could never be erased from memory. Well might their voices have echoed the Irish poet's lament:

Farewell to thee, Erin mavourneen,
Thy valleys I'll tread never more;
This heart that now bleeds for thy sorrows
Will waste on a far distant shore.
Thy green sods lie cold on my parents,
A cross marks the place of their rest—
The wind that moans sadly above them
Will waft their poor child to the West.

Notwithstanding, there was an allure in the very word *America* which helped remove some of the sting of parting. Here was a land so rich, so immense that there was opportunity for all to make their dreams come true.

But when the ships bearing them landed, practical obstacles of a more difficult nature had to be faced. Suddenly they were alone, cast upon their own resources. Now they had to discover their own inner resources. Those who pulled themselves up in the face of insurmountable heartbreak were able to forge a new life for themselves in this new land. Others failed. But rarely did the reality match the idealism of the dream.

For those increasing numbers who sought their life to the west of the Ohio Valley and the Mississippi River, in the expanding American West, the ties to the past were usually severed completely. Communication was severely limited. Many were illiterate, and mail was slow and undependable.

Still they came—undaunted.

From New York they moved slowly west, the more adventurous by wagon train to the wild American frontier. Some, indeed, discovered the green pastures they had come seeking. Others found further disappointment, and even death. For this was a raw and untamed land. The life of the midwestern prairie offered no pot of gold at the end of a mythical rainbow. And rare, indeed, was the opportunity to look back to the homelands they had left. When their hearts yearned once more toward the lands of their birth, the practicality of struggling for life in the new west was always more pressing.

Yet by their very ability to wrench themselves away from home and kin and heritage, to courageously face the hurdles thrown in their path, they proved themselves a special breed. Out of their sorrows, their hopes, their dreams, their valor, their private exultations and agonies, a nation was forged. Each one lived out his personal and unique drama and so carved out a future in what became his new homeland.

Thus the proud Ramsey lineage, one of Scotland's ancient and honored names, sent a new strain of the noble dynasty across the sea to root itself in a new land. As former generations of the Ramsey descent had given their lives and blood to Scotland and to the family estate of Stonewycke, so now would future generations give themselves to this new land.

1

The Father and the Vicar

❖

IT WAS GOING to be one of those pale days of autumn in which the chill hung almost visibly in the air. A breeze portended from the ocean, as yet a mere hint that somewhere over the horizon to the north winter had already come and would soon engulf this coast in its icy grip. Before this day was over the breeze would increase and rush over the forested cliffs overlooking the craggy coastlines of northeast Scotland. But for now the morning was a quiet one.

In the distance the sound of galloping horses intruded into the stillness. As they approached the village the hoofbeats grew louder, and now and then a shout could be heard. The three riders were oblivious to the tranquil scene into which they tore in a frenzy of speed and determination. As they crested the hill and came into view, the pulsating rhythm of pounding hoofbeats thundered down the hill unheralded by dust clouds, for the road was still wet from days of rain.

The lead rider, a slight man, sat his horse firmly, like the lord he aspired to be. James Duncan's shoulders were square, his back straight. And as his black eyes bore down on the road in front of him with a steely malice, one sensed he was not the sort to let anything stand in his way. He was clearly not a man who would swerve from his purpose. His mission on this chilly fall morning was to find the man who had had the audacity to block the success of the scheme he had been working toward for years. The man he sought had not only run off with his daughter, he was also in hiding for the murder of the man Duncan had planned to make his son-in-law. Now Falkirk was dead, removing from James' reach the Falkirk fortune which Duncan had been greedily eyeing for the furtherance of his financial empire. And the man who had thwarted his ambitions and seduced his daughter—the son of his hated cousin, the Earl of Landsbury—must be found and brought to justice.

The horses rounded a bend in the road and were suddenly upon the environs of the little Scottish village of Fraserburgh. The town was awake, to be sure, but the wild pursuit of the three horsemen caused such a storm as they sped through the normally quiet street that the few persons who happened to be out quickly took shelter; children's hands were grabbed and the youngsters yanked to the safety of whatever buildings were closest at hand. The look in the leader's eye could be felt as much as seen, and no one dared impede his flight.

Through the streets they raced, and around two corners; then the pace slackened. Their destination was at hand. They rode up to the front of a homely stone manse standing within thirty yards of the ancient parish Presbyterian church, "the muckle kirk," as it was referred to by the local inhabitants. Duncan leapt from his foaming bay gelding, and stalked briskly toward the house. He lifted a clenched fist, but before he had a chance to begin pounding on it, the door opened.

The elderly vicar had heard the approaching commotion, had risen to investigate, and now stood facing a glaring James Duncan.

"Oh, dear me!" he said, nervously straightening his spectacles.

"I'm looking for a man," James bellowed without pausing for any of the common amenities, "—a scoundrel trying to pass himself off as a gentleman! I have reason to believe he may have come to you."

"I have seen no such man," returned the vicar, regaining his composure. "Though in truth, it is well he would seek out the church, and I hope that I may have the opportunity—"

"He was with a girl!" James broke in, ignoring the vicar's speech. "The impudent—they would have wanted to be married!"

"Oh-h-h," breathed the vicar slowly and thoughtfully. Now he knew the couple, but he was less than certain he should tell this man, whom he was all but certain could be none other than the girl's father. He was clearly in a very dangerous mood.

For a moment his mind spun. He liked the young couple who had come to him two nights earlier to be married. Not only were they well-mannered and obviously in love, in addition the vicar had been given to believe, through a note from the girl's mother, that they had the parents' blessing. Jeremy Littlefield was an inch or two shorter even than James Duncan, and a good many inches rounder. But while his figure and ready smile were considered jolly by the people of his parish, the vicar was a staunchly principled man, and once his mind was set he could appear as stiffnecked as several of the hearty fishermen who listened to him preach on Sunday. For all he knew, this man might *not* be the girl's father, or might, indeed, be the scoundrel himself. The look in his eye told clearly enough that his was not an errand of love.

"Well?" James demanded. "Have you seen them?"

"Sir, I must tell you," Littlefield began cautiously, "there are certain privileges of my calling . . . certain, shall we say, confidentialities—"

"I give not a bloody hang about your calling! I am James Duncan, laird of Stonewycke—and the girl's father. You will tell me *now* all you know!"

"Sir," replied the vicar, the back of his neck growing stiffer by the moment, "the authority of Stonewycke does not extend to Fraserburgh."

"Why you contemptuous old . . ." as he spoke James stepped forward toward the vicar, still standing in the open door, raising his hand slightly as he did so.

"Your lordship!" said the vicar sharply. "I must warn you that even though I am not a strong man, I am well respected in this town, and there are even now on the street men observing our conversation—men who would come swiftly to my defense, and ask questions later. I caution you, for your own safety, nothing more."

If James had intended to harm the little man, he made no further move in that direction. "Sir," Littlefield continued, "I can see you are distraught. Please come in, and we can discuss the matter privately over a cup of tea."

"I want none of your tea," James replied in a lower but no less menacing tone. "Tell me what you know, or I swear you will never see the inside of a church again."

"I do not take kindly to threats," stated the vicar firmly, rising to his full height.

"And *I* do not take kindly to your stalling!" rejoined James sharply. "I must warn you of the repercussions of your unprincipled harboring of a man who has kidnapped an innocent girl." James paused, allowing time for his words to have their full impact on this stubborn clergyman. "Besides which," he went on, "the man is a fugitive from the law."

Though he did not let his face show it, the angry man's statement did indeed impress the vicar and stimulated a reevaluation of his position. Although the girl, Lady Margaret Duncan, had appeared in no way coerced into the marriage, there was still the point to be considered that she had acted in disobedience to her father's will. Yet, the marriage had apparently been arranged by the girl's mother. And if the boy was indeed fleeing from some crime, how could he—as an agent of God's righteousness—withhold what he knew? The thing had come to a most confusing pass!

Deep in his heart the vicar saw good in his fellowmen. Evil existed in the world, to be sure, but it was found in dark and disreputable drinking houses and back alleys of large cities, not in the hearts of fathers toward their children. Littlefield was the father of three daughters, whom he loved and had doted upon since their earliest days. What father could feel differently toward a daughter? Furthermore, the marriage he had recently performed was over, in the eyes of God and man a legal and spiritual reality. Thus there was little this man Duncan could do to change that fact. Undoubtedly the children would be able to reason with the overwrought father, and in light of the fact of the marriage, he would in the end follow the mother's blessing with his own. And if there was some difficulty with the law, the father, as laird, certainly possessed every legal right to look into the matter on behalf of the authorities.

When Littlefield at length spoke, his words came from a heart which was certain he was doing the right thing, given the unusual circumstances facing him. "Your lordship," he said, "I will direct you to where I believe they may be, though I cannot guarantee they will still be there—it has been two days since I last saw them."

"Where, then?" James barked, moderating his cold tone but slightly.

The vicar hesitated. There was something in this man's eyes he could not identify, a hard emptiness he had never seen before, something which reminded him of the angry sea in the middle of the winter.

Their eyes met for a brief instant, then the vicar glanced quickly away. *It must be nothing,* he thought to himself. *The man is merely worked up, and it will pass. Soon all will be mended and healed.*

He directed James Duncan to the humble little cottage some four miles down the road. Without a word of thanks James spun around, jumped onto his horse, and rode off with his companions in the manner in which they had come.

The vicar stared after them, exhaled a long sigh, closed the door of his home, and turned back inside.

2

The Daughter and Her Man

THE MORNING SUN pierced the wood with fragments of light dancing against the leafless birch and rowan and the green stands of fir. The face of approaching winter was evident, but a few tenacious orange and yellow leaves still clung to their branches, flickering colorfully in the sunlight. Most of the foliage, however, lay on the ground, a dying bed of autumnal splendor.

Laughter rang through the wood overlooking the sea, roaring far below the top of the bluff. The three riders heading eastward on the bordering road did not hear the happy voices, perhaps because the laughter blended so sweetly with the serenity of the wood; perhaps, too, because the reverberating hoofbeats of their steeds drowned out all other sounds as they passed.

Two figures, concealed from the riders' eyes as their laughter had been from their ears, stood at the far end of the wood, at the very edge where the tall cliffs began to fall away to meet the beach below. They had heard the horses approach, pass, then die away in the distance. The galloping rang with urgency. But they could not have guessed that they were themselves in the very eye of the storm whose fomentor was now disappearing toward their own honeymoon cottage over the next rise—a storm whose thunderclouds threatened to engulf them and destroy the bliss they had shared so briefly. The man and the woman stood hand in hand overlooking the sea, gazing toward the distant horizon. Had James Duncan known that the very people he was searching for stood so close within his grasp, the peaceful little grove would have rung with dissonant sounds of strife. As it was, Lady Margaret and her new husband Ian Duncan stood alone, taking in the scene before them, as if by peering far enough they might see far ahead into their own lives.

"It's out there, you know," said Ian at last. "That's where our future lies."

"That's north, silly," replied Maggie, still in a cheerful mood.

"You know what I mean," returned Ian. "Away from Scotland. Not north, maybe, but over the sea."

"I know," said Maggie with a sigh. "But I want to go, Ian. As much as I am torn about having to leave this land I love, our future is westward, in America."

"And you're still sure?"

"Ian . . . we made the right decision."

"No second thoughts about fleeing the country with an accused killer?"

"Of course not! When Falkirk's murderer is found and once my father gets used to our being married, we can return, just as we agreed. Maybe in a few years. But for now, this is best. We must get away and start our life together afresh. There's no other way."

She paused and looked her new husband full in the face. Then, as if to divert his attention from forebodings about their future, she grabbed his hand. "Come, I think I know a way down to the beach!"

"You do know this whole coastline!" exclaimed Ian in disbelief.

"I told you, before you came into my life, I rode every inch of this ground with Cinder and then with Raven."

She laughed, then tugged at his hand and led the way to a steep, narrow path strewn with rocks and dead leaves and debris. It was clearly seldom used. And no wonder, for it wound steeply downward back and forth down the edge of the precipice.

When they at last reached the bottom, with only a few smudges on their faces and a scratch or two, they turned back to look up at the wood from which they had come. From this perspective the trees looked as if they had rushed up to the cliff and then frozen before hurtling over the edge. Their attention then turned out to the sea, where a lone fishing vessel was fighting the rising sea about a mile offshore. The surface of the water was glassy calm, but its pale gray seemed to indicate that it was only holding the grand storm in check for a few moments more. And indeed, on the horizon a mass of dark clouds threatened to swallow the blue which remained overhead. A solitary gull winged overhead, swooping down to the water for a moment, then quickly arching upward again.

"I can hardly believe we're actually married!" said Maggie with a sigh.

"Believe it, my dear. 'Tis true," said Ian, bending over to kiss her.

"It's so peaceful here. Just think, Ian, not a soul knows where we are." Maggie paused, then added, "I wonder if he knows?"

"Your father?"

"Yes. What do you suppose he thinks now that it's too late to stop us?"

"It matters little what he thinks," stated Ian. "We are married, and I love you." Suddenly he jumped to his feet from where he had been sitting. "Do you hear!" he shouted toward the cliff and along the shore, "I love her!" The sound of his voice was quickly lost in the crash of the surf on the rocky shoreline.

Maggie laughed. "You always did believe in expressing yourself to the fullest, didn't you, my goose of a husband!"

"Of course," replied Ian gaily. "If you have something to say, everyone might as well know it."

"Digory was right," remarked Maggie. "He said all things work out for good when you believe God. It's true. It's happened for us."

Ian smiled and merely nodded. The mention of God suddenly brought back to him the painful memory of that desolate ride to Stonewycke Castle only a few days ago when, thinking he had lost Maggie forever, he had shouted curses at the very God Maggie now spoke of. It would not be easy for him to regain his hold on that God—whoever or wherever He was. Even at its best any belief he had once possessed had been fragile. He was glad Maggie could forget those days so easily and know everything had worked out for good. But he still had to live with the horrible burden that perhaps he was, in fact, the murderer of the heir to the Earl of Kairn.

He could laugh with Maggie and speak of the future. But that cold fear was never far from him—fear that his mind had blocked out what he did not want to remember. Yet for her sake he masked it, as he had masked his deepest feelings all his life.

"A storm is moving in," he finally said. "I hope that little fishing boat makes it back to shore before it breaks." He continued to fix his gaze on the white sail in the distance, bulging in the mounting wind.

"The sea can be so friendly one moment," Maggie said, "and the next—"

She left the sentence unfinished. As with Ian, the sea had made her pensive and her thoughts had wandered. She had lived her entire life within sight of this mighty Scottish coast. And now the thought of sailing to America, living away from the sea, perhaps never to—

No, she told herself. *None of that matters. The important thing is that Ian and I are together, and safe. We can live anywhere and be happy.*

Suddenly Maggie became aware that Ian was staring at her.

"Confused?" he asked. "Having more doubts?"

"No," she answered. "Perhaps a little sad, but never confused. We have done the right thing. I am happy, and my future is with you."

They climbed back up the rugged path, but the ascent was far more taxing than coming down, and when they finally reached the top they both fell onto the soft floor of the forest, breathing hard. They lay for some time as the shadows shifted in the swaying treetops. When they stirred into activity again, the sun had reached the midpoint of its arch.

Ian pulled Maggie to her feet and they walked toward their horses, the silky black Raven and Maukin, the chestnut mare. "You probably thought we were never coming back," Maggie murmured into the ear of her friend from childhood, her closest companion since she had been fourteen. So many changes had come into her life since then, but Raven had been an important and deeply loved source of stability. A momentary stab of bitterness raced through her at the thought of Cinder, the first horse she had loved, and what her father had done. But just as quickly it passed, and they mounted and rode out of the forest and back onto the dirt road which wound along the high coastline.

The highway was empty now; it had been two hours since the three riders had passed. Maggie and Ian rode eastward, the way they had come, in silence. The few belongings they had brought with them on the night of their hasty wedding in Fraserburgh were tied to their saddles. Yet as if by common consent they followed the road back toward the cottage where they had spent the last two nights. The wind had picked up, and conversation was difficult. At length Ian reined Maukin to a stop.

"Maggie," he said, "I think we should ride straight to Aberdeen and seek passage immediately."

"I wish we could go back to the cottage for a few days longer," said Maggie.

"So do I. But I have an uneasy feeling about it. If your father does try to follow us, he won't have far to look. Our presence there was not altogether unknown."

"The vicar would never tell, do you think?"

"Perhaps not. But word spreads in a place like Fraserburgh. And your father can be very persuasive. I think we should ride for the coast without any further delay." Ian knew what he was asking of his new wife. Yet Maggie had shown herself strong, and he knew the time had finally come for decisions. "Maggie," he said at length, "if this is going to be too difficult, we don't *have* to go to America. We could be happy closer, someplace—"

"No, Ian. It's our only hope. It's the only way. I *want* to go, to be safe and with you. But . . ."

"What is it, my love?"

"When I said good-bye to my mother, I hadn't known it might be forever. Maybe that's what is making me hesitate, the thought of never seeing her again."

"We can go back to Stonewycke," Ian broke in quickly. "Besides, maybe they have found the killer by this time."

"Oh, Ian, you would risk going back, for me?"

"Of course."

"But it's too dangerous. What if—?"

"Nonsense!" said Ian, reeling Maukin around in the road. "I'd do anything for you! Besides, we'll just slip in, see your mother, tell her of our plans, and be gone before your father lays an eye on us. We'll go to the inn. Queenie will help us."

"We'll have to be careful," cautioned Maggie.

"Don't worry. Everything will be fine. But you're right, we do have to be careful. And if your father is looking for us or hears any rumor of us in connection with Fraserburgh, this very road is the one he'd use to follow us. Is there any other way back to Port Strathy?"

"There's a road—hardly more than a trail actually—a mile or two west of here that cuts across to the Inland Highway. That would be a long way around though."

"Better than being seen," said Ian. "Lead the way!"

Maggie swung Raven around, dug her heels into the mare's flanks, and the two galloped back up the hill, passed the wood where they had spent the morning, and in less than fifteen minutes were heading south away from the sea on the trail Maggie had spoken of.

They had scarcely left the Coast road when three riders, returning from the abandoned cottage, thundered past the inland cutoff and descended once again upon Fraserburgh. Their second interview with the vicar was brief and terse.

Satisfied that he knew no more than he had told them earlier, the riders spurred their exhausted mounts back through the streets and again toward Port Strathy, to the estate of Stonewycke, where the leader of the three would have to rethink his strategy against the son of his hated cousin.

3

Flight from Stonewycke

QUEENIE RANKIN MOVED her stout bulk deftly among the tables of the Common Room of her inn. With a strong arm she polished each one until it shone. She was proud of the inn she and her husband had built, and all the more now that he had died so shortly after its completion. Perhaps the *Bluster 'N Blow* stood as a memorial to the only man that had ever loved her, and the only man she had trusted enough to love in return. Some characterized the woman as cold, and the hard businesslike gleam in her eye attested to that image. But there was more to Queenie than most of her customers ever guessed, for she had kept what lay underneath hidden from all except her husband. Even he had seen only glimpses of it.

Evening shadows had begun to fall across the glistening tables. Queenie stood back from her work, cast a quick eye about, and deemed the place at last fit for her evening patrons. With winter coming on and the herring season completed, times at the inn were busier; they would be coming soon. There was just time to clean up a bit behind the counter where the glasses and most of her cheaper stock of liquor were kept. But she had barely reached the counter when the door unexpectedly opened behind her. Turning around, her eyes opened wide and the glass she had been holding nearly dropped to the floor.

"I canna believe my auld eyes!" she exclaimed, hurrying out to greet the new arrivals. "An' the leddy too!" she added. "Whatever ye'll be doin' here I don't know, but a hearty welcome t' the both o' ye!"

Ian glanced quickly around and was obviously relieved to find the place empty.

"Hello, Queenie," said Ian almost in a whisper, as if he feared being heard despite the fact that the three of them were alone in the inn. "I don't want to bring more trouble upon you, but—"

"Hold yer tongue, lad!" interrupted Queenie. "I'll be the one t' say when trouble's bein' brought upon me. Now, come in an' sit ye doon."

Queenie led them to a secluded bench near the hearth. A cheerful fire was blazing away in anticipation of the evening guests, and the two travelers welcomed its warmth. Noting the anxiety on Ian's face, Queenie was reluctant to be the one to confirm the news Maggie and Ian dreaded most to hear: the murderer had not been found, rumors were still circulating (rumors which had grown to conviction in the minds of many of the townspeople) that Ian was the guilty party, an incriminating knife had been discovered, and James Duncan had been ravaging the town for three days in search of any stray clue that might lead him to wherever Ian was hiding.

Maggie fell back heavily against the wall. How desperately she had forced herself to believe that all would be resolved once they returned to Stonewycke! Now it seemed to return at all would be suicide if they encountered her father. Once again, there seemed no alternative but to get as far away from Port Strathy, and Scotland, as possible.

Into the blur of Maggie's consciousness drifted the urgent sound of Ian's voice, hurriedly making arrangements with Queenie. She struggled to pay attention but could barely concentrate; her confused brain could only tell her that he was making arrangements with Queenie for Atlanta, her mother, to come to the village to see them. *I have to see her,* she thought. In that instant nothing else mattered to Maggie except being able to see her mother one last time.

". . . an' I'll fix up a room fer ye upstairs, until then," Queenie was saying, but Maggie scarcely heard.

A full moon illuminated the tall grasses behind the inn. The clouds that had hung threatening in the sky all day parted for a time, allowing the night light to shine through. A short distance away the waves crashed against the shore, their foamy tops an eerie phosphorescence in the moonlight. Atlanta Duncan quickly surveyed the scene. But her mind was not on its beauty, but upon the clandestine reunion with her daughter. Her heart ached; she, too, had hoped it would not come to this. Yet when she had sent Maggie and Ian off to be married, a dark premonition had told her their flight would be more permanent than any of the three had dared openly admit. She was a pragmatic woman, and had hardened herself against that possibility. Still, she had hoped. Now she knew the inevitable moment had come. Why else would they send for her so soon? And in the dead of night? Why else but to say good-bye? So Atlanta had prepared herself to bid her only daughter farewell, knowing she might never see her again.

Maggie stepped out of the cover of the grasses when she saw Atlanta approach.

"Mother!" she said in an urgent whisper.

"Oh, dear child!" cried Atlanta, turning toward her and taking her daughter in her arms.

"I had to see you again," Maggie said.

"I know," Atlanta replied, holding her close.

"Mother," began Maggie, "we're going—Ian's still in danger . . . we have to—"

"I know, I know. Ian's note said you were going away."

"Mother, we've decided—we're going to America."

"Oh, Lord!" gasped Atlanta.

"It's the only way."

Recovering herself, Atlanta brushed an unseen tear from her eye, took a deep breath, and replied. "You are married now. You and Ian must begin a new life. He will take care of you."

"I wish you could come with us."

"No, Maggie. My life is here. Yours is with Ian now. You will be happy."

"I know," said Maggie, clinging to Atlanta. "I am happy."

Atlanta eased Maggie away from her, then held her at arm's length and gazed into her face. She reached up and arrested a tear that had begun to drop down her daughter's cheek. "You are strong, my dear daughter. And you have a husband who loves you. You will have the happiness you deserve. And perhaps you will return some day, when all this is—"

A sob caught in Atlanta's throat. Even as she spoke, she could feel the hollowness of her words. She swallowed hard and closed her eyes for an instant in an attempt to regain her desperately needed reserve.

Maggie embraced Atlanta again. "Mother," she said, "we'll let you know where we are—we'll write."

"That may not be advisable at first," said Atlanta, the practicality of her nature speaking out before the urgings of her mother's heart. She drew a deep breath. "Only until this thing with Ian is cleared up, of course."

"You can reach us through Drew Mackinaw," said Ian, speaking for the first time. "You should at least know that much. He has a small farm in Chatham, New York."

"Thank you, Ian," said Atlanta, turning to her son-in-law. "I want you to know, regardless of what has happened, that I have faith in you. I know you will do what is best for Maggie."

"Thank you, my lady," Ian replied. "That means a great deal to me. I will try to be worthy of your trust and—"

The rest of his reply was lost in a wild volley of shouts which erupted behind them.

"I swore you would not get away with this!" shrieked James as he approached hurriedly, his eyes flashing. His outstretched hand held a pistol poised dangerously at Ian's head.

"Father, no!" screamed Maggie.

"You'll thank me for this later!" Turning toward Ian, James continued his threats. "The constable may not have thought there to be enough evidence to hang you, but, by Jove! I'll not have a murderder abducting my daughter!"

"Don't be a fool, James!" Atlanta interrupted.

"Trying to undermine me again, my dear wife?" James sneered. "But you'll not win this time."

Ian stood gaping in shock and disbelief. When at length he came to his senses, a resolve rose within him. He would stand his ground and make James Duncan know that he was not a murderer. He opened his mouth to speak, but all the words he would utter caught in his throat.

"I'm—I'm no killer," he stammered out, but the speech was weak and strained. How could he convince this man of something he was not even certain of himself?

"Ha!" returned James with a fiendish laugh. "And whose blood was that on your hand, your own? Ha! ha!"

Unconsciously Ian shot a quick glance at his hand as if the blood might still be clinging to his skin. His eyes saw only the remaining bandage over the wound he had received that awful night—the wound he could not remember how he had received.

"I'm warning you, Duncan," James went on. "Leave this town immediately! I'll not give you another chance. If I ever see your face around Stonewycke again, I'll kill you, do you hear?"

"Father!" cried Maggie, running to Ian and standing by his side, "you cannot shoot my *husband*!"

At the word a fury of rage swept over James's face.

"Husband!" he shrieked. "He's a scoundrel!" Again he raised the pistol and took deadly aim down its barrel.

"Run, Ian!" Maggie screamed, rushing toward her father. "Run!"

For a brief instant Ian stood transfixed. Maggie slammed into her father, sending him reeling backward. Without further thought, Ian turned and sprinted toward the chestnut mare. He was barely astride when a shot range out. Astonished by the suddenness of her attack, James had been dazed by the jolt of his daughter's body. Coming quickly to himself he threw her aside and let fly a hasty round after Ian. The crack of the gun made the horse bolt forward just as Ian had found his seat.

"You'll not destroy my family again, Landsbury!" James yelled, firing once more, this time nearly finding his mark. In his wild frenzy he never realized he had called Ian by the hated name of the lad's father.

Quickly James reloaded. Just as he was setting himself to fire a second round, Atlanta rushed to him and grabbed his arm. The shot went wild.

"Go after him, Maggie!" Atlanta cried.

Maggie cast a forlorn glance of farewell toward her mother, then sprang onto Raven and bolted in the direction Maukin had taken Ian.

James easily broke free from Atlanta's grasp and flung her viciously to the ground. The gun shook in his hand as he glowered like a crazed animal at his wife.

For one of the few times in her life, Atlanta trembled with fear. But she directed a cold, penetrating stare at her husband.

"Would you kill me, James?" she said softly. "Or your own daughter? Has your madness gone that far?"

The shots had been heard, and by this time a small group of locals were straggling down the path to investigate. The surprise was evident on their faces finding Lady Atlanta lying on the ground with the laird above her holding a gun. Realizing the delicacy of his position, given the local tendency toward gossip, James hastened to explain that the fugitive who had killed Master Falkirk had dared to show his face and that he had frightened him off. No one thought of questioning the laird, although not a few wondered to themselves why they had heard the sound of two horses.

Atlanta silently rose as the group disbanded, saying nothing—for she could hardly refute her husband's word in public. She was only glad that Maggie and Ian had escaped safely and soon would be out of danger for good. How fortunate it was that James knew nothing of their plans!

4

A Knife in the Night

RAVEN AND MAUKIN galloped through that entire night, carrying their masters faithfully despite their exhaustion. The few stops for rest were all too brief before their riders once more urged them on. For another day Ian and Maggie continued their urgent flight, stopping to sleep but twice, and even then only for an hour or two.

Ian was sullen and morose. Maggie tried to bring back his merriment, but her efforts proved useless. He refused to say what was troubling him.

"I just have to think," he had insisted.

"But can't you tell me, Ian?" Maggie pleaded. "I am your wife now."

"I can't talk about it, that's all. I just can't! I have to work it out myself."

Finally she stopped pressing him.

On the second evening out, just as the sun was setting, they stopped the haggard horses and dismounted. For the first time in days Ian looked at Maggie. He suddenly saw how pale she had grown. Dark circles outlined her lovely eyes.

"Oh, my Maggie!" he said. "I'm sorry. It's been thoughtless of me to push you so hard, as tired as you are."

"I'm fine," she replied, trying to smile. But in truth she had never been more exhausted in her life. Twice she had nearly fallen asleep in the saddle.

"We'll stay here tonight," he said. "We've covered enough ground to relax somewhat. No one's after us."

A small search revealed a secluded spot some hundred feet from the roadside, nestled among the trees. The ground was soft with fallen leaves, though moist from a shower the day before, but rain did not appear likely tonight. They spread out the blankets Queenie had provided, and brought out a half-eaten loaf of bread, several oatcakes, a round of cheese, and the last of two bottles of wine—all of which had also been graciously provided by the innkeeper. They enjoyed their dinner greatly; if not the most luxurious they had partaken of in their lives, at least one of the most appreciated. The two horses munched peacefully at what grass they could find, as if they too sensed that this stop would be a little longer than the others.

At length, darkness having fallen in earnest, Maggie lay out on one of the blankets and stretched to her full length. "This *is* nice!" she said dreamily. And scarcely had the words parted her lips before she was sound asleep. Ian gently laid two more blankets over her. The night was chilly and a steady breeze whistled through the trees. Perhaps they should have sought out an inn, but Ian judged it better that they not take that risk. Especially with Aberdeen so close, then America, and their freedom!

Yet what good would it be if Maggie became sick? he argued with himself. *What good was anything?* he thought with despair.

In those days of silence, his tormented mind had not given him a moment's peace. He was beginning to hate himself as he never had before. He had *run* from James Duncan! Like a coward, he had left two women to defend him, and he had *run away*! The mere memory made him recoil in shame.

Yet his cowardly flight was not the only memory gnawing at him. For as he had galloped away in terror, the thought had driven itself into his brain that James had won, after all. In his panic the conviction shouted out to him that Maggie would stay with her father. She would realize she had married a hopeless weakling, unable even to speak like a man to her father. When he had looked back to see his new wife riding up behind him, he had actually found himself surprised. And thus what troubled him more than anything was the simple fact that he had not believed in Maggie. He had forgotten how strong she was.

Ian lay down next to Maggie and put his arm around her as if to protect her from the cold—the only danger he had any power against. Tossing and turning in the confused corners of his tired mind, he soon fell into a deep sleep.

A sharp cry pierced the night, and Ian started awake. His protective arm was no longer around Maggie, and his shoulder ached, for it had been pressed against a rock underneath him. Groggily he rubbed it, then lay his head back down, forgetting the cry as if it had been part of some hazy dream.

But again a terrified scream rent the air and this time Maggie's voice pulled Ian fully to his senses.

"Maggie!" he yelled, turning around where he lay.

A huge form hovered over her. Ian could see the gleam of steel in the darkness. He sprang on the enemy with a howl, knocking the man away from his prey. Maggie leapt to safety while the two men rolled on the ground, the crude knife looming inches from Ian's throat. Whoever the man was, his intent was clearly evil, and he would stop at nothing short of the death of his antagonist.

With all the might he could muster, Ian held the murderous weapon at bay. Somehow he forced the attacker onto his back, then smashed the wrist of the hand holding the knife against the ground. At last the man's grip loosened and the knife fell to the ground. Unconsciously Ian relaxed momentarily and the attacker quickly seized the advantage, sending his fist into Ian's face. Stunned, Ian staggered backward. The man bent down to look for the knife, caught its gleam in the moonlight, and reached for it. His hand never reached its target, however. With a dull groan he fell backward from the weight of Ian's booted foot in his midsection. Crying in pain, his hand sought his two cracked ribs, then he lumbered forward like an angry wounded bear. But Ian had followed the line of the man's hand to the knife and now held the treacherous weapon. Not seeing the advantage his enemy held, the man threw himself toward Ian, and the knife sliced his arm.

"Bastard!" he yelled, then tore off into the shadows.

Ian took two steps after him, then stopped. He turned and sought Maggie where she stood alone in the darkness, sobbing with terrified relief.

"Maggie, my dear!" Ian cried, enveloping her in his embrace. He shuddered at the thought of what might have happened. Hardly realizing that he had saved her life, he could only berate himself that he had not waked sooner.

At length Maggie's panic eased and she found her voice.

"It was him, Ian," she said in tremulous tone. "The man from before. That voice! I would know it anywhere—it had to be him!"

"Oh, God!" wailed Ian. In the seconds since the attack, he had hoped the man was nothing but a passing vagrant, a thief or marauder passing along this same road. But Maggie's words confirmed what he had been afraid of all along: they had been followed, and by the man who had already attacked her once, on the very grounds of Stonewycke. If it was indeed Falkirk's money he sought, he would try again, and again. He would not leave them alone until he had it. And even then, would their lives be safe?

He must get Maggie away from this place! Far away! But he groaned within himself at the conflict in his heart. For now he knew a decision must be made, a decision Maggie would never willingly accept. Yet he knew it was the decision he must make if he would be the man he longed to be.

5

A Change in Plans

MAGGIE TRIED TO focus on Ian's words, but her mind screamed out against them.

". . . *Alone* . . ." She heard nothing else he had said. Riding along the quiet road late the next morning, it seemed as if the terrors of the night were far behind them. She would have no fear as long as he was beside her. But now he was telling her he couldn't be there.

"Don't you see?" he had just stated. "I can't run anymore."

"You said we would both go away together until we were out of danger," Maggie argued.

"I know . . . *I know!*" he replied, his voice revealing the strain from the decision he felt compelled to make. "But I despise myself for running from your father. What kind of man—what kind of a husband is such a coward?" The muscles in his neck rippled with tension, and there was an emptiness in his tone and bearing.

"Ian, please don't say that. You're not a coward. My father had a gun!"

"But *you* faced him. You ran at him—to save me."

"You would have done the same," she replied with urgent tone. "And you stood up to that awful man last night."

"Maggie," he said, paying little heed to her arguments, "I had no choice last night. And maybe I could stand up to your father now. Anyway, I would rather he kill me than to run again."

"Ian, how can you say that?"

"Try to understand. I have to learn to be a man, to stand on my own two feet, to face what comes at me—to face your father."

"What does all that matter, Ian? As long as we are together, the opinion of my father means nothing."

"Maggie," said Ian in a more thoughtful tone, "there was a time when I tried to bring derision on my name. I hated it. I hated my father, my family. I suppose I hated myself, too. But it's different now. Since meeting you, something has risen within me—a pride, a self-respect. For your sake—and for my own sake too—I must restore the integrity of my name . . . of who I am. I cannot be a coward. I have to face whatever comes squarely—like a man."

Maggie was silent. There was no other sound in the morning than the gentle clop-clop-clop of the hooves of the two horses on the hard-packed dirt road.

At length she reached over toward Ian and placed her hand on his arm where he rode beside her.

"Ian," she said, "I am proud of you. You *are* a man—a good man—a strong man. We can face this—together! If you want to stay until you are cleared, I'll stay with you. If you want to go, I'll go with you. But please, don't send me on without you. I can't bear it."

"There's no other way. I am afraid for you. Your life is in danger."

"If I'm with you, I won't be afraid of anything."

"I'm your husband now, Maggie. I must protect you. And getting you away from here is the safest thing. We know one man followed us. There could be others. What if your father—"

"Oh, Ian!"

"It's the only way, Maggie. If that man finds you, he will kill you. I can't let you stay here after what happened last night."

"Then come with me," Maggie pleaded, "like we planned!"

"No, Maggie. I have to clear my name. Please try to understand. I *must* restore my honor. Besides you, all I have left is the integrity of what I stand for. All my life I've amounted to nothing. Now I'm accused of a murder I don't even know if I committed. If my life is to mean anything, if my love for you is to mean anything, then I have to stay until my name is cleared. There is nothing a man has left but his honor."

"But isn't our love just as important?"

"Maggie," insisted Ian, "I won't expose you to danger because of me. I must know that you are safe. Then I have to face this alone."

"Oh, Ian," begged Maggie, "don't do this to me. Don't leave me alone!"

Ian focused his eyes straight ahead, fighting within himself to control the tears and the screaming agony in his soul. How he wanted to find some way to avoid inflicting this pain on the one he loved so dearly! Yet in the depths of his heart he was still driven by another fear which he could not tell Maggie, and barely could face himself: that if Maggie did remain behind, somehow James would find a way to wrest her from him—or kill them both trying.

"It's the only way," he said, swallowing hard and closing his eyes to shut back the tears of desperation. "And you will not be alone. Drew Mackinaw will be there to help you until I come. Hector says Drew has been longing to see someone from the homeland for ten years. He knows he will be anxious to open his home to us and put us up until we are settled on our own. He gave me a letter to take to him."

"I've never ever met Drew Mackinaw."

"Maggie, you're from Stonewycke. That's all that matters. They will welcome you as family."

"But—"

"And I will be there before you realize it! Almost before you set foot in New York a month from now, I'll getting ready to board the next ship. We'll be apart a month or two at the most!"

"If I stayed with you, I could help," insisted Maggie.

"No, my Maggie. It's too risky. Please—trust me. It's only because I love you."

"Two months, and no longer?" she questioned, evoking a promise.

"No longer," he replied with more confidence than his sickened heart felt certain of. "You take the train up to Chatham, stay with the Mackinaws until the next ship arrives, and I will be there to meet you. Think of it, Maggie—America! A new life for us!"

"It will seem like forever," she replied, still far from convinced about her husband's optimistic words.

"But it won't be forever," he said. "The time will pass so quickly you'll hardly realize we're apart."

He drew Maukin up close to Raven, stretched out his arm and pulled Maggie gently toward him. He leaned over and kissed her as the two horses walked peacefully side by side. Then he released her and they rode along together in silence.

Maggie wiped her face, looked toward Ian, and forced a smile, but a vague apprehension still lingered in her eyes.

6

Aberdeen

IT WAS ANOTHER day to Aberdeen. Their stops continued brief, and though Maggie dozed occasionally Ian never once allowed himself to sleep. His mood vacillated between carefree joviality and intense disquietude; the spirit Maggie had seen in him when first he came to Scotland gave way to the opposite melancholy half of his personality.

Twice on the road he had sensed they were being followed. But try as he might, without giving away his suspicions and alarming Maggie, he could never gain a clear sight of anyone tracking them. Eventually they reached the city without incident.

Darkness had closed in upon the streets by the time of their arrival, and the sound of their horses' hoofbeats echoed crisply into the stillness of the night. They easily located an inn, but they could not make time stand still; morning arrived too soon for a couple dreading their parting.

Ian had slept fitfully, never escaping the gnawing anxiety that all was not well. When they descended the staircase for breakfast, the innkeeper casually mentioned a stranger who had arrived in the middle of the night.

"But I gave the two o' ye my last room," he said, "so I had t' send the bloke away. Dinna ken why folk canna arrive at a decent hour o' the evenin'."

Ian was relieved Maggie had not heard these words, and that she did not comment on his restiveness. He could hardly eat and continued to glance about nervously. When breakfast was over Ian rushed Maggie to the waiting horses, anxious to complete the final leg of their journey to the dock before anything could happen to stop them. When they arrived, passengers were already mounting the gang plank while seamen busily hoisted the riggings, loaded luggage and stores onto the deck, and made the final preparations for departure.

Suddenly Maggie thrust her hand into the pocket of her cloak and realized her mother's envelope was missing. This couldn't be! It had been in her pocket constantly since the night she and Ian had left to be married.

"Ian . . . it's gone!" she exclaimed as her hand frantically searched the empty pocket.

"What?" asked Ian in the detached tone of one whose mind is on other matters.

"The envelope. My mother gave it to me before I left," she answered. "It's not here. I took it out for a moment at the inn, just to look at it. I thought I put it back in my coat. Perhaps it fell out somewhere in the room. I have to go back for it."

"But the ship is ready to sail!" replied Ian, forcing his attention now on this new crisis.

"I have to have it! Mother said it was important."

"I'll go," said Ian.

He mounted Maukin and wheeled her around.

"Ian," cried Maggie. "Hurry! I can't leave without it . . . nor without seeing you. Hurry!"

Ian dug his heels into the mare's sides and galloped off through the streets, hounded by a growing sense of foreboding. But his fears proved groundless. He easily found the packet on the floor beside the bed. He caught it up quickly, flew back down the stairs three at a time, and ran across the inn's common room to the door. He hastened toward Maukin, and almost instantly felt a pair of eyes on his back. Yet he forced himself forward, never once betraying the stab of dread which hit him.

Maggie had climbed the gang plank for a better vantagepoint. Most of the passengers had boarded, and from all indications the crew's final preparations for departure were underway. She paced back and forth anxiously.

Ian, where are you? She couldn't sail without seeing him. The packet hardly mattered now. She had to hold him in her arms once more and feel his reassurance that this was indeed the best way. Something inside still shouted out to her that she should refuse to go. Even as a child she had always made up her own mind, never letting people tell her what to do. But however strong her doubts, he had been so insistent that this was best. She had to hear once more his promise that they would again be together in two months.

The final call for passengers to board was given.

Oh, Ian, Maggie thought, *where are you? Please come!*

"Miss!" one of the sailors yelled. "I've got my orders t' pull away the plank. Are ye stayin' or goin'?"

"Please," Maggie answered, "just another moment."

Her eyes strained down the dirt street she and Ian had come down only a short time ago. All about the dock there remained a bustle of activity, though by now all the passengers were on board.

She alone remained—uncertain, staring over the crowd into the maze which was Aberdeen.

Oh, Ian . . . why don't you come?

Ian hesitated momentarily when the stranger called his name. Then without glancing back he broke into a run, racked to Maukin, leapt onto the mare's back, dug his heels into her sides, and galloped off. He did not look back, but heard the immediate flurry of footsteps in quick pursuit.

His impulse was to run directly for the dock. But he could not bring the danger there. Maggie's safety remained foremost in his mind. If this was indeed the man whose dagger sought to end her life, he must not let him near her.

Instead, he wheeled Maukin to the right, through a short street, then left, across a broad thoroughfare, down several blocks, right again into a deserted alley, out the far end, and left. Back and forth through the unfamiliar streets he raced, desperately hoping to elude his pursuer.

At length he stole a backward glance over his shoulder. It appeared he was not being followed—for the moment at least. Now if only he could find the pier in time. He turned toward the sea and sped in that direction, not daring to slow his pace. He remained oblivious to obstacles, wagons, other riders, and passers-by and allowed Maukin every inch of the wild freedom she desired. As he came in view of the dock his heart gave a leap: the ship was still anchored firm! Still he did not slow his frenzied ride until he nearly collided with a loaded vegetable wagon.

Reaching the edge of the gathered crowd, he hastily dismounted and flailed through on foot. His eyes darted back and forth until he saw her standing peering in a different direction. She had been looking elsewhere and had not yet seen him.

She spotted the mare first. Then she heard Ian's shout.

"Maggie!" he cried.

She rushed down the empty gangplank, heedless of the warnings of the sailors who had been trying to urge her aboard. She was only aware of her husband's outstretched arms; she cared for nothing else until they were firmly around her.

"Ian," she said, "I was so afraid . . ."

"It's all right now, my little Maggie," he said, trying to calm her, as he handed her the envelope. Yet both were painfully aware that their hurried words could never convey the depth of the feelings hidden in their hearts.

"Ian . . . there's so much I want to say—so much I want to give you."

"We will have time," Ian reassured. "But it will have to wait. We must just hold on to the promise of the future."

With her head pressed against his chest, Maggie could tell Ian had been riding hard. But she asked him no questions; neither did he tell her of the man outside the inn. They only remained locked in each other's silent embrace.

At last the moment came.

In the background rose the urgent cries of the seamen. Still Maggie wanted to scream, "No, I can't leave you . . . I won't go!"

But this bitter parting was Ian's wish. There was danger at home, and this was the course he had chosen. He was now her husband; from the very beginning she had known she was willing to sacrifice all for him. This, then, would be her sacrifice of affection for the man she loved. And she must do it joyfully, leaving the memory of a smiling face in Ian's heart.

She gazed deeply into his brown eyes one last time, then held her face up and kissed his lips. He returned the kiss fervently, squeezed her close once more, then released her and choked out the words, "It's time for you to go."

"Ian . . ."

"Two months," he said, forcing a cheery smile reminiscent of old. "I'll be on the next ship."

Reluctantly Maggie took her place on the ship's deck as Ian slowly descended the gangplank. She stood clutching the rail until her hand ached, and watched as Ian dragged his sleeve across his brow. She knew his tears were flowing as were hers.

Suddenly she felt the movement of the ship, its first jerky motions causing her insides to lurch in one final moment of uncertain anguish. Gradually it moved away from the dock. She tried to call out, but her husband's name caught in her throat. Words were no longer possible. Thoughts were no longer possible . . . save the one piercing realization that he was slipping farther and father away.

At last she could bear the torment of his gradually shrinking figure no longer. The ship was out of the harbor now and gathering speed. She would rather remember his face standing there reaching out to her than to see it fade slowly into oblivion. She turned away from the rail. Immediately she wheeled around and ran back. A glimpse—any glimpse—was better than nothing at all!

The crowd had now become but a distant blur. To one side she saw a horse speeding away from the pier, leading another which had no rider. Ian's face was nowhere to be seen.

At last she turned away, walked to the bow of the ship, and cast her eyes out toward the open sea and what lay ahead.

7

Capture

STANDING ON THE dock, Ian stared after the retreating ship. The desolate gray of the sea suited his mood, but he was scarcely aware of it. Already the crowds had begun to disperse and the crew of longshoremen were hard at work lugging several giant crates from the pier.

Still he remained transfixed, gazing after the ship as if somehow his intensity might bring it back. He could just barely make out what seemed to be a single figure standing on the ship's deck. Was it his imagination, or was it returning his wave?

At length, when the ship had receded into the distance, appearing the size of a child's toy, he turned, mounted Maukin, took Raven's reins in his free hand, and said, "Come on, you two, it's time to go."

If Ian Duncan had ever known tragedy in his life, he had faced it with a hard laugh and a cynical sneer. But in the mere three months since he had come to Scotland, he had learned that life could be sweet, and with that realization the hard veneer which many had thought to be his true personality had been stripped away. He hadn't known, however, that happiness and sorrow were reverse sides of the same emotion. With the joy had also come an inroad for pain, for the greater one's joy, the greater the capacity for sorrow. Hence, when the painful tragedy had assailed him, it had come so suddenly that there had been no time for him to pull his protective shield around him. As his heart opened to the joy of love, so too he had become vulnerable to the devastation of loss and heartache. Now, the strength and determination he had possessed only a short time ago slowly drained from him. For all his confidence and reassuring words to Maggie, he wondered how he could go on. Half his being and all his soul had disappeared over the horizon on that ship.

Oh, Maggie! Why did I let you go?

He shook his head as the reality of the truth dawned upon him. *I did not let you go; I made you go,* he thought. *How could I have been such a fool!*

He rode aimlessly from the dock, hardly caring in which direction he proceeded. He had formulated no plan to free himself and restore his honor, as he had told Maggie he would do. On he rode, letting Maukin determine his direction while his mind wandered equally at random. Storekeepers were setting out their wares on the sidewalks, shoppers were beginning to gather for the morning's activity, children were darting in and out of open doors. But Ian was only vaguely cognizant of the city's bustle.

Maggie was gone!

Yes, they were going to meet again in two months—everything had been arranged. But that hope seemed all too tenuous to him, like a man grasping at a branch to keep him from falling over a cliff. The branch might break at any time, and what then? For what purpose had he stayed behind in Scotland? To restore his integrity? What honor was possible when even he could not be certain he *was* innocent! The night of the murder was still a horrible blur in his mind, and he looked down at his wounded hand—another reminder. It was healing now, and Queenie's fears that he would lose two of his fingers were unfounded. But the wound called out to him again and again, reminding him he could not recall where the gash had come from. *Could he have had another fight with Falkirk?* What if this second fight had involved a weapon which had cut his hand and fatally wounded Falkirk? Surely he would be able to remember such a thing—surely! But he had been drinking . . .

Dear God! The words caught like bile in his throat. There could be no God. It was all a cruel joke, a twisted irony with him at its center. The world was mad!

Yes, he thought, *perhaps I could have murdered that night.* But Maggie's father would have been the more likely victim. For did not James Duncan stand irredeemably at the core of his pain? He had forced Ian and Maggie apart and had threatened to kill him. James had tried to manipulate their lives as if they were mere pawns in his grand business schemes. He was no doubt at this very moment plotting further how he might destroy his own daughter's husband.

But you won't touch Maggie, thought Ian grimly. *She is out of your reach now. And although I may have lost her too, for a while, at least you won't turn her love for me away.* In his misery Ian, even after she had left her beloved homeland for him, sorely underestimated Maggie's love for him. Her very act of obedience in leaving her dear home stood as everlasting proof that she placed her love for her husband above whatever affection may have remained for her father. But Ian had no way of grasping the depth of such a love, for in all his twenty years never had such devotion been expressed toward *him*. No wonder, then, that he could little understand such a giving and sacrificial love.

Ian continued on through the town, so absorbed in his thoughts that he took no particular notice of the three horsemen approaching him. One of the three cut sharply in front of him, bringing him up short; Maukin reared in alarm. Ian pulled in the rein, brought her under control, and then stared at the riders with a gaze which registered neither emotion nor question. He recognized none of them. They were dressed in coarse woolens and wore wide-brimmed hats and heavy coats.

"Ye be Theodore Duncan?" asked the man who had directed his horse to cut in front of Ian. His voice was gruff with the tone of one who was tired and most likely hungry. "That's right?"

"Yes," answered Ian.

"I'm the constable up Strathy way, Tom Lancaster. Ye led us a merry chase this mornin'. But 'tis o'er now."

Ian had all but forgotten his frantic ride through the city trying to elude the stranger who had tried to accost him at the inn. Now he recognized that this was the very same man.

"What happened to Duff?" asked Ian, dull fear rising to panic within him.

"Seems the laird thought it time fer him to be thinkin' o' retirin'," Lancaster replied. "Too old t' do his job properly's how I heard it. But I'm none too old, ye see, an' I don't plan on retirin' fer a good long time. So ye jist come along wi' us nice an' peaceable."

"What—what for?" asked Ian, knowing all too well the man's mission. Again James Duncan's hand had reached out toward him. Suddenly he realized that with Maggie gone, James could do anything he pleased. He would have no more strength to resist the man if he did not take it now. Without waiting for an answer to his question, he let go of Raven's rein, jerked Maukin's head around, and dug in his heels. But the constable's two men were on the watch, drew up the same instant, and wrenched Maukin's reins from his hands.

"I was hopin' ye'd be a reasonable man," said Lancaster.

"You can't do this!" cried Ian. "You have no proof against me! Duff knew that, and let me go."

"Well, Duff's not the constable anymore. An' since I came to the job, I've uncovered new evidence."

Lancaster paused for effect, then went on. "Seems we found the murder weapon—right where his lordship was killed. Guess Duff's failin' eyesight o'erlooked it. 'Twas a real handsome-lookin' dirk too." Lancaster fumbled in one of his saddlebags for a moment, and finally withdrew a jewel-handled dagger. He held it toward Ian triumphantly while an evil grin spread over his face.

Ian stared in disbelief. It was his own knife. His father had given it to him years ago. The best one, the family heirloom, had of course gone to his brother. But though only a cheap copy, Ian had nevertheless treasured this knife and had discovered it missing shortly before he and Maggie had left Stonewycke. Then he shuddered—the tip of the knife was stained with dried blood.

"Well, I can see, Mr. Duncan," Lancaster continued, "without yer sayin' a word, that ye hae seen this afore."

"What are you planning to do with me?" asked Ian coldly.

"Why, I thought ye knew, lad," replied Lancaster with a laugh. "I'm puttin' ye under arrest. I'll be takin' ye to the choky here in Aberdeen, since there's no jail in Strathy. Ye made my job a bit easier in comin' here yersel' so I can forgive ye fer givin' me the slip this mornin'." Again he laughed, this time without restraint, joined by his two companions. "Abner," he directed one of the other men, "I think ye better tie Mr. Duncan's hands behind him." Then he looked back at Ian. "Jist so ye don't get any more ideas aboot diggin' yer heels into that frolicksome mare o' yers."

Abner did his deed. He yanked the rope tight, apparently enjoying his assignment, until the cords cut into Ian's wrists.

Ian offered no resistance. James Duncan had indeed won, after all. It was useless to fight against a man whose power was so vast it even controlled the law. Submissively he sat while they turned and led him back toward the middle of Aberdeen.

Maggie! he cried out inside. *Maggie, I'm so sorry. But how could I ask you to spend your life with a murderer? At least this way you are safe.*

Ian's heart sank, and any last hope that things would work out died within him. For what hope was possible now but a belief in a power greater than the futility of this life? And Ian no longer possessed any such belief.

8

Mid-Sea

❖

M AGGIE DREW IN deep gulps of the tangy salt air. For three days she had remained cabinbound with violent seasickness. Longing for fresh air, this morning she had forced herself out of her bunk and dragged herself onto the deck. But she could hardly keep her feet under her, and the gentle swaying back and forth of the ship in rhythm with the swelling sea was more than her queasy stomach could handle.

She had been fine at first. The voyage to London was uneventful, and the seas were calm around and through the channel and westward. Six days out of Brighton they had encountered a brief but blustery autumn squall; the ship had pitched about unmercifully, and she had been unable to recover. When the captain had looked in on her last night, she had asked how long the storm would go on.

"Why, we left that little tempest behind yesterday morning, my lady!" Captain Sievers laughed. "Why, we haven't begun to see anything like a real storm yet!" Noting the dismay on Maggie's face, and recalling that the purpose of his visit was to console his young passenger, he hastily added, "But no doubt we'll avoid any other completely, so you need not worry yourself."

This morning the sea did seem somewhat gentler. But whatever the change, it apparently had no effect on her tormented stomach. She had scarcely eaten in three days and even the captain had grown concerned.

But today she would fight this thing. With determination she gripped the cold metal railing until her knuckles were white, repeatedly breathing in deep draughts of the healthy sea air as if it were a medicine she had been ordered to take. Her mind cast up rumors she had heard of people dying on such voyages, but she was not going to be one of them! *Oh, Lord, please, I'm not . . . I refuse . . .* A new wave of nausea assailed her and she lurched over the rail in silent agony.

A few minutes later Maggie raised her eyes and tried to focus on the horizon. Everywhere was the sea, in all directions. *Oh, Ian,* she thought, *why did we part?* She had to stay healthy, for soon she would see him again! The handsome visage of her husband rose before her face—his laughing brown eyes and tender lips and disarming smile. The hint of an involuntary smile crossed her mouth as she recalled their first meeting. How his brash impudence had galled her! But he had been able to make her laugh at the same time. He had opened his troubled heart to her, and taught her to open herself in return. Together they had grown, and discovered strengths and a love neither could have believed possible.

How I need you, Ian! Maggie thought. Yet as the very thought formed, the nightmare of her departure from Scotland flooded through her like the remembrance of a half-forgotten dream. How could such horrors happen? The murder . . . the man who had attacked them in the forest . . . having to part from the man she loved? Yet all dimmed beside the treachery of her father's contemptuous outburst. His incensed threats against Ian made her shudder. What wellsprings of maniacal self-centeredness could cause any man to so hate his own flesh and blood?

Perhaps Ian was right, leaving Scotland was the only way. But she would never forgive her father for making it come to this!

Then out from the depths of the past crept that old gnawing uncertainty, the question that had so often plagued her. *What did I do to make you hate me so?*

"I see you're coming a bit more to yourself, my lady." Captain Sievers' resonant voice drew her back to the present. His eyes, above sun-reddened cheeks, smiled, revealing deep crows' feet at the corners of each.

Maggie turned, relieved to be diverted from her melancholy thoughts. "I'm trying." Her voice was thin and weak.

"Well, you're still a bit pale, but you look a mite less green about the gills, as we say on the sea. I'll wager by tonight you will be able to join me at my table for dinner."

The mere thought of food brought Maggie's stomach halfway back up her throat. She forced a smile and said, "Thank you, Captain. I'll make my best effort."

"Don't feel you're alone in your misery, my lady," Sievers went on cheerfully. "Why, I remember my first voyage. I was but twelve, and stowed away in the hull of a clipper bound for the Barbados. I don't know which is worse during a storm, to be up top-mast or down in the belly of the ship. But at the time I was sure it was the latter. Finally, I didn't care if they hung me up by my thumbs—anything was worth the risk of a breath of fresh air. I crawled up on the deck and was nearly washed overboard by a wave which crashed over the starboard side right at the moment."

"But you stayed with the sea?"

"I got better about a week later and figured it would be foolish to throw away all that agony for nothing. And besides, I'd always loved the sea. It gets under your skin, you know."

"I do know what you mean," said Maggie, warming to the captain's enthusiastic manner.

"Do you, now?" Sievers replied, leaning forward on the rail and giving his stubbly beard a scratch, fully interested in any tale this young lass might have to share with him.

"I live—that is, I used to live by the sea," began Maggie. But before she could go on she felt warm tears rising in her eyes. She turned her gaze back to the open sea. The pain was still too raw. Maybe in time she would be able to talk about her homeland again with composure. But today she could say no more.

"Whereabouts was that, my lady?"

"I'm sorry, Captain—I'm afraid I'm not feeling very well. I think I had better return to my cabin and lie down." Maggie turned and hurried away without awaiting further response.

Would she ever be able to think of her wild and rocky seashore again, or see the heather bloom, or look into the face of a lovely yellow primrose . . . How Ian had loved them!

Dear God, she wept into her pillow, *how can I do this thing? Everything I love is in Scotland! Why must I leave? Why couldn't you help us?*

Maggie did not make it to the captain's table for dinner that evening, and for two more days lay on her bunk. Even death, it seemed, had to be better than the misery of the constantly pitching ship. On the ninth day of the voyage she emerged from her cabin again, noticeably thinner and her face drawn and pale. But her nerves had quieted down and the hint of an appetite sent occasional stabs of hunger rumbling through the empty cavities of her stomach. The thought of solid food was for the first time in nearly a week an appealing notion.

If only her heart might heal as quickly! But in her mind she could find no peace, not even in the joyous prospect of her reunion with Ian. For there was always the fear—though she fought against it whether it threatened to take shape in her mind—the fear that something would go wrong.

9

Chatham

N EW-FALLEN SNOW LAY in drifts against the little farmhouse. Staring out the kitchen window, Maggie could not help wondering if the first snows of winter had yet fallen in Port Strathy. Right after a snowstorm was one of the few times the massive stone towers of Stonewycke could be truly beautiful.

Winter had come early to Chatham, the little village in eastern New York where Maggie's journey had come to an end. Snow did not usually fall until after Thanksgiving, the townsfolk said; this year it was already ankle-deep with the autumn holiday still two days away. But the weather was of little consequence to Maggie. Let it snow, let it rain, let the wind blow, let it do whatever it liked, just as long as it did not keep Ian from arriving on schedule!

She herself had arrived only three days ago. How intimidated she felt the moment she first stepped off the ship in the vast harbor of New York City! How different the people sounded, how fast everything moved—and not a single familiar face. But at least the ground was not moving under her feet! She had recovered from her seasickness; fortunately, Captain Sievers had been right and they had encountered no more stormy weather. Nevertheless, the journey had not been an altogether pleasant one, and she was relieved it was over.

What she would have done had it not been for the assistance of the cab driver, she didn't know. An old man with a cherry-pie face and a broad, toothy grin, his mission, it seemed, was to help foreign strangers get over their initial fears after setting foot in America, the great land of promise. Taking the uncertainty on Maggie's face as a challenge, he stepped toward her, assisted her with her things, and within moments had won over a new friend. He took her to a respectable boarding house, with whose mistress he was apparently on good terms, helped her make arrangements for travel to Chatham by train, and investigated for her the timetable for all future arrivals in the harbor from England. She breathed a deep sigh and smiled her thanks. Just knowing that information was all the world to her!

Maggie was in such a daze from the rapid flow of events that it was not until the following morning that she realized she did not even know the man's name. Too weak from the effects of the sea voyage, she had hardly stopped to consider how it seemed her path had all been prepared for her in advance—everything had progressed as smoothly as clockwork ever since her farewell to Ian on the Aberdeen dock.

Perhaps the most difficult hurdle would be facing the Mackinaws themselves. There had been no time to send word of her arrival, and while Maggie knew very little about them, they knew nothing of her. Drew had been forced to migrate from Scotland some twelve years earlier; three harsh winters and poor harvests in succession had not left enough to feed the mouths of the scraggly Mackinaw homestead on Braenock Ridge. As the eldest of the children, his lot had been to seek a new beginning elsewhere, and he had chosen to do so in America. As Maggie had neared the village of Chatham, she wondered if Drew Mackinaw harbored any resentments toward the lordly family of Stonewycke who knew no want, yet did so little to help the people of the land.

As the train began to slow, Maggie's misgivings rose defiantly to the surface, telling her to stay in her seat and keep riding . . . riding . . . But where else was there to go? As disagreeable as was the idea of imposing upon people she had never met, there were no other options open to her. Therefore, when the clickety-clack of the wheels on the iron rails finally ground to a halt and the shrill whistle blew, Maggie rose from her seat, picked up her belongings, made her way to the door at the front of the passenger car, and then timidly stepped down.

How strange and foreign everything looked! The hilly region probably compared in many ways to her native Scotland, but it was somehow different. She glanced about the small town. There were only a few buildings and not a great deal of activity. Chatham was probably even smaller than Port Strathy, she thought with relief. Just as long as all American cities weren't like New York!

Well, thought Maggie, *here I am. I might as well make the best of it.* She took a deep breath, then walked toward what appeared to be the center of town, if town it could even be called. She passed a feed store, then a livery stable. Most of the activity seemed to be coming from within one building. "S-A-L-O-O-N," Maggie read. "Whatever can that mean? I suppose it could be the proprietor's name," she speculated. "Still, it is a rather odd-sounding name for a store."

At the end of the street, running out of buildings, Maggie walked into a friendly looking establishment whose sign called it a "General Store." A couple of farmers were milling around and chatting with a man behind the counter.

"Howdy, ma'am," he said, leaving his friends and approaching her with a broad smile. "What might I help you with today?"

"I just got off the train," Maggie began. "I'm looking for someone in your town, and I wondered if you might be able to help me."

"I reckon Jeb here knows just about everybody in these parts for miles," put in one of the farmers, nodding toward the owner of the store.

"Well, I'll sure help you if I can, ma'am," said the man they called Jeb. "I been selling goods to the farmers hereabouts for nigh onto twenty year, so I guess I know most of 'em."

"I am looking for the Mackinaws . . . Drew Mackinaw."

"Oh, sure, Drew's a good man. Walked into town twelve years ago with nothing to his name but a few dollars and a strong back and willing heart. A good worker, that man. He's built him up a nice place. Lives out yonder, mile east of town, past the bridge over the wash."

"I'm headin' out thataway, ma'am," said the third man, who had not yet spoken. "Drew's my neighbor. Mine's the spread just yonder o' his'n. If you'd be likin' a ride, my wagon's got a heap o' spare room. I just have to load up my supplies here from Jeb, then I'm on my way."

"Why, thank you. Thank you all," said Maggie. "That's very kind of you. Yes, I would like a ride."

Warmed by the genuine hospitality of the three men, Maggie enjoyed the fifteen-minute ride on the bumpy wagon. Her host pointed out all the landmarks he deemed interesting, and by the time he drew rein on his plow horse at the gate to the Mackinaw place, Maggie felt she knew almost as much about the little farming village of Chatham, New York, as she did about her own Port Strathy. When he drew the horses to a stop she descended, thanking him again, and with a carpet bag in one hand and smaller parcels under each arm, Maggie approached the house.

The farmhouse was not exactly what she had anticipated. She had half expected every dwelling in America to resemble the drawing of the one-room log cabin she had seen in a book one of her childhood tutors had shown her. Instead, the four-room house was constructed from rough-hewn pine, whitewashed and trimmed with brown around the windows. A dozen chickens pecked about in the yard, scattering wildly in all directions as she walked up. Besides the house and barn, there were two or three smaller outbuildings. Had she been able to identify them, she would have known them as a chicken coop, a smokehouse, and a woodshed. Though she knew absolutely nothing about American farming, by Scottish standards at least, humble as the dwelling was, it appeared to be a farm with plentiful provision. In addition to the chickens, Maggie caught evidence of cows, goats, and a few pigs as well. She could not help but compare this sturdy house with the poor one on Braenock Ridge Drew had been born in. It certainly seemed the elder Mackinaw had benefited from his move.

The only train to Chatham came in midafternoon two days a week, and Drew was out in the fields when Maggie arrived. All Maggie's last-minute fears of intruding were quickly dispelled by the greeting she received from Ellie Mackinaw, Drew's wife.

After Maggie's awkward attempt to explain why a stranger was standing on her front porch with bags in hand, the light suddenly seemed to dawn on Ellie's face.

"All the way from Scotland!" she exclaimed. "Why . . . I don't believe— but how . . . ?" she stammered through beaming eyes that sparkled with all the welcome Maggie needed. She placed a strong, loving hand around Maggie's shoulder and drew her inside while Maggie attempted to explain the circumstances as best she could. Ellie's immediate warmth reminded Maggie of Bess Mackinaw, and she could not help noting the coincidence that Drew had married a woman so like his own mother. But the comparison between this American housewife and the mother-in-law she had never seen ended with their warm personalities. Unlike the large-framed, plain-looking Bess, Ellie was short and plump. Soft blue eyes highlighted a pretty face, with creamy skin and full lips that never ceased either smiling or laughing. Ellie had been raised but twenty miles on the other side of the Hudson, high in the Catskill mountains, and was as thoroughly American as Maggie was Scottish.

Immediately Ellie began preparations to find a place for Maggie in their home. The four rooms were spacious, to be sure, but with five children, ranging in age from three to nine, living quarters were already tight. Conscious of Maggie's uncertainty, Ellie simply laughed and said, "Why, with five young'uns running about, you're a gift right from the Lord!"

The home was snug and warm despite the gathering signs of approaching winter. The large potbellied cookstove was the hub of household activity where Ellie spent a good portion of her time. The kitchen opened into a huge room containing a table, a great stone hearth where a fire would be blazing later in the evening, a bench which sat under the only window, and three rockers.

"The children sit on the floor, me and Drew each sit in one of the rockers, and the other one's for a guest," Ellie explained with a smile. "If there's more'n one guest, we make do some other way."

One by one the children made their appearance: Bess, 7, and Darren, 5, from their chores outside; the two older boys, Bobby, 9, and Tommy Joe, 8, home from school; and finally little three-year-old Sarah, wandering in sleepily from her afternoon nap.

Despite her protests against displacing Bobby and Tommy, a little loft above one of the bedrooms was prepared for Maggie's sleeping quarters. The two boys were eager for the opportunity to sleep out in the barn and ran out excitedly to begin their boyish preparations.

When Drew walked in just after sunset, his welcome may have been less exuberant than his wife's, but in no way would it be called less sincere. He was a large hulk of a man with red hair and beard. Young wiry Stevie flashed through Maggie's mind, and she wondered if she were seeing a vision of what he would look like as a full grown man. In many ways Drew resembled old Hector. Quiet and reserved like his father, it seemed to require the greatest part of his bodily energy simply to keep his large frame in motion. And like Hector, Drew was a compassionate man of few words. Had Maggie known of his widespread local reputation for never turning his back on a man or woman or child in any kind of trouble, she would never have spent a moment worrying about her reception into this big man's home.

Maggie's report of Bess Mackinaw's death was the first of it they had heard. Observing the reaction of her loving son, Maggie could not keep herself from weeping. As the color drained from his ruddy cheeks, at first he merely stared blankly ahead, the knuckles of his hand turning white as they gripped the arms of his wooden chair. Back and forth he slowly rocked. The only sound in the somber room was the gentle creaking of the chair on the hardwood floor.

He had known when he had left Scotland that it was unlikely he would ever see any of his family again in this life, and his struggling faith often doubted whether he would see them in the next. Therefore, when the news came, his human heart was torn. At length he heaved himself up and walked outside without a word. Whether he wept or not, no one would ever know. But when he returned an hour later, his voice was husky and strained.

"I'm glad ye were wi' her, my leddy," said Drew. "It means a lot t' be able t' talk wi' one who was there at the last. I'm happy that now we can see our way t' do ye a small favor in return. Although just havin' ye here in our home is a great pleasure fer us all!"

"I need nothing in return," Maggie replied. "It was a privilege to be with her. She was a special woman. But if there is any other favor I could ask of you, it would be that you simply call me Maggie, and not *my lady.*"

"But ye be a leddy, aren't ye, an' not folk like us?"

"This is America, and I am no different than anyone else. I left Scotland and any claim to title behind. In fact, while I am under your roof, it is you who are the master."

The grief seemed to have done its work, and the sorrow had passed. Drew laughed, so deep it rumbled like a roll of thunder.

"Hoots!" he said. "Wouldn't my auld daddy get a chuckle out o' that? His son a laird o'er a Duncan!"

"I'll stay under no other condition," Maggie persisted.

"Well," he agreed at length, "let's just say we are equal an' leave it at that. An' I'll try t' call ye Maggie."

"The Lord is the only master we need in this house, anyway," added Ellie buoyantly.

Her husband tossed her a curious glance as if to say, "Not now, dear." Then he threw another log on the fire and stood staring as it crackled into bright orange flames. Maggie wondered if perhaps Drew had abandoned the faith of his parents when he came to America. But she took no time to dwell on the thought, for it seemed enough that he was warm and kind and had welcomed her, a stranger, into the home of his family with open arms.

Now, three weeks after her arrival, Maggie was jolted from her reverie by the scamper of a light-footed young deer across the fresh meadow of snow. She gave a sigh and turned her eyes from the kitchen window back into the house. Thanks to Ellie's open heart and Drew's generosity, she had been made to feel as much at home as could be expected under the circumstances. The gentle snowflakes again began to fall and the sound of rising activity indicated that breakfast was nearly at hand. *I wonder what Ian is doing now,* Maggie wondered. But of course, he was on the ship. There were only two weeks yet to wait. She hoped he didn't get seasick. But no matter, she would take care of him when he arrived!

"Child," called out Ellie's voice into the midst of her thoughts. "Watching won't make the snow stop, nor make your man get here one day sooner. Besides, the ship will float along with or without the snow."

Maggie turned and smiled. "You read my thoughts, Ellie."

"Well, I know you're thinking of that husband of yours most of the time!" Ellie chuckled.

"But my daydreaming certainly isn't helping much with breakfast, is it?"

"Never you mind about that," said Ellie. "You'll still be our guest, for a little while yet. But if you really want something to do, you can help little Bess with the dishes. They're a mite too heavy for her to carry."

Maggie lifted the stack of plates the youngster was attempting to carry and took them over to the table. Bess, a pale, willowy child of seven, followed with the flatware. The girl's hair was deep auburn like Maggie's; perhaps it was this similarity that had drawn her to their visitor from Scotland. Since Maggie's arrival Bess had been her shadow, following her everywhere. She was a quiet child, her large eyes ever attentive.

As the two set the table, Ellie busily hovered around the cookstove. Suddenly a sharp crackle set the kitchen ablaze with sound as she tossed a handful of bacon ends into a large cast-iron skillet. The fragrance of frying bacon filled the room, but as the pleasing aroma drifted past it had just the opposite effect it was meant to. The same awful nausea she had experienced on the ship assailed her. She threw her hand over her mouth and dashed outside into the snow. A few moments later, pale and trembling, she returned.

"Good heavens, child!" exclaimed Ellie with a questioning look on her face.

"I must not be quite over the seasickness," Maggie said weakly.

Scrutinizing her, Ellie momentarily forgot the bacon. Then, catching a whiff of burning edges, she quickly returned her attention to the stove, stirred the bacon in the rising grease, then removed it from the heat. Finally she wiped her hands on her apron.

"Maggie," she said, "I doubt that's seasickness."

"What do you mean?"

"When was it you and Ian were married?"

Puzzled, Maggie answered, "About two months ago."

"Dear girl!" Ellie grinned. "You're—"

She stopped suddenly.

"Boys!" she called to her sons who were in the next room. "Go out and tell your pa breakfast is ready."

"All of us?" nine-year-old Bobby protested.

"Yes, all of you. Now scat!"

The three boys grabbed up their coats and marched obediently from the house.

Ellie approached Maggie, took her hand, and led her to a chair at the table. Still grinning from ear to ear, she seemed hardly able to contain the excitement which had suddenly risen within her.

"Dear," she began, "have you ever considered that you may be—in the family way?"

"Family way?" Maggie repeated.

"You know . . . with *child!*"

Unable to keep calm a moment longer, Ellie giggled as if she were a girl again and threw her arms about Maggie's neck.

Bewildered, Maggie sat as if in a trance. The thought of being pregnant had never so much as crossed her mind. She tried to open her mouth to speak, but words refused to come. Instead, she felt tears rising in her eyes.

"Why, Maggie," laughed Ellie, "you're going to have Ian's baby!"

Now came the tears in earnest, to both women. And Maggie would not have stopped them even if she could. Her womanly instincts knew that Ellie was right, and she let the tears of joy flow, for this was the first moment of real joy she had felt since she and Ian had been together.

Ellie slackened her embrace, sat back, and smiled radiantly at Maggie.

"I'm so happy for you!" she beamed. "There's nothing more wonderful for a woman—and I should know!"

"Oh, I wonder what Ian will think," said Maggie.

"He'll be delighted," assured Ellie. "What a wonderful gift for you to present to him when he arrives!"

They laughed again, then Ellie said, "Now let's figure out when you're going to be due."

Maggie provided the knowledgeable wife the necessary information, then Ellie spent a few moments counting on her fingers, and finally announced, "July!" Then she added as an afterthought, "Maybe your first child will be born on the Fourth of July—the birthday of our country. That would make him a true American baby!"

Beaming as if the child-to-be were her own, Ellie could hardly keep from sharing her great practical wisdom, and for the first time could see a hint of happiness shining in Maggie's eyes—eyes which till this day had always seemed haunted and sad. Feeling well-satisfied with the turn of the day, Ellie rose and continued with her breakfast chores, singing softly the verses of "Rock of Ages."

Maggie remained at the table in a contented daze. The nausea had passed for the time, and suddenly she felt Ian's presence with her in a way she hadn't since their painful parting on the dock. The words *first child* echoed in her mind. She and Ian would have such a wonderful life here with their children! For the first time since leaving Scotland the hope of a new life seemed actually possible. This life around her seemed so inviting; how could even the title of marquise compare to it? Maybe she and Ian would even out-do the Mackinaws and have six or seven "young'uns" of their own. Lots of children and a cozy farm like this . . . with Ian beside her in his own oak rocker. It was all Maggie had wanted and yearned for.

10
Giles Kellermann

☘

THE MAN STOOD gazing out his large picture window over the expansive valley of green farmland. On a clear day the slowly moving Hudson River could just be seen in the distance to the west. In the other direction an afternoon's ride on horseback brought him to the Massachusetts border. It was good land, he thought, and he had done well for himself. It would not be long before he owned a great deal more of it. His name was already prominent in Columbia Country, and if this drought continued another year his dream of occupying a position in Albany's legislature could become a reality. He would by then hold power over a large financial base of prime land. And what he didn't want to keep for himself, he would resell for a handsome profit.

He could hardly believe his good fortune. When he had begun diverting some of his investment capital into mortgages for local farmers, his goal had merely been the high interest he was able to receive on notes for their farms and equipment. Too poor to obtain loans from any bank in the area, many immigrants had seen his Mortgage Company as a way for them to expand, get new tools and equipment, and plant new crops they wouldn't have been able to afford otherwise. Times had been plentiful, hopes ran high, and even though the 7% interest of his terms was almost double the 4¼% being offered by the banks in Hudson, Albany, and Catskill, most of these people had no collateral with which to secure financing any other way than with him. He required no cash investment on the part of the farmers, as the banks did. The poor were more than willing to place whatever they had—homes, livestock, acreage, future profits on crops— on the line in exchange for capital to expand.

But with the drought the bottom had fallen out, and one by one the local farmers had been forced to the painful realization that their visions of prosperity had been only dreams.

A tentative knock on the door to his office interrupted his reverie. He turned, walked across the floor, and opened it. There stood a farmer in his faded blue dungarees with suspenders, plaid workshirt, and heavy worn boots. "I brung you the wagon, Mr. Kellermann," he said with his hat held between both hands. Seeing no response on the face of the man opposite him, he nervously went on, "It's out back. I unhitched the team. But I got t' keep them oxen, Mr. Kellermann. Surely you kin understand. I got t' have 'em or I can't nohow plow my fields."

"Yes, yes, of course, I understand, Homer," said the other, finally speaking but revealing no other sign of communication. "As we agreed, you have another month before the oxen are—well, you understand."

"Yes, sir! And don't you worry, I'll have the money by then. Yes, sir, I'll git it sure!"

"Good, Homer. That's just fine. Now you give my best to your wife."

He closed the door and the farmer slowly walked outside, untied the team of two oxen where they stood at the side of the building, and let them home on foot.

Inside, Kellermann watched Homer Wilson through the window. He didn't like to have to repossess something as small as the poor man's wagon. But business was business, and Wilson was already two payments behind. He could never allow word to get out that he was soft.

At length he went to his desk and sat down. Giles Kellermann carried a frame of average height with dark brown hair, tinged with gray. His build, in his younger days, would have been termed stocky. But the life of comparative ease with which he had accustomed himself had turned him soft, and now instead of athletic he simply had the appearance of one comfortably overweight.

But what arrested one's attention more than his build was the piercing look of his face. His deep-set dark eyes were surrounded by a firm, square face; his mouth, on the rare occasions when it lent itself to a smile, seemed to resist every movement of the exercise. The natural resting place of the facial muscles set the wide mouth and strong chin in a perpetual look of hard-boiled offense. Whether this stern visage, with just a hint of cunning about the corners of the lips, had been physically inherited or had been acquired through years of practice as a crafty businessman would have been difficult to determine.

Kellermann had started his investments in the financial centers of Boston. But competing with men older, wiser, and more unscrupulous than himself had proved too upsetting for his vanity. Realizing he could achieve his ends to greater purpose where he held a superior advantage over those he had to deal with, he migrated westward, working for a brokerage firm in Albany for a time. A brief sojourn south a few years ago had alerted him to the unlimited possibilities for gain among the farming community. When he settled here in Chatham, his coming had at first been viewed by the inhabitants as a godsend. But with the failure of the crops two years ago, they first began to realize how much power they had foolishly given him. By then, of course, it was too late, the documents had been signed.

Another knock on the door followed, but this time the door opened without waiting for Kellermann's answer.

Glancing up, the businessman's face broke, not into a smile, but at least into a sign of recognition.

"Oh, it's you, Harry. What did you find out?"

"Old man Simpson doesn't have a cent to his name. It looks like we'll be moving on his place next month."

"Good! Add it to the auction list. I want to get that list of properties over to Albany by next week. There are some prized plums on it this time. We should get handsome prices. What about the widow Rodman up in New Lebanon?"

"She paid me. Everything, in fact. Two months back interest, and next month's besides."

"Blast it! How'd she come up with that kind of money?"

"Rumor had it some of her friends chipped in. They're really upset around there. They hate us. There's talk of banding together."

"Let the clodhoppers talk!" said Kellermann. "There's nothing any of them can do. They signed the deeds over to me and if they don't pay, the law's with us. By the way, Homer Wilson was by to leave his wagon."

"Fine," said his associate. "I'll take care of it."

"You know I don't like dealing with these people face-to-face, Harry. I don't want you to let this kind of thing happen again."

"I'm sorry. I was going out to Homer's for the wagon this afternoon. I suppose he thought bringing it here himself might make us more sympathetic about his oxen."

"Yes, he did mention them. And I can be as sympathetic as the next guy, as long as he keeps up the payments on his loan. And what about that Scottish fellow?"

"Mackinaw?"

"Yes, Mackinaw."

"He has some time left."

"But what does it look like?"

"He's not doing well. His should fall in time, like the others."

"Good. That farm of his is a choice piece. I want it. And I'd like to get rid of him anyway. That phony accent of his drives me crazy. He's been nothing but a nuisance, always taking people in, trying to help them. It goes against what we're trying to do. Things will run a lot more smoothly when he's gone."

"They've just brought in someone else from what I hear."

"Who?" asked Kellermann.

"I don't know," answered Harry. "I'll try to find out. Someone said it was a noble lady from Scotland."

"Just so long as she doesn't get any ideas about making his payments for him. Find out what you can, Harry. We need to be ahead of him on this. We can't take any chances on getting his acreage."

"I'll see what I can find out. In the meantime, I think it might be a good idea for you to talk with him, sir."

"Why?"

"I've been out there a few times, for payments, half-payments, and so on. He's none too cordial with me."

"You expect him to be cordial when we're about to repossess his farm?"

"The folks hereabouts don't like me none too much since I went to work for you, Mr. Kellermann."

"Do you want to be liked or rich, Harry?"

"I just think Mackinaw could be a problem, if it gets into his mind to challenge you. He's pretty highly thought of. He could raise the rest of the folks around here. So I thought if you talked to him—firmly and decisively—it might lay any ideas he might have to rest. I think he'd be afraid of you if you really laid it down to him."

"I understand, Harry. I'll talk to him and we'll make him see the futility of trying to fight us on this. He either pays or he's off the land."

11

The Long-Awaited Day

❈

I T W A S A L L Maggie could do to still herself long enough for Ellie to offer thanks for the breakfast.

". . . and now, Lord," Ellie was praying, "we ask that you watch over us while we travel down to the big city, and bless Drew and the children till we get back. And thank you, Lord, for your bounty and provision in this food you have given us. Amen."

The day had finally come!

Somehow the interminable weeks had passed; now it seemed it had not been so long after all! And in one hour she and Ellie would board the train which would take her to New York and—

Oh, the thought was too wonderful!

"I declare, Maggie, you're in another world!" laughed Ellie.

"I know," beamed Maggie. "I'm sorry. I just can't concentrate on anything else. I've forgotten everything you've said these last couple days and—"

"No need to apologize, dear. We all understand. We're excited about Ian's coming, too. Have you considered Allen Smith's offer of his springhouse for the two of you?"

"Oh, yes," Maggie replied. "I'm sure it would be perfect. It's so kind of him."

"Nothin' fancy," Drew added, "I mean, fer the likes o' ye an' yer gentleman husband. 'Tis a rough-hewn place."

"It's just what we want, Drew. We've left the other life behind us. I only wish," she added, a serious look crossing her face for the first time, "I only wish you would be here to share our new life with us."

Ellie glanced toward Maggie, then quickly away and down at the floor. Drew also said nothing. It was clear the subject Maggie had opened was a painful one to both of them.

"'Tis fer the best, Maggie. We have no choice," said Drew.

"Oh, Drew," said Ellie, almost in a pleading tone, "we could manage, we could find a new place. My family would—"

"Ellie," interrupted Drew, "I know how ye're feelin', but I thought all that was settled."

"It is," replied Ellie with a submissive sigh.

"I've told ye before," Drew went on, but the firmness in his voice was touched with his own uncertainty, "that I dinna want handouts from yer family. If we can't keep up the mortgage on the place, 'tis best we move on. An' ye know as well as I that old Kellermann's been lookin' fer a way t' get the place back from us."

"I know, but it just seems that there must be something—"

"I've been t' the bank down t' Hudson, an' everyone in Chatham's in the same fix as us. It's jist been a poor two years an' there's nothin' more we can do aboot it."

The remainder of the meal continued in subdued silence with only the sound of the chattering of three-year-old Sarah, who was oblivious to the vague tension about the table. As soon as breakfast was over everyone scurried in different directions. Ellie remained subdued and Drew went outside to bring the wagon around for the short trip to town.

"I'm sorry, Maggie," Ellie said at last, "for spoiling your special day."

"Nothing can spoil it, Ellie," Maggie replied, gently stroking little Bess's hair; the girl had shyly sidled up for a farewell hug. "But," she went on, "if there's anything I can do . . . I mean if you think you ought to stay here, I can go to New York—"

"No," Ellie answered quickly. "This is the best thing for me. There's no way I could sleep knowin' you were off on that train in that huge city by yourself." She sighed. "Besides," she added, "a couple days away will be good for me, give me a chance to think. And this is somethin' I have to work out for myself, I suppose. The Scriptures talk about a woman leavin' her kin to become one with her husband. Maybe it's a choice all women have to face some time or other. And maybe this is my time."

"Moving west you mean?"

"I knew it was comin'. He's been a wantin' to go west since he set foot on this land. Then he married me, and I kept gettin' in the family way. I had two stillbirths besides these five. Well, he kept puttin' it off, an' then we got this here little farm, which was a good thing them first few years. And he kept puttin' it off and puttin' if off, but I knew it was always on his mind. Then these last two years were so bad. The crops nearly failed completely and all the smaller farms around these parts are in trouble. Drew tried to keep it up. He worked hard, fourteen hours a day, and he tried to find money to keep up our payments on the place."

Ellie paused and sighed, then rushed on, "But when there's no rain and when you've got little mouths to feed, sometimes there just ain't much a body can do. I see the strain on his face. I know he's just trying to do what's best. And he has his pride as a man, too. I try to be a good Christian wife—but my whole family's here, and we're awful close, and I sometimes think I can't bear to leave. I might never see 'em again."

She stopped and glanced away and Maggie felt the tears she could not see. She set Bess down and stretched out her hand to Ellie's shoulder.

"But listen to me!" said Ellie after a moment, wiping her eyes with her sleeve and forcing a smile. "That's exactly what you did, isn't it? Why, *you* are the good Christian wife."

"It was much different for us," replied Maggie wistfully. "We had little choice."

"But still, you did it."

"It wasn't easy for me either, Ellie. Leaving to follow your husband can't be easy for any woman when she's got to leave her family and home behind. And here I had to leave *without* my husband," she laughed, trying to lighten the mood. "But the wait's almost over!"

"Your trial's nearly past; mine's just beginnin'," said Ellie.

"But when the time comes you will be strong for it. And perhaps something will happen . . . maybe Drew will find a way for you to stay."

"I don't know, Maggie. It's gone so far now I think there's no turnin' back. I can see the far-off look in his eyes. He's saddened by the turn of things here. But at the same time I can tell he's buildin' with excitement about what may lie for us west somewhere. California and Oregon—that's all he and Evan McCollough seem to talk about anymore. Evan's got picture books of how it is. And he says the ground there is so rich anybody can grow anythin' they like."

"And you think it's certain, then?"

"Might as well be. All we're waitin' on is to find out the *when*. Mr. Kellermann was by the place two days ago. I saw him and Drew talking out in the fields. Drew, he didn't say nothin' about it later. But I could see it on his face. I knew it was all settled."

Just then the sound of the wagon interrupted their voices. As Drew brought the horse up to a stop in front of the house, the four older children ran outside and scampered up into the large flatbed. Drew jumped down, picked up little Sarah and set her up. Lastly he offered Maggie his hand, then Ellie, and in a few moments the seven Mackinaws and their new friend from the old country were on their way into Chatham to meet the New York Central on its way south.

"Maybe the two o' ye will be wantin' to come west wi' us," said Drew, trying to make conversation. "That's where the opportunities in America are now, they say."

"I don't know, Drew," replied Maggie. "I don't want to get too far from New York. You know, we're going to want to return to Scotland someday, after . . ." Her voice trailed off and she fell silent.

"After what?" asked Ellie.

"It's a long story," replied Maggie. "Let's just say we won't be able to return for some time. But after a few years, hopefully it will all have blown over by then and it will be safe to go back."

No one felt inclined to pursue the conversation further, and the rest of the ride into Chatham was dominated by the sounds of the five happy children in the back of the wagon.

12

New York

ALL MAGGIE WOULD ever remember of that train trip was its length. When she had taken it a month ago, it hadn't been slow enough. She had blankly stared out the window, neither noticing nor caring as they passed through Jersey City, Rockland, Newburgh, Poughkeepsie, and Hudson. Now the south-bound train could not move fast enough, and the miles seemed endless.

They did not arrive until late afternoon, as dusk was starting to descend on the great metropolis. The ship was not scheduled to arrive until the following morning and the two women stayed at the boarding house where Maggie had spent her first night in America, close to both the train station and the harbor, a four-story brownstone on Vanguard Street. The stairs creaked as they climbed to the second floor behind the tall, austere figure of the elderly landlady.

"She reminds me of an old teacher I once had," giggled Ellie once they were alone in their room. "You couldn't blink without her knowing it. And believe me, you didn't try!"

"I'm so glad you came with me," said Maggie. "Somehow the city isn't quite so intimidating with someone to share it with."

"Do you suppose," asked Ellie, "that we could have a look around the city after we meet Ian? I've only been here once before, and I was only ten. We have to wait till day after tomorrow for the train north, anyway."

"Oh, that would be fun," agreed Maggie. "But to tell you the truth, all I can think of now is seeing him again!"

"I know. Perhaps he will want to stay here a little longer. He's from London, didn't you say?"

"Yes."

"Well, the big city won't be anything new to him. He might want to wait until the train four days from now. You know how men are—sometimes they're attracted by all the lights and bustle of a city."

"What about the children?"

"Drew'll be fine. Besides, didn't I tell you? My mother's comin' over for a visit, and to help him out a bit. And maybe I'll just go back to Chatham myself and let you and Ian be alone."

"Oh, Ellie!" said Maggie. "Stop teasing!"

"Come now, child, I remember what it was like bein' just married!"

"Your Drew is a good man," said Maggie. "You must feel very fortunate."

"Yes, I do," replied Ellie with a long sigh. "Only it's such a heartache to me that he can't bring himself to share my faith."

"What? He's such a kind man. I assumed . . ."

"Drew's a good man. The best. And he accepts my faith in God just fine. Down in his heart I know he believes. There's somethin' gnawin' at him that keeps him from bein' able to accept it fully. But his day will come."

"I'm surprised," said Maggie. "If only you could have known his mother. She positively radiated her love of God."

"Oh," exclaimed Ellie joyfully, "that's so wonderful to hear! Drew doesn't talk much about his family."

"It was Bess Mackinaw who got me really thinking about spiritual things. She and our old groom, Digory."

"Maggie, you don't know what that means to me, to know that Drew comes from a godly background like that. I pray for him, of course. But that helps me know that somewhere down inside he must believe. The Word says, you know, that when children are raised in the faith they won't depart from it. Who knows but maybe that's why the Lord's wantin' us to be movin' west. Maybe a change like that's what's needed to rekindle his faith."

Maggie found herself touched by her new friend's openness. Would she understand if Maggie told her about her own father? As they dressed for bed, twice she opened her mouth to try to share some of her own feelings and uncertainties, but each time found that she could not make a beginning. The words, along with the painful resentments of the past, remained locked inside. Perhaps when she and Ian were finally together—maybe then all the hurts would finally heal. Maybe she would be able to forget what her father had done, once she and her husband were out of his reach forever.

Only a few hours left to wait! Maggie thought.

A flurry of light snow fell on New York during the night, and when the two women woke, the dingy city streets were covered with a thin layer of purity. Maggie sprang out of the old four-poster feather bed as if she hadn't slept at all. Ellie yawned, stretched to her full length, and lay back again, thinking what a change it was not to have to get up, stoke the fire, prepare breakfast, change a diaper, or dress children.

"Oh, this *is* nice!" she groaned sleepily as she rolled back over on her pillow.

"No more sleep, Ellie," said Maggie cheerfully. "This is the day!"

"You're right. And I suppose I ought to go downstairs to help that dour old landlady prepare breakfast."

"Ellie!" Maggie laughed. "This may not be an expensive hotel, but even in a boarding house like this they do those things for you. Have a bath instead."

"A bath! They charge extra for that."

"This is New York, Ellie! How many chances do you get to do something like this? I'll pay for the bath. Enjoy yourself!"

Reluctantly Ellie complied.

"That was the most wonderful bath I've ever had," she said as they sat down to breakfast, "except for when I was a kid up in the swimmin' hole on Gorsett's Creek. Just think, I didn't have to hurry so one of the kids could use the water."

"Mine was nice too," said Maggie, "but rather cold."

"All we try to do is take a little of the chill off," said the landlady, who had overheard the last of the conversation. "And that's only for the women. Men have to wash in the cold as best they can. Can you imagine the cost of providing *hot* baths!"

Sheepishly Maggie glanced toward Ellie and grinned.

"You look so nice," said Ellie. "Ian won't be able to keep his eyes off you. You're just beautiful today."

Maggie had been relieved when she awoke to find that most of the wrinkles had fallen out of the navy blue taffeta she had hung up as soon as they had arrived. The dress was so plain despite its pearl buttons. She thought of all her lovely dresses back in her wardrobe in Scotland. But they had left in such haste, there had only been time to pack three. And these had to be practical and versatile; there was no room for the colorful silks and satins with their yards of lace and ruffles. She had wanted to buy a new dress for this important occasion, but she knew she and Ian were going to have to conserve their money in order to make a start in America. Besides, there weren't many fancy dresses to be found in the rural shops in Chatham or any of the nearby villages. This taffeta was her best, and might have to remain so for a long time.

"Thank you, Ellie," Maggie replied with a smile.

"Before long you'll be havin' to borrow some of my dresses," giggled Ellie. "That is, when your young'un starts pushin' out."

"I appreciate the offer, Ellie, but I'm glad I'm not showing just yet. I want to look my best for Ian."

"Oh, child! Do you think he'll care what you look like? Remember, he's been countin' the days just like you." Then she added brightly, "But you do look lovely, just the same!"

After breakfast they informed the landlady that they would need a second room when they returned that evening. Then they opened the door and walked out into the glistening sunlight of the new day. The thin snow cover and the clear, wintery brightness could not have matched the exuberant mood of Maggie's heart more perfectly.

"Oh, it's a glorious day!" she exclaimed.

Travel through the streets, however, was slow. Twice the hired carriage nearly skidded out of control on the icy streets, and thereafter the driver refused to listen to Maggie's urgent appeals to hurry.

"Look, lady," he said, "I take people down to the dock all the time, and I tell you that ship don't arrive till 11 o'clock."

"But I don't want to be late," Maggie insisted.

"Late! You got almost two hours before those passengers are even going to see the harbor."

Maggie said nothing more, thinking instead of the kindness of the driver she had had on her first day in New York a month earlier.

At last the shipyards came into sight. The streets here were so alive with activity that the snow had been long since trampled away. The driver obviously knew the harbor well, waving greetings to other carriage drivers and directing his horse straight to the pier where the great steamer, *H.M.S. Fairgate*, was expected from London.

"Well, if that don't beat all!" exclaimed the driver. "There she is heading in already."

Maggie looked in the direction he pointed. To her great excitement she could see the ship in the distance. By the time they had reached the roped-off waiting area, the ship had covered half the remaining distance and was already beginning the gradual turn which would end as the captain maneuvered her gently into the waiting slip.

Anxiously Maggie scanned the faces onboard. The passengers crowded about the railings, as eager to get off the ship as Maggie had been to meet it, but she could not find Ian among them. It took nearly another hour for the dock hands and ship's crew to make the *Fairgate* secure. Frantically Maggie continued her visual search, but there were so many faces.

At long last the gangplank was slowly lowered, and in a surge of bodies the passengers made their way onto land. Maggie and Ellie found themselves nearly smothered in the confusion. Customs officials ushered the great rush of humanity into narrow roped-off lines and began the tedious process of checking each one's papers. Some were allowed to go their way quickly. The greater number, however, those who had come third or fourth class, were subject to close scrutiny, disinfection, even de-licing. Maggie knew that Ian would be holding a second-class ticket, as she had, and concentrated her attention on those who were passed through customs most hurriedly.

One by one, men and women passed by, and the growing uneasiness became more and more apparent on her face. Once or twice she cast an apprehensive glance toward Ellie. The older woman tried to remain calm, returning Maggie's pleading looks with as much calm and reassurance as she could muster. But inside she could not ignore her own concern, visibly mirrored on Maggie's panic-stricken face.

Finally, after more than an hour, the gangplank was empty. In a frenzy of agitation Maggie turned this way and that, scanning the ship with the imploring eyes of a caged animal.

"Oh, Ellie!" she cried, "I'm—I'm so afraid. I don't—"

"Best go speak to one of the men on the ship," said Ellie with measured calm. "I'll go ask him if you like."

"No," replied Maggie. "I can manage. But come with me, please."

Desperately hoping that Ian had been somehow detained on board and would any moment wander from somewhere within the ship with the other laggers who one by one were disembarking, Maggie and Ellie tentatively approached the ship, walked up the steep gangplank onto the deck.

"Hoy, ladies," hollered out a crusty voice with heavy Irish accent. Maggie turned to see a grizzled sailor with a deep scar across his forehead. "Ready t' set sail again, are ye?" He laughed good-humoredly, but it did little to ease her anxiety. His banter was joined by several of his shipmates before being abruptly cut short by a commanding voice approaching behind Maggie and Ellie.

"All right, you lubbers!" it snapped. "Any more of that sort of rudeness and I'll dock your pay. Now get back to your chores!"

Recognizing the voice, Maggie turned quickly.

"Captain Sievers! I didn't expect to see you!"

"We made good time on the return voyage, Lady Duncan, after we left you in New York. The Captain of the *Fairgate* took sick, so I filled in for him, turned right back around, and here I am."

"Oh, I'm so glad you are," said Maggie, seeming to suddenly remember why she was here. "I'm here to meet my husband, Captain. He's supposed to be on the ship, but I haven't been able to find him."

"Well, my lady, give me a name and I'll check the roster," he replied. "You're sure it was this ship?"

"Yes . . . well, this was the day I thought he was to arrive. You've taken on the passengers from Aberdeen, haven't you?"

"Aye, just as when you made the voyage."

"Then he has to be here."

"Let me check the list—what was the name?"

"Theodore Duncan—perhaps Ian Duncan."

The captain turned, disappeared for about ten minutes, then returned carrying a sheaf of papers. The frown on his face revealed the news Maggie had dreaded to hear. She could not even bring herself to ask the question.

"I'm sorry, Lady Duncan," he said.

"Ellie, could he possibly have got past us? There were so many passengers."

But then without waiting for an answer, she turned again to the captain. "Did you check the entire list? Maybe he was in steerage."

"I hardly think so, my lady."

"He could be!" returned Maggie sharply, forgetting the captain's kindness.

Sievers checked the list once more, then shook his head.

"You must have missed his name! He *has* to be there. I'm going to look—I know he's here!"

In tears Maggie pulled herself away from Ellie and began running along the deck of the ship.

"My lady! Please . . . Lady Duncan!" the captain called out after her. But Maggie was heedless of his voice. Ellie attempted to follow her, to calm and comfort her. But it was no use.

Hysterically Maggie ran along the deck, then inside and along the inside corridors of the ship, toward the kitchen, then to the sick bay. Weeping she ran, calling out his name between choking sobs, "Ian . . . Ian . . . please—please be here!"

At last, exhausted and broken, Maggie slumped to the floor in the middle of a deserted hallway on the second deck, and—still weeping—murmured the words, "Oh, Ian . . . Ian—where are you?"

It was there Ellie and the captain found her some time later, still on the floor, weeping and calling out Ian's name in a barely audible voice. Gently Ellie eased her to her feet and led her off the ship and home.

13

Incommunicado

✴

SOMEHOW HE HAD to keep the panic from overpowering him. He couldn't lose his grip on reality.

Ian jumped to his feet and once again began pacing the tiny cell. It was cold and dark, and the ancient stones indicated that he was being held in some massive city prison of great age. He supposed it was Glasgow but had no way to be certain. What did it matter where he was, anyway? He was not on board the ship, and that is all Maggie would know. Somewhere around this time—but how could he keep track of the passage of days and weeks?—she would go to New York expecting to meet him.

God, he thought, *I've got to get out of here! Maggie will think I've deserted her!*

He paced for a few more minutes, then sat down again on the floor. He had been here only two days. But he could not escape the growing obsession of panic which threatened to master him. All he could think of was Maggie in New York, waiting . . . waiting.

For three or four weeks they had held him in Aberdeen. He had seen no living soul other than the jailer. At first he had been angry. Then he had grown morose and despondent. But as the days passed into weeks it finally began to dawn on him that he was in serious trouble which could well keep him from Maggie. The time dragged by slowly and there was no word, no sign of release, no sign of a trial or official charges. No lawyer was sent to interview him or review his case. There was no sign of anything whatsoever! He had been allowed to send no communications to the outside—nothing!

Then one night four or five days ago something did happen. Two men came for him, dragged him from the jail and outside where a light rain was falling. How delicious the fresh air had tasted! But he had little time to enjoy it. Rudely they shoved him into the back of a carriage, his hands tied, and immediately took off into the night. Only minimal stops were made during the journey; each time he was given a new jug of water and half a loaf of dry bread. Sleeping while jostling about was impossible, but he did manage to doze off frequently.

The destination was reached in the dead of night. He heard voices he did not recognize talking outside in subdued tones. Then the carriage door was opened, he was pulled roughly outside, and with the words "We'll show ye how we takes care o' low-life aroun' here!" Ian was hauled into the great stone building, down several flights of stairs, and at last deposited in the tiny cell in which he now sat. From the length of the trip he judged himself in Glasgow. There was no window, and when the terror of his position overcame his attempt to remain calm, he was alternately seized by the cold sweat of dread or the hysterical desire to scream his way to freedom. But whenever the latter took hold, his voice echoed against the dull stone walls and fell again to silence, and Ian knew no living soul had even heard. He had been used to brief stints in London, but never in a place like this. There was an evil irony about this turn of events which did not look hopeful.

The sound of the jailer approaching from the end of the dark passageway interrupted his despondency. The decrepit old man was his only link with the world, and each time he heard the jangle of the guard's keys mingled with the faint shuffle of a leg that had gone lame, his spirits came to life. He leaped to his feet and pounded on the great, unyielding iron door.

"Get me out of here!" Ian shouted. "I'll do anything—I have money!"

"Ha!" replied the jailer with a cruel laugh as a key fumbled in the rusty lock. "I've heard that one afore, guv'nor. Ye tell me that every time I come an' I no more believe ye than t' think ye could fly through these walls. Now, get back against the wall so I can bring ye these fine victuals!"

The door swung open and the man slipped a tray in on the floor. Ian stormed toward him, kicked the tray, scattering the contents, and threw himself against the man. In other circumstances he would surely have overpowered such a one. But he had grown weak and his despair had not been accompanied by prudence. The wary jailer was experienced and cannily on his guard. He whisked the heavy cudgel from his side and swung it deftly at Ian's head. Ian fell senseless back against the wall.

"Now ye gone an' done it, ye rotter!" swore the man.

Still dazed from the blow, Ian felt himself being dragged toward the adjacent wall where a thick chain hung from an iron ring. He clasped the manacle around

Ian's wrist. "Why don't ye take t' some manners, yer lairdship! I got my orders t' keep ye chained as long as ye've a mind t' cause trouble!"

"Please!" Ian pleaded, coming to himself, "help me! For God's sake, at least let me have some paper to write a letter. No one knows I'm here."

"Oh, I'll help ye, guv'nor!" the man laughed, shoving the tray toward Ian with his foot. "There, enjoy yer supper! Ha! ha!" He turned to go, then called out after him, "Ask me fer help again, yer lairdship, when ye got some o' that money jinglin' in yer pocket! Ha! ha!"

The door slammed shut with a final metallic thud. Ian fell back on the dirty straw mattress, while a bold rat approached the sour oatmeal which had spilled on the floor.

As the days passed, Ian's body continued to weaken and his mind wandered. Often his imagination convinced him he was back in his own room in London and the crippled guard was his butler. More frequently he awoke to find himself calling out Maggie's name, having dreamed himself with her again in the little cottage near Fraserburgh. And each time his mind wandered, it was more difficult to pull himself back to reality. For whenever his wild-eyed countenance focused with renewed reality on the filth and squalor about him, and when his nose brought his senses fully awake to the stench of his own private dungeon, the horror of this utter helplessness nearly drove him mad.

Days, weeks passed. There was no change. There was no night or day, no light or darkness; only a pale glint of faded yellow from the candle-flame down the corridor seeped in through the small barred opening in his door. He lost all track of time. The guard came and went, bringing the nauseating provisions designed merely to keep him alive, of which the rats took more than their fair share. At length the iron wrist bar was removed and Ian accepted his newfound freedom with indifference. His body was depleted and his tormented brain plagued with forlorn thoughts of Maggie and his own impotence; more often than not the guard found him sitting in a heap in a corner, staring straight ahead into the darkness, mumbling incoherently.

Honor! He cursed the thought. What a fool he had been! If only he had gone with Maggie all this would never have happened. What an imbecile to think he could throw away the past and suddenly become an honorable man. Then the face of Maggie rose in the vision of his blurred consciousness. Her face was despairing, looking this way and that. As the vision faded in and out he could see her standing forlorn on a dock, peering toward an empty ship, looking, searching, tears of anguish streaming down her face. *Oh, Maggie! I never meant to put you through this. What will you do . . . can you ever forgive . . . Maggie, I'm still coming—don't desert me—Oh, Maggie, help me! Maggie . . . Maggie . . . I'm sorry—I'm so sorry!*

Guilt assailed him. Not only was he a stupid fool, he was a rogue, possibly even a murderer. He had killed Falkirk, and now he had ruined Maggie's life besides, forced her away from her homeland, her family, her inheritance, and from a marriage and a future with a gentleman. Perhaps she would have been happy with Falkirk. But he had ruined it all! What was honor to such a wretch as he? For so-called honor he had given up happiness and ruined lives besides.

Why did I send Maggie away! Why? Why . . .

The familiar sounds slowly penetrated his dazed brain. *Jingle . . . shuffle . . . shuffle . . . jingle . . . jingle . . .*

It was a sweet sound, a gentle sound. Soon his mother would be back in to tuck him in. She always set the little bell ringing in his room just before she came in to say good night. Usually with the ringing came a bedtime story, a special moment, for even his brother didn't often get one. He hardly needed it, with the attentions showered upon him by their father. Then when the story was over, she would pull the satin comforter over him and gently kiss his forehead. *Good night, my little Theodore . . . pleasant dreams . . .*

Jingle . . . jingle . . . shuffle.

The cell door creaked open. Ian looked up. The face standing over him wasn't his mother's. He couldn't quite remember . . . he had seen it someplace before . . . if only he could remember. *Mother . . . where are—Mother, won't you come back? I heard the little bell . . .*

"Don't ye know me by now, yer lairdship?" the face asked. It wasn't his mother's voice at all, but a gruff masculine one.

"Huh?" said Ian, staring blankly ahead.

"Ye're lookin' at me like ye never seed me afore."

"Get me out of here," said Ian dully, through the parting fog of reality.

"Same ol' story, eh, guv'nor?" stated the guard, shoving the tray toward him on the floor.

"At least tell me what day it is."

"Tuesday."

"The date," said Ian sleepily. "What is the date? When is my mother coming for me? She said she'd be back soon—"

"Yer mother!" roared the jailer. "That's a good one, guv'nor! But seein' as they call this the season o' good will an' all, I guess no harm could come o' tellin' ye. Mind ye, I'm breakin' strict orders, for we're s'posed t' tell ye nothin'. But if ye'll have it, why 'tis Christmas Eve!"

Ian started forward with a wild look in his eyes. The jailer jumped back, his hand instantly on the handle of his cudgel. But he did not have to use it. For just as suddenly Ian slumped back against the wall and slowly fell again to the floor.

"Oh, God, no!" he wailed, hardly aware that he had long since told himself he no longer believed in such a being.

"'Tis the season t' be jolly, yer lairdship!" mocked the guard.

With sudden energy, Ian grabbed the tray, which today in addition to the customary gruel and dried bread contained something resembling a slice of meat. He flung it at the man.

"There you go again! An' I was just about t' tell ye that if ye behaved yersel' I had instructions t' take ye up fer an airin' outside. Now ye can rot in this stinkin' miserable cell!"

Ian heard nothing of the jailer's words, nor did he even notice when the door clanged shut with the finality of death. He only heard the echoing ring of the words he had just heard.

Christmas Eve!

He and Maggie were to spend Christmas together. He had *promised* he would meet her. What must she think of his honor now that he had broken every vow he had made to her? Oh, the cruelty of this fate which seemed to be punishing him for trying to change his ways and start a new life! Now there was no way to tell her that he had meant every word, that he truly loved her. What futility lay ahead! *Oh, Maggie, what have I done to you? Can you ever forgive me? Will I ever see your smiling face again? Oh, gentle, sweet Maggie . . . I never meant to hurt you. I love you! Maggie, how I loved you! Oh, why did I do it, why did I send you away? What a fool I was . . . I didn't trust your love for me, and yet you went to a strange land because you trusted me. And now you are alone. I failed you, Maggie!*

Ian fell back against the stone wall, pressing his hands against his head. At length his eyes rested on the tray and the food scattered about the floor. He crawled across the cell and retrieved the crusty hunk of bread and slowly raised it to his mouth. As his teeth bit into it he suddenly realized to what pathetic depths he had sunk—he had scarcely bothered to brush off the dirt and mold. He looked down at the frayed rag which had once been a white shirt, and his filthy breeches which had come from one of London's finest shops.

This was his true self! He had finally sunk to the reality to which he had been destined since birth. He had tried to cover it up through the years with his quick wit and winning smile and fine clothes—playing the part of a gentleman. But he had played false with the world. He was no gentleman. He was not even a man! All the while, deep inside, lurked this ghastly illusion of manhood—wasted, impotent, waiting for the right moment to surface and destroy him and those around him.

In the distance the familiar sound of the jailer's shuffle again approached, but this time Ian detected the additional sounds of someone with him. Probably another prisoner, he thought. Christmas or not, it could certainly be no visitor. Who would visit him? His father? Ha! If his father ever found out where he was, he would probably rejoice, thought Ian cynically.

The steps drew closer, then stopped. Ian heard the jingling of keys outside the cell door. His heart quickened!

All at once an unbelievable thought pierced the fog. This *was* Christmas Eve. Perhaps this was the season for miracles after all! Could someone have finally realized it was all a mistake? Had the real murderer been found? It could only be a matter of time before this horrible mistake would be undone. Yes, of course, they were coming to release him! *Maggie . . . Maggie . . . I'm coming after all! Don't give up, Maggie—I'll be there!*

The door opened and a man entered, well dressed; although of slight stature, he carried himself with a straight back like a military officer. He was attired in an impeccable brown pinstriped suit, probably of cashmere, clearly not the usual garb of a prison official. His shirt was snowy white and boasted a silk tie. There was something in his bearing of authority Ian recognized, but the light was poor and his visitor held a handkerchief to his nose, partially obscuring his face.

Coughing lightly, he lowered the handkerchief and finally spoke.

"How do you stand the stench?" he asked.

At the sound of the man's voice, the scales fell from Ian's eyes and his ears were opened. He started forward, uncertain whether his mind was not playing another vile trick. But he could never mistake that voice, and the loathsome face was unchanged. This was no Christmas miracle, only a shattered mirage of justice.

"What do you want?" snarled Ian, flooded with anger at the remembrance of past cruelties.

"I heard of your . . . er, your misfortune," James began in measured tones. "You can imagine my dismay. I felt it my duty, as this trouble befell you while you were under my roof, to inquire into your welfare. I see I have come none too soon!"

"*What do you want, I asked!*" repeated Ian, still doubting whether the figure before him might be but some fiendish specter of his insanity.

"I wish to do what I can for you," James replied, and coughed again, as if to further punctuate the magnanimity of his gesture. "Of course, I can do nothing to alter the facts of your guilt, but you need not remain in"—he waved his hand disdainfully in a circular motion about the cell—"in such abject straits."

Ian continued to stare blankly at Maggie's father.

"I have here a document," James continued, removing a paper from the vest pocket inside his coat. "You need only to sign it, and I'm certain funds could become available and certain, shall we say, *arrangements* could be made to—ah—procure such comforts as might make your stay here more tolerable." James stepped forward toward Ian and handed him the paper.

Mechanically, Ian took it from his hand, opened it, and tried to focus his eyes in the dim light. Mingled anger and apathy combined to make him resist anything James Duncan might suggest, while at the same time he felt that he had little recourse but to act in a foreordained manner as events came to him.

Then his eyes fell on the single word—*annulment*. Nothing more was necessary to stir the passion simmering within him. In one swift motion he crushed the paper, dashed it under his foot, and flew at his adversary's throat.

For the first time in weeks Ian felt fully alive. He threw James to the floor, his blood boiling hot within him. If he would rot in this hole for murder, then let it be for good reason!

The jailer had stepped into the corridor to allow the distinguished visitor privacy. And even when he heard the first sounds of trouble, he still waited before interfering. If the gentleman wanted to rough up his prisoner, what was that to him? But at length he realized the sounds from within the cell were not what he had expected.

He rushed inside and found James on the floor struggling wildly, Ian beating at him with clenched fists.

"You fool! Didn't you hear me yelling at you?" shouted James enraged. "Get this bastard off me!"

The guard rushed at Ian, knocking him aside, then turned to help James to his feet. But Ian, awake now, turned, and rushed the guard, kicking him to his knees, then made another lunge at James. But his fury was ill-advised, for the guard, recovering himself quickly, sent him sprawling backward with a punishing blow to his midsection with the brutal cudgel.

James stood, brushed off his clothing, and attempted to pull his coat back into some semblance of order. Once he had put a safe distance between himself and this wild man, he cast Ian a hateful look of scorn.

"You shall regret this!"

"I regret only that it was Falkirk who died that night, and not you!" cried Ian.

"You shall die a thousand deaths in this stink-hole as payment for that error!" replied James with a sneer. "I'll not try to help you again!" With these words he spun and stalked from the cell, followed by the jailer.

Ian slumped back onto his cot. Every ounce of strength was drained from his limbs, and with the fight had gone his fleeting Christmas hope.

Slowly Ian's head sank onto his hands. Every fiber of his being told him that James was right, that he would die in this miserable pit and never see Maggie again. The tears rose in his eyes, and Ian wept.

14

Evil Designs

THE PERCEPTIVE EYE of any who knew James Duncan well would have seen that the preceding months had taken their toll. But few, if any, knew James well. Atlanta had noticed, but said nothing.

The gray streaks in his black hair had grown more pronounced, and a hollowness about the eyes had shown itself. He was thinner and there was a slight slump to his formerly poker-straight shoulders. Despite all this, the fire of his former self still burned in his eyes and the hard force of his drive was ever present.

George Falkirk's death had been a difficult blow. Not that he cared a trifle for the man, either as a friend or as a suitor for his daughter and potential son-in-law. The real blow had come because the anticipated funds from the lad's father— intrinsically linked to the marriage of the young couple—would never be forthcoming. When he had exchanged his daughter's hand for certain financial gratuities, James had never dreamed the intended bridegroom would be violently struck down. So certain had he been of the match that he had stretched his resources to the limit in prospect of laying his hands on the elder Falkirk's investment capital, foolishly putting up earnest money for a new brewery. When the marriage, and thus the deal with Falkirk, fell through, the deposit had been lost and James suddenly found himself in financial difficulty.

Times have definitely not been good, thought James. He reflected on his own father who had squandered a fortune and brought ruin on the whole family. Of course, James stood to lose only his private reserve; there still remained his share in Atlanta's inheritance. But it bitterly galled him to crawl to her for help. As yet he had avoided having to do so. But every farthing of the profits from the old brewery was now having to go toward paying off debts incurred in the loss of the earnest money. Lord Browhurst had turned surly and demanding. Sales of his fine Scottish ale had dropped. His reputation in economic circles had grown shaky. And he had even been forced to dip into the profits of his shareholders in order to keep things afloat, though he remained confident he would be able to turn the business back around and repay these amounts before he was discovered.

James rose from his chair and walked toward a small table which held a tray and two crystal decanters. He opened the one containing brandy and poured out a generous portion into a glass. He took one swift gulp, then began coughing.

"What in heaven's name is in this brandy!" he said, trying to catch his breath.

He managed to force down another swallow as the fit subsided. "Terrible stuff," he reiterated. "If only I could have got that brewery for myself."

James had been drinking a bit more than usual of late. He was an intensely proud man and could not face the erosion of his self-confidence. But if anything within James Duncan was giving way, it was not yet evident to others—and was certainly something he would never admit to himself. He remained a powerful man, but he was walking a narrow ledge.

Stonewycke had begun to mean more to him than ever. Of course it would never be for him what it was to Atlanta. But now, for the first time, he saw the estate and his presumed standing as its so-called *laird* as his only link to a future in the world of the rich and powerful.

The face of Maggie came before his mind. Her leaving had been one of the few positive events of late. But so surrounded was her departure by the whole predicament concerning that cousin of his that his blood boiled just to think of it. He had actually been surprised she would go so far. Had it been fatherly compunction and regret he had felt when he had heard the news? Whatever it may have been, the feeling was overshadowed by the thought that she had actually spurned him for that scoundrel of a lover! She—his own daughter!—had practically ruined him.

Any remaining glimmer of fatherhood was quickly put to rest in the memory of that thought. How dare she! *Regrets are for the weak,* James thought. *A strong man takes tragic events and disappointing setbacks and turns them to his advantage.* Maggie knew how to take care of herself; she would not suffer in America. Meanwhile, James could see how her absence might prove fortuitous indeed. Would it not make Stonewycke all the easier to secure for himself—not to mention his son? Atlanta would no doubt prove as difficult as ever. But a present husband and heir would be able to exercise a great deal more power than an absent heiress.

There remained sticky details to work out, however. James reminded himself he had often faced greater obstacles than these, and had surmounted them. The challenge would be invigorating! He had already taken care of the one crucial detail, and he was confident the news he had arranged about Ian would have just the impact Atlanta feared most. But if it put any ideas in Maggie's head about returning, he would just have to come up with something else.

He tossed his head back and emptied the brandy glass, then poured himself another.

There was always a way to get what you wanted. He was as confident that Maggie would never return as he was that this was inferior brandy. Unless, of course, she returned to put a gun to his own head. He laughed a dry, barking laugh which quickly gave way to another fit of coughing.

No, he thought, *she has that Ramsey pride flowing through her veins, and it would never let her return to the arms of the people she will most certainly despise!*

He would just have to wait and see. It was a nasty turn when that blackguard of a boy refused to sign the annulment papers. That could have made things so much easier. When he had first been informed of their intentions to marry, he had been certain he would have little difficulty effecting a swift end to any such plans. But he had underestimated Atlanta's power. And when she had threatened to bare that power and use it against him, James realized his only recourse was to force that criminal cousin of his to agree to an annulment. Thus, James had arranged for a change in magistrates, had planted evidence against the lad, and thereby forced an arrest.

It had not been difficult, with his remaining influence in the lower circles of the law, to delay a trial and keep Ian incommunicado, while at the same time preventing any information about him from reaching Atlanta. He wanted her to hear nothing until the time was right. He had judged the boy weak-willed enough to agree to anything in order to escape from that rat-infested dungeon of a prison where he was being kept. But he had been wrong, and that miscalculation would cost Ian Duncan dearly.

In his heart, James did not believe Ian a murderer. Certain factors which only James knew pointed in other directions. In addition, James simply didn't think the boy man enough to commit such a brutal act. Cold and calculating as he was, James wanted to avoid the stain of innocent blood on his hands. His future—and whatever the temporary setbacks, he still had the future to consider—demanded that his record be as unblemished as reasonably possible. But though the evidence leading to Ian's arrest had been entirely fabricated, James still hoped further evidence—*true* evidence!—would eventually be found against him, sufficient to hang him. So much the better if he actually *was* guilty!

And soon it would not matter anyway whether the boy was alive or dead. By then Stonewycke would be firmly within his grasp.

15
A Letter to America

❈

IT HAD BEEN well over a hundred years since the careless laird Iver Ramsey had nearly lost Stonewycke. His poor management had in the end reduced the awesome stone castle to an empty shell dominated by cobwebs, empty hallways, and scavenger rats.

Why should Atlanta Duncan, the mistress of Stonewycke, be thinking of these things today? Surely on this winter's day in early 1864 the house stood as grand as ever, reclaimed in all its glory from Iver's carelessness. The walls were adorned with flocked red and blue paper and golden sconces. Velvet hung from the windows. The furnishings were the best to be found in Europe. Though at times an overlooked cobweb might be found in some dark corner, no scavenger rat dared show its face in those halls these days.

But for Atlanta the house might as well have been as empty as in Iver's time. She walked down the hall, her black taffeta sending a ghostly echo into the damp air. There were duties to be performed as mistress of a grand Scottish estate, and she would never have dreamed of shirking even the most trivial. But her heart had gone from her. She had once considered Stonewycke her heart and soul. But when her daughter had left, Atlanta gradually began to realize that Stonewycke was only part of what gave her life meaning. The greater part had been Maggie. She had been the reason for it all. Without her, everything suddenly had grown meaningless.

The vague melancholy which had settled over Atlanta stemmed no doubt from the uneasy conviction that Maggie might never return and that the land would instead go to her brother Alastair, who cared nothing for it. It was bad enough that not a drop of Ramsey blood flowed through the boy's veins, but infinitely worse was the obvious fact that Alastair was cut straight from his father's mold. The boy was only fifteen, but Atlanta could already see that his sole interest in Stonewycke lay in gaining prestige, power, and wealth. When he came into the inheritance, Stonewycke would at first fulfill such temporal cravings. But the moment it ceased to enhance his schemes, she was certain he would have no qualms about disposing of it.

At first Atlanta had harbored the hope that Maggie would return. But when Mistress Rankin had brought Maggie's letter written after her arrival, the inferences from her daughter did not bode well. Clearly it had been written when she first arrived in America, for Atlanta had received it a mere month after the girl's departure. Atlanta had been staggered by the news that Maggie had at the last minute sailed alone and that Ian had remained behind to clear his name.

The news had been inconceivable! Especially since in that time she had heard nothing from Ian. Certainly he would have tried to contact her despite James's threats. Yet even now, over a month later, she had still received no word from him. What it all meant, she dared not guess. Had he sent Maggie on alone, only to desert her, as part of some cruel revenge against her family?

Of only one thing could she be certain: the fact that Maggie had gone to America alone signified a depth of devotion and loyalty to her husband which was unequaled. Whether Ian was, in light of his disappearance, worthy of that devotion was perhaps a question to be considered. But the point was that in Maggie's heart all ties with Stonewycke had surely been severed. The mere suggestion brought a wince of pain into Atlanta's well-controlled face. There was a pride in Atlanta's bosom of motherhood for her daughter's courage, but it was a pride not unclouded with agony. Maggie was a Ramsey, with roots in an ancestry which had maintained the family continuity for over 300 years. She exhibited the same strength that had carried other Ramseys through war, poverty, and betrayal. Yet now that very strength had wrenched her from the beloved land.

Atlanta turned down another corridor and paused by a closed door. Gingerly she reached for the knob. Her hand trembled slightly as she gripped the ornate brass. Slowly the door swung open to reveal the room which had been Maggie's. Atlanta had not entered it since the day Maggie had left.

She stepped into the room and tears rose quickly to her eyes as she glanced upon everything just as Maggie had left it. It had been a night of hasty flight—Atlanta, being forced without preparation to sever the ties of motherhood all too quickly; Maggie, excited yet terrified, beginning the adventure of her new life with the husband she loved.

A dress still lay across a chair where Maggie had tossed it when it wouldn't fit into her carpet bag. The bed was rumpled where she had sat sifting through her belongings trying to decide which to take and which to leave behind. Now it was all so still; the silent ghosts of that night flitted to and fro through Atlanta's memory. Maggie seemed so very present in the room. And yet the dim intimation of her presence made her seem even farther away.

"Oh, Maggie," Atlanta sighed. "Did we do the right thing?"

Atlanta's gaze fell on the tapestry hanging over the bed. She recalled so vividly the day she had given Maggie the intricate needlepoint of the Ramsey family tree. Her daughter had been glowing in her newfound love for Ian and had at last found the courage to share the secret with her mother. Fresh tears rose in Atlanta's eyes at the remembrance of the tender moment between mother and daughter—a moment all the more touching in that for so many years there had been such distance between them.

When Atlanta had presented the tapestry to Maggie, she had not known how much it would mean to her daughter. When she had suggested moving it to Maggie's present room, Maggie had been reluctant.

"But it has always hung here," she had said. "It seems like it belongs in the nursery."

In the end they had moved it, and here it still hung.

Suddenly Atlanta reached up and took the large tapestry from the wall. She was not an impulsive woman, and later might well look on her action as silly and sentimental. But right now she felt sentimental! For this moment, in her present reminiscing mood she wanted to again see the tapestry in the place where perhaps it was the most natural—in the room where Maggie would always be remembered. Maggie was a grown woman now, married and far from home. But for her mother, she would always think of her daughter in relation to those happier times before womanhood and sorrow closed in upon them.

Still holding the great framed tapestry between her hands, Atlanta turned, left the room, and made her way to the nursery.

Later that afternoon, sitting at her desk sorting through some papers, Atlanta was interrupted by the butler knocking softly at her door.

"A message just came to the house, my lady," he said.

"A message? From whom?"

"'Tis from Glasgow, my lady. It came on the schooner this morning."

Atlanta took it, dismissed the man, then broke the seal on the envelope and unfolded the letter inside. The only sign of reaction as she read was a gradual whitening of her lips and increasing tautness in her composure. The message was brief and took but a few seconds to read.

She immediately rose, went to the door, and called out to the butler retreating down the corridor, "Where is my husband?" she asked sharply.

"I saw him last in the library, my lady," he replied, half turning toward her.

Atlanta swiftly made her way down the stairs to the second floor and to the library, which she entered with a single rapid motion. James was seated at his desk. He glanced up casually, but immediately a look of concern passed over his face.

"My dear, whatever is wrong? You look positively ashen. Are you ill?"

"Since when were you concerned with my health?" she snapped in return, her voice shaking as she tried to maintain her composure.

"You are being unfair, Atlanta. I *am* concerned. You need to take things more in stride. You have seemed so overwrought of late."

"And I have no reason to be?" she fumed. "You have driven away my daughter, your bastard son stands to inherit my land . . . and now this!"

She flung the letter down in front of James.

He replied with nothing more than a puzzled look, then picked up the paper, and briefly scanned the lines.

"My God!" he breathed, appearing shaken.

"You knew nothing of this?"

"What do you take me for? I confess I did know the boy was in prison—"

"And you said nothing?"

"I knew how upset it would make you," replied James. "And there was nothing we could do."

"You knew I would tell Maggie and were afraid she would come home!"

"How dare you!" James retorted. "She is my daughter, too. The last thing I wanted was for her to leave. I fully intended to inform her of his . . . his—plight. But she was so worked up over this whole thing. The boy turned her against me. I had hoped to give her enough time to reconsider her actions, to cool off, as it were, and to get fully over her silly infatuation."

"That *silly infatuation* was her husband!"

"It's no secret I bore the boy no love. But this news grieves me as much as anyone," James's tone had calmed and over his face spread a look of grief. "I am deeply sorry for the boy, especially in that he was so troubled. But I cannot say I am equally sorry that our daughter is once and for all free from him. Now maybe she will come to her senses and come home where she belongs. If you know where she can be reached, you should notify her of this news at once."

"Yes, I will have to write her," Atlanta said with a candor in her tone not often displayed for James. "But I am afraid . . . I'm afraid my letter may produce just the opposite effect. What if it drives her further from us? But she must be told."

Slowly Atlanta turned and walked heavily from the room. Gradually the terrible burden facing her came to focus in her thoughts. She must write a letter that could be her only and final hope of getting her daughter back. Yet at the same time it could push Maggie into self-imposed oblivion. Maggie was a strong-willed girl; she could well blame everyone for Ian's fate. And she would be well within her rights to do so.

Dear Lord, Atlanta prayed, *please give me strength and wisdom to do this thing I must do.*

16
Thoughts of the West

THE WEEKS FOLLOWING her futile trip to New York were anguish for Maggie. To have anticipated a moment with every fiber of her strength, only to have its joyous object dissolve into nothingness, was a crushing blow. Had she not been physically strong, it is doubtful her emotions could have withstood the devastating impact of that awful moment. Now she was truly alone in a strange land, with the hope which had sustained her thus far crumbled into doubt and apprehension. Worst of all, she did not know *why* Ian had not come, and was left to the confused and frenzied nightmares of her vivid imagination.

With every approaching rider or wagon, she found herself stopping in the middle of her drudgery, heart pounding wildly. Each time she would jump up, rush to the window and look out, only to return again, each time more disappointed than before. The days passed on and on, one into the next. She gave scarce a thought to her future, only built back her hope again, one tiny piece at a time, that Ian would be on the next ship, and would notify her however he was able. She could wait, she thought. Even if it took two or three more ships from Scotland without Ian, still she could wait. Any wait was worth the joyful thought of once again holding him in her arms, of seeing his smiling face, of listening to his exuberant laugh. Just so long as he arrived before their baby was born!

One afternoon shortly before Christmas, Drew burst into the house, his face red—not only with cold but with excitement.

"Evan's got himsel' a Conestoga!" he announced. "Why, 'tis the prettiest thing ye ever saw!"

The response on the part of his wife was considerably less enthusiastic than Drew had anticipated, and his expression quickly sobered.

"What's a Conestoga?" asked Maggie.

"It's a covered wagon. Remember, I showed ye a picture o' one the other day."

"So that's what they're called," replied Maggie. "And you put all your things in them and that's where you live?"

"A *few* of your things is more like it!" said Ellie, speaking out of her cool silence for the first time since Drew had burst in. "Mostly folks have to decide what to leave behind."

"That doesn't sound very appealing," said Maggie.

Ellie merely nodded, while casting Drew a knowing glance as if to say, "You see, I'm not the only one who thinks the whole idea's hair-brained!"

Not to be put off so easily, Drew went on enthusiastically, "It's not so bad. Especially for a new life out west. His wagon'll be Evan's home for several months."

"His whole family!" Maggie exclaimed. "But they're just tiny little things!"

"Ye'd be surprised, Maggie. 'Course, 'cept in poor weather, most o' the folk sleep outside under the wagon itsel'. But when it's cold or rainin', they're right cozy an' snug."

"Well, I don't envy them," Maggie replied. "But I suppose it's no worse than that ship I sailed on."

Drew laughed. "They call 'em *prairie schooners*," he said. "An' maybe that'll be just why. Ye an' yer husband ought t' give it some thought."

Maggie exhaled a sharp sigh. She was silent and everyone in the room, most of all Drew himself, realized he had opened the painful subject of Ian's absence with the word *husband*. In spite of her own troubled and subdued spirit, Ellie walked to Maggie and placed a reassuring arm about her.

"Who knows?" said Maggie at length, "it may be just the thing for us . . . you may be right."

"So," said Ellie, with forced nonchalance, "the McCollough's are movin' out west?"

"They're leavin' in a month," Drew replied. He was in no way oblivious to

Ellie's reluctance and spoke cautiously, keeping his enthusiasm in check for the moment.

"Seems a foolhardy thing to do," remarked Ellie, "in the dead of winter and with a war goin' on."

"Ellie," answered Drew, trying to reason with his wife without arguing, "ye know the war's not goin' t' have any effect on that, so long's they stay far enough north t' avoid the fightin'. Why do ye think they passed that Homestead Act? They want t' make sure the west is solidly Union."

"Sometimes these American terms are completely foreign to me," Maggie interrupted. "What is the Homestead Act?"

"'Tis a law the Congress passed," Drew answered. "Say's they'll give ye a hundred an' sixty acres o' land if ye but work it an' live on it fer five years."

"Just give it to you? Free?"

"Aye! Ye see, Maggie, America is a huge land. There's millions o' acres just lyin' fallow belongin' t' the government. 'Tis nothin' like in Scotland wi' all its estates. It would be impossible fer the government t' control that much land. An' they figure the best way fer it t' be productive is fer each person t' own his own piece. A man will work his life out on his own parcel o' dirt—take real pride in it."

"That may explain leavin' in the middle of a war," Ellie said briskly. "'Course, that doesn't bother me so much since I nearly lost you at Bull Run. Nothin' could be like that again. But what about the winter? You explain that, Drew Mackinaw!"

Drew smiled, for he had been waiting for the opportunity to explain that very thing.

"Seems crazy, I ken," he began, "but if we don't leave now, we won't get t' Independance in time t' hook up wi' the wagon trains. Ye got t' cross the prairie in a caravan, Ellie. Wouldn't do no other way, what wi'—"

He stopped short, realizing suddenly what impact his words would likely have on the force of his argument. Yet he was not a deceptive man and would not persuade others by telling them only half-truths. Especially those he loved.

"Well," he continued after a moment, "what wi' Indians an' all. Ellie, I'll not lie t' ye. 'Tis a dangerous trip, an' maybe folks are a wee bit off their chump t' make it. But think o' what's waitin' at the other end! The pick o' the choicest land in the whole country—an' a hundred an' sixty acres is just the start. The land is so cheap, we'd be able t' buy more in no time. Rich pastures an' fields o' wheat as far as the eye can see!"

"The land of milk and honey," said Ellie, more in the tone of a reflection than a criticism.

"Oh, yes, Ellie! Can't ye see it? We're not makin' it here, with the drought an' Kellermann an' all. It's a chance t' start over."

Maggie could not help noticing the similarity of Drew's arguments in favor of moving west with those with which she and Ian had convinced themselves of the wisdom of leaving Scotland for America.

Ellie found herself gazing steadily into Drew's face, alive with the fire which comes with a man's vision. An intense joy gathered in his countenance and she could not help being moved by it. She was, after all, his wife and partner, the woman given this man by the Lord to share the adventure of his life. Gradually she felt her doubts dissolving in the strength of his fervor. She stepped toward him and placed a loving hand on his arm.

"Drew," she said softly. "I think I'm beginnin' to understand how you feel. Can you forgive me for holdin' you back? Wherever you go, I'll follow."

"It wasn't ye holdin' me back, not really. The time just hasn't been right. But now—if ye're willin', I mean truly willin'—I think the time is right. I told ye, Kellermann's given us notice. So I think that's just some kind o' sign that this be the time."

"I'm willin'," answered Ellie simply.

Maggie watched, happy for her new friends. She knew Ellie had taken a great step forward and she was glad for her victory. She wondered if she would ever be so lucky as to have the opportunity to surrender to her own husband in such a loving manner. And she wondered, too, what Drew and Ellie's decision would mean for her own future.

17
A Message from Atlanta

CHRISTMAS CAME TO the little farmhouse in Chatham with mingled gaiety and sorrow. For Ellie it signified the last she would spend with her mother and father and the rest of the family for a long time, if not forever. And despite the fact that she had begun preparations for their move with preliminary packing and arranging, she insisted on having her parents and her two sisters with their families—a total of twenty people—to their home for Christmas Day. Besides, she thought, it would give her the chance to dispose of some of their belongings, for she was certain her sisters' families would not turn down any handouts. Having made up her mind that moving west was indeed for the best did not, however, keep Ellie from occasional outbursts of tears at the thought of never seeing her loved ones again.

Maggie welcomed the bustle of the festive day because, for her, Christmas was merely one more lonely day without Ian—one more day of waiting, one more day of wondering where he was, one more day filled with dreams of their being together once again. She was thankful for the furor of activity to keep her mind occupied. For several days before there had been constant Christmas baking. Even with their precarious finances, Ellie had wanted to hold nothing back for this very special holiday. And when Maggie went to the store for her, she added several things to her list of purchases which she knew the Mackinaws would be unable to afford. It was the least she could do to repay their hospitality and kindness. She only wished she had enough to pay their mortgage. *If Ian would only come,* she thought. *He might be able to help.*

All in all, the two women baked mince and pumpkin pies, fruit bread, and four varieties of cookies, in addition to the staples of a magnificent Christmas feast. Ellie's mother brought a ham, her sisters fresh yams, carrots, and potatoes, and Ellie's father supplied the arm-power—one of the few things he could contribute, he said—to make fresh-churned butter out of the cream from Drew's cows. It was one of the last meals they would contribute toward, for the livestock were scheduled to be sold at auction the following month, the proceeds from which Drew would use to settle his accounts in town and outfit his Conestoga for the journey west.

Both Ellie and Maggie tried, through the activity, each in her own way, to forget the individual trials of their hearts. Yet neither could keep the tears from occasionally flowing in the midst of the frantic pace.

Seeing his wife brush back the tears as she stood in front of the stove on the day before Christmas, Drew went to her and gently drew her aside.

"I'm sorry, Ellie," he murmured softly, "t' be bringin' this on ye. I know 'tis a hard time."

"This is what the Lord wants for us," she answered firmly, sniffing and wiping her eyes and nose with her apron.

"Well, I'm glad He an' I agree fer a change."

"I'll get over it, Drew. Once we're on our way I won't have time to give it another thought."

Ellie turned to return to the kitchen but was stopped by Drew's hand on her arm.

"Ellie," he said hesitantly. "I know I don't say this t' ye enough, but . . . well, ye're a good wife—an' I'm thankful fer ye—an'—an' I love ye."

He turned quickly and lumbered from the house before Ellie could throw her arms about his great frame and give him the kiss her heart felt. Ellie smiled and watched him go, her tears now tears of joy. *He is a good man too,* she thought, *and I have much to thank the Lord for.*

Maggie had not been prepared for the difficulty of Christmas Day. Her stoic facade had served her well up till then, masking much of the pain in her heart. But surrounded by Ellie's family, with children and happy shouts all about her, she was barely able to keep from weeping every moment. But her protection gave way entirely when little Bess stepped up to her from the tree with a carefully wrapped package tenderly tied with a single strand of blue yarn.

"What's this?" asked Maggie huskily as tears began to fill her eyes.

"It's for you," the girl said shyly, staring down at the ground.

Suddenly the image of Lucy Krueger rose before Maggie's eyes. This was so like that humble gift she had received so many months ago—in another lifetime, in another world—a gift from a poor peasant girl who had begun to be Maggie's friend.

With trembling fingers, Maggie slipped off the yarn, then opened the paper, her eyes blinking rapidly in order to see. Inside was a pale blue knitted neckscarf. Instantly Maggie realized the girl had made it with her own hands and the last wall of resistance broke. The flow of tears broke through, and she wept in choking sobs, pulling the slender child into her arms as she did.

"Well, I declare, Bess!" Ellie exclaimed. "Aren't you full of surprises? Whenever did you manage to make that?"

"I seen her hidin' out in the barn doin' somethin'," said Tommy Joe.

At last Maggie released Bess and smoothed the girl's hair away from her face. "Bess . . . Bess," she said, trying to stop her crying, "don't you know you could have caught a dreadful cold out there in this weather?"

The girl merely stood and nodded with a half-smile on her face.

"Well, I thank you even if you do," said Maggie, hugging her again. "This is the most special Christmas gift I've ever received. I will treasure this always."

The climax of the day came in midafternoon, after the Christmas meal had ended, when Ellie's sister stood and cleared her throat.

"I have an announcement," Leila said.

Ellie clapped her hands. "Another baby!" she cried.

"At my age!" laughed Leila, not embarrassed at the subject in mixed company. She was taller than Ellie and older by five years. Her appearance was more imposing and her face wore a look of austerity, but she retained the family trait of good humor.

"No, I'm just waitin' for grandchildren now," she replied. "My announcement is this—" She took a deep breath, then turned to her husband. "Maybe you want to tell this, Frank?"

"You're doin' just fine," he replied.

"Well then," she continued, "Frank and I have been a-talkin' an', well . . . we've decided—that is, we think we'll move out west with Drew an'—"

She never had the chance to finish for the scream of joy coming from Ellie's mouth as she jumped up and clasped her hands over her mouth in disbelief.

The remainder of the day proved to be one of renewed mayhem in the little house. Suddenly everything had changed for Ellie—she would have *kinfolk* with her, and that made all the difference in the world. God had answered a prayer, she told Maggie later, that she hadn't even dared to pray. She would still miss her parents and her other brother and sister. But with Leila, the best friend she had ever had, besides being a good sister, the journey would be more wonderful than ever.

* * *

The first weeks of the new year were full of anticipation and excitement in the Mackinaw household. Ellie and the children proceeded with the slow progress of deciding what could go and what couldn't, while Drew sold, gave away, or traded for provisions what he could of his livestock and equipment—those items which weren't pledged already to Kellermann. For Maggie, however, the weeks were more difficult than ever. Another ship had been scheduled to arrive in January and she fought within herself the urge to travel again to New York to meet it. She knew Ian would come immediately to the farm the instant he set foot in America, but somehow she longed to be standing on the dock when he sailed in.

Ellie talked her out of the journey, however, realizing that another disappointment would devastate her already fragile emotional state.

"He'll come, child," she reassured. "And when he does, he'll be *here* the next day. One afternoon you'll look down the road, and there'll be your Ian runnin' toward you with open arms!"

Maggie tried to smile her thanks for Ellie's comfort.

"And you know we won't leave you here alone. We'll wait as long as we can before we have to go, till he comes. We'll find out every ship due in if we have to, so we will know when to be a-lookin' for him."

Maggie nodded her appreciation, but was unable to say anything.

One afternoon toward the middle of January, Drew approached Maggie, hesitated a moment, then said, "Why don't you and Ian come with us . . . out west?"

Maggie merely looked down toward the ground.

"That is," Drew went on, "I just wanted ye t' know that ye'd be welcome, and that we'd love t' have ye join us, fer as far as ye'd want t' be goin'."

"Thank you, Drew," Maggie answered. "Perhaps we will, that is if—" Maggie's voice caught on the remainder of her sentence, for she could not bring herself to say *if he comes.*

Approaching them where they stood, Ellie had heard the last of the conversation. She put her arm around Maggie and said, "He'll come. I know he will. And like I told you before. Don't you worry. We're not goin' to leave you all alone. Drew an' I've decided we're goin' to wait till your Ian's here."

Maggie thanked them both, then turned and walked toward the bare winter fields to be alone and to think. Ellie's words were comforting, but Maggie could find little hope in them. Aside from the farfetched fear that Ian had simply decided not to come, there were other more awful considerations which Ellie and Drew knew nothing about. She had tried to push them from her mind, but they refused to go. What if Ian had not been able to clear his name of that terrible crime? What if her father had had his way? What if he had been tried and convicted, even hanged? *Oh, Lord! no . . . please no!* Maggie wailed in bitter agony.

She thought of returning to Scotland. But the risk that Ian had already set out for America was too great. If they missed one another on passing ships, the torment of uncertainty would be magnified all the more.

Oh, God, what should I do? Help me, Lord. Help me!

In the confusion of tormenting thoughts and half-prayers, Maggie threw her shawl about her shoulders and continued down the dirt path. Remnants of the last snowstorm lay in the fields, but on the walkways it had long since turned to mud. The chill bit through to her skin, and Maggie shivered. Yet the crisp air felt good; it reminded her of home, and she suddenly realized how little she had been out-of-doors since arriving in Chatham. Maybe this was just the sort of exercise she needed. In Scotland she had spent nearly every possible moment outside. She thought of Raven, the sleek black mare that had carried her for years over the endless miles of moors and hillsides and sandy beach west of Port Strathy. She could almost feel the Scottish wind whipping through her hair and the spray of salt-water in her face.

Those were wonderful times, she thought, *even though often those long rides had been designed to escape life at home.*

Home . . . Maggie smiled wanly as she thought of the place she had called home. A grim, three-hundred-year-old castle with more rooms and corridors than even she had been able to explore in her entire childhood. She had alternately hated and loved it. A tear dampened the corner of her eye. It may never have been home, not in the same sense that this little place in Chatham was home for the Mackinaws. But Stonewycke was such a part of her. *Stonewycke will always be part of me,* she had once told her mother. *I will never forget it.* And what was it her mother had said the day they parted—"It will always be *yours,* Maggie!"

What is a home? she wondered. Was Stonewycke her home? Was it part of her, as she had told her mother? Was that what Atlanta had meant when she said it would always be hers?

Or was her home now with the Mackinaws? Yet they didn't even have a home at all—at least they wouldn't in a few months. Their home would be nothing but a tiny wagon covered with canvas.

When Ian had asked her if she could leave her beloved homeland, Maggie had replied that her home was with Ian. She loved Stonewycke, but it meant nothing without Ian. She loved Scotland, but it too held no meaning apart from him. And now here she was in America, with a family she had known only two or three months. How could she make this her home without Ian?

"Oh, God," she prayed, "are you so cruel that you would take it *all* away from me! Am I to go back? *Oh, what are you trying to tell me!*"

Yet she could never go back. Not without Ian. The strife at Stonewycke, with her father in its midst, was too great. Since her earliest memories she had always had the sense of being caught in the middle, the root of the family contention. Who could tell, perhaps now that she was gone, things were happy again at Stonewycke. How could she ever go back? How could she face her father again? That would be the most bitter pill of all, to go to him, hat in hand, and admit his victory over the love she and Ian had shared. No, she would never do that! She would never forgive him for what he had done to them!

Ian *would* come. They *would* have the life together they dreamed of. And *this* new land would become their home!

As Maggie returned to the house and approached the barn, she saw Drew talking with a man she recognized from her first day in Chatham. The man then turned, climbed onto his wagon, and headed back toward town.

"Maggie!" called Drew as he saw her in the distance.

He ran toward her with something in his hand. "Funny ye should be out here," he said. "I was just headin' into the house t' get ye."

"I needed some fresh air."

"'Tis a fine day fer it," he replied, reaching her, then stopping to catch his breath. "I just had a visit from Jeb Cramer o'er at the General Store. He brought this fer ye. Looks like it came all the way from Scotland."

Maggie's heart leapt and she took the envelope from Drew's hand with a face that radiated hope.

"Figured ye might feel that way," Drew stated with a smile.

Maggie quickly scanned the envelope. It was smudged and crumpled, and had obviously passed through many hands before finally coming to rest in Maggie's cold, pale fingers. She studied it for a moment, then realized with a sinking feeling that it was not Ian's but her mother's handwriting she recognized.

"Maybe ye'd be wantin' t' be alone," added Drew, sensing her hesitation.

"Yes . . ." she replied. "I think so. I'll go into the barn."

She turned and walked in that direction; Drew gazed after her, then went toward the house.

The familiar smells of animal flesh, manure, and hay greeted Maggie like old friends from the past and she welcomed them. She thought of old Digory with his kind visage and soft, loving voice; a fleeting remembrance of all the time she had spent with him crossed through her mind. She found a mound of hay and nestled down into it.

She looked again at the letter she held in her hand. The precisely elegant script was so descriptive of her mother. Slowly she tore an edge of the paper and then opened the rest of the envelope. Two sheets of fine paper slipped out into Maggie's hand.

With trembling fingers she lifted the pages and, with emotions surging through her, began to read the words which had caused Atlanta such agony to write:

My dearest Maggie,

I was not certain if I could write this letter, but it had to be written and it is best, though it pains me more than you can imagine, that I be the one to impart this news to you.

I thought when you left that your troubles would end and you would finally find the happiness I longed for you to have. I had prayed and hoped for it more fervently than I had ever desired anything in my life. But now I must place upon you instead the greatest of all sorrows. I must tell you, my dearest daughter, that your husband is gone. Gone, I hope, to a final peace, into a final rest for his troubled spirit.

I doubt that it has come to your knowledge that he was arrested shortly after your departure. (What a shock it was for me to learn that you had sailed for America alone!) It appears that while Ian was in prison he refused all attempts at assistance. Even your father made an attempt but it was violently rebuffed (and who could blame the poor boy after the things your father said to him!). Finally there was an accident—a fire.

Oh, dear child! How my heart aches! When the news came of his death, I could not make myself believe it. It simply did not seem possible. But, alas! There can be no doubt—he is gone.

Oh, dear Maggie, I so regret that you must be alone at this terrible moment. How I yearn to put my arms around you and give you what comfort it is within my power to offer. If I cannot do this for you now, let me at least do it for you soon. You will find that I have enclosed some money to secure your passage home. Please come as soon as you can—there is no need for you to be alone. Ian may be gone, but your family is still here in Stonewycke.

With all my love,
Mother

The letter fell from Maggie's hand onto the hay-strewn dirt floor. For endless moments she sat motionless, staring straight ahead as if into a void of space. Her brain ceased to function. There were no feelings, no sensations, no tears. All within her had gone numb.

How long she sat there, Maggie could not tell, and whether at last she fainted or simply fell into a stupefied sleep she never knew. But just before she slipped from consciousness, the visage of her father rose in her mind.

An hour later Ellie found her curled up in the straw. She awakened her gently, realizing at once from the deathly pallor of her face that some dreadful calamity had befallen her. Maggie stared blankly up at her out of dull, unseeing eyes, and when Ellie reached down to help her to her feet, Maggie could barely stand, her strength spent. Leaning on the mature woman like one of her small children, Maggie allowed Ellie to lead her from the barn. Neither woman spoke as they walked slowly back toward the house.

18

A Grief-Stricken Resolve

❈

FOR THREE DAYS Maggie neither spoke nor rose from her bed. Little Bess tended her friend, brought Maggie meals which remained mostly untouched; often she just sat next to the bedside offering her childlike comfort.

On the fourth day, Maggie awoke to find Bess beside her again; only this time the child's head was bowed as she softly murmured what Maggie recognized as an innocent childhood prayer. Keeping still so as not to disturb her, Maggie listened as the child said, "Dear Jesus . . . please help Maggie to be happy again."

As simple words often do, Bess's prayer somehow penetrated the shell of Maggie's pent-up grief. But from beyond the words came the realization that they would never be fulfilled. She never *would* be happy again. The child's faith was naive and misplaced. *All faith was misplaced!* Maggie thought, as tears at last swelled in her eyes. She covered her face with her hands and wept.

Thinking she had caused the outpouring of Maggie's grief, Bess jumped up and scurried downstairs in alarm. Ellie climbed up into the loft and looked upon the scene of heartbreak with relief. She knew there was good in the release of tears, and that often healing could begin no other way. But what she did not realize was that with Maggie's tears of mourning for Ian were mingled the bitter tears of anger and hatred.

"Bess," Ellie called back down, "fetch Maggie a cup of tea. I think it'll help her feel better. An' watch them steps comin' back up."

Ellie turned and sat down on the edge of the bed next to Maggie. She placed a gentle hand on Maggie's shoulder. "Cry, dear Maggie. Just go ahead an' cry it all out."

Still sobbing, Maggie turned a tear-streaked face toward Ellie. "He killed him! It was no fire—my father killed him!"

Knowing practically nothing of Maggie's former life in Scotland, Ellie hid her momentary dismay at the harsh words and continued to soothe the young widow the Lord had placed in her care. In the anguish of the moment, she thought, the girl was raving. She would settle down and accept the reality in time. Until then, she would minister to her as if she was her own kin. Still, Ellie could not hold back an involuntary shiver from the cold tremor of loathing she had detected in Maggie's voice.

Sleep did not come to Maggie that night to block out the pain for a few blessed hours. The tears which had begun in the afternoon continued to flow. Whenever a moment of respite came and she began to doze off, almost immediately a vision from the past would follow and crowd out the moment of calm. Dominating the confused torment of her overwrought brain was not the face of Ian and the awful emptiness she felt, but rather visions of her father. The vague sense of bitterness she had carried through the years intensified, and before the night was through she had heaped upon him blame for every bad thing that had ever happened to her. Visions of Cinder exploded upon her memory, mingled with her father's words to Ian—shouting vicious, threatening, evil words—the night of their flight from Stonewycke. She tried to force herself to think of Ian, to remember his laugh, his voice, the tenderness he had shown her. But always James pushed Ian from her mind, just as he had tried to push him from her life.

And had he not now succeeded? In the end, James Duncan had *won,* just as he said he would. He had always been set on destroying her. His wrath had not been set against Ian at all—it had been directed at her! *It was always me you despised, wasn't it? Me, not Ian.*

The face of her father loomed large in her mind, laughing, toasting his success with his friends . . . laughing, laughing. The vision took on grotesque proportions as the lips grew and grew—laughing still—taking over the whole face, and turning evil in their intent. Still he laughed . . . she could hear the sinister voice as if it were in the same room.

Of course! He *was* in the same room, for there she sat in the corner. She could see herself just like it was yesterday, sitting in that old wooden chair in her nursery, sitting in the corner watching. Her father was talking with a big man about something. They were talking about Cinder! Now she could hear them perfectly. He was giving the man her horse! *No, Daddy . . . no!* she cried. But she could not speak. She couldn't open her mouth or move from the chair. *No, please—Daddy don't!* she shouted. But he didn't hear her. He just threw back his head and laughed, then glanced in the direction of where she sat, gesturing toward her, and said to his companion, "You see, my daughter won't mind. She doesn't care about horses!"

Suddenly the laugh changed and an evil sneer took over her father's face. Still she sat immobile, watching—watching . . . powerless to move, to speak, to stand. He was no longer laughing with the horseman but shouting threatening and horrible things. But who was that man he was yelling at? His face was too obscure. If she could just get a little closer. Unable to move from her chair, she squinted, and—yes, it was Ian. *Ian, Ian!* She opened her mouth and tried to force out the words, but they strangled in her throat in a chilling, stifling silence. Still her father was yelling, screaming. Ian was backing away, pleading with him in gentle tones. Suddenly her father pulled a gun from his pocket. *No! no! Daddy, please . . . no!* But it was too late. A deafening explosion sounded and Ian slumped to the ground.

At last her muscles were freed and the little girl sprang from the chair and ran toward the dying form. He lay in a pool of red blood, still flowing from the open wound in his chest. On his face was a look of peace, but there was no life left in it. She spun around to face the villain, but the room was empty. She was alone . . . alone with the corpse of the only man she had ever loved.

She turned again toward the dead man, but the face which only moments ago had looked so contented to have passed out of the world of the living was fading . . . fading. She reached out to touch the beloved face one more time, but her hand sunk to the floor and she was left with only the red pool of blood, still wet where he had fallen and now was no more. From above and around her came the hateful voice, the sound of death—laughing . . . laughing . . . laughing in his triumph, laughing in his final victory. *I hate you . . . I hate you!* she screamed, and now her voice returned—*I hate you!*

Suddenly Maggie started awake in her bed, roused from the nightmare by the sound of her own voice, cold sweat dripping from her body. *Oh, God!* she cried silently, *God . . . help me!* Then she lay back down as new sobs shook her frame.

Maggie turned on to her side, aching for sleep—peaceful, dreamless sleep—to enfold her and deliver her from the prison of her thoughts. All at once a strange fluttering stirred within her.

The child! Her hand sought the place where the new life was growing inside, eager to feel the tiny movement again. Then she realized for the first time—*this child will never see its father.* "Oh, why?" she moaned. "It should not have been this way. We were supposed to have a happy life together. Oh, God, why? What purpose can there be in this heartache and anguish?"

Now Atlanta intruded upon her mind, urging her to return, to come back to the home of her childhood, to the land of her ancestors, to return to be comforted by her family. But what comfort could there ever be at Stonewycke? Yes, she longed to feel the embrace of her mother's arms again. And perhaps there would be some small comfort there. But there would also be the abhorrent presence of James Duncan hovering over her, no specter from her dreams but a living and malefic presence, bent on completing his destruction of her in order to further his own ends. And would not his treacherous intent extend—as it had begun with her and reached to Ian—to her child? Her child! No, she could never let him near the child of her marriage. He would destroy the child as he had destroyed them! He did not care for family, ancestry, the estate, or the future of Stonewycke. He only wanted to secure his own empire, whose future he would place in Alastair's hands. Should her child ever stand in his way, he would stop at nothing to remove any barriers to the execution of his plan. Had he not already demonstrated how far he was willing to go?

But she would not let this child stand in his way. He had won. He could have Stonewycke! But she would keep this baby as far from James Duncan's lethal tentacles as possible, even if it meant keeping the child from Atlanta. For if Atlanta knew where the child was, surely James would find out, and would seek to destroy it. Maggie had been helpless to save Ian, but she would let nothing happen to his child.

"You will never," she determined, voicing her thoughts, "lay eyes on us again!"

Verbalizing her resolve silenced Maggie's trembling thoughts and stilled the flow of her tears. An icy calm stole over her, followed by an uneasy sleep.

She awoke just as the first streaks of dawn were breaking through the night sky. Downstairs the hushed voices of Drew and Ellie filtered up to the loft where she lay.

". . . but I don't want to press the poor child," Ellie was saying. "She's already been through so much."

"But—" Drew hesitated in his uncertainty.

"I know, I know," Ellie went on. "The time is drawing so near."

"Harry was by yesterday. He says if we're not out, Kellermann's goin' t' send men o'er t' pack up our things an' haul 'em away. An' we just can't hold the others up much longer."

"I'll talk to her today," promised Ellie.

Maggie slid from the bed, wrapped herself in a blanket, and descended the steps. As the wood floor from the loft creaked beneath her feet, the voices immediately ceased. Drew and Ellie both glanced up, more surprised that she had at last risen from her bed than that they had been caught talking about her.

"I didn't mean to eavesdrop," said Maggie.

"We weren't likin' t' talk about ye," said Drew sheepishly. "But—"

"I've been a real burden for you," interrupted Maggie. "And I'm sorry."

"No, no, my leddy—I mean, Maggie," Drew answered quickly. "Never that. 'Tis just that . . . well, we're wonderin' what ye'll be doin' now. I ken 'tis a terrible time t' be thinkin' about such things."

"It may be a terrible time for me," said Maggie, moving fully into the room where the light of the fire seemed to accentuate her pale frailty all the more. "But I realize you have to decide what you're going to do."

There was something in Maggie's tone which was new to her. Ellie saw the same look in Maggie's eyes that Atlanta had seen on the night of their mother-daughter farewell. There was in the set of her face a strength, a determination, a fearlessness of new resolve. It both alarmed and relieved Ellie, for it was a resoluteness of will which could either carry her victoriously forward or plunge her into destruction.

When Maggie opened her mouth to speak again, her voice was steady and clear. "If you are willing to put up with me," she said, "I want to travel west with your family."

19
Dermott Connell

DERMOTT CONNELL RESTED his chin in his folded hands. On the desk before him were piled several huge law books, their leather spines brittle with age, and a half-dozen scattered sheets of paper. They represented, however, not merely a great deal of work but a perplexing legal dilemma. He sighed deeply, rubbed the sleep from his eyes, and looked once more at his desk.

A tall, muscular man in his late thirties, he might easily be mistaken for a common laborer. Indeed, he was no stranger to Scotland's factories and coal mines. But he had given them up long ago to follow the profession of a lawyer. One of the city's most respected yet misunderstood lawyers, Dermott Connell had the reputation in the legal community of a maverick, a loner whose penchant for exposing falsehood and proclaiming truth went beyond the bounds of propriety and tradition. The moment Connell caught the faintest hint of a compromise of the truth, his high-principled instincts sprang into action—no matter whom he opposed in the process. To him, principles were everything; practical considerations, if they could not be carried out with integrity, were nothing.

Today, on this gray Glasgow morning, his mind was focused on the dismal state of one of his clients. He had spent half the night obtaining the troubling bit of information; now perhaps it would be better if he had never found out—or never taken the case in the first place. His client, one Harvey Bidwell, was a poor man whose work in the shipyards was more off than on, and whose large family depended on him for their sustenance. Not a man given to hasty conclusions, Dermott had finally come to believe the man's pleas of innocence and had committed himself to his defense when no one else had given him so much as a nod. Harvey's crime was not an especially heinous one—he had been accused of embezzling a few shillings from his employer, A. P. Carey. Now he was locked up in prison, and doomed to remain there for some time unless something was done to help him.

For half the night Dermott had trudged about the grimy back alleys of the Glasgow Saltmarket. He had questioned dozens of the city's more seamy inhabitants, hoping to find a witness to corroborate Harvey's story that he was nowhere near Carey's Coffee House on the Trongate at the time of the burglary. But he had, in fact, learned just the opposite. Harvey had been seen slipping into the shop's rear door a short time after closing. The witness seemed reliable. But in that part of town, of course, virtue was not always the motivating factor in things that were said.

All at once Connell's door burst open and the lawyer's head jerked up from its tired reverie.

"Didn't mean to startle you, old boy," said the visitor, a stocky well-dressed man about Dermott's own age.

"I'm afraid I was deep in thought," Connell replied with a smile. "Though I admit after last night it wouldn't take a great deal to put me to sleep." He ran a hand through his thick black hair and leaned back in his chair.

"You waste too much time thinking, Connell," laughed the visitor.

"Time spent thinking is never time wasted, Langley," he replied, the serious, almost intense timbre of his voice contrasting sharply to the other's light joviality. "The Lord gave us minds to think with and wills to move mountains with. But you can't move the mountains without thinking first what to do."

"Well, I still say it's no way to start out the day—so serious and pensive."

Connell smiled, but his upturned lips seemed to oppose the melancholy depths of his cobalt-blue eyes. He bore heavily the troubles of Harvey Bidwell and those of a half-dozen others in similar straits.

"You've been up all night, haven't you, Connell?" Langley went on. "No doubt tromping after one of those poor devils you call clients." Langley Howard was a competent barrister, and in his own way given to compassion now and then. But he would never dream of staying out past seven o'clock on a case.

"They have as much right to representation as any," replied Connell calmly, "and perhaps more need of it than most."

"I only wish I could afford your benevolence," Langley said. "But I'm a family man now, and I need more from my clients than promises of good faith."

"Not everyone is called to follow such a course, Langley, my friend. But he would be a fool who spurned his calling."

"Quite right," Langley replied more thoughtfully. Then resuming his jovial tone, he continued. "Now, as to why I barged in on you in the first place. Agatha has asked me to invite you to dinner this evening. It would seem my wife's calling is akin to yours—taking in stray cats and poor bachelors!"

"Then it would be foolish indeed of me to refuse Agatha's kindness and her wonderful cooking!" replied Connell with a good-natured laugh. "I would not want to stand in the way of *her* calling."

Langley opened the door to let himself out, then as if only remembering an afterthought, turned once more toward his friend.

"One more thing," he said, then hesitated before going on. "You've heard that Lord Crowley has been making inquiries into engaging a permanent advisor to manage the affairs of his estate?"

"I heard nothing of specifics," Connell answered. "Though I did understand he was in Glasgow."

Langley eyed his friend a moment before speaking. "You're not capable of false modesty," he said at length, still with a hint of the question in his eye, "so you must indeed not have heard." He closed the door, stepped back inside, and approached Connell in a confidential manner. "Rumor has it that Crowley has his eye on you."

An amused flicker awoke in Connell's eye, which grew, giving way to a wide grin, then a mighty laugh. Almost immediately his serious look returned, but the twinkle in his eye remained.

"Me?" he chuckled. "What use could a man like him possibly have for a malcontent like me?"

"Go ahead, laugh, Dermott," said Langley, taking his turn to be sober. "But it is true. He was observing you yesterday in the courtroom, and I've heard he was impressed. It's no secret that it would be a highly prestigious position. This could be quite a coup for you, Dermott—a real advance in your career."

"Langley, you said I was not one given to false modesty, and I thank you for that compliment. And in that light, I can only assume that Crowley must certainly have been eyeing someone else. And even if what you say is true, can you imagine a man more unfit for such—a—calling? My methods would not fit in with the sort of thing he is used to. And I most certainly would not alter my convictions. Lord Crowley's circles are a bit removed from my realm. I can assure you, I possess no such career aspirations as you allude to."

"Your realm being the back streets and gutters where—"

"Where people need help," replied Connell almost sharply. "Certainly more good can be done there than in advising a wealthy lord how to make still greater fortunes."

"I have a feeling you would be able to do great good there, for I doubt you would be intimidated or bedazzled by it all. A man like you would—"

Langley stopped, suddenly realizing that arguing Connell against his conscience was futile. He smiled and turned the conversation into a light vein.

"You'd surely set the Glasgow Bar a-talking, that much would be certain!"

"Well, regardless of that," Dermott replied good-naturedly, "Crowley will have to look elsewhere for his pigeon. I have no intention of denying the calling the Lord has given me. And I have more important matters to occupy my time as it is."

When the door finally closed behind his friend, Connell returned his thoughts to the predicament which had been occupying him before Langley's visit, the news of Lord Crowley dimming perceptibly in light of the hard luck of a penniless embezzler.

He had always known the day would come when he would find himself in just such a scrape, though he had tried to avoid it by judiciously reviewing every potential case beforehand. It had always been part of his creed never to take on a case he did not thoroughly believe in, so that there would be no disparity between his client's success and his own convictions. But now here he was facing that dreaded dilemma he had sought to avoid: Could he defend a man he knew was guilty?

Certainly he could aid his family and offer comfort to them. And he could do his best to lighten the rigors of the man's prison sentence. But he faced a more pressing question: Could he use his lawyer's wiles and deductive skills to fight for the release of a man, knowing all the while he was arguing against justice and truth? He had given the man his pledge; he had *taken* the case.

Was not doing his best to secure the man's release inherent in having taken the case upon himself? Was not that the essence of being a lawyer? Had he not so pledged himself when standing before the judges of the Bar? Was not that how every lawyer in the land viewed his calling? Was not that principle at the root of a free society where every man, however guilty he may appear, deserved the right to a solid defense?

To every question he would answer *yes*. Then why was this uncertainty still gnawing at his gut?

As he turned the dilemma over in his mind, arriving at no apparent solution, gradually his thoughts awoke into prayer.

"What would you do, Father? Your Son knew the hearts of men and knew what was best for them. And you must constantly face this situation, for all men are to you as Harvey Bidwell is to me. How do you respond, Lord? You forgive, you love. How I wish all society could respond thus to Harvey Bidwell! Oh, Lord Jesus, show me what *is* in Harvey's best interest. Show me, Lord, what you would have me do."

Dermott sighed, inwardly calmed by the prayer, though he knew an answer would not come easily. He removed his watch from his pocket, glanced at it briefly, then replaced it. He closed the books, straightened the papers, and rose to leave.

His office was located on the second floor and toward the rear of the drab but stately stone building on the Trongate. This particular street represented the hub of the Glasgow business community where sat dozens of such buildings containing hundreds of offices, Connell's being undoubtedly one of the least pretentious.

He often mused that he had not been placed toward the back of the building by mere chance, but rather by the specific design of the more respectable clients. And it suited him perfectly, for most of his clients were glad to be able to slip in and out, using the back stairway unnoticed. Yet in truth, very few of Dermott's *people,* as they were sometimes called, ever came near his office. Most were either already in prison, or close to it, and had all but given up hope—never even considering the luxury of professional legal counsel. Dermott usually sought out his clients rather than the reverse.

Today he would have to visit the tollbooth again. But this time it would be to confront Harvey Bidwell with the truth.

Dermott stepped out into the street, then stopped briefly to button his old tweed coat against the winter chill. A fine mist fell from the sky, destined to soak his thick dark hair long before he reached his destination. He had never been able to develop the habit of wearing a hat, though Dr. Townsend, his landlord and a retired physician, had often remonstrated him for this. He had tried to do so early in life, but found he was forever removing his hat and leaving it someplace or other. Townsend would laugh over his excuse, saying a forgetful memory when it came to the misplacements of hats was at least one sure way of keeping poverty from the door of the milliner's. But the good doctor realized Connell's mental lapses rarely extended beyond the loss of hats, and had come to greatly respect the keen instincts and sharp mind of his young friend. The thought of Townsend reminded the lawyer that he must inform the doctor that he would not be in for dinner this evening. He would send a message when he finished at the prison.

Even at this hour of the morning, traffic was heavy along the wide street. Public horse cars, carriages, and people with an infinite variety of business on their minds pursued their daily activities despite the steadily increasing drizzle. Dermott walked briskly east past the row of great stone buildings darkened by the perpetual soot of the city. Within fifteen minutes he had reached the Saltmarket at the fringes of the slum where Harvey Bidwell lived. How fitting that the tollbooth should be located so near, to house the city's ne'er-do-wells until a more permanent place could be found for them. The building itself was far less noble, a structure of hewn stone with a tower considerably too lofty and imposing for the infamous place.

Dermott breathed deeply before entering. This would be his last breath of fresh air for some time and he used it to full advantage, filling his great lungs full. More, however, he used the moment's pause to whisper a quick prayer for grace and wisdom. *If ever I needed the mind of Christ,* thought Dermott, *now is that time.*

The main entryway bore the appearance of many similar buildings on the Trongate, conducting their enterprises from day to day with various clerks and employees milling about. However, the business of this place was of a considerably different nature.

Dermott paused to speak with the chief wardman who then called another wardman to assist Dermott to his destination.

"Well, guv'nor," the second man said as he led the way down a long corridor, "ye think the rain'll gi' us a breather?"

"It doesn't appear so, Willie."

"What wi' the snow an' all a fortnight past, my wife's near her death o' cold."

"I'm sorry to hear that. If there's anything I can do . . ."

"Thank ye, sir. We jist need a few days o' sunshine t' dry out her bones."

"Well, you and your wife say your prayers then, Willie."

"Are ye thinkin' the Lord'd trouble himsel' wi' the likes o' such a prayer?"

"I'm more sure of it than I am of anything, my friend. And you let me know if I can be of help to you."

They had by now walked along the main hall and passed through two great iron doors into the heart of the gaols. The stone walls and floor became increasingly dingy as they walked and the fresh outside air had given way to an inundating stench. They passed a stair winding steeply downward into the belly of the building, and at last Willie unlocked and shoved open another heavy iron door. This opened into a large room where several men were variously lying about on mats or pacing aimlessly to and fro. No man without a strong constitution could long have withstood the sight and smell of such deprivation.

"Bidwell!" Willie called. "Harvey Bidwell, ye got ye a visitor."

From the far end of the room a man slowly stepped forward. He was tall and gangly, stooped at the shoulders, and with his tousled hair and squinted eyes, he looked easily twenty years beyond his age of thirty-one. The ankle-irons prevented him from approaching more than a step or two toward his visitor.

"Harvey," Dermott said, stepping toward the man and extending his hand. "How is it with you?"

"Fair t' middlin', sir," Harvey replied without enthusiasm.

Willie unlocked the ankle-irons and the lawyer led the prisoner to a bench in the hallway where they could talk in semi-privacy. As they sat down on the ancient splintered wood, Dermott caught an uneasy glance from Harvey, as if he had some premonition of the sort of pointed questions which were about to be put to him. It was a difficult, even agonizing interview for Connell.

Midway through he suddenly came to the realization that Harvey Bidwell was indeed one of Glasgow's most skilled actors. He still refused to admit guilt, but now Dermott could see and hear in him those subtle signs betraying true motive which he had missed on previous occasions. There was in the convict's voice a timbre of belabored sincerity and in his eye a nervous glint. The light was so dim he could scarcely see it. Yet he could somehow *feel* it all the while they talked.

Dermott had long since risen above the petty feelings of insecurity over his own initial mistaken judgment of the man's intent. Lawyers were taken in. It had happened before and it would no doubt happen again. He was not hurt or angered by Bidwell's dishonesty; he was profoundly saddened by the man's inability to see his own folly.

When he finished the interview and was waiting for Willie to lock him back into the dingy room, he still had come to no decision regarding Bidwell's disposition. Forever clouding his judgment was the impoverished picture of Harvey's wife and three innocent children. He could perhaps leave Bidwell to the mercies of the state, but then what of the family that depended on him?

He and Willie were progressing down the dim corridor when they heard a jangling of keys and a mild commotion. All at once two figures emerged from the stairwell rising from the lower depths of the building. The one in the lead, though clearly not the leader, was pushed headlong into Connell.

"Watch yer step, ye miserable cuddy!" shouted the other, a jailer. "Sorry, yer honor," he added in Dermott's direction.

The lawyer barely heard the hasty apology, for his attention had been arrested by the prisoner who had stumbled into him. Like all inmates in this place, he was lean and gaunt. His light sandy hair was unwashed and hung to his shoulders as his clothing hung in rags from his body. He would have remained to Dermott indistinguishable, expect that as he was pushed, their eyes met. In that passing instant Connell saw a different kind of desperation than he had ever seen. There was something in those silently pleading eyes that spoke, not just of innocence, but of heartbreaking confusion. And there was the hint of a spark of love which had not yet been fully extinguished.

This indefinable something arrested Dermott's gaze caused him to take in additional details which would otherwise have slipped by him. The prisoner was little more than a lad. Even in his wretched state it was clear he could be no older than nineteen or twenty. Then there were his clothes. Rags to be sure, but they had once been the garb of a gentleman. And still those eyes—a mute appeal, a hopelessness, the look of life slowly fading, but not dead yet.

Before Dermott could say a word or offer even the hand of hope the man so desperately needed, the jailer nudged the prisoner forward with a sharp poke from his cudgel and away down the corridor he shuffled with his guard limping after him.

"Who was that?" Connell asked as if waking from a daze.

"I dinna ken," replied Willie.

"Surely you must know his name," the lawyer persisted.

"Not that one," said Willie. "Everythin's real hush-hush about him."

"Why?"

"I axt na questions, but jist do my job."

"What do they call him?"

"Well, Jerry there is in charge o' the de'ils doonstairs. He'd be the one fer ye t' talk to. I heard Jerry call him yer lairdship sometimes."

"What is he in here for?" Dermott asked as he watched an iron door clang shut behind the two retreating figures with a finality that made him shiver.

"Now *that* I can tell ye, sir," Willie answered, glad for the chance to vindicate his appearance of ignorance. "He's here for murder!"

"Murder!" Dermott exclaimed in an astonished voice. "But why is he *here*? He's obviously been here a long time. Has he been brought to trial?"

"I'm afraid I canna answer any more questions, Mr. Connell. Ever since the fire down in that part o' the prison, they been keepin' a closer guard on that bloke than ever, an' nobody's sayin' nothin'. Maybe ye ought t' talk wi' Jerry—though I'm doubtin' he'd be knowin' more'n me."

That evening Dermott was a less than entertaining dinner guest. He could not erase the young prisoner's eyes from his memory. At length he broached the subject with his host.

"Langley," he said, "have you heard of any gentleman being imprisoned down at the Saltmarket? I'd say in the last two or three months?"

Langley laughed. "Some of them are in and out of it constantly."

"I don't mean for disturbing the peace or welching on a debt. Have you heard of a murder?"

"Hmm," Langley pondered, sipping his brandy slowly. "A murder . . . no—and I doubt that something of that magnitude would slip past me. I say, Connell, are you finally giving some thought to the upgrading of your clientele? A gentleman, you say?"

"I would certainly never dream of prejudicing myself against our nobility," Dermott replied soberly, without the slightest hint of a jest. "I would take on the defense of any king's son as readily as any beggar's if the man turned to me for the sort of help I could give. And of course, if I felt the Lord's prompting me to do so."

"Yes, yes . . . quite. Well, in any case, have a brandy, Connell?"

Dermott shook his head while Langley poured himself another. Suddenly he thumped his head. "That's it!" he cried. "I knew it couldn't get by me! Surely you remember? Lord Byron Falkirk's son—you know, the Falkirks from the estate of Kairn up north. It happened about four months ago. He was murdered under very odd circumstances. I was in Aberdeen shortly after it happened. Perhaps that's why I heard about it. Now that I think of it, it is rather strange how the whole thing was kept so quiet."

"You think intentionally so?"

"I don't know. The whole affair dropped quickly out of the news. I know there were suspicions floating about which the authorities couldn't substantiate. There was another local laird involved too. There was something about his daughter being involved with the younger Falkirk."

"What happened?" Dermott asked, leaning forward in his chair. "Do they know who killed him?"

"I don't believe it was proven conclusively, but the rumor I heard involved the Earl of Landsbury's son—a typical love triangle, a fight over the girl. I suppose we never heard more because he died in prison after they finally caught up with the boy."

"Died?" Dermott queried. Again the visage of the bedraggled youth rose in his mind. "He was never brought to trial?"

"I never heard anything of it."

Dermott pondered his friend's words. Yes, there could be no doubt that a trial such as that would have been widely publicized and could hardly have escaped the attention of the two barristers. He thought about the evening's events over and over as he walked home later that night. He climbed the steps of Dr. Townsend's stately residence near George Square, then suddenly remembered he had never sent the good doctor a message about his dinner plans.

20

The House at George Square

⚜

A TINY SLIVER of pale light in the gray sky was the only sign that morning had ascended over Glasgow. The light struck the high dormer window in the garret of Dr. Elijah Townsend's ancient brick house at just the proper angle to reflect down across Dermott Connell's bed.

He started awake, and for a man who had had one nearly sleepless night followed by another late one, he greeted the morning energetically. He swung his feet out of bed in order to gain a better look out the window. The light had fooled him into thinking the sun had broken through. But what he saw was only a small streak of sunlight across the sky, surrounded by the massive gray clouds that had hung over the city for days.

He smiled and softly murmured one of his favorite passages from the twenty-eighth chapter of Deuteronomy: "The Lord shall open unto thee his good treasure, the heaven to give rain unto thy land in his season, and to bless all the work of thine hand."

The rain had its good work to do and Dermott could therefore welcome it gladly. The night had been a restless one, disturbed by dreams of haunted youths and gloating judges and penniless thieves. But as the rain washed the dingy city, so the new morning renewed Dermott's spirit.

The room was small but comfortable in its plain way. In addition to the bed with its quilt which Mrs. Townsend had made him some years ago before her death, a desk and chair sat under the dormer, and a bookcase stood against the wall, jammed with an assortment of volumes: *Ivanhoe* and other favorites of Sir Walter Scott's, poetry, some sermons, a first novel by a fellow Scotsman by the name of MacDonald, and a number of ancient volumes on Roman law. On the desk, Dermott's Bible lay open where he had left it the previous night on returning from Langley's. The particular passage which had sparked his interest had not been on forgiveness, for he had already resolved to do whatever he could for Harvey Bidwell, in or out of prison, if for no other reason than because he could not yet give up on the man's spiritual regeneration. Whether his help would come in the courtroom or after Bidwell's probable conviction, he didn't know. But he would continue to pray, and the Lord would do His work; Dermott Connell was again at peace in that regard.

But instead of Harvey, Dermott's mind had been elsewhere, and the book was still opened to the fourth chapter of Luke. The desperate image of that poor youth he had seen so briefly in the prison had never once left his mind during his every waking hour since, and had even intruded into his dreams. As Dermott dressed, he paused to look at the passage once more. *The Spirit of the Lord is upon me, because he hath annointed me to preach the gospel to the poor; he hath sent me to heal the brokenhearted, to preach deliverance to the captives, and recovering of sight to the blind, to set at liberty them that are bruised . . .*

Here certainly was hope for the despairing. And if he never again saw that young gentleman, at least Dermott was comforted that hope existed for such as he. Those very words had comforted Dermott as he neared the end of his own search for faith.

He finished dressing, then descended the three flights of stairs to the main body of the house. He could have had any other room in the great place, many with much finer appointments than the garrett. But he had chosen his present quarters because of their simplicity and because he liked its high aspect, with a broad view of the city reaching, upon occasion, even as far as the Clyde.

Dr. Townsend was already in the dining room, seated at the table in his usual place near the hearth.

"Up with the chickens as usual, Elijah," said Connell, greeting the old gentleman warmly.

"Yes," the doctor replied. "But on my feet before you as well, and that is not so usual!"

"I have been something of a sluggard," said Dermott, seating himself at the table.

Dr. Townsend laughed. He knew Dermott all too well and did not even attempt a response.

At sixty-two, Dr. Elijah Townsend was one of those rare individuals who combined a youthful vitality with such a depth of wisdom and venerability that he was both respected and loved by all whom he met. Beneath thick white brows, his eyes sparkled with life, and the white fringes of hair circled his balding head like a halo. Spare in girth, his slightly bent frame stood only a few inches shorter than Dermott's. The lawyer had lived with the older man for eight years and still could not say whether Dr. Townsend was more a father, a brother, or a best friend to him. For it was the doctor who knew Dermott best, who had been part of his past struggles and victories. It was the doctor who had nurtured him through more than one crisis as he was slowly gaining his spiritual feet. It was the doctor who had laughed with him, cried with him, talked him through times of weakness, and more than any other single person was responsible for the man of God Dermott Connell had in the end become. And it was now the doctor to whom Dermott could most fully open his heart and share the burdens of his vision of service to Glasgow's downtrodden.

"You were in late last night," Dr. Townsend commented, noting a hollowness in the lawyer's eyes that perhaps only he could have detected.

Before Dermott could reply, Tillie, the housekeeper, scurried into the room carrying two steaming bowls of porridge on a tray.

"Och! 'Tis you is it, Mr. Connell. There ye be at last!" she said with no attempt to disguise her scolding tone. "Yer dinner still sits untouched on the sideboard there, as cold as stone."

"I'm sorry, Tillie," replied Dermott with true contriteness in his voice. "I will try to repent of such thoughtless actions in the future."

"Hoots! 'Tis rich, that!" Her round face changed in an instant from the former sternness to a look of good-humored embarrassment. "Ye were no doubt out doin' some good, an' what's a cold dinner t' that!" She set the bowls down in front of the men and returned to the kitchen, calling over her shoulder as she went, "I'll hae some fresh bannocks for ye in a minute."

The men turned their attention to their meal and nothing was said for a few moments. At length Dermott was the first to speak. "I apologize to you also, Elijah," he said, "for failing to send you word that I planned to be absent for dinner. I was with Langley."

"No need, my boy. Such things happen, and we have over the years learned to remain flexible with the rise and fall of circumstances."

"Yes, but this was simply pure thoughtlessness on my part." Dermott paused to sprinkle salt over his porridge, then stirred the hot cereal before continuing.

"But I must admit, though, something has happened which has quite overtaken my mind. I can seem to find no mental rest since it happened."

"I could tell there was some trouble behind those eyes of yours."

"The incident itself covered the span of merely a few seconds. Yet I still cannot escape the impression it made on me."

"There may be good reason for this," said Dr. Townsend. "Is not that frequently how *He* speaks to us?"

"Exactly! And that is precisely why I have been wondering—"

Just at that moment Tillie burst into the room again bearing a tray of bannocks and thick slices of cheese. She served her two charges, then poured out for them cups of the strong black coffee they both enjoyed. Dermott commented on the wonderful nature of the meal and Tillie beamed as she again retreated into the kitchen.

"I don't know what I'd do, Dermott," mused Dr. Townsend as he lowered his cup from his lips, "if you disdained my preference for this foreign drink as so many of our countrymen do."

"There are moments when a soothing cup of tea is the perfect thing. But on a morning such as this, I heartily endorse the coffee for which this house is known!"

"I suppose you're right; they each have their place. Now, go on with what you were telling me."

"I was at the gaols on Saltmarket yesterday visiting one of my clients," Dermott resumed, "when I *chanced* to bump into another prisoner. Elijah, I shall never forget that face! So tragic, so hopeless, yet with the ray of something unknown, the glimmer of love and the life he had left behind. So desperate were the eyes crying out, yet they seemed to know they would never be heard. Without hope, yet with a glint of life that could not be extinguished."

"Nothing is *chance* in our lives, my friend," said the doctor with a smile.

"How well I know! Don't forget, you taught me to see the Lord's hand in every circumstance."

"You should say, we learned it together. Please go on. I am intrigued."

"Mind you, everything I have just recounted transpired in but a few seconds. Later that evening I dined with Langley Howard and questioned him about the youth I had seen."

"How did you come to question Langley?"

"I forgot to mention, the bearing and aspect of the man, despite his ragged appearance, indicated high birth. Langley would be likely to know of such a one being imprisoned."

"A gentleman in rags, imprisoned in the Saltmarket gaols!" Townsend exclaimed. "The case grows more and more curious. That alone could well pique the curiosity of such a one as you. Did you learn who this unfortunate is?"

"Now comes the puzzling part of the whole question. One would think that the imprisonment of such a one would have come to our attention, especially for a crime as hideous as murder, of which this youth has been accused. But neither Langley nor myself could recall any talk of it among the legal community of the city. And when I asked Willie, one of the wards of the place, about him, he said things had been kept secretive about the young man and his case."

"Hmm," voiced the doctor with a puzzled expression. "I think I begin to understand why your inquisitive mind latched onto this and can't seem to let it loose."

"Langley remembered a crime up north several months back. A certain George Falkirk was killed."

"Certainly," said the doctor. "I recall reading of it, the heir to the estate of Kairn, up near Aberdeen somewhere—nearer Banff, actually. I have heard the old earl has accumulated a sizeable fortune. Though with his son gone I doubt it will bring much happiness. Money never does, as the Lord said. But I am beginning to ramble. Back to your prisoner. You think he is connected somehow to the death of Falkirk?"

"That is one of the troubling elements. The son of the Earl of Landsbury was arrested for the crime."

"Are you certain?" asked the doctor. "Landsbury is a powerful man. He is not unfamiliar to me. And he would certainly have the power to keep something like this out of the papers. So you think the lad you saw might be Landsbury's son?"

"The thought did occur to me. But Landsbury's son is reported to have died in prison. There was a fire shortly after Christmas."

"Then you do have something of a mystery on your hands," Townsend remarked with a sigh, settling back on his chair to reflect on the full implications of all he had just heard.

"Yes—and I am afraid it is definitely on my hands," said Dermott with a curious mixture of humor and sobriety, "for I doubt I shall find a moment's rest until I get to the bottom of it." He made another attempt at his meal, growing cold like its predecessor on the sideboard. But the doctor could already see the signs of restlessness overtaking him. "What do you know of Landsbury?" Dermott asked after a lengthy pause.

"I met him last year in London," Dr. Townsend replied, thinking over each word as he spoke. "I can think of nothing particularly striking about the man. He sits in the House of Lords and is quite influential, from what I understand. Much of the talk, upon that occasion, did in fact turn upon his sons, though none of the talk was in Landsbury's presence. It seems the elder has distinguished himself in the Navy and will no doubt follow his father into Parliament. The younger son, Theodore, was something of a troublemaker, the subject of the unquenchable gossip of those London circles. The father has on numerous occasions bailed his son out of difficulties which were an embarrassment to his reputation."

"Then the earl is the benevolent sort?" Dermott offered.

"Not the Landsbury I met, I'm afraid to say. Quite the opposite, I believe. It is far more likely it is the mother who has championed the son's cause."

There followed another lengthy pause, during which neither man touched his food and both sat absorbed in thought.

"I wonder why Landsbury's son would kill Falkirk?" Dr. Townsend mused, half to himself.

"Langley said there was a girl involved."

"Ah! Not an unfamiliar motive for murder."

"Not unfamiliar. Yet not common among gentlemen. And from such well-known families."

"If I might offer you some counsel, Dermott," said the doctor seriously, "I would say that if you choose to follow this course—that is, if you feel the Lord prompting you forward in it—you must prepare yourself for stiff opposition from Lord Kairn, or perhaps Landsbury himself."

"Yes, I know," replied Connell, drawing the words out slowly. "But I sense that my hand is already set to the plow, and that it is too late for me to alter the course before me."

"I thought as much," said Elijah. "Then I will pray all the harder for you."

21

Stone Walls

"I TELL YOU, Connell, the man you're looking for isn't here!"

"You're sure there is no chance you overlooked—"

"None whatever!" interrupted the warden belligerently. "No murderer would sit here for two months without my knowing it!"

"I simply thought that with the unusual circumstances of the case—"

"How many times do I have to tell you, Connell? He's not here!" the man replied with steadily rising anger. "That's the trouble with you independents, you think you can just walk in and have the run of the place. Well I know your kind, Connell. And it won't work with me. Do you hear? It won't work!"

"I'm sorry, I didn't mean to—"

"Just get out!"

Slowly Dermott rose and left the warden's office. All morning he had been battling various authorities connected with the Saltmarket gaols. No one would admit to the presence of such a prisoner as he described. He had finally worked his way up to the warden himself, with the same result. Under no circumstances would they allow an arrogant young lawyer to roam about among the prisoners with nothing more to go on than a few hazy notions of thwarted justice and an unnatural desire to help society's outcasts.

Stepping from the warden's office, Dermott hesitated momentarily, trying to decide what to do next. The best thing, he concluded, would be to go home, take stock of the situation, and ask the Lord for guidance. With that resolve, he made his way toward the end of the hall toward the main entrance. About halfway down the corridor he heard a voice.

"Mr. Connell!" The tone was a labored whisper, as if the speaker wanted to be heard by no one but Dermott.

"Yes, sir," said Dermott, turning around to see the warden's assistant poking his head halfway out his office door, glancing about nervously.

"I . . . that is—this is," the man began to reply as Dermott approached; "—please come into my office," he said finally, still speaking in little more than a whisper.

Dermott did not hesitate. The man closed the door behind him, saying confidentially, "This is a very delicate matter. We mustn't be heard."

Dermott did not reply, but sat down in the chair indicated by the man. He looked quickly around the office. J. Ellis Withers, the man who had summoned him, looked about thirty, with thick spectacles and thinning brown hair. He was clearly agitated, but whether that was the result of his nature or the nature of his present business was unclear.

"I have heard of your inquiry," he began, his eyes continually darting about, as if the three offices between his and his superior's were insufficient separation. "I don't know if I can help you, but . . . I have kept my eyes closed long enough."

"At this point, Mr. Withers, anything would be a great help," said Dermott.

"I know you are a respectable lawyer. There are others who think your views of justice, shall we say, misplaced. They think if a man is born to poverty, then it's nothing more than he deserves if he happens to wind up in here. But I wanted to work for the prison system because I wanted to help these kinds of men. I'm sure you can understand—"

"Yes, Mr. Withers, I think I do. Perfectly, in fact."

"But there are just too many . . . that is, there is no way I've found to help—the system is . . . but I want you to know I have never been a party to what has happened. At first I was afraid . . . now of course, I am ashamed of myself . . . but with the security of my job—though it's not much of a job, now that I think of it—but I was afraid to lose it."

He paused, struggling to find words to express what was on his mind. At length he went on. "But I finally feel compelled to do something."

"Please, I don't want you to jeopardize yourself for me."

"No, Mr. Connell. I respect and admire what you do with these men. It's what I have wanted to do myself, to serve, to make a difference."

"Follow your conscience, Mr. Withers. I can ask nothing more."

Withers took a deep breath, sat down behind his desk, then began slowly in a voice of resolve and decision.

"I believe, Mr. Connell, that the man of whom you have been inquiring *is* in this prison, though I have no idea who he is. He was brought here in the dark some months ago. I did not lay eyes on him personally, but—as much as they tried to keep the matter quiet—I got wind of it through a guard. I inquired; the warden told me not to concern myself, said he would handle all the details with this prisoner, and that was the last I knew of it. But if you knew our warden you would know that he is never personally involved with any of the inmates. So I could hardly help being curious. I tried to see the prisoner myself, but was barred at all points by the guards and referred back to the warden. He left me no doubt that my job would be affected if I meddled in the affair again."

Throughout his speech, Withers fumbled with a pen on his desk, rolling it in his fingers and tapping it on the dark oak surface. All at once he rose, began pacing the room, and went on, "I fear something is amiss. And I have allowed it to continue too long. There are principles involved here. I don't know what can be done to remedy the situation . . . I don't know if I—or perhaps you—I'm not really certain of—the way to . . . proceed. But perhaps you—that is, you seem like a man who could do something."

"First, Mr. Withers, it is imperative I see the man. That is where we must begin if the truth is to be obtained."

"Naturally," Withers replied. He stopped his pacing, stood still for a moment, then turned toward his desk with face brightening. Hastily he pulled a paper from his drawer and began writing. When he had finished in a few moments he handed it across the desk to the lawyer. "This," he explained, "is the name of another prisoner *downstairs,* as we call it. It is also an authorization to see him. That will at least get you in the general direction of the man you seek."

"I do not like you endangering yourself—"

"I am not exceeding my authority," Withers replied, a look of satisfaction, almost enthusiasm, spreading over his face.

"I know you are acting on the best of motives. And whenever truth is served, the man upholding it cannot be hurt. I am confident the Lord will bless your intentions to help."

"Now," said Withers, "the men downstairs are brought up for an airing twice a week. I am certain the man you want is never with these, but generally two or three guards accompany this group. At these times the downstairs cells are left manned with only one guard for a space of about half an hour."

"That should give me time to make a beginning at least. Thank you, Mr. Withers. I will be in touch with you if there is news. And I will pray for the safety of your job."

"Don't worry about me. Perhaps it's time I had a new position anyway."

"Then I will pray you are led into one of service, where you clearly belong."

22

A Downstairs Interview

❧

THE DESCENT INTO the bowels of the Saltmarket prison was narrow and steep. Where the stone steps were not worn smooth, they were broken and jagged and in the dim light could be treacherous to unfamiliar feet. It was not a pleasant journey under any circumstances, but Dermott felt a deep sense of purpose and satisfaction. Not only did he finally have hopes of actually laying eyes again on the wretched youth who had so occupied his thoughts of late, but also he was penetrating yet deeper into the heart of his ministry. Here were imprisoned souls he had till now never been able to reach, men so miserable that their unfortunate counterparts above trembled at the mere thought of being sent *downstairs*. The prison system was so appalling that short sentences were a blessing, even when they ended at the gallows. Death was preferable to a long sentence in one of these dungeons where even a month was considered a living death, not to mention years. The words of his Lord ran through Dermott's mind: *I was in prison and you came to me*. "Help me, Lord," he breathed. "Help me be your instrument to this man."

He strode down the narrow, dimly lit corridor at the bottom of the stairs, following Withers, while a strange mingling of fear and anticipation filled his heart. For his own safety he was not concerned. He knew he had a Protector fully equal to Daniel's of old even in this dark pit. Rather, his fear sprang from a sense of inadequacy to meet such evil as resided here. But then he reminded himself of Paul's words: *My strength is made perfect in weakness*. As always, from his personal inadequacies sprang strength—strength from One beyond himself. And from this sprang anticipation.

All at once Withers' voice broke sharply into Dermott's thoughts, though the words were not directed at him. The man had definitely changed during the preceding hours. His step was purposeful and he had mustered a certain ring of authority in his voice that had not been there earlier. In his eyes was the look of a soldier who had finally proved himself in battle.

"You, Barnes!" he commanded. "Look alive! I've a visitor for Phelps."

Barnes' head snapped up at the unexpected sound of Withers' voice. He had not been dozing, but very nearly so. Scrambling to his feet, he said, "He ain't here, they all gang up fer a airin'."

"Blast! I forgot," replied Withers. "Well, we can't keep an important man like this waiting. Go fetch him!"

"Phelps?"

"Yes, and be quick about it."

"But I'm the only one here," protested the guard. "I canna be leavin' my post—"

"Are you insinuating that I'm not capable of manning your post?" Withers retorted, his eyes flaring with outrage.

"Well, I wasn't . . . what I meant was—"

"I'll have none of your excuses. Just do as you're told!"

Barnes began to stumble away down the hall as Withers bellowed after him, "And don't come back without Phelps!"

Then he turned to Dermott, cast him a knowing, almost sheepish glance, and said, "We won't have much time."

"Which is his cell?" asked Dermott.

Withers led the way down the hall a few more cells, then came to stop in front of a locked door. He fumbled through his keys, finally settled on one, and shoved it into the rusty keyhole. The door groaned as he pushed it open.

"You will have to make haste," said Withers before the lawyer disappeared inside the cell. "But don't worry about Barnes. He will slow down the minute he's out of sight."

As Dermott stepped inside it took some moments for his eyes to accustom themselves to the darkness. A cold chill crept through his body. He had seen such things before, but it was a sight he would never grow used to. A thin form of a man lay on the wooden pallet at the far end of the tiny room. The head turned slowly toward the bright light of the open door. The face was as pale as a hundred deaths, and the eyes were the same unforgettably hopeless eyes Dermott had been haunted by since he had first seen them in the corridor above. The lawyer stepped fully inside and shut the door behind him.

For a moment Dermott stared at the wasted form in silence, uncertain what beginning to make. At last he spoke, and in the silence of the ancient and foreboding walls around him, his softly spoken words seemed to resound like thunder.

"I'm Dermott Connell," he said. "May I speak with you for a moment?"

"What do you want?" the prisoner asked with a voice that rasped and grated like a rusted door.

"I'd like to help you—"

Suddenly the man lurched to his feet. The dullness of despair was suddenly fired by a fierce ember of life. "I know what you want!" he tried to shout. But his voice could not muster the force to succeed. "He sent you, didn't he?" he said, in scarcely more than a whisper.

"No one sent me," Dermott replied calmly. "I bumped into you in the hall the other day. The look in your face seemed to say you needed help and I—"

"I won't sign anything!" he yelled, half crazed, then flew at Dermott. He had been so subdued of late that the chain had been removed from his ankle. Dermott was momentarily knocked off balance, but he easily repelled the attack and held the youth firmly, but gently, in his grasp.

"Please listen to me," said Dermott urgently, still holding him by the shoulders.

"I haven't much time before the guard gets back. Let me help you. I have nothing for you to sign. I have come completely on my own. I am a lawyer—"

At the word the youth tensed and struggled to free himself from the large man's grasp. But his strength was not what it had once been.

"Perhaps you have no reason to trust me," Dermott continued, "but can it be any the worse for you? Now, I'm going to let you go. You can do what you will. But would it do any harm for you to talk with me, if there is even a small hope in it for you?"

Slowly Dermott released his captive. The lad glowered at the lawyer for a moment before slumping back down on his pallet.

"Tell me your name," Dermott said.

"My name?" he asked, his voice quiet and remote. "When was the last time I even heard my name? *My God!*" he groaned. "Was it in Aberdeen when she said good-bye?"

He paused and Dermott waited patiently in silence. At last he spoke it like an anathema. "Ian," he said. "My name is Ian—how I despise it."

"Then you're not Lord Landsbury's son?"

"Ha! ha!" Ian scoffed dryly. "Now I see your game. You hope to curry my father's favor by helping me. Ha! You are as much a fool as I, for my father doesn't care a straw for me. He would sooner see me dead than lift a finger for me. No, Mr.—Mr.—whatever your name is—"

"Connell."

"Well, Mr. Connell, as I said, my father will only scorn you for trying to help me."

The words tore at Dermott's heart and a lump rose in his throat at the thought of this man's feeling deserted by his own family. But time was too precious. If he wanted to help, he would have to use the few moments he had wisely. He swallowed hard, but the words which came from his mouth were not the ones his heart ached to speak.

"Your father? And who is your father?"

"You said you knew."

"I know only that the Earl of Landsbury has two sons, neither of whom is named Ian."

"Ian is my middle name. I am Theodore. And I am finally out of my father's hair, which must be an enormous relief to him at last," he added with a bitter laugh.

"Then you do not know," said Dermott. "Your father . . . everyone—they all believe you are dead."

"Dead!"

"That is if you are Theodore Duncan, the son of the Earl of Landsbury—"

"My God!" cried Ian. "Everyone? How . . ." He stood up, wringing his hands and looking frantically around as if he must do something. Then suddenly realizing his impotence, he crumbled back down onto his mat. "Then she must think so also . . . he would have told her . . . just to punish us. Oh, God, no!"

He buried his face in his hands and silent tears trickled through his fingers, tears perhaps more for his own loss than anything.

Just then a sharp rap came on the door.

"Mr. Connell!" It was Withers' urgent voice. "Are you almost through? Time is short. Barnes will be back any moment."

Dermott looked across the cell at the heap of defeated humanity which had reached out to him from the depths of some unknown bond of love. He knew that as of this moment the troubles of this young man had been placed irrevocably upon his own shoulders by the One who was the guiding power of his life. But he realized he would never learn all he needed to know in the short time left today. His final question was crucial, yet there was so little time to weigh every word in the balance of forethought.

"Ian," he asked, "did you do what they said you did?"

The lawyer felt he already knew the answer, but he had to hear it from Ian's own lips.

Ian looked up, his dirty face streaked with the tracks of his tears.

"I don't know!" His groan revealed that he had asked himself that very question a thousand times. "I could have . . . I—"

He held up his left hand, showing a thick white scar across the palm. "There was blood there . . . was it only my own? Why can't I remember? If only I could make the blood go away . . ."

"I will help you, Ian—" But Dermott's words were cut short by Withers' sharp appeal. In the distance Dermott thought he could hear the sound of faintly approaching footsteps.

"If you would help, then find *her!*" Ian implored. "Tell her I'm alive. What a fool I've been . . . tell her that I need her."

"Who, Ian? Who do you want me to tell?"

But before he could answer the muted echo of voices could be heard outside and the door swung open.

"Come!" whispered Withers urgently. "They're almost here!"

"I'll be back," said Dermott. "I'll try to find her for you. Don't give up, Ian. Trust God."

Withers pulled Connell free of the door, hastily shut and locked it, and the same moment the guard Barnes and a pitiable old man, who could be none other than Walt Phelps, came into view.

Barnes swore freely and angrily at Withers' insistence he had brought the wrong man. But not about to trudge back upstairs, he locked Phelps back in his cell while Withers and Dermott made their exit. Though Dermott had promised Ian he would return, he wondered how he would keep his word, for this first visit had been difficult enough to manage. Then he remembered he was not alone—that there was Another who also cared for the lad in the depths of the Saltmarket gaol.

23

A Second Visit

❈

THREE INTERMINABLE DAYS passed before Ian's strange visitor returned. From his initial suspicions and mistrust, the quiet lonely hours worked on Ian's imagination. For the first time in what seemed an eternity, he had something hopeful to occupy his thoughts. He had no reason to, of course, but what would it hurt to trust the man? He did not seem the sort to be party to a cruel hoax, but appeared strong and reliant, even compassionate. And in his deepest heart, Ian realized he needed someone.

Thus by the end of the third day, Ian's despair had gradually changed to anticipation. When he had said, "I'll be back," there was a ring in the tone of his voice which told Ian he could trust in that promise—that he *would* return. In his wildest fancies he began to imagine freedom again. And best of all, he dreamed that somehow—defying all reason and all of James's schemes—the lawyer would be able to reunite him with Maggie.

When at long last the door once again creaked slowly open, Ian leapt to his feet.

"I'm sorry it has taken so long for me to come back," Dermott's familiar voice spoke through the dim light of the open cell door. "I have never had such difficulty getting in to see a prisoner. But God has proved faithful once again."

"How did you do it?" asked Ian.

"We have won the assistance of one of the guards," Dermott replied. "I'm afraid Withers has bribed the man, though they both deny it completely. I'll accept Withers' word for now—he has a great heart." Dermott strode over to the pallet where Ian was seated. "May I sit down?" he asked.

"It's dirty."

"I'm no stranger to a little grime. It's better than standing, and we shall have more time today."

A shot of hope filled Ian's face. "You mean there's a chance . . . ."

Reluctantly Dermott had to shake his head in answer to the unfinished question. He had labored constantly for three days on Ian's behalf but had immediately come to see that he would have to be discreet if he hoped to see the lad again. Pushing too hard would only drive Ian further into isolation and further from any hope of release. Progress would be slow, and would be made all the more painful from the hope his activity was bound to raise in Ian's heart. In this tiny cell each hour would seem as a week, while on the outside Dermott realized that weeks, even months, could go by without a single step made in the right direction.

Ian sank back against the wall, the momentary color draining again from his face.

"You didn't find her."

"No, I'm sorry," Dermott replied, wondering how much good he was going to be able to do this lad if he just raised his hopes only to dash them to pieces. "Tell me about her," he said.

Slowly Ian began to talk about Maggie. A year before, sitting in one of the many cells of London, he would never have opened his heart to a stranger. But just the thought of Maggie brought her nearer again. At times during the past months he had wondered if she had not been just some cruel figment of his imagination, a dream, a taunting vision of loveliness. But now—speaking of her, reliving in his mind their conversations and plans—she began to come alive again. And as she came near again in his memory, his heart opened and he found himself sharing more intimately with this stranger than he ever had with anyone but Maggie. There was something in the man's eyes which gave Ian confidence, confidence that all would somehow be made right in the end.

Dermott listened, reaching out at times with a comforting hand on the weeping lad's shoulder as he recounted the events of the night of the murder and then the terrible day in Aberdeen when he had sent Maggie away—alone.

"Do you understand?" Ian sobbed. "She trusted me . . . she loved me . . . she gave up everything for me—and I sent her away. God, how I hate myself! Will she ever be able to forgive me? Will I ever see her again?"

Dermott said little, comforting when he could, listening a great deal. When at last he had to leave, it was with anguish of soul that he rose and said, "Ian, I know it's but little comfort to you, having to stay in this cell and my dragging you back through all these unpleasant memories. But you have my solemn promise that I will pray earnestly for you. I know the Lord loves you far more than I do, even more than Maggie does. And He will show us what to do. I know He has sent me to you, and He will turn this all out for your best. I do not know how, but I will pray He will show us."

Over the next several weeks, Dermott's visits increased and he listened with growing interest to Ian's story—his former life in London, his weeks at Stonewycke, his newfound love with Maggie, the altercations with Falkirk, and finally all about James Duncan, his plots and threats and machinations against them. Dermott balanced the conversation by sharing about his own life and ministry with those in dire circumstances. Ian grew to look forward to his stories about his lively friend Langley and the buoyant housekeeper Tillie as if they were his own friends, and clung to the lawyer's words as if they were givers of life—as indeed they were.

Dermott continued to pray for an opportunity, not only to help the lad find justice and possible release but also to share the meaning of Life with him—to the lawyer an even more vital necessity. Yet whenever he began to approach the subject, a wall of ice sprang up around Ian! Dermott did not press. He knew the Giver of that life would do His work in His good time.

One day, to Dermott's great satisfaction, a momentary laugh escaped from

Ian's lips—slight, yet it could have been the very music of angels. Even Ian himself seemed surprised when he heard what had come from his own mouth, then stopped short and grew quickly somber.

"Don't stop," said Dermott. "You know what they say about the healing virtues of laughter."

"I used to laugh," Ian said, "to hide the pain. That was before Maggie showed me I could laugh for pure joy."

He stopped as his lip began to quiver. "Oh, God! Will I ever know joy again? How can I laugh again without seeming to be unfaithful to her?"

"Perhaps she would rather know you are laughing than dying inside," suggested Dermott.

"But I *am* dying!" cried Ian. "I can't hide from it any longer!"

"I wouldn't ask you to hide from it. But joy can exist next to heartache. Perhaps that is even its purpose. Don't shut Him out when He desires to give you His life to sustain you in your time of pain."

"*Him!* I want nothing from God!" retorted Ian with unexpected anger, rising from the pallet and stalking across the cell. "I want none of that whitewash you try to pass off as *joy*. It only proves God is helpless to take away this agony."

"Sometimes merely removing our difficulties is not for the greater good in our lives, and the Lord knows—"

"Greater good!" spat Ian at the floor. "Ha! That's a stinking excuse! If there is a God, He can't bring Maggie back to me, and you gloss over it with that drivel about it being for the best."

"As much as you feel you need Maggie," Dermott replied, "there is even a higher need. How the one might prevent the other, only God knows. He has nothing but your good in His heart—and Maggie's also."

"Get out of here!" Ian shouted. "I'm not better off without her and I won't listen to any more of your religious nonsense. Get out! I'm sick of you!"

"I'll leave when I'm ready," Dermott replied calmly. "But I have one more matter to discuss with you."

"I was wrong to think you might be a friend," said Ian scornfully, swinging around to face the lawyer.

"I am as distressed as you over my failure to help you," Dermott replied. If Ian could have seen the pain in the lawyer's eyes, he would have known the face of true friendship. Realizing it was useless to argue against the man whose mind was made up, Ian sat back down and said nothing further, listening with disinterested resignation. "That is why I feel compelled to take more aggressive action," the lawyer went on. "Up till now I did not want to risk making things worse for you by stirring it all up. For if I was to expose this hoax that has been played upon you, it could mean an immediate trial—a fact which might not bode well for you in your present circumstances. You have sworn me to keep your family out of this, and so that avenue is closed as well—though if they knew you were alive, it might help me to—"

"My father wouldn't care," muttered Ian.

"Perhaps some other member of the family?"

"It would kill my mother to know what has happened to me."

"And what do you think it has been like for her thinking her son dead?"

That very question had crossed Ian's mind several times of late. He tried to convince himself that they were all better off without him. But in reality his steadfast refusal to contact any of his family was only his way of avoiding having to face another painful rejection. What if he appealed to his parents only to be ignored and left to rot in jail? It was better to be thought dead than to be turned away. The risk of such renunciation was too great.

"There must be another way," said Ian at length.

"If there is," Dermott replied, "perhaps I shall find it in Port Strathy."

"Port Strathy?"

"Yes. I've decided to go north. Your only hope of release may be in forcing a trial. Before that time, I must find some answers. For if it does come to that, I will have to be prepared. There is only one place I can learn what I need to know, and that is where this all took place."

"James Duncan will maul you if he discovers what you're about."

"No doubt he is a strong man. But there is power on my side, and I can be strong too."

"Not in the way he is," Ian warned.

"And he not in the way I am," Dermott replied, a smile tugging at the corners of his mouth.

Dermott rose to take his leave. As he reached the door, Ian called after him in the most despairing voice the lawyer had yet heard, seeming by his tone to apologize for his earlier outburst. "Will you . . . ?" he said, then hesitated a moment. "Will you—still try to contact her?"

"Of course, Ian. I will do everything I can," replied Dermott, then opened the great iron door and let himself out.

24

The Journey West Begins

MAY WAS WELL in bloom before the sparkling expanse of the Missouri River came within view of the small party made up of three covered wagons. They had set out from New York later than planned and the snow-encrusted roads had slowed their pace considerably. Then two severe breakdowns in Pennsylvania and Indiana had cost them an additional three weeks.

The three wagons—carrying Drew and Ellie's family, Evan McCollough with his wife and three children, and the Wootons (Frank and Leila and their two teen-age sons)—which would later become known as the Mackinaw Party, reached Independence feeling already seasoned and travel-weary. Yet the bulk of their westward trek still remained before them. Up to this point they had traveled largely through long-settled and friendly farmlands with towns and villages and other signs of civilization all about them. Once they crossed the Missouri, however, all that could change. On the Kansas plains they might easily go days—perhaps weeks—without sight of civilization. And though the trails west were well charted by now, the dangers of desert sun and Indian attacks and barren waterholes were ever-present concerns. But the spirits of the three men remained high on the crest of anticipated adventure.

With a dull countenance Maggie absorbed the changes of environment as a matter of course. The decision to travel west in this huge and strange new land had been the one supreme effort of will which had enabled her to get past the bitter shock of Ian's death. Once that decision had been made her once energetic emotions sank into apathy and despondency. Dressing in the morning, helping Ellie with a pot of beans for the night's meal around a campfire, bathing one of the young children in a nearby stream—Maggie did everything by rote, as if walking about in a half-dream. She spoke little, cared nothing for the changing sights of the terrain, and was the only member of the party who displayed no anticipation for what lay ahead.

Yet as impassive as her empty stare was, a look deep into her eyes could not hide the truth that Maggie was running away—away from her past, away from the memories of pain. Setting sail into the unknown world of America's western frontier was her way of severing the ties to her former life—a life at one moment she hoped she would one day forget, a life at other times she longed to run back to.

At this moment the arduous journey served her need to forget and could be nothing else for her. Only *One* greater than she could cause it to serve her highest need. But His ways take time, and Maggie could not see His hand at work. Yet as they approached the desert which would before many months burn its heat down upon their wagons, the Master's hand was lovingly moving closer to Maggie's heart through the parched and barren desert of her soul.

The three wagons entered Independence, Missouri, as the afternoon sun was melting into evening. Drew did not pull back on his reins until about a mile on the other side where they found eight covered Conestogas like theirs camped in a haphazard circle.

"Ho, there!" called out a barrel-chested man with long arms and a bushy beard. "Pull up anywhere. We got lotsa room."

Drew was first to leap down from his perch, then he helped Ellie to his side. The children needed no invitation to scurry from the confines of the wagon and join the new children already presenting themselves from behind the circle of stationary wagons. Maggie remained where she was, watching the proceedings with indifference as the others of their small party followed Drew's example.

"I'm Drew Mackinaw, and this is my wife, Ellie," Drew said, thrusting out his hand. The big man took it and shook it vigorously.

"Glad t' make yer acquaintance," he replied in a brusque, deep voice which contrasted with his obvious friendly nature. "Pete Kramer's the name. Everyone else can take care of their own introductions."

"A man in town said we'd find ye oot here," Drew went on. "If ye be goin' west we thought ye might like the company o' three more wagons."

"I declare, where'd you all hail from, Mackinaw?" said Kramer with a booming friendly laugh. "You don't strike me as the pioneerin' type!"

"I'm from Scotland years ago," answered Drew, "but we just left New York a few months ago, where we been livin' fer ten years."

"Well, wherever you're from and whatever kind of accent your tongue's comfortable with, you're welcome t' join us. This here land's big enough for us all, I reckon. And three more wagons couldn't hurt none. Fact is, we been hung up here more'n a week. No one's willin' to take such a small train of wagons cross them plains these days."

"We were just about ready to strike out alone," put in a tall, slim man several years younger than the bearded Kramer. He ambled forward and offered Drew, Evan, and Frank his hand.

"Maybe *you* was, Williams, but I ain't so sure," said Kramer.

"What's the problem?" said Evan.

"A few weeks makes a big different here," Pete explained. "If we'd have arrived a little sooner there wouldn't have been no problem. But it's near the end of May and we—and now you folks—why, we're just about the last of the emigrants heading west this year. Most of the big trains left last month, on account of the fall snows and such like. You can't make it unless you start before June. So you see, we can't keep waiting to see if any others show up. But we've been warned to stay in large groups—twenty, thirty wagons at least."

A pause followed; the question *why* seemed to hang unspoken on the lips of all in the recently arrived Mackinaw Party. Finally Drew spoke the word.

At first Pete seemed reluctant to venture an answer. "Well, there's always rumors like this flyin' around," he began. "It's right hard to tell just what a body should put stock in and what you should just put out of your mind altogether. Word is, there's been some Indian trouble. Seems the stage line to Denver's been attacked a couple of times. And there was a couple of wagons from the last train headin' out of here that came back with some stories to tell that'd shiver your hide."

"Come on, Pete!" interjected Williams, his voice laced with the frustration of youth toward their elders. "If anyone listened to that batch of hog feed, there'd be no settlers west of the Missouri!"

"I know you and the other young bucks around here think nothin' of a scrape with some renegade redskins," said Kramer. "But those of us with families is bound to exercise a bit more caution."

"Weel," said Drew, "eleven wagons be more'n eight."

"Maybe we can get someone to take us on now," said Kramer hopefully. "But most of the experienced wagon masters have already set out with full trains," he added, almost as an afterthought to himself.

"Stoddard's still in town," put in a new voice joining the small crowd.

"I thought we voted him down," said another.

"That was a week ago," came the reply. "Things are different now."

"We can't sit around here forever!"

As the discussion continued, Ellie, Leila, and Rebbekah McCollough glanced toward one another with some apprehension. The subject of Indian raids had come up before. But suddenly the danger loomed much closer than they had dared allow themselves to think about.

Long before the discussion between the men grew heated, Kramer's commanding voice interceded.

"This ain't gettin' us nowhere. Maybe it's worth another vote. But first, I reckon' these newcomers are plumb beat and lookin' for supper."

Two hours later, once dinner was behind them, parents began settling their excited but tired children into bed. Between the Mackinaws and McColloughs there were eight youngsters, in addition to Frank and Leila's older boys. Evan was but twenty-five, and Frank was the oldest member of the group. But the party revolved around the Mackinaw wagon and around Drew Mackinaw himself. His quiet strength and vitality represented a maturity that both the other men willingly looked up to. Yet each man and woman contributed to the total fiber of the group which had already grown into a close, compatible unit. Only Maggie remained outside the circle of their oneness—by her choice, not theirs.

Once the children were asleep and the dinner gear put away, Pete Kramer sauntered over, the aromatic smoke from his pipe preceding him, and invited them all to join an impromptu meeting with the rest of the small camp. They followed him toward the large campfire already blazing away. He introduced the few who hadn't already met, then cleared his throat several times until he had the undivided attention of the group.

"Well now," he began, "it looks to me like we gotta decide what we aim to do. And soon. It's nearly June, and summer's no time to be settin' out across the plains. Some of you been talkin' 'bout goin' it alone. But since none of us has ever been across before, and with Indian trouble brewin', it strikes me that we oughta be thinkin' of somethin' else."

"There's Stoddard," said one of the men.

"Yes, there is him," returned Kramer thoughtfully.

"He's been across four times."

"Knows his stuff, that's sure."

"But we voted him down," put in another.

"Who is this Stoddard fellow?" asked Evan.

"We only know what we heard," began Kramer, but he was interrupted before he could go on.

"And what we heard is that the last train he led was massacred while he was drunk!" said one of the men.

"Is that true?" asked Drew.

"Like I told you before," Kramer replied, "rumors hereabouts are thick as swamp mosquitos on a balmy night. But the train was massacred, that's a fact."

"Seems a man ought t' have the chance t' defend himsel'," said Drew. "Things like that happen an' ye canna be holdin' it against a person the rest o' his life."

"Would you want him responsible for your wife and children?" asked the man who seemed to be head of the opposition.

"That I couldna answer till I met the man face t' face," answered Drew. For a moment there was no reply, for none of those present had yet met Gil Stoddard personally.

Before the discussion had ended some time later, it had been decided that their situation was desperate enough to merit giving the man Stoddard the benefit of an interview.

The next morning Drew, Pete, Kramer, and the man who had spoken against Gil Stoddard rode into Independence in search of the man who had been the object of their discussion. Their search was rewarded, for shortly before noon, four riders approached the small cluster of wagons. The fourth sat in his saddle like one weary with riding, weary with life. His wide-brimmed hat was tattered and dusty, tipping downward over his eyebrows so that it cast a melancholy shadow over his face. Yet that was perhaps only an illusion; a deeper and more permanent shadow shrouded his eyes even when his hat was removed. It might have been a handsome face once. No doubt in its younger days it had turned the eyes of more than one frontier woman. But all those past glories were dulled by dust and a three-day stubble of beard, and dark eyes that seemed to have forgotten how to smile. His clothes hung shabbily from his large but weary frame, and one could only wonder what had caused this once mighty man of the west to age before his time.

A somber group slowly gathered about the riders as they dismounted. Somehow they had hoped all the rumors were wrong about Stoddard, but one look told them this was a man about whom such rumors could certainly be true. Still, why else had Pete brought him back to camp unless he thought they should hire him to lead their group of wagons west?

"Folks," said Pete addressing the group, "this here's Gil Stoddard. He wanted to come out and have a look around before he made any decisions."

No one spoke as Stoddard began to amble in and out among the group, eyeing the wagons, seeming to count the children with growing disgust, never relaxing the scowl on his face. Suddenly he stopped in front of Maggie, who had edged toward the fringe of the onlookers.

"Good Lord!" he exclaimed rolling his eyes. "That's all we need—a pregnant woman!"

"You don't need to worry about me," Maggie replied haughtily. The defiance in her voice came as a surprise even to her. But she resented this man's tone. She'd been pushed around by circumstances enough, and she wasn't about to let this rude and dirty horseman insult her. "I can manage myself just fine!"

"A foreigner, too," he mumbled as he moved on. Finally he stopped and swung around to face Kramer. "I'll tell you all something right now. You're going to be paying me good money to do that—*worry*, that is. And you just well better let me do my job. I expect you to do what I say and when I say it. There's no room on the prairie for a bunch of greenhorns arguing with the only person around who knows what he's about. Those are my terms. I'll want a hundred and twenty-five dollars. Fifty now and the rest when we get there."

A murmur rippled through the group, and a few suppressed gasps of astonishment could be heard.

"The going rate's only fifty dollars," complained one of the men.

"That's in April," stated Stoddard roughly, "and that's not for no ten-wagon train with more kids underfoot than grown men, and pregnant women besides," he added with another glance toward Maggie.

"We have eleven wagons," said one of the wives.

"Ten . . . eleven, what's it matter?" said Stoddard. "It's not enough."

"What about the rumors of your last train?"

In reply, and without a word, Stoddard swung back up on his horse, wheeled it around, and began to ride off.

"Wait!" shouted Kramer. "Where you goin'?"

Stoddard paused to shout back over his shoulder. "That's another rule I forgot to mention. If there's no trust, there's no use even making a beginning."

"We're only askin' fer a reason t' trust," answered Drew, gazing steadily after the man.

Stoddard's horse stopped; the weary trail boss returned Drew's stare, seeming to sense the younger man's desire to trust him if only he would let down his hard-bitten exterior.

"I wasn't drunk," Stoddard said at length, his voice as steady as Drew's gaze.

A moment of silence followed, during which the only sound was the shuffling of Stoddard's horse's hoofs in the dust. At length Drew's voice broke the silence: "The Mackinaw party will put in forty dollars."

With his words the trance-like hush was broken and others of the small group began likewise to pledge themselves to the task at hand. Whether they had more faith in Drew's assessment of Stoddard's character, or in Stoddard himself, no one could tell. But it did not take long before the full amount had been committed, so anxious were they all to get moving again.

In the midst of the general commotion Maggie stood, still angered over Stoddard's arrogant words. As she turned to move back toward their wagon she was startled by the presence of another man who had come up quietly behind her. Not expecting the mingled look of anger and surprise on her face, the stranger stood speechless for a brief moment.

"I hope I didn't startle you," he said at last.

"No, you didn't," Maggie replied crisply, hardly noticing that her body had stiffened again.

"I'm Dr. Carpenter," the man said. In the awkwardness of the moment, his words were reticent, yet there was also in his voice a quiet, soothing quality which could not help but dissolve a little of Maggie's tenseness. "Mr. Stoddard's less than sympathetic words compelled me to speak to you," he continued.

"Mr. Stoddard's words meant nothing to me," said Maggie coldly, hoping her lie was convincing.

"I'm glad to hear that," Carpenter said. "Still, I want you to know that I am available to assist you when it becomes necessary."

The man before Maggie was at least two inches beyond six feet tall, with most of his height in his thin gangly legs. Yet he did not appear clumsy but carried his tall frame easily, as if he had long ago conquered his lanky build because there were more important things for him to concentrate his energies on. In his mid-thirties, he had brown hair streaked here and there with strands of gray. However, the gray tended to soften his lean, angular face, almost handsome in its rugged irregularity.

"Thank you, Dr. Carpenter," said Maggie, relaxing by degrees. "That is very kind of you." She continued on her way without further word.

She did not look back again until she had reached the wagon, then cast one backward glance at the retreating doctor. A momentary pang of guilt reminded her that she had been less than courteous to him, but she brushed it aside quickly. She owed the man nothing, she thought. Still she was uncomfortable with the memory of the encounter. It had given her an almost forgotten glimpse of her old self—the child Maggie enclosed in self-imposed walls of protection, the Maggie who had shut out all love before finally allowing Ian to break through to her heart.

She thought that she had changed, but in reality the change had not worked into her fully. Perhaps the brief change had been worse than no change at all. For now Maggie felt that her childhood rejection by her father was made complete by the one man she had allowed herself to love. Even Ian—through no fault of his own—had deserted her at last, through death. Her father had had the final victory over her and the final revenge over Ian. As she climbed up into the wagon, the lonely child deep within her heart still felt the bitterness of a father's rejection, and if the woman in her refused to admit it, the child nonetheless hid once again behind the stone walls of her soul, thicker and more impenetrable than the walls of her girlhood home.

By the time Stoddard had returned to town for the few possessions he would need, a hasty lunch had been prepared and camp had been broken. By one o'clock in the afternoon, eleven wagons with billowing white canvas were creeping toward the Missouri, where a ferry was waiting to carry them to the west bank and the beginning of their long journey.

25

An Unexpected Encounter

※
☆

MAGGIE TOSSED A sweaty strand of hair from her face. But it was no use—another immediately took its place. Had she ever been so hot in her life? She inhaled the tepid air, but it only stung her parched throat. Gazing out the back of the wagon, Maggie strained her eyes to see some change in the terrain. But as far as her eye could see, as it had been for days now, was nothing but the monotonous expanse of dry, grass-covered plain—barren as a desolate heath moor. For a moment her mind wandered back to the solitary wasteland she had known and loved called Braenock Ridge.

"I've heard some call it godforsaken. But I'll not be believin' that. A place like Braenock Ridge holds a tender place in His heart just because it never gives up." Digory's words rushed unbidden back into her mind. She had not thought of the old groom in weeks.

Maggie sighed. But as the sigh caught in her throat a sob rushed in to replace it, suddenly jarring her back to the present. She could not think of the past! She had to forget. Forget Digory. Braenock Ridge, Stonewycke . . .

"Oh, Ian, I can't forget you!" she murmured into the dry air.

Suddenly the rear wagon wheel jostled over a rock, almost knocking Maggie off her hard wooden seat. She glanced quickly at the bed opposite her. The three youngest Mackinaw children still slept soundly. Maggie marveled, for the constant jolting of the wagon did not seem to disturb them; yet last night, when all had been still and quiet, they had hardly slept a wink.

Perhaps last night had been too quiet. Almost eerie. If the children's cries had not kept her awake, she would undoubtedly have found sleep difficult all the same.

There had been talk of them all day. And about an hour before sunset they had actually seen four Indians on a ridge about half a mile in the distance. The Indians sat tall and proud on their brown and white horses, all except for the leader whose magnificent white stallion Maggie had particularly noticed. Still as statues they remained, watching the train in silence as it passed until slowly it had rumbled out of sight. Maggie knew she and her friends were under special scrutiny, and the incident had had a disquieting effect on everyone in the wagon train.

For some unknown reason Maggie did not feel afraid of these savages, as all the men called them. In an odd sort of way they reminded her of her own Viking ancestors—proud and mighty warriors who would spare neither blood nor tears for the land they loved. Could these very natives of the land called America have sprung from the kindred blood of exploring Vikings who ventured to the New World centuries before the Spaniards?

Yet in the end the Scotsmen were subdued—some called it unified. Maggie supposed that these Indians, as well, would be subdued one day. The thought made her more sad than before. Yet glancing back toward the four grand warriors, she knew they would not allow their people to be subdued without a struggle.

Now the children were asleep, for the fears of the night had been dispelled. Another day's welcome light had arrived safely. For Maggie it meant another day to go on living, another day to watch the children, to *watch* the progress of their train and the lives that were bound up in this adventure, but never to feel a part. She wondered if she would ever feel a part of anything again.

As her thoughts drifted back to the present Maggie realized the wagon had stopped. Scrambling forward she poked her head out through the canvas opening.

"What is it, Ellie?" she asked.

"Soldiers," Ellie replied with some alarm in her tone. "Drew," she went on, turning toward her husband where he sat at her side holding the reins, "you don't suppose the war's come this far west?"

Drew did not answer for a moment, then spoke thoughtfully. "Fort Laramie's none too far from here. 'Tis most likely they're from there. I doubt 'tis the war."

With the words he swung his large hulk down from the wagon. "I'd best be goin' over t' see what it's all about. Ye stay here," he added firmly.

Most of the other men had also climbed down from their wagons and were walking toward the cluster of eight or ten mounted soldiers where they sat conferring with Gil Stoddard. As Drew came within earshot he could hear the voices of Stoddard and one referred to as Captain Henry.

"We heard talk of that in Independence," Stoddard was saying. His voice, naturally low and gruff, sounded even more serious now.

"That looks like only the beginning," replied the captain, a young man in his mid-thirties with a clean-shaven face and eyes that seemed unable to focus long on any one object. At first Drew thought him nervous, then wondered if the constantly roving eyes were actually alert and vigilant, always on the lookout for possible signs of danger.

"Evans has sent out a proclamation to the Arapaho and Cheyenne—" Captain Henry began, but was cut off by one of the men who had gathered.

"Who's Evans?"

"He's the governor of Colorado, you dimwit!" yelled another before the captain could reply.

"That's right," Henry went on. "He's warned all the friendly Indians to collect at the various forts so they don't get killed along with the bad ones."

"They're not likely to take too kindly to that," said Stoddard in the tone of one who knew his business.

"That's why we're out on patrol," replied the captain. "Evans' message just got out a couple of days ago. So far none of the Indians have responded except a few of the old and sick. The worry is that they're mixing with the Sioux from up in

Dakota. And they're a bloody bunch, always inciting the more peaceful tribes into war."

"You don't think the Cheyenne will listen to Evans do you?" asked Stoddard cynically.

"Not hardly. That's why we're expecting trouble. Evans is determined to put a stop to all the pillaging and raiding. He'll retaliate and the redskins will fight back."

Henry's eyes deliberately scanned the distant horizon. Unconsciously the eyes of the onlookers all followed his gaze, but all that met their looks was the dry, blazing-hot prairie grass.

"Evans has had enough," Henry went on, almost to himself. "He's vowed that no more Little Crows will turn up in his territory, even if it takes a repeat of what happened at Mankato to keep them in their place."

"Mankato?" asked one of the men.

"A small town up in Minnesota. Little Crow and thirty-nine of his followers were all hanged from a single scaffold a while back. They had killed over 700 whites before the army tracked them down."

A murmur rippled through the men as the captain wheeled his horse around. "So you all stick together, and watch yourselves," he warned. "These are perilous times to be heading across the plains, and there's not enough soldiers to defend every one of these trails."

Before the men had concluded their informal meeting with the army officer, Maggie shifted uncomfortably in her seat and realized how stiff and cramped she had become. And the sun beating down on the immobile wagon had made it like an oven inside. It was time for a little walk and some fresh air.

Without a stepping stool on the ground outside to assist her, it took Maggie some moments to maneuver her cumbersome, swelling body out of the back of the wagon. But finally her feet touched the ground, and she sighed with some satisfaction. Several of the other women were stirring about the wagons. There were no children about.

The still air outside the wagon gave Maggie little respite from the heat, and she could not help being drawn to the river less than a stone's throw away. She didn't think to tell Ellie where she was going, nor did it occur to her how foolhardy it was to wander away from the train alone. If the wagons should start up again, who would know she was missing? Still less was she aware of the tiny furtive figure that climbed out of the wagon and followed.

Before her lay the Platte, a broad expanse of muddy water running swiftly within its low banks. By summer's end it would in many places be little more than a trickle, but in this spot in early June, still swollen from the last spring runoff, it bore a strong resemblance to the more mighty rivers of its kindred land. It was certainly not the Lindow, Maggie thought carelessly, then braced herself against the pain of whatever memories the thought of that lovely Scottish river would give birth to in her mind. In defiance of those memories she sucked in a deep breath of the warm air and marched boldly down to the bank. The few cottonwoods scattered sparsely along the shore offered little promise of shade from the intense June heat. Cautiously Maggie lowered herself at the water's edge, reached down with a cupped hand, and began to splash water onto her dry face. She couldn't remember when anything had ever felt so refreshing.

Suddenly a twig snapped behind her. She froze, arresting her hand halfway to her face. She turned slowly, then let out a relieved sigh.

"Bess! What are you doing here?" she asked in a scolding tone despite her relief.

"I don't know," the child replied simply. "I just followed you."

"You shouldn't have left the wagon."

"No one told me."

Maggie eyed her for a moment, then smiled and held out her hand.

"Oh, dear little Bess," she said, "I suppose neither of us should be out alone like this. But since we are, come and let me splash some of this cool water on your face."

Bess approached her and, in a sudden playful mood, Maggie threw out a handful of water toward the young girl. Giggling, Bess ran to the water's edge and retaliated with two small splashes of her own. Maggie threw her head back and laughed, and in the brief moment of unusual abandon felt almost like a child again herself. She was, after all, only seventeen, and it had been so long—too long—since she had actually giggled. Dripping with the cool water, Maggie threw her arms around Bess and kissed her.

The brief moment of affection ended a second later with a sharp gasp from Bess as she stiffened in Maggie's arms.

"Bess, what is it?" asked Maggie with alarm.

The girl's mouth moved but she was unable to utter a word, continuing to stare over Maggie's shoulder. Maggie turned, and to her horror saw a young Indian girl not much older than herself inching toward them. Just as Maggie turned the Indian slumped down to the ground against one of the scraggly cottonwoods. Overcoming her initial shock, Maggie glanced hastily around, afraid that others might be following. She grabbed Bess by the hand and rose to leave. Still the woman sat motionless, leaning heavily against the tree. Her worn buckskin was old and dirty with several dark splotches on it. Maggie paused to stare a moment longer. The young woman was clearly too exhausted to warrant Maggie's initial fear. Her bronzed skin and large dark eyes set in a moon-shaped face must surely have once been lovely to look at. But now her features revealed only weariness and pain. Her eyes stared blankly ahead, taking no notice of the two whites who had intruded into her land. Still Maggie stood, little Bess clutching her skirts.

All at once Maggie saw that a small baby lay on the woman's lap, wrapped in rags which must have once been an Indian blanket. How she could not have noticed it sooner, despite her fear, Maggie did not know. The child remained very still, then as Maggie took notice of it, seemed to stir slightly.

Maggie took a tentative step toward the girl and her baby, and then the Indian turned her head slightly and stared toward Maggie's swollen abdomen. A sudden kinship of motherhood stirred within Maggie, the first of its kind even though her own time was drawing near.

"My—my—baby is almost due," Maggie said at last, with tentative voice.

The woman gave no indication that she understood the words.

"Ellie thinks it may be only two or three more weeks. And she's had five children, so she must know." As she spoke, Maggie took a step closer, with Bess still clinging behind.

"Is this your first?" asked Maggie. "Seems like a good sleeper."

The woman's eyes seemed to search Maggie's face, as if beseeching Maggie with her eyes because her mouth had no words.

"I don't know if I want a boy or a girl," Maggie went on, trying to put the other woman at ease. "Ellie says God knows what is right for us."

All at once the woman held the child up toward Maggie in her two hands, as if making an offering. She spoke a single word, which was as unintelligible to Maggie as Digory's Gaelic utterings of her childhood. But as with that gently spoken Gaelic, Maggie did not need to understand the words to know what was being said. The woman's pain-ridden eyes and the soft wail in her voice was interpretation enough. She was pleading for help.

Maggie approached cautiously and reached out to lay a hand gently on the baby's cheek. But even before her touch revealed the burning fever, she could see it in the flushed skin.

"Oh, dear! he's so hot," she said with alarm.

The woman repeated the word she had spoken before, imploring Maggie once more, then lowered the child again into her lap as she fell back against the tree.

"Bess!" said Maggie. "Go get the doctor!"

Bess did not move but continued to press up against Maggie's back.

"Go on, hurry!" Maggie urged. "This is important . . . do you understand, *important!*"

Bess began to edge away.

"Run, Bess, run!" Maggie called. The young girl took one last hesitating look at Maggie, then at the Indian woman, then shot up the bank and back toward the wagons at a full run.

In less than five minutes Samuel Carpenter appeared trotting down the shallow slope of the bank toward Maggie. He took in the entire scene with a single glance, not appearing in the least disturbed at the object of his call.

"What's the trouble?" he asked, kneeling down beside the two women. As he reached toward the child's reddened cheeks the mother drew her infant back, hugging the baby closer to her with a look of panic growing in her eyes.

"He wants to help," said Maggie softly. "He's a doctor. He will help . . . help . . . do you understand? *Doctor.*"

She paused and glanced helplessly at Dr. Carpenter. Then an idea struck her.

She hastily repeated the single word she had thus far heard the Indian woman say. She said it over several times, and gradually a dim light seemed to dawn in the young mother's countenance and she slowly relaxed her grip on the child and allowed the doctor to touch him.

"Dear Lord!" Carpenter exclaimed. "He's burning up!"

Moving closer he peeled away the blankets and wrappings and began pressing the baby's abdomen and flexing its limp arms and legs.

"He's dreadfully dehydrated," he said, then turning to the woman, "When was the last time he ate something? Have you any milk?"

She stared back at him blankly.

"Milk," he repeated, touching his chest, then the baby's mouth, "milk!"

The woman dismally shook her head. Maggie saw tears inching down the poor woman's cheeks. But the doctor's urgent voice was oblivious to the woman's inner sorrow. He was intent on saving her child.

"Mrs. Duncan, have you a petticoat?" he asked, then continued on before she had a chance to reply. "No . . . never mind. I'll use my shirt." As he spoke he tore the shirt from his back.

"The sun will burn you to a crisp," objected Maggie.

"Never mind that. Just take my shirt to the river and get it wet, mud and all, if you have to. It'll be better for the child then nothing."

Finally understanding, Maggie complied. "How could such a thing have happened?" the doctor said to himself in frustration. "I only hope we've found her in time to do some good—"

But the rest of his words were lost on Maggie as she plunged his shirt in the dirty Platte and ran back to where the doctor still knelt at the woman's side.

He took it from her and brought the moist cloth to the baby's parched lips. Maggie placed a hand under the tiny head and before she knew it was cradling the baby in her arms. The child's mother had fallen back unconscious. Carpenter bent over her and, picking her up in his strong arms, carried her to the water's edge.

Meanwhile Maggie held the Indian child closer to her breast, as if to afford it extra protection now that its mother had gone from sight. The child made a feeble effort to suck at the wet shirt. Unconsciously she began to softly sing an old poem Digory had taught her which she had hardly thought of in years:

Ane by ane they gang awa;
The getherer gethers grit and sma':
Ane by ane maks ane and a'!

Aye what ane sets doon the cup
Ane ahint maun tak it up:
A' thegither they will sup!

Golden-heidit, ripe, and strang,
Shorn will be the hairst or lang:
Syne begins a better sang!

She sang the tune softly again, then again, until Dr. Carpenter's heavy footstep sounded behind her. She turned, surprised to see him approaching alone. His face was pale in spite of its sunburned skin, and the strain of failure was evident in his deep-set eyes.

"She's gone," he said with a husky, strained voice.

"Gone?" repeated Maggie, confused.

"She's gone . . . dead," he answered, his lips trembling slightly. "She was the one who was really sick, hemorrhaging. I saw it when I carried her to the river. She must have known she was dying and was probably trying to get to Fort Laramie for help."

He dropped to his knees beside Maggie where she sat holding the baby. "It must have depleted all her strength and dried up whatever milk she had for the poor child."

Overwhelmed with a greater sorrow than she could understand, Maggie listened dumbstruck to the doctor's words. She felt she had lost a friend. And indeed, in those brief moments, Maggie and that poor lovely Indian woman *had* shared an intimacy of sorrow and loss as perhaps no other two friends could have. A choking sob struggled to explode from her throat, but generations of Ramsey breeding kept it back and prevented the hot tears from escaping to the surface.

Maggie merely held the baby closer, and—as if to remind her of the preciousness of life—her own unborn child moved within her. It was also a reminder of sorrow.

In the midst of her private thoughts Maggie realized Dr. Carpenter was speaking, but when she looked up at him she saw that his head was bowed. He had not been addressing her.

". . . in your wisdom. Protect this child with your strength, Lord," he said earnestly. "He is in your hands, for I have no power to help him without you. Let his mother's dying wish be fulfilled."

"Did—did she say something to you?" asked Maggie when he paused.

"No. But I don't doubt that her last thoughts were for the survival of her son, even that her own death might somehow buy back the life of the child."

Maggie merely nodded. There were too many questions. Why should such an exchange of life be necessary? Why couldn't both be spared? Life could seem so cruel!

Dr. Carpenter watched her for a moment as she concentrated her attention on the small Indian child. He could detect a hidden purpose in her eyes—she seemed to be coming to life again. The doctor had observed this young Scottish mother-to-be frequently since the wagon train had left Missouri. And though the dormant beauty of her face was not lost on him, what had truly drawn his attention was the tragic sadness of her countenance and being. She seemed but going through the motions of life. He had learned that she was a recent widow and his heart ached that this joyous time, the anticipation of her first child, should have been so marred with grief.

Yet now he could almost detect a small spark igniting within Maggie. Just as the helpless little Indian child was struggling for its very life, so also the spirit which had once given life its joy and zest was fighting within Maggie to remain alive. He hoped the spark in her eyes would ignite and grow. For as she sat holding the motherless child, Dr. Carpenter could see that the success of the one struggle was intimately bound up with the progress of the other.

26

Samuel Carpenter

❈

VOICES AND THE clamor of approaching feet suddenly broke in upon
the gentle silence of the two kneeling figures. Dr. Carpenter looked up to see
several of their train companions coming toward them.

"What's keepin' you?" Gil Stoddard asked with an impatience that had clearly
been simmering for some time. "We thought you musta drowned!"

"Maggie here found an Indian woman—"

"Indians!" shouted one of the others while the rest looked frantically around.

"Only a sick squaw and her child," Carpenter replied calmly, but with a hint
of exasperation in his voice. "The poor woman just died and the child here is very
sick."

"It ain't contagious, is it, Doc?" Stoddard asked.

"No. You needn't worry."

"Are you sure?"

"I'm a physician, of course I'm sure!" Carpenter snapped. "We'll have to take
the child on—at least as far as Fort Laramie. And we need to bury the woman."

"We'll take the kid," Stoddard replied. "But we ain't stickin' around for no
buryin'. There could be warriors not far behind her."

"We can't just leave her here."

"Didn't you hear those soldiers, *Doctor* Carpenter?" said Stoddard, emphasizing each syllable. "We're right plum in the middle of three or four tribes of
hot-tempered redskins. We've already given them time to surround us twice over
lookin' for you and the lady here."

"Surely you're not suggesting we leave the poor woman to rot in the sun?"
demanded Carpenter, pulling himself to his feet. "That's inhuman."

"If you think we're going to risk our necks for a dead savage who would have
thought it nothing to stab you in the heart if she had the strength—"

Carpenter stepped up to Stoddard and faced him squarely. "Then you go on
ahead. I'll catch up."

"You're a crazy fool," said Stoddard spitefully. "And I thought it was *good*
fortune you was with us." With the words Stoddard turned and hurried back up
the bank toward the wagons. In a few moments he returned with four shovels and
a scowl on his rugged face.

"Well, Kramer, Williams, Wooten," he shouted at the other men present, "if
I'm goin' to lose my scalp buryin' a redskin squaw, I ain't about to do it alone!"
He walked away, cursing loudly.

"Mr. Stoddard," the doctor said, his voice beginning to lose its usual even-tempered patience, "I'll also remind you there is a lady present."

Stoddard's mumbled reply was lost to the doctor's ears as he slammed the tip of his shovel into the hard, dry earth.

Samuel Carpenter was not a frontiersman. Born and raised in the Lower East side of New York City, the son of a dock-worker, Samuel was a good deal more familiar with brick and crowded tenements and noisy markets than with the dusty wagon trails, lawlessness, and sage brush so typical of life on the open prairie. Practically from the moment he could walk he had worked, first as an errand boy, then a newspaper assistant, and finally by his father's side on the grimy docks of the greatest city in the land. In his meager spare time he read incessantly and while reading about the discovery of the smallpox vaccination in England, he had been inspired by the courage of English physician Edward Jenner and decided he wanted to become a doctor. He loved helping people more than anything else. Raising himself up in society, however, especially with illiterate parents who considered his desire for an education to be frivolous, proved to be a long and strenuous achievement. But when he graduated from one of New York's medical schools as second in his class, their pride knew no bounds. Shortly thereafter he married the daughter of a wealthy New York businessman whom he had met during his hospital residency. Samuel Carpenter seemed well on his way to what was destined to be great achievement and worldly success in his career and in the glamorous life of New York society.

He was just on the verge of being appointed chief-of-staff at Bellevue when his well-ordered life began to crumble. After six childless years his wife had finally become pregnant. But their ecstasy was short-lived. The blessed news was followed shortly by the devastating revelation that she had contracted leukemia. Within six months the doctor's wife and unborn child were both dead.

For a year Carpenter's shattered life lost all meaning. Even the spiritual values which he had considered part of his life were unable to sustain him. He resigned his position at Bellevue and took to traveling—wandering throughout the east, searching for the inner strength he had thought he possessed. The tragedy of his wife's death drained away whatever scanty reserve of fortitude he had, leaving him with the firm conviction that God had deserted him altogether.

But when he finally came to terms with his loss, he realized God had never left him at all. The moment came as he stood in the biting cold before a solitary white-steepled church in the snowy Vermont hills. For the first time he was empty enough to be able to yield himself fully to the God he had kept at arm's length all this time. Coming in from the cold into the humble boarding house where he was lodging, his mind was suddenly alive again. Suddenly he saw that he could make something of his life again if he would begin relying on God rather than himself. He knew he could never return to the comfort of his previous life as a successful physician in the high society of the city. For the first time he realized that in the glamour of his success, he had forgotten his original dream to help people in need. But he determined to forget it no more.

A week later, in Boston, he chanced to hear a lecture entitled "Medicine in the Wild West." Here was a need he never knew existed! The thousands of easterners and emigrants pouring across the American plains were finding medical services in short supply. When a doctor was to be found he was often a charlatan with little or no medical training.

But the moment his talk turned to thoughts of going west, again he met with opposition. His family and friends considered him crazy even to think of turning his back on his well-established career. But more than ever before in his life he knew he was being *called* to a cause greater than himself and he would let nothing stand in his way. He was accustomed to fighting for what mattered to him, not perhaps in the manner in which a rough westerner like Gil Stoddard would fight, but nonetheless determined. His battles were not fought with fists but with a strength of will and even, as his mother might have said, "with a streak of stubbornness a mile wide." Yet he remained a soft-spoken man who never relied heavily on words to win his battles, but rather on his immovable convictions.

Having made the decision to go west, Samuel Carpenter became more single-minded than ever in the pursuit of his goal of helping the sick. That passion had drawn him away from the city life he had known since birth with the destination of California before him. But he was in no hurry, for was there not plenty to do along the way? His sensitive nature had surfaced in his rugged surroundings more than it would ever have been able to in the confines of Bellevue. Not only did he minister soothing words and comfort to the ailing, but their cares ministered healing to his once-troubled soul in ways he was only beginning to see.

Maggie gladly took charge of the Indian child when Dr. Carpenter asked her. She had hardly considered any other course of action. In fact, she found herself surprisingly disheartened when he explained that they would give the child to the Indian agent in Fort Laramie when they arrived in two days. It hardly crossed her mind that she would soon have a newborn child of her own to care for; the mothering instinct simply reached out to the helpless little infant who had so unexpectedly dropped into her arms, and she wanted to love him as her own.

Ellie dug out a bottle from a small box of baby things she had brought along for Maggie, and their cow was still yielding a scanty supply of milk. By the end of the day the baby had taken enough to insure his survival at least through the night. By morning his fever had dropped and his eyes seemed more alert.

"It's amazing how quickly they mend," remarked Maggie as she cradled the infant in her arms.

"It is that," replied Ellie, pausing a moment in her repacking of their gear for the day's journey. "But he didn't do it alone," she added, noting the look of pride on Maggie's face. "I've been prayin' for him."

Maggie smiled. "Thank you," she said. She could not bring herself to confess that she had never once prayed for the dying child. The thought of prayer had come to her, but the words would not form on her lips. And she could not admit, especially to Ellie, that she was rapidly losing any assurance that God even heard whatever prayers she might offer.

As the two women spoke, Dr. Carpenter ambled up to the Mackinaw camp and was carefully eyeing Maggie and the baby.

"You're doing a fine job with him," he encouraged.

"It's the prayers, like Ellie said," Maggie replied, looking away.

"Yes, Mrs. Duncan, but you are the answer to those prayers. You have given the boy something he needed far more than milk. Let me examine him a moment."

The baby protested mildly as the doctor took him in his arms, and smiled. "He's getting some fight back. That's good."

"I thought we should give him a name," Maggie suggested.

"He will be here only until tomorrow."

"Yes, I know. But he ought to be called something besides 'the baby.' "

"You don't want to become too attached, Mrs. Duncan. You do know that taking him to the agency is the best thing for him."

"How can some agency take better care of him than I—we—than Ellie and I could?"

"They will return the child to his people. He deserves to be raised among them. I'm afraid, Mrs. Duncan, that it would be neither an easy nor a happy life for him among white men."

"I understand," Maggie resigned. "But I shall call him my little *Indian bairn,* nonetheless."

Dr. Carpenter tried to restrain the smile that crept to his lips. She, too, had a stubborn streak, and he realized it would serve her well as she tried to forge a new life in this rugged land.

Before anything else could be said, Drew approached with the announcement that they were ready to be on their way. Dr. Carpenter returned to his wagon, and Maggie, carrying the baby, climbed into the back of theirs, followed by Bess, Sarah, and Darren. By now Tommy Joe and Bobby had all but taken up residence in the roomier Wooten wagon.

With a shout from Gil Stoddard and the answering commands from each of the men to their teams, the wagons plodded forth into another wearisome day. The following day dawned in the same manner, each moment bringing them closer to Fort Laramie. Though Maggie understood, when the moment finally came it was no less difficult to relinquish her Indian bairn. The Indian agent was a kindly man and said the boy would be returned to his tribe to grow up among his own people, perhaps to even be reunited with his father or grandparents.

It was the best thing—Maggie knew that, but that knowledge could not keep away the empty feeling within her. That emptiness was beginning to be so ingrained in her that she wondered if she had ever been without it. The child had filled the void, but only for a few days. Now the hollow pit in her heart seemed larger than ever.

Samuel Carpenter could sense Maggie's need and tried to find ways to involve her in the needs of others. Caring for the child had been good for her, he thought, even if the parting was painful. At least she was feeling again. Even pain could be beneficial in the right doses. *Yes,* he thought, *she just needs some time, and enough opportunities to help others.* He would continue to try to draw her into his work whenever she might be useful.

West of Fort Laramie the road brought the weary train to the ascent of the Black Hills. Stories of previous trains passing through the Dakota mountains were enough in themselves to sober any overconfidence which might still have remained in the minds of any of the western migrants. Already they had seen evidences of earlier difficulties and heartbreaks strewn along the road—treasures cast aside as the stresses of travel had mounted: a weather-worn carved secretary, a rusted iron plow, an equally rusted cookstove. Stoddard had insisted that all the wagons be repacked before they left Fort Laramie, and many had found parting with at least one precious keepsake necessary.

Though low in comparison to the Rockies which the travelers would eventually cross, the road through the Black Hills was nevertheless rough and barren, surrounded on all sides with craggy bluffs and with many steep inclines. They negotiated one of these bluffs and began making their descent at a point called Mexican Hill.

Stormclouds had been massing throughout the day, and as they crossed the rolling plateau that led to the descent, cracks of thunder began splitting through the still, humid air. Almost immediately the deafening sounds were accompanied by great pounding drops of rain. The jagged streaks of lightning and strange explosions terrified the bewildered animals. The oxen pulling the wagons were easily brought under control, but the fifty or sixty head of cattle following behind bolted with the first peal of thunder. Despite the attempts of the men on horseback to bring them under control, they rampaged through the train and the oxen followed suit. The declivity of Mexican Hill gave the oxen unexpected freedom, and several of the wagons, including Frank Wooten's, were caught in the middle. For a few tense minutes, a flood of dust, animal flesh, and billowing white wagons seemed bent on racing toward certain destruction.

Tommy Joe poked his head out of his uncle Frank's wagon to catch a glimpse of all the excitement just at the moment when the wagon wheel struck a protruding rock in its wild dash down the hill. The jolt sent the boy flying from the wagon. He would almost certainly have been trampled to death had he not been thrown clear and landed in a narrow gully some ten feet off the path of the stampeding livestock.

Drew Mackinaw had managed to keep his team in tow where he followed behind Frank, but the horror of seeing his son flung to what certainly must be his death was far worse than the terrors of any stampede. With shaking arms Drew reined his team to a halt as quickly as he could and ran to where his child lay. Two other wagons, including Samuel Carpenter's, stopped as well while the remainder continued down the hill to give what aid they could to the stampeding wagons.

Near hysteria, Ellie climbed from the wagon and followed her husband. Maggie ordered the little ones to stay inside, and then joined her friends. When they reached the gully where Tommy Joe's broken body lay, they found Drew kneeling at his side, tears streaming down his cheeks, holding his son's limp head gently in his hands. Ellie's tenuous control gave away.

"He's dead!" she screamed. "My boy's dead!"

Scrambling down the gully Dr. Carpenter ran to the scene, knelt down, felt about his neck and shoulders, leaned over the boy's chest with the side of his face against his heart, then rose slowly.

"He's alive," he said, but the words were lost on Ellie's screaming mind. A moment later her form, limp and unconscious, fell into Drew's arms.

"Oh, God!" Drew wailed. "It's my fault! What have I done?"

"Stop it, Mackinaw!" the doctor said firmly. "Your son is alive! And I'm going to need you strong if you're to help me bring him around. Now, see to your wife while we get the boy back to the wagon."

Then he directed his words to the two other men who had followed them off the trail. "Help me carry him out of here. But be gentle. I still can't tell if there might be some broken bones."

The three men eased Tommy Joe's body off the ground and worked their way up the embankment, now slick with mud. Drew carried Ellie back to the top, but Maggie found that she could not climb out of the gully alone. Glancing back as he reached the top, Dr. Carpenter saw her predicament, ran back to where she stood, and gave her his hand. He did not speak until they reached the top.

"Mrs. Duncan, go to my wagon and prepare a bed for the child. And we'll need a fire," he added to no one in particular, "if one can be lit in this rain."

They carried the boy to the doctor's wagon where Maggie stood by, watching and wondering what else she should do. But the doctor did not leave her standing thus for long.

"Mrs. Duncan, come here," he said. "Sit beside the boy and speak to him—he needs someone he knows nearby. I've got to see about the fire."

Maggie sank down next to Tommy, and laid a trembling hand lightly on his head. "Tommy . . . Tommy . . ." she said with shaky voice. "It's . . . you're going to be fine. The doctor's—"

"Mama!" the boy cried. "Mama!"

"Your mama will be here soon," Maggie soothed. "Here, take my hand."

The boy seemed to calm down and in a moment Dr. Carpenter returned. "The leg appears broken," he murmured. He began to probe gently with his hand, but when he reached a point three inches below the knee, where the skin was lacerated and his trousers were wet with blood, Tommy Joe screamed out in agony. "If only I had ether."

Just then Stoddard's voice could be heard outside. The wagon boss had galloped back up the hill after bringing the runaway wagons and stock under control. The weariness of his visage seemed even more pronounced.

Carpenter jumped from his wagon and hurried up to the trail master, who had dismounted and was barking orders to the few who were still standing out in the rain.

"Stoddard," the doctor asked without prelude, "have you some whiskey?"

Stoddard glared at the doctor.

"I need it for the boy."

Still Stoddard hesitated. The moment he and the doctor were alone, he reached into his saddlebag and withdrew a battered canteen. He shoved it into Carpenter's hand, but before the doctor could retreat to his patient, Stoddard said, "You ain't going to tell no one?"

"I'm a doctor, Mr. Stoddard. I know how to keep secrets."

"I only keep it around for times like this," the trail master added lamely. But the doctor had barely waited to hear and was already hastening back to the wagon.

Immediately Dr. Carpenter busied himself with preparations for the task ahead. He gave the whiskey to Maggie with instructions to administer it to Tommy Joe in whatever amounts he could tolerate.

It was a grueling two hours before the shattered leg was set to the doctor's satisfaction. Tommy Joe had long since passed out, both from inebriation and shock, and Maggie had been pressed into assisting the doctor more directly. While the leg was the most immediate concern, there was also a broken arm to be tended, as well as numerous cuts and scrapes. A badly bruised head also indicated the likelihood of a concussion, but Dr. Carpenter was at least relieved that no internal injuries were apparent.

When a pale and grief-stricken Ellie finally appeared at the doctor's wagon, Maggie assured her that Tommy Joe was sleeping soundly, and doing well, considering what he had been through.

"I was so scared," Ellie whispered. "I couldn't even pray. But the Lord will see him through. I know He will."

Maggie smiled and put an arm around her friend.

"I'm afraid, Mrs. Mackinaw," said the doctor in a soft voice, not wanting to disturb the sleeping boy, "that the worst may still be to come. Once he wakes up, for several days the pain is going to be excruciating. He's going to need lots of comfort and sympathy, and probably a good deal more whiskey to relieve the pain. And there's always the possibility of infection, but I'll watch him closely."

"Oh, dear!" said Ellie. "Poor Drew. He worries me almost as much as Tommy Joe. He keeps blaming himself, for letting the boy go in the other wagon, for dragging us all out west. I can't seem to say anything to him."

"He'll feel better when he sees that Tommy is all right," said Maggie.

"I don't know. I've never seen him like this."

Suddenly Gil Stoddard's shout could be heard outside. "Come on, let's get movin'. We're wastin' precious time!"

Maggie's initial reaction was outrage that the man could be so insensitive. She had no way of knowing that the soldiers had decidedly warned Stoddard against even starting out through the Dakotas. The Black Hills were Sioux country. Only two weeks before, a train had been attacked and suffered many casualties. A full-scale massacre had been averted only because an army patrol had happened along. But there could be no such guarantee of good fortune for other travelers. And Stoddard wanted to take no risks by remaining in one place too long.

Within five minutes the wagons began lurching forward and down the slope of Mexican Hill. The two women remained by the side of the injured boy in Dr. Carpenter's wagon. He awoke once and, after being comforted by the sight of his mother, fell back into a fitful sleep.

As the day progressed, Ellie and Maggie took turns remaining with Tommy Joe. Maggie made every attempt to relieve Ellie's anxiety by urging her to return to their wagon to be with Drew. And by the next day Maggie was tending the boy almost single-handedly while Dr. Carpenter eased his wagon along the rough and rocky trail as gently as he was able. Whenever he had the opportunity he turned, poking his head back through the opening in the canvas, to smile reassuringly at Maggie. He knew there was more healing taking place in the back of his wagon than in Tommy Joe's body and was gratified whenever Maggie returned his with a smile of her own. And not only was Samuel Carpenter concerned for the hurt in Maggie's heart, he knew her time was rapidly approaching; it was his responsibility to keep an ever closer eye on her condition.

After two days, the train made camp beside a grove of cottonwoods near a spring of pure, gushing water known as Warm Springs. Tommy Joe had gradually improved, and Dr. Carpenter was optimistic. He did not say, however, although the thought was heavily on his mind, that they still had to brace themselves for the possibility of infection.

Maggie climbed wearily out of the wagon. Even in her fatigued state it felt wonderful to stretch and walk about. The storm had long since passed, but it had left clouds in its wake and the respite from the earlier heat had indeed been welcome. She had hardly left the wagon in the past two days, and the fresh air and the scent from the trees and water invigorated her spirits.

"It's a wonderful place," she voiced, almost to herself.

"I wish we could stay here and recuperate for a few days," said the doctor, walking up behind her.

"Oh, Doctor," said Maggie, glancing around. "I didn't know you were there."

"The boy's sleeping. I needed to stretch my tired legs. But you must be exhausted, Mrs. Duncan. You've been so attentive to the lad. I appreciate your help."

"It's the least I could do. After all, his family's my family now too."

Just then Stoddard approached. As he passed she heard him muttering to one of the other men, "Too many trees here. I don't like it," he added in his gruff, laconic manner.

"All the wagon trains camp here," offered the other.

"Yeah. It's a fine place if the Indians don't—" He cut his words short the moment he saw Maggie nearby.

Maggie forced a thin smile. "Good evening," she said awkwardly.

"How's the kid?" Stoddard asked.

"About the same," Maggie replied.

"He'll be fine, Mr. Stoddard," added the doctor.

"Shouldn't have kids out on the trail," Stoddard muttered.

Maggie turned to walk back toward the doctor's wagon, but Stoddard addressed her once more. "Where you from anyway, Mrs. Duncan, with that peculiar accent of yours?" he asked bluntly.

"Scotland," she replied, wondering what had prompted his sudden interest. "Why do you want to know?"

"Just curious." He paused, then went on. "You about ready to have that there kid of yours?" he asked.

Maggie's cheeks reddened at his plain-spoken manner. Her embarrassment heightened because, even in the twilight, she could see that he had noticed her reaction.

"Look here, ma'am," he said. "This is a wagon train. Things are a mite different here than you may be used to. We gotta cut through all that propriety they hide behind in the East. If you're going to have a baby in the middle of Sioux territory, it's important that I know."

"Thank you for your concern," Maggie replied, still dubious but realizing he was right.

"My concern is for the whole train."

With the words Stoddard strode off in the direction he had been heading, leaving Maggie to ponder what he had said. *He'd be the last person I'll tell when my baby comes,* she thought, defiantly ignoring the sharp twinges of pain she had been feeling for the past three hours.

27

Ian's Child

A S IF GIL Stoddard's words had been prophetic, that night Maggie's labor came in earnest. As she lay on her bed wide awake, her eyes seemed to bore a hole through the canvas ceiling, now black with night. When the first sharp pains began to assail her with regularity, her muted cries were lost on the sleeping children. Drew and Ellie were asleep in the doctor's wagon to be near Tommy Joe. One after another the pains came and she lay awake wondering if it were the real thing or a false alarm.

Oh, Ellie, she thought, why aren't you here when I need you!

Beads of perspiration gathered on her forehead and the joints of her hands ached as she gripped the bedclothes. Finally there could be no doubt. Maggie pulled herself up, rolled over, and crawled to the end of the wagon. Just then another contraction hit. She waited until it had passed, then eased her cumbersome body down from the wagon and onto the ground.

The night was still all about her. How she dreaded the thought of waking the whole train! If she could only suppress the screams that seemed bent on forcing their way out of her mouth! Slowly she walked toward the doctor's wagon, pausing every few steps to catch her breath in anticipation of the next pain. They were coming sharply now, and more quickly.

It was not far, but it seemed to take an eternity to traverse the few yards. Every step made her dizzy and nauseous. At length she fell against the wagon and tried to whisper, "Doctor . . . doctor . . ."

Dr. Carpenter was asleep under the wagonbed. A light sleeper by nature, he was awakened by the soft footsteps shuffling toward him. Pulling his suspenders over his shoulders, he crawled out just as the words reached his ears. There he saw an ashen figure braced against his wagon.

"Mrs. Duncan!" he gasped softly.

She made no reply but stepped forward as if she would continue her quest, but almost immediately she crumpled into the doctor's arms. He picked her up lightly, carried her back to the Mackinaw wagon, roused the children, and laid her back in her bed. Bess was sent to wake her father and mother, and while Drew carried Sarah and Bobby from their beds, half-asleep, and deposited them in the doctor's wagon, Ellie and Dr. Carpenter began hasty preparations which soon became a very furor of activity. A baby is not born on a wagon train in the middle of desolate Indian country without causing some stir, and before many more minutes had elapsed, several of the wives had arrived, drawn by the common bond of dawning motherhood, to lend what assistance they could.

Desperately Maggie tried to maintain the control that years of breeding had taught her. But as night wore into morning, her energy for propriety diminished. The other women at her side recalled the pain of their own labors and encouraged her with every cry, rejoicing in the agonizing ecstasy of the struggle for new life.

"Ian!" she screamed, hardly knowing what she said.

But Ian was not there. Even before the word left her lips, another cry forced its way into her throat—but this cry was not from the pain. *There was no Ian!* She was alone in this precious moment, with no one to hold her hand and caress her tangled hair.

"Oh, Ian!" she sobbed, and turned her face away from the women who were trying to comfort her.

Just then a strong hand touched her head and brushed back her hair. She looked up into deep-set, dark eyes gazing down on her with love and compassion.

"You're doing fine, Maggie," said a voice. "Just fine. We're all here to help you."

It was a voice she recognized, and the gentle eyes of Samuel Carpenter were eyes that cared. She closed her eyes and tried to relax. Ellie was there too, never leaving her side. Now her mind began to come clear again. Now she remembered. Of course, these people cared! They were her friends now. This was a new life. That other life was a long time ago, in another place.

Oh, but how could she forget the land and all it meant! Her child should have been born in the place where generations of Ramseys before it had been born. Not in this godforsaken, barren strip of land. Not out on the ridge. Nothing could grow there. It was windy and cold. And the child should have a father to receive it lovingly into its arms. And what about the child's grandmother . . .

"Oh, Mother!" Maggie cried, breaking into sobs again.

Was there to be no singing the child to sleep in the arms of a smiling grandmother? Was the proud Scottish matriarch Atlanta Ramsey to have no opportunity to look into the face of another generation of this mighty family?

Outside the sun continued its steady rise, and its head began to penetrate the canvas roof of the wagon. Before ten o'clock the air had become stifling.

Dr. Carpenter lifted her head and placed a cup to her lips. "Here, Maggie," he said gently, "take a sip. That's good . . . good. We're close to the end now. You're doing wonderfully!"

He set down the cup and silently prayed. "Lord, speed her along. Comfort her. And may this precious child work healing in the wounds of this family."

"It will be over soon,"he said, "and you'll have a fine child—"

Maggie interrupted him with another scream. One look told the doctor all he needed to know.

"Mrs. Mackinaw!" he shouted to Ellie who had left the wagon for a moment, "Mrs. Mackinaw . . . the moment has come!"

By late afternoon Maggie finally drifted into a sound sleep as the wagon jostled beneath her. In her arms lay her tiny daughter, as fine a child as the doctor had assured her it would be. As she had lain there before falling asleep, so many of her cares seemed to dissolve in the sweet awe of motherhood. This was *her* child, her own daughter! And for the moment, at least, all the painful memories were forgotten.

When she awoke the wagon was still and she could tell they had already made camp for the night. The voices outside were a blur, but as consciousness gradually returned she became aware that a heated debate was in progress.

"She just better be ready to go in the morning," declared Stoddard's unyielding voice.

"I tell you," began the voice of Dr. Carpenter in a measured, but less than patient tone, "there is too great a danger of another hemorrhage. She has to remain still until I can control it. The movement has already taken its toll. If the trail is rough tomorrow, there could be fatal consequences."

"I'm willing to risk it," came Stoddard's gruff reply.

"You're willing to risk it!" the doctor returned, his voice rising angrily. The past three days had been tense, sleepless ones for him; little reserve of patience was left for this mulish trail master. "No one is risking anything, do you hear! You refused to stop for the boy—"

"And I'm refusing again," Stoddard rejoined flatly.

"Then go on. I'll be staying. And that is no idle threat! We'll catch up with you as soon as we can."

Drew had walked up and heard the last two remarks of each of the men. "I know my party'll be stayin' behind wi' the doctor," he said. "An' I heard some o' the others complainin' it were time fer a rest. The oxen's hoofs are wearin' raw, an' they need t' be shod. If it's Indians ye're afraid o', ye're na goin' t' get fer wi' lame animals, nor wi' only a han'ful o' wagons."

"You greenhorns just don't understand, do you?" stated Stoddard with disgust. "You don't understand the danger. You hired me to get your carcasses through safely, and that's what I'm trying to do. Okay, I give up!" With the words he turned. "Women!" he muttered as he stalked away. "They're always trouble."

Though Maggie heard fragments of their words, she was too absorbed in the daughter sleeping in her arms to care, or even to notice the pains of her own weary body. The tiny infant had given her a joy she thought she would never experience again. Words from her childhood floated into her mind, and for the first time in many months she found she could almost believe them: *"Every good gift and every perfect gift is from above, and cometh down from the Father of lights, with whom is no variableness, neither shadow of turning."*

Could it be that God had given her this wonderful gift? That was what Digory always called Him, the giver of pure and lovely gifts to His children. Ever since news of Ian's death she had been cursing God in her mind. How could He be both the giver of life—pure and innocent as this new child—and the author of death and heartache?

Could it be that God had *not* taken Ian from her? Could the sadness and destruction and death in the world be not His doing at all? Was it possible that in the midst of her heartbreak, God himself was trying to shower His love into her heart to sustain her and help her to stand in the midst of evil forces operating to destroy her life? Could He, after all, really *be* a God of love as Digory said? Might this child be more truly from Him than the heartache she had laid to His charge?

Ellie's cheerful voice, oblivious to the deeper struggles within Maggie's heart, suddenly washed away all Maggie's thoughts as she burst into the wagon.

"As Drew would say, 'She's a braw lass!' "

"How's Tommy Joe?" asked Maggie weakly.

"Moanin' something fierce. But the doctor says he's on the mend. Have you decided on a name yet?"

Maggie had hardly given naming her child a thought. But all at once she knew what it would be. "Her name is Eleanor. After you, my dear friend."

Ellie fell to her knees by Maggie's side, and stretching her arms around Maggie, wept great tears of joy.

Later that evening, as Maggie dozed in and out of consciousness, her thoughts drifted again to Ian. How he would have loved this baby! Tears welled in Maggie's eyes at the thought that little Eleanor would be robbed of knowing her own father.

Father.

With the word, confused and bitter images tumbled into Maggie's mind. *He* was the one who had brought this ruin on her and Ian! It hadn't been God at all! He was the cruel man responsible—her own father!

How she hated him for what he had done!

But even if he had brought destruction to the love that she and Ian had shared so briefly, at least he would be powerless to reach out and take this precious child from her.

Maggie hugged her daughter close.

No, she thought, *you will never see this child, James Duncan! She will never know how cruel your selfishness can be. I will protect her! I will love her. And you can never take that away from me!*

28

The Master of the House

DIGORY WAS A good deal slower these days. It took twice as long for him to move his arthritic body about the stable to feed the horses. But every morning, without fail, he was there about his tasks, and never was a single animal slighted. If he seemed to dote particularly on the coal-black Raven and the chestnut mare Maukin, he could perhaps be forgiven. They were reminders to him of happier times.

Digory had never been a man to dwell on the past. He knew that God's hand was in every season of life, regardless if the weather of the soul was sunny or frostbitten. But Stonewycke had become so bleak of late that he often was reminded that, truly, God's ways were not his ways.

"An' fer that truth I do truly gi' ye thanks," he murmured that crisp, late-spring afternoon. "I'd hae things all braw an' pleasant, an' then we might ne'er see oor need fer ye, Lord."

The depth of his own dependence on his Father above was a truth never far from aging Digory's mind. Thus his old heart ached when he saw others reject his Lord. And how his heart did ache every time he looked upon his master!

If a man's inward degeneration could be denoted by his outward appearance, then James Duncan was truly a lost man. Each time Digory's loving eyes rested on the laird of Stonewycke, he seemed to have aged several years. The hollowness about his visage reminded Digory of a grand cathedral gutted by a raging fire. Digory knew the fire which was slowly consuming James Duncan was an internal one no eyes would ever see. But he was not one to speculate on what was in his master's heart. All he could do was pray that the laird would one day yield to the purifying fires of Love's forgiveness before the self-willed fires of hell took him to his death.

Digory hobbled up to the black mare's stall, carrying a pail of oats which he poured liberally into the trough. The mare gave his arm an amiable nudge before she began the business of devouring her lunch.

"Ye're a braw one, Raven," Digory said softly to the animal. "'Twas a glad day when ye an' yer chestnut friend came back home. I only wish . . . eh, but what's the use o' it? Yer mistress is gane an' if the Lord wants her back, then 'twill be. A fine day like this is when I'm missin' her the most, an' I don't doubt but ye'll be missin' her too. Ye're needin' a good run, ye are. If only the master—"

"What about your master?" came an icy voice behind Digory. If James had intended his words to impart scorn to his groom, Digory did not notice.

Digory slowly turned his bent frame to face the laird. "I was jist wonderin' when auld Raven here might get oot fer a run, my lord."

"I told you, no one's to ride that horse!"

"An' no one has, sir," Digory replied. "Not since—well, not since the lass hersel' gang away."

"That's over and done with, do you hear?" James barked. "And I'll not hear any more of it. Nor will I stand for your turning around and disobeying my orders behind my back!"

"That I couldn't dream o' doin', sir," Digory replied earnestly. "'Tis just that sometimes I canna help thinkin' aboot those happier times."

"So, now you're complaining?" James accused.

"Oh, no, yer lairdship, at least no fer mysel'."

"For whom, then?" James's question was phrased as a challenge, and a man with less humility and more guile would have backed down from it. But Digory knew only how to hear a question, and answer it, from his heart.

"I canna help but t' see that ye yersel' hae seemed sorely troubled since the Lady Margaret left. An' my heart truly hurts fer ye, an' I wish there was somethin' I could do fer ye."

"You leave that little tramp out of it!" James exploded. "It'll be a cold day in hell," he spat, "when a measly groom could do anything for *me*! Except saddle up the bay—which is all you're good for." His dry laugh was unmistakably full of derision, and might have indeed stung the groom if it had not immediately been followed by a pathetic fit of coughing.

Digory could feel no malice toward his master, only regret that he had himself brought it on. "Are ye sure, sir, that ye ought t' be oot wi' sich a cough?"

"And I'll not be treated like a doddering old man, either!" shrieked James in a rage. "Especially by an old fool who can walk no better than you!" Without awaiting a reply James stalked outside to await his servant's compliance to his orders.

Digory left Raven's stall and shuffled with all the speed he could muster toward the bay. He hitched on the reins, then led the horse to the saddle rack where the laird's finest English saddle lay. If he had not had so many other things occupying his mind, he might have wondered that the laird had come to the stable with such a request at all.

For three weeks James had not set foot outside the ancient stone castle. The servants had more than once discussed the peculiarity of this change from the man who had previously seemed bent on remaining away from his home as much as possible.

But Stonewycke had become a place of refuge for James, a shelter where he did not have to face the wagging tongues of his business associates, nor embarrassment from his creditors. Rumors had begun to spread about the laird of Stonewycke. Many had begun to guess the truth about his pilfered funds from the accounts of the stockholders. Others had noted his alarming increase in alcohol consumption. Still more wondered when long-overdue accounts would be settled.

Stonewycke had become a convenient hiding place. But for James it symbolized more than that. Here he could hold his head high, here he could still maintain the ruse of his lordship. If his ambitious dreams of grandeur and power had slipped because of these temporary setbacks, his servants and these locals need never know. He was still the mightiest man in Strathy. This was his domain, and he still ruled with an iron hand and a word which was the law.

Yet such assurances did not completely mollify his apprehensions about his difficulties outside Stonewycke, for in the depths of his soul James knew the foundations of his lordship remained in place only through the sufferance of his wife. He couldn't help wondering why she was suddenly allowing him to have his way so easily. Had she stopped caring? Had the disappearance of their daughter affected her so greatly that she had even ceased to care about who controlled her beloved Stonewycke?

It didn't matter. He was beyond trying to analyze it. He never looked things straight in the eye anymore.

All that was important to James was that he never had to come face-to-face with his horrible failure. And to maintain this thin gloss over what remained of his life, another requirement became tantamount—Atlanta must never know that he had fabricated the entire story of their son-in-law's death.

To this end went a good deal of the money James had not already lost on his erstwhile brewery. Bribes were costly, and he prided himself on being able to keep it a secret this long. If only that blackguard son-in-law *would* die in prison! But now it only mattered that Atlanta never find out. For James knew with cold certainly that if she did, her recent lassitude would explode with more vengeance and wrath than a dozen generations of Ramseys could contain.

To this end his current ride had become necessary. More money had to be sent to Glasgow. An assistant wardman had found out about Ian—how close he was to the truth James hadn't been able to determine. There were rumors another man had become involved as well. He couldn't let it unravel now. He would have to buy their silence; every man had his price, and these men were no different. But it came at a difficult time. He hoped their price was not too high, for he was drawing dangerously near to the end of his resources.

What James did not know was that one of these men had no price. And he was at that very moment in temporary residence at the inn less than two miles from Stonewycke.

29

The Lad on the Moor

DERMOTT HAD BEEN in Port Strathy only two days and was becoming more and more convinced that his task was not going to be easy—not that he had ever expected it would be.

This was a small, closely bound community, and he had immediately discovered that it was unwise to barge in with questions which might be taken to be accusations. Especially where the laird's family was concerned. The day after his arrival he had asked an innocuous question about Ian of the innkeeper. The woman's small eyes had sharpened and her hands sought her hips in unconscious defiance.

"What d'ye want t' ken fer?" she asked in something less than friendly tones.

"I made his acquaintance some time ago," Dermott replied honestly enough. "I heard he stayed in Port Strathy for a time, and I hoped I might avail myself of his friendship while I was here."

"Well, he had precious few friends," she said gruffly. There was an odd catch around the edges of her voice, as if she knew more than she was telling. But before Dermott could comment further, she scurried out of the common room where they had been talking, and disappeared into the confines of the kitchen.

Further queries among other townsfolk yielded similar responses. The few who acknowledged Ian acted as if there were some ban on revealing anything about him. With every encounter Dermott probed the eyes of each person he met, trying to ascertain whether this might be someone in whom he could confide his purpose. But a voice inside kept saying, *Wait.* From scattered remarks the boy had made, Dermott had assumed the woman known as "Queenie" was his friend. However, upon arriving in Port Strathy he wasn't so sure. Her eyes had contained a suspicious glare since the moment he walked into the inn, and Dermott had been reluctant to open his mind to her. *Time will tell,* he thought, *whether this past acquaintance of Ian's is truly to be relied on as an ally.* For all he knew she could be part of the elaborate frame which had caught Ian in its grip. He would have to be discreet with his questions and watch that whatever plot that was afoot did not ensnare him as well.

For the next several days he walked about the village, listening, observing, learning what he could of its people and their ways. He learned a good deal about the family of Stonewycke and heard many reports—not always consistent with one another—concerning the laird, the James Duncan Ian had spoken of. But nothing came his way which revealed where he should direct his attentions. Finally, after a week, a chance conversation with a feisty old fisherman down at the harbor yielded a bit of information which he thought worth exploring. The man told Dermott he had seen a young couple the previous fall on horseback heading toward a desolate moorland ridge south of town.

"Used t' visit wi' a fellow by the name o' Kruger, I did," the man said. "Kin o' my wife's. They lived on a sparse patch o' ground two or three mile from here. They was havin' trouble wi' a couple o' their animals last year. My wife an' me, we rode oot t' see 'em every week or so, t' see if we could help. That's when I seen the young lad from Lonnon, wi' Lady Margaret. More'n once I saw 'em ridin' out toward the ridge."

The following morning, having received what directions the man had been able to give, Dermott decided to ride out into the countryside. The solitude would be restful; he needed time to seek guidance for what he should do, and in addition, he thought, an idea might unfold as he followed Ian's paths of the previous autumn.

He headed south on the old, slow-plodding gelding Queenie Rankin, the innkeeper, had provided. As she had handed him the reins a puzzled look came over her face, and she opened her mouth as if she was about to tell him something. Then apparently she thought better of it and turned away. If she had something to say, Dermott thought, she would have to learn to trust him first—and he her. If it was meant to be, that would come in time. They would have to continue testing the waters of each other's loyalties.

About a mile out of the village, the terrain began to rise slightly into gently rolling meadows. Summer was gradually revealing its face to the land held so long in winter's harsh grasp. The meadow lay green before him with the soft yellow faces of wild daisies and an occasional clump of primroses or daffodils gleaming up at the crisp blue sky overhead. To Dermott's left he could just make out the stone turrets of Stonewycke jutting up proudly into the northern sky. The thought crossed his mind of letting the old horse take him in that direction, for he knew his path must ultimately lead there, but instead he rode on, for the time for a confrontation behind the massive stone walls was not yet come.

He continued over the meadows another mile until their greenery began to give way to the moor called Braenock Ridge. Dermott had grown up not far from a moor very similar to this one. It was not unusual he was drawn to the desolate heath. As a boy he had often sought the somber comfort of the lonely countryside to be alone and work out the difficulties of growing up. As he rode, the way became rockier; he directed the gelding up the rocky ridge to the dreary peat bog.

At length he stopped his horse and gazed all about him. No thoughts of Ian were present just now, only nostalgic memories of his own past and of long walks on land just as this. He sighed deeply, then urged his mount slowly forward, aimless in his destination, soaking in the essence of his aloneness. *Lord,* he thought silently, *what do you have to say to me today? What would you have this place tell me?*

The heaps of granite boulders lying in seeming haphazard fashion escaped his notice as he passed them at a distance of some hundred and fifty yards. Instead, his eyes caught sight of a lonely figure crossing the moor some quarter mile distant. His drab, peasant garb and browned skin would have made him blend perfectly into the landscape had it not been for the wild shock of wiry red hair. From a distance Dermott could not rightly judge his age, but wondered if the figure was one, like he himself had been so many years ago, who sought comfort from the land, beautiful—as the old groom had maintained—in its sheer tenacity.

Dermott flipped the reins and moved toward the distant figure. As he drew closer and the shape took on more definition, Dermott saw it to be a tall gangly lad of about fifteen. But he carried himself like an old man with the cares of the world resting upon his shoulders. Immediately Dermott's heart was drawn to him.

Stevie Mackinaw had also sought the peculiar peace of the moor that day. And as the man and the boy approached one another, both would probably have been surprised to discover their thoughts flowing in a similar current. Stevie thought often of those past days when the healthy bleating of sheep followed him home to his dear mother and father, where also on an especially bright day he might be blessed to find the sweet countenance of Lady Margaret. But now such happy thoughts were gone and he, too, was struck with the loneliness of the place. Yet where else could he go for strength? This land was all he knew.

He looked up at the tall stranger approaching on horseback. And if his wary look was less than friendly, perhaps he could be forgiven. Gentlemen such as this one seemed always to bring nothing but trouble. Yet this man's eyes bore something different than he had been accustomed to lately, something that told him perhaps his mission was different, too. If Stevie had known the man better, he would have known it was love which looked out of those eyes upon him.

"If ye'll be wantin' directions," Stevie said as they met, "ye'd best be veerin' t' the left away from the boulders and takin' the road back down there off the ridge. There's nothin' up here but moorland, an' it'll lead ye no place."

"Why would you think I'd want directions?" asked Dermott.

"Any gentlefolk sich as yersel' who get this far up on the moor are usually lost," Stevie replied honestly, taking in a closer look at this stranger as he spoke.

"Perhaps you are right," Dermott said. "But in my case," he went on, strongly compelled to continue the conversation with this burdened young man, "I have come here to think. The place drew me simply by its solitary loveliness."

"Ye maun hae strange sight, sir," replied Stevie. "I've only known the moor t' be lovely once . . ."

His voice trailed away and his eyes seemed to scan the horizon as if he expected that lovely vision to appear once again.

"Then you must not be too familiar with this country," Dermott suggested, hoping to lead him into further speech.

"Na famliar wi' it! I were born an' raised but three furlongs from here, as were my daddy and his daddy too. Here all those years we were, until the laird turned me oot twa months past."

"I'm sorry to hear that," said Dermott, dismounting and taking the reins lightly in his hand.

"I thought ye was one o' his men when I saw ye ridin' up."

Dermott laughed. "No, not hardly. I have business of my own. But tell me, what could have happened to end all those long years of service?"

"My daddy died," Stevie said, his voice bleak as the moor itself. "An' fer the laird, I'm guessin' that be crime enough." The bitterness of his last words were unmistakable.

"And then the moor lost its loveliness?"

"Somewhat, maybe, but 'twas long before when the life was taken awa'— when my mither died and she on her black Raven no mair rode o'er this country."

"Your mother was a horsewoman, then?"

"Na, na. Not my mither. The *lady*. She was the rider."

As they spoke Stevie's initial wariness had subsided. If he had asked himself why, he would have decided it was something in the quality of the man's voice, in addition to the look in his eyes. Almost unconsciously they began walking together over the rocks through the wiry, bare heather brush whose blossoms were yet dormant. As Dermott gently questioned him, Stevie told about the days when his mother and father were both alive, about tending the sheep for them. The boy talked of his mother's faith and how it had always seemed to carry them through even the hardest times and coldest winters. Dermott said he would like to have known her, wondering silently if she did not somehow symbolize the essence of what was good on the Stonewycke estate. Then Stevie told of the day she died.

"The lady were there wi' us that day," he said wistfully. "My mither loved her. Some o' her last words were fer the lady. 'Always keep the hope o' the Lord in yer heart,' she said. I'll ne'er forget that day."

"Who was the lady, Stevie?" Dermott asked, realizing now that God had indeed led him out onto the moor for a purpose.

"The Lady Margaret, o' course."

"Lord Duncan's daughter?"

"Aye," he replied. "An' 'tis a sorry thing that an angel like as her maun call sich a man her father. If she would hae been here, he wouldna hae turned me oot. She was always friend t' the likes o' us. But she wasna here."

"What happened? Where is she?"

"She went off wi' him."

"Ian Duncan?"

"Aye. But I canna say mair aboot it," Stevie said pointedly, the former sadness returning to his tone.

"I am a friend of Mr. Duncan's," Dermott said. "I have come here to try to help him."

"He'll be needin' na help whaur he rests noo."

"Stevie," Dermott said, pausing and placing a firm hand on the boy's shoulder. "You must tell no one else this. But Ian is alive, and I have promised to help him. And I have promised to try to find her for him too. She has disappeared somewhere in America. Stevie . . . can you help me?"

Stevie stared blankly at the lawyer. They stood for some moments as the wind blew over the moor, tousling red and black hair alike.

At length Dermott spoke again, gently but urgently. "Do you hear me, lad? I need you . . . *they* need you."

When Stevie spoke again, the shock had disappeared from his face and his voice droned on sadly. "We didna see her o'er much after he came. An' she didna come t' oor cottage. She still rode her fine mare, but mostly wi' him. Then one day he came t' oor place."

"The young Mr. Duncan?"

"Aye. He came by himsel'—alone. He asked my daddy an' me t' tell na a soul—for her sake, he said."

Stevie stopped, as if he would say no more.

"I know why he came," Dermott said. "Ian told me himself that he sent Maggie to your brother in America."

"Then why would ye be needin' me?" asked Stevie.

"There was a great deal Ian could not tell me," Dermott replied. "Both time and his memory prevented him. He has been badly mistreated in prison and it has not been good for his mental powers. If I don't help him soon, I fear for what might happen to his mind. That is why I have come here, to try to fill in the gaps of what happened. And there is one most important thing that only you can help me with. I have tried to contact your brother in New York. But it seems he has left, moved west. If Margaret Duncan ever did reach him, I must find out where she is now. But there is no hint of her whereabouts. If you know anything . . ."

"I hae na heard from my brother in nigh t' four years."

"Didn't you notify him of your parents' deaths?"

"I ne'er wrote a letter in all my life. My mither used t' write sometimes. But I ne'er could learn. An what good would it hae doon anyway?"

"It might have gotten us closer to Lady Margaret," Dermott replied thoughtfully. "But I will have to pursue another direction for that."

They began walking again. Both remained silent as they pondered their own thoughts. Gradually their steps led to the foot of a small rise, over which sat the sod hovel where Stevie Mackinaw had been born. As they approached, Stevie veered away from the rise and back toward the road, for in the two months since his eviction he had never returned to the old cottage with its bittersweet memories of happiness and loss.

It was some time before Dermott finally spoke. "Did Mr. Duncan ever speak to you of anything else besides going to America, Stevie?"

"Na o'er much," Stevie replied, glad to have his thoughts diverted from the painful memories of his home. "He didna come t' visit wi' sich like us, not a London gentleman like himsel'."

"Do you remember anything about the death of Master Falkirk?"

"The likes o' me!" Stevie said with something resembling a smile on his weathered face. "The lairds keep even their deaths t' themselves. That's what made the Lady Margaret so special. She wasna afraid t' be one o' us, if ye ken my meanin'. But I do recall, noo that ye mention him, askin' the laird Falkirk the same question once that I asked ye a while ago."

"What was that?" Dermott asked.

"Weel, I asked him if he was lost."

"Do you mean out here on the moor?"

"Aye. But like yersel', he said he wasna lost. But he wasna as kind as ye were, sir. He told me t' mind my own business an' tore on past me on that golden stallion o' his. It wasna the only time I saw him here. But 'tis a free country an' a man, 'specially a laird, can ride whaur he wills. 'Tis the only time I laid eyes on Master Falkirk up close. I dinna ken what might hae been between him and Mr. Duncan. But Mistress Rankin might ken aboot that, fer Mr. Duncan stayed at the inn fer a spell. He said that if we ever had any messages t' git t' him, he told us t' leave them wi' the mistress o' the inn, that she could be trusted."

Dermott's face brightened. "So she *is* an ally! I thought as much."

"A friend t' some, na doobt," remarked Stevie. "But not a woman t' be crossed when she's standin' her ground. But Mr. Duncan thought she was a friend o' his, that much is certain."

"That explains her cool reception," said Dermott almost to himself, reflecting on Queenie's hostile looks the moment he had begun asking questions about Ian. Undoubtedly the woman was only being protective of the lad who had become her friend while staying at her inn, and had assumed him an enemy.

By now they had reached the road again, if that narrow rocky path through the peat bogs and over the rough landscape could be called a road. When Dermott extended his hand, large and warm and grateful, the lad responded awkwardly and shyly. But Dermott took the coarse, dirty hand and uttered a deeply felt *thank you.*

"Do you have a place to stay, lad?" Dermott added before they parted.

"Whaur the heather be soft an' dry, 'tis good enough fer me," Stevie replied earnestly.

"But the heather won't be in bloom for months. And it's hardly the dry season yet."

"An' till then, 'cept when it *is* warm enough t' be oot, I stay wi' friends in Strathy who was kind enough t' open their home t' me."

Dermott studied the boy for a long moment, satisfied at least for the present that the boy had a dry roof over his head. The bitterness he had occasionally seen rise to his face had now been replaced by a guileless simplicity. It was as if both emotions were struggling within him, even as boyhood still continued its losing battle against coming manhood, and young Stevie did not know which to give place to.

Finally Dermott took a sovereign from his pocket and handed it to Stevie.

"Nay, sir," Stevie protested. "I'll na take what I hae na worked fer."

"Neither would I expect you to." Dermott answered. "But you have been of immeasurable help to me, and I expect to call upon your service again. And so this is payment for those services. You will make yourself available to me in the future?"

"Weel," Stevie replied, rubbing his chin thoughtfully. "Since ye put it that way . . . I suppose I could that."

"Thank you," Dermott said, swinging himself up on Queenie's horse. "What's the name of the couple you are staying with?"

"'Tis the Hawkins. Their place is aboot a half mile east o' the village, on the road up t' the summit."

"I shall be in touch," said Dermott.

He turned and directed the gelding north and toward Port Strathy on the road by which he had come. His keen lawyer's mind was already working meticulously over the details of his conversation with Stevie. By appearances he had learned very little. Yet he had a strong sense that this would prove to be of inestimable importance later. For now at least it had directed him to another who might help still further. The next order of business would certainly seem to be a candid talk with the mistress of Port Strathy's inn.

Dermott did not forget that he had been led out to the moor. God had indeed been faithful in providing the guidance he had sought. And on the way back toward the village Dermott Connell, in the quiet of his own heart, gave thanks to his Lord that he was not responsible to order his own steps throughout the perplexities of life.

30

An Evening at Queenie's

THE CHEERY FIRE of the Bluster N' Blow's common room was inviting after the chill of the moor. Dermott settled down before the hearth and gratefully accepted a steaming mug of coffee from Queenie.

"We don't get much call fer that drink in these parts," the inn's mistress said as she stepped back to watch from Dermott's expression whether she had prepared it to his satisfaction.

"It tastes as if you are quite an expert with it, nevertheless," said Dermott after a sip.

She smiled, one of the first Dermott had seen, and said, "I learned it in the city, where they go fer such strange customs. Dinna touch it mysel', but I've always kept a small supply from those days. I'm surprised it didna lose its flavor."

At that moment the door of the inn opened and three fishermen walked in, diverting Queenie for some time. Before long, however, she returned to her soft spoken customer where he sat in front of the fire.

"Would ye be wantin' more?" she asked.

"Yes, I'd like that," Dermott replied.

Queenie left him and returned with another mug of the brew. She tarried a moment longer than was necessary, then made to leave, but then turned again, clearly indecisive, and said in a casual voice. "Were—were the horse t' yer satisfaction, Mr. Connell?"

"Quite so, Mistress Rankin," Dermott replied, noting the uncertainty in the innkeeper's bearing. "I should like to make use of him once or twice more in the next few days if he is available."

"That it will be," she replied. "Then ye'll be stayin' a bit longer?"

"Yes, it seems so, for I have not yet been successful in my purpose. I had hoped to locate some friends of a certain lad in grave trouble. But it begins to appear I may be his only friend."

As he spoke Dermott registered the woman's reaction to his veiled words with his keen lawyer's eyes.

"'Tis a sorry pass," she replied noncommittally. "I had a friend in a fix like that mysel' once," she continued, still offering no clue to what lay beneath her thick black eyebrows. "In grave trouble, as ye put it. But where that lad is now, he needs no friends. Still, if he was alive, a body mightn't be able t' trust a man's words—fer anyone can *say* he's a man's friend."

As she spoke Dermott thought he detected an imperceptible squinting in her inquiring eyes.

"But if someone had tried to convince everyone that a lad was dead," Dermott argued softly, "and another came along to declare that he was alive and in dire need of help, would that not be proof enough of the latter's sincerity? Who else but a friend would risk provoking the powers which had feigned the man's death?"

"But no one has yet declared the man of whom you speak to be alive," Queenie said, fastening her shrewd gaze on Dermott now more fixedly. As she did so, she slid her bulky frame onto the bench next to the lawyer. Dermott held her gaze and spoke in measured, precise tones. "I declare to you, Mistress Rankin, that Ian Duncan is this moment alive. I have seen and spoken with him less than a fortnight ago."

Yet even with the words Queenie did not relent of her wary suspicion. "Why then were ye lookin' fer friends, sir?" she asked as if she had caught a thief in his own trap. "Fer if ye had known this Mr. Duncan, ye would hae known where t' look fer his friends."

"He spoke to me of you, Mistress Rankin. But after your initial reception, I too felt caution was necessary. Deceit abounds in this case. Even old friends can turn—or be turned—away."

"Not I!" Queenie exclaimed, showing her emotions for the first time. "There's nothin' that laird up on the hill could do t' turn me against the lad!"

"Then let us put aside our caution," Dermott entreated. "Let us trust one another, for the sake of him whom we both care about."

"He's truly alive?" Queenie breathed. "Somehow I was sure all along he was."

"What can you tell me about him, Mistress Rankin?"

"First, I can tell ye, he called me Queenie, an' if ye be a friend o' his, then ye can call me that also," she said as she propped an elbow on the table and began rubbing her ample chin. "He enjoyed a good time, he did. But I always had the feelin' there was more t' it than jist that. Mostly I only saw the lad after all his troubles began. That is, the troubles here in Port Strathy."

"He told me of the day and night of the murder," Dermott said. "But it was so sketchy, as though he was remembering it through a fog. What do you remember of that day?"

Queenie glanced around hastily toward her other customers. Satisfied that they were well provided for and were paying no attention, she lowered her voice and said: "He had that sprattle wi' Master Falkirk, an' everyone swore t' the constable later that the lad had blood in his eye. But I ken that's no true. He couldna kill—not murder wi' oot good cause. But what's an auld innkeeper's opinion against what came oot o' the lad's mouth? Fer he swore he'd kill Falkirk if he touched the lady again."

"But neither of us believe he followed through on that threat."

"We're the only ones, Mr. Connell," said Queenie gloomily. "Time was when I thought it'd all turn oot right. Constable Duff seemed t' be believin' the lad. But then suddenly he was gone."

"Constable Duff?"

"Used t' be the constable o'er in Culden. But then jist aboot the time I thought he an' the lady was aboot t' get free o' their troubles, some new man's sniffin' around an' no one's heard o' Duff since."

"What happened?"

"No one's sayin'. But I hae my suspicions," returned Queenie.

"It seems no one is willing to speak of Ian Duncan at all, either for good or ill."

"'Tis the laird, sir," said Queenie, lowering her voice still further. "He controls everythin' an' the people are afraid o' him. I sure wish I knew what Duff knew, an' that's fer certain, fer Ian told me the last time I saw him that Duff believed him. But the laird won't tolerate even the sound o' Ian Duncan's name in his hearin'. An' so most folk jist as soon na speak o' him at all. The laird has eyes an' ears everywhere."

She paused for a moment deep in thought, and when she began again, it was slowly and cautiously. "Noo that I think o' it, maybe he's better off wi' folks thinkin' he's dead. The laird's got people t' believin' 'twas Ian that killed Falkirk an' made his daughter run off. If they knew he was alive, I'm thinkin' he'd only end up at the gallows."

"I can't figure why Lord Duncan—for it is certainly he who has perpetrated this hoax—has done this to Ian, his own son-in-law," said Dermott thoughtfully. "What could he have against him? What motives are hidden from our view? But whatever the cause, Queenie, no man should be forced to live under the awful pall of guilt and shame that Ian faces with each new day. And though I fear exoneration alone will not give Ian the peace he needs, it might at least set him on that road. But for true healing to come to his soul, the changes will have to go much deeper."

"Deeper? What changes would ye be speakin' o', Mr. Connell?"

"Forgiveness, Queenie. I'm speaking of forgiveness, the one true road to forgiveness for all men and women."

Queenie did not respond, lost in her own silent reminiscences which Dermott's words had triggered. When she did speak, it was to ask perhaps the most practical question of all. "An' what if he's na cleared o' the crime?" she said, voicing the fear that had always haunted Dermott.

Silence once more descended upon the two and they sat staring into the fire for some time. Dermott's thoughts sought both comfort and guidance in silent prayer. At length he spoke. "He will be exonerated, Queenie," he said. "Only a moment ago, I was not so sure. But I now believe God has given me assurance that such is His purpose."

"Weel then," Queenie said, her practical nature once again asserting itself, "if that's t' truly be, then God might be wantin' a suggestion from an auld woman."

"And what would that be?"

"As things stand wi' the lad, it appears t' me the only way he'll be cleared is when we find who *really* murdered Master Falkirk."

At that moment several of Queenie's customers began clamoring for refills of their ale. She rose and busied herself about this task for most of what remained of the evening. Dermott finished his coffee and leaned back against the wall, his eyes focused on the dancing flames in the hearth. His mind ranged in many different directions, but before long it could not help settling on the conversation between certain of Queenie's guests whose words had grown too loud to ignore. A small group of farmers and fisherfolk, they were seated in a cluster about one of the larger tables in the room, bandying about small tidbits of daily news and local happenings. Dermott doubted he could learn much concerning the affairs of the laird or the neighboring gentry from their talk, which centered mostly on the state of their crops or the running of the fish. However, after some time, as their voices became louder, Dermott could not help his interest being drawn in their direction.

"He's got nerve comin' back after a' these months!" one was saying with mild indignation in his voice.

"I'm plumb surprised his wife had'm back, leavin' her as he did t' the mercies o' frien's an' neighbors," put in another.

"Weel, I'm tellin' ye straight oot," added a large imposing man with graying beard, "I'll na take the likes o' him on my boat again! He's a no account guid fer nothin' — an' them's the *kind* words I hae fer'm!"

"What goads me," one offered, "is jist afore he slithered oot o' here, he was actin' so high n' mighty like — "

"Aye!" agreed another. "Braggin' aboot becomin' a wealthy man an' all that talk about wrappin' some gentleman 'round's finger."

"That's Marty Forbes fer ye!"

"Tellin' tales. All yammer an' little t' back it up."

"Why do ye think he left so almighty hurried like?"

"I saw him the day after that young lord from Lonnon killed the Falkirk fella. He looked none too good that day, I can tell ye."

"Aye. That's when he left, it was. I never saw him after that, until — "

The speech was stopped suddenly as the door of the inn opened and in walked a tall, bedraggled man. From the looks on the faces of the men he had been listening to, Dermott could only conjecture that the very object of their conversation had entered. They welcomed him, if a bit stiffly, to their circle and the conversation slowly regained its momentum, drifting toward other topics.

Dermott paid little heed, soon rose and stretched his tired limbs, and decided it was time to turn in for the night. Before he climbed the stairs to his room, he took Queenie aside for a moment to apprise her of his intentions.

"Sometime I'm going to have to ask you what you know about this Marty Forbes who's now seated in the other room. And I think it's of some importance that I locate the man Duff to learn what he might be able to shed on this."

"If he's to be found," added Queenie with cautious concern.

"Yes, you're right," said Dermott with a grave sigh. "But tomorrow," he went on, "I intend to ride out to Stonewycke."

"An' what can that accomplish," she argued, "but t' maybe incite the laird t' further injustices against the lad?"

"Sooner or later I must confront the man and try to find out what happened that night, from the laird's own mouth. I have delayed meeting him as long as possible. I had hoped to obtain some solid evidence first, to see how things stood. But if he knows more than he would readily admit, then it may be that I can discern it from his speech."

"Weel, I wish ye godspeed," Queenie replied with resignation.

"Thank you. I shall need it."

Dermott turned and mounted the steps to his room. He fell asleep some time later to the sound of crashing waves on the shore, a prayer still lingering on his lips for the man he must confront in the morning. In so many ways he was the man who seemed to be at the very core of all the events which had swept him into their path. *Was he,* Dermott wondered, *destined to be the man who in the end will prove to be my fiercest adversary?* Only the Lord could know that. So with a prayer for the Lord's hand to prepare his way, he drifted away from the world of the waking.

31

The Laird's Match

D ERMOTT STUDIED THE castle a long while before beginning the ascent up the wooded hill to where it sat—somber yet majestic in its strength. The mighty estate known as Stonewycke had stood thus for some three centuries. It had weathered the awesome currents of history—the rise and fall of kings and chiefs, the victories and defeats in gruesome battles between Scotch and English, the passing of great and lowly alike. Dermott's present business might seem insignificant in comparison to the magnificent and inexorable march of history. But such a mission could never be insignificant to one like Dermott. For no matter how great a building or the persons within its walls, nothing was to Dermott more significant than the life and soul of a single human being.

As he rode up the hill and through the great iron gates standing open as if welcoming an honest breath of air, Dermott's mind and heart had never been more firmly set upon an unwavering purpose. Earthly might did not stir him, for beside the grandeur of his God this ediface before him was the same as a broken-down hovel. He kept the image of that God before his mind's eye, for he knew from years of hard experience that his own strength would avail him little.

A white-clad maid, breathless from hurrying down from the second floor, answered the brisk clap of the door knocker.

"I wish to see Lord James Duncan," Dermott said crisply.

"An' who might I be sayin' is callin'?" asked the maid.

"I am Dermott Connell of Glasgow," he replied, and as he did so he took a small card from his pocket and handed it to the woman.

She studied the card for a moment, then said without much enthusiasm, "Weel, I'll give him the card, but I canna say he'll see ye. Keeps t' himsel' these days, he does."

"Kindly tell him I am here on prison business," Dermott said.

She sighed heavily at the prospect of having again to negotiate the stairway, motioned for him to enter, closed the door, then turned and left him.

Soon she reappeared at the top of the stairs and beckoned him to follow her. With mounting anticipation Dermott took the stairs two at a time, then followed as she led down the wide corridor past several rooms, till they at length paused before two thick double oak doors. The maid opened one and stepped aside for Dermott to enter. He saw immediately that he was in a finely appointed library. Shelves of countless volumes lined the walls, in several places two books deep. The furnishings were as rich as he had seen, and for a moment he failed to note the slight figure seated behind the huge carved desk.

As his eyes fell upon his host his attention was instantly diverted from its external trappings to the source of Stonewycke's power. Here was a man who had unleashed all the wrath of his person and position against his own family and still held them firmly in his grasp. And yet to the first-time observer he seemed withered and spent, a mere shadow, a poor misguided wretch rather than an evil tyrant.

But James Duncan had not lost all his fight yet.

"I have never heard of you," James began without benefit of any social preludes. "What business could you possibly have with me?" If he quailed inside it was only because he feared a creditor may finally have caught up with him. But he maintained his outward composure without flinching an eyelid.

"If your maid relayed my message correctly," Dermott said, trying to ignore the man's haughty manner, "I said I have come on prison business."

"I have nothing to do with prisons," replied James, somewhat confused.

"But I have," Dermott stated. "I am a lawyer."

"What is that to me?" James stated, pulling himself up straight in his chair.

As he spoke Dermott began to see that this man could indeed pose a threat.

"During the course of my duties," he went on, "I made the acquaintance of a poor unfortunate young man imprisoned some months ago in the tollbooth in Glasgow. Imprisoned, I might add, for a crime he did not commit."

James laughed lightly, almost delicately. "Excuse me, Mr. Connell," he said with something of a half-smile on his face, "but don't *all* those malcontents *claim* to be innocent?" He was so greatly relived to find the course of the conversation moving in directions other than toward his own debts that James's first reaction was toward an attempt at humor.

"Be that as it may, Lord Duncan," Dermott continued, "this man has not even had the benefit of a trial. The right to a speedy hearing is guaranteed to all British citizens, is it not?"

"Sounds like that freedom drivel from the colonies in America!" replied James, gathering strength for the resumption of his anger once he saw that the barrister's attacks were apparently not going to be aimed at his weak financial underbelly.

"But true, nonetheless," Dermott persisted.

"And?" was the only acquiescence James made.

"I should like to see justice done by my client."

"So see to it!" The finality in James's voice indicated that the interview had ended as far as he was concerned.

But Dermott had only begun. "That is what has brought me to Stonewycke."

"I fail to see how either I or Stonewycke could be of any assistance to you," said James, his impatience growing. If this man had not been sent by Browhurst or the others, then he needn't bother himself with him.

"My hope would be that you would offer your assistance for the aid of your *son-in-law*."

Dermott said the words slowly and calmly, letting them fall over James with the subtle power of understatement.

James's poker-straight body sagged slightly, nearly escaping Dermott's notice. But he could not fail to note the growing agitation in the man's eyes.

"I have no son-in-law!" James replied with only a hint of the emotion churning inside.

"And you have no daughter either?" Dermott rejoined.

"How dare you bring my daughter into this?" cried James, rising from his seat. "Whatever ill-advised commitments she may have innocently been duped into, they have all been annulled."

"Legally?" queried Dermott.

"Yes, legally! Of course legally!"

"By the court?"

"I am the court around here, do you understand?" retorted James, unable to mask his anger.

"Then perhaps you might be able to direct me to where I might find a certain constable by the name of Duff?"

"Duff! What in the name of—what could he possibly—why you—" thundered James. "What could Duff possibly have to do with—why, I replaced Duff months ago! The incompetent fool!"

"Well, I intend to find him with or without your help," said Dermott.

James turned back toward his desk, swallowed hard, and walked to a nearby sideboard where a decanter and several crystal glasses sat on a silver tray. This man would not so easily be intimidated. As his initial anger receded, a different approach occurred to him. He grasped the decanter carefully to conceal his shaking hand, then poured a portion into two glasses.

Handing a glass to Dermott, he said, "I hope we may be able to discuss this— ah, this, er—this case like gentlemen."

Declining the drink, Dermott answered with great earnestness. "That is very much my wish."

James tossed back his head and did away with the contents of his glass in one gulp, set it down on the table, then took the one meant for Dermott and began sipping it more easily. "This is most excellent brandy," he said. "You really should avail yourself of at least one small glass," he added in his most gracious social tone.

"I like to keep a clear head about me," Dermott replied.

"Yes, yes, I see your point," said James, taking another swallow. "Now," he went on, as if the brandy had renewed his strength, "you have come upon someone claiming to be my erstwhile son-in-law. Very interesting, indeed. Especially in light of the fact that he was declared dead by the prison authorities some months ago. For no matter what you may think, Mr. Connell, I have been genuinely concerned for the boy and have kept close track of him."

"You and I both know that not to be true. You know as well as I that the boy is alive." Dermott's eyes, like blue ice leveled on James in an unrelenting grip.

At that moment, perhaps for the first time, James noticed that the stranger's imposing figure towered over his own by some ten inches. In addition to his stature, the lawyer's muscular frame was nothing to be disregarded even by one who held lofty notions of his prowess in less physical realms. James had always prided himself in his uncanny ability to stare down an adversary, and he tried desperately to hold Dermott's eyes. But after several moments he dropped his eyes to the table, finished off his drink, and poured another. Carefully avoiding Dermott's piercing gaze, he spoke.

"I see your game now, Connell," he said. "And I see no reason why we cannot arrive at some sort of mutually beneficial agreement. You see, this so-called son-in-law of mine has not only proved an embarrassment to all concerned, but he has also shown himself to be of most unstable character. His sole purpose has been to get his hands on my daughter's inheritance. It was especially for my daughter's sake—"

"Have you no conscience?" Dermott exclaimed, at last losing his patience with the pointless verbal sparring. For as the other had spoken, a picture had risen in his mind of Ian's wretched agony in his dungeon cell. But almost the same moment he calmed, breathing a hasty prayer that he would—in the midst of heated emotions—be able to see this man as Christ saw him.

"Come now, Mr. Connell," James said in his most condescending manner, "I thought we were going to be gentlemen. And in that vein, I think, and indeed I hope, you can understand my position. I greatly regret the circumstances which have led me to do what I have done. But I can assure you it was all necessary. If that alone is not enough to insure your—ah—your discretion in the matter, then I'm sure more, shall we say *tangible* inducements can be made available."

"You cannot understand, can you, Lord Duncan?" If Dermott felt deep pity for this man, he did not let it escape in his tone. "A man is dying, if not in the physical sense as you would have everyone believe, then surely he is dying in his soul. He has lost all hope and believes that the one person whom he feels has ever loved him is lost to him forever—as perhaps she may be. Can you feel nothing in your heart for him? Or at least for his wife—your own daughter? Imagine how deserted and alone she must feel? How can you in good conscience allow this deception to continue!"

"There are some matters," James replied without hesitation, as if he had not heard a single word of Dermott's impassioned speech, "that are more important than the *feelings* of a murdering reprobate."

Dermott gasped. The words were to him as bitter in his face as a physical blow. He was not innocent of men with such cold and callous motives. But his nature could never confront such evil intent without it stirring a passion toward righteousness within him. If he had prayed to view this man with the mind of his Lord, even Christ would not tolerate the falsehood of the moneychangers in the temple. If the lawyer's sharp response sprang from this passion, none could blame him—none except perhaps Dermott himself.

"There is no reprobate," he seethed, "except the one who refuses to turn from his selfish ways! And you, James Duncan, are dangerously close to occupying that position! For if you had a heart within you, it would this very minute cry out against the agony of one so helpless, if not innocent!"

"How dare you!" James shrieked in a rage. "You have no right—"

"Do not speak to me of rights!" Dermott cried. "For if Ian Duncan dies—as surely he must, in that miserable hole to which you have condemned him—his blood will be upon *your* head. As surely as if you had cut him down with a sword!"

"Then I'll live with it! Why you godless—"

"If you can live with such a thing, then you truly are a lost man," Dermott replied, cooling noticeably, then sighing with heavy anguish. He turned on his heel and started toward the door. If James had shown but the tiniest flicker of repentance, Dermott's heart remained so hopeful that he would have turned back immediately and made every effort to minister to the man. But the sounds which reached his retreating ear were far indeed from the sounds of a repentant heart.

"How dare you turn your back on me? You—you—By Jove, I'll see you—"

"I'm sorry, Lord Duncan," Dermott said, turning as he reached the door. "I'm sorry it has come to this. But I must do as my conscience—and my God—lead me. I can do no other."

James's only further response was a violent stream of imprecations at Dermott's back as the door closed behind him, ending with one final and pitiful attempt to regain the upper hand. "Do not set foot in my house again, Connell!" he yelled. "Do not even let me hear of you setting foot on my land, or I'll have *you* arrested and see you hanged!"

James Duncan shook with his own kind of passion—a passion far different than what drove Dermott Connell into the thick of battle. After so many years spent striving for the wrong things, being right was the only thing that mattered to the laird of Stonewycke. For if he once admitted to being wrong about anything, his life itself would instantly begin to erode from beneath him. How could he know—after all these years looking in the wrong direction for the happiness he had never found—that the only way out of the dungeon which so tightly imprisoned him, the dungeon of his *self,* was death to that very self which had sustained him in its evil ways all his life? How could a man in his advanced state of spiritual decay summon the courage to lay the axe to the old foundation in order to begin forming a new? To take even the first small step forward out of his bondage, the admission of one insignificant wrong, would have been of incalculable difficulty to one such as he. Such is the point where repentance must begin, but for a man like James Duncan, such an admission would have been to swallow a vial of pure gall.

The moment the lawyer was out of the room, James turned toward the silver tray and crystal decanter. The liquid sloshed into the glass as he filled it to the rim. Even now, completely alone, he made a vain attempt to steady his hand before grasping the glass with eagerness. The ruse of his life was as much a show for himself as it was for outsiders.

Slowly, purposefully he brought the glass to his lips. Then, as if his steady patience had worn thin, he tossed it back and emptied it with two greedy swallows.

"The nerve!" he spat, slamming the empty glass onto the table. It splintered beneath his hand. Quickly he drew back, but the shattered glass had done its work. Blood dripped from several gashes in his palm.

"Curse him!" James cried.

Not even pausing to bind up the wounds, James stormed from the room. He sought the passages leading to the back of the house so as to avoid any chance of meeting the lawyer or any of the servants, but his menacing pace did not slacken until he reached the stables. There he ordered Digory to saddle the chestnut mare.

"But, my lord . . ." protested Digory, knowing the prowess of the chestnut, especially since she had not held a rider since her last master had fallen into such misfortune.

James shoved the groom aside and began to saddle the horse himself.

Seeing that his master was not to be dissuaded, Digory stepped back, while James mumbled that "the old fool of a groom would take too long about it anyway!"

He mounted Maukin with a vengeance, as if riding the horse which had been so dear to the man whom James had wronged was the final assertion of his lordship. He would keep the man in prison! He would destroy this lawyer Connell! And he would prove his superiority by mastering the murderer's own horse! He was lord! No one else. And more than anything, that made whatever he chose to do right.

"You'll see who's right!" he cried as he lashed the mare's flank and lurched forward into a frenzied gallop. *Right . . . right . . .* the words echoed in his mind as he tore from the stables.

The iron gate was but a blur as he passed it. Somewhere in his confused mind must have been the thought of getting the constable in order to follow through on his threat to have Connell arrested. For James was a calculating man, even in the midst of his present frenzy. Yet his one-time cool character was presently on the verge of cracking.

He turned sharply to the left a furlong past the gate, away from the road into Port Strathy. At breakneck speed and for no apparent reason he tore down the steep path, normally a footpath leading into a rocky gorge and thence to the valley.

It was here, while negotiating the gorge, that Maukin stumbled. A rider of James's caliber would have had little difficulty maintaining his seat under normal circumstances. But Maukin hit the trail at a full gallop, and besides being in a white wrath, James had had far too much brandy already that day. Both horse and rider fell hard onto the stony ground. Maukin pulled herself up and shook her head with a horsey whinny, fortune indeed to still have four unbroken legs beneath her.

The rider had not been so fortunate. James lay still, his face pressed against the dirt and stone of the path. Digory found him some time later. As the groom hastened down to where he lay, James had just begun to come to himself. He groaned in agony, rudely rebuffed the groom's efforts at assistance, and attempted to pull himself up, only to fall helpless back onto the ground with a dull moan.

In the end, Digory had to hobble back to the house for help. And thus the once proud James Duncan, lord of Stonewycke, was borne back to the castle in the arms of his servants, with his old groom constantly by his side.

32
Maggie and Stoddard

As THE SMALL wagon train had left the rugged hills, many had been the prayers that their fortunes would improve. Tommy Joe had some color back in his face, and the day's rest had worked magnificently upon Maggie. Though Gil Stoddard would never have admitted it, the stop had proved a boon for the entire train. However, the cheerful spirits about the camp did not sense the menacing thunderclouds of fate hanging just over the horizon toward which they were headed.

Truly, God's providence shields the future from the eyes of His children. As Ellie had prayed for her son and had assumed he was on the mend, she had no way of knowing how serious the injury had really been. No one, not even Dr. Carpenter, had known that. But since the day of the accident, infection had been masked by more outward symptoms, and by now it was surging through the boy's weakening frame. Even as Ellie prayed, she had no way of knowing that before they had traveled another day, he would be dead.

That night they camped again within sight of the Platte. It was like returning to an old friend, for they had followed the river on and off for weeks. But this night it held no comfort for the weary train. Its only contribution was the soil from its bank for their first grave.

If grief over the loss of their son were not enough, Drew and Ellie had to face the harsh reality of their situation, which prevented even a crude outward release of their pain. Drew attempted to fashion a cross for his son's grave. He had not wept since the boy's death, but as he worked, his face was drawn and taut, his lips pressed firmly together in mute anguish.

"What're you doin?" asked Stoddard.

"I'm makin' a marker fer my boy's grave," Drew answered simply, continuing on without looking up.

"Listen, Mackinaw," Stoddard replied, making a genuine attempt at sincerity, "this here is Sioux country an' we all know they're on the warpath. If you want your kid to rest in peace, you'll toss that thing in the river."

Drew glanced up, puzzled. "My wife wants a proper cross on his grave," he answered listlessly.

"I'm just givin' you advice," Stoddard said. "Take it or leave it. But I'll say this much—them Sioux is just as liable to destroy the grave as leave it alone if they see a marker. I don't think your wife'd be wantin' that, neither."

Drew stared blankly at the wagon master, then heaved his frame slowly up to his feet and lumbered to the river. He stood for a moment on the bank, perhaps in indecision, weighing Stoddard's words, perhaps offering a silent prayer of awkward grief and frustration. Then with one mighty motion he flung the wood far into the gray depths of the surging water. There was no one to see, but then and then only did the tears glisten on the rims of his eyes. To Drew this was one further reminder of the tragedy he had called his family to. He had brought hardship and death upon them, and now his wife was robbed even of the shallow comfort of a grave for her child. By the time he returned to his companions and the wagons were ready to move forward, Drew Mackinaw's tears were dry and he was ready to take command of the task that remained ahead.

But perhaps there was, after all, some latent sensitivity deep within Gil Stoddard's heart, for after the wagons were moving smoothly along, he fell back and brought his horse alongside the Mackinaw wagon. Normally a taciturn man, he managed to keep up a steady stream of conversation with Drew. Even Maggie, listening from inside the wagon, could tell he was purposely trying to distract the grieving parents with the only sympathy of which he was capable.

"Ain't much to look at on the surface," Stoddard was saying, "but that river can be a real—" He paused with a glance toward Ellie. "Well, it can be a killer. We're lucky there's a bridge now, but I crossed three times by ferry. I was there back in the summer of '52 when fourteen Mormon men from one train were swept away in one shot! That water's cold and ugly this time of year."

"Why do we have to cross the river, Mr. Stoddard?" Ellie asked.

"For one thing, the grazin's better on the north side for the animals. But you'll soon see even that ain't much to speak of."

"How so?" asked Drew. Were there *more* hardships in store for them, he wondered?

"Well," he replied, noting the concern in Drew's voice, "it's best to take one day at a time. And now we got at least one day of smooth traveling ahead."

It was well the trail master said no more of what lay ahead. By this time tomorrow they would embark across fifty miles of the worst terrain yet—high bluffs, broken and barren, combined with a semi-desert of endless scorched brush. But this was not all. Heat and dust would choke the travelers and their animals. Alkali filled the dust and stung the eyes and throats. Any water to be found along the way was a sheer deathtrap to the unwary or unprepared. Stoddard made certain that all the water receptacles were filled from the Platte before beginning the trek across the arid wasteland. But even he could do little to prepare against the hot, thirsty stock trying to drink the poisonous water. It was a constant battle, and littered along the trail were innumerable carcasses of animals whose masters had lost that battle in times past.

Fifty miles. Stoddard was determined to make it in two days—nothing less than a forced march. This time the travelers gave little resistance to the hard-bitten but experienced trail master. Once the stinging, stifling air began to assail them, they quite agreed it was necessary to get past the desert as rapidly as possible.

Hurrying over one of the slate-gray bluffs, the Kramer wagon lost one of its front wheels. For an awful moment the wagon teetered precariously and would surely have slipped to disaster over the edge had it not been caught by the jagged teeth of the rocks beneath it.

The nearby wagons stopped immediately and Stoddard rode up in a cloud of dust.

"Get a rope!" he yelled, dismounting and running forward. "Kramer," he instructed Pete, now standing on the ground after getting his family out of the wagon, "you get back up in the wagon and take the reins. We'll need a few more men. Williams, run back down the trail and get as many as you can."

By the time reinforcements had arrived, Stoddard had a rope attached to the undamaged side of the wagon with a crew of four men pulling. He and another were bracing the other side where the wheel was missing, while Kramer was furiously *geeing* and *hawing* his weary oxen.

Steadily the wagon inched toward level ground. Just then Stoddard's companion lost his footing on a piece of loose rock, fell, and slipped several feet down the edge. At that same moment, while Stoddard's attention was distracted by the falling man, the wagon suddenly lurched forward throwing the unprepared trail boss under the wagon. The shouts of the onlookers warned Kramer of the trouble and the wagon ground to a halt, but not before Stoddard's arm was caught under the rear wheel.

The lurch had brought the wagon up onto level ground. But there was no way it could now back up to free Stoddard's arm without repeating the earlier mishap. Now the men had to lend their strength to lift the cumbersome wagon straight up while one dragged their leader out from under it.

Shouting all manner of oaths and curses, Stoddard lay on the ground while several of the men milled around him, the others assessing the damage to Pete's wagon. In Stoddard's defense, most of his curses were aimed at himself and the wagons and any other inanimate objects within sight. When Dr. Carpenter arrived at the scene, the curses began wandering in his direction also, but he took no heed of them.

"That's my arm, Doctor!" he yelled. "You let *me* move it! I tell you, I can move it!" But one attempt forced him back with a groan and a curse. "This is going to set us back all day. Kramer, you get that wheel fixed! We still got four or five hours of daylight left." Then turning to the doctor, he said, "I want you to know, Doc, I practice what I preach. We ain't stayin' no longer on my account than it takes to repair that wheel."

Dr. Carpenter made no comment, but signalled three of the men who weren't immediately occupied to help carry Stoddard clear of the wagon and out of the others' way.

"It's my arm!" Stoddard grumbled. "Not my legs! I can walk!" He tried to pull himself to his feet, but immediately his vision blurred as objects began to spin before him. Catching himself from falling by grabbing for Samuel's arm, he let loose another string of frustrated oaths.

Supporting him between himself and Drew Mackinaw, Samuel at length managed to transport the surly wagon master to his own wagon—the closest thing on the train to a hospital wagon—where he could begin setting the crushed arm.

"I'm sorry," Samuel said as he began his work, "there's no more whiskey."

"Just my luck! The one time I could have a drink for all to see. But I been through worse—without whiskey," he added.

Before long Stoddard succumbed to the pain. His cuts were not severe, yet the blood lost contributed to his weakened state. He awoke several hours later to the eerie glow of a lantern illuminating what must certainly have been an angel. Even in his groggy condition he knew it was not the doctor standing over him. For an instant of disorientation his blurred mind was sorely perplexed. Then almost immediately his vision began to clear and he realized the ministering angel was none other than Mrs. Duncan—a fact perplexing enough in itself.

"Why ain't we movin'?" he asked with a hoarse attempt at a shout. "Never mind," he added almost immediately as if he had just realized the fact, "it's night. We couldn't get far, anyway."

He lay still for a moment as if deep in thought, then continued, as if Maggie had answered him. "Yeah, but *what* night? How long have we been sittin' here? If that dang fool doctor—"

"Mr. Stoddard," Maggie interposed. Though she had intended to greet him softly and gently when he awoke, she could not now keep a scolding tone from her voice. "That doctor saved your arm—and probably your life. I'll thank you to speak more respectfully about him in the future."

Suddenly Stoddard shot a glance at his injured arm. "I half expected it to be gone," he said in a moderated tone—relief mingled with some apparent esteem for what the doctor had done.

"Well, it's not," replied Maggie, and her tone also softened. "Dr. Carpenter worked very hard to make sure it would heal properly."

"What're you doin' here?"

"The doctor had to tend Mrs. Keys. She burned her hand on the cookfire tonight. He asked me to watch over you. Are you thirsty?"

Stoddard licked his dry, dust-caked lips. "Yeah, as a matter of fact."

Maggie brought him a cup of water and placed one hand under his neck, lifting his head to help him drink. "And to answer your previous question, this is the same day as your accident—or rather, night. Mr. Kramer's wheel is repaired and we should be able to move on in the morning. We are all no less anxious than you to get through this wretched place. Though I doubt we've anything better to look forward to anywhere else."

Maggie's final words were spoken almost before she realized it, and then only because they had been an ever-present thought in her mind.

"No one ever said it was goin' to be a picnic out here," Stoddard said. "It takes some doin'—yeah, and some hardships sometimes—to be able to start a new life in a new country. And that's what this is all about, isn't it? But when we get through the stretch, we got the Sweetwater and then the Pass. And as places go, they ain't half so bad. There ain't hardly a sight to match the Rockies! Nothin' like 'em in Scotland, I don't imagine."

He paused as if his mind were trailing back over the four other times he had crossed the Continental Divide. In a moment he brought his attention back to the new young mother sitting at his side, and focused an intent gaze upon her. "But that weren't what you meant, was it?" he asked after a moment of silent reflection.

"What do you mean?" Maggie replied, taken somewhat aback by the question, especially coming from one such as Gil Stoddard.

"Well, it sounded like maybe you figured that with your husband dead and all, you sort of didn't care anymore. 'Course, maybe it's none of my business."

"I don't mean to be rude, Mr. Stoddard"—Maggie was not quite sure how to take this unusual display of interest on the part of the rough westerner, and she was in no mood to discuss Ian with anyone—"but you're right: it isn't any of your business."

"Oh, I know you ain't the rude type," he said airily, apparently ignoring her previous words. "You won't offend me by anything you say. But it seems to me that with a kid and all that you'd have a mighty lot to be lookin' forward to." Then his voice fell into a pensive tone. "I used to have a kid—two of 'em, in fact. Can you picture that? Me, a father. I was never much cut out for it, though."

"What happened to them?" asked Maggie tentatively. She hesitated to pry into another's life, especially as she was unwilling to discuss the inner turmoils of her own. Yet simple curiosity drove her on.

"Things . . ." he began evasively, yet thoughtfully, "things is different out here. It's a hard life. People get torn apart. Things happen, you know. Sometimes you have to leave your past behind. That's what it takes to build a new country like this."

He paused, clearly not having intended to say so much. "Yeah . . . things happen," he resumed at length. "But you got your kid. And it seems to me you got everything to look forward to, a reason for living, for starting over."

Perhaps Maggie would have agreed with Gil Stoddard's coarse wisdom. But just at that moment Dr. Carpenter poked his head into the wagon and Maggie's mind was diverted for a time.

Later that night, as she lay in her own bed nursing little Eleanor to sleep, her thoughts once again were drawn to the trail master's words.

Had she indeed given up on life, without even realizing it?

She gazed down at the child, a constant wonder to her. The tiny round face was so smooth and soft. And those sweet eyes with their long pale lashes, closed now as she sucked contentedly with her little hand grasping Maggie's nightgown.

Here was a part of her own self . . . a part of Ian . . . cradled now in her arms.
And as she stared at the newborn child a well of joy surged within her. Was this
baby indeed reason enough to go on, to face the future in a rugged new land?
Even without Ian?

Yes, she thought. *I did give up when I had learned of Ian's death.* And yet she
was moving forward. Living again. Now here was little Eleanor in her arms as
a sign that all does not end with death. Life goes on. Ian still lived, even if only
through their daughter. Did she not owe it to him, to the child, and even to herself,
to go on, to make something of her life, to maybe give Eleanor the chance to find
love, even if she and Ian had lost it? Could not the love she and Ian had shared
be passed on to the next generation . . . and then the next? Was their love
meaningless because they had shared it so briefly? Or could she not still—even
though Ian was dead—add to its meaning by passing it along to their descendants
to come—to Duncans and Ramseys yet unborn?

How can I feel this joy in my heart over this tiny child, she thought, *in the midst
of my grief and this wilderness?* And yet the moment Eleanor had been born,
something had begun to change. Maggie hardly knew what the change was, but
the bitterness which had so filled her heart had begun to subside that day. Without
Maggie's even realizing it, the words of a tough, half-disoriented, thick-skinned
trail boss had somehow triggered a yearning after a deeper inward life, a yearning
to start new again.

*But with a kid and all, it seems to me you'd have a mighty lot to be lookin'
forward to.*

She could not erase Gil Stoddard's words from her memory.

All at once Maggie recalled her thoughts immediately after the child's birth:
Eleanor was a gift from God.

Was this precious little gift, this bundle of life, meant not merely to give her
joy—for that she had already begun to do—but to awaken the numbness which
had consumed Maggie, to give her a reason to go on? Before she reached any
conclusions, Maggie had drifted to sleep—the peaceful slumber of one who is
beginning to feel the approach of dawning freedom from the bitter chains of the
past.

When she awoke in the morning the joy remained, and so did the questions. A
vision of Atlanta rose in her mind, and with it came tears at the memory. Maggie
loved her mother. Yet she knew, too, that her mother had allowed herself to shut
off her deepest feelings—especially those toward her children—and had in the
end become a hard woman, unable either to give or receive the delights of love
which should have been able to pass between her and her daughter. What had
caused this, in addition to the codes of her upbringing, Maggie could not guess.
But the marchioness of Stonewycke had kept her emotions steadfastly hidden to
the very end, and the love which she and Maggie harbored each for the other had
never found vent for its expression.

Tears rose in Maggie's eyes. *Yes,* she thought, *I love Mother dearly, but I do
not want to be like her.* She did not want to become a hard woman, growing old

with the bitterness she knew she had every earthly right to cling to. No, she wanted something different for herself. And for her daughter!

Maggie rose, laid the sleeping baby down in the bed, and left the wagon. The bustle of morning had begun. She strolled about, unconsciously seeking the closer approach to some kindred soul to whom she might draw near in order to give expression to the vague feelings rising within her. After a short walk she returned and approached the wagon. All was silent even though Ellie and Drew were making preparations for breakfast. The thought of opening herself to Ellie about her own thoughts in the midst of her friend's grief was inconceivable. Therefore after lending what assistance she could, Maggie found herself— almost without realizing it—wandering toward Samuel Carpenter's wagon.

The bustle of activity about the train grew steadily; parting preparations multiplied the closer the moment came. Samuel had just completed checking the harnesses on his brace of oxen and looked up, smiling at Maggie's approach.

"Good morning, Mrs. Duncan," he said cheerfully. "You look well today. I'm glad to see it."

"Thank you, Dr. Carpenter."

"And how's little Eleanor?"

"We had a restful night. She's sleeping now."

"A restful night? After I had to compel you into service so late last night here in my makeshift hospital!"

Maggie laughed. "and how is our patient this morning?"

Samuel answered with a knowing look of exasperation, then said, "I can't remember when I've had such an ornery man under my care!"

"Now that the arm is splintered," said Maggie, "will he have to stay in bed all day?"

"It would be best if he kept it immobile for a week. But I doubt that's possible. In Stoddard's case, if I let him up, he'll be out driving the cattle and loading the wagonbeds and carrying on within an hour. My only hope is to keep him under my thumb at least for the rest of today." He sighed. "And Lord help me!"

Maggie laughed again. "He is an unusual man, isn't he?" she said. "Last night while you were gone, he spoke rather freely to me. There's more to him than I would have thought."

"I've seen that, too. I think he's suffered a great deal in his life. People who carry about a gruff exterior like that usually have. They're only hiding deeper hurts they don't want to expose."

"Why do people suffer?" Maggie asked reflectively.

"Everyone suffers," replied Samuel. "That's part of life. The Bible says that man is born to trouble."

"But why? Why does it have to be that way? Why does life have to be cruel? Why does man have to be born to trouble?"

"Because we have turned from God's ways. Apart from Him, there can't be anything but grief."

"But couldn't God erase the pain and trouble and grief of life?"

"That's not His way," replied Samuel. "Besides, the troubles of this life aren't really that significant to God, I don't think."

"That doesn't make them any easier to bear," said Maggie. "Just think of what poor Drew and Ellie are going through right now."

"I know," said the doctor. "And my heart grieves for them. But the Lord has Tommy Joe in His hands. And Drew and Ellie's loss will pass and they will go on from this time of mourning."

"But then, what's the purpose of it all? How can you say the troubles we face don't matter that much to God if He's supposed to love us so?"

"It's not that God doesn't care; He's interested in what we do with our difficulties. Time heals the pain of our hurts and eases the anguish. But only the Lord can heal the deepest wounds. He wants us to take our hurts and griefs and bitter memories to Him so He can wash them from our hearts. Trouble comes to all of us; God wants us to give them to Him. That's how He is able to fashion us into the kind of receptacles which can then contain the love He has to offer us."

Maggie was silent a moment. "Then why do you do what you do, Dr. Carpenter," she asked at length, "if God is the only healer?"

"Because I care about people's hurts and pains. And if by tending their surface wounds—their cuts and bruises and infections and broken arms—I am sometimes able to pray for them and point them toward the Healer of their deeper hurts, then I will be a happy man. I offer what healing I can on the physical plane, and as I do I always pray that God will take care of the inner man or woman. Because that's where true life is lived. The troubles of this life are only the means God uses to get us to face the real weighty issues of pride, unforgiveness, and selfishness. Once we have faced those, we can be reborn into the life of joy He wants for each of us. But no man—or woman—can truly face the need to forgive without first experiencing bitterness and hurt. There is no other way."

Maggie looked down at the ground and did not reply. The doctor's words had suddenly probed dangerously close to home in her own heart. They had been talking so earnestly that they had all but forgotten the clamor of activity in the background. Gil Stoddard jarred them back into the present realities.

"Hey, why ain't we movin'?" he yelled.

Maggie turned toward the voice to find the irascible trail master standing outside the wagon with a scowl on his face, clad only in his long underwear, his arm hanging limply at his side, its sling dangling around his neck.

"Stoddard!" Samuel exclaimed. "What do you think you're doing?"

But before Stoddard could answer, Evan McCollough raced up to the doctor's wagon.

"Doc," he said, gasping in the stifling dusty air, "my missus is taken poorly. Do you think you could come and have a look at her?"

"Of course," the doctor replied. "Is it an emergency?"

"I s'pose it can wait a bit."

"I should see to getting Mr. Stoddard's arm tended to first. What are her symptoms?"

"Just kind of weak, you know, and a bellyache."

Samuel had learned that all internal complaints were referred to as bellyaches. From Evan's description it could be anything from indigestion to premature labor.

"I'll be there in a moment, McCollough," he said. "It could be the alkali in the air."

"Okay, Doc," he sighed wearily. "But I don't know what I'm gonna do. I got to get the wagon hitched an' the young'uns are runnin' all about . . ."

"Mrs. Duncan?" Samuel turned to Maggie. "Could you possibly lend a hand?"

"Yes, of course," Maggie answered without hesitation. "You go on back, Evan. I'll be right there. I just have to make sure Eleanor is still asleep."

Within a few minutes Maggie was seated in the McCollough wagon with the three McCollough children next to her as she read them a story. Rebbekah McCollough looked dreadful, lying motionless on her bed. Maggie mused that they had spent nearly four months traveling together, and yet she still barely knew the young woman who was now so frail and sallow in appearance. Yet she had to admit to herself that the fault had been entirely her own. She had been so withdrawn and unapproachable. But she determined that would change.

She had little time to dwell on such thoughts, however, for the children were agitated, and Rebbekah's "bellyache" was in reality stomach cramps so violent that when the woman did move she was assailed by severe nausea.

Maggie did whatever she could, which amounted to keeping an eye on the children, cleaning up after Rebbekah, and bringing her water which she demanded frequently. Still the doctor did not come.

At length the wagon jolted forward. It was not like Dr. Carpenter to neglect a patient, although there could be no telling what complications Gil Stoddard had thrown his way.

Maggie had no way of knowing that while Samuel was finishing with the trail master, two more freak mishaps had occurred. In the rush to get underway, one man had been pinned against his wagon by a nervous ox and had suffered a cracked rib. Another received a nasty gash in his arm while securing a loose wheel. These two men had barely been tended to when the first of the wagons began to move. And in the flurry Samuel, who indeed was not a man to forget a patient, did forget Mrs. McCollough and the nurse he had sent to help.

33

New Crisis

THE TRAIN PLANNED to stop at a spring Stoddard knew of, the one supposedly good spring in the fifty mile stretch of desert. The water there, however, turned out to be as foul as the rest and two more cows were lost from drinking it. After conferring for a few minutes, the men decided to move on. Willow Springs was still a day and a half distant, the next water source of which they could be certain. Their water reserves were getting low; the sooner they got to the springs, the better.

It was not till the wagon had stopped that Samuel remembered his oversight. He hurried to the McCollough wagon, calling out a greeting, and climbing up and inside before even receiving an answer. The experiences of his profession notwithstanding, the putrid odor that met him nearly sickened him.

"Dear Lord! Mrs. McCollough, I'm so sorry it's taken me so long. And Mrs. Duncan—can you forgive me?"

"Doctor," Maggie said, "she's so sick."

"And your own child?"

"I'm sure Ellie is caring for her, though it's long past her feeding time and I ought to go to her soon. I'm afraid I haven't been able to do much for Rebbekah."

"You've done more than you know," Samuel replied. Then he turned his full attention to his patient. It was immediately obvious that she did not have long to live. Her skin tone evidenced dehydration, though Maggie assured him she had been drinking water despite the fact that it only seemed to make her all the more ill. He listened to Maggie's description of Rebbekah's other symptoms with an apprehension which grew into horror. The past several days had been so tragic it seemed impossible they could cope with another crisis so soon. Yet the doctor feared this could be the beginning of something far worse.

He laid down Rebbekah's hand, whose bluish nails finalized his awful diagnosis. He sighed heavily, but it seemed more a shudder than a sigh. Only one word could he utter: "Cholera."

He needed to say no more. Maggie fell back against several crates in the crowded wagon, the color drained from her face. But Samuel Carpenter was a medical man; his acute instincts were only temporarily daunted, but not overpowered by his complete dismay. Before another moment passed he sprang into action.

He did not know how to cure cholera, not even what caused it. No one did. But he did know that it could spread like a prairie fire, and he was determined that should not happen. If it did, the entire wagon train would be wiped out and the hopes and dreams of its members along with it.

"Mrs. Duncan," he said, "go to my wagon and draw some water and wash very carefully. Then go get your Eleanor and return to my wagon immediately. You must stay there, do you understand?"

In a daze Maggie obeyed.

The moment Maggie had left, Samuel called Evan and calmly explained the situation facing them. "I will inform the rest of the train, but you and your family must keep to your wagon." Samuel did not relish the task of carrying such tidings to the others, for he had more than once seen superstition and panic overcome good sense and prudence. And if there was one thing they didn't need out in this wilderness, it was to have panic split the train apart.

Making sure Rebbekah was comfortable, Samuel left the wagon. He found Stoddard in the process of mounting his horse. The doctor suppressed a rebuke at the man's flagrant neglect of his orders, but there were suddenly much more urgent matters on his mind. *It's just as well, anyway,* he thought, *now that Margaret and Eleanor will have to stay in the wagon.* When he imparted the news to the trail master, even Stoddard blanched.

"Good God!" he swore. "That's all we need!"

"Only our good God will protect us through this," Samuel responded.

"Well . . . are you going to tell the rest of them, or am I?" Stoddard asked, choosing to ignore the doctor's statement. Without waiting for an answer, Stoddard rode off to round up the men for another conference.

Samuel presented the information medically, logically. For the moment at least he pushed from his mind the fact that the woman would soon die an awful death. He tried to convince the others that if they worked together they could isolate the dread disease to the McCollough wagon. But even if it proved too late for that, there was still no reason to panic.

"They're all going to die anyway!" someone cried. "It's best to save as many as we can right now."

"That may not help," Samuel tried to reason. "We can't even think of splitting up the train, not in this wilderness."

"That's better than all of us dying!"

"We've got our own families to think about!"

"Folks . . . please!" implored the doctor, but by now the general confusion had spread to the wives, who had gotten wind of the trouble and were approaching one by one.

"Listen to the doc!" commanded Stoddard.

"We've got to stay calm," urged Samuel. "Now, how many of you have been in close contact with Rebbekah McCollough these past few days?"

Rebbekah was a quiet, retiring woman and kept mostly to herself; no hands went up. Samuel could not help breathing a sigh of relief, but this did nothing to bolster his argument. Inside he was sure the train would reject his pleas and would, in the end, move on. He recoiled at the thought and would fight against it. But perhaps the others had that right. Yet even if the McColloughs did manage to survive the plague, how could they possibly hope to survive long in the middle of hostile Indian territory? And what of Margaret's exposure already, and his own? Only a miracle would keep the cholera from spreading.

It was an unexpected voice that assured the decision. "Listen, folks, I don't want to get too close . . ." It was Evan McCollough, standing some distance from the group. "But I ain't expecting you to make such a hard choice. We been through a lot together, helpin' one another out of one scrape or another, and, well . . . now it's my turn. My wife just died, and now my daughter's ailin', and I don't know which one of us might be next. You gotta go on ahead. Maybe when this thing's run its course, what's left of us will catch up. But that's the way it's got to be."

He finished his speech, overcome by the tears which were rising in his eyes, turned sharply away, and walked back toward his wagon, saying not another word and clearly expecting no argument from his companions.

A somber silence settled over the group, only to be broken by another voice that spoke as if it felt no pain at the man's terrible sacrifice. "Weren't that Duncan woman with the McColloughs all day?"

"Yeah, Doc," said another. "Ain't it possible she got it too?"

"It's possible we *all* could catch it!" shouted Samuel in frustration.

"Well, maybe she ought to stay with them."

"This is madness!" Samuel cried, rubbing his hands across his face as if when he removed them everything before him might have changed.

"Dinna worry, Doc," came Drew Mackinaw's slow foreign drawl. "We come wi' Evan an' Rebbekah all the way from New York—" As he spoke there was a certain mournful ache in his voice. "We've all had our hardships. We knew when we set out t' find a new life that it wouldn't be none too easy. That's the chance we took. Now we both have lost someone dear t' us an' I don't intend t' leave my friend here alone, even if it means my dyin' by his side. We Mackinaws ain't leavin' them. I'm na sayin' this t' make ye others feel obliged t' stay but what e'er ye do, I ken my own duty, an' we're stayin'."

Sorry as they were to lose a good man like Drew, very little resistance was offered. Bound as they had been together, suddenly life and death confronted them. Though such decisions were loathesome, they had to be made for the greater good of all, each tried to convince himself. As if in unspoken agreement, the party of travelers began to silently disband and husband and wives slowly made their way back to their families. Before ten more minutes had passed, the line of wagons was again moving on under the scorching prairie sun. Only Stoddard and Frank and Leila Wooten remained with Drew and Samuel Carpenter.

"I thought you would move on with the others, Stoddard," said Frank.

"Thought I'd be worryin' about savin' my own skin, is that it?"

"I just thought that with seven wagons goin' on ahead, and only four stayin' here, you'd figure the others would be most in need of a guide."

"Not to mention getting the rest of your money, Mr. Stoddard," put in Ellie. "If you stay with us, we may all be dead before two weeks are out."

"It's become more than for the money by now," said Stoddard slowly. "Before I agreed to sign on, I said this'd be my last train. I said to myself I was going to make this one count for something—make myself count. Well, now I've decided this is where I do something that matters. So I've got to stay with the people who might need me the most, no matter how many of you there are."

"Weel, Mr. Stoddard," said Drew with a smile, approaching the trail boss with outstretched hand, "we're proud t' hae ye with us. An' we thank ye!"

When Maggie heard what had taken place, she could hardly speak. Since she had come into the Mackinaws' lives, a complete stranger, they had never ceased from the first moment to give to her. What she would have done without them she hardly knew. But now she knew she could ask no more of them.

Climbing down from the doctor's wagon, little Eleanor in her arms, she spoke out, "No," she said with a hard edge of determination in her voice. "I can't allow you to jeopardize your families like this. Not for me."

"Maggie, you've got little choice if we decide to stay," said Ellie, speaking more firmly than anyone had heard her since her son's death. "And we're not just doing it for you alone, although I'm sure we all would. But we must stand by Evan now too. He needs us more than ever."

"Drew," Maggie said, turning her argument toward him. "If it were just you and Ellie, maybe you'd have the freedom to do such a thing. But you have your children to think of. And, Dr. Carpenter," she now looked in the doctor's direction, "isn't it true that they could well escape it because their contact has been limited?"

The doctor nodded reluctantly.

"But I have been close to Rebbekah. I'll probably come down with it, won't I?" Maggie pressed.

Samuel swallowed hard. He could not forget that it was he who had in ignorance sent Maggie to the McCulloughs' wagon in the first place. "No one can be certain . . ." he offered at length.

"Please!" Maggie pleaded. "Go on with the others. You have to protect your children. Let me stay and be of what help I can to Evan. But there need be no one else. There is more danger for me. Whatever is going to happen to me is already determined. But you—Drew, Ellie, Frank, Leila—you must go on!"

Maggie turned and in the silence that had fallen upon her friends, she climbed back into the wagon. She feared that if she remained a moment longer she would allow them to stay, even beg them to stay. It was some moments before she heard another sound, and then it was Ellie's broken, sobbing voice.

"At least let us say a proper good-bye!" she cried.

"We will see each other soon," Maggie replied. "It won't be long. If we ever have to say a proper good-bye, let it be later. For now we will just have a brief parting."

"No . . . not long," Ellie managed to say. "Oh, Maggie . . . I love you! God be with you!"

Maggie could not reply. Her voice was strangled with tears. Worst of all, she could not even give her friend one last hug. She simply held her hand up and watched them slowly turn toward their wagons. They realized, painful as it was, that Maggie had spoken truthfully. They did have to consider their children, even more than their friends.

As the two wagons finally rumbled down the road, Maggie saw quiet little Bess waving vigorously from the back of the wagon. Maggie tried to smile, then waved back so the child could see. She was glad Bess could not see her tears. For she wept in the conviction that it would be the last time she would ever see the sweet little girl who had been her dear companion through the most difficult months Maggie had ever faced in her life.

As Maggie turned her head away and swept her sleeve across her eyes to dry the freely flowing tears, her attention was quickly arrested by the two remaining figures standing beside the wagon. Dr. Carpenter and Gil Stoddard remained side by side, an unlikely match in any but the most tragic of circumstances.

"You had better not let them get too far ahead of you," Samuel said.

"And what about you, Doc?" Stoddard asked.

"I'll be staying," Samuel answered. "A doctor will be needed here, hopefully not with the others."

"That's fine," Stoddard stated. "I was plannin' to stay, too. You'll need another gun."

Both Maggie and Samuel stared in unmasked surprise.

"What're you gawkin' for?" Stoddard snapped. "What'd you take me for, a dirty sidewinder that'd leave you to the vultures?"

"We never doubted your intentions," said Samuel, clearly touched. "But the train still needs you."

"They'll manage," he replied, glancing toward the cloud of dust that was by this time all that remained of the retreating Mackinaw Party. "It's like this, Doc. I owe you. And you too, Mrs. Duncan. After the way I treated you, you still sat by me when I hurt my arm. And you, Doc, you kept me in your wagon. Not many folks through the years have stuck by me, or shown me such gratitude. So now I got a chance to pay you back."

Samuel opened his mouth to speak, but Stoddard hurried on, "There's more, Doc. You got a right to know. And, anyway, I think I want you to know. I lied back there in Independence when I said I wasn't drunk the day of the massacre. I was, or at least hung over so bad I couldn't see straight. We'd just lost my son to the smallpox. And when he died I just couldn't handle it and went out on a bender to try to drown my sorrows in the bottle. But even that don't give me no excuse, 'cause I was the boss and they were all depending on me. There'd been rumors of Indian trouble. I was just plain stupid . . ."

He paused and looked away from his two listeners as if he could not continue if he had to face them.

"My wife and daughter were still with me—and I lost them too. I lost *everything!*" He sighed deeply, fighting back the tears that were none too familiar to this tough-skinned man of the prairie. "But I can't let that happen again," he resumed, "—not where there's something I can do about it. Maybe you don't want me to stay, and well . . . I couldn't blame you."

"Mr. Stoddard." It was Maggie who spoke, her voice shaken anew with emotion. "I am honored that you would want to do this for us . . . for me. But I could never ask it of you."

"No one's asked," Stoddard replied gruffly, attempting once again to bury the emotion which had surfaced beneath the tough exterior. Then he continued more briskly, "Well, I expect we got work to do."

With that he strode to the wagon box where he took down a shovel, then walked some distance away and began digging a grave. This one would be Rebbekah McCollough's permanent resting place. He hoped he didn't have to dig too many others.

Samuel gathered up Maggie's carpetbag and few other belongings where Ellie had left them. And after stowing them in his wagon, went to continue his vigil at the stricken McCollough wagon.

34

Attack!

THE FOLLOWING DAY was one of waiting. For what, the little party did not know. Death, perhaps. Indians, maybe. But certainly there would be more suffering and grief.

Two McCollough children were now sick, and it looked as though the youngest would not make it through another night. Samuel kept all but himself and Evan as far removed from the wagon as possible. Maggie had taken up residence in the doctor's wagon, while Samuel and Stoddard slept in the open air.

Stoddard kept himself occupied foraging about the area. He returned late in the afternoon with the announcement that he had discovered some good water. The remainder of the day he spent filling up every available container, a job which took him twice as long since he still had the use of but one arm. He had also located a more secluded campsite down the road, but the idea of harnessing the oxen and repacking all the gear was so overwhelming to the weary band that they unanimously decided to stay put. As it turned out, that decision would save their lives.

In the morning another grave had to be dug; during the night Evan's youngest daughter died. Maggie wondered how Evan could hold up under the mounting loss, but she knew how apt men were to hold their painful thoughts inside. She prayed, as she hadn't prayed in some time, for Evan and what remained of his family.

After the others had dispersed from the little graveside service for Evan's daughter, Maggie spoke out to Dr. Carpenter.

"Dr. Carpenter," she said, then hesitated.

"Yes, Mrs. Duncan, what is it?"

"I wanted to tell you that I was encouraged by the things you said the other day; you remember, when I was asking about suffering?"

He nodded.

"I was really asking as much on my own behalf as I was for Mr. Stoddard."

Here a smile tugged at the corners of Samuel's lips. Maggie reddened slightly, realizing he must have guessed at the truth all along, but something in the situation also pleased her, and she continued. "I must be extremely dense. Of course, you knew all the time."

"Perhaps. But what I said applies to us all. And I didn't want to embarrass you by—"

He paused with apparent uncertainty.

"—but it appears I have done so anyway," he concluded at length.

Maggie laughed. "I can tolerate a little redness in my cheeks from time to time," she said. "But I want you to know that I appreciate your honesty—both then and now. It's—it's very difficult for me to talk about myself to others. Especially since—well, you know, since my husband's death."

"It's understandable. I'm a complete stranger."

Now it was Maggie's turn to smile. "Here I am living in your wagon, completely at your mercy. I would hardly call you a stranger any longer, Dr. Carpenter."

For a brief moment, the thought of Ian came into Maggie's mind. How amusing this awkward little interview with the doctor would have been to him! He had always laughed at her feminine discomfiture, and she would have become angry at him. Later they would have laughed over it together. But this time, the memory of Ian had come into her mind, unaccompanied by the awful, sickly emptiness which had so characterized her mood for the last six months. She found herself almost smiling at the thought of his laughing eyes and merry wit.

"You would have liked my husband, Doctor," she replied finally. "And I'm sure he would have liked you."

"I'm sorry I couldn't have met him," replied the doctor. "I'm sure he must have been quite something for you to love him as you did."

"He was unlike you in many ways—so boyish and gay. There was almost a delightful immaturity about him. But, then, I was young, too—only seventeen when we married. It seems I have grown ten years since then."

"Age and maturity are not always measured in years," he remarked. "Perhaps you have grown far more in the past than you realize, although it'll probably take years to appreciate it."

"If I live that long," replied Maggie with a sigh.

"Don't worry," said Samuel. "You'll make it through this, you and your little Eleanor."

"How can you be so certain?"

"There's a certain tenacity about you, Mrs. Margaret Duncan. Nothing's going to keep you down forever. God has things to do with you, in you, perhaps through that beautiful child of yours. I have no doubt of that. A spirit like yours comes along only once in a family in many generations. No, I'm quite sure the Duncan family will live on and on through its American line."

Maggie was silent a moment, and her thoughts returned to Ian. When she spoke again it was about him once more, as if to pick up the thread of conversation which had been dropped a few moments back. "He was not like you . . . and yet, in many ways, he was. He had such a deep sensitivity and a strong yearning after right. I know he would have respected you. For you stand up for the things you believe in."

"When there is something I believe in," Samuel said, "then I consider it worth fighting for."

"You believe in God like that, don't you?"

"Yes."

"I've been so confused these last months. There was a time when I could pray and feel I was being heard. But that was long ago. And I want to pray again, and I've tried. Little Eleanor has brought me such joy. I think that's a gift from God. But it's all so hard to understand."

"Perhaps understanding it isn't as important as we make it. Perhaps the most important thing is simply allowing the love God has for us to flow over us."

"But it's not something you can see or touch."

"Perhaps it's like renewing the acquaintance of an old friend, a friend with whom we may have had a bitter parting. The first steps toward coming together are slow, almost painful. But we know the friendship will be worth the wait, so we persist, and ultimately are rewarded."

"Maybe I just don't have enough faith."

"I don't think so," replied Samuel. "I don't think God cares so much how big our faith is, but whether we are willing to trust Him the little bit we are able. A little faith put to use is much better than a big faith sitting on the shelf doing nothing. No, I think we all have plenty of faith if we'll just put it to work."

By now they had walked a little distance from the wagons along the jagged rocky path. It was odd, Maggie thought. Traveling in the wagon with the awful alkali-laden dust all about, hot and dry and bumpy, this road had seemed ugly. But now it had become rather peaceful. Around them all was still and quiet. Even the dry sage and jagged rocks contained a certain beauty.

"Only you can judge your own faith," Samuel continued. "And only you can know how God expects you to use it."

"But how can I *know* if I have faith?" Maggie asked, her eyes intent on him for an answer.

"I'm afraid I can't answer that question," he replied. "Perhaps *desiring* faith is all we need do—all we *can* do, in fact. God alone is the giver of faith. If we desire it, and ask Him for it—"

He stopped short, for suddenly Maggie had grasped his arm. Her face had turned white and she leaned heavily against him.

"Margaret . . . !" he could hardly force the word out. "You're ill?"

She only nodded, barely cognizant of the fact that he had used her given name. He caught her up in his arms and raced back to the wagons.

Immediately new sleeping arrangements had to be contrived. Maggie knew she would have to be separated from her daughter, but she insisted that Eleanor be kept in the wagon out of the day's intense rays of sun. Stoddard rigged up a tent for Maggie nearby, for none could bear to put her in the McCollough wagon, now rank with the odor of death. Samuel and Stoddard shared the doctor's wagon and took turns caring for Eleanor as best they could. As she could now have no more of her mother's milk, they had no choice but to soak dried biscuits or jerky in water and then attempt to force some of the liquid down her through the bottle which Ellie Mackinaw had provided. Both men shared equally the inevitable task of changing diapers.

Had Maggie been able to observe the tender care given her daughter by the two men, she would have rested without a care. Samuel was not altogether inexperienced, for physicians often find themselves commandeered into a variety of motherly chores while caring for the sick. Not so with frontier wagon masters! But Stoddard accepted his duties gamely, picked up the tiny bundle of life with fingers no less delicate in that they were hard and calloused with years of hard work, and even—when alone—murmured little bits of encouragement to the infant in high-pitched fatherly tones. During and after feeding times, being the more experienced of the two, he was often in the position of tutoring the doctor.

"Give her back a good firm rub," he instructed. "Down low—that's it—down where it'll bring up the burp."

But if the good doctor was unsuccessful at the fine art of burping a baby, he was an expert at singing to it and rocking her to sleep as he hummed soothing tones. During one such moment, as he walked slowly about the camp crooning to the child, he heard Maggie calling him from her tent.

"Samuel," she said feebly as he approached. "Look in the bottom of my carpetbag. I have a small music box I brought from home. It plays a sweet little lullaby. Eleanor might like the sound."

The doctor did as instructed and found, indeed, that the strains from Brahms' most famous tune quieted the baby as nothing else could.

That evening another of Evan's daughters died and by morning he and his remaining daughter had been taken ill. But Maggie—perhaps mercifully—was unaware of all this. The dreaded disease—so feared by everyone—had indeed struck her down.

At first her consciousness could only focus on the pain, the fever, and the shock of her hopeless plight. Then suddenly it seemed to dawn on her that she would probably *die* from the disease. Rebbekah had died, and her daughter had died, and far back in her memory Maggie recalled the cholera epidemic in Port Strathy when she was a girl. Drew Mackinaw's sister had died at that time, and many others besides.

People *die* from this thing! Her mind seemed to pulsate with the thought.

Oh, God, I don't want to die! she said half aloud. For so long after Ian's death she had longed to die, but now she knew she felt that way no more. She had reason to live now. *Oh, God . . . please don't let me die! I want to live, God. I want to know you if you'll just show me how!*

All at once the words she had heard so recently tumbled into her fevered brain: *Desiring faith is all we need do . . . God is the giver of faith if we desire it and ask Him for it.*

"Dear Lord," Maggie murmured, "I *do* desire faith. Let me live long enough for you to give me faith. And let me use whatever little faith I have already."

Not far from where she lay, Samuel also prayed. Perhaps he prayed no more for Maggie than he had for any of his patients. But there was a fervency in his prayers that surprised even him. He trembled at the thought of Maggie dying. Why, he did not know, but being left without her, though he had known her so briefly, scared him as much as the dying itself. He had felt the same during the months of his wife's illness. On the other hand he told himself that he hardly knew young Margaret Duncan. She was but half his age. Yet through the rugged circumstances of chance they had been thrust together, he felt, to minister and strengthen one another. She could not die now.

"Oh, Lord," he prayed earnestly, "in the name of Jesus, the healer of bodies as well as souls, I ask you to spare her life and heal her of this dread affliction."

Maggie's sickness continued throughout another terrible day, during which Evan's last daughter died. Still Maggie did not know that only she and Evan remained, and that for reasons undoubtedly miraculous in nature, Eleanor, Samuel, and Stoddard had thus far been spared. The lack of activity was beginning to craze poor Stoddard, although the rest allowed his arm to heal nicely. But on the fifth day since their separation from the rest of the wagons—just as he was about to crack—cholera suddenly became the less significant of their problems.

Stoddard, ever the vigilant wagon master, first spotted the Indians shortly after sunup. Like a dreaded nightmare, they had appeared on the rise of a rocky bluff a mile or two south of their position. He had rubbed his eyes several times before he could be certain that the sight was, in fact, real and not a hallucination brought on by another unrelenting day in the burdensome heat. But there could be no mistake. There on their spotted horses sat a half-dozen Sioux warriors, outfitted, by all appearances, for war—regal feathers upon their heads, buckskin quivers hanging from their bronzed shoulders, paint adorning their stern tan faces. The sweat stood out on Stoddard's face, for he knew better than anyone what lay in store for them. He instantly roused Samuel and shouted warnings to Evan to stay hidden while he and the doctor quickly moved Maggie to what they hoped would be a safe position behind two large rocks. They had barely eased her onto the ground and readied their weapons when the warriors swept down upon them.

Stoddard had always been a crack rifleman, and even with but one good arm he picked off two of the attackers before the first arrow pierced through the canvas wagon top where Eleanor still lay sleeping. The remaining warriors raced through the camp with ear-splitting yells and continued past them and disappeared over a rock rise on the other side of the trail. Perhaps the rapid diminishing of their numbers discouraged them, or perhaps they had not intended a massacre in the first place, but for whatever reason, they were gone, and the two men fell back against the wagon wheel where they had taken cover. Samuel had not yet fired a shot.

"Thank God, they're gone!" he sighed.

"Don't be thankin' your God yet, Doc," Stoddard replied as he hastily reloaded his Winchester. "More'n likely they've gone for reinforcements."

"Maybe we should move away from here," Samuel suggested.

"Yeah, we might, but . . ."

He paused for a moment as he looked sharply out toward the horizon. Were those more war cries he heard in the distance?

"We'll have no time for that," he said grimly. "If only we could get the lady and her kid to safety."

But there wasn't time. Almost before Stoddard could finish his sentence, the Indians were on top of them again. This time the descent from the hills was made by ten warriors, two of whom were armed with rifles, the rest with bows.

"If you can't shoot straight, Doc," said Stoddard, "then maybe you better do some mighty fast prayin'."

"I'll do both," Samuel replied as he lifted his rifle in readiness. He had never killed another human being before. His hands trembled, for in fact he had never even hurt another, not even in a fist fight on the rowdy docks where he had worked with his father. But he would kill now, forsaking for a brief moment of time his calling as a healer of men, in order to save the lives of those he had grown to love. And as the attackers drew within range he began to empty his rifle at them, remembering whom he was protecting and that he would die before he allowed them to be harmed.

Samuel's first shot missed its mark. But Stoddard's did not and another painted warrior fell. Behind them a shot rang out from Evan's wagon and the doctor and trail master shot looks of hope toward one another with the addition of Evan's gun to the battle. How effective Evan would prove was debatable, for he could barely hold the rifle in his arms. But it at least served as one further distraction for the Sioux. But even this could not hold them off indefinitely.

Quickly they were approaching on horseback now, too rapidly and too many to stop. As one of the band rode past the campfire which the doctor had maintained for the sterilization of water, he swooped down with a torch in his hand. Instantly it jumped into flame. Brandishing the blazing wood aloft and screaming a hideous cry, he pitched it toward Samuel's wagon. The next instant the Indian fell from his bewildered horse, fatally wounded by Stoddard's shot. But the brand still found its mark. It landed on the front seat of the wagon and instantly the canvas top was ablaze, fanned by a light breeze.

Samuel and Stoddard both jumped up and leapt forward in horror. Stoddard was the quicker of the two and reached the flaming wagon first. Inside he could hear Eleanor crying and his heart pounded against his chest in fear he could not get her out in time. All around him arrows continued to fly and shots explode, while he beat against the flames with his jacket.

Just as he climbed up to reach into the back of the wagon he heard, rather than felt, one of the arrows pierce his back. The thud and awful screaming pain which followed stunned him momentarily and brought an unspoken oath to his lips. But he refused to collapse; he would not die in that manner. If he must die, it would be in a manner worthy of those who had become his friends. As his mind grew blurred and the sounds around him distant, the only other thought which remained was that he must save the child.

No longer could he heard the sounds outside—the shots, the pounding of hoof-beats against the dry earth, the shouts and yells. All around had grown dim and quiet, all except the faint sound of a crying child.

He stumbled toward the infant, oblivious to the fire raging all about him. "There, there," he gasped, as tenderly as his failing voice would permit. "No need to cry. Uncle Gil's got you now."

Quickly he picked her up and backed out of the wagon. The pain in his back was gone now. In its place there was only numbness. He could not feel his legs, though he could tell he was standing on them. The wagon was engulfed in flames and all around he was exposed to the attack. A piece of burning canvas floated down and landed on Eleanor's blanket. Stoddard brushed it away and tried to run, keeping his back always toward the attack.

Suddenly people were running about. Vague shouts penetrated Stoddard's dim consciousness. He could hear no more shots or warcries; all was a blur. He began to slip. He clutched Eleanor to his chest more tightly.

"You ain't touching her!" he cried in a barely audible voice, then crumbled to the ground.

When he awoke, Samuel was kneeling over him, his great tender eyes wet with tears. Eleanor was gone.

"Where's . . . ?" he tried to say, but his mouth was dry and his tongue too swollen to move.

"It's all right now, Gil," Samuel replied. "It's all right. You just rest."

"Did you kill 'em all, Doc?" he asked weakly.

"I didn't have to. A small company of soldiers heard our trouble."

Stoddard tried to laugh. "Your—your God . . . He does okay after all, huh, Doc?"

Samuel nodded as tears flowed unchecked down his sunburned cheeks. Stoddard did not have long. The arrow was too deep and the shaft had broken off in the fall. There had been a good deal of death this week, but this was going to be one of the most difficult of all for the compassionate doctor. But though he could do nothing for the body of the dying man, he gave him something more important than what lay in the power of his medical skills.

"He's your God, too, Gil," Samuel said.

"You think so? I never had much use . . ."

"I know He is." Samuel replied, the certainty of his statement broken only by his trembling emotions. "And He always has been."

"It kind of makes dyin' easier, knowin' that, you know, Doc?"

"I know." But the doctor by now could hardly speak himself.

"And the kid? You sure she's okay, Doc?"

"She's fine, Gil, thanks to you. You saved her life."

Stoddard smiled a thin smile. "And the woman. You'll take care of her, too, won't you, Doc?"

"Yes, of course I will, Gil."

"And no whiskey, either, Doc . . ." Stoddard said with a smile.

Samuel slowly shook his head and forced a smile to his lips also. But the weary wagon master did not see, for he had already slipped into eternity.

35

Respite

𝕏

MAGGIE RECOVERED SLOWLY. Even after the contagion passed, weakness clung to her. The soldiers had been kind enough to provide protection to the stranded travelers—at some distance, to be sure. July was drawing to a fiery close before they deemed it safe to move Maggie and Evan to the safety of the garrison along the Platte. Although most of the contents of Samuel's wagon had been spared, the wagon itself had been burned beyond use and the oxen from both wagons had been scattered by the Indians. So the four made the trip on spare Army horses, brought out from the fort during the last exchange of those who had been on duty staying with them to guard against another attack.

On the morning of their departure, Evan began to succumb to the loss he had experienced. Six soldiers and the four civilians had departed the campsite, while two soldiers had been left behind to burn the wagons, eliminating the possibility of the Indians returning to pillage and picking up the disease. About a hundred yards away, Evan turned back, saying he had forgotten something. When he reached the two soldiers where they stood lighting their torches, he grabbed one away, and with a wild gleam in his eyes flung it upon his wagon. Then he stood as if in a trance, watching the flames hungrily licking at the last remnant of his earthly possessions. The two men finally had to carry him from the scene.

They reached the Platte Bridge Army Garrison late that afternoon. It was a flimsy fort-like structure, a log wall encompassing barracks for approximately a hundred soldiers in addition to all the other buildings necessary to complete such a wilderness complex. Maggie and Eleanor were put up in the captain's quarters, hardly plush by aristocratic standards, but welcome and comfortable after months in the back of a crowded wagon. Space was made for Samuel, Evan, and Captain Hodges in the barracks.

Samuel ordered Maggie directly to bed where she was to remain for at least a week. Maggie did not protest. With Eleanor at her side and with strength once again beginning to flow through her weary frame, she was at rest. Samuel brought her meals and dropped in at least four or five other times throughout every day, ostensibly to check her condition; more often than not, he spent the time holding Eleanor or conversing with his patient. Maggie looked forward to each of his visits and could even tell that little Eleanor had developed an attachment to the kindly doctor.

On a bright morning during the first week of August, Samuel paid one of his frequent visits to Maggie's bedside. He wore a cheerful, almost buoyant expression and his step was unusually light. He caught up Eleanor with a single motion, and his mood seemed to infect her as she broke out in a grin.

"Look, she's smiling!" he exclaimed. "Why, that must be her first smile!" He lowered the child to the bed, where Maggie could also appreciate Eleanor's marvelous achievement. Maggie smiled and said nothing. He need not know that she had smiled the previous day for her.

"She's such a pretty baby!" he went on exuberantly. "She must be a month old already."

"She is. Today, in fact," Maggie replied, but her voice seemed far away.

"Well, I have a one-month birthday present for you, Eleanor," said Samuel with a grin. "How would you like to go for a walk with your mother today—outside in the sunshine?" He turned toward Maggie, anticipating her reaction to the news that her confinement was drawing to a close.

"That sounds nice, Samuel," Maggie said. But even as she spoke there was something missing in her tone.

"Aren't you feeling well today, Margaret?" he asked, peering at her with something more than medical concern.

"Oh, yes. I'm much better," Maggie replied, trying to put more enthusiasm into her voice. "It's just that I was thinking of . . . well, today is my birthday, too. And I was . . . thinking of what it was like this time last year."

Samuel drew up a chair and sat down at Maggie's side, still cradling Eleanor.

"Much has happened to you since then, hasn't it, Margaret?" he said.

"Yes . . ." Maggie replied, drawing out the word thoughtfully. "It's hard to believe that only a year ago I was whirling around a ballroom, dressed in an elegant gown, without a care in the world—"

She stopped abruptly as a sudden and unexpected vision of her father came into her thoughts. He danced with her on that night, she recalled, and even in the innocence of the remembrance, the thought was like a grim cloud passing momentarily over the sun. "There were cares, even then," she mused, nearly forgetting Samuel's presence. "But it seems like so long ago."

"I know it is said that with the passing of time, pain is eased and grief is softened," Samuel replied, his words expressing the depths of his own heart as much as they were intended to ease Maggie's burden. "But I believe there is some pain which never leaves us entirely; perhaps it is intrinsically wrapped up with much that is good within us. I wish there were something I could *do* for you to help lighten your load, if only it was to direct you to the One who can bear the whole load for you."

"You have already done that, Samuel," Maggie replied softly. "Each day, each moment you are here brings me closer. God is giving me faith. I know it. I know that's why He saved me from dying."

Then, as if visibly shaking herself into a new mood, Maggie began again in a less pensive and more cheerful tone, "But the day of my first walk is quickly slipping away! Take Eleanor out with you now, Samuel, while I dress. Then I shall meet you in a few moments."

So the time passed, one day inching lazily upon the next. Each was filled with its own peculiar kind of peace even though very real burdens and fears still lurked on the edges of life. For when one can do nothing about one's own troubles or the troubles of friends far away, peace often forces itself upon us. And at such times, though the cares of life do not evaporate, such peace can be accepted, even enjoyed. For Maggie, this time of respite was a soothing balm to her soul, an unexpected break from the cares which had for so long engulfed her. In total isolation from any remnant of what she had known, she was able to look around her, as she and Ian had learned to do together, saying, "This rock, this flower, this horse, this tree, this land . . . they are beautiful. And life can be good again!"

Only one shadow crossed the tranquility of those fine days. Evan McCollough had gone to bed one night in the barracks with all the other men; in the morning he was gone, and with him one of the poorer horses in the stable. A few dollars, probably all that Evan possessed, had been left by the captain's bunk for the animal. A small party of soldiers immediately set out on a futile search. But he was never found.

And if that desolate Army outpost had a spell over it, the peace continued to cover Samuel and Maggie; Evan's loss seemed to blend in with all the other losses they had weathered together. The heartaches stood at bay like a threatening wave held in place by some miracle—never far from crashing down, but for the moment at least, its fury checked.

If anyone had asked Maggie later what her clearest memory of those days was, she would have immediately replied, "The leisurely walks about the grounds." Morning and early evening would usually find the pair, with Samuel carrying Eleanor, strolling just outside the flimsy enclosure of the garrison. Captain Hodges permitted them to proceed no further, for the Indian unrest was still at a high pitch. The tortuous, murky river and the barren, sage-covered hills surrounded the two as they soaked up all the peace that God had to shower down upon them.

As they walked, and talked, the ground of their lives was softened and before long they were able to tread the paths of their hearts as if the gates had long been open and the ways well-worn.

One day Maggie laughed at Samuel's abandoned play with Eleanor. They had begged permission from the captain for a picnic. Hugging the safety of the wall, they sat upon a blanket in the questionable shade of a scrawny cottonwood. Samuel was doing everything within the powers of his masculine persuasions to induce delightful smiles from the two-month-old baby.

"You are very good with Eleanor," Maggie remarked.

Samuel laughed. "I'm afraid Gil Stoddard would never agree. But I hope I succeeded in learning something from him." A cloud of sadness momentarily replaced the laughter in his eyes.

"I was so sick," Maggie replied. "I had nearly forgotten how you both cared for her. I wish I could have seen Gil with her."

"He was so gentle. He treated her like the most delicate flower on earth. And if she *looked* out of place in his scrapping arms, I know she never *felt* out of place there. It was a wonderful sight."

"How terrible that he had to die!"

"Yes. It was awful—but in a way, perhaps it was marvelous, too."

"How can you say such a thing?" Maggie exclaimed.

"I'll always miss Gil," Samuel began, then he paused. When he resumed there was a smile in his eyes. "When I first met the man, no one could have convinced me I'd ever feel a fondness for him. I will greatly miss him, and yet I cannot begrudge him the happiest moment in his life since he lost his family—a moment that seemed destined to come to him only in death."

"Do you think a man like that could ever, you know, be with God?"

"Do you think he could *not* be, Margaret?"

"I know he died saving Eleanor, and he shall always hold a high place in my heart for that. But isn't there more to it? Going to heaven, I mean."

"Yes, there is," Samuel replied. "And I believe that somewhere in those last moments, Gil Stoddard made his peace with God."

"Someone could go along his whole life scorning God," Maggie mused, "and in the end come over to His side."

"Have you not heard of the eleventh hour?"

"I suppose so—like the thief on the cross who repented?"

"Exactly! But how much better to turn to Him sooner if we have the chance. For as happy as I am for Gil, he missed so much that he could have had here on earth—if only he could have opened himself to let God cleanse him. Then he would have been able to forgive himself for his past."

"It always seems to come back to that, doesn't it?" stated Maggie. "Forgiveness."

"That's often what stands in our way before God," said Samuel. "Either not being able to forgive ourselves, or another. And sometimes not being able to forgive God. Yes, the approach to intimacy with God often does hinge on being able to forgive."

"But what if we're unable to?"

"Maybe I should have said being *willing* to. For like faith, forgiveness begins with the desire to make things right."

Maggie did not reply. The words hit too close to him.

She did desire faith. She knew that now. God had spared her life; to Maggie that was a sign He was with her and loved her. Since then she had tried more diligently to exercise the limited faith in Him she possessed. She had tried to accept His love and to pray and ask Him what He would have her do. But so many of the spiritual things Samuel spoke of remained a mystery to her.

Am I holding something back?

Yet even as she asked herself the question with Samuel's words still ringing in her ears, she recalled vividly the day she had shouted out—about one who was thousands of miles away but whose image could still bring a trembling to her lip—that she would *never* forgive.

With the memory rose an inner emotional wall to shield her from its pain. If approach to intimacy with God, as Samuel had said, did indeed hinge on being willing to forgive, then perhaps she would just have to settle for a faith smaller and shallower than his. For that was a step she simply was not yet able to take.

Whether she wanted to take it was a question Maggie was unprepared to consider.

Soon September came, heralding autumn and the distant whisperings of winter. And as if the change of season contained deeper significance, the peaceful respite of those days at the garrison also drew to a close and the impending wave of trouble was at last released. But it seemed to fall more gently on the two who had been greatly strengthened and refreshed by the weeks of God-given peace.

36
The Winds of Change

A S THE COLD autumn rains descended upon the high country around the Platte, the Indians began to take more seriously the Governor's call to them earlier in the summer. In gradually increasing numbers they made their way to the three forts deemed as *safe*. Many on their way to Fort Laramie, mostly women and children and old men, traveled past the garrison on the Platte. The soldiers stood watchful and not a little nervous on the rickety ramparts, guns poised. But there was no trouble. Some who were sick would stop, and there they found a compassionate physician in Samuel Carpenter. But most chose to ignore the outpost of the "long knives," perhaps praying to their Great Spirit that they might also be somehow spared the indignity of facing the white man further on at Fort Laramie. But the rains were heavy and the snows would be deep this winter, and the white man had medicine for the terrible diseases that had come to the Sioux these past five years.

On many days Maggie watched the sad migration, often wondering if one of the brown Indian babies could possibly be the one she had cared for early in the summer. Occasionally she would assist Samuel in his work among them and she always found special joy in this—both from being needed and finding a great satisfaction in ministering, and simply from being with Samuel, who was such a source of peace to her. Throughout the weeks their friendship had grown and deepened. They had come to share things with each other that neither had ever expected to share with another human being again. In the end a mere word or nod or sigh was enough to communicate what the other was thinking.

One afternoon Maggie sat at the secretary in the room which had all but become her own since their arrival. She was reflecting on a conversation she had had that morning with Samuel. For one of the first times he had asked about Scotland, and for the first time in many months she had found herself speaking of her home. Samuel had known about James and Ian and their terrible conflicts. But somehow it had been more difficult to talk about the land itself. That morning, however, through tears of bitter joy and loss, at last she did. And now, alone again, she could not erase from her mind the visions of the heather hills and the craggy bluffs overlooking the sea.

Suddenly Maggie rose to her feet and found the carpetbag where she had shoved it underneath the bed upon their arrival. How vividly she remembered the day so long ago when she had packed it! She had wept, thinking she would never see her homeland again. And how much worse might it have been had she known those fears were to be true? Carefully she pulled out the stitchery she had sewn as a child.

"Oh, Mother . . ." she murmured, trying to visualize the grand tapestry she had tried so hard to copy. It was still so clear in her mind hanging regally above the little canopied bed in the nursery.

"But we moved it, didn't we . . . ?" she thought absently.

With deepening nostalgia sweeping over her, Maggie reached in and removed the brown envelope her mother had been so careful to give her the day she left Stonewycke. She had not yet opened it. But now, a year later, the time all at once seemed right. Out of respect for her mother and the heritage of Stonewycke in which her memory was steeped, rather than from sheer curiosity, Maggie carefully opened the envelope and pulled out the contents. Inside were two papers, both apparently very old, yellowed with age, and written in ancient script and archaic language. One was clearly a description of the Stonewycke properties and estate, for Maggie recognized names of many familiar places in the description of borders, boundaries, and distance. The other was . . .

She could hardly believe her eyes.

It was the deed to Stonewycke!

She had never even known such a thing as a written deed existed. Why had her mother taken such pains to give it to her? Obviously this explained her cryptic words before their departure—that Stonewycke was *hers*. Was this Atlanta's way to insure her daughter's return?"

But, Mother, I cannot return! she thought, tears rising in her eyes. *There is nothing there for me now . . . without Ian. Even you . . . and the land . . . without Ian they—nothing left—Oh, Mother! . . . there would be no meaning to life for me there now . . .*

Maggie dropped onto the bed and wept.

At length, after her grief had subsided for the moment, Maggie sat up, wiped her eyes, returned the papers to the envelope and returned it to the carpetbag. Her hand struck another object. She wrapped a trembling hand around it and pulled it into the light.

"The music box!" she cried softly.

Slowly she opened the lid and turned the key, and instantly the delicate Brahms lullaby floated out as clearly as it had the first time she had played it as a child. Before the tune had played itself out Maggie had once again crumpled onto the bed in a rush of tears.

She was only vaguely aware of the soft knocking at her door; at length Eleanor, stirring from her nap with growing cries of hunger, awoke Maggie from the sleep of her sorrow.

"Margaret . . . Margaret . . . are you all right?" a voice was calling.

Maggie opened her eyes and gazed around, bewildered for a moment at her strange surroundings; then, coming to herself, she rose, picked up the crying baby, and went to the door.

"I'm sorry, Samuel," she said. "I was asleep. I had just . . . been . . ." But the tears had not finished their work with her yet and began to flow again in earnest.

"Margaret," said Samuel, taking Eleanor in his arms and placing a tender hand on Maggie's shoulder, "is there anything I can do?"

Maggie shook her head, then caught up the music box from the bed where she had dropped it. She handed it to Samuel.

"Something from home?" he asked.

"My father . . . on my fifth birthday . . . he gave it to me. It came from London," she managed to say. "Oh, Samuel," she cried in an anguish of fresh weeping, "I wanted to adore him and for him to be my papa . . . that's all I ever wanted from him!"

"And you want it still, don't you, dear?"

"Yes!" said Maggie as she broke down into an agony of convulsive sobs.

Managing Eleanor as best he could, Samuel put his arm around Maggie's shoulders. She laid her head on his chest and continued to weep. Neither spoke for several long minutes.

At length Maggie came to herself and said, "Is there ever anything else that a daughter wants from her father?"

"Probably not," Samuel replied softly.

"Is it so wrong to want a father's love?"

"No," he said. "A father's love is at the center of everything. It's just that our earthly fathers don't always reflect the love of their heavenly Father as God intended they should."

"But it will never be, not with my father," said Maggie. "I'm afraid after what he did, the hate has gone too deep. Even if he were here I doubt I could love him again. I wish it weren't that way. But I know it is."

"Forgiveness can begin to cleanse away the hate."

Maggie was silent a long while. She knew Samuel's words were the key to the closer life with God and the growth of her faith which she desired. But the struggle in her heart could not let go of the past. Finally she did speak.

"What good would it do now, anyway?" she asked softly. "I'll never see him again."

"The healing of forgiveness begins in your own heart," replied Samuel tenderly. "Your father will have to answer to God for himself. And you are responsible for the attitude in *your* heart. To draw close to Him, your heart must be clean. He alone can cleanse it, and the process begins with forgiveness."

"Oh, I can't," wailed Maggie. "I'm afraid . . . the pain is too deep!"

"My dear, dear girl," said Samuel, holding her close to him. "Don't you know," he continued in a barely audible voice, "that God requires only what we are ready to give? You need only take a small step, as long as it is in the right direction. And He requires nothing of us that isn't for our best, because He loves us so dearly. It is for your sake, and for the sake of the love He would shower upon you that He requires such a difficult thing from you."

He pulled his handkerchief from his pocket and dabbed Maggie's wet eyes. She looked up, smiled, and whispered a soft, "Thank you."

"I'll help in any way I can," he encouraged.

"I must write . . . somehow. I don't know what I would say, but the beginning must be a letter home," said Maggie.

For the first time since they had begun, Maggie seemed to notice her daughter. "Oh, Eleanor!" she cried, taking her from Samuel's arm.

"She must have known her mother needed more care right now than she did," remarked Samuel. "She stopped crying the moment I picked her up."

Maggie laughed and dried her eyes further. "Thank you, Samuel," she said warmly. "You are so good for me. I don't know how I could have made it through all this without you."

Before he could reply a knock came to the door. It was Captain Hodges.

"I'm sorry to intrude," he stated. "But I thought you'd like to know. A rider has just arrived from California. He's carrying mail east, and if you have anything, this will likely be the last opportunity before winter sets in. He'll be leaving in the morning. And he also has news from the West, if you'd like to come over to the mess hall and hear his report."

About thirty minutes later Samuel and Maggie entered the room with the captain. Clustered about one of the long, rough-hewn tables were eight or ten soldiers. At the center of the group was a dusty civilian dressed in well-worn buckskin with a battered hat still on his head, despite the fact that he was about to dig into a steaming bowl of stew.

"Hello, Jack," the captain called. "Getting enough to eat?"

"Sure am, Capt'n," the rider answered. "Best grub I've had in months!"

"Folks," he went on to his companions, "this here's Jack O'Reilly. He's been a sort of unofficial Army scout for years—best in the business, too. Jack, these are a couple of our other guests, Dr. Carpenter and Mrs. Duncan. They got separated from their wagon train a while back and we've been putting them up until they are strong enough to move on and have decided what they want to do."

"Pleased to make your acquaintance," returned the scout, rising partially from his chair and touching the rim of his hat toward Maggie. "What train was you with? If it wasn't too long ago, I might of run into 'em."

"Oh, if you could tell us anything about them!" Maggie exclaimed.

"We started out as Gil Stoddard's train, but he was . . . he was killed—" Samuel began, but O'Reilly cut in with a whistle.

"Stoddard, you say? I didn't think he was in the business anymore. Killed, was he?"

"An Indian attack," said the doctor.

"He was one of the best. That is until he lost that train out on the Humboldt . . . but anyway, you was sayin'?"

"Pete Kramer would probably have been in charge of the train," Samuel replied.

"Kramer . . ." O'Reilly rubbed his chin, trying to recall.

"Perhaps it might have been Drew Mackinaw," put in Maggie impatiently.

Gradually O'Reilly's face darkened and he dropped his fork onto the tin plate with a clank. "Them's your friends?"

"Yes . . . yes!" cried Maggie.

"Then I'm sorry I got to be the one to bring you the news," stated Jack with a somber face.

Maggie held Eleanor tighter and clutched at Samuel's arm.

"What news?" asked Samuel in what was barely more than a hoarse whisper.

"I'm surprised a small train like that made it as far as it did. It don't make no sense. They got clean through the Sioux territory without a scratch, but Bannock country's even worse these days. There ain't been many to make it through without at least a skirmish or two. But your friends' train . . . well, bad timin' is all you can chalk it up to. And too few of 'em to hold off the savages. Only six survivors in the whole train."

"Dear Lord, no!" Samuel breathed. The look of shock on Maggie's face was her only response. There could be no words.

"I talked to 'em myself," Jack went on. "They wanted me to get word back to some of the relatives."

"Who . . . who were they?" Samuel asked. "Whom did you talk with?"

"Mackinaw and his wife, though Mackinaw was wounded pretty bad in the shoulder. Then there was a fellow named Williams, a woman by the name of Wooton, and a couple of young'uns."

"What children?" Maggie asked urgently, finding her voice at last.

"I don't know. We just passed on the trail. They was pretty friendly with them Mackinaws though. Seems as though I remember a little girl called him Pa. What I can't figure is how the man and his wife, and their wagon, and their young'uns—if they was theirs—all came out of the scrape when most everyone else was wiped out."

As he spoke Maggie recalled, with tears in her eyes, how many times since their separation she had prayed for the Mackinaw family and their safety. God *had* heard her!

"But the other children . . . the Wootons' sons," said Maggie, her voice pale with shock, ". . . I just can't believe it."

"I'm sorry, ma'am. But I helped the survivors hook up with another train. Least they're all safe in California by now."

"You mean they went on?"

"No choice, ma'am. Out there you either go on or turn back. It happened in the Bear River Valley. When you get that far, already across the Divide, there's no way you can turn back then. Even if you have the supplies, you can't risk traveling alone."

O'Reilly pushed his chair back from the table and stood. "Well, I'm going to get me another bowl of that stew and then turn in. I'll be leavin' before most of you are even thinkin' of wakin' in the morning. So if you have anything for me, I'll leave a sack right here and get it before I leave."

Later that same night, Maggie left the room and walked briskly across the compound. The night air was chilly and she had left Eleanor alone on the bed. There were a few soldiers about and they tipped their hats to her as she passed on her way to the mess hall. She opened the door and spotted O'Reilly's waiting pouch in the candlelight. She walked across the floor, opened it, dropped her letter inside, then turned and left.

As she walked slowly outside and looked up at the rising moon over the distant Rockies, all she could think of was the heather moor from which Drew Mackinaw had come. The news of that day, as well as her talk with Samuel, had prompted the letter she knew she must write. She hoped Atlanta would write back, although how the letter would reach her she couldn't think. But she missed her mother at moments like these, though she doubted she would ever see her again.

Braenock Ridge was so far away now. Drew would certainly never go back. And probably old Hector, if he still lived, and little Stevie would go to their graves never knowing what had become of their eldest son and brother.

Land of opportunity, they called it. She and Ian had thought it would be the place of new beginnings. But it was a hard land and it took its toll. For Drew and Ellie, though the price had been high, they had made it west, their bridges forever burned behind them. *And for me,* Maggie wondered, *what does the future hold?*

Even as she framed the question, she knew her bridges were burned behind her as well.

There would be—there could be no turning back. She had come too far. She had crossed the Great Divide of her soul. Scotland was another lifetime ago.

37

The Laird and the Marchioness

GRAY CLOUDS, HEAVY with impending rain, massed around Stonewycke's even grayer stone towers. But rain and the approach of winter were far from James Duncan's mind that dreary morning. He lay between silken bedclothes and could only reflect despondently that he felt weaker by the day. He cursed aloud, though there was no one in the room to hear him. He swore at the chill emanating from the very walls themselves and cursed the fact that he could not even rise to toss another log on the fire. He cursed the sluggard of a servant who was supposed to be watching out for the state of the fire. And finally, he cursed that "devil of a horse" that had landed him here in the first place.

"That animal's had a spell on her since the day I first laid eyes on her!" he said, as he had many times before.

But all James's cursing only masked what he really felt like doing—cursing himself for such a foolhardy stunt. A broken leg had, miraculously, been his only injury. But it refused to heal, and inflammation had set in. Several doctors were called in, whom he had thrown out with their dour prophecies of gloom. Although when he tried to walk the pain was frightful, on numerous occasions he had disobeyed orders to remain in bed, thus thoroughly impeding any potential progress. And there was also his cough. It had grown worse since the fall, and now came from the deepest parts of his chest.

It had never been James's character to accept illness. And it was even more impossible for him to think of death. He would hang onto life with a desperate grip, for it was all he had. There was no hope of afterlife, and James had not even the small hope of immortality in being remembered fondly by loved ones. He was a practical man. He knew no one loved him. He had never sought love and he did not care that it would be missing at the end of his life.

Or so he told himself.

But lying in bed as the days dragged wearily on, robbed of everything which had once made him feel important, reminded every day of the swelling in his leg, and having to face the raw realities of his own impotence and mortality—his circumstance was beginning to work in an imperceptibly positive way upon James. He was just as liable to shout all manner of fierce imprecations to any soul who ventured near. But, simply, James Duncan was gradually beginning to believe less and less in himself.

This particular morning found him more surly than usual. His weakness was so acute that he either had to admit his failing condition or gloss over it with a harsh attitude toward everything in sight. He chose the latter and tugged angrily at the covers, finding a new victim upon which to vent his anger.

"Rotten bed!" he muttered. "It never stays in one piece! I say, where's that maid? If she—"

A knock at the door arrested his attention, and though he answered it gruffly he was in fact glad for the diversion. Part of him even hoped it might be the old fool of a groom. Digory had come to visit the laird every day since the accident. James would never admit that he was fond of the old fellow or that he ever listened to his religious babble. Instead, he tried to convince himself that the old lout was good for a laugh or two, which, in his condition, he needed from time to time.

The visitor this morning was not Digory, but the butler instead.

"Well, what do you want?" James barked.

"This came to the house a few moments ago, sir," the butler replied, holding out a dull white envelope. "The Lady Atlanta was in the kitchen with the maid and didn't see it, sir. I thought you'd be wanting it . . ."

"And what else do you think I've been paying you so handsomely for?" James snarled. Indeed, the man had been receiving generous gratuities from James to insure that any correspondence coming to Stonewycke arrived in James's hands first. For even in his weakened state the laird still kept up the precarious game of duplicity with Atlanta, a tug-of-war which had characterized the whole of their marriage, and even to the present day he fully believed he was maintaining the upper hand despite the serious handicap of his leg.

"Well, give it to me!" James snapped.

The butler stepped forward and placed the envelope in his hand.

Instantly the scant remaining color drained from his master's face.

"Are you feeling well, sir?" asked the concerned butler.

"Get me a brandy!" was James's only reply.

"But the physician said—"

"Do you think I give a bloody farthing what that rascal of an absurd doctor thinks? Get me a brandy, you swine, and be quick about it!"

The butler retreated from the room, knowing full well the futility of trying to argue with the laird.

The moment he was gone James looked again at the letter.

It couldn't be! Yet the fine hand and the return address—the absurd name, *Platte Bridge Garrison*—left no doubt.

Margaret . . . in America . . . writing to *both* him and Atlanta! What could it mean? What scheme was the little devil concocting now? No doubt something Atlanta had contrived. Was she now planning to return to stake her claim?

A cold sweat broke out on his forehead. His heart began pounding in his throat. Why else would she now break her long silence? *She will ruin everything!* he thought. He could never stand against Maggie and Atlanta if they joined forces against him.

"You'll not take it from me now!" His voice trembled.

More than anything he feared what would be exposed if his daughter returned. To be publicly disgraced would be worse than death; no one must ever discover the terrible lie he had perpetrated against the so-called husband of his daughter. He could not even imagine what retributions Atlanta would levy against him were she to find out. He had only just begun to be able to manipulate her. The return of their daughter would only strengthen the terrible resolves of the mother once again.

It must not happen!

He flung the bedcovers from him. With all the effort he could muster he edged his infirm body from the bed, groaning as he swung his injured leg over the edge and wincing in pain as he lurched to his feet. Bracing himself beside the bed, he staggered toward the table, then holding onto the back of a chair he made his way to the hearth.

Standing in front of the crackling logs, he hesitated with the unopened letter poised in his hands. The part of him that might once have been called a conscience—the part of him which subconsciously longed for love—that part of the father wanted to read the letter from his little girl. For the briefest of moments, as he had first glanced at the familiar handwriting, something had leapt inside him, touched by the fact that she had addressed the letter equally to him.

But fear overpowered the longing in his heart. He understood greed and ambition and deceit, but love was an unknown and fearful entity. To open the letter might somehow force him to look at things differently. James Duncan was not ready for that yet.

He pitched the envelope into the flames.

"I do not hate you, Margaret . . ." he murmured. "But I have gone too far to change now."

The creaking of the door behind him startled James. Nearly losing his precarious balance, he reached out for the chair behind him. Atlanta quickly rushed to his side and caught his arm.

He stared at her for a long moment, more stunned at the proximity of her body than at her sudden arrival. *When was the last time she touched me,* he wondered?

"It is just like . . ." he began, then paused, unable to find the proper words within him.

"You shouldn't be up," said Atlanta like a stern parent, but with a measure of concern in her voice.

"What do you care?" asked James, more sadness than bitterness registering in his tone.

"I am concerned for your health," she replied.

"Concerned?"

"What do you expect me to say, James, that I feel affection for you?"

"Have you ever had affection for me?" James asked distantly. "And whatever the past, isn't pity what you feel now? But I suppose all of that matters little now, even if it is contempt you feel."

"I have never felt contempt for you, James," Atlanta replied, almost forgetting in that moment all the bitter emotions of the past.

"It's odd," James remarked. "But despite what we have said and been to one another through the years, neither have I felt contempt for you—"

He stopped short, seized with a fit of uncontrollable coughing.

"Come back to your bed," Atlanta entreated.

Leaning heavily on his wife, James hobbled painfully back to the bedside.

"I, too, have maintained a respect for you, Atlanta," he said, settling himself between the silken covers.

"And yet ours has been the mutual respect of adversaries," she said, almost regretfully.

"Do you think it could have been different between us?"

"I don't know, James," she replied. "But such speculation is useless now," she added, with more finality than she had perhaps intended, for the same fears which had assailed her husband a moment ago were at that instant surging through Atlanta.

"So much for sentimentality . . ." sighed James as he laid his head back heavily on his pillow. "Where's that butler with my brandy?"

38

Unraveling the Mystery

DERMOTT HAD NOT expected it to be so long until he returned to Port Strathy. He had left the little village several months ago, feeling as disheartened as he had ever been. He had made the trip with such high hopes, yet the only success he could point to was the finding of two worthy allies in the innkeeper Queenie and the lad Stevie Mackinaw. But all three together had not been able to penetrate the mystery surrounding the night of young Falkirk's death.

There was only a handful of persons who knew anything about that night. Of these, one was dead, one was lost in America, one would sooner die than aid the hapless youth in prison. Dermott had managed to see Lord and Lady Falkirk. But Lord Falkirk had degenerated into a senile old man whose only lucid moments came when his eyes glowed with the memory of his youth in the faraway world of India. And when he had temporarily wrested Lady Falkirk away from her bitter denunciations of the Duncans, it was clear that she knew nothing which could possibly be of help to her son's accused murderer. And even if she had, Dermott doubted that she would have revealed it anyway.

Dermott had counted heavily on the possible support of Lady Duncan, but she had been away during his visit—in Aberdeen on one of her extremely rare absences from Stonewycke. But though Atlanta Duncan may have been able to lend moral support to Ian's cause, Dermott doubted she could offer any concrete evidence. Had she known any pertinent facts, she would have brought them to Ian's defense long ago.

Now more months had passed. Several other cases had demanded Dermott's attention. He continued his visits to Ian, but it was clear the lawyer's unsuccessful excursion to Port Strathy had been hard on the lad. He, too, had counted greatly on Dermott's success. Many a dismal day had he occupied with daydreaming of the moment of his release—the moment when he would begin his own search for his love. He would book the first ship to New York and within two months she would be in his arms! He knew he would find Maggie, and he would never rest until he did! The brilliance of the dream kept him alive.

But every day since Dermott's return, the lawyer had seen him grow more and more detached. Not only from his friend, but from reality itself.

At last, however, there was a break.

Working late in his office one evening, a stranger came to Dermott's door. The man was coarsely dressed, a sailor—not an uncommon sight in Glasgow. But this seaman had just arrived in town, he said, by way of Aberdeen. He bore a message which had been more than a month in route, first upon the schooner running between Banff and Aberdeen, where it came into his hands. He was on his way to a new job at the Broomielaw, the great quay upon the Clyde, and had brought it the rest of the way himself. The faithful messenger handed the note—for indeed it was little more than that, now crumpled and soiled—to Dermott, who amply rewarded his great efforts.

Dermott opened the single sheet of thin yellow paper, held it up to the candle, and looked on the printing, which was as coarse as its bearer. *You are wanted*, it said, *urgently . . . in Port Strathy. Something important has turned up. Should say nothing more until your arrival.*

It was signed, *Queenie.*

Saying nothing to Ian, Dermott was en route north again the following morning. Within a week he was standing on the deck of the Aberdeen schooner watching the small harbor of Port Strathy draw near.

He walked immediately to the Bluster 'N Blow, and Queenie greeted him as an old friend. Looking around he was both surprised and delighted to see Stevie Mackinaw standing near the kitchen holding a broom.

"She has you working for her, eh, Stevie?" he said with a laugh.

"Mistress Rankin's been very kind t' me," he replied.

"Just some small-time employment," said Queenie. "I needed some help, an' the lad's a hard worker. But, Mr. Connell, I thought ye'd never get here!"

"I received your message less than a week ago," Dermott replied. "But I'm afraid its route from you to me was rather circuitous."

"I was afraid o' that. I knew I should o' delivered the note mysel', but I thought my goin' t' Glasgow might o' caused undue suspicion."

"Well, I'm here now, in any case," Dermott said. "What is your news?"

Queenie cast a look around the inn to assure herself they were alone. "'Tis Stevie here," she said, "who should tell you, for it was his own discovery."

"Come then, lad, and tell me about it, for I have been waiting a week."

Stevie stepped forward and, clasping his hands behind his back as if about to recite his lessons, began. "Weel, Mr. Connell, 'tis a simple enough bit o' news. But when I made mention o' it t' Queenie here, she nearly flew through the roof. If ye remember when we talked oot on the moor, I made mention o' seein' Master Falkirk ridin' upon the ridge on his bonnie golden stallion. It all came back t' me sometime later when I was here in the inn and I seen auld Martin Forbes takin' his ale as he does some too much, if the truth be known. For I recalled that twice I had seen old Forbes himself ridin' on the ridge wi' Master Falkirk. And when I seen them I said t' mysel', 'What would a blighter like Forbes be doin' ridin' wi' the likes o' a laird?'

"Weel, it all came back t' me an' I made mention o' it t' Mistress Rankin. An' didna she go an' ask the very same question I had asked up there on the moor! *What would the two o' them be doin' t'gether?*"

"I did," Queenie put in. "I asked that very question. Sorry, lad. Go on wi' yer story."

"Weel, ye ken yersel', Mistress Rankin, that's aboot the end o' it. Except that mysel' an' ye, we been keepin' a hawk's eye on Martin Forbes."

"Have you approached this Forbes?" Dermott asked.

"Oh, no! I didna want t' risk him flyin' before we knew what ye would make o' this information."

"Is it so out of the ordinary for these two to be seen together?" Dermott asked. "Perhaps this Forbes was in the employ of Lord Falkirk. Or perhaps they met by chance on the moor and were simply riding together."

"I don't like the looks o' it, whether ye can use it or not," said Queenie a little stubbornly.

"I'm simply trying to look at it from a legal standpoint," said Dermott. "Two men riding together is not enough upon which to base an accusation. And it offers far less evidence than, say, one man's verbal threats upon another's life in front of witnesses—which is the predicament Ian is in."

"'Tis lookin' like we made a mistake callin' ye all the way from Glasgow," said Queenie.

"Forgive me, Queenie," said Dermott. "And you also, Stevie. I know you meant well. And it may turn out significant in the end. But what you have discovered is purely—in legal terminology—circumstantial. Before we can level any accusations against anyone, we must examine this from every angle. At this point the only one with a motive for killing George Falkirk is Ian. If only we could establish a motive for someone else! But I'm afraid riding together on a lonely moor is *not* a motive."

"Then we still have nothing," sighed Queenie.

"We may have more than we did a week ago, thanks to you and Stevie," said Dermott with an encouraging smile. "We will just have to see where this leads us. If Falkirk's body had been found upon the moor, we would certainly have opportunity, if not motive. But instead, it was found in the stables at Kairn."

"Forbes could o' been there as easily as Master Ian," Queenie said. "And," she went on, her face brightening as if suddenly remembering something else, "it strikes me as odd that Martin Forbes all at once turned up missin' less'n a week after the killin'."

"Now that *is* interesting!" Dermott mused. "And who would have thought anything of it since no public connection had ever been made between the two? You say whenever they met in the inn they acknowledged no acquaintance?"

"Like perfect strangers, they was."

"Curious. I wonder why they were so careful to conceal their relationship?"

"I'll warrant they was up to no good," said Queenie with a disgusted snort. "That Martin Forbes never did an honest day's work in his life. An' Falkirk—weel, I seen but little o' him. But what I did see, I didna like."

A short silence followed.

"I think I'll ride out to Kairn," he said at length. "Perhaps someone there might have seen something. The last time I only spoke with Falkirk's parents. And I must try to locate that man Duff, the former constable. Where did you say he was from?"

"Culden. But I haven't heard aboot him in a year."

"I must try, though. There may be a reason for his disappearance as well."

Queenie's old gelding plodded determinedly along the tree-lined road leading to the stately manor of Kairn. Dermott was making this trip uncertain how to proceed, for his parting with Lady Falkirk upon his last visit had been none too cordial. But if there was anything to uncover here he must not miss it.

Soon the manor sprawled before him. Unlike the austere Stonewycke castle, Kairn looked the part of the country estate it was. Never had an army been mustered here nor a battle fought on these grounds. Nestled among its oaks and surrounded by its expansive green lawns, it offered the picture of peace and solitude, certainly no visible setting for a terrible murder.

Veering away from the front courtyard, Dermott steered his way toward the stables, where the young lord's body had been found. A year had passed, so clearly no clues were still to be found, but it was a place to begin at least. He dismounted and slowly walked inside the stone structure, where the dull winter's midday sky emitted a few streams of light through high narrow windows. The lazy snorts of horses mingled in a pleasant way with the drone of flies. A lad of perhaps thirteen or fifteen was busy currying the gray coat of a fine mare.

"Mornin' t' ye, sir," said the boy.

"Good morning," Dermott replied. "Do you mind if I have a look at the stock?"

"I'm seein' no harm in that," the lad answered, then returned, unconcerned, to his task.

Dermott ambled down the aisles between the stalls. Probably eight or ten animals were housed here, not as many as the stables of the larger estate of Stonewycke could boast, but each was a thoroughbred.

Then Dermott was struck with a thought.

"Lad," he called, "where is the fine golden stallion that used to be housed here?"

"Oh, him," the boy answered. "The laird had him put away right after the young master were killed."

"Dear Lord," Dermott breathed. *How much more anguish must there be?* he thought. *It has to stop. I must get to the bottom of this and end the heartbreak! Dear God, guide my steps through this maze.*

"Lad, how long have you worked here in Kairn's stables?" Dermott asked.

"Two . . . three years, sir."

"Then you were here when the young master Falkirk was killed?"

"Aye, sir," replied the boy, squirming perceptibly before this powerful stranger. "But I didna see nothin'," he went on—too quickly, Dermott thought. "Honest! Ye must believe me. I didna!" His voice had risen dramatically as he spoke.

"I always believe the truth," said Dermott slowly, fixing his eyes with all their intensity on the boy.

"Oh, God!" the boy wailed.

"What is it, son?" asked Dermott, fully intrigued. His bearing revealed more fear than could be accounted for even by the lawyer's steady gaze.

"He sent you, I knew it!"

"No one sent me, boy."

"Please don't hurt me, sir!"

"What are you talking about?"

"Ye can trust me. I won't say a word," the lad went on in the same high-pitched voice, ignoring Dermott's question. "Tell him I ne'er said a word t' nobody."

"I won't hurt you." Dermott's voice softened as he perceived the terror in the _ boy's appeal. "I don't know who you are talking about. Who is it that wants to hurt you?"

"He said he'd kill me if I told."

"But another may die if you do not," said Dermott. "If you are shielding a criminal, it will be God to whom you will have to answer."

"Oh!" the boy wailed mournfully. "I should o' told the other man an' then I wouldna had t' live wi' it all this long year!"

"What other man?"

"The constable what came aroun' right after, ye know, talkin' t' all the servants an' me an' the master an' lady."

"And you told him nothing?"

"I couldna, mister . . . I *couldna*! Oh, god!" the boy cried, "I was scared! He said he'd kill me!"

"So the constable left without any idea of the truth?" asked Dermott.

"He left, but I think he suspected me o' lyin'. I could tell from his questions that he guessed it all. But he said he had t' hae proof an'. . . Oh, God! I just couldna tell him! I was so scared!"

"And has this other man been around threatening you recently?"

"Na. I hanna seen him in a year."

"Well, the time may have come, boy, for you to tell what you know. Others are suffering because of your silence. Do you understand me?"

The lad stared blankly at Dermott, trembling. Then he slowly nodded.

"I am a lawyer," said Dermott. "I think I can protect you."

"But what'll I do if he finds oot an' comes after me?" wailed the boy.

"God will also be your protector. He always honors the speaking of truth."

A long silence followed. At length the boy slowly began to speak.

"I canna name the man," he said, his voice steadying. "He came here once before . . . before that night. He left a note fer Master Falkirk an' told me t' give it t' him. Then another night—it was real late. I was asleep in Donnie's stall—he's one o' my favorites an' was a bit collicky that night. The voices woke me—they was talkin' awful aboot each other, aboot deceivin' an' lyin'. Master Falkirk spit in the other fellow's face an' told him t' git oot an' t' ne'er come back an' that he'd git nothin'. The other fellow flew off in a murderous rage. Then I heard a struggle an' a groan an' then all got deathly quiet. I'd been listenin' so intently that I was payin' no attention t' Donnie, who was restless and kind o' movin' aboot. All at once she stepped on my foot an' I couldna help lettin' oot a yell, as much as I tried t' hide it. That was when he found me. He came int' the stall an' held a knife t' my throat—still red wi' blood it was—an' I knew he was goin' t' kill me right then. But he jist threatened me an' said if I didna keep my mouth shut, he'd come back an' find me an' run me through wi' the knife right through my heart. An' I was so scared I couldna hardly sleep for a week." He stopped, tears streaming down his cheeks.

Dermott placed his large hand on the boy's shoulder.

"I ne'er meant fer anyone else t' be hurt," said the boy, breaking into a fit of sobbing.

"I believe you, lad. And did the man ever bother you again?"

"No, I never seen him again."

"Only the constable?"

"He was here the very next day. But I was so scared, I couldna tell him. Then when the new constable came aroun', that was some while later, he didn't much seem t' care aboot talkin' t' any o' us."

"And you never saw Constable Duff again?"

The boy shook his head.

Dermott thought a few moments.

"What is your name, lad?"

"Neil, sir."

"Well, Neil, would you help me find this man and bring him to justice?"

Neil shrank back a step. He looked at Dermott a long moment, then sighed deeply. "I'm thinkin', sir," he finally said, "that I best help ye noo, so he won't come back an' kill me"

"That's fine, Neil," said Dermott. "You'll be safe. I just need you to identify the man with the knife. You're the only one who can."

By the following day, as he returned along the solitary country road from the inland village of Culden, a plan was forming in the keen lawyer's mind of Dermott Connell. After much searching and many questions, he had succeeded in locating former constable Angus Duff, exiled to what Duff had termed an "enforced retirement from public service." Dermott's suspicions were confirmed; he had gained Duff's first-hand account of how things stood the day after the murder—including Duff's own inclinations. Now Dermott returned to Port Strathy armed not only with what he hoped would be enough to free his client but with information sufficient to extract concessions, if not admissions, from James Duncan himself.

39

The Beginning of Justice

❖

DERMOTT'S PLAN WAS to commence at sunset two days later. When all the necessary arrangements had been made, he sent a message to Martin Forbes. He had to meet him, it said. Forbes could choose the place.

Forbes was initially suspicious. Then it crossed his mind that perhaps his fortunes had changed and that the appearance of this impressive gentleman from the south boded well for him. It was, therefore, with mixed and not altogether pure motives that he chose as their meeting place his favorite haunt at Ramsey Head. Many was the time he had retreated here with his jug of ale, and after the discovery of Falkirk's body he had hidden out in the cave for several days. If for any reason events should turn against him, he could easily elude the gentleman, who would be unfamiliar with the craggy caves and cliffs on the Head. Besides, if all else failed, he had his dinghy tied up on the rocks below. He didn't trust any man in gentle garb, but he was willing to take a chance if it might—for reasons unknown to him in advance—mean a few extra shillings in his pocket.

Dermott was unfamiliar with the place, it is true. But as soon as he had received Forbes's message, he had sent Stevie and Neil to reconnoiter the place and report back to him. He arrived, with Angus Duff and the two lads, an hour before sunset and easily found the mouth of the large cave—more a tunnel through the rocks, as daylight could be seen through from the other end—which Forbes had specified.

Nestled in one of the dark crevices midway through the tunnel, Neil trembled with fear.

At length he heard the scraping of heavy boots.

"Hey you . . . Connell!" Forbes shouted from just outside the cave's opening.

"I'm in here, Mr. Forbes," Dermott answered. "Come closer. I must talk with you."

He heard the approach of Forbes's unsteady footfall, and even before he could see his silhouette in the dim, fading light, the stale smell of Queenie's ale assailed him.

"Where are ye? I can't see ye in the dark. Come oot where I can see ye!"

"No, Mr. Forbes. It is I who want to see you. Come in still farther."

"What're ye talkin' aboot?" said Forbes, his confused and muddled brain growing wary of the commanding voice in the darkness. "Hey . . . what is this? Connell, ye blighter, let me see yer face!"

"All in due time, Mr. Forbes."

"Where are ye, Connell? . . . Why ye jist let me git my hands on ye—"

Forbes's words were cut short as suddenly a brilliant orange shaft of light shot through from the opposite end of the tunnel. Momentarily stunned, Forbes stood stock still, but the light of the setting sun which had receded to a point exactly on a line with the other end of the tunnel fully illuminated his face.

"It's him!" cried Neil. "It's him that killed my master!"

"Why you lyin', double-crossin'—" Forbes began. But he took no time to finish. He spun around to make a retreat, but Dermott stepped quickly forward and loomed in his path. Rage and the growing effects of the alcohol in his body combined to produce terror. Crying out at the sudden sight of what must be a giant in front of him, Forbes turned again and ran toward the western exit where the shaft of light was already fading. But Angus Duff and Stevie Mackinaw blocked his way.

Forbes stood momentarily at bay, his hand seeking the crude dirk at his side.

"Why did you do it, Forbes?" called out Dermott's voice behind him.

"He's a dirty liar!" Forbes snarled. "I didn't kill no one!"

"The lad will swear it was you."

"He didna see nothin'. He was asleep in a stall—" Hardly realizing his blunder, Forbes stopped.

"Perhaps you had your reasons," Dermott said. "George Falkirk was a hard man."

"A dirty, cheatin' rotter—but I'll git what's comin' t' me yet!"

"What did he do to you, Forbes?" Dermott asked, determined to get as much of the story as possible, his voice still calm, though his heart was pounding.

"What'd the likes o' ye care? Ye can't trap me. I know ye can't prove a thing!"

"You've already trapped yourself, Forbes," said Duff, speaking for the first time. "I've heard all I need to bring you to justice. And we have more than enough witnesses."

"I know that voice," snarled Forbes, but even as he spoke he dodged to the right and straight toward Angus Duff. In the darkness, Angus could only barely make out the approach of danger. He dived toward Forbes, but miscalculated the distance and landed only inches from the fugitive. Bumping his head on a projecting rock, the former constable fell unconscious while the fugitive shot through the opening made by Duff's courageous blunder. He had just made it to the western opening of the cave when Dermott caught up with him. Dermott threw his full weight against Forbes, knocking him to the ground.

"He deserved what he got! An' I'll kill ye too!" Forbes yelled. The gleam of metal flashed in his hand.

He slashed wildly with his knife, aiming it upward toward Dermott. In the darkness Dermott saw nothing until he felt the sudden pain of a deep gash in his arm. Forbes was on his feet now and running from the tunnel. By now Stevie and Neil had reached Dermott and were following the wild man where he was making his escape along the top of a precipice toward a trail leading down to his boat.

"No! Boys, stay here! See to Duff. The man's too dangerous. I'll go after him!"

They obeyed. Clutching his arm to stop the flow of blood, Dermott took up the chase.

Forbes had already reached the top of the steep path and was scrambling down the loose rocks toward the sea some fifty feet straight below him.

"Forbes . . . Forbes. Stop!" called Dermott. "I didn't come here to try to hurt you. I'm a lawyer. Let me try to help you."

"Help me t' the gallows, ye blighter!" yelled Forbes. "I'll kill ye before I'll go with ye!"

Dermott reached the top of the cliff and could see Forbes struggling down the dark incline inch by inch. He dared not follow. In the gathering darkness it would be too dangerous.

"Forbes," he called out again, "even if you escape from me, you will never evade your crimes. *God* will always haunt you until you repent. Lay yourself at His feet, Forbes, where you will find peace!"

For a brief instant Forbes stopped in his descent, the sentiment of Dermott's unexpected words catching him by surprise.

"It's never too late with the Lord, Martin!" shouted Dermott.

"Ha!" yelled Forbes back up the cliff. "Who'd believe my side o' the story?"

"I would," replied Dermott. "I would try . . . and would do all I could for you."

"An' I believe in Broonies!" scoffed the fugitive.

"Think of your family—they need you, Martin!"

Forbes had begun his perilous descent again, but suddenly the rock beneath his foot began to give way. Dermott could hear the rush of loose stones falling into the stormy sea below.

"It was fer them I did it all!" shouted Forbes as he scrambled frantically to regain his foothold, "that they might hae somethin' better in life than me! But now if they canna hae the fortune," he went on, his voice trembling in panic and desperation, "they are better off wi' oot me!"

"What . . . Martin! Don't let this keep you—"

But Dermott's words were cut short by a long scream as Forbes's flailing arms and furiously struggling feet lost their hold altogether and he plunged down the side of the cliff into the violent and rocky water below.

Dermott lurched forward, then realized any attempt to descend was futile. He stood for a long moment gazing down into the darkness, staring into the foaming grave of the poor, dejected man, uttering a prayer for him even now. Then Dermott turned and, wrapping his shirt tightly about his wounded arm, plodded back toward the tunnel where the others were waiting for him. His quest was over; Ian would at long last be freed; but he could feel no elation at the successful conclusion of his mission.

40

The Truth Comes Out

THE LAIRD HAD called for Digory.

The long weeks of his illness had stretched to months, and he had never once done so. It had always been Digory knocking tentatively on James's door to ask how he fared. Sometimes the laird's only response was a rude insistence that the groom leave immediately. On other occasions, more and more of late, he would speak to the groom for a few moments.

"Well, come in," he would growl, "before you let all the heat escape into the hall."

Oftentimes James would carry the burden of conversation, talking mostly of the old days. What to him were the "good" days were the times when he was a lad before his father lost his fortune. He also reminisced about his days as a rising young bank executive. His speech became inflated with the arrogance he had carried as a young man. And yet such lapses were not total, for there were other moments when the laird grew pensive.

"That was all before I came to Stonewycke," he might say. "Ah, what hopes I had for this place! But look where it landed me. A fancy bed with silken sheets to die in!"

And Digory would gently reply, "Didna the Book tell us that the rich hae already received their consolation?"

"And so that is all I am to expect?" James would retort.

Then Digory would seize upon such an opportunity to turn the conversation toward the things most dear to his heart, speaking to his master about the love of the God he served. And if James did not fall asleep during the groom's speech, at least he would generally allow Digory to have his say, then gruffly dismiss him. How much he really heard, Digory had no way to guess. But he could not let his master die without having the opportunity to hear and repent.

This morning, as he answered the laird's summons, Digory expected more of the same. He never took offense at the laird's gruffness, especially now. He knew the Word of God would never return without accomplishing the work God had intended for it.

He knocked on the door and the feeble voice which answered from inside the room was noticeably weaker than usual.

"I was afraid," James said after Digory had entered and closed the door, "that if I waited for your next visit, it might be too late."

"What can ye mean, my lord?"

"I mean, I doubt I shall see you tomorrow."

"Oh, my lord, can ye be so sure?" Digory stepped close to the bed and knew when he saw the ghastly pallor on the laird's face that he might indeed have spoken prophetically.

"I doubt it will inconvenience anyone, except that they will have to hastily convene their celebrations."

"Ye canna mean that!" Digory exclaimed, a tender pity in his voice.

"You have been a faithful servant," James said. "Perhaps you shall feel some sorrow . . ."

"An' Lady Atlanta," added Digory hastily, the tears of grief rising in his eyes. "She will mourn ye."

"I doubt that, Digory. And why should she? I have been a monster in her eyes."

"Oh, my lord," implored Digory. "Ye mustn't talk so."

"It's true. You know it."

"But if ye feel so, then ye still hae time t' make it right, na only wi' Lady Atlanta, but wi' the Lord God also."

"Ha. An old rotter like me? Come now, Digory. I know you've had high hopes for me, with all your preaching. And I haven't minded it so much. But you know my heart is hard as stone."

"Only the heart that's dead, my lord, can be that hard. An' I know yer heart's na dead. I hae seen the longin' fer somethin' more in yer eyes, my lord. Why else would ye hae listened t' all my ramblin's so many times?"

James was silent for a long moment.

Through eyes that glistened with the mingled tears of sadness and hope, the faithful groom looked on, praying for this soul struggling so hard against the birth which would allow him to face death as his Maker had intended.

"If only I could die knowing someone cared," he said at length, in a tone which Digory had never heard from his lips before, a tone which reminded him of sorrow—not sadness, but genuine, remorseful, almost repentant sorrow at what he had been. But before he could continue, a paroxysm of coughing overtook him. When it was finished he lay back on his pillow exhausted. He could not speak for some time.

Digory reached down and took the feeble hand of his master and bowed his head. "Oh, Father, ye only know the mystery o' this moment yer Son called birth an' hoo it prepares us fer the other moment called death. Strengthen yer child, Lord, this child o' yers that ye love. Strengthen him t' give birth t' yer life within him, an' strengthen him t' meet ye t' yer face when that moment o' crossin' the river comes t' him . . ."

When he lifted his head, James was staring at him.

"Ah, I should be happy that at least you care, my friend," said James, his voice now barely audible. "But it is not enough . . . go, will you . . . and find Atlanta . . ."

"Of course, my lord," said Digory rising.

"You'll probably find her crying somewhere. She's become so touchy and sentimental lately . . . God help me, I swore at her this morning . . . Bring her, will you, Digory . . . please . . ."

Atlanta had completed her morning duties. After leaving James several hours before, in tears, she had buried herself in meaningless tasks for distraction's sake to divert her attention.

There had been a time she had believed that Stonewycke could not survive without her. For so many years, especially since her father's death, she had thought that the very earth itself depended upon her for its sustenance. But lately she had not been so sure. She had even begun to wonder if she were nothing but an old matron deceived by her own self-importance. It therefore did not surprise her when she realized that she needed Stonewycke even more than it needed her. The heather-covered hills would continue long after she resided beneath its black loam.

Mortality, she sighed, *is such a hard fact to face.* But at least with it comes the hope of the cares of life ending one day. *I do not deserve more than that,* she thought. But she longed no less for more—for the hope of eternity which makes mortality easier to bear.

"I *am* growing old," Atlanta murmured, shaking her head. "Now I have forgotten what I was about to do."

At that moment a maid hurried up to her.

"M'lady," she said, breathless from her climb up the stairs. "There's a gentleman at the door. He wanted t' see the laird, but I told him his lairdship were seein' na visitors. He said it were important."

"Thank you, Abby," Atlanta replied, "I will tend to it."

The tall, broad-shouldered man standing in the entryway was a stranger to Atlanta, but he knew her immediately. The stately woman in her austere black taffeta stood exactly as Ian had described her to Dermott on many occasions. But even had the lawyer not had the benefit of these descriptive introductions, he would nonetheless have known the marchioness of Stonewycke, for this woman could be no less than the mistress of such a grand estate. Her very bearing reminded Dermott of the stately walls of granite over which she presided.

"I was told you wanted to see Lord Duncan," Atlanta said as she reached Dermott where he stood in the entryway.

"I did, my lady," he replied. "It is a matter of some urgency."

"He is quite ill and receiving no visitors."

"I am truly sorry to hear that he is ill."

"Perhaps I can help you," Atlanta offered.

Dermott quickly appraised Atlanta as she stood awaiting his reply. He wondered how much she knew of James's deception, both with regard to Ian's plight and Duff's disappearance.

"I don't know if you can, Lady Duncan," Dermott replied after a moment. "Or if I would be within my rights to beg for your help. You see, my business concerns your son-in-law, Ian Duncan."

Atlanta sighed heavily. "Even in his death, he will not give us peace. But I suppose we little deserve it."

"Then it is as I supposed, that you are in the dark concerning Ian's condition. I had hoped after my last visit, the laird might have been induced to tell you."

"My husband is dying, sir," Atlanta replied. "We have not . . . talked . . . about Ian in some time. How can you be apprised of situations in my family of which I am not?"

"Forgive me, Lady Duncan. My name at least I can give you. I am Dermott Connell, a lawyer from Glasgow."

"Then, Mr. Connell, perhaps you should acquaint me with these conditions, as you call them, of which you are so well informed."

"I am reluctant, because I would not want it to appear I have come to speak ill of your husband behind his back."

Atlanta's taut lips bent into a slight smile, whether from humor, bitterness, or sadness Dermott could not immediately discern.

"You need not spare me, Mr. Connell," she said. "I well know my husband's shortcomings. And as he is thus indisposed, it is time I became familiar with his affairs, especially where they concern my late son-in-law."

"My lady, I came here to inform the laird that I have found George Falkirk's murderer. And it is not, as many have supposed, your son-in-law. Young Falkirk was killed by one of Port Strathy's more unsavory characters, who was apparently in the employ of Falkirk—although the motives are still obscure."

"Thank God!" said Atlanta, closing her eyes and showing more emotion than she yet had. "At least we can take comfort that she did not marry a murderer. But little good it will do her—or poor Ian—now."

"I do not know about your daughter, my lady. But Ian shall benefit greatly from this discovery. He is not your *late* son-in-law, Lady Duncan. Ian lives, and will be free the moment I reach Glasgow."

"Alive!" exclaimed Atlanta. "But we were so certain! There was an official document . . . a fire . . . How can this be?"

"It was carefully conceived—"

"Say no more, Mr. Connell," Atlanta interrupted, as the full impact finally struck her. "I understand now. I will not place you in the position of, as you say, 'speaking ill' of my husband."

She turned toward the stairs to hide her rising emotions. She laid a trembling hand on the oaken rail. "Even I could not guess at how far he was willing to go in order to secure his ambitions," she said softly. "And yet, I can feel no rage. Knowing he is dying . . . somehow I can no longer look upon him as the evil man in reality I know he was. And perhaps it is because I can scarcely any longer feel . . . anything."

"Perhaps it is also that you feel tender toward a man who now only has death to look forward to."

"How can you know that, Mr. Connell?"

"I can only guess."

"You are not far from the mark."

At that moment, Digory appeared at the top of the stairs. Atlanta glanced up at the bent frame of the trusted servant. She knew even before he spoke why he had come.

"The laird, my lady," Digory said. "He's wantin' t' see ye."

Atlanta closed the door softly behind her. She wondered if James was already dead; he appeared so gaunt and shrunken. A knot formed in her throat, but she bit back the rising emotion and inched forward. What were these feelings? Was it pity at seeing her once powerful adversary now so helpless, so wasted? It surely could not be affection for the man.

"Atlanta," came James's feeble voice. "You have come."

"Of course," she replied. "You called for me."

"But you did not have to come. I should hardly have expected it."

"James, let us not spar just now."

"I would not . . . not now . . . wife . . ." James lifted his white hand to her. "Come and sit by me."

Atlanta moved a chair near the bed, then seated herself and took the proffered hand.

"I have been the devil to you," he whispered at length. "Is it enough to ask forgiveness?"

"Don't James. It is not necessary."

"Ah, but nothing is more necessary. I have been cruel. I grasped for all the wrong things—"

His voice caught on a cough. He gripped Atlanta's hand as if to gain the strength from it to live just a moment longer.

". . . But I threw away the best things. And now . . . I shall never have them back . . . and that . . . is my terrible punishment."

"God shall make it right," Atlanta heard herself saying.

"Yes. So Digory assures me. And I can almost believe it now. But there is one more thing . . . I have—have . . . deceived you about—our son-in-law . . ."

"I know all about that," said Atlanta tenderly.

"And still you came? . . . will he . . . can it be—how can I undo it now?"

"It's all taken care of."

"Atlanta . . . will you see that Ian . . . is provided for?"

Atlanta nodded. It took all her strength now to maintain her composure.

"And Maggie . . ."

James swallowed as the words had become almost impossible to form.

"Little Maggie . . . what did I do to you? . . . how shall I ever . . . Atlanta . . . wrote us . . . I've got to—"

"Yes, yes. James, I'll write her," assured Atlanta, now choking back the sobs.

"No . . . no—she . . ." he murmured. "She—oh, Atlanta. I'm going—I have to tell you . . . apology to make. Atlanta, she—"

He could not finish the sentence. The glow faded from his eyes as the last breath of air left his body forever. He was dead.

Slowly the grip of his bony fingers loosened on Atlanta's hand. But she kept her fingers wrapped around his, though she knew all life had gone from him. Finally, as a single desolate tear inched down her cheek, she bent over and kissed her husband.

41

Securing the Future

JAMES WAS GONE. Atlanta could accept that. But what continued to gnaw deeply at her was the awful reality that from the moment she had known James, she had never once told him she loved him.

Perhaps she never *had* loved him. But what consolation could there be in that? That only made the ache of the realization more painful. What might have been if they had loved one another? If only . . .

Atlanta sat in her dayroom and looked about.

Everything was empty now, barren of life. Even the elegant furnishings which surrounded her brought pain. She remembered when she had purchased them so many years ago. She and James had traveled to Italy—before Maggie was born. James, of course, had been absorbed with business and she had spent her time in the shops. She was younger then, and such things had held a magnetizing allure for her. After searching through a great many shops she had at last found a set she had fallen in love with and immediately ordered the delicate furnishings for her own little dayroom. James found the purchase frivolous but was indulgent.

Were we even vaguely happy then? Atlanta wondered.

No. For instantly she recalled how piqued James had become with her less-than-amiable reception of some duke whose favor he had been currying. The fat, double-chinned man was a pompous fool, and Atlanta had had no intention of patronizing such a person.

No, there could have been no love between them. They were pursuing their own interests and stubbornly refused to budge from their own ways to accommodate the other.

"Oh, dear Lord!" Atlanta agonized. "Why was I so selfish? If only I had given just a little then, I would have more than some spindly furniture to comfort me now . . ."

But she could not finish, for a choking sob rose in her throat, followed by another and another until terrible sobs shook her entire body. Atlanta held out her hands in confused supplication as one totally unaccustomed to the agony of tears. As they mounted she could not control them, and they issued forth unchecked. Tears continued to wash down her face as her shoulders convulsed. She clenched her hands and unconsciously began pounding her fists against the desk where she sat. But still the tears would not abate.

All her past failures rose to confront her. And now the most terrible thing of all glared at her with a stark reality she had never seen: For the sprawling parcel of dirt and trees and moorland and valley called Stonewycke, she had sacrificed everything—love, children, husband, friends, happiness. *Everything!* And in the end would even the cold earth comfort her? No, for she had sacrificed her right to be comforted. She had nothing!

If only she had been able to say the simple words *I love you.* Would James then have fought so hard to protect himself? Would he then have needed to strip her of his greatest threat—their daughter?

Oh, Maggie, it was my fault, not his! For I drove him to it. He was my husband and I refused to love him . . . all for what?

Suddenly Atlanta pulled her distraught frame straight in the chair. She allowed one more sob to escape her lips, then she tightened those white lips and would cry no more. I have been mourning too long . . . a lifetime, she thought. Now I must give it up for at least one act of love.

She rose from her chair, went to a nearby secretary where she pulled out a clean white sheet of paper. Taking her pen and dipping it into the jar of ink, she began to write. How it would find its way to her daughter she did not know. She would have to think of that later. For now all she knew was that the letter must be written.

"My dear daughter Margaret . . ." she began.

*   *   *

Thirty minutes later, Atlanta rose from the secretary. Tears had once more assailed her and she could not finish the letter. She carefully folded it and, glancing about the room for a suitable place to put it until she could return to it, finish it, and send it, her eyes fell upon the old family Bible on her shelf. She walked toward it and laid her hand upon it.

"Oh, Lord," she thought, "you know we didn't make much use of this. But Maggie used to enjoy my reading to her from it."

Slowly Atlanta opened the Bible. It fell open in the Psalms. She tenderly placed the half-completed letter to her daughter inside. "Protect her, God. And keep this letter in your care until it shall find its way to her. Amen." Atlanta closed the book, turned, and walked to a bookshelf on the opposite wall where she retrieved a key from among the books. She then returned to the desk she had been at earlier and unlocked the bottom drawer. She took from it an envelope containing a single yellowed document. Then she dropped the key in the drawer.

"No need to lock this; there is nothing to hide anymore," she said.

The paper she held in her hand was very old. She had discovered it a number of years ago hidden in an ancient chest. At first it had appalled her and frightened her. Yet it had also intrigued her.

As she had examined it and investigated its origins, she more and more realized what a powerful document it was, especially as a weapon against one such as her own husband. Ever since, she had held it over James as a constant threat and an ever-present reminder of the lengths she was prepared to go in order to keep Stonewycke intact, safe, and out of his greedy clutches. He had never seen the paper, and she had only hinted of its contents to him. But it had served her purpose well, and had kept James and his schemes in check. Her own grandfather Anson had drawn up the document, and Atlanta trembled each time she realized that he would have invoked it had not sudden death prevented him. The date on the paper was merely a few days prior to his untimely accident.

What made Atlanta tremble even more was how close *she* had come to using it. But now, as her final, perhaps her only act of love toward the man she had married, she would destroy the paper altogether. For James's sake she would allow Alastair his share in the inheritance. He had been a son to her almost since the moment of his birth; even he himself did not know she was not his mother. He was James's son, so if Maggie did not return one day to claim Stonewycke as Atlanta had promised she should, then Alastair would have it. For James's sake, she would not invoke the powerful document against his son.

From a drawer Atlanta took a match, struck it, and held it to the paper, poised to reduce to ashes all evidence of Anson's deed.

Anson . . .

Suddenly the thought of her grandfather swelled in her mind. She had always had such a deep loyalty and respect for him, though she had never known him. How could she destroy his legacy, how could she destroy something he had held dear? This paper was a constant reminder of how deep the love for the land ran in Ramsey blood—and a reminder, too, of the capability that very love had to destroy. She could never let it destroy again.

Atlanta blew out the match.

No, she could not burn this paper. Anson was blood of her blood, bone of her bone. He was a *Ramsey*, as she was a Ramsey. Whatever amends she might make in death to the husband she had despised in life, she could not thereby destroy the deepest petitions of her own grandfather.

Another sob of anguish caught in Atlanta's throat. She was torn between strong conflicting motives, uncertain where to turn. "Dear Lord," she cried, "if only my Maggie would return . . . But she is in your hands. Oh, God! And so is my Stonewycke. You love this land and its people, and you will always do right for them. If only I could have realized that long ago . . . *Oh, Lord, take care of Maggie and Stonewycke!*"

Suddenly a resolve came to Atlanta. She would neither destroy the paper nor invoke it. She would hide it! But not among her own things, where it would be looked for and could easily be found.

She left the dayroom, still clutching the paper. In the hallway she glanced in both directions, and finding it deserted, she stole down the short distance to the next room. There she opened the door and entered the room where Maggie had spent her childhood. The room sparked in Atlanta all the emotions she had been fighting so hard to ignore—pain, bitterness, love, loss . . . and now longing.

But this room also represented the small bit of happiness she had known. What better place to seal up the past and step into a future where love might somehow be found?

42

Ian

DERMOTT REMAINED IN Port Strathy long enough to attend James's funeral. He was buried quietly with only immediate family and household servants in attendance, laid in the Ramsey crypt—at which even the vicar registered some surprise. But Atlanta was firm in her resolve that at least his body should rest peacefully in the one place which had remained elusive to him during his life.

So the man was laid to rest and Dermott set out to fulfill his final wish concerning Ian's care. Atlanta considered going to Glasgow herself, but in the end she chose to stay. "The most I can do for him now," she sighed, "is to allow him the chance to forget Stonewycke and those of us who so misused him. Let him begin his life anew, perhaps even find his Maggie."

Inclement weather had beached the schooner, and Dermott was forced to take the snow-encrusted inland roads. The trip was a long and weary one, and a fortnight passed before he finally beheld the pleasant house at George Square. What a contrast to the grim granite walls of Stonewycke!

It was late evening but still a lamp burned in the drawing room. Elijah was sitting by the fire, a book in his lap, his head nodding in a restless doze. At the sound of Dermott's step he raised his head and turned toward his friend.

"Ah, good evening, lad!" The doctor greeted Dermott as if he had only stepped out for several hours rather than having been gone a month. "I've always been so intrigued by Apuleius's *Metamorphoses*, but I'm afraid in my old age it sometimes only puts me to sleep."

"It's good to see you, Elijah," Dermott said. Unconsciously tears rose in his eyes. He possessed so very much, and at this moment he realized how often he took it all for granted.

"Come and sit down, if you are not too fatigued."

"I have never been so fatigued," Dermott replied, taking a seat near Elijah's. "So tired that I long for the rest a conversation with you always affords."

"So . . . you had a difficult time of it then?"

"Sometimes I forget the hellish depths our separation from God can bring us to," sighed Dermott wearily. "It is both the price and reward or redemption to forget. Yet in His mercy God occasionally allows us to see again how those outside His love suffer, to remember how we suffered when we were without Him."

"But you and I both know the suffering does not end the moment we give our hearts to Him," said Elijah.

"That is true, my friend, but at least it is a suffering with hope. But for all the difficulty of my trip, God was glorified in a most marvelous way. I have confidence that one of the hardest of hearts turned to Him in the end. And"—here Dermott brightened as some of the weariness fell from him—"the best piece of news is that my young prisoner will be free!"

"God be praised!" said Elijah.

They both fell into a restful silence for some moments until Elijah suddenly jumped from his chair. "I nearly forgot! A message arrived for you some days ago. I set it on the mantel over there." He retrieved the letter and brought it to Dermott.

The message had clearly traveled some distance to reach him. He was reminded of the last letter he had received from Queenie. It too had been travel-stained and had borne good tidings. Perhaps this would do likewise.

He broke the seal and removed the pages of the letter. As he read his face grew somber. When he finished, he leaned heavily back into the chair while his hand dropped limply at his side, the paper falling to the floor.

"When will the heartache end?" he sighed deeply. "How can I bring this news to the woman I just left behind! It will crush her. Yet she will have to be told. Oh, Lord!" Dermott sighed again, then closed his eyes.

When Dermott had first met Ian, he had enlisted the help of an acquaintance in America to conduct a search for the young man's wife. After many dead ends and false leads, the man had at last learned of Margaret Duncan's fate through relatives of the Mackinaws whom he had located in central New York state.

She had, indeed, traveled west in a covered wagon with the Mackinaws. But they had been beset by Indians somewhere west of the Great Divide and, saving for a handful of survivors, all had been killed, including Margaret Duncan and her child. A list of survivors had been printed in an eastern newspaper, which was included in the correspondence to Dermott. Drew Mackinaw and his family were listed. Margaret Duncan was not. *At least the news will comfort Stevie,* thought Dermott.

"I had hoped to bring a man the joy of freedom," he said at last, "and the hope, however slim, of being reunited with his wife. But now, what can I tell him? This will destroy him altogether!"

"Is he not in God's hands?" Elijah said. "You once said that God's higher purpose went beyond restoring Ian to his wife."

"Yes, but that was before . . ."

"Before you knew of a certainty that was not God's purpose?"

Dermott sighed. "Yes . . . you are right. My own shallow faith is revealed again."

"God cares more to reconcile Ian to himself than to his wife. God's purpose is higher, further-reaching. Who can know what healing He will work in Ian's heart through this heartache? And who can fathom what He might have done in Margaret Duncan's life through this tragedy? Many prayers have been prayed. And none will go unanswered. Forgiveness, Dermott, is one of the great lessons of life. People like Ian, or Margaret Duncan . . . people like you and me. All people, Dermott, most humbly come to the point of being able to forgive others the wrongs they have done them, forgive themselves for their own sin, and even forgive God for what we perceive as the cruel hand of fate working against us."

Elijah paused and looked intently at his young friend. "It is this forgiveness which lies at the root of repentance and opens the way for the life He would give us. This is now Ian's great opportunity. After such forgiveness, out of the ashes of the fires of bitterness and remorse, one is able to rise up with new light in his eyes, then to move forward into the abundant life spoken of by the Apostle John."

"But how does one such as Ian forgive? Only God in a man's heart can make such a miracle happen. Yet without forgiveness, who can approach God?"

"Another of the mysteries of our faith, Dermott," Elijah said, his eyes reflecting the glow of the dying fire. "We *can't* forgive without God's help. Yet to avail ourselves of His power requires a letting go, a turning away from the past, an attitude of forgiveness. I suspect God's help is already there before any change is made—prompting, urging, strengthening. And then His presence grows ever more keen the more of our *selves* we lay at the altar."

"Ah, Elijah," replied Dermott, "deep indeed are the mysteries of walking with Him in faith. Deep, yet practical. The choices remain ours, do they not?"

"We shall never understand God's ways. But you are right, it is practical. The lad must have a chance to make his own choice in life, Dermott. And perhaps the lesson God desires to teach him is that to choose God during and in spite of adversity *is* the higher purpose. At least for this lad who seems so much like the 'wave of the sea' spoken of by the Apostle James. He has been driven to and fro with every variance of the wind. And the time has come for him to learn to stand firm in the midst of the storm. Perhaps he never could have learned that any other way. Only the Lord knows that. But is that not what life really is about, rather than fleeting happiness and worldly peace?"

"Thank you, Elijah, for speaking truth," responded Dermott humbly. "I think I fear telling Ian about his wife as much for the pain it will cause me as it will cause him. But he must know."

Dermott rose, left his friend, and climbed the steps to his room. There, notwithstanding the weariness of his body, he spent the next hour in prayer for the task which he would face with the dawn of morning.

Dermott glanced around him as he neared the corner of Trongate and Saltmarket. The stone walls of the shops and businesses with their soot-blackened walls were almost appalling in their ugliness compared to the lovely countryside he had recently left. Yet even their filthiness reminded him of Elijah's words and he was strengthened. A man's heart need not be affected by such temporal things as his surroundings or his lot in life.

Dermott had learned all too graphically that even a lovely countryside could breed pain and suffering. The circumstances of life were *not* in themselves life, but only the means through which a person finds true Life. Every person's unique life breeds distinctive circumstances—some pleasant, others painful. But it was the response of each individual heart to the circumstances confronting it which was the substance of life—the very essence of what that person was and was becoming.

Dermott turned into the ancient prison where first he sought out the warden. Feigning shock at Dermott's presentation of the case, the man denied any part in the deception. But once having seen the affidavit from the ex-constable, two or three other signed eyewitness accounts, and a brief letter from the marchioness of Stonwycke herself, the man quickly scurried about to make himself agreeable to the lawyer—especially after learning of James's death. Dermott had suspected the warden's role in the duplicity all along, but that was hardly his primary interest at present. It was enough that he gave Dermott permission to see the prisoner while he arranged the details of his release.

Jerry shuffled ahead of Dermott down the narrow, worn stairs, then through several long dark corridors until they stood before the iron door of Ian's cell.

The door creaked open and Ian looked up sluggishly.

"I thought you had deserted me," came his dry, rusty voice from the dim interior of the cell.

"No, lad. I would never do that," Dermott replied, his voice already choked with emotion at seeing Ian once again. "I have some good news for you, but there is terrible news as well—heartbreaking news."

"I have come to expect it," said Ian with forlorn resignation.

Dermott sighed, then went on. "Ian, I have been to Port Strathy again. That is why you have seen nothing of me for these past several weeks. I didn't want to tell you before I left for fear of raising your hopes. But, Ian, I have at last found George Falkirk's murderer."

Ian started forward. "Then I am *not* guilty! Thank God!" He bowed his head in his hands and began to weep. "I shall be freed?"

"Yes, Ian. As soon as the proper authorities are notified and the details are all arranged. I have already seen to it."

"Free! I can find her now . . ."

Ian stood, his weakened body pulsing with sudden energy. "We'll be together at last. You were right . . . about God, you know. You were right! He *does* have His hand on us." A smile lit his face. "How can I ever thank you, dear friend?"

Dermott could not respond. His mouth had gone dry in the agony of what lay ahead.

"When shall I get out?" Ian went on.

"Ian . . ." Dermott tried to say, ". . . Ian, please sit down . . . there is more."

Surmising impending ruin from his tone, Ian slowly sank back to his chair.

Dermott drew a deep breath and tried to continue. "Ian, I have received a letter from America—from an acquaintance who was searching for Maggie . . ."

He closed his eyes, but the tears had already risen in them. He sighed again. "Ian . . . your wife and child have been killed."

For a moment there was no response. Then slowly Ian began to shake his head in bewilderment.

"No . . . no . . . it can't be true. There has been a mistake."

"I'm sorry, Ian. Here's the letter."

"I don't want to see any letter!" Ian shouted. "*It's not true!* It's someone else! I had no child . . ."

"The letter explains it. The child was born after Maggie reached America."

"Oh, God . . . no!" Ian wailed.

Dermott rose and went to Ian, but Ian shoved him away.

"Leave me alone!" Ian cried. "You were supposed to find her. You liar! He has bought you, too! I knew it! You want to keep me from her. But you won't! He won't win!"

"Ian . . . please," Dermott implored. "No one wants to keep you from Maggie. James Duncan is dead—he has nothing to do with this. Oh, Ian . . . I'm so sorry."

Once more he reached out to the desolate young man.

But Ian tensed and moved away slowly until his back pressed against the cold stone.

"God!" The word choked past his lips with loathing.

"Don't, Ian!" Dermott pleaded. "God loves you. He will help you through this. He is the only one who can."

"Don't talk to me of love!"

But even as he spoke a terrible look of reproach stole onto his face. Even in the dim light Dermott could detect the anguish of some horrible guilt passing behind Ian's eyes in the window of his soul. "I'll tell you about *love*," he went on in a dramatically altered tone. "Love sent her away, alone, helpless . . . to her death. It was *me*. I killed her!" he cried, and the words reverberated against the cold walls of the prison.

But before the echo had died away Ian crumpled to the floor. "I killed her," he whimpered. "I killed her . . . I killed her . . ." At last the only sounds from his mouth were helpless, moaning sobs and inarticulate whimpering.

Ian was released the following day. He had not spoken since Dermott had left him. The lawyer dressed him in the new clothes he had provided as if he were a child, then led him out of the prison as he might a dumb beast.

He was taken to the house on George Square where he was surrounded by all the love Dermott and Elijah Townsend could give. But still Ian did not speak. Guided by Dermott, he went through the motions of living. For two weeks there was nothing in his face or eyes to indicate life.

One night as Dermott drifted off to sleep, a vision rose before his eyes—a vision of himself, walking slowly through a cemetery shortly after dusk. All was still and quiet. Through the ancient tombstones he walked, not pausing to read the inscriptions, moving straight ahead as if with some mission. In the distance he saw a mound of earth. Closer Dermott walked. The mound of earth was freshly dug; beside it was a deep grave, awaiting its new owner. Near the grave was a long, flat, cold slab of white marble. But as he moved closer he saw that a body lay flat on its back on the slab. The body was cold as the night and as deathly still as the air around him. It had been laid out for burial. Closer he came. All at once he saw the face. It was Ian!—his youthful frame shrouded in death. On his chest were great splotches of blood! In his anguish at the sight Dermott tried to cry out, but no sound would come. Like Ian, his tongue was held in check. He reached out his hand toward the pale face . . .

Dermott suddenly woke, breathing deeply, sweat pouring off his face and chest, his body trembling.

He jumped from his bed and raced from the room to that on the next floor where Ian slept. Dermott flung the door open and saw Ian poised on the edge of his bed with a knife aimed at his chest.

"No, Ian!" Dermott screamed, rushing forward.

Ian raised his head and turned toward the advancing form. In his eyes glowed the same confused desperation which had first arrested Dermott's attention the day he had come upon him in the hall of the prison.

Gently Dermott pried the knife from his clenched fist, then held the weeping boy in his arms. It was a long while before Ian's tears subsided. Finally Dermott helped him back to bed, where he fell into a troubled sleep.

Dermott did not leave his side again that night, or thereafter for three weeks.

One morning the sky dawned blue and the air was crisp with the hope of spring. As the sun streamed in upon him Ian sat up in his bed. He glanced toward Dermott, reading at the opposite side of the room. Without warning he swung his feet out of bed and walked over to the window and threw open the shutters.

"Ah, the sun is shining!" he exclaimed. "Soon the flowers will be in bloom!"

Dermott stared speechless.

"It was a dreary winter," Ian continued. "I shall be glad to see it behind us." Then turning to Dermott, he said, "Have you my breakfast ready yet? I'm starved."

Seeing no visible motion from Dermott's chair, he added, "See here . . . are you awake? I'm not paying you to just sit there, you know."

Finally Dermott forced himself to speak. "Ian, are you . . . are you all right?"

"Never better, my man!" Ian replied with a boisterous laugh. "Never better! But it must have been some drunk I was on last night—I can't remember a thing! Tell me, what time was it when they brought me in?"

Dermott rose to his feet and descended, followed by Ian's light step behind him.

"Funny, I don't exactly recognize this place," he said. "But I suppose it must be some design of my father's to keep me off the streets. Well, no matter, it seems pleasant enough. Do you work for my father, my good man?"

With noncommittal reply Dermott arranged for Ian's breakfast, then went to Elijah's room to explain the latest developments in Ian's behavior.

They concluded, at length, simply to continue caring for Ian as tenderly as possible, allowing time for his subconscious to work its way through the trauma and slowly back to present reality. For the remainder of that day Ian's mood remained elated yet subdued, and he spoke freely of past events in his life as if they had taken place that very week.

So day after day, in days that eventually stretched into weeks, Ian's conscious mind had obliterated an entire year and a half of his lifetime. He could not face the pain of loss; he could not face God; thus he went through the motions of life as if his sojourn to Scotland had never existed. At times he might lapse into terrible bouts of despondency, at which times he threatened violence, both to himself and to others. But like his youthful binges, these were usually slept off and were replaced by an exuberant mood the following day. He showed little inclination to read, yet seemed content to loiter about the house, taking walks from time to time. As spring gave way to summer Dermott exposed him to more and more of Glasgow, even taking him on an occasional call to the prisons. But no recognition showed on the lad's face, even there.

His father would not have him back in London, so he continued on for some time in Glasgow. In late summer Atlanta came for a visit. He greeted her as a stranger. His forlorn condition tore at the woman's heart. When she was about to leave the following day, he said, "I shall have to visit this Stonwycke of yours one day." She turned her face and nearly wept.

They did not often mention Stonewycke or Port Strathy, but when the words came out in conversation, they appeared to have no effect on him. One afternoon he walked into the library as Dermott and Elijah were speaking of Maggie.

"Who are you talking about?" Ian asked, and only a slight wrinkling of his brow in momentary confusion gave indication that anything had stirred within him at the mention of her name.

But along with the pain, Ian had also obliterated the good—that which might have been able to comfort him and lead him to the One who would never stop reaching out to him, no matter how far he tried to hide within his mind.

43
Maggie

MAGGIE GAZED OUT the window.

What a wonderful sight it was to see Samuel and little Eleanor together! He rolled a bright red ball across the grass, and with squeals of delight she grabbed it—whenever she didn't tumble over in the attempt, giggling more then ever—to toss it back.

At two she was a beautiful child, with deep brown eyes and golden curls so like her father's. Sometimes Maggie's heart fluttered with a dull ache when she looked on her daughter. But more often she would just delight in her, thankful to God that she had been given such a blessed heritage from the man she had loved.

Three years was a long time. But it was not long enough to quell the pain that still surfaced in Maggie's heart. Yet healing was taking place—a healing of her heart *and* her spirit. With Samuel's help and the growing delight of little Eleanor, it was happening.

They had left the little garrison on the Platte the spring following the news of the Bannock massacre and had returned to the surer and somewhat more civilized protection of Fort Laramie. The Indian trouble that year had been so severe that it was unthinkable to leave the confines of the fort. During the winter of her first year, Eleanor had come down with pneumonia, and travel from the plains was again impossible.

Samuel had gradually developed a ministry among the Indians, teaching them what medical practices they could grasp. Although the majority of the Sioux were hostile, many came to trust Dr. Carpenter. But Samuel would no doubt have remained even without such work, for a great bond had developed in his heart for Maggie and her daughter. The terms of their relationship had remained unspoken, each gaining comfort and security from the other without burdening themselves with attempted definitions.

This hot, dry land was certainly nothing like Maggie's Scotland. But perhaps that change further hastened the healing process. For some time after her letter to her parents she had waited, first in anticipation, then in growing despair, for an answer. But as the months had passed and no return letter had come, a startling realization had slowly dawned upon Maggie; perhaps she really *could* begin a new life here in America, with all the pain from the past erased! Perhaps, after all, she was now a woman—able to stand fully on her own with the ties completely severed to homeland, house, even parents.

She continued to tell herself that someday she would return to Scotland. But yet when she learned of the death of the marchioness of Stonewycke from a Scottish immigrant working on the new railroad several years later, she realized there was no longer any reason to return. She would always love Stonewycke. But with Ian gone and her mother gone and her daughter growing up as an American, the estate would have no life for her any longer. Her future was here.

There remained, however, a dull ache in her soul. Something was still not right. She could not identify it. And though she asked the Lord to remove it, almost as a "thorn in the flesh" the melancholy remained. She had learned to smile again, but the smile was incomplete and still did not touch her innermost heart.

On this summer day Maggie was quietly reflective as she watched the play on the scraggly lawn draw to a close. Exhausted from chasing the ball, Samuel had caught up the child and was carrying her in his arms toward the house.

"This little bundle of energy has worn her old Uncle Samuel out!" he exclaimed, then sank into a chair at the table. To the accompaniment of Eleanor's pleasant chattering they ate lunch; though toward the end of the meal the doctor grew unusually quiet. When they had finished, Samuel pushed back his chair with a look of purpose on his face.

"Margaret," he said, "I have something I must speak to you about."

"What is it?" asked Maggie as she began cleaning up after Eleanor.

"We have known one another for some time now," he began. "It is amazing how circumstances—though of course we know *Who* controls circumstances— bring things about that might never have happened otherwise."

He paused, searching for the right words.

"Well, in the time we have been together, I have grown closer to you than I have been to anyone since my late wife."

Slowly Maggie returned to the table and sat down.

"What I'm trying to say, Margaret, is that—I—I wish to take care of you."

"You *have* taken care of Eleanor and me," Maggie said. "We could never have survived out here without you."

"But times are changing," he went on. "It was different when this frontier was peopled with only Indians and soldiers. But with the gold strike on, the Sweetwater has brought in hordes, not only prospectors, but families. Nebraska's near statehood. Wyoming's now a territory. More people than ever are moving west to settle. Don't you see what I'm getting at . . . people tend to talk—"

"And you care about the opinions of strangers?" said Maggie.

"No, of course not!" he burst out. "Oh, I'm afraid I'm going about this all wrong," he sighed. "I don't care about what others think of *me*. It is *you*, Margaret, and *your* reputation I am concerned with. But it's more than that . . . *Maggie, I love you!*"

With the words he leaned back in his chair, seemingly more exhausted than he had been from his play with Eleanor.

"I—I don't know what to say, Samuel." Now Maggie's color had paled too. It was lost on her that for the first time since the birth of Eleanor, he had called her by the name Ian had always used.

"Perhaps," said Samuel cautiously, "it is too much for me to hope for. And I know I can never take Ian's place. But, Maggie . . . do you think—that is, could you ever want to spend the rest of your life with me? Could you . . . would you be my wife?"

Maggie took a deep breath, but it did little to clear the whirling emotions inside her brain. She cared for Samuel, but this was something she had never expected. She had loved Ian so much that even after three years she could not let go of that love. She didn't *want* to let go of it. How, then, could she give herself to another?

"Otherwise," Samuel went on, "it seems that perhaps the time has come for me to move on. You and Eleanor are situated here and it might be best for you if I—"

"Move on!" interrupted Maggie. "Samuel, you're not thinking of leaving us if . . . if I . . .?"

"I just thought it would be in your best interests, you know, so you and Eleanor could get on with your life without having to worry about me."

"Oh, Samuel, we need you. I —I don't know about marriage. It's so unexpected—but don't you know how much you mean to me? I don't care what people might say."

The doctor leaned back in his chair and was silent for a few moments. At length he spoke in a quiet and thoughtful tone.

"It's strange," he said, "how God brings people together. Here we are out in the middle of the American wilderness. I'm years older than you. You're in a foreign land trying to raise a daughter thousands of miles from your family. We're both so alone. And yet here we are. God has given me to care for you, and both you and little Eleanor to add a sparkle of joy to my life. Margaret, I know neither I nor anyone else can ever take Ian's place. But if you'll have me I would be honored to watch over you—either as a husband, or like the father and brother you left behind."

The mention of her father and Alastair sent Maggie's thoughts spinning once again. Suddenly she realized that she had grown closer to Samuel than anyone except Ian. Her real family had been left behind, and all at once she was aware of how deep had grown the bonds of attachment she felt toward Samuel.

But she still loved Ian and could never let go of that love. How, then, could she commit herself to another?

But almost the same instant a tiny voice inside her seemed to say: *It will never be required of you to let go of your love for Ian. Just as I gave you this good doctor to see you through a difficult time, though you did not know he was sent from Me, so I will yet—though you know not how—use your love for Ian in that work I intended for it. In the meantime, I have given you into the care of this righteous man, who will watch over you and protect you in this new land which is now your home.*

"Please stay," said Maggie at length. "But can you just give me some time? I just don't think now is . . . that is, perhaps the time will come when—"

He reached out and touched her arm. "I understand," he said. "You don't have to explain."

"But do stay," Maggie continued. "I don't think I could face life here without you."

"You want me to keep being little Eleanor's 'uncle'—whatever people may think?"

"Of course I do," replied Maggie. "You are our family now—more a father and brother to me than even blood can make. You have helped me find contentment in my life. But if you should go away . . ."

"I don't want to."

"Then stay—if you do not mind sharing a part of *us* with Ian."

"I would be content to occupy whatever small corner he would leave me," said Samuel.

"Oh, Samuel!" said Maggie, "thank you. Thank you for understanding."

44
Journey's End

THREE MONTHS PASSED, and Samuel sensed a storm brewing in Maggie's spirit. Then the crisis broke.

For two days the distress in her soul had been growing. Whatever lay at its root was clearly coming to a head, though Maggie was still at a loss to know the source of trouble.

She awakened in the middle of the night, breathing hard, overcome with a great sense of depression. In vain she tried to recapture the peace of sleep, but instead tossed about until the gray dawn of morning began to light the eastern sky.

Throughout the morning the oppression grew. She became sullen and morose, irritable both with Samuel and Eleanor.

By midafternoon she became restless, almost frantic. She had to get out of the house—away. She asked Samuel to watch Eleanor, then headed toward the creek, running like one in flight trying to elude hounds on her trail. Across the footbridge she flew and up the rise on the other side, toward the distant hills.

Halfway up the nearest in the succession of steepening hills, she knew *Who* was chasing her. But still she did not slacken her pace. By the peak of the second hill she knew *why* He was pursuing her, His surgeon's scalpel poised to inflict the mortal wound in her heart which she so long had feared.

Still she ran on. *No . . . no!* she thought. *I can't do it! I shouldn't have to do it!*

A hundred yards farther she stopped.

She knew she could no longer hold His insistent Spirit at bay. She had told Him, in numerous prayers during the past two years, to do His work in her, to give her more faith. But whenever He had suggested *this,* she had quickly shut the door to His intrusions. Samuel had told her that the one thing we hold back, the one thing we refuse to give Him, is the one thing which can open the door to the richness of further blessing.

Still she had resisted.

But He was now finally—today—bent on having His way with her.

Maggie turned from the path and walked slowly toward a small grove of trees which shaded the grassy hillside.

"Oh, Lord," she whispered in quiet desperation, "I can't . . . I can't!"

With the words came the answer she dreaded. Yet she knew it was His voice, and that she could not escape.

You must, my child. It is the only way into the fullness of the life I have prepared for you. It is the only way.

On Maggie walked, groaning inwardly at the weight of the burden she must release to the One she had made her Lord.

Each step grew heavier than the last. At last she reached the trees.

"Oh, Lord, help me!" she pleaded.

I will help you, child, came the immediate answer. *Trust me.*

"I cannot do it, Lord! I have no strength to face it."

But I do, child. In your weakness is my strength. I have put my power in you. It is a cross you must bear alone, though I will be at your side.

In an agony of despair Maggie sank to her knees at the foot of a small birch tree, stretching out her hands above her.

"Oh, Lord . . . help me!" she cried.

Then, bowing her head to her knees, she prayed: "God . . . with you helping me—I—I—will try to . . . to forgive him."

She jumped to her feet and screamed, *"Oh, God—I forgive my father!"*

With those words all heaven seemed to explode about her ears. She fell prostrate on the ground and burst into an agony of uncontrollable weeping such as she had never known.

An hour later Maggie slowly approached her house. As Samuel watched her through the window, he could tell by the composure of her demeanor that the crisis was past. He opened the door and went to meet her. Though tears streamed down her face, her eyes sparkled with the radiance of peace and joy.

Without a word she approached him, gazing up into his understanding eyes, while she continued to weep tears of gladness and freedom.

"It is over," she said softly. "God has released me from the terrible burden of bitterness I have carried all my life. I have at last—I should say, at last the Lord has enabled me to forgive my father."

"I knew the day would come," said Samuel tenderly. "I have been praying that He would give you the strength to face it."

"He has been so faithful, Samuel. And now it is past."

"I am happy for you, Margaret."

"Thank you, Samuel. Now with the Lord's help, perhaps I can begin to do more to pay back all the patience you have shown me."

The doctor simply smiled, his eyes saying, "There is nothing you could do that would mean more than the pleasure of your companionship."

Together they turned and walked back toward the house, where little Eleanor's unmistakable chatter beckoned them.

Later that night, while Eleanor slept, Maggie rose and went outside onto the porch. The warm night sky was filled with the sparkling brilliance of the heavens. Across the compound the occasional snort of a restless horse revealed the nearness of the livery stable. Next door, Samuel's office was dark, as was the single room adjoining it to the rear where he kept his quarters. She smiled at the thought of what went on in that office from time to time—everything from veterinary emergencies to infant care among the Indians.

Then her thoughts turned toward Ian. Upward into the stars she gazed for some time, at last breaking out in spontaneous prayer: "Oh, Lord, I thank you for crucifying my bitterness on the cross of my pain. And now, God, somehow in some way I pray for Ian. In your infinite ways I pray he will be drawn into your presence, even as I have been. Let him release his bitterness to you, so that he might know the freedom of forgiveness—"

Suddenly she stopped, trembling.

"Do prayers avail the dead?" she finally breathed. "Only you know, my Lord . . . only you know!"

Still looking upward, in the new silence of peace within her soul, Maggie seemed to hear the Lord say, *It was I who gave you and Ian your love. And it is I who will perfect it in each of you. Trust me, Maggie. For Ian is now in My hands. And I will never forsake him.*

Content at last, Maggie turned back inside—to Ian's daughter, and to the promise of a new life with the God who had made her.

THE LADY
OF
STONEWYCKE

To Judy Phillips,
from whose ideas
The Stonewycke Trilogy was born.

CONTENTS

Introduction

LIFE IS NOT lived without heartbreak, loss and tragedy; such is the human condition. As Job said, "Man is born to trouble."

But a person's moments on earth are merely a flicker. The joys and miseries of circumstances ultimately fade into nothingness, and all that remains is the character one carries from this life into the next. The physical world provides the training ground for the deeper life as we learn to respond to the God who made us. Temporal loss can be the price of timeless gain.

How could Maggie know that an eternal destiny called her to America, there to discover the forgiveness which would allow His healing to wash over her? How could she have seen that in the agony of her loss, the hand of God was drawing her to himself? God's way is often beyond man's understanding.

How could Ian, in his bitterness, perceive the loving Hound of Heaven stalking his spirit as it tried to hide from its sorrow?

Temporal suffering clouds our sight and limits the scope of our heavenly vision. But the story for Maggie and Ian does not end with their farewells. Their history is not one of earthly happiness, but of eternal gain. It is a saga of God's unrelenting pursuit after the heart of man, a chronicle of healing. It is a trilogy of three intertwining lives who experience the threefold nature of God's forgiveness.

The drama does not end with Maggie's parting from Ian on the docks of Aberdeen. In the infinite provision of God's wisdom, the story of their love comes full circle to its victorious conclusion through His work in the generations who come after them.

God's plan for reconciliation is never exhausted. The prayer of a broken young woman on the prairie of the American West resounds through the heavens, awaiting the arrival of the moment when its fulfillment is at hand.

Prologue

THE SUN HAD begun its ascent in the east. In the harbor the large schooner readied itself to sail with the tide. As the morning's pale light rose on the Aberdeen skyline and farewells were said, passengers slowly separated themselves from family, friends, and well-wishers.

The bustle of activity on the teeming dock seemed incongruent with the early hour. Only a short distance away in the heart of the city, the town was barely beginning to stir. One by one storekeepers opened their doors to display their wares to the day's customers. A wagon laden with sweet-scented hay meandered into the dirt street from a side alley and made its way toward the waterfront, heralded by the tired groan of its iron-rimmed wooden wheels.

Without warning, the clatter of horse and rider shattered the tranquillity of the morning. The horses reared. The farmer jumped to his feet, grasping the reins firmly in a desperate attempt to keep his frightened team from overturning the load.

"Hey, ye curs'd bla'guard!" he shouted. "Keep yer de'il o' a beast oot o' my way!"

But the horseman was oblivious to all obstacles in his path. He slashed the leather straps mercilessly across the chestnut mare's neck and galloped on down the street.

Reaching the dock the rider yanked back viciously on the reins; the mare flailed savagely in an attempt to bring her huge frame to a halt.

Amidst trailing dust from the thundering hooves, the horseman dismounted and hastened toward the schooner. Frantically his eyes searched the deck of the ship, but too many bodies blurred together. He turned to scan the faces of those scrambling up the wooden-planked gangwalk but could not find the one he had ridden so hard to see. In desperation he rushed toward the ship, his face drenched with perspiration and splotched with dirt from the dusty road, his eyes recklessly probing the crowd before him.

The young auburn-haired woman did not see him at first.

She had been occupied briefly as he stampeded up. Turning toward the dock, she first spied the chestnut mare, flanks heaving from the exhausting gallop.

He had come!

She had nearly given up hope . . . but the mare could be none but his!

All at once she heard her name above the clamor, and at last their eyes met.

For a moment the girl forgot the voyage before her and ran, pushing her way through the crowd. As she reached the gangway a grizzled sailor called for her to stop.

"We'll be castin' off, lady. Ye better stay aboard!"

She heard nothing—neither sailor nor crowd nor the deafening clang of the ship's bell tolling its scheduled warnings. She shoved her way down the narrow ramp, heedless of all else, and ran into the arms she had feared would not hold her again.

"I thought you weren't coming," she said, as she took the packet from his hand.

He clasped her tightly as if to prove that her fears were unfounded. "I would have hated myself if I had been too late." He gently kissed the soft tresses of her hair. "It's bad enough that you must go—"

"Then, please, let me stay and stand beside you."

"No. We already agreed this is the best way . . . the danger is just too great."

"I know," she replied. The tension in her voice hinted at previous conflicts. "But what good is honor if it forces us to part?"

"A man's honor is all he has."

She swallowed hard and fought back the gathering tears. A sick feeling stirred in the pit of her stomach, but she would not let the evil premonition take shape. Yet she knew only too well what she feared—that she would never see him again.

"We could talk to my father again, maybe—" she began, her eyes pleading at him helplessly.

"Your father! Don't you realize that he hates me?" He stopped short, and when he began again, though his words were soft, they seemed but a thin veil over the passions surging within him. "Oh, my love . . ."

He cupped her face in his large gentle hands and looked down tenderly at her slight girlish frame. "Let's not spoil these brief moments. Let's only think about when we shall be together again. The weeks will pass before we know it. Then we will begin anew. It will be a good life we will share in America."

"If you could but come with me now . . . they would never find you."

The innocent hope of her naive words stung at his resolve.

"I'll not provide a life like that for you," he replied. "We will be free . . . able to hold our heads high, not cowering in fear of the past."

"But—"

"I know this sacrifice is hard. I know how you love this land."

For a brief moment the girl reflected that her mother had said those very words before she left. The heartbroken woman had placed the envelope in the girl's hands and spoken emphatically, almost desperately: "In this, find the hope of your return. But more than that, the safety of this land we love. No matter what happens, my dear child, *it is yours!*"

The girl's hand unconsciously sought the pocket where she had tucked the envelope. She had not yet even had a chance to look at it. But whatever it contained, she knew it would always serve as a bitter reminder of the tragedy that had torn her life apart.

"All aboard . . . last call!" shouted one of the ship's mates.

He drew her close and kissed her. "I love you, Maggie," he said through trembling lips.

Then she knew she must go. It was his will, after all, that she go. She loved him, and she would obey.

She turned and walked slowly toward the ship. As her foot touched the gangwalk a chill gripped her. With each step up its incline the agony of misgiving increased. Reaching the deck she looked away out toward the sea she would soon cross. Tears rose quietly to her eyes. Before her loomed . . . she knew not what. The great unknown.

She turned and looked back toward the man she must leave. If only it could have been different!

"I love you!" she shouted from the deck. "Ian . . . do hurry!"

He waved, but could find no words. She saw him lower his arm to sweep a sleeve across his tear-filled eyes.

On the deck the riggings had been loosened and the signal to cast off given. Beneath her she felt the first signs of motion. She opened her mouth to speak his name one last time, but could not. Her lips were unable to form that beloved name again.

Soon his form faded to a speck in the distance. She turned toward the far side of the ship where she tried to divert her attention to the sails, the outriggings, the movement of the sailors. She wiped her eyes with the back of her hand, then sucked in a deep draught of the clean salt air. The wind whistled through the masts and sent her long hair flying. She could not hear the beat of the mare's hooves retreating into the distance.

The schooner eased its way out of Aberdeen harbor, and the girl did not turn and look again toward her homeland until only the white-capped open sea met her gaze.

1
From Out
of the Past

❖

JOANNA WAS GLAD when they finally cast off.

The tranquillity she now felt, however, had not come upon her immediately. As the excited throng of passengers boarded, most had pressed against the ship's rail, shoving and straining for a better view of the crowd on shore. A stout little man in a checked, double-breasted suit had turned on her with sharp words.

"No need to push!" he snapped.

"I . . . I'm sorry," came her timorous response as she eased away.

Where she stood mattered little. There was no one waving to her from the dock. Her future and her hopes lay in the opposite direction, out to sea. A moment later the great horn of the *Atlantic Queen* blasted, shattering both her ears and thoughts. The tremendous girth of the modern liner, the pride of the new century's shipbuilding excellence, cleared its moorings and powerfully eased its way eastward.

As their speed mounted and the last view of New York's harbor and receding skyline thinned to the horizon, the passengers slowly dispersed to the many corners of the vast ship, leaving Joanna alone at the railing.

There she still stood an hour later, gazing out upon the watery expanse before her. The *Queen's* prow plowed through the swelling waves, sending churning whitewater spraying before it, mesmerizing her in the infinite dance of salt and foam, spray and wind.

A gradual sense of calm surged through Joanna's spirit as the sea quieted her soul. For the first time in weeks she found herself thinking in a realistic way about the adventure events had launched her into. She—reserved and cautious Joanna Matheson, who had never set foot out of the Midwest in all her twenty-one years—was sailing on a luxury ocean liner for Scotland, the land of her ancestors!

What would she find?

All she had to guide her were her grandmother's imploring deathbed words and the enigmatic puzzles she had discovered in her great oak secretary.

I wonder what kind of ship brought Grandmother to the States? she thought. *What it must have been like forty-five years ago! Times were so different then. And she was so young!*

Unconsciously Joanna clutched the pendant hanging from her neck—one of her few remaining links with the heritage which had brought her into the world. Lost in retrospection, she thumbed the golden locket.

Grandmother, she mused. *Grandma . . . if only I had taken the time to know you better.*

Joanna's thoughts trailed back . . .

Only a few weeks earlier she had returned from Chicago after her grandmother's accident. Nearing the house on Claymor Avenue where she had lived as a teenager, Joanna found a flood of memories rushing through her. As she walked up the broken sidewalk, she gazed with new awareness at the dilapidated two-story structure. She'd never realized how run-down it was—the paint peeling and chipping away, the shutters hanging sideways, the screen door torn, the rotting picket fence missing nearly every third board. The memory of that drab Denver house contrasted starkly with the glamor of her present circumstances aboard the magnificent vessel, sailing with what was doubtless a wealthy crowd.

A tear rose in Joanna's eye as she remembered those last days with her grandmother.

She shuddered at the recollection of the cold chill and the antiseptic bleakness of the hospital where her grandmother lay.

"Grandma, I'm here now," Joanna recalled saying as she pulled a chair next to the bed.

"I'm glad you've come . . ." returned a thin, strained voice. Joanna's grandmother had always been slight, but extremely energetic and youthful for her age. Yet now she lay almost motionless. A week earlier she had been walking to the market, as was her custom. But on this particular day as she crossed the dusty intersection, a child had darted into the street, ignorant of the dangers of the horseless carriage. As the driver swerved to miss the youngster, the car had careened toward the cross street, hitting Joanna's grandmother. The woman lay unconscious on the hard-packed dirt, her leg broken. At the hospital, the doctors found serious internal hemorrhaging. They fought the bleeding and managed to keep her alive, but their prognosis for her recovery was grim; the damage was too widespread. She awoke for a feeble moment, insisted they send for Joanna, then immediately lapsed back into unconsciousness.

"They won't tell me . . . but I know I'm dying," she said weakly.

"Don't be silly, Grandma," Joanna returned, trying to sound more confident than she felt inside.

"Think what you will, child," continued her grandmother. "But I have to make my preparations. I've very little time left, and there's something you have to do for me." Her voice trailed off and her eyes closed.

"Anything, Grandma," responded Joanna. "You always took care of me; now it's my turn." Even as she said the words, Joanna could not tell whether her grandmother heard her.

Almost as the words were out of her mouth the door of the room opened.

"The doctor would like to see you, Miss Matheson," the charge nurse informed her. "He's just down the hall."

Joanna turned to follow the nurse from the room.

Suddenly the ailing woman's eyes jerked open. Even in the dim light of the hospital room, they flamed with intensity. "You mustn't let them take it, Joanna," she cried out. *"It's yours . . . !"*

"It's okay, Grandma," said Joanna, turning again and leaning toward her. She reached out an uncertain hand toward the bed and gently let her fingers rest on the trembling arm, now limp on top of the bedcovers. "Everything will be fine."

Once again the older woman's eyes closed and she lay still as Joanna left the room. Outside the doctor approached and introduced himself.

"I have to be candid with you, Miss Matheson," he said. "Your grandmother is dying. We've been very fortunate to keep her alive this long. She's lapsed in and out of consciousness many times already, and every time we think we've lost her. But she has a resilient body, and her faith seems to be sustaining her beyond reason."

"And there's nothing more you can do?"

"It's up to the Almighty now, my dear. And of course your prayers would avail much."

Joanna's gaze dropped suddenly and awkwardly to the floor. When was the last time she had prayed? If her grandmother's survival depended on her prayers alone, then it was indeed hopeless.

The doctor caught the shifting of her eyes and sensed the meaning of it. He laid his hand on her shoulder. "We will both pray and hope," he said. "I've known your grandmother for many years, and she is a fighter."

"How long do you think it will be?" asked Joanna with a faltering voice.

"As I said, it is in God's hands. It could be any day. Medically speaking, there has been extensive internal damage, not to mention the broken leg and three fractured ribs. The surgeon did as much as he could, but she's lost so much blood, and I'm especially concerned with these lapses in consciousness. Every time she fades out, I fear for a coma. But she keeps fighting back."

"What would happen then?"

"Once a patient is comatose, then it's just a matter of waiting. There's nothing medically we can do at that point to bring them out of it."

That evening Joanna returned to the old house. How different it seemed, how empty of life! Perhaps for the first time she realized just how much her grandmother meant to her. She crept upstairs to what had once been her room, intending to arrange the few things she had brought with her, but instead she sat down on the bed and glanced about. A lump rose in her throat, and she found herself choking back tears for the woman who had practically raised her.

She wept, not for her grandmother alone, but for herself, because not until now did she find her love for the woman surfacing. She had gone to live with her grandmother at the difficult age of thirteen. Whatever was troubling the girl the grandmother could never quite tell, and Joanna was careful to keep her young emotions tucked deep inside. How could she ever tell the older woman that her own now-departed daughter Eleanor was at the root of Joanna's troubled spirit?

Joanna's mother Eleanor died in childbirth, just three hours after Joanna had been born. Eleanor was one of those exquisite creatures found so rarely in life—not only because of her fine-featured, flaxen-haired beauty, but also in her gentle, godly spirit. She loved and gave freely of herself without even knowing she did so. Stephen, her husband, loved her completely and was devastated by his wife's sudden and unexpected death.

In life she would have been a strong guiding light and example to her daughter. But in death, the child's thoughts and the husband's memory of the gentle woman became a source of pain and enmity between the two she left behind. For some time Stephen could not even function rationally, and his dead wife's mother cared for the baby for several months until her son-in-law could take the responsibility on his own. But he never could fully accept the child whose life he felt had been traded for his beloved Eleanor's.

Perhaps things would have been different if Joanna had been allowed to remain in the care of her grandmother. But shortly before she was a year old Stephen Matheson moved from Denver, ostensibly because of his job. If he could have admitted it, the truth was simply that he could no longer bear the memories in their Denver home. First Wichita, then St. Louis, and finally Minneapolis— Stephen could settle nowhere, because in one form or another the memories always followed him. In Minneapolis his sorely neglected health failed him at last, and he died one snowy morning in his own bed. Thirteen-year-old Joanna could never shake the awful conviction that somehow she had caused his death, just as she had her mother's.

Because Stephen Matheson had no family of his own, Joanna's grandmother gladly welcomed Joanna into her home. But it was impossible for the older woman's love to penetrate the shell that had by that time hardened around the young girl's heart. The cool distance separating them simply could not be overcome. The grandmother did not know how; Joanna, on her part, was unable to let down the walls of her defenses to see that all her grandmother wanted to do was love her. The inner child within Joanna's heart was still too tender. The guilt and unworthiness she felt blocked her ability to receive the love which might have been shown her.

Had her thoughts been formulated more distinctly, Joanna would have asked how anyone could love her—especially her grandmother, the mother of the woman whose death she had caused when she came into the world. She knew what a saintly woman her mother had been—had she not heard it constantly from her father? Whenever she was naughty, did not Stephen rebuke her by reminding her she would never grow up to be like her sweet and beautiful mother?

"I hate my mother!" the child had exploded once, in the bitter confusion of mingled guilt and longing for the mother she had never known. How could she possibly cope with the conflicting emotions of love for her mother on the one hand and self-blame on the other? She, after all, was responsible for the death of the one person her inner child so desperately needed.

At those words Stephen slapped her face in anger. Never again did Joanna speak ill of her dead mother; she could control her voice, but she could not control her thoughts. Her yearning for her mother was mixed with equal portions of resentment—a paradox her immature mind could not sort out. She resented her goodness and grew to despise the angelic picture that her father kept on the piano. Yet at the same time she hated herself for feeling as she did. What kind of an awful person must she be? Thus if her father did not love her, his disdain was no more than she deserved. And as Joanna's childhood years progressed, the twisted, confusing emotions, rooted in self-condemnation, drove her more and more deeply into the shell of her aloneness. She could find no place of belonging and began to feel as an alien, even under her father's and grandmother's roof.

The kindhearted lady tried to do what she could for her granddaughter. She taught her to bake and sew. But nothing could spark the girl's interest. She read the Bible with her each morning at breakfast and prayed with her as often as possible. But while Joanna showed courtesy to her grandmother's faith, she was never able to embrace it fully. For its foundation was the single element Joanna could neither understand nor accept—love. She was unable to forgive herself for the grief she felt she had caused. How, then, could she accept God's love and forgiveness when she herself stood condemned?

One Saturday morning when she was sixteen, Joanna entered the kitchen to find her grandmother sitting with her sewing basket beside her. Joanna ambled toward the stove in an aimless manner and held her hands over the wood fire to warm them.

"Joanna dear, would you like to embroider a sampler?"

"Oh . . . I don't know, Grandma," replied the girl with indifference.

"Come on—sit down here with me. I'll show you how."

With lukewarm interest Joanna shuffled to the table and sat down. Her grandmother handed her a fresh piece of cloth and proceeded to instruct her on the rudiments of embroidering her name.

After fifteen minutes Joanna threw down the needle and cloth in frustration. "It's no use! I can't do it!"

"You're doing fine," said her grandmother, encouraging her to continue. "You should have seen the first time I tried it. I was much younger than you. I'm afraid I bit off more than I could chew—"

"Oh, Grandma," interrupted Joanna, rising to her feet. "I'm just not interested."

"It takes practice, dear. I'm sure if you—"

"Not now . . . I'm sorry. I just don't want to do it anymore."

Joanna hurried out of the kitchen, leaving her grandmother alone at the table.

If only I could find something to interest her, the older woman thought, reflecting on her own first efforts to stitch her name on a piece of linen. "That was so many years ago," she whispered to herself. "It seems like another lifetime."

She rose slowly, walked toward the large kitchen window, and stood staring out. Her thin shoulders and graying head cast a shadow into the small sunlit room. Yet in spite of her years, her eyes revealed the inner strength and fortitude passed on to her from her own Scottish mother. The image of Joanna's dejected young face rose in her mind. Gradually her thoughts drifted back to her own teen years. *I suppose her life has been no less turbulent than my own,* she thought. *But at least I had someone who loved me to share it with—if only briefly.*

As if unconsciously drawn by the memory, her hand sought an antique golden medallion which hung around her neck underneath the faded pink sweater. She had worn the locket almost constantly since that sweet day in her youth when it had been given to her. Now, gently stroking it with her thumb, the memory of the miniature pictures inside brought a lonely tear to her eyes.

Sunk in a reverie of faces long past and places far away, she stood motionless—for how long, she did not know. At length, Joanna's footsteps on the stairs brought her back to the present, and she turned from the window with a sigh and returned to the kitchen to begin supper.

Joanna never knew how many hours her grandmother agonized over her. As she grew older and things did not seem to improve, the older woman became troubled about the girl's future. Perhaps, the grandmother thought, there might be one step she could take to improve the girl's feelings about herself. Joanna had always been a good student; perhaps she might excel in some career. As a last hope, the woman scraped together her meager savings and sent Joanna off to college in Chicago. Women were beginning to make their place in the world. In the city, perhaps, Joanna could discard the shackles of her past and develop a sense of her true worth and abilities.

Joanna complied with her grandmother's suggestion, not because she cared about women's achievements or even her own, but simply because she ached to get away—from the house, from Denver, from the painful memories of years she would like to forget. She had few other opportunities from which to choose.

The time away had indeed matured Joanna in many ways, though the walls still remained closed around her deepest self. Not until she returned home after her grandmother's accident did some small inroads begin to penetrate her pent-up heart. In the time she had been gone, not a single repair had been made in the house, which had always before been well maintained. The cupboards contained but the barest of necessities, even for a woman living alone. The icebox was empty except for a bottle of sour milk.

What had happened?

At the hospital, the nurse explained that her grandmother was on public assistance. Joanna was appalled. Certainly they had not by any means been wealthy, but money had never been scarce. But when she sought out the family lawyer, Joanna learned of the self-sacrifice which had been made on her behalf.

Her grandmother had poured every available dollar into her granddaughter's education. Had Joanna known, things might have been different. But she hadn't known. For her, college merely represented an escape from the one-dimensional world of her upbringing. Completely oblivious to the cost required in sending a young woman into the predominantly male world of higher education, she had never given the expense a second thought.

Now jolted into reality by her grandmother's sudden accident and by the lawyer's revelation, Joanna found her attitude immediately altered toward the woman who lay dying in her white hospital bed. Perhaps by attending to her grandmother faithfully in these days of her greatest need she could, if not equalize the scales, at least perform a portion of the duty she should have acknowledged much sooner.

2

Memories

IN THE DAYS that followed Joanna gave herself completely to the care of her grandmother. She went daily to the hospital and relieved the nurses of many of their duties to the lady in bed number six.

Each day the woman grew weaker, her mind floating in a dream world of semi-consciousness. Yet as incoherent as they often were, her spasmodic ramblings offered Joanna her first glimpse into her grandmother's early years, previously shrouded in silence. Her grandmother's girlhood in Scotland had ended abruptly in a youthful flight to America, and there the past seemingly vanished from memory—until now. During these moments at her grandmother's bedside Joanna realized that, with her own parents gone and with neither brothers nor sisters, her only tie with her heritage hung by the slenderest thread to her grandmother's ebbing life.

If only I had been more interested in these things before! she thought to herself. Half of what her grandmother said made little sense and now Joanna painfully admitted that her curiosity had likely come too late.

On the third morning after her arrival, Joanna came to the bedside. She was suddenly struck with how different her grandmother looked. This woman who had seemed to laugh at the advancing years, to exhibit an energy which could keep pace with women twenty years younger, now lay injured and helpless. The accident had changed everything.

The moment the tired face saw Joanna a gleam lit her eye and she stretched out her hand. Joanna vacillated a moment then took it, smiled, and felt a weak squeeze on her fingers. The older woman was attempting to say something but couldn't get the words out.

"That's all right, Grandma . . . I'll be right here. Take your time."

She continued struggling to make herself heard. Her ethereal voice was barely audible and her breathing labored.

". . . you here . . . I've waited . . . must tell you . . ."

"Just rest, Grandma."

"The house . . . I gave it up . . . had to leave . . . my family . . ."

The words were so soft and indistinct Joanna could barely make them out. She leaned closer and turned her ear toward the feeble voice. As if grasping a lifeline, the woman clutched Joanna's hand.

Just then her voice rose with passion and her head lifted off the pillow. *"It's yours!"* she cried. "Don't let them take it. . . ." She fell back, exhausted by the sudden exertion.

A nurse approached with a breakfast tray. "She's been going on like that all night," she said. "I don't know what's gotten into her." She set the tray on the bedtable. "Don't bother waking her to feed her. She probably wouldn't eat anyway."

Her grandmother slept until the cold breakfast was replaced with a lunch tray. Joanna was debating within herself whether to wake her when the frail woman's eyes shot open.

"It's there . . . !" she cried, hoarsely pulling herself nearer her granddaughter. ". . . the treasure . . ." Now her voice came out in labored gasps. ". . . in the nursery . . . find it . . . hidden away all these years."

Once the words were out she seemed to relax. Joanna tried to get her to eat some of the bland food the nurse had brought, but she pushed it away. Then her hands went to her neck; she fumbled a few moments until her efforts were at last rewarded, and she lifted up the gold locket. Her mouth moved silently as she tried to put her thoughts into coherent words.

"I'm going to die . . . you must take this . . . I never . . . never forgot him . . ."

Joanna hesitated a moment. "No, Grandma," she said through her tears. "You're not . . . you can't . . ."

But before she could finish her grandmother took her hand and dropped the locket into it with the words, ". . . yours now . . ."

With tears in her eyes Joanna took it, then with trembling fingers placed it around her own neck.

"Joanna," her grandmother went on, struggling desperately to make herself understood, "the treasure's in the nursery . . . the house . . . yours . . . I always loved it . . . but now it's time for me to pass it on to you . . ." But her mumblings grew incoherent, and at last she fell asleep.

That night when she returned to the lonely house on Claymor, Joanna felt emptier than she had ever felt in her life. Her grandmother's words seemed little more than delirious ramblings, but they caused Joanna to realize that there was much more to the woman who had given birth to her own mother than she had ever allowed anyone to see. A sickening fear gripped Joanna, the realization that she might never have the opportunity to know her grandmother as she suddenly longed to.

She stared silently out of the dirty window toward the railyards, now shrouded in the pallor of a wet, smoky dusk. Tiny raindrops clung trickling to the windowpane, adding to the gloom her spirit felt.

What would become of her once her grandmother passed away?

She had certainly never been a compassionate granddaughter. Now she chided herself for thinking of her own future while the last vestiges of life seemed to be slipping from her grandmother's weakening grasp.

Still . . . she had to face the fact that she would be left completely alone—probably penniless as well. Of course, there must be work she could do. She wondered if there was anything of value in the estate. But even as she framed the question, she chastised herself for thinking of money at a time like this.

Was what her father always said about her right after all—that she was callous and unfeeling? Yet as she thought about it she realized he had never actually said such things to her. But somehow she had always *felt* that he thought it—words or not.

Stephen Matheson never purposely hurt his daughter. Beyond losing his temper that one time, he had never so much as spanked her. Nor were his words ever harsh. It probably would have pained him to know how deep were the hurts in his daughter's heart as the result of his unintentional actions, and worse, his lack of action toward her. His attitude revealed itself in offhanded comments of which he undoubtedly remained completely unaware. He probably would have scarcely even remembered the piano recital, but the memory still stung painfully at Joanna's heart.

Her mother had been an accomplished pianist, which undoubtedly contributed to Stephen's encouraging the lessons for their daughter. If anything remained symbolic of the woman Stephen loved, it was her piano.

Joanna had practiced hard, wanting to surprise her father with her progress. For the recital Joanna chose "Three Waltzes" by Franz Schubert, a somewhat complicated piece for a nine-year-old, but she mastered it well. On that day she donned her prettiest dress of pink organdy and lace, tied a pink ribbon in her auburn hair, and went to get her father. He was sitting in his chair reading the newspaper, still dressed in his work clothes.

He had forgotten. She prodded him to his bedroom where he changed his clothes and together they went to the auditorium. Joanna was too excited to sense his reluctance. This was the first time in her life she had ever felt proud of herself.

She played the cheerful waltzes flawlessly. But her father's only comment was, "You should have heard your mother play Schubert. She could make his pieces sound like the very music of heaven!"

He had wept during the performance, but whether from sorrow for his wife or pride in his daughter no one—especially Joanna—would ever know. All she knew was that she had done her best and it hadn't been good enough. Still she fell short. The phantom of her mother had caused her to be rejected again.

Soon thereafter Joanna gave up the piano. But from that day onward she gave up more than music. She retreated ever deeper into her protective shell, building resentments she could not voice, insecurities she thought she deserved, guilt she could not understand.

3

A Captivating Stranger

❖

THE BLARING OF the *Queen's* horn jolted Joanna from her reverie.

She heaved a deep sigh and looked about. All remained the same as before her lapse into reminiscence, except for a small fishing vessel off the port side. That must have been the object of the great horn's signal.

How much time has passed? she wondered.

She ought to get back to the cabin to check on Mrs. Cupples. Her matronly employer and companion had mentioned taking a nap after coming on board. But she should peek in to see if she might be needed for anything.

Joanna turned and walked along the railing toward the stern of the ship. All about were excited travelers—many, she assumed, like herself, voyaging on the Atlantic for the first time. Some already occupied themselves with the classic shipboard activity of shuffleboard. Others lounged in folding wooden deckchairs, soaking up the warm sunshine and gentle May breezes, reading their favorite books and magazines.

Taking the long way back to the cabin in order to have a quick look at her new surroundings, Joanna continued toward the rear of the ship. She stopped and looked out behind her toward the land she was leaving. A great white wake widened into the distance, stretching as far as the eye could see.

"There's nothing more thrilling than setting out on a journey," said a masculine voice behind her. Joanna turned slightly, uncertain whether the comment was directed at her, nodded doubtfully, and returned her gaze to the sea.

"Don't you agree?" he persisted.

"Oh . . . oh yes, I suppose," Joanna halted, glancing toward him briefly, then diverting her skittish eyes toward the ocean.

"I've been on many cruises," the man continued, "and the thrill is always there. Is this your first?"

Joanna nodded again.

Her mood was far from conversational, but the handsome stranger could hardly help but draw her attention away from solitary reflections. Not particularly tall, his square, broad shoulders nevertheless gave the imposing appearance of towering above her own 5′6″ build. The impeccable gray, pin-striped suit covered a physique any girl would definitely look twice at. An elegant derby, angled perfectly atop his head, outlined the well-sculptured features. Below the brim showed neatly clipped black hair, distinguished with streaks of gray. But most conspicuous were the piercing jet-black eyes, striking in their intensity.

He flashed a disarming smile.

"I'm sorry to have intruded. I can see you have other things on your mind." He turned to go.

"Wait," faltered Joanna, "it's okay. I'm just . . . not very talkative."

"And you do have something on your mind?" he queried, with another good-natured grin.

"I suppose you're right. My life's rather . . . well, everything's uncertain right now and I can't help thinking about it."

"Anything you'd like to share with a stranger?"

Joanna said nothing but shifted her gaze once more to the open sea.

"No," she replied at length, with a sigh. "It will fit together in time—once I get there."

"Where's that?"

"Scotland."

"Is that so . . . ?"

"Yes—Aberdeen first."

"What a coincidence," he said with a calculated gleam in his eye. "Traveling alone?"

"Yes . . . well no, actually," she added. "I mean, I'm traveling with an older lady, as her maid and companion. But I scarcely know her."

Joanna squirmed under the investigating stranger's eyes. But she could hardly escape the charm of his apparent interest, and something inside her tingled with excitement. Her shyness, however, could never allow such a feeling to show. After all, she hardly knew this man. Yet she found herself wishing she had followed Mrs. Cupples's advice and worn her fashionable navy and white chemise and the dark blue felt hat adorned with its daring red feather. In this severe brown tweed suit she felt like an old schoolmarm!

Joanna's soft-spoken reserve, however, only added to her mystique. Though hardly a showy dance-floor beauty, she was certainly no schoolmarm. Her abundant auburn hair, now pulled back into a bun, could be positively alluring when allowed to drape over her shoulders. She gave her thick-lashed brown eyes and creamy soft skin little credit. And she would have considered her shapely figure far from perfect. Yet they were sufficient in themselves to draw most any man's interest, and would have done more than that had she given encourage-ment—which she never did.

Notwithstanding her restraint, Joanna's new shipboard acquaintance was not accustomed to waiting for opportunities to unfold; instead he created his own.

"I hope you don't think me too forward," the man said, "but I would like to introduce myself."

Somehow Joanna knew her consent was a mere formality which wouldn't alter his plans one way or the other.

Weakened under the discomfiture of his gaze, Joanna replied, "I . . . I don't know—I really should be getting back."

"I sense you are a young lady not given to talking with strangers. But I assure you I am respectable enough. The Captain will vouch for me. And I am hoping you will make an exception in my case."

He paused, removed his hat, and with a slight bow and smile, proceeded.

"I am Jason Channing. And I do hope I'll have the good fortune to see more of you on this voyage."

"Thank you, Mr. Channing," returned Joanna, summoning the courage to put aside her reticence for a moment and respond in the demure manner she knew was called for. "I am flattered."

She could feel the color rising in her cheeks.

"But I really must get to my cabin," she went on. "I left Mrs. Cupples there immediately after we boarded and haven't looked in on her since. Good day."

Joanna turned and walked briskly away, hoping to maintain her confident composure at least until she was around a corner and could relax. The probing eyes of Jason Channing followed her every move till she was out of sight.

Once in the cabin Joanna sat down on her bunk and exhaled a long sigh. Mrs. Cupples stirred from her nap, and Joanna spent the following hour attending to her needs as the two women acquainted themselves with their stateroom and made themselves as comfortable as possible in their limited surroundings.

About four o'clock in the afternoon a knock came on the cabin door. Joanna had dozed off momentarily. She started up, rose, and answered it. There stood the ship's steward.

"Are you Miss Matheson?"

"Yes." Joanna, still groggy from her brief nap, frowned in confusion.

"I've been asked to give you this," the steward said, handing a personalized card to Joanna.

She took it, reflecting that she hadn't given her name to anyone on the ship, and closed the door.

The card she held simply bore the name *Mr. Jason Channing*, printed in fine script. Turning it over she read the handwritten words: "I pray you will do me the honor of dining with me this evening at 7 p.m. I will be at the Captain's table."

It was unsigned.

4

Advances

"**P**LEASE," SAID JOANNA, "you're embarrassing me."

"Miss Matheson, surely I'm not the first to tell you how lovely you are?"

The pink that rose still higher in Joanna's cheeks was undoubtedly all the answer Jason Channing needed. But she felt compelled to make some response.

"Not quite like that." She smiled nervously.

"I didn't think the men in Chicago were so blind."

"I didn't often mingle. I'm not much of a social butterfly."

"Let me change all that."

Joanna looked down toward her plate and made a pretense of stabbing another chunk of the tender beef with her fork. But she was not hungry. For three successive nights she had accepted his dinner invitations. But tonight his compliments had progressed a bit further than she had anticipated, and certainly further, if they continued, than she knew how to handle comfortably.

He was not a man easily disregarded, nor were his blandishments easy to sidestep. His was, admittedly, a dashing personality. She liked him; indeed, it would have been extremely difficult not to be enchanted with his magnetic charm. No man had paid such attention to her before. Who was she to refuse the admirations of such a distinguished and handsome gentleman of the world?

Yet, why was such a man interested in her?

Jason Channing, for his part, had made a point of isolating Joanna the moment the voyage had begun. What had been calculated to come across as a chance meeting was in reality nothing of the kind. He had consulted with the Captain, as he always did prior to sailing, for a look at the passenger manifest. It was his custom to know what eligible, unattached young ladies would be aboard for his enjoyment. On this particular occasion Joanna fit the bill. He found her to his liking, invited her to dinner, and had been slowly moving in on her affections ever since. And at forty-one, Jason Channing—self-made millionaire, real estate developer, and entrepreneur—was a man whose plans eventually were fulfilled to his satisfaction. He was not in the habit of failing in anything he undertook.

"Miss Matheson," he said, "you've been drifting off again."

"I'm sorry."

"I was saying that I'd like to change that timid image you have of yourself. Come to London with me when we dock."

Joanna did her best to conceal her astonishment. Was this dubious proposal what it appeared?

"I . . . I really couldn't," she said in a wavering voice.

"Why not? This is the time to cast aside your sheltered past," Channing urged. "This is 1911; times are changing."

"I have plans . . . I must get there."

"Change your plans. What difference will a few days make?"

"But . . . aren't you going to Scotland too? Didn't you say that?" she asked.

"Only for a few days. I have some dreary business in a godforsaken little village. The people there are such bores, speaking a ridiculous dialect no one can understand. You'll never fit in there, Miss Matheson. London is where the life is. Piccadilly Circus, Buckingham Palace . . . perhaps I could even get you an audience with the King."

"The King of England!" exclaimed Joanna. "You don't really know him?"

"Well, actually," Channing laughed, "I've only met him once. But I have several contacts in high places. I think I could arrange some sort of an invitation from the royal family for my special lady-friend from the United States."

"I . . . I don't know, Mr. Channing." Joanna's head was spinning. "I suppose—"

"You must come, Miss Math—"

He stopped, reached across the table, and placed his hand gently on her arm. "—Joanna."

She looked away momentarily, then back toward him. Her uneasiness was clear to Channing's trained eye. It was not his first venture into such a situation. He derived a certain masculine pride in confronting inexperienced young women with daring overtures, even if he did cause them to squirm. "It's good for them," he rationalized. "They need to grow up and face the world eventually."

But even if Joanna were contemplating his offer, a decision was forestalled temporarily. She breathed a sigh of relief as a man approached, whispered briefly in Channing's ear, and then retreated as abruptly as he had come.

Channing rose, excused himself, and hastened away.

From her table near the edge of the outdoor dining area, Joanna looked out over the railing of the ship's deck. The rising moon cast a golden reflection on the surface of the calm sea. Hardly a breeze stirred, and Joanna felt as if she were on a South Sea island rather than a moving ship. Her midwestern origins had offered little exposure to the sea, and she had been apprehensive about the trip. But now she found she loved it.

Her thoughts strayed across the sea to the Scottish village that was her destination. She knew nothing about the place except that it was situated on the northern coast and that she made a vow to her grandmother that she would go there.

She glanced toward the interior of the dining room and saw Jason Channing returning. She had to refuse his invitation; even if Scotland were not tugging at her, how could she do such a thing? But she feared it would not be easy to turn him down. Had he not told her he always got what he wanted?

And now, it seemed, he wanted her!

Part of her wanted to shed the schoolgirl image, cast caution to the wind, and accept his offer.

Dare she?

He approached, conversing with another of his business associates, a short, balding man Joanna had seen before. Judging from Channing's gestures the discussion had grown heated. About ten feet away they stopped. Channing turned abruptly on his companion.

"Look, Ed. I don't care about all that!" he said sharply.

The short man retreated a step or two, his face twitching under the tongue-lashing of his superior.

Then in a measured tone, controlled, but stern with intensity, Channing went on: "You just get it done. Whatever you have to do—just get it done! If you're going to work for me, that's the only thing I care about. Do you understand?"

. He turned and made his way toward the table, broadly grinning. Behind him she saw the man he called Ed hesitate a moment, and then walk away slowly in the opposite direction.

As Channing sat down, the conversation resumed, but she could detect a smoldering glint of anger flickering in his eyes. "I should know better than to mix business with pleasure," he said.

"Is something wrong?" Joanna asked.

"No, not really. One in my position just has to be firm, that's all. But enough of that—let's get back to the pleasure."

Rising from his chair he walked around the table and took Joanna's hand. "Come with me, will you?"

She complied.

He led her to the ship's deck, then moved close beside her and slid his arm around her waist.

"Do you see that moon?"

Nervously Joanna nodded.

"Do you know what moonlight shimmering on the water represents?"

She remained silent.

"Romance, Joanna, romance! Come to London with me. Let me show you the city. It's time you free yourself to experience what life has to offer. It can be wonderful!"

Joanna could feel the heat rising in her neck and cheeks; even in the cool breeze she was perspiring.

He grasped her shoulders firmly, turned Joanna toward him, and gazed intently into her eyes.

"But . . . but what if I—"

"Refuse?" he said, completing the sentence for her.

"That's not what I was going to say . . . exactly."

"But it's what you meant, is it not?"

Joanna said nothing.

"I wouldn't like that, Joanna." He paused. "It would mean I'd have to work that much harder to convince you."

He drew her to him and kissed her full on the lips, once, then again, this time more fervently. His kisses were warm and intense, leaving her little room to respond.

Overwhelmed, she tensed and raised her hands to separate their bodies.

"Mr. Channing . . . please! Not here."

"Then come to my cabin."

"I couldn't. I'm not—"

She stopped and turned away, breathless. She couldn't bring herself to say she wasn't "that kind of girl." It seemed such an unsophisticated thing to say in the presence of someone so . . . so worldly and experienced. Would she ever meet another his equal?

He took her hands. "I'm sorry to appear forward, and to make you uncomfortable. But when I see something I like, I see no sense pretending otherwise. And, Joanna . . . you are so beautiful—"

"Please," she interrupted. "I just . . . don't know . . ."

Thoughts of her grandmother and the unclear mission before her tried to crowd into her mind, but they were dimmed in the immediacy of Jason Channing's powerful presence.

Then Joanna became again aware of his soft words whispering into her ear. She was once more in his arms, though she scarcely remembered him embracing her.

"I could make you so happy, Joanna, if only you'd let me."

He kissed her again, this time gently and tenderly.

Again she stiffened. "I . . . . I can't think right now . . . we have plenty of time . . . I should go . . ."

"The present is all the time anyone has, Joanna. There is no tomorrow."

His arms encircled her waist firmly. She felt her body crushed against his powerful torso as his lips moved against hers. Her head swam. But by degrees she relaxed and yielded to his passion. Even as she did her own desire mounted. She found herself returning his kisses with more emotion than she would have thought possible.

For a moment Joanna felt not at all like herself. Could she indeed be the sophisticated woman Jason deserved? But the thought lasted only a moment. When she heard voices in the distance, she stiffened and pulled away.

She managed a smile before retreating several steps, then turned and hastened down the deck toward her cabin.

When she arrived, to her great relief, Mrs. Cupples was sound asleep.

5

Clues from the Past

✠

JOANNA THREW HERSELF on the bed and fell to dreamy dozing. Someone cared for her! She had experienced little caring in her life. Asked if she was in love with Jason Channing, she would have hesitated in finding a response. But that couldn't change the fluttering in her heart.

Amid these thoughts, Joanna fell asleep, and in the dim phantoms that accompany light slumber, dreamed about Jason Channing throughout the night.

Dawn woke her.

She had all but decided to accompany Jason to London. What could a few days matter one way or the other?

Yet as she lay reflecting in the early morning hours, her mind continued to focus on her destination. A gray morning fog had settled in during the night, and as she peered through the tiny porthole Joanna found herself wondering if last night's interlude with Jason had been but the wild fancy of an active girlish imagination.

No! she corrected herself. *I am not about to lose this moment of happiness. Scotland or no Scotland, I will go to London!*

Why shouldn't she have a good time? She wanted to be shown the city. She wanted a man beside her—a man with experience, style, and gallantry. A man like Jason Channing!

Then her thoughts turned again toward that unknown northern coast of Scotland. How curious that a place she had hardly even heard of could suddenly loom so important. She simply could not rid herself of the deep gnawing urgency to press on immediately. Try as she might, Joanna could not get her grandmother's imploring words out of her mind. Whatever she was supposed to learn of her grandmother's family apparently had to be discovered before her death, if that was possible. Time was crucial!

Time. The word triggered such a deep response in her brain.

There was never enough when you needed it; too much when you didn't.

Time . . . time . . . time, she mused.

As her grandmother lay dying, Joanna had become so aware of time's pull. Constantly she was haunted by her careless squandering of the years she had had with her grandmother. And now it was too late. There was no time left. No time to build the relationship which had been so one-sided. She could not redeem the minutes and hours in the bond she had earlier neglected. As Joanna sat by the fading woman's bedside, she began to find within herself a capacity to love she had never known existed. Her grandmother's need drew her and made her forget all else. If only there was something she could *do* to demonstrate her love!

By the eighth day, her grandmother actually seemed a little improved. The rain had temporarily stopped and a thin beam of sunlight slanted across the room, brightening the woman's face. She gave Joanna a smile of recognition as her granddaughter sat down in the familiar chair. She reached toward the bedside table and awkwardly fumbled about. The exertion was clearly fatiguing, and Joanna stepped forward quickly to help.

"What do you need, Grandma?"

"My book," she answered.

The only book on the table was a black cloth-covered Bible. It was the hospital's, for when Joanna had brought a few of her grandmother's personal items from home she had not thought to bring the woman's old worn leather-bound Bible.

Once the book was in her hands, the grandmother opened it immediately. Her fingers turned the pages with difficulty but at last she appeared satisfied and handed the open book back to Joanna.

"Read . . ." the words formed soundlessly on her lips, but Joanna understood clearly enough.

She knew immediately the passage her grandmother had been seeking. There were four psalms on the page, but Joanna knew without question that she wanted to hear the 23rd. It had always been her favorite, and many times she had read it to Joanna, though the girl had usually listened with polite detachment.

"The Lord is my shepherd," Joanna began, "I shall not want. He maketh me to lie down in green pastures: he leadeth me beside still waters: He restoreth my soul: he leadeth me in the paths of righteousness for his name's sake. Yea, though I walk through the valley of the shadow of death—"

Suddenly Joanna's voice caught on the lump forming in her throat. Unexpected tears rose to her eyes; her lip quivered as she tried to continue.

But it was her grandmother's faltering voice that took up the words:

"—I will . . . fear . . . no evil. For thou . . . art with me . . ." Her voice trailed away. She seemed too tired to go on.

"Thy rod and thy staff they comfort me," Joanna went on, forcing out the remaining words past her emotion.

Did her grandmother genuinely not fear death? Did she truly believe God was with her?

How Joanna longed to ask her those questions! But she knew the woman had not strength to form the answers. How many opportunities she had once had to ask them. But no more. The realization heaped still more regrets upon her burdened shoulders.

By the time Joanna finished the psalm her grandmother was asleep. The rays of sunshine waned and deepened into evening shadows. Joanna knew she must leave before the streets were dark, but still she lingered.

After a while her grandmother's eyes opened once more. Immediately Joanna could tell something had changed in her countenance.

"Joanna," she said, ". . . mind clear . . . want to tell you the story."

Joanna leaned forward in her chair.

". . . it's there, do you understand? . . . yours now . . . in the house somewhere . . . the paper . . . I have to give you . . . just help me get up . . . important . . . my mother . . . the day I left . . . gave me . . ." She struggled to rise, then winced in pain and fell back again.

"No, Grandma," Joanna protested, "you mustn't. We'll find it another time, maybe tomorrow."

". . . find it . . . it's in the nursery . . . you must go there and find it . . . you must go *now!*"

"Go where, Grandma? What do you mean?"

"Strathy, child. You have to go . . . before it's too late, before they find out I'm gone . . . always caused so much grief . . . if only the land had belonged to the people instead of our corrupt family . . . I couldn't have it . . . didn't want . . . but you . . ."

"Grandma," urged Joanna, "calm yourself. We can talk about it again tomorrow."

". . . might not be a tomorrow. I'm dying, Joanna. It was mine, but I'm now passing it on to you . . . have to promise me you'll go—*now*. It's the only thing

I ask of you . . . mustn't wait for my funeral. I've neglected it too long . . . I love—"

She stopped, choking back the tears.

"—haven't even said the name in years . . . Oh, Lord, have I neglected what you gave me? . . . how I loved Stonewycke! Now you must take my place . . . must go back and find it. *It's yours now* . . . want you to have it. I'm not rambling. My mind is clear. Promise me, Joanna. You must *promise* me you'll go!"

"All right, Grandma, I promise."

"Promise me you'll go. Before I die I need to know you'll have what is yours . . . who knows what my brother has done? . . . should be yours . . . *you must go now!* Don't wait for me to die. You are my only hope, Joanna. Remember your promise. You must go *now!*"

Further words failed her and she fell back against the pillow, exhausted.

When she spoke again after several minutes of silence, the lucid quality had departed from her voice. Instead she sounded weak, worn, as if now that she had spoken her last urgent message she could relax and let death take her.

". . . wind the music box, Mommy . . ." she murmured in a childish voice. "Such a pretty melody . . ."

"Yes, it is," replied Joanna softly, not knowing whether to speak or keep silent.

". . . doesn't matter anymore . . ." said her grandmother, again with her normal voice. "Won't be much longer . . . the paper . . . Strathy . . . my mother . . ."

"Oh, Grandma," Joanna sighed painfully.

"The nursery, Joanna . . . *it's all there* . . . won't be long before I'll see *his* face again!"

She closed her eyes with a radiant smile on her lips, and fell back into silence.

Joanna took her hand, held it tenderly, and stroked the soft, white skin. The hand felt so lifeless, thought Joanna. Yet it too had once been young and supple like hers. Soon her grandmother was sleeping soundly. Joanna sat by the bedside another thirty minutes, gazing on the tranquil face that lay barely breathing, cradling the warm, thin hand in hers. At length she laid the bony hand across her grandmother's body. She rose quietly and left the hospital.

The following morning Joanna arrived at the hospital to find that her grandmother had slipped into a coma.

"I'm afraid there's nothing we can do," the doctor told her, "other than wait . . . and pray."

"Wait for what?" asked Joanna.

"As I explained," the doctor began, then hesitated. "You must understand, Miss Matheson . . . her injuries were just too severe. It's only a matter of time . . ."

"Before she dies," said Joanna, completing the doctor's unspoken words. Tears welled up in her eyes.

"Yes, I'm afraid that's it."

"And there's no chance of recovery."

"None whatever that I can see. Of course there are isolated cases on record . . . and who can say what the Lord might choose to do? But medically, no. I see no possibility of recovery." As he spoke he led Joanna to some chairs in a small waiting room.

"You spoke to the nurse of her urgent plea for you to go to her homeland?" he went on.

Joanna nodded.

"I see no reason why you shouldn't fulfill that wish. Who knows what might come of it—for her sake and for yours. This thing may draw out interminably, and you have your own life. I will keep you informed of her condition. And if the inevitable happens . . . well, at least you can know you were fulfilling her final wish."

Joanna was silent. Her grandmother's words of the day before came back to her. She had hardly understood anything she had said. There could be no doubt that her voice had stressed the urgency of Joanna acting quickly. Yet how could she leave her grandmother, knowing she might die any day? On the other hand, if she was in fact dying, her one last wish was that Joanna go to the place called Strathy immediately, not even waiting for the release of death.

". . . no chance of recovery." The words rang in Joanna's ears. What good would it do for her to wait at her grandmother's bedside if by doing so she neglected the woman's last appeal to the only living relative she had left?

And what if, despite all the doctor had said, she did somehow miraculously recover? Would it still not then have been best for her to go, for her grandmother's sake?

"I promise, Grandma." Joanna's words came back into her mind. She had spoken them with no inkling of what they truly meant, merely to satisfy her grandmother's imploring entreaties. Yet now all at once the words took on solemn implications. She had committed herself to fulfill her grandmother's final desire, perhaps her deathbed wish. How could she not honor it? And if she waited until her grandmother was actually gone, then it might be too late. The nature of the urgency she could not imagine. But there must have been something her grandmother had left undone that she was now depending on Joanna to set right—something which she might not be able to rectify if she waited too long.

That evening, still full of conflicting thoughts about what to do, Joanna entered her grandmother's room. She had not done so since her arrival from Chicago, and now a shiver ran through her body. How cold and lifeless it seemed! There was no spirit left; only possessions. She opened the closet door. There hung clothes which had once held meaning. Now they seemed ghostlike. With a sigh Joanna closed it. She walked to the window. The rain had stopped and the sun was making an effort to shine. But the room remained dreary.

Against the far wall, opposite the window, stood an ancient oak secretary. Joanna could never recall a time it wasn't there, a mute reminder of the past. There it had been, for years.

She walked toward it. The fine oak surface was engraved with intertwining carvings of leaves and primroses. Never as a young girl in her grandmother's home would she have dreamed of opening it. In fact, she could never recall seeing anyone open it.

Now, alone in the chamber where its owner had lived for so many years, Joanna approached, then reached out to run her hand along the smooth texture of its polished oak finish. What a beautiful piece of furniture! What secrets it could tell!

With reverence she rolled up the top and peered inside. A dozen or more small drawers and compartments met her gaze. Opening several at random she found the usual hodge-podge of bills, receipts, stationery, pencils, pens, article clippings, rubber bands, thread, needles, paper, envelopes—years of accumulated miscellany.

To the right beneath the roll-top were four larger drawers. Joanna worked her way from top to bottom, opening drawer after drawer and sifting through a similar assortment of an old lady's collection. Reaching the bottom drawer, she gave it a tug. Locked! The only locked drawer in the entire secretary!

Hadn't she run across a key somewhere already?

Her curiosity piqued, she retraced her steps through the drawers once again till she came to a tiny compartment, one of several of the same size, in the upper-left section of the desk area.

Now she remembered.

The drawer had been empty, and she had inadvertently pulled it all the way out of its frame. And there, attached to the back of the drawer, where it never would have been visible, was a very old-fashioned key.

Hastily she loosened it and inserted it into the keyhole of the locked bottom drawer.

It opened.

Joanna trembled with excitement and awe.

She knelt on the floor and gazed with wonder at the contents. Here was an altogether different collection of possessions. Unlike the other compartments in the secretary, in this drawer every item was packed carefully. Catching her eye first was a very old, hand-carved music box, small enough to fit in the palm of her hand. How lovely it was! With great care Joanna lifted it out, wound it, and set it down on the wooden floor beside her. In ancient, crisp metallic tones it played Brahms' lullaby, perhaps for the first time in countless years. The nostalgic strains sent Joanna into a reverie lasting several moments; the simple melody repeated itself over and over in an ever-diminishing tempo.

Was this the music box her grandmother had been mumbling about the day before she lapsed into a coma? It must have been a childhood heirloom of her own.

As its resonant sounds wound down, Joanna came to herself. She next lifted out two oval-shaped pictures from the drawer. They were considerably faded, but the likeness of a man and woman remained clearly discernible. The man was adorned in full Scottish dress: tartan kilt with small leather sporran in front, broadsword gleaming to one side, a great brass shoulder-brooch, high stockings, leather brogues, and round bonnet to match the kilt. The woman's dress was exquisitely old-fashioned, high-necked, reaching to the floor, and fully laced all around. If she could but see the colors!

Were these her grandmother's parents? Her own great-grandparents? Joanna's pulse quickened as a thrill surged through her spine.

Hastily she removed from her neck the locket her grandmother had given her. She had scarcely found time to examine the faces in it. But now as she looked—no, they could not be the same persons as the two miniatures she had just discovered in the drawer. But there could hardly be a doubt that the one face in the locket was her grandmother, though it was small and faded. Who was the young man in the other picture? Joanna had not a clue.

Returning to her task, Joanna came upon an aged packet of heavy brown paper. Slowly she opened it. Several official-looking documents were inside. Though well preserved for their age, she could nevertheless decipher nothing of their meaning; the old script appeared to be in another language. On one of the documents, however, she could clearly make out the name of a certain town—a "Port Strathy" in the county of Banff, Scotland. As her eyes strayed further, a single date leapt off the page—1784. Her mind reeled momentarily. This paper was almost a hundred and thirty years old! Examining it further she could just make out what appeared to be the single surname—Ramsey.

Immediately Joanna's thoughts turned to her grandmother, about whose past she knew so little. Why had she always kept her background so veiled? Were these the papers she had been talking about yesterday?

Eyes straining from the effort, Joanna refolded the papers, carefully laid them back into their pouch, and reached down to the last of her grandmother's personal treasures that she had hidden in this most private and cherished vault. There lay a folded piece of fine linen, no larger than fourteen by ten inches. Joanna opened it and gazed in amazement on a finely embroidered sampler displaying four generations of a family tree. Though obviously stitched by a young girl, it had been sewn with care and tolerable precision. Along the top the name *Ramsey* had been stitched in flowery old English script. A colorful band of primroses and forget-me-nots bordered the linen, and all the names for four generations were carefully worked into a pyramid design.

Names . . . they seemed to shout out at her. But what stood out most blatantly was a blank spot where a name had been torn out. The fabric had faded slightly around where the letters had been, but she could still make out the vague outline of the single name—*Margaret Isabel Duncan.*

With a knot rising in her throat Joanna recalled that day not so many years earlier when her grandmother had tried to interest her in embroidering a sampler and she had thrown it down in frustration. This was no doubt the very cloth she had mentioned that day.

A tear fell from Joanna's eye as she sat gazing upon her own genealogy preserved by her own grandmother as a young girl—a heritage she never knew existed until this very moment. She stroked the fabric gently, still exquisite after all these years. Then absently she rewound the music box.

As it repeated the haunting melody, Joanna sat fondling the linen, rocking back and forth, a child at heart once again. She had already forgotten the other items in the drawer. For this discovery transcended all else. Just seeing those names pierced her heart with a sense of belonging such as she'd never known, more permanent, more secure. Even if they were all dead, even though her own parents were dead, even though her only remaining relative—her grandmother—was now on the verge of death, somehow, she still belonged to a family. Though she knew nothing about them, she had roots.

She sat as one entranced, caught up in the dying tones of the lullaby. Her mind drifted back to those faraway days she had never known, to that Scotland she had never seen, to those people to whom she might belong.

From that moment of discovery in the secretary everything changed for Joanna. A purpose began growing deep inside, but its progress was so gradual that at first she did not realize it or understand it.

That night she slept fitfully, waking frequently, always with the impression of having left something undone. Once she arose to check all the doors to make sure they were locked. Another time she climbed out of bed and surveyed the kitchen to assure herself all was in order there.

Later, in one of her dozing dreams, a fragmentary vision of waves crashing against a rocky coastline came over her. Set back from the water's edge she could make out a small village with crude buildings of stone and brick sparkling in the sun.

When she awoke the following morning, without quite realizing it, Joanna had crossed an important threshold.

A decision had been made.

She could not even say she had actually made a decision. Rather, she sensed that one had been forced upon her by some power greater than herself. She knew she had to follow her past, wherever it led her. She had to find Port Strathy. She had to be faithful to the promise she had made. She had to honor her grandmother's wish.

She had to go to Scotland!

Telling her plans to one of her grandmother's friends, though it felt good to vocalize the decision, was far from encouraging.

"Do you have any idea how much it costs to sail to Europe?" the neighbor had asked.

"No," Joanna had replied. "But I'll get there. I'll find a way."

As it turned out, this same acquaintance opened the door. The aunt of a friend was traveling to Europe; because of poor health she had been in search of a companion—a maid, attendant, and friend all rolled into one. For a suitable person, she was prepared to pay the expenses of passage. Joanna could hardly believe her good fortune when Mrs. Cupples engaged her for the voyage.

And now, less than a month later, here she was, aboard the *Atlantic Queen*, on her way to Scotland, perilously close to falling in love with a millionaire. It all seemed like a fairy tale. Her grandmother still lay in a coma in the hospital, unchanged. Joanna only hoped whatever she was to find at the end of her journey would not come too late.

Joanna lay dreamily in her bunk and sighed. Two months ago she had no purpose in life, no goals other than to float along with whatever came her way, hardly caring what it was. Now, all that had changed—perhaps she had changed, too. Whatever happened, this trip was an adventure she would never forget.

6

The Storm

HOW QUICKLY THE sea could change!

The following morning the sky, once clear and blue, cast a gray pall over turbulent whitecaps. A heavy dampness hung in the air stirred only slightly by the warm breeze.

By midafternoon the temperature had dropped fifteen degrees and the wind had intensified as it swung around from the north. Great waves slapped against the huge white hulls of the ship. Toward evening the wind had grown to a full gale accompanied by a heavy downpour. The *Atlantic Queen* was more than up to the assault, but nonetheless the liner's great bulk found itself tossed by the wind and great swelling waves.

Joanna's stamina during the voyage surprised her. Not once during the trip had she felt even a twinge of seasickness. Mrs. Cupples, on the other hand, was not so fortunate. From the first moment of the storm she had grown ill and by evening had taken to bed.

For the next three days of the tempest, Joanna's hands were full running errands for her bedridden mistress—a bit of broth from the galley, some seltzer from the dining room, a concoction of ginger tea or a hot-water bottle from the dispensary.

Joanna did not see Jason Channing for a day and a half—although he had been in her thoughts. His invitation had been constantly on her mind. While attending to Mrs. Cupples's needs she had fantasized herself on his arm, in the midst of London's gayest society. She had almost convinced herself she was ready to lay aside her timid personality in favor of confidence, self-assurance, and charm. She would lure him and bedazzle him with her wit, her coy glances, her disarming smile. Yes, the time had come to step out of the backwoods. She was ready to become a woman—his London lady. She would find him, seek him out. She would tell him. Yes, she would go.

Scotland could wait a few days; her grandmother would understand.

On the afternoon of the storm's second day, Joanna found herself walking to the galley. Her slicker was dripping from traversing the port deck where the fierce wind blew in unhindered. Leaving the deck she entered a short corridor, shook off as much of the rain as possible, and headed through a set of double swinging doors into the dining room.

Quickly she scanned the sparsely populated room for Jason Channing's face. Unsuccessful, she turned her steps again toward the galley. All at once he stood right before her, in front of the door through which she had to pass, arms folded nonchalantly on his chest, head tilted to one side, eyes gleaming.

Starting, Joanna looked at him casually in a manner intended to communicate the self-confidence she was determined to muster.

"Why, Mr. Channing," she said in a measured tone, "what a surprise!"

"Mr. Channing, is it?" he answered with mock alarm. "I thought we had gone beyond that, Joanna." He flashed a knowing smile intended to convey what his words had left unsaid.

"I . . . I don't know what you mean," her voice faltered.

"Come now, Joanna." He stepped toward her and took her arm firmly in his own. Without a word he led her to an alcove just off the dining room.

He drew her toward him, slipped his arms around her waist, and kissed her several times, each kiss hungrier than the last. Finally he held her at arm's length.

"That's what I mean."

Joanna found herself too dazed to speak. For the past two days she had secretly looked for him with every errand. She had even worked herself into feeling bold and sophisticated. She had carefully orchestrated in her mind exactly how this meeting would take place. She would lead him on, force him to beg her to come to London. At the last moment she would accept. Then together they would disembark the ship.

But now her words caught helpless in her mouth. Her clammy hands trembled. She was nothing but a simple country girl after all. She had fooled no one but herself.

"I thought perhaps you had been avoiding me," Channing broke into the silence of her thoughts.

"N—no. I . . . I was," Joanna attempted awkwardly. "I mean, Mrs. Cupples has been sick. I've been nearly cabin bound. But I have . . . well, I've thought a lot about what you said."

"So, Joanna, have you decided to throw aside those old-fashioned values of yours and come with me? I believe, Joanna, that it's what you really want."

She looked away.

"Your first step," Channing continued, "will be London. I won't take no for an answer."

"Oh, Mr. Ch—, Jason," she said. "I would love to go to London with you."

She hesitated again, searching frantically in her mind for a reason, after all, to abandon logic and say yes. But at the last moment, uncertainty and fear overpowered her indecision.

"But, Jason," she said finally, "I . . . I just don't think I'm ready for that right now. Please understand. I would love . . . to be with you. But I can't—not now. My ticket is for Aberdeen. And something tells me I must go on without delay."

Joanna's voice trembled. She knew she sounded uncertain and hesitant.

". . . perhaps after I've been in Scotland a while I could arrange to come—"

"I may not be in London that long."

"You said you were coming north also," suggested Joanna.

"I don't know," replied Channing, whose voice suddenly seemed to grow cool.

"If we met later," said Joanna, "I . . . I—"

She struggled for words.

"I might be ready . . . then."

"As I said, I don't know. It may not be convenient then." Cool distance supplanted Channing's previous passion. "Now, Miss Matheson," he added, stepping back and offering a slight bow, "I must bid you good day. I have several people I must see this afternoon."

He turned and walked briskly down the corridor.

Joanna's eyes followed him.

Oh, Jason, she thought with a sigh, *I might be in love with you. But, I just don't know.*

She turned, walking toward the sheltered starboard side of the ship, went out to the railing, took a long breath of salt air, and looked out on the gray, stormy sea.

"Next stop, Aberdeen," she murmured as a gust of wind blew through her hair.

After several more moments, she turned and continued her errand to the galley.

7

MacDuff

THE LAST POTHOLE nearly jarred Joanna's teeth loose.

Unfortunately, the road wasn't getting better. The empty haywagon gave every evidence of searching out the largest, deepest, and muddiest holes before determining which direction to go. Then its steel-rimmed wheels bisected each with uncanny precision, sending its two occupants into the air and down again.

The unyielding, straight-backed wooden seats offered no cushion, and muddy water from the puddles splashed up freely.

"I'm thinkin' ye might ha' doon better waitin' fer Monday's schooner, mem," said the driver—a tall, gangly Scotsman about fifty years old. "Makin' the drive over wi' me two horses there an' a sweet-smellin' load o' cut hay ahin' me in the ol' wagon, 'tis a right comfy ride. The hay keeps the wagon settled doon a mite, ye know."

Joanna nodded as best she could between bumps.

"But," he went on, "the return's always tolerable tougher on me sore bottom an' bones, the wagon jostlin' up an' doon the way she do." His reddish-blonde hair revealed hardly a trace of gray, but life in the severe northern climate had weathered and wrinkled his pale, freckled face like a dried apple doll. His pale blue eyes seemed always to give the impression of looking through rather than at you, but his hands and muscular arms revealed a certain time-worn strength as they gently fingered the compliant leather reins and maneuvered the wagon down the rain-soaked road.

"I don't mind," said Joanna through clenched teeth, bracing herself for the next jolting bounce into the air. "I was fortunate to find you, Mr. MacDuff."

Joanna had arrived in Aberdeen on Tuesday. From there a coach bore her to Fenwick Harbor on Thursday, where her intention had been to catch the schooner sailing north around the coast to Inverness. It would have taken her to her destination just beyond Troup Head. However, once she learned of the schooner's scheduled two-day layover at Peterhead, not putting out again until Monday, and another stop at Fraserburgh, she considered her chance meeting with MacDuff fortuitous. He had assured her the overland drive would take only two days and that he could put her in the village a full three days ahead of the schooner. At the time it seemed the sensible thing to do. Of course, she hadn't foreseen the condition of the road.

"Ye jist missed the storm," MacDuff was saying. "'Twas a bad'n fer this time o' year. But we sometimes get a late spring outburst tryin' t' sneak all the way t' June or July."

"Well, it's lovely now," said Joanna.

"Aye, 'tis that," beamed MacDuff, proud to hear the weather of his native land extolled by a foreigner.

The bright blue sky peered down upon them as a testimony to their praise. Great white puffs of clouds dotted the blue, but as decoration, with no threat in mind. The rain had washed the landscape clean, bringing every blade of grass and tree leaf into crisp, brilliant focus. Joanna thought she had never been so close to such beauty. She could not distinguish ash from oak, birch from pine, or larch from fir—her world had always been too closed for an appreciation of nature's splendor. But the woods and pasturelands, even the desolate moors through which they had to pass, all combined in her heart to give her the sensation: "This is what I came to Scotland to discover!"

She recognized the dainty faces of white, purple, red, yellow and blue primroses breaking through their rough shells among the country grasses. The sight of their delicate faces kindled the memory of her grandmother.

She was actually in Scotland! It still took awhile to sink in.

Then she pondered her purpose in coming here. *Grandma,* she thought, *this is as much for you as it is for me. If I can find your people, whoever and wherever they are, I will have fulfilled—*

Her thoughts came to an abrupt halt. She didn't know what she would have fulfilled exactly. Maybe that, too, was part of what she had to discover here in her grandmother's native land.

Another bump jarred her thoughts back to the present and to the sound of MacDuff's craggy voice.

"Ye'll no doobt find oor wee village a bit backward after all the big cities ye've traveled through. But 'tis a bonny place, all in all. Though maybe ye'll be thinkin' I'm a mite prejudiced, havin' lived there most o' my life. Ye must ha' thought I were from the wee toon up the coast bearin' my name. An' maybe my people had some association wi' the toon o' MacDuff way back, but 'tis beyon' my recollectin'."

He attempted to edge the horses around a small pond in the middle of the road, hitting two rough-edged potholes in the process.

But soon he resumed his irrepressible talk. "Canna see what would be in oor village t' bring a lass like yersel' clean from America. 'Course I dinna mean t' pry . . ."

"That's all right. Mr. MacDuff. My grandmother was from Scotland. I don't know much about her past. But she left to come to the United States when she was a young girl, and I have reason to believe she may have been from Port Strathy."

"Why don't ye ask her, mem?"

"Oh, I should have explained. She's had an accident and is now in a coma," said Joanna. "She's not expected to live."

"I'm sorry, mem."

"I never had the chance to find out more before . . . She didn't talk much about her early life."

"Hmm," muttered the driver. "So ye're comin' here t' find relatives," he went on, "t' settle her affairs . . . the will . . . an' so on—is that it?"

"No," Joanna laughed. "No . . . I'm here, I suppose, as a last favor to her. I promised her I would come. She seemed to think there was something for me to find or do here. But I don't really know. I guess I'm here for myself too, to discover what I can about my own heritage."

Joanna paused.

"Takes a heap o' money t' travel so far jist t' gaze at the countryside," said MacDuff in some astonishment. "Yer parents must ha' some bank account t' sen' ye all this way, mem."

"I'm sorry to disappoint you, Mr. MacDuff," Joanna said with a tender smile at the talkative man. "I really have nothing. I worked my way here on a ship and

I've only got enough money with me for a few weeks' lodging. After that, I have nothing. You see . . . my parents are both dead."

Rebuked by her response, MacDuff fell silent, staring at the road that wound ahead of them as far as the eye could see.

"And who knows?" resumed Joanna, "I may still have some relatives living in the area. I suppose down deep, that's what I'd like to discover, Mr. MacDuff. That would make the trip worthwhile. Be it a twelfth cousin or what," Joanna sighed at the thought that she had for the first time put into words. "And perhaps if it's not too late, it might still help her."

"Weel," the old man said, falling back into his talkative mood. "Ye're comin' at a gran' time. Big doin's up oor way these days. 'Tis lookin' as if some real prosperity is comin' t' oor toon."

"What's the cause of it all, Mr. MacDuff?"

"Weel, the laird died na too lang ago, an' since there be no heirs, the estate's t' be sold. Talk has it that some o' the proceeds from the sale will be put right back int' the toon an' the surroundin' crofts. Maybe even some outright cash fer the tenants. Mind ye, the laird weren't so ill a man, as lairds go. But this weren't his regular home, an' well, it seems he let things go a bit o'er much."

MacDuff paused while he coaxed his horses over a particularly tricky stretch of road. After a time he resumed.

"Ye'll be seein' yer first Scottish gloamin' no doobt, Miss Matheson," said MacDuff as the sun lowered toward the horizon.

"Gloamin'?" asked Joanna.

"This far up north, mem, late in the summer, the sunset lasts all the night long. Jist goes right over t' sunrise it does."

"It must be beautiful!"

"Aye, it is, mem. Pink sky all the night long. An' we call oor long summer sunsets the gloamin'."

"Will I see it tonight?" Joanna asked.

"We'll have the gloamin' all right. But it'll be gettin' prettier later in the summer."

MacDuff explained they would spend the night at an inn in a little hamlet called Northhaven. He judged they would complete their trip by midday tomorrow.

At that point the wagon collided with another pothole, sending MacDuff's hat flying into the wagonbed behind him.

"These roads aren't nothin' t' brag aboot, as ye can see, mem," MacDuff said. "That's why most folks, travelin' folks like yersel', mem, prefer the sea roads."

"Perhaps some of the funds from the laird's estate should go for road improvements," said Joanna.

"Aye," said MacDuff. "They should put ye in charge o' the estate, mem!" He laughed good-naturedly.

8
Port Strathy

✣

THE FOLLOWING MORNING dawned fresh and crisp with a lingering chill of the spring just past. The wagon proved even more uncomfortable as Joanna climbed aboard, rubbing her sore hindquarters, hoping somehow the road would be smoother today. But her spirits remained undaunted; her destination now lay close at hand. As she looked around, the frost clinging to the grass reminded her that she should have been cold. But instead she tingled with the warmth of anticipation.

"A tip top mornin', 'tisn't it, mem?" said MacDuff as he hitched up the horses.

"It couldn't be lovelier!"

"Aye, 'tis a gran' day t' climb Strathy summit t' look oot on the sea."

As they settled into the ride the sun gradually thawed the frozen earth and by midmorning had blanketed the surrounding countryside in sunny brilliance.

The terrain grew increasingly rocky and woodsy, with trees coming up to the road on both sides as the pastureland ceased. Hardly noticing the difference—it had come about so slowly—Joanna was surprised when her guide pointed out to her:

"If ye'll look behin' ye a bit, mem," he said, "ye'll see we've climbed a considerable height."

Turning around, Joanna was startled.

"Why, Mr. MacDuff, I had hardly noticed! But you're right, the road is definitely dropping off behind us, for as far as I can see it."

Joanna took everything in with a flush of excitement.

"She said she loved it," Joanna murmured aloud, "and now I see why . . ."

"Mem?"

Embarrassed that she had been caught voicing her thoughts aloud, Joanna blushed, then stammered out a quick explanation. "I—I was thinking of my grandmother."

"There is somethin' mighty special aboot yer own kinfolk," he replied. "Ye say she was from aroun' here?"

"I'm reasonably certain she may have been."

"How long's it been since she left?"

"I'm not sure," Joanna replied.

"Hmm," he mused, ". . . ye say yer name was Matheson?"

Joanna nodded.

"Can't say as I recall any Mathesons from these parts," he said after he had brooded on the name for a moment, "'cept it be the dry-goods Mathesons down in Aberchider . . ."

"Matheson was my father's name, not hers."

"An' what was her name, then?" asked MacDuff.

"Margaret Duncan."

"Duncan!" exclaimed MacDuff, making an attempt at a whistle. He paused, then—in a noticeably subdued voice—said, "*The* Duncans?"

"You've heard of them?" asked Joanna, momentarily oblivious to the bumps in the road.

"Who hasn't, bein' the laird o' the land an' all? But who am I t' be tellin' ye aboot that?" he replied, in which seemed to be a cooler tone.

"I know nothing about my grandmother's family, if these Duncans you're talking about should be the same Duncans at all."

"Then ye were na comin' fer the funeral?"

"Funeral? I . . . I don't understand?"

"The laird's, like I were tellin' ye aboot, mem. Guess it matters little noo, since ye missed it. The buryin's lang since come an' gone. An' meanin' no disrespec', mem, an' everyone's sore distressed aboot it. But 'twill no doobt turn oot best fer the toon."

"Because of the sale of the estate?"

"Jist like I said, yesterday, mem. Jist how are ye related, mem?"

"I don't even know that I am," replied Joanna. "I'm sure it's just a coincidence of names."

"Could be . . ." MacDuff ruminated softly. "Could be . . ." He said not another word for some time.

Joanna also grew pensive and silent. What had caused the silence of the loquacious man, Joanna could not tell, and she was reticent to ask. For the first time, she began to wonder if this whole thing had been a mistake.

Joanna turned her attention once more to the countryside and at length commented, "We're still climbing, aren't we, Mr. MacDuff?"

"Aye, fer jist a couple furlongs more, mem," he replied, seeming his old self again. "We're almost t' Strathy Summit. An altogether peculiar name fer a mountain."

"Why do you say that?"

"Why, 'tis a complete contradiction o' terms. *Strathy* means valley, mem. Hoo can ye ha' a valley summit?" He chuckled at his wit.

"How did it come to get such a name, Mr. MacDuff?"

"I suppose the toon got its name first. Since this here's the way int' it, more than's likely the first folks must o' climbed this mountain, come doon the other side int' the valley—that's where the toon is noo, mem—an' called the place Strathy. Then someone later must o' named this mountain after the toon. 'Tis all I can figure."

"I'm sure you're right. That makes all the sense in the world."

After a few minutes more, the wagon rounded a curve, cresting the summit, and Joanna suddenly caught sight of the sea in the distance, far below them. It lay spread out like a radiant sapphire, at the end of a vast green carpet of trees descending from the peak of the hill, down to a hundred feet above the water's surface. There the sea lay spread out at the foot of a sheer rocky cliff.

Joanna jumped up in the wagon, excitedly straining for a better look.

"Oh, Mr. MacDuff . . . it's absolutely beautiful!" she exclaimed.

"Aye, mem, an' so are ye yersel', an' I dinna want t' lose ye jist yet. So take it easy an' hold yersel' in the wagon. 'Tis a steeper climb doon the fellside, an' then a narrow road doon the edge o' it t' toon. Ye'll ha' time t' see it all."

Joanna resumed her seat but kept her eyes riveted on the coastline, though the trees continued dense and frustrated her view.

As they wound down the hill the trees began to thin until the wagon emerged at the top of the great cliff.

"What's that?" Joanna asked, pointing toward a huge protruding rock that came into sight. "Is it an island?"

"'Tis Ramsey Head. An' no, mem, 'tis no island."

"It looks like a small mountain. You mean it's connected to the shore?"

"Aye. But too rocky an' steep t' do folks much good, though some take the path up it noo an' then. From the top ye can see Strathy Harbor clear as a bell. I'm guessin' the Head's mainly there jist t' let the sea-fearin' folk know Port Strathy's aroun' the next bend."

Joanna wished she were one of the graceful gulls so abundant about the Head—she wanted to fly from the wagon, off the cliff's edge, to the huge rock bearing the Ramsey name. The moment MacDuff had said the word a thrill had surged through her; she instantly remembered it from the embroidered sampler she had discovered among her grandmother's things. She kept her thoughts silent, however. At the first mention of her grandmother's name she had detected a curious change in MacDuff's bearing. She did not want to bring up anything more just yet.

Keeping her seat, Joanna was disappointed to find the road veering away from the cliff, leaving the sea momentarily, as they began the descent down into the village.

Her disappointment was short-lived, however, for almost immediately she spied on their left the first sign of habitation since leaving Northhaven that morning. A small hut with thatched roof was nestled snugly in a grove of tall firs. So thoroughly did the tiny cottage blend into its surroundings that Joanna would have missed it altogether had it not been for the bright red flannels hanging from a tree branch in front.

As the wagon rumbled past, a stone skittered across the road behind them, striking a tree to their right.

"'Tis Mackinaw's place," explained MacDuff, reining the team to a stop. "Likes his privacy . . . an' his red underwear."

"Why would he build his house so near the road then?" asked Joanna turning to get a better look at the ancient hut.

"'Tweren't no road here when that hoose were built, mem." Then over his shoulder MacDuff's voice rose to a shout: "Look here, Stevie, dinna ye go bein' so unsociable!"

"I meant nae harm," yelled back a voice as ancient as the house. No face appeared. "Jist wantin' t' see wha b' trouncin' 'pon my yard!"

"Got a visitor all the way from America!" returned MacDuff. Then when no response was forthcoming, he turned to Joanna. "Dinna be mindin' him," he said. "'Tis really a friendly place, Strathy is. Ye'll soon see fer yersel'."

It was hardly the sort of reception Joanna had anticipated. But every place must have its eccentrics, she told herself.

As the wagon moved on past the hut, Joanna was unable to see the cavernous eyes peering out from a crack in the shutters at MacDuff's retreating wagon. Nor did she hear the faint whistle emitting from the wrinkled lips. She had no way of knowing that Stevie Mackinaw, for all his advanced years, remained sharp as ever and never missed his mark unless it was his intention.

At increased intervals cottages and houses came into view along the roadside. Not all were as old as Mackinaw's, but most were small and impoverished. In some yards chickens scratched about; others displayed a pig, a goat or two, with here and there a family cow. The seeming poverty of the place, however, was offset by lovely attempts at gardens. Bright nasturtiums and daisies, along with climbing vines of morning glories, bedecked many a porch. Bushes of rhododendron and azaleas, alive with springtime, appeared around nearly every corner. And each house, it seemed, had its own private little crop of primroses.

A woman dressed in a simple flowered house-frock stepped onto her porch, shaded her eyes from the sun with a hard-working hand, and waved. Her wide, unassuming smile eased Joanna's heart, and she returned the greeting.

"Mornin' t' ye, MacDuff," the buxom young woman called out, but her friendly eyes rested instead on Joanna.

"Mornin', Mistress Creary," shouted MacDuff in return. "I've brought a visitor t' oor fair village all the way from America!" he went on, giving every indication that he had personally conveyed Joanna the full five thousand miles.

"Welcome t' ye!" Mrs. Creary called out to Joanna as the wagon passed.

"Thank you," replied Joanna, noticing two smudge-faced little children peeking out from behind the woman's full-length working dress. Joanna could not help laughing.

As the wagon continued down the widening lane, other curious folk—mostly good-natured women—peered out from their houses, while a few stepped boldly out to offer their friendly welcomes and exchange a greeting or two with MacDuff and his passenger.

Before long the houses bunched together and the badly pitted country road grew into a tolerably smooth lane winding its way through the small town toward the water sparkling two hundred yards away. The smells of salt, sea, and fish mingled together to tell Joanna she had finally arrived.

"Does the road take us right to the water's edge?" Joanna asked in delight.

"The Bluster 'N Blow is next t' the wharf," MacDuff replied. "Ye'll ha' yer fill o' the water soon enough, I'll warrant!"

"The Bluster 'N Blow?" inquired Joanna, ignoring for now the rest of MacDuff's words—she could never have enough of the sea.

Visions of waking to the crashing of the waves and the shrill squeals of gulls filled her heart with anticipation.

"The inn. 'Tis where ye said ye'd be stayin', 'tis it not?"

"Oh yes," Joanna nodded. "I didn't know the name."

"'Tis the only one in toon, regardless. 'Tis where all the visitors t' Strathy stay—when we ha' 'em."

9

Local Speculations

"WEEL, MACDUFF, ARE ye goin' t' stay tight-lipped ferever, man?"

"Can't a man ha' a bit o' drink in peace?" MacDuff put his hand to his mug of ale and proceeded to lift it to his mouth, but Rob Peters' large hand reached across the thick oak table and restrained him.

"Not every day this town o' oors sees someone all the way from America," Rob persisted.

"Come, MacDuff," put in another of the men at the table, who had emptied his first two tumblers of the strong local brew rather too quickly and whose head was growing hotter by the minute. "No more o' yer cat-an'-mouse games wi' us! Oot wi't or we'll drag't oot o' ye!"

"I ain't a man given t' gossip."

A ripple of laughter through the group indicated they knew MacDuff only too well.

"'Tis only gossip when womenfolk do it," returned Peters. "What we're doin' here's discussin' the welfare o' oor town." Rob could not keep back the hint of a mischievous grin around the corners of his mouth even as he said the words.

"My wife says she's some awful bonnie—though a mite on the scrawny side," offered Douglas Creary.

"Weel, MacDuff," put in several in unison. "Oot wi' it!"

MacDuff freed his hand from Peter's grasp and slowly lifted the frothy mug to his lips, leaving a foamy remnant on his overgrown moustache. He well knew he would reveal all he knew to the small gathering of friends in the Bluster 'N Blow's common room. But he rather enjoyed being the center of attention and desired to stretch the moment out as long as possible. Thus his delays and shadowy allusions to knowing more than the others achieved their maximum design. He took two long swallows of the strong Scottish beer.

"'Tis a top-notch ale ye ha' oot today, Sandy." MacDuff savored another slow draught.

"Ay . . . top-notch!" MacDuff continued. "Fittin' fer such an important day. 'Course, I expec' such a highborn lass would be goin' fer nothin' so ordinary as what we commonfolk be drinkin'."

"What d'ye mean, highborn?" came a chorus of voices at once.

MacDuff had his friends exactly where he wanted them.

"'Tis only speculation, o' course," he said solemnly, leaning forward in his stiff-backed chair and lowering his voice perceptibly; "—not likely t' be true," he added. "But it do make a body think."

"What are ye talkin' aboot?" snapped Peters, beginning to think the news might not be worth the frustration of drawing it out of one so coy as his friend.

"The lass says she's a Duncan." MacDuff at last dropped the full weight of his revelation into the midst of his companions, then folded his arms and rocked back on his chair as if to say, "Noo . . . wasn't that tidbit o' news worth the wait!"

The various reactions around the small gathering ranged from astonishment to disbelief. This same group of men drank ale, played cards, regaled one another with stories (the truth or falsehood of which was rarely important to their full enjoyment), and shared the latest town gossip (which they steadfastly insisted was *news*) every Saturday evening in Port Strathy's only establishment of its kind. But rarely had there been much of note to report until the laird's death had stirred up the nest of speculation about the town's future. Coming on its heels, this latest piece of information was fraught with possibilities for discussion.

"Her name's Matheson," said Sandy Cobden, the innkeeper, firmly. "Got it written in my register clear as day."

"What says ye t' that, MacDuff!" laughed Creary.

The conversation would undoubtedly have continued on in this vein for some time, growing ever further afield in its range of individual conjectures, had not the object of their discussion at that moment made an appearance. MacDuff opened his mouth to speak once more, but stopped the moment he heard a creaking on the stairs above him.

All heads turned to see Joanna walking slowly down, seeming to test each one of the rickety steps with her toe before easing her weight fully onto it.

Sandy jumped from his place at the table and hastened over to her as she descended.

"Evenin', mem," he said. "Trust ye had a pleasant rest in yer room. Bed weren't too hard?"

Joanna shook her head. "No," she said. "The room is fine."

"I hope it'll be warm enough fer ye."

"I'm sure everything will be perfect."

As she spoke, Joanna tried to conceal the awkwardness she felt from the hush that had come over the room. Leaving her room she had heard sounds of friendly conversation from below. Now, however, the common room had grown still as a tomb. Without looking up she instinctively knew all eyes were turned upon her.

"Ye'll be wantin' some supper," Sandy continued. "Come o'er here an' set yersel' doon."

"Just something simple will be fine," said Joanna with a smile. "I'm still rather tired and would like to retire again to my room early tonight."

The innkeeper led her to a table on the opposite side of the room. She sat down while he bustled off toward the kitchen. Joanna fidgeted uneasily on the hard wooden seat while the conversation between the men across the room resumed by degrees into other channels of talk. When the eyes of one would glance Joanna's way, she would offer a smile and her greeting would be returned with a slight tip of the hat. The awkwardness gradually subsided, and the ale, stories, and "news" once again flowed freely.

After Cobden returned with a hearty loaf of brown bread, butter, a slab of sharp cheese, and a pot of steaming tea, Joanna began eating with the uncomfortable notion that each bite was being scrutinized by an anxious cook. At length she finished and, excusing herself, returned to her room.

The men removed their hats and said, "A good evenin' t' ye, mem."

Their conversation, however, never turned in her direction again.

The following morning Joanna once more descended the broad staircase. The previous evening's bright and cheerful fire had grown still, replaced by gay morning sunlight streaming through the windows. Already two of the tables were occupied with village folk come to the inn for breakfast. Sandy and his wife were both busily engaged in the kitchen and with their guests.

Joanna sat down. As she waited for her meal her eyes scanned the room, taking in more details than she had been aware of the day before. Coarse wooden furniture stood on bare wood floors in plain but homey surroundings. She noted with surprise that the only windows in the room were high on the wall, and none faced the sea.

"I'll have a fire goin' afore ye know it," said Sandy, entering with an armload of fresh wood. "'Tis the only warmth we get in here, an' I keep a few embers most days from the night before. But this time she went oot on me."

After a sound night's sleep, Joanna could hardly sit still long enough for breakfast. She was anxious to see the town, the sea, the shoreline, to explore her new surroundings. The Scotland of her ancestors beckoned her!

When she had arrived at the inn the previous afternoon, Sandy Cobden's plump, good-natured wife had led her to her room to settle in. Joanna planned to have a look around Port Strathy that very day. She had lain down on the bed, just for a moment. But the weeks of traveling had taken their toll. When she awoke, hours had passed, and a glance outside told her the "gloamin'" had come. There would be no walking about her new environs today. After arranging her few belongings, she had gone downstairs for her bread and cheese and then back to her room for the night.

Now as she sat watching the struggling fire take hold, Sandy Cobden appeared with a tray laden with two fresh biscuits, a pat of butter, a bowl of steaming oatmeal, and a small pitcher of fresh, local cream.

"I hope all is t' yer likin', mem," he said. "I'll bring ye some tea too, if ye like."

"It looks delicious, Mr. Cobden," said Joanna.

With that word of approval, the innkeeper made the rounds to his few other morning guests and then to the counter-bar where he began cleaning the tabletop, wiping glasses with the bottom of his apron, and straightening up. He was a large man, both in height and girth. One hardly expected such quick movements from such an oversized frame. But he worked quickly and gave the appearance of constant motion.

Joanna listened to the clinking of glasses and bottles, continuing to take in the scenes about her, until she had made a hearty inroad into her meal. Sitting near the counter, she looked toward Sandy still busily engaged in his work.

"Do you know any Duncans around Port Strathy?"

"Mem?"

"The Duncans—I'd like to go visit them, if there are any still around. Do you know where anyone by that name lives?"

Sandy set down the mug he had been wiping. "Weel, mem," he said, "the ol' laird died a month ago. 'Twould be him ye'd be asking aboot?"

"I heard about the laird," Joanna said. "But no, I'm just looking for anyone by that name, possibly not even in this laird's family at all. Surely there must be other Duncans about?"

"He were the last. The auld hoose be empty noo, 'cept fer the factor an' the hoosekeeper—an' o' course, auld Dorey. All the other servants been sent away."

"Perhaps I could go to the house and speak to one of them."

"The Duncan affairs'll soon be a closed book aroun' here, mem."

Were Cobden's words a mere statement, or was there a subtle warning in his cool tone? Whatever it was, Joanna recognized the same distance she had noticed when she mentioned her grandmother's name to MacDuff.

"I'm sure it is no concern of mine," Joanna assured him.

"Hmm," muttered Cobden, more to himself than to her, but with still a trace of hidden suspicion in his tone, as he returned to the glass he had been wiping.

"Could you direct me to their house?"

"*The* Hoose," the innkeeper corrected. " 'Tis up on the hill . . . *the* Hoose on the hill," he added.

"And which direction is—"

But just at that moment Mrs. Cobden appeared and called her husband to the kitchen.

With the words, "Best see what the missus wants," Cobden made a hasty retreat. But before he disappeared behind the kitchen door, he paused and said to Joanna, "Ye might enjoy yer day more if ye spent it lookin' at the fishin' boats, mem." Then he was gone.

Giving little thought to his parting words, Joanna rose and walked outside. In a town this size, it shouldn't be difficult finding "*the* House on the hill."

10

Olive Sinclair

✼

EXITING THE BLUSTER 'N Blow for her first thorough walk about Port Strathy, Joanna thought she had never seen a bluer sky. And the sea, only a hundred yards away, reflected a perfect match. Of course from the inn's name and the limited knowledge she possessed of the winter storms on Scotland's north shore, she knew today's calm must be the exception rather than the rule.

She walked slowly toward the harbor, practically outside her front door. Maybe she should follow Sandy's advice. All the boats were securely docked. But as picturesque as were the many varieties of large and small fishing vessels bobbing gently in the clear salt water, Joanna's mind remained occupied with other things.

She turned, crossed the street, and proceeded back the way she had come on the other side of the street. She had ridden this very way on MacDuff's wagon yesterday, but somehow she had missed so much. Today she was more immediately conscious of the shops and houses crammed tightly together, bordering the street on both sides.

This was clearly Port Strathy's chief region for commerce and activity. Joanna noticed a number of shops, old and a bit run-down, but nonetheless pleasant: a dry goods dealer, a chandlery, a cobbler's shop, and several others jumbled together in uneven profusion. Interspersed were houses, large and small. Not until she saw the shops were closed did Joanna realize that today was Sunday. That accounted for the relative sparseness of any crowd, although a number of people were about.

Reaching the end of the straight thoroughfare, a quarter mile inland from the water's edge, the street ended at a broad thoroughfare running at right angles in both directions. Arriving the previous day from the east, or left, today Joanna chose to follow the road—obviously intended as a highway through the small town for travelers moving along the coast—to the right.

Quickly she realized, however, that the town—whose nucleus clustered tightly around the precincts of the short street between the harbor and the intersection— soon came to an end. The houses became less numerous, shops disappeared, and in the distance Joanna saw farms and fields coming down to the road on her left. To the right of the road stretched sandy beach grasses down to the water's edge. A narrow beach, no wider than twenty or thirty yards, glistened with smooth, white sand. Some five or six hundred yards away the sand turned rocky, and gently waving grasses quickly gave way to a cliff shooting high in the air, bordering the small natural harbor to the west.

Taking in this scene at a glance, Joanna vowed to return to this magnificent stretch of coastline another time. Turning, she made her way back into the town, angled left at the intersection, crossed to the right of the street, and walked leisurely back toward the inn.

Church—which was situated about a half mile south of town—had by this time dispersed, and more and more of the townspeople were about. A barefoot boy ambled by carrying a crude handmade fishing pole and burlap bag, obviously heading for an afternoon's fishing from the pier. Two men clad in overalls sat chatting in front of one of the houses; they stopped as Joanna approached, tipped their hats as she passed, and then went on with their conversation in subdued tones.

Down the wooden sidewalk in front of her Joanna saw a stooped old woman, carrying a rather large basket, enter the market. Deciding that to be a logical place to obtain the information she sought, she increased her pace and followed the woman inside.

In the cluttered little room Joanna was inundated with a score of smells; the first two she was able to identify were dried fish and mint. On the counter stood a row of tempting glass jars full of peppermint sticks, gum drops, and several varieties of fish and beef jerky. All about the walls, stacked twelve feet high, stood shelf upon shelf of merchandise of every imaginable type—salt and flour, corn and wheat, seed, chemical fertilizers, kitchen utensils, bacon, and miscellaneous household adornments. A marvelous variety!

As Joanna stood staring about taking it all in, a voice interrupted her thoughts: "Be with you in a moment, dear!" it boomed.

Glancing up, Joanna spied a grayish-black head looming over the clutter on the counter. The shop's proprietor, a middle-aged woman of above average height, her face dominated by protruding eyes and a large roman nose, stood helping the elderly woman who had preceded Joanna into the shop.

"Thank you," replied Joanna. "I'm in no hurry."

When the other customer in the small establishment had completed her business and gone, Joanna stepped forward.

"Actually," said Joanna timidly, "I'm rather surprised to find you open today."

"I always open for a couple hours on Sunday afternoon," the lady said in an intimidating voice, loud enough to match her imposing stature. "The folks sometimes needs things and can't wait till the morrow, you know."

"Well, I'm glad you are," replied Joanna. "I'm new here and—"

"You'll be the lass from America, no doubt!" echoed the voice. "I'm Olive Sinclair."

She thrust out a large hand across the peppermint sticks and grasped Joanna's firmly. "Pleased to make your acquaintance at last. I knew I would sooner or later. Everyone ends up in here. Especially am I glad because seems like you're all a body's heard about these last two days. Like I say, everyone ends up here—and more so when there's news to spread."

A flush rose to Joanna's cheeks.

"I don't see why I've caused such a stir," she said.

"We don't get many visitors up our way, you see, miss. Was a Frenchman visiting the laird a few years back. 'Course, we common folk didn't see much of him. But you didn't come in my shop to listen to me ramble on, now did you? What can I do for you this bright day?"

"I don't mind listening," said Joanna. "But I was wondering if you could direct me to the Duncans' house?"

"You mean *the* House?"

"That's just what Mr. Cobden the innkeeper said. You both make it sound as if it's the only house in town."

"In a certain manner of speaking . . . sorry, Miss—Matheson, isn't it?" Olive Sinclair asked, casting Joanna an interrogative glance.

"Yes . . . Joanna. Joanna Matheson."

"Well, like I said, in a certain manner of speaking, Miss Matheson, Stonewycke Castle *is* the only house in town. Leastways, the most important. Been that way for over three hundred years."

Joanna's eyes widened in surprise. A small smile stole onto Miss Sinclair's thin lips as she realized how old that must seem to an American, especially as wide-eyed a young girl as now stood before her.

"'Tis a fine sight for travelers to see," Miss Sinclair offered. "The rare foreigner that came to our town was often given a tour of the place. But things'll no doubt be changing with the laird gone . . ." A hint of regret was obvious in her final words.

"Well, I hardly expected a tour," said Joanna, "only possibly to talk with some of the servants."

"Is it true what folks have been saying about you?"

Joanna tensed, wondering if she should keep her reasons for coming to herself. Yet she did not sense the same discordant tone in Miss Sinclair's voice as she had in others with whom she'd talked. Instead, there was a sincere friendliness. A certain warmth emanated from the loud and imposing woman.

"I don't really know. My grandmother is a Duncan. She wanted me to find her home. She's very ill. That's practically all I know."

Suddenly Miss Sinclair leaned over the counter, drew her alarming features close to Joanna's, and said, "If she was born here . . ."

She stopped abruptly, glanced around to make sure the shop was still empty, then went on in little more than a whisper, ". . . there could be no doubt she'd be related to the laird. The Duncans *is* Port Strathy, if you know what I mean. I never heard mention of any other family by that name in these parts. No, if you be a Duncan, dearie . . ." and here the animated shopkeeper simply let a long, low whistle complete her thought. Then she nodded her head with lips squeezed tightly together as if to add still more force to her unspoken conclusion.

"Well, dear, you go on to the house," she went on. "Who knows what may come of it. I'd take you there myself, but I can't leave the store. I left for a bit yesterday while Tom was cleaning up the back room for me and the place was a mess when I got back. I don't know how his wife puts up with him. I only thank the Lord He saw fit to endow me with brains instead of beauty. Leastways I don't have to worry about keeping a no account like that in tow."

"Where exactly is this . . . Stonewycke Castle?" Joanna asked, the name feeling awkward on her tongue.

"About a mile northeast of here. The road crosses the one you came in on—you can't miss it."

"Thank you so much for the directions," Joanna said, turning to leave.

"If I might just leave you with a bit of advice, before you go, dearie," the woman said, following her to the doorway. Then she motioned Joanna closer and lowered her voice again. "I suggest you keep all this about your grandmother, well . . . to yourself for a spell—at least till you know something for certain."

"But . . . why?"

"Folks are a mite touchy these days. Since the laird's death, you know. The old town's changing. New people coming in. Important folks from London, even the States. You're not the first. No. I'd just not stir anything up unnecessarily."

"That's not my intention. But how will I find anything out unless I ask questions?"

Joanna stopped. Suddenly her grandmother's words raced through her mind.

She turned and looked at Miss Sinclair standing at the door, then smiled. "Thank you, Miss Sinclair, for your advice. I'll try to do what you say. I know you mean well for me."

"Folks has to do what they have to do," she replied. "But take it from me. 'Tis best you walk warily for a while. And if you do make it up to the House on the hill, you'll be seeing old Walter Innes. He's the factor. Bit of a grouch at first. But he means no harm. He'll help you out."

11
The House

AFTER LEAVING THE main road into town, the approach to the estate wound its way through a moderately wooded, hilly country for perhaps three-quarters of a mile. Joanna crossed a stream on a rickety little wooden bridge, then came among some small hills covered with larches. Other hills displayed cultivated crops, and still others bore only bright yellow broom and the wiry heather shrubs which now held in secret their purple flame, waiting for the outburst of autumn. The avenue had been well-maintained and lacked the deep swampy ruts and broken stones of the road she had traveled with MacDuff.

Joanna strode down the middle of the road, sucking in the warm pure air and taking in the lovely sights. Dwarfed oak or mountain ash or silver birch occasionally extended down to the edge of the road. Then the trees gave way to green fields, fenced with walls of earth or stones overgrown with moss, stretching away on both sides, dotted with grazing black and white cattle.

With no sign of human life, the solitude at length began to grow eerie; Joanna began to wonder if she had mistaken Miss Sinclair's directions and taken a wrong turn. But just as she was about to reverse her course, the road turned sharply and a towering gray castle suddenly loomed in front of her. Caught off guard, Joanna realized that the imposing structure had been shielded from view by the particular approach taken by the road winding its way through a tight grove of trees. The still, sullen place was surrounded by woods, young and ancient firs interspersed with beeches.

A great iron gate stretched across the road before her, from which extended a thick, ten-foot-high hedge in both directions. Through the iron bars she saw a cobblestone courtyard immediately in front of the house. In the center stood a fountain with a rearing horse at the center, whose open mouth—presumably intended to greet guests with an impressive spray of water into the air—now stood empty and dry as a silent reminder that death had taken the head of the Duncan clan.

Joanna wavered a few moments before summoning the courage to lift the heavy iron latch of the gate, which appeared to be unlocked. She could not shake the feeling that she was an unwelcome interloper.

The latch creaked as she moved it upward in its unoiled slot. With a slight shove the gate swung open and Joanna stepped inside. Her steps were timorous as she walked toward the great carved door of the house. The place seemed possessed of another time, another world in which she had no part. She tried to conjure up visions in her mind of automobiles and factories to remind herself that this was indeed the twentieth century. But she felt like Alice entering some ethereal, fairy-tale realm.

A brass bell hung on one side of the door with a rope dangling from its center. Joanna reached up, hesitated momentarily, then pulled the rope.

The clanging of the bell echoed in her ears. She waited, scarcely breathing, wondering if perhaps some spectre from out of the past was going to open the door.

No one answered the bell.

She tugged at the rope again, but the sound so shattered the solitude that she stepped away from the door. Slowly she backed away, glanced around again, descended the three stone steps, and began walking timidly around the right side of the house in order to circumvent the ivy-covered stone walls.

After rounding a projection in one of the walls she came upon a grassy area extending from the house toward the hedge. It was so pleasant, like a miniature well-tended meadow, that for a moment she almost forgot the awesome castle on her other side. Neatly pruned azalea and rhododendron bushes bloomed with bright splashes of lavender and orange and vermilion. Rose bushes clung to the bleak stone of the house, and their red and pink buds heartened Joanna with a spirit of newness and hope.

In the distance beyond the lawn she spied a structure detached from the house, constructed of stone and wood. She continued walking toward it, wondering if she might find someone there. However, before she was halfway toward it, some movement among the roses caught her attention out of the corner of her eye. She turned sharply to see a man standing less than twenty feet from her. She had not noticed him because he had been kneeling down among the bushes. He was an elderly man, by appearances well into his sixties.

"Hello," she called. "Are you Mr. Innes?"

For a moment he did not reply, just stared toward her with a strange intensity in his eyes, as if he were trying to bring her into focus.

At length his voice uttered a single word. "No." The sound was toneless, as if it had come from far away.

After an awkward silence Joanna was about to walk closer, when from behind she heard the loud rumbling sound of an approaching vehicle, the first such sound she had heard since her arrival. The gardener's eyes rested on her with that same disconcerting hard gaze one instant more, then he turned and bounded away with more speed than she thought could be possible for a man of his years. But she had little time to ponder the brief encounter, for a new voice was already shouting out behind her.

"Ye dinna *look* like a common trespasser!"

Joanna spun around to see a tall, gaunt man, perhaps in his late forties, glaring at her as he climbed down from a plain, serviceable-looking automobile. Though her heart was pounding from his sharp words, her first thought was of Abraham Lincoln without a beard. The image was heightened by his dusty black frock coat and pin-stripe trousers. The man's small, close-set eyes were not altogether welcoming.

"Weel?" he said, coming fully out of the auto and stalking toward her. "Who give ye leave t' come aroun' here scarin' auld Dorey?"

"No one . . . I mean, I had no intention of trespassing," Joanna stammered, trying her best to conceal her uneasiness. "There didn't appear to be anyone about and . . . I came to visit, and—"

"Visit, ye say! Who would ye be comin' t' visit? I ken o' no invitations bein' sent out!"

"I wasn't invited. I only—"

"Then ye're trespassin'!"

"No—I mean . . . I didn't know I had to be invited. I only wanted to speak with the servants or the factor."

"What for?"

"I—I thought they might be able to tell me about the Duncans that used to live here. The laird's family. Or any other Duncans in the area."

"There are no others. An' the laird is dead," he returned, with more gruffness than sadness in his voice.

"I just thought—" Joanna began, then hesitated. She reflected on Olive Sinclair's parting words to her.

"I'd like to know more about him," she continued at length. "It's important."

"I'll be the judge o' that, mem. Jist what is yer business here, if I may ask?"

Joanna's only answer was silence. What did she dare say that would keep her from alienating everyone?

"Look here, mem," said the man, softening his tone almost imperceptibly, though not relaxing the force of his words. "I'm the factor here, an' anythin' that concerns Stonewycke concerns me. The place is mine t' take charge o'er, fer the time bein' at least."

"I understand," said Joanna, attempting a smile. Then she held out her hand. "I'm Joanna Matheson. I'm new here and I don't know the rules and customs yet."

"Name's Innes," replied the man, apparently touched by Joanna's admission yet unwilling to relax his tough stance and chilling gaze.

"If you're Mr. Innes, then perhaps you can help me. Miss Sinclair at the store recommended you."

"She did, did she?"

"You see, if you know the Duncan family, then . . ." Joanna hesitated, choosing her words carefully, "I'm trying to find out if there might be some common blood between these Duncans and myself. You see, my grand-mother—"

"So that's it!" Innes' eyes narrowed as he bristled once more. "Come t' see if ye can grab a piece o' the pie, no doobt! Weel, it won't work, young lady!"

"No . . . that's not it at all, Mr. Innes," insisted Joanna. "I don't know anything about the estate . . . or the laird . . . or any of that." A lump rose in her throat.

"It's entirely personal," she added, her lower lip quivering.

"Noo, dinna cry, lass," said the factor. The tears that had begun to gleam in Joanna's eyes seemed to support the truth of her claim to the surly Scotsman, and his former gruffness dissolved by degrees into an apologetic tenderness.

"It's jist that I heard o' some lass come from America makin' all kind o' claims. So naturally I thought ye be jist another o' the vultures come t' lay yer hands on the spoils o' death."

Through her tears, Joanna said in a soft voice, "I haven't made any claims at all. I came here never having heard of the laird."

"I dinna mean t' cause ye grief. I jist knowed what I been hearin' an' when I seen ye, an' seen poor Dorey runnin' off like that, weel, I was naturally on my guard."

"But I mean no harm."

"Weel, I have a job t' do here. This muckle hoose 'tis kind o' like my responsibility noo. I already failed him once. An' failin' him at the end o' his life, I'm not goin' t' fail him in death. So ye see how I canna be lettin' jist anybody in. Maybe ye mean no harm, but even wi' the laird dead, I do have my orders, ye ken."

Joanna dried her tears, sniffed, and said, "Can you tell me about the laird's family? I only want to know——"

"Maybe I can, maybe I canna. 'Tis best ye go t' Mr. Sercombe first. If he gives ye leave . . ."

"Mr. Sercombe? Who is that?"

"Palmer Sercombe. He's the executor o' the Duncan estate. Been the family's solicitor for years. He'd be able t' tell ye more'n anyone. His office is in toon, only two doors from the store."

Indicating her appreciation Joanna began to walk away. Before she had gone three or four paces, Innes called to her:

"Would ye like a ride back into toon?" he offered. "I'm a wee bit unhandy wi' the motor car. The laird brought the contraption from Glasgow. But I reckon I'll get ye there."

"Thank you, Mr. Innes," returned Joanna. "But the walk will be nice. I enjoyed myself on the way out and have nothing else to do this afternoon."

She turned and gave one more parting look upon the great house. Suddenly her eyes were diverted to a small tower, high on the north side. At the window a lean figure stood gazing out. But the moment Joanna's eyes turned toward him, the form vanished inside. She continued to stare in the same direction, but no one reappeared. Finally she turned and continued on. She did not look back again.

Walter Innes raised a bony hand to his chin as he watched her until she was out of sight. "An interesting pass this'll be," he muttered to himself; then he strode back to the automobile, climbed in, ground it into gear, and drove in the direction of the stone outbuilding which was, in fact, the stable. Still mumbling, he parked the car in front of the building, a symbol of the modern industrial age strangely out of place so near an ancient castle.

The stalls needed mucking out, but he couldn't do that in his Sunday best. Instead, he dug a pail of oats from a burlap sack and carried it to the stall which held the only horse in the stables.

"Here ye go, lad."

He dumped the oats into the trough.

"The laird said ye was always t' have the best—nothin' but the best for his Flame Dance." The factor's voice caught momentarily.

"Weel, 'tis the least I can do now," he went on, "takin' good care o' ye—so ye'll hae all the oats ye can eat."

The great roan stallion snorted and stamped his hoof in anticipation. Innes wiped a hand across a damp eye.

"Yer in sore need o' exercise, lad, but I canna help ye there, stubborn beast that ye are."

Innes patted the horse's nose and for a moment the animal's savage eyes seemed to soften.

*　　*　　*

By the time Joanna reached the main road, her feet were throbbing. Beautiful though the countryside was, if she continued such traipsing about, she was going to need either different shoes or tougher feet!

She was relieved to find the streets of Port Strathy empty. She had had enough of the place for one day. All she wanted to do was go to her room and rest, and perhaps read one of the books she had brought along with her.

But just as her foot touched the threshold, Mrs. Cobden's cheerful voice rang out.

"Back at last," she said. "Ye missed tea, but I'd be glad t' fix ye somethin'. The biscuits are warm an' there's still some broth on the stove."

"I think I'd rather just go upstairs and rest awhile, Mrs. Cobden. But thank you."

"My Sandy said ye were goin' oot t' the Hoose."

"Yes, I did."

"Did ye talk wi' anyone?"

"I saw Mr. Innes, who was nice enough, and there was an old man named Dorey, who didn't talk much at all."

"Ah," the innkeeper's wife intoned, nodding her head knowingly. "Too bad ye ran int' him—noo, there's a strange one."

"Who is he?"

"The gardener—leastways he's done up the grounds real bonny since he's been there. Even come in t' the toon once or twice an' got most o' the folks plantin' flower gardens. But, weel . . . he sort o' gives a body the shivers t' talk personal like wi' him."

"What's wrong with him?"

"Who can say? Jist leanin' a bit t' port, as the fishers say."

She chuckled at her wit.

"Been like that ever since I can remember, an' we been here near twenty-five years. He's been oot t' the castle since then an' weel before, from what I hear. But I can see ye're tired an' so I dinna want t' bother ye no further. Would ye be wantin' me t' call ye fer dinner?"

"Yes, thank you. I'd like that."

Joanna continued up the stairs to her room. She headed right for the bed, took off her shoes, and lay back on the soft feather mattress. Why had she even bothered to come? She was never going to find out anything. If this had all been for naught she might as well find out quickly and set about to find some means to get back to the States.

She sighed heavily and all at once the face of Jason Channing filled her mind.

Maybe she should have gone to London after all. This trip to Scotland wasn't working out. There was no family here. Only people with something they didn't want spoiled, whispering words behind her back.

At least Jason would have been able to get her back home. But now here she was stuck in the far north of Scotland!

Unconsciously Joanna's hand sought her purse, and her fingers felt for the documents she had kept carefully with her since discovering them in her grandmother's secretary. Along with the music box, the locket, the linen embroidery, and a few photos, she had brought these mementos with her, as her only solid reminder of the past she was seeking to uncover.

Perhaps in these papers lay the place to start. Instead of asking questions and making a nuisance of herself, it would be best simply to show someone the documents and ask what they meant.

This Palmer Sercombe, a lawyer of some sort, she gathered, would be a likely place to begin. She had seen his office on her way back from Stonewycke, just as Walter Innes had described it. The words *Mr. Palmer Sercombe, esq., Solicitor* were painted on the window in precise black script. Venetian blinds on the window had been closed so she had been able to see nothing inside. The Duncan family attorney would surely be able to tell her about the documents and perhaps even about her grandmother. It would be good to get everything settled once and for all.

She would visit him first thing the following morning.

12
Palmer Sercombe

PALMER SERCOMBE SHUFFLED briskly through the aged papers. One bushy black eyebrow was cocked slightly.

"These are your grandmother's, you say?"

Joanna nodded.

"I found them among her things after her accident."

"Yes . . . I see." He drew the words out thoughtfully. "They do appear to be genuine."

He continued perusing the documents. "What did you say your grandmother's name is?"

"Margaret . . . Margaret Duncan."

"Hmm," he responded, more to himself than to Joanna. He was clearly deep in thought.

The office in which Joanna found herself—surrounded with rich, dark walnut, plush red velvets and china lamps, with a fine Persian rug covering the floor—stood in stark contrast to the rough fishing village she had thus far seen. But no less a contrast was the eloquent, impeccably dressed lawyer himself. His thin, pale lips articulated almost perfect English with scarcely a trace of the

Scottish brogue her ears had already grown accustomed to. The eyebrows and lips were perhaps the only notable features on his rather unexpressive clean-shaven face. His countenance conveyed no warmth or friendliness, neither antagonism nor villany. It remained utterly devoid of feeling. Either Palmer Sercombe was a totally impassive man or he was exercising great restraint in Joanna's presence to conceal his emotions. But for whatever reason, Joanna was growing more convinced by the moment that she could learn little from his expressionless countenance.

"You say your grandmother went to America when she was a girl?" he asked at last.

"Yes."

"But you have no proof—er—documents indicating her parentage?"

"No. She spoke very little of her past. I was hoping maybe you'd be able to tell me something . . . from these papers."

"Well, Miss Matheson, these documents—if they indeed are genuine—"

"What are you saying, that they may not be?"

"Not at all, I am merely posing the question in its broadest terms. As I said, these documents really tell us very little. Now you are certain your grandmother's name is Duncan?"

"I . . . I never actually saw her birth certificate if that's what you mean, but I—"

"I see," interrupted the lawyer, "and you say you are not absolutely certain her birthplace was Port Strathy?"

"Again," said Joanna, growing uncomfortable with the challenging direction of Sercombe's questions, "I know nothing for *certain*. I have nothing to go on but my grandmother's last words . . . and these papers. She spoke of the family and about Strathy and the house."

"What exactly did she say about the family and the house?" asked Sercombe leaning closer and revealing a deep furrow in his brow.

"Well, nothing, actually. She just used those words—the *family* . . . the *house*."

"She didn't specifically identify either?"

"Not exactly . . . no."

"Ah . . . I see," he said, leaning back once more in his chair and appearing to relax somewhat. "So we don't actually know if she—as a Duncan—came from the laird's branch of the family, or from Port Strathy, or what. For all we *know*, these documents—"

"But, Mr. Sercombe," insisted Joanna, "surely you can see that all the signs indicate that—"

"I admit, Miss Matheson, that on the surface things look rather, shall we say, intriguing as to the possible connection between your grandmother and the laird's family, the Port Strathy Duncans that is. But when we—I'm speaking of lawyers, of course—when we settle the affairs of an estate, we have to have proof of these things, solid, documented proof."

"But it's not the estate I'm so much concerned with," said Joanna. "I simply want to know who my grandmother is, where she came from, if there are any living relatives still here."

"Of course, of course," he replied with the hint of a grin.

"Have you never heard of my grandmother . . . of a Margaret Duncan?"

"It was so long ago, my dear."

"But if you've been the family lawyer for some time, surely someone would have referred to her, at some time."

"I've been with the family only some fifteen years, Miss Matheson. How old did you say she is?"

"In her early sixties. Surely there must be someone still in the area who might have known her, or known of her."

"I am well acquainted with all the families around here and I doubt—"

"There must be any number of townspeople sixty-five or seventy or older who would remember what happened, especially if it involved a family so important as—"

"My dear," interrupted the lawyer in soothing tones, and rising from his seat, "I'm afraid this may be little more than a wild goose chase for you. I'm sorry you have gone to so much trouble and expense, but these papers really say very little—and then, too, we have no way of knowing how your grandmother came by them."

"You're not implying—" began Joanna, growing uncomfortable with Sercombe's insinuations.

"No, my dear, I'm not implying anything. I wouldn't think of casting suspicions on your grandmother. It may have been someone else. The point remains that the documents, knowing no more than we do about their origins, raise more questions than they answer."

"Well, they must say something," said Joanna, biting a quivering lip. She wasn't about to lose control of herself in front of this man. "As a lawyer, could you at least interpret them for me? I want to know if there's anything for me to pursue, if I'm heading in the right direction. All I want to know is if I have family here—is that asking too much?"

Sercombe had made his way slowly around his huge desk and approached Joanna in a manner indicating his gracious attempt to show her to the door, responding to her last question even as he did so: "As I have said, Miss Matheson, these papers would offer little help in that direction."

"Surely there must be someone—"

"Alastair Duncan was the last of his line. Of course, Duncan is a very common name here in Scotland. There would be literally thousands with that surname."

"But I heard her say the word Strathy."

Sercombe nodded his head sympathetically.

"It would be impossible to contact everyone with that name in other localities!" Joanna said, her voice nearly breaking with emotion.

"I'm sorry I can't offer more encouragement."

At length Joanna rose from her chair. "These are all I have to go on then," she said, reaching for the papers the lawyer still clutched in his hands. He made no move to yield them, appearing instead to withdraw almost imperceptibly from her.

An awkward pause followed momentarily, until he answered, "Perhaps I should hold on to them awhile . . . for safekeeping."

"I assumed they were essentially worthless," said Joanna, eyeing him questioningly.

"Of course they represent no monetary value," he said, "as historical or antique documents, but I recognize the sentimental value they possess . . . for you, that is, and I wouldn't want anything to happen to them."

"Is thievery a serious problem around here?" asked Joanna with the slightest hint of sarcasm in her voice.

"No, of course not," Sercombe assured, "but there is the poverty which cannot be ignored. And well, we must face it—poverty can drive men to do anything."

"And greed?" suggested Joanna.

"Yes . . . of course, that too. All the more reason it might be best for me—"

"Still, I don't like to part with them," insisted Joanna, stepping forward once more and reaching her hand toward the papers.

Again Sercombe retreated a half step. "Then, too . . . it may give me a chance to have a closer look at them."

"From what you said I assumed you were certain—"

"You never know," he interjected. "I may have the opportunity to speak with someone who is more familiar with this sort of thing." His impassive exterior could not hide his reluctance to yield them.

"Nevertheless," she found herself saying, "I do want to keep them myself for a while longer."

She held out her hand, this time with more certainty, and at length the lawyer relinquished them. "Of course, of course . . . if you insist so strongly on it I have no objection." He shifted uncomfortably and glanced from Joanna's face to her hand holding the ancient documents.

Replacing the papers in her bag, Joanna left the office and turned toward the inn. Just now she did not feel like returning to her room, or enduring the silent, staring faces of the townspeople. She simply wanted to be alone . . . to think . . . to decide what to do. Without consciously framing a decision, she found her path leading toward the sea.

Her mind was filled with only one thought—her grandmother. *Is it my destiny to fail everyone who loves me?* she wondered.

Her own life had been traded for her mother's; how many times had the pangs of guilt caused her to wish she could have reversed that process! How gladly she would have died twenty-one years ago in order that her mother could have lived. Then everyone would have been happy.

But instead she had come into the world. She had lived . . . her mother had died . . . and grief had been the result. She had killed her mother, she had failed her father, and now it seemed she could not even honor the last request of her grandmother. Was she destined to fail her too?

Oh, Grandma, I wanted so badly to do this—for you; for once in my life to do something for someone else! But everyone is determined to block me and I'm just not strong enough to know what to do.

I ought to just demand that those people tell me something!

But, she realized with a sigh, *I won't. I'll probably give in under the pressure rather than push it.*

She thought of Jason Channing. His presence had overpowered her, too. Whatever her resolve had been when alone, once his eyes fell upon her she became her fainthearted self again. And in many ways Palmer Sercombe had the same effect on her. Would she be able to stand her ground against him?

Joanna made her way slowly toward the sea and then westward along the beach. She avoided the harbor where a group of fishermen were tending their boats. For the present she had nearly had enough of this town and its people.

She found she had to negotiate some distance of rather rocky terrain before gaining the wide expanse of flat sand which she sought. Once her foot slipped, twisting her ankle. She let out a little cry, but the pain only increased her frustration. She would be glad to leave this place! It had been a mistake to come.

When at last she was rewarded with the feel of soft sand beneath her feet, Joanna removed her shoes and wiggled her toes in the warmth of it. For a moment, she stood staring about her. Then she took a few tentative steps. The sand was warm in the sunlight, comforting, inviting. Throwing down her shoes, Joanna ran toward the water's edge where six-inch-high waves lapped gently against the sand. Cool, salty water splashed against her feet and soaked the fringes of her dress. She stopped, walked a few feet farther, then turned and ran back onto the beach, water splashing about her feet in all directions. The sea could be a great healer. Her cares receded in the joyous ebb and flow of the foamy tide.

Joanna reached down, scooped up a handful of water, and sent it flying into the sunlight. The water receded and she ran toward the beach, then turned and followed the water's edge, farther away from the town, making a straight row of footprints in the wet sand. She stopped and turned, watching the incoming water fill the impressions and gradually erase them. Unconsciously her toe spelled the name D-U-N-C-A-N in the sand. Then another silent wave rippled in, washing the letters away. Did the motion of the seas represent her efforts to discover her heritage? Were her grandmother's past and her desperate request destined to disappear into the silent vaults of history even as these waves obliterated any memory of the footprints she had made but a few moments earlier?

She ran farther down the sand, then stopped and looked toward the vastness of the ocean to the north. On the right, Port Strathy's harbor and buildings faded into the distance. An urge overcame her to throw caution to the wind and rush headlong into the oncoming waves. Summoning her courage she held the bottom of her dress above her knees and ran a few steps. But when the water reached her knees, the boldness disappeared and she bolted for the safety of the shore.

Suddenly the unwelcome sound of a man's laughter interrupted her childlike play.

"If ye be intendin' t' have a swim in oor icy water, mem, I'm afraid ye'll spoil such a bonnie dress as ye be wearin'." His words were followed by another chuckle, this time more subdued.

Standing some fifty feet up the beach, on the gradual rise of a small dune, was a man dressed in worn overalls and faded blue cotton workshirt. That he was broad-shouldered she could see immediately, but Joanna could not judge his height because of his vantage point on the dune above her. He appeared to be tall. Straw-colored hair was blown by the wind, though he did not appear to be the type who would worry about keeping it combed under calmer circumstances. His face, for all its roughness, bore a youthful look, beaming in good-natured laughter. He looked no more than twenty or twenty-two, but was in reality twenty-seven.

Crimson crept into Joanna's cheeks.

Her first thought was to ignore him. She was in no mood today to pass the time of day with a stranger who seemed intent on making sport of her.

"Please," he went on, seeing her silently standing still at the water's edge, "don't stop yer fun on my account. I dinna mean t' interrupt ye, mem."

His tone and her downcast spirits filled her with indignation.

"I think I've entertained you enough!" she snapped, angry and embarrassed.

"I'm sorry. 'Twas rude o' me not t' let ye know I was there. But truthfully, mem, I only jist this second came over the rise o' the dune here an' saw ye. An' ye was havin' such a wonderful time in the water."

His laughter faded but there remained a twinkle in his azure eyes. That he appeared to be enjoying this made it all the more exasperating.

"How dare you!" said Joanna with growing perturbation. "Why aren't you out fishing or mending your nets with the others?"

"Deed, I am sorry, mem," he said, chuckling again but trying to conceal it, "but ye don't understand—"

"What makes you think you have the right?"

"I'm no fisherman, mem. I was only makin' my way back t' the town. I beg yer pardon again," he said, but his tone conveyed that her pardon meant little to him. He clearly did not take the encounter with the seriousness it carried to Joanna. He then turned and disappeared on the other side of the dune as quickly as he had come.

Joanna stood stock-still, staring after him a full minute after he was gone from her view.

Then, the earlier spell of the morning gone, she gathered up her shoes and bag and walked back to Port Strathy in somber uncertainty over her future.

13

Foul Play

❧

JOANNA STARED IN disbelief.

The whole room had been torn apart—ransacked!

She blinked back the tears. The mess she could clean up, but why would someone do this to *her*? Why was she so unwelcome?

"How can we make this up t' ye?" exclaimed Mrs. Cobden, wringing her hands together.

"We've never had anythin' like this happen before," said her husband. "'Tis a disgrace! Ye can be certain the magistrate'll hear o' it!"

Joanna climbed over the upturned mattress and picked up a few of the belongings which had been scattered from her suitcases. Clothes were strewn about the floor, her bags had been recklessly emptied, the drawers in the dresser were pulled out, the bed was in disarray, and the clothes she'd hung in the closet lay scattered about the room.

"Can ye tell if anythin' has been taken?" asked Sandy.

"I had nothing of value," Joanna replied.

Nothing of value, she thought, grasping her purse which still hung from her shoulder. Fortunately she had her only possessions of value with her. Apparently the burglars hadn't considered her grandmother's music box valuable enough to take, for it sat undisturbed on the dressing table. She reached out and picked it up, winding the silver key, then replacing it, relieved in mind once again just to hear the delicate strains of the lullaby.

"Let me fix ye a nice hot cup o' tea," said Mrs. Cobden, placing a tender arm about Joanna. "I'll help ye clean all this up later."

Reluctant to face the ominous task of putting the room back in order, Joanna accepted the offer and descended the stairs to the common room. She found a seat while Mr. and Mrs. Cobden went into the kitchen to prepare the tea. There were no other guests.

Joanna sank deep into thought, lamenting this latest turn of events.

After some moments her consciousness woke to words drifting out from the kitchen, whisperings clearly not intended for her ears but which had grown loud enough for her to make out.

". . . not her fault . . . she doesn't know . . ."

". . . more'n she's lettin' on . . ."

"She's just an innocent lass."

"Serves her right, that's all I'm sayin'." It was Sandy Cobden's deep bass voice.

"What a thing to say!" came Mrs. Cobden's voice, now raised above a whisper.

"I'm not sayin' I think it's right t' go tearin' her room apart. I can understan' the poor lass's plight. I'm jist sayin' that's what comes o' comin' into a place an' stirrin' up trouble."

"She's caused no trouble, an' ye know it, Sandy. She's oor guest!"

"I know, woman. An' I like the child," returned Sandy. "But I venture even ye yerself'll be singin' a different tune if she takes the laird's money an' the sale o' the land falls through."

"She wouldn't do such a thing!"

"And why not, I ask ye? This town means nothin' t' her. She can jist turn around an' sail back home t' the States. An' I don't have t' tell ye what the new harbor would mean t' us. If that sale falls through, it's not goin' t' do oor inn any good, an' that's God's truth."

"Keep yer voice down, Sandy!"

But the innkeeper's wife need hardly have worried. Long before their conversation had reached this stage they had been left alone in their inn. When they reentered the Common Room with preparations for Joanna's tea, their guest was nowhere to be seen.

Joanna left the inn to continue what she had done for most of the day—wandering about the town, thinking, pondering, weighing what to do. She had had very little to eat all day, and had considered walking again out to the Duncan House but decided against it. That she had stirred up speculation in this little fishing village could hardly be doubted. She hadn't intended it when she came. But it seemed her grandmother's very name was a goad to the people who had for so long lived under the Duncan hand.

Maybe all this was what came of poking in where you weren't invited. More and more she felt she didn't belong in Port Strathy. But she didn't belong in London with Jason either, or in Chicago, or even in Denver if her grandmother died.

Somehow she had hoped here it might be different, that . . . but no, it was no use. Tomorrow she would spend what little money she had left to book passage back to London. She still had Jason's card. She would look him up and ask him to help her get back to the States. Even if she had to borrow the money at interest, he would help her. She just hoped he didn't expect too much in return.

Immediately Joanna felt a sense of relief.

Having decided what to do removed the burden of uncertainty. She would put her things in order tonight. Then in the morning she would make arrangements to leave at the soonest possible moment.

Joanna wandered westward from the town. The road ran parallel with the shore but lay removed from it by some hundred or two hundred yards, separated from the water by a huge dune. Though she could not see them, Joanna could hear the crashing of waves, growing louder now with the incoming tide. They beat against the large rocky base of a cliff-like precipice which rose at the westerly end of the broad sandy beach about a mile from the town's sheltered harbor. Likewise, the road along which Joanna walked rose gradually until it, too, bordered the edge of a great cliff which overlooked the beach, the harbor, and tiny Port Strathy in the distance.

Breathing hard from the climb, Joanna stopped and looked behind her. The pink and yellow glow of the early summer's "gloamin'" took her breath away.

"It's beautiful!" she said softly to herself.

Away below her the sea stretched out in a dull evening blue-gray. Gulls squawked as they flew swiftly along the surface of the water hoping for an easy catch. Silent-sailed fishing boats drifted leisurely out of the harbor for the night at sea.

Joanna then began the walk back down the road to town for what she hoped might be her last night in Port Strathy. If only she could be lucky enough to find some means of transport tomorrow—either overland as she had come, or on a vessel bound around the northeastern head of the country toward Fenwick, Peterhead, or at best Aberdeen. By the time Joanna reached the first cottages at the town's edge, it was past nine o'clock and the sky had grown as dark as it intended to get, a deep bluish gray with fringes of the endless pink sunset in the west. As the night progressed, the light would imperceptibly shift around to the east and eventually give way to a brilliant sunrise.

Port Strathy was closed tight.

Its fisher families were either in their homes or beds by this hour, or their men toiling out on the water. Joanna saw no living soul as she walked through the streets toward the intersection which would lead her back to the Cobdens' inn. A quarter moon had risen from the horizon in the direction of Stonewycke and added to the silent, eerie enchantment of the solitary evening. Again Jason Channing came to her mind. It would be a lovely night for a walk through these quaint streets with him.

She wondered if he took moonlight strolls. Perhaps, if things fell right, within a week she might find out for herself.

Well, regardless . . . she had no one to walk with tonight—and nowhere to go but back to the inn where her room, still in shambles, awaited her corrective hand. She passed Miss Sinclair's store, now darkened and still. She had liked Olive Sinclair. Out of all the people she had met, she would be one Joanna would miss. She would like to have gotten to know her better. And MacDuff, whom she would probably not see again.

Joanna stepped down off the wooden walkway to cross an alley. The inn lay only about fifty yards in front of her, yet already appeared darkened for the evening. The only sign of life lay in the thin wisp of smoke reaching from the chimney straight into the windless night.

Suddenly a hand shot into her midsection!

She felt another rough hand close over her mouth as she struggled to free herself.

In the confusion she could not make out the features of the man who had been waiting in the shadows of the alley, hidden behind the corner of the building. The moment she stepped down onto the dirt of the street, he pounced.

"Ye won't git hurt if ye jist gi' me yer purse," hissed the assailant, holding her fast.

She felt the man tug at the strap of her purse. Unable to scream for help, she kicked at him. Finally, fighting frantically, she partially freed her mouth.

"Help!" Even as she shrieked, a strong, fleshy hand clamped down once more over her mouth. Clinging desperately to her purse, she worked her teeth into position, then bit down into the hand with as much force as her jaw could summon.

"Ow!" hollered the attacker. "Ye bloody shrew! Take that, ye good fer nothin'!" he cursed at Joanna, and he allowed his grasp on her to slacken just enough to punish her with a fierce slap across the face.

The blow sent her reeling backwards, temporarily free.

Just then a voice from behind called out: "Hey! What's goin' on there?"

The attacker swore in frustration, then darted down the alley and disappeared as quickly as he had come.

Joanna tried to turn toward the voice that had frightened him away, but everything seemed to whirl around her and she felt herself becoming faint. She struggled to retain consciousness, but the blow had been a hard one.

Her knees buckled, her head spun, and the hurriedly approaching footsteps faded into hazy nothingness.

She felt she was falling forever in a slow motion as the night around her grew steadily blacker.

Then she knew no more.

14

Friends

A FLICKERING AMBER glow first touched Joanna's senses.

Where was she . . . what had happened? If only she could remember!

She struggled to rise but found the effort too taxing and lay down again. Her bewildered mind remained in a foggy blur as she sank back into the bed.

Why did her head hurt so?

Wakefulness crept gradually back into her confused brain. The pain in her right cheek grew more severe. She reached toward her head, and the moment her hand touched her face she realized the throbbing came from her hot swollen jaw. Then first the memory of the attack on the street returned.

Joanna twisted her head slightly to the left.

Even her neck muscles were sore. Her whole head felt ready to explode. From her vantage point in a corner of a dimly lit room, she saw the hearth opposite her, from which the glow and warmth radiated. The fire was a small one but had been burning for some time, and its fiery coals emitted a pleasing heat. She was lying on the soft cushions of a drab brown couch.

As the haze began to lift, Joanna took in the rest of the room in which she lay. Faded chintz curtains hung from the windows. A worn Persian rug lay before the hearth. The furnishings were Victorian, several polished oak pieces no less beautiful in that they had clearly been chosen for their practical and functional value. She immediately thought of Palmer Sercombe's office and an involuntary chill ran through her. Momentarily she wondered if that was where she now lay. Yet she quickly realized that here the trappings of refinement had seen better days. Unlike the lawyer's office, this room possessed an air of charm and simplicity if it lacked elegance, if its beauty were perhaps more humble.

To take all this in took scarcely a moment before Joanna's attention was drawn away by soft, yet heated, conversation in the background.

"Jist let me get me hands on the filthy bla'gard!" came a masculine voice. "They may be auld, but they're hard-workin' hands, an' strong!" Though its owner kept his tone subdued, the voice seethed with passion.

"The lass'll be fine, Nathaniel," came another, a voice Joanna recognized but couldn't place.

"But the rascal must be punished, Olive. Ye must see it!"

"You know what the Lord says . . . vengeance is mine." Now she remembered; the voice belonged to Olive Sinclair.

"But sometimes the Lord's wantin' jist a wee bit o' help from His people doon here, ye ken."

"You've already helped Him plenty by drivin' him off and bringin' the poor lass here," said Miss Sinclair. "Don't be making it worse by runnin' off and doing somethin' foolish."

"Ah, but it makes the blood in my auld Highland veins boil!"

"The Lord'll not let the scoundrel go unrewarded, that you can count on, Nathaniel," said Miss Sinclair, gently moderating his anger by degrees.

Just then Joanna's stirring attracted the attention of her hostess.

"Well, dearie, are you awake? You just lie still a while longer. How's the head? You took quite a blow, from the looks of it."

Joanna looked toward the shopkeeper and attempted a smile. "I . . . I'm fine—I think. My head does hurt awfully . . ." She glanced in the direction of the other face, now gazing silently on her. He appeared friendly enough. "Have I been here long?" Joanna asked.

"Nathaniel brought you in only a few minutes ago."

The man with Olive Sinclair was large framed, in his fifties Joanna guessed from his sparse graying hair. His deep-set, small brown eyes were framed with crow's feet, the inevitable reward of long years of hard work outdoors. The denim trousers showed signs of heavy wear and appeared a little large. The plaid work shirt was a faded red.

"Then it was you," Joanna said, "who came to my aid?"

"Weel, mem, I dinna do much," he replied. "That no good, cowardly brute jist ran off as soon as he heard an honest voice."

"And it's a good thing for you, Nathaniel Cuttahay, that he did," put in Miss Sinclair with a touch of irony.

"Hoot, mem!" exclaimed the man with animation, "I only wish I could ha' caught 'em. But at the time I was tryin' to keep this young lassie's head from fallin' against the street."

"I'm indebted to you," Joanna said. "I don't know what I would have done—" Her hand suddenly jerked to her side as her face blanched. "My purse!" she cried. "He didn't get my purse—?"

"Don't fret, lass. It's right here." Miss Sinclair picked up the bag from the table where it lay and handed it to her. Joanna grabbed it hastily and plunged her hand inside. Everything was where she had left it. She breathed a sigh of relief.

"He was after my purse," Joanna explained.

"The thievin' scroundrel!" exclaimed Mr. Cuttahay in a fresh outburst of Scottish anger. "The idea o' tryin' t' rob a visitor t' oor toon!"

"I doubt they were after my money," said Joanna. "I have precious little left."

"You must have a low opinion of our town," said Miss Sinclair, bringing Joanna a hot cup of tea as she sat up on the couch. "Why don't you just sit there a spell and relax and sip this good strong tea. It'll bring the life back into you."

"I'm afraid there's nothing wrong with your town," said Joanna at length. "I've brought it all on myself. I've caused offense from the very moment I arrived."

Joanna closed her eyes and took a swallow of tea. It felt good warming her deep within.

"But . . . excuse me," said Miss Sinclair as if suddenly waking from a reverie. "I've been amiss in my introductions. Joanna, this is Nathaniel Cuttahay . . . Nathaniel, meet Joanna Matheson from the United States."

Joanna smiled.

"Pleased t' make yer acquaintance," said Mr. Cuttahay, "although a formal how-do-ye-do hardly seems necessary after what we went through t'gether, eh?"

Miss Sinclair laughed. "Right you are there, Nathaniel!"

"But I dinna understand how ye could be thinkin' ye brought yer troubles on yersel'—a harmless an' honest-lookin' lass ye seem t' me," Nathaniel added.

"I just meant maybe I had no right to come here, asking questions, trying to find out about the past."

"Joanna has come here hoping to find some of her grandmother's long-ago kinfolk," Miss Sinclair explained, directing herself to Nathaniel. "If indeed this was her grandmother's original home."

"I don't know what to think," said Joanna. "Earlier today my room at the inn was broken into and searched . . ."

She stopped and turned her head away, unable to continue while she composed herself.

". . . I really think coming to Scotland was a mistake," she went on in a tremulous voice. "I was going to try to find passage to London tomorrow—"

"My dear," interrupted Miss Sinclair, "you must just try to rest for a few days. You're not up to traveling now. We'll have to find you someplace safer to stay though, and that's the truth."

"'Tis jist a sore disgrace!" exclaimed Mr. Cuttahay. "Makes me ashamed t' call this toon my home . . . e'en though 'tis usually not such a bad place. But why should a body aroun' here care that ye be seekin' yer kin?"

"Joanna's grandmother was a Duncan," put in Miss Sinclair.

"Ye don't say? A Port Strathy Duncan."

"So I thought," said Joanna. Then she briefly told them of her grandmother's condition and last words. "But Mr. Sercombe thinks I'm on a wild goose chase," she finished with a sigh.

"What was her name?" asked Nathaniel.

"Margaret Duncan," Joanna answered.

"Lord preserve us!" exclaimed Nathaniel, and the color drained from his face.

"What is it, man?" asked Miss Sinclair in alarm. "You look like you just saw a ghost returning from the grave!"

"Maybe I have, Olive," he said, sinking deeply into the chair and shaking his head in disbelief. Then he shot a penetrating glance at Joanna and eyed her intently. "I jist canna believe it," he finally said at length. "I jist canna believe it!"

"Well, don't keep us in suspense, man!" demanded Miss Sinclair. "What's given you such a start from hearing the name? Come on, out with it!"

He hesitated, then drew a deep breath.

"Ye're new around here, Olive—what is't, twenty years since ye came here from Leeds? So ye wouldn't hae had cause t' hae heard o' Margaret Duncan. But time was, that was a name what caused quite a stir in these parts. 'Course I was but a wee lad myself so I dinna really ken much o' what happened."

"What do you mean, Mr. Cuttahay?" asked Joanna impatiently. "What about my grandmother . . . you didn't know her?"

"No, no. I was only eight or ten at the time."

"But you knew of her, is that it?"

"Everyone knew o' her . . . an' ye dinna ken hoo she came t' leave Scotland?"

"I know nothing about her past. She only made a few delirious references to Port Strathy before the coma. Please . . . tell me about it."

"'Tis not a pretty tale, lass," he began. "An' as I said, I know but fragments o' the story. 'Twas so lang ago. Maybe she left for America because her heart was broken. Suddenly she was jist gone. No one in the toon knew why. 'Course, it was no secret that her father, the laird, an' her had a great falling oot o'er an ill-fated romance; her father was determined t' put a stop t' the affair. The scandal was kept quiet an' the next thing anyone knows Margaret is on her way t' America. Nothin' more were e'er heard o' her. What e'er it was atween Marg'ret an' her family, it must've been somethin' great for her t' walk away from her inheritance like she did an' turn her back on all that would hae been hers someday—she was the eldest o' the laird's children. The auld laird, that is."

"The laird that just died?" asked Joanna. "Who was he?"

"The auld laird's son; Marg'ret's younger brother Alastair."

Joanna sat stunned.

"So that's what everyone's so suspicious about," said Miss Sinclair. "Don't you see? They think Joanna's come to claim the estate."

"I never knew a thing about any of this," said Joanna with a numbed sigh. "I can't even get into the place."

"You had no luck at the big house up on the hill?" Miss Sinclair queried.

"None," Joanna replied. "I spoke briefly with the factor, but he said nothing of consequence; said he couldn't speak without permission from Mr. Sercombe. And when I went to him, he told me my papers were worthless."

"Papers?" asked Cuttahay with interest.

"Some documents I found among my grandmother's things after the accident."

"Do ye hae them with ye?"

"They're in my handbag," said Joanna. "I showed them to Mr. Sercombe early this morning. He said they didn't mean anything, but he did offer to have someone else examine them."

"Hmm . . ." drawled Nathaniel.

Joanna set her cup on the table and took up her purse and removed the brown envelope containing the documents. She then spread them out before her two new friends.

"They 'pear mighty important," said Nathaniel.

Olive Sinclair looked closely at them without saying a word, studying the details carefully. After a few moments she said, "Perhaps my own ignorance is deceiving me," she said, rubbing her chin thoughtfully. "But it doesn't look as though it would take much to interpret them—once you get past the archaic language and all. And that would be no obstacle for a lawyer."

"What do you make of them?" Joanna asked.

"This one looks like a surveyor's report . . . wouldn't you say so, Nathaniel?"

The man drew closer, looking over Miss Sinclair's shoulder, and at length nodded and mumbled an uncertain assent.

"You see there," went on Miss Sinclair with her finger pointing the way, "all these property lines and various distances, so many furlongs from such-and-such a line. And here's the starting point of it all—the Firth of Lindow. That's the border of the laird's lands—where the River Lindow opens into the sea, some ways down the coast west of here. What this—this, Rossachs Kyle means, I don't know that one."

"'Tis gone now," put in Nathaniel. "'Tis all covered wi' the sea. 'Twas a strait o' land some three miles east o' the harbor up the coast. In ancient days it was a harbor o' sorts, but its ownership was always in dispute wi' the laird o' the adjoinin' land east o' here. Finally the laird—"

"Which laird?" Joanna asked. "I'm confused."

"Talmud Ramsey, lass. He would o' been Marg'ret's grandfather, her mother's daddy. Anyway, he took legal possession o' it when he was laird. I suppose 'twas so important back then because it provided a natural line o' defense fer the toon."

"And what happened to it?" asked Miss Sinclair.

"'Twas a muckle storm at sea, back in '60. Near destroyed the whole toon. The fierce tides that whole winter jist pulled doon that narrow spit right back int' the sea. Brought the inn doon that year too, if I remember aright. I wasna e'en five at the time, but old-timers talked aboot it fer years."

"Well, maybe this surveyor's report was made to settle some dispute after that."

"No, it couldn't have been," Joanna pointed out with growing interest. "Look at the date—1845."

"That would be jist aroun' the time Atlanta Ramsey married James Duncan— that would be yer grandmother's parents, lass," said Nathaniel.

"James Duncan must have had the report made to confirm the extent of the property," said Miss Sinclair. "Marrying into the family like he did, and property lines being kind of uncertain, he probably wanted to be sure how much land he held."

"Or how much his wife held," suggested Nathaniel. "Remember, James Duncan only married int' the Ramsey estate. Some said he was a sly ol' fox who only wanted t' get his hands on the land. An' o' coorse Atlanta was the only survivor o' the Ramsey name at the time."

"Nevertheless," went on Miss Sinclair, "this other paper might even be of greater interest. Look here, Nathaniel. Can you make out any of this Old English?"

"'Tis written in such a fancy script t' make it all the more illegible. I don't see why they dinna—"

"Never mind," interrupted Miss Sinclair, anxious to proceed with her investigation. "It seems to be a deed of some sort. Just look—'The lands heretofore known as Port Strathy . . .'—the ink is smeared there but that could be a reference to a survey report or some indication of boundaries. And then it says, '. . . Ramsey and all legal heirs, by royal decree shall govern and possess . . . by the grace of King George III and his Almighty God . . . this 17th day of April, 1784 . . .'"

She stopped and exhaled a long sigh.

"What does it mean?" asked Joanna.

"Who can say for certain?" replied Miss Sinclair. "But if it was up to me to decide, I'd say this was the deed to the Ramsey estate—the Duncan estate now, that is."

"I should probably explain what you've told me to Mr. Sercombe," Joanna said. "Maybe if he took a closer look and I told him about—"

"Joanna," began Miss Sinclair, "'tis not my habit to be speaking ill of another, especially as he's practically my neighbor. But if I were you, I'd say nothing more to him for a while. If he had anything to tell you, he'd have done it this morning."

"In any case," said Nathaniel, "'tis far too late t' settle anythin' tonight. Letty will be worryin' hersel' o'er me by now."

"I'm sorry to have kept you so long," apologized Joanna, but before the words were scarcely out of her mouth both her newfound friends silenced anything further in that direction. "In any case," she added, "I must be getting back to the inn. I have to put my room in order and get some sleep. Then tomorrow I'll try to decide what to do about leaving."

"We'll have no more talk of you leaving town," insisted Miss Sinclair as she gave Joanna a friendly hug, almost smothering in its gentleness. "And your going back to the inn alone is not a good idea. Whoever went through your room—"

"Lass," broke in Nathaniel, "my Letty an' I hae a wee croft only aboot two miles south o' town. 'Tis far from fancy, but we've a spare room an' we'd consider it a great honor if ye'd bide a wee wi' us, leastways till yer rested or until some course o' action presents itsel'."

"I . . . I don't know," stammered Joanna as Miss Sinclair readily nodded her approval, "you hardly know me, and I don't want you to get into trouble from befriending me."

"Hoots, lass! It'll be best fer all concerned, gettin' ye oot o' town and away from the glare o' gawking eyes watchin' ye. Ye'd do the same fer me if I was a stranger, wouldn't ye now? An' ye know what the Lord says about bein' a stranger and takin' him in? No, lass, ye must come, I couldn't sleep myself fearin' tonight's incident might be repeated, an' me not nearby t' help."

The fire had burned low and the light in the room was now dim. The night was silent around them. Joanna gazed at her two companions across from her—Nathaniel's homely simple, brave face, and Miss Sinclair's stout, honest, true countenance.

"You don't know how much this means to me . . ." she said through tear-filled eyes. "Thank you both . . . so much."

Was their gentle compassion and goodness part of what she had come to Scotland seeking?

15

A New Home

❧❧

THE MEADOW SPREAD out before her like a blanket of rich green dotted with countless white and yellow daisies. In spots the grass reached as high as her knees as she made her way purposefully through it, plucking a bouquet of flowers as she went. Looking back, the Cuttahays' cottage had already faded into the distance and was just barely visible.

Joanna had awakened early. Lying on the straw mattress, she attempted to place where she was. But the sunlight streaming through the window, the homely sounds of Mrs. Cuttahay singing hymn after hymn in the kitchen, and the hazy memory of her ride home the night before in Nathaniel's wagon soon restored order to her brain. As did the pain in her jaw!

She lay quietly a few moments, listening to the rustic alto voice singing "Blessed assurance, Jesus is mine. . . ," and gradually a great peace stole over her.

Later that morning, after Nathaniel had returned to town for some of her things, Joanna remained at the farmhouse, trying to help Mrs. Cuttahay.

"Oh, I've only a wee bit left t' do, lass," the cheerful woman had said. "Ye jist rest an' dinna trouble yersel'." Letty Cuttahay was several inches shorter than Joanna and, as Nathaniel was apt to say, "nicely filled oot." Her brown hair, amply peppered with gray, was always braided and the braids neatly wrapped over the top of her head. Her small brown eyes seemed to twinkle constantly with merriment. This morning she was wearing a blue flowered cotton dress covered with a crisp white apron.

The house appeared immaculate, yet the energetic woman never stopped with her chores. "Ye've been through plenty, lass," she said. "Ye jist take yersel' easy." So Joanna sat on a small wooden stool while Mrs. Cuttahay peeled and cut up a pile of potatoes. She tossed them into the three-footed iron pot suspended by a heavy chain within the chimney of the fireplace, where they boiled and frothed in anticipation of midday dinner. It was not long before the older lady's unpretentious cheerfulness put Joanna completely at her ease.

They had only chatted briefly the previous night, but the reception could hardly have been more gracious. Letty Cuttahay's first reaction to her unexpected houseguest was a warm, welcoming hug; she blinked not an eye at having to ready a bed in their spare room at midnight.

Shortly before noon Letty said, "Why don't ye have a look aroun' the place? We'll be havin' some dinner as soon as Nathaniel gets back, an' ye'll be gettin' bored stayin' inside on such a bonny day."

Therefore Joanna had set out on a walk from the little cottage. Her destination was a small knoll she had spotted that morning from the kitchen window. It was hardly high enough even to be called a hill, but from it Joanna gained a wide view of the surrounding countryside. She could not see the town, but away eastward— where the terrain rose steadily—she thought she caught occasional glimpses of the sun reflecting off the towers of Stonewycke. Beyond to the north lay the glistening expanse of the sea. To the west, but out of sight, she knew from Nathaniel's description of the surrounding terrain, lay the River Lindow. A thin line of lush green trees lay off in the distance and Joanna wondered if they bordered the river as it wound to the sea. An afternoon's hike in that direction would be an adventure to undertake one day, she thought . . . if she was here that long.

I was going to make plans to return to London today, she thought suddenly. She had nearly forgotten.

Joanna looked again toward the outline of the great house. It could only be a couple of miles away, but it may as well have been in another world. Did the secrets of her grandmother's past lie hidden there? Should those secrets be left alone?

Joanna lay back in the grass, closed her eyes, and allowed the sun to bathe her in its fragrant summer warmth. How long she lay thus, half dozing, half daydreaming, she could not tell.

All at once she heard a great bounding, and something wet and scratchy brushed against her face. She opened her eyes in terror to find herself face to face with the largest, shaggiest sheepdog she had ever seen. He stared at her, tongue hanging out, eyes alive with the joy of being, when a sharp whistle sent him flying back down the hillside.

Joanna stood up and saw Nathaniel crossing the pasture toward her.

"Hello, lass," he called. "I'm afraid auld Reiver must hae disturbed ye. Hope he didna give ye too much a fricht—he's harmless enough, though."

"He is rather big!" laughed Joanna.

"The missus sent me oot after ye. She was wonderin' if ye'd be ready fer some dinner wi' us?"

"That sounds nice," Joanna answered, ". . . that is, if you don't mind?"

"Mind!" rejoined Nathaniel in something like disbelief. "Why, lass, ye're oor guest, practically family by now. Ye jist put all such thoughts oot o' yer head!"

Joanna smiled. As she descended the hill, Reiver ran toward her once again. She stooped down and ran her fingers through his shaggy mane, encircling his neck with a hug.

"I think he's already taken a special likin' t' ye," said Nathaniel.

Watching the dog dart off after a butterfly, then return to walk a few steps with her and Nathaniel, Joanna realized she felt more secure and at peace than she had in days.

"I stopped by the inn," said Nathaniel at length.

"Will everyone know where I am?"

"Won't matter much, I think," he replied. "I let it be known that ye were plannin' t' leave Port Strathy soon, t' see some o' the rest o' the country before returnin' t' the States. I didn't know yer plans fer certain, but maybe that'll take some o' the pressure off ye fer a while, if folks dinna think yer tryin' t' stir up trouble."

Dinner proved a pleasant occasion at the Cuttahay home. They sat down and Mr. Cuttahay offered thanks. "Oor Lord, we thank ye fer yer special care, an' especially fer bringin' young Joanna safely t' us. Lord, protect her an' give her guidance in these troubled times an' may she feel welcome in oor humble home as long as she like. And now, Lord, we thank ye fer the provision o' this food an' fer the roof over oor heads. We thank ye fer the life ye hae given us. Amen."

Touched by the man's words, Joanna looked up. Both husband and wife were smiling at her. She knew the words were no mere tokens but sprang from genuine love. Was there something in that prayer to explain what made these two people so special, what set them apart from so many others Joanna had known in her life? She recalled similar words and prayers from her childhood and youth. Her grandmother had spoken such things from the heart. Why hadn't she listened then as she was now?

The hearty oatcakes, which Mrs. Cuttahay referred to as bannocks, broth, boiled potatoes, and dried herring were served with pride and enjoyed with gusto. That life's simple pleasures of nourishing food, good company, and warm conversation could be surpassed by anything seemed impossible to Joanna at that moment. The Cuttahays spoke openly of everyday life in Port Strathy and plied Joanna with questions about America. When the meal ended, Nathaniel stood, stretched his long legs, then ambled toward his favorite chair. Sitting down, he lifted his legs to a three-legged wooden footstool and lit his favorite pipe.

"Jist time fer a wee smoke before I hae t' git t' work," he said.

The room fell silent for a few moments as the two women cleared away the dishes and Nathaniel puffed contentedly on his pipe.

"There was one thing I dinna tell ye aboot my trip t' town this mornin'," said Nathaniel after a moment. Joanna and Letty stopped their work and looked toward him expectantly. "Dinna ye say, lass," he continued, "that ye bit the hand o' that man last night?"

Joanna nodded.

"Weel, I saw Tom Forbes at the inn an' he was sportin' a fresh bandage on his hand."

"Oh, poor Tom," said Letty with dismay.

"I hate t' think o' it bein' him," Nathaniel went on. "But I'm afraid I couldna put it past him, either."

"An' after all that sweet Olive has tried t' do fer him too," Letty sighed.

"Sometimes the likes o' him are beyond help, Letty."

"Beyond oor help, maybe," answered his wife. "But not beyond His help who made him—so we mustn't give up on 'im, either. An' all this time I thought he was doin' so good, gettin' over his accident."

"He's been spendin' an uncommon amount o' time at the Bluster 'N Blow lately—I hear none o' the boats will hae him on."

"His poor family!" said Letty. "First thing tomorrow, I'm goin' t' call on Annie . . . maybe take her some preserves."

"That'd be nice o' ye, Letty. Ye're always tryin' t' find what the Lord'd do, aren't ye, my bonny lady?"

Watching the man gaze on his wife, Joanna thought she had never seen a man look at a woman with quite that same look in his eyes before—a look of admiration, not a little awe, and certainly a deep and reverent love. Here was simplicity itself. For the first time Joanna found herself wistfully desirous of something like this from a man, a love she wondered if someone like Jason Channing could ever give, or would even recognize or care about if he saw it.

"But all the trouble he's been through," Nathaniel went on at length, "still canna account fer such a deed."

"I still don't understand it," Joanna said. "What reason would he, or anyone, have for doing it?"

"I'll warrant it has somethin' t' do wi' them papers, or at least wi' ye bein' a Duncan," Nathaniel said.

"But Mr. Sercombe said they were worthless."

"Lawyers!" Nathaniel scoffed. "They're sly rascals, an' Palmer Sercombe's no different."

"Why, Nathaniel," Letty chided gently, "you forget about dear Mr. Ogilvie doon in Culden. He's a real nice man."

"I ken, Letty, but they're few an' far between. I'll na be surprised if Sercombe doesna stand t' make a tidy sum fer himsel' oot o' the sale."

"How can ye be sayin' such aboot the man?" Letty said. "Wi' all the things he's arrangin' fer the town?"

"Calm doon, Letty," Nathaniel returned in a tender tone. "Holdin' folks up t' Christian virtues may be one thing. But sometimes ye trust people too far, even gowks like Tom an' Sercombe. I'm goin' to give every man the benefit o' the doobt. But the Lord warned us t' be wise as serpents, ye know, an' we be boun' t' keep oor heads clear an' no be gowks oorsel's."

"What is Sercombe doing for Port Strathy?" asked Joanna.

"Weel, since there is no legal heir," Nathaniel said, "Sercombe's arrangin' fer the estate t' be sold. An' supposedly the man's agreed t' improve the harbor. An' there's been talk that a share o' the proceeds will be passed on t' each o' us tenants t' improve oor houses an' invest in oor crops an' fishin' boats an' the like."

"Nothin' like it's happened since I can recall," Letty added. "'Tis all folks hae been talking aboot. These last two winters were rough ones. An' this is jist the sort o' thing t' give this auld village a boost."

The small household fell silent for a few moments.

Soon Nathaniel stood, knocked his pipe clean in the hearth, put on his red wool cap and, bidding the ladies a pleasant afternoon, went outside to tend to his chores.

Letty took a kettle of hot water from the hearth and filled the dishpan in the small adjoining kitchen, humming softly. As she watched, Joanna could not help wondering what life was like in Port Strathy fifty years earlier. Could this very house have been standing then? What were times like for her grandmother? And what had happened to drive her away? She tried to imagine Port Strathy two generations earlier and wondered if the look of the town had changed.

"How I wish I could have been there then . . ." Joanna mused out loud.

"Child?"

"I was just wondering what it was like when my grandmother was here," Joanna replied.

"Ah . . . the Lady Margaret was a bonny lass."

"Did you know her?" came Joanna's startled reply.

Letty smiled as warm memories filled her head. She dried her soapy hands and sat down at the table with Joanna. "I only ken what my mama would tell me aboot her o' an evenin'. She was the one who knew Lady Margaret. I guess they were as much friends as their different stations in life would allow. That was one thing that was sure different in those days t' be sure. Folk had their place, an' the lady o' the estate had her place an' a poor crofter had hers. But my mama said Lady Margaret was different. 'Twas like she *wanted* t' be like the crofters."

Letty sighed and fell silent for a few moments; the far-away look in her eyes told Joanna that the older woman had been transported to that time so long ago. At length Letty began again. "When I was born, the Lady came t' see me. Ye see I wasna expected t' live through the night. But she came jist t' look in on my mama an' me—that's hoo much she cared . . ."

"Did your mother ever say why Lady Margaret left Scotland?"

"She only liked t' tell me o' the good times," Letty replied with a note of sadness in her voice. "When the Lady left, weel, I think my mama felt like a piece o' the heart had been cut oot o' Stonewycke. No one really knew what happened. Some said it were the romance. But the laird forbid anyone t' speak o' his daughter in his hearin'. An' soon folk jist found other things t' interest them. An' though I hate t' say it, through the years most jist forgot aboot her. Not my mama though, an' there were perhaps a few others o' the folk that loved her. But they werena given t' gossip."

"Could it—" Joanna began, but then paused as if she was afraid to frame the question that so dominated her mind. Finally she blurted out: "Is it truly possible that this . . . this *same* Margaret is my grandmother?"

In answer, Letty clicked her tongue thoughtfully, then said, "It appears t' me, child, that there's jist too many coincidences if she's not. Aye, I'd say 'tis more than likely."

Joanna knew, however, that one way or another she would have to find out—on the basis of more than mere coincidence. Wasn't that why she had come to Scotland?

The remainder of the day passed leisurely. Though her first day at the Cuttahays' had been a wonderful change and relief, when evening came Joanna found herself nearly exhausted. The emotional drain of her few days here had finally taken its toll.

That night she retired early. Drifting slowly into sleep, her final thoughts were of her grandmother and the gray stone walls of the "muckle hoose" on the hill. She dreamed during the night, and that was a vision of a tall thin man in gardener's clothes running through a broad field of yellow daisies, chased by a shaggy sheepdog.

16

An Unexpected Meeting

JOANNA AWOKE EARLY.

It was full daylight, but a quick glance at the clock in her room revealed that it was only 5:30. Knowing further sleep to be impossible, she crawled out of bed, dressed, then crept from her room. She found Nathaniel sprawled out in his chair, fully dressed but sound asleep. She couldn't tell if he had never been to bed or had slept, risen some time before her, and fallen asleep once again. She stole past him and outside into the sharp morning chill.

Reiver lay next to the chicken coop as sound asleep as his master. The frosty air was quiet and Joanna felt as though she should walk on tiptoes so as not to disturb its tranquillity. How strange it seemed for the sun to rise so early in that northern land!

All at once the silence was torn by an inhuman blood-curdling cry.

Joanna froze!

She told herself it was nothing but one of the many usual animal sounds one grows accustomed to on a farm. But her assurances couldn't quell the thumping in her chest. Looking toward the barn, from whence the awful sound had come, Joanna crept slowly in that direction.

She approached the open door and peeked inside.

All she could make out were dark shadows. She stepped tentatively in and looked hurriedly to her right, then to her left. Nothing appeared amiss. Her eyes slowly adjusted to the dimness, but she saw the stack of empty milk pails a moment too late.

Toppling to the ground they crashed and clanged against one another until each rolled to a stop.

"Yow!" answered a loud yell from the opposite end of the barn. "Nathaniel, what are ye aboot? Keep quiet, man!"

"I'm sorry . . . it's not Nathaniel," Joanna's answering voice sounded so small.

"Weel, keep quiet will ye, whoever ye are! The noise frightened the bo an' she nearly crushed my arm."

Knowing she was unwelcome, yet driven by curiosity, Joanna inched forward toward the last of a group of stalls in which Nathaniel's cows spent the night. A dim light from that direction drew her, and she slowly made her way across the dirt floor strewn with dry straw. Reaching the end of the row of stalls, she saw a man kneeling on the ground next to a great prostrate form. The man's back was toward her as he tended an unmoving beast; his muscular frame was stripped to the waist and dripping with sweat despite the morning's cold. Steam rose from his shoulders, accented by occasional silent puffs from the animal's wet nose.

"I'm sorry," said Joanna again, "I thought I heard a strange sound, and—"

"And what do ye expect from the poor beast!" he interrupted, spinning around. Catching full sight of Joanna for the first time, his frustrated face flashed recognition. "You!" he exclaimed.

Joanna started in dismay.

It was the man she had seen on the beach. Only this time the tables were turned and she had disturbed him, an occurrence which had clearly upset him.

Before she had a chance to say a word the cow let forth another heart-wrenching low wail. He patted her flank and whispered some soothing Gaelic words Joanna could not understand.

"Is she sick?" she asked, glad to have the attention diverted away from the disturbance she had obviously caused in the proceedings.

"Jist tryin' t' give birth," he said. "And no doubt all this racket has set her back hours!"

He stood and walked over to a bucket of soapy water. His right arm was caked with dried blood and Joanna's stomach lurched uncertainly for a moment. He dipped both arms into the water and attempted to scrub the blood away, but most of it still clung to his skin.

"An' what might ye be doin' roamin' aboot the Cuttahays' byre at such a time o' day?" he asked with a tone of authority. The fact that he had been awake most of the night had shortened his usual degree of tolerance.

"I told you," she answered defensively, "I heard a noise."

"That ye did . . . ye'll be the girl from America?"

She nodded.

"Stayin' wi' the Cuttahays, are ye?"

"Well, I have for a couple days. That is, I don't know what—"

Her words were cut off by the whines of the cow.

"Back t' work," he said, hastening to the cow's side. "Ye run an' fetch Nathaniel . . . quickly!"

"He's asleep."

"Must've dropped off—the man's been oot here wi' me most o' the night," he said, then hesitated as he thought for a moment.

"Weel," he went on, "'tis no time noo. Ye'll have t' help me yersel'."

"Me!" exclaimed Joanna. "I don't know anything about—"

"Don't argue! There's no time!" In his exhaustion he was in no mood to debate with a fainthearted female.

"But I—"

"I'll tell ye what to do," he said, and without waiting for her consent, he took a rope from where it lay next to his bag of instruments and quickly tied a slipknot in one end. Kneeling down he slipped his arm into the straining animal.

Joanna gasped as his hand and arm, still clutching the rope, disappeared inside the hindquarters of the cow.

This was no time to be sick, but she felt her stomach giving way!

For the first time she noticed the pungent stench of manure and stale urine in which the cow was lying.

"Stand ready when I call!"

Joanna's hand unconsciously sought her mouth. She had to keep her queasy stomach in check. She couldn't lose control of herself now!

"If only I can get that head around . . . " the man was saying. "I think the calf is still alive."

He paused, concentrating on his task. "Aye . . . it is!"

Long moments passed.

Joanna found herself—in spite of the nausea which threatened to erupt at any moment—awed not only by what she was witnessing, but also by the man kneeling on the hard, dirt-packed floor. For all his homespun appearance, his features managed to retain a certain boyish gaiety. She recalled his unassuming laughter on the beach—which annoyed her so. And though he certainly wasn't smiling now, his eyes were alive with excitement—as though he were a boy on a wonderful adventure.

But it wasn't his taut muscles or craggy features that captured her attention, but the gentle intensity with which he devoted himself to his task—his comforting murmurs to the cow and his determination to deliver a healthy calf no matter what . . . no matter whose help he had to enlist. He appeared totally consumed by the event.

"I've got it!" he exclaimed at last. The strain in his voice masked the triumph he felt.

"Noo, lass . . . grab the end o' this rope!"

Joanna hesitated.

"Noo!" he barked. "Kneel doon here . . . take the rope."

Joanna stepped forward and reluctantly knelt down. Her knees oozed into the soft layer of muck coating the floor of the stall. He forced the rope into her hands and her fingers slowly closed around it. She was grateful that in the dim light she could not tell if the slime she knelt in was brown or red.

"Don't yank it, jist pull slowly . . . a nice even tension on the rope."

Joanna obeyed.

"That's it . . . nice an' easy."

Joanna could feel the calf struggling on the other end. A surge of wonder shot through her frame. She was holding a new life! An unborn being was attached to this rope she held, and she was pulling it into the world.

In that instant she forgot her dress, buried from the knees down in a smelling black mess. She forgot the putrifying reek which would have sent her into a deathly faint only a week earlier. She forgot her dainty pride and feminine dignity. She forgot about her grandmother and Jason Channing and deeds and papers and plans and problems.

She only knew she was helping to give life!

"Ah, lassie . . . ye're doin' great!"

Joanna smiled and still held on, arms and shoulders beginning to ache from the pressure.

"Thank you," she said.

"I was meanin' the cow," he said. "But ye're doin' jist fine too!"

The cow's movements and the vet's words of encouragement increased in intensity. Joanna's heart pounded and her throat had gone dry. Then she saw the tiny pink muzzle emerge into the open air. The man eased back to Joanna and grasped the rope with her.

"Now she's right where we want her. Together . . . let's pull her on oot!"

Before Joanna knew it, the bloody, wet newborn calf lay on the floor.

But the vet's job had not ended. He grabbed up a handful of clean straw and began rubbing it over the brown and white spotted calf, lying there limp and lifeless. Still it made no move. Hurriedly he pried open its tiny mouth, scooped out mucus with his fingers, and blew several forceful breaths into it. He continued to massage the little animal's chest until its eyelids flickered. Suddenly the calf jerked wildly and struggled to gain footing. He was still too weak for that, however, and slumped back to the ground.

"I've never seen anything so beautiful!" said Joanna, through tears streaming down her cheeks.

He continued to rub the newborn calf down with straw, then dragged him to his mother's head. The listless cow lay exhausted, but as he drew her new baby near, her nostrils distended, she sniffed, then began to lick the tiny young face vigorously.

"Aye . . . it never fails to stir me!" he said. As Joanna turned toward him she thought she detected the faint glistening of moisture in his eyes too. And such deep blue eyes they were!

They each stood in silence for a few moments, observing the tender spectacle being played out before them. They hardly noticed the rising sun's attempts to penetrate the cracks in the walls of the ancient barn as it now poured in through every available slit. A sound of clomping boots behind them hurrying through the barn interrupted the peaceful morning silence.

"Hullo . . . Alec . . . how's she doin'?" called out Nathaniel, fearful he had overslept the time when he was needed the most.

"Relax, Nathaniel," the vet called out. Just then the old man burst through into the crowded stall.

"Ye have a fine new bull, Nathaniel," beamed Joanna's unknown companion. "Jist what ye were wantin'!"

"Weel, the Lord be praised! An' it certainly is alive, too. What would I do wi' oot ye, Alec? An' me off asleep whilst ye did all the work! How'd ye manage it?"

"This new guest o' yers, Nathaniel. She did the work o' a stout woman!"

"Why, lass!" exclaimed Nathaniel, seeming to notice Joanna's presence almost for the first time. "Jist look at ye, all dirty an' wi' the sweat standing on yer brow . . . ye been workin' hard!"

Nathaniel's pride could not have beamed more brightly had Joanna been his own daughter. He threw a strong arm around her and gave her a tight squeeze. Joanna blushed, then laughed outright.

"I never had the chance to thank ye fer all yer help," said the vet, the earlier edge to his voice softening as he turned toward Joanna standing at Nathaniel's side.

"Certainly," she replied. "I wouldn't have missed it . . . even if I did stumble in here by accident and upset all the milk cans."

Now it was the young man's turn to laugh. "No harm done," he said good-naturedly.

"Weel," said Nathaniel, "I'm glad t' see that the two o' ye hae made such fine acquaintance."

"Actually, there was hardly time fer a fit introduction. Yer lass walked in on me and I put her t' work."

"Weel then, Joanna, I'd like ye t' meet, official-like, oor young vet'narian in these parts, Alec MacNeil. Alec, this here's Joanna Matheson, oor visitor from America."

Alec extended his hand, but then remembering its appearance and where it had recently been, quickly withdrew it. Joanna laughed. "My dress isn't in much better condition, Mr. MacNeil," she said.

"Now. Come," said Nathaniel. "Wash yersel's up. Letty's fixin' up a hearty breakfast fer us all. I'll fetch ye some fresh water from the well."

Holding up the edges of her ruined dress as they walked out of the barn together, Joanna felt happier than she had ever been in her life.

17

A Peaceful Afternoon

JOANNA SLIPPED A jar of Letty's bread-and-butter pickles into the basket. Only one or two more items and all would be ready.

This was wonderful! A real picnic in the country!

She had been awake almost since dawn waiting impatiently until she heard Letty stirring in the kitchen.

The morning had progressed at an interminably slow pace while Nathaniel hurried through his day's chores to free himself for the afternoon. But at long last Letty asked Joanna to fetch the basket and begin the preparations.

She had fairly skipped to the pantry!

"This jar o' marmalade an' those four plates there, an' that should do 't," said Letty, handing the jar to Joanna.

At that moment Nathaniel walked into the kitchen. He plucked off his cap and ran a sleeve across his brow. "Weel, the stock's all fed—we can go when Alec gets here." He reached into the basket for a biscuit but Letty gave his hand a gentle swat.

"Those are fer later," she scolded.

"Jist thought I might lighten the load a wee bit," he said with a laugh. Letty looked at the twinkle in his eye, weakened under his smile and handed him his prize.

"'Tis a grand day fer an afternoon in the meadows," he said as he munched on the fresh-baked oatbiscuit.

"We're ready," said Letty.

"Oh, where is Mr. MacNeil?" said Joanna, trying to conceal her impatience but not wanting to lose a single moment of the day.

It had been two days since Alec MacNeil had been to the Cuttahay farm to deliver Nathaniel's new young bull. Since that morning—which had proved nearly as momentous for Joanna as for the calf—she had scarcely thought once about leaving Port Strathy. Something had changed for her that morning. Seeing the sights, smelling the smells, and getting on her hands and knees and participating in such a fundamental experience of Scottish country life had established a bond deep in her soul with this lifestyle which earlier had been so foreign to her. Suddenly London seemed distant, far removed from these earthy values and priorities of simple existence.

The Cuttahays accepted her so totally and shared their humble life and provision with her so entirely that after just two brief days, Joanna felt as if she had belonged there all her life.

It was another half hour before Alec MacNeil finally arrived, out of breath as he galloped up the dirt road and hastily dismounted, sweaty and disheveled.

"Sorry I'm late," he said. "I've spent the mornin' wi' the Kerrs' bull, an' he wasn't the most cooperative o' patients."

"We're jist glad ye could come, Alec," enjoined Letty heartily.

"Nathaniel, could I put my horse up in yer byre? He's in sore need o' a rest after the way I ran him."

"O' course," Nathaniel replied. "I'll go oot wi' ye. I have t' bring the wagon 'round."

At last the little party assembled, loaded into the wagon, and was soon rambling along behind Nathaniel's two trustworthy horses. The dirt trail they followed led from the Cuttahays' cottage south and west, across mostly flat terrain, toward the neighboring county across the Lindow. It would take them most of the way toward their destination, a secluded little meadow of soft green grass abundant with wildflowers and surrounded by a dense growth of pine trees. Nathaniel and Letty had discovered the spot quite by accident when they were courting, and it had remained a special place ever since. Jostling along the bumpy road Alec held the reins, with Nathaniel perched on the seat at his side. Letty and Joanna half-reclined on blankets in the wagon bed behind them, chatting away, enjoying the wonders of early summer.

The morning was in full flower and gave promise of continued clear skies and warm sunshine. "If only ye could see the heather in bloom," said Letty to Joanna with a sigh. "Right here," she said, sweeping out her hand toward the low-lying hills to their left, "'tis absolutely stunning, a thin mat o' purple as far as ye can see."

"When will it bloom?" asked Joanna.

"Later . . . not till September or so, depending on the weather."

"It's beautiful now," said Joanna with a satisfied smile, drawing in a huge breath of the sweet fragrance born on the southerly breeze. "I can't think of any place I'd rather be."

Letty returned her smile and placed a motherly hand on Joanna's arm. "An' I'm glad ye're here wi' us, child," she said.

Alec directed the two bay mares along the barely passable road, first in a southerly direction, then veering gradually toward the west. They had been riding nearly an hour when Nathaniel said, "Weel, here's oor stop. Pull the horses up over yonder, Alec. There's plenty o' fine grass here t' keep 'em occupied."

Tying the horses and gathering the blankets and basket, the small group began to traipse through high grass, over a rocky, rugged hill and finally through a tiny wood. At last their efforts were rewarded.

"It's . . . it's lovely!" exclaimed Joanna in mingled delight and wonder. "Such a magnificent tiny meadow, hidden away from the world like this!"

"It's oor own private little hideaway," said Nathaniel with pride.

"Aye," said Letty, "we been comin' here fer years and never saw another soul."

"An' do my ears mistake me, or do I hear the river?" asked Alec, equally taken with their scenic discovery.

"Aye, ye do, Alec," said Nathaniel, "trees on three sides an' the river on the fourth. 'Tis a perfectly protected little spot."

The older couple proudly showed the youths all about, at last making their way to the far side. The river was still swollen with winter runoff and rumbled along mightily on its way to the sea. In late summer the banks would drop away nearly ten feet to the water. But now the water reached the top of the rocky edge.

"In my younger days," said Nathaniel, "I tried t' impress my leddy by comin' here, rippin' off my shirt in one motion, an' divin' into the water t' swim across."

"First time he did," laughed Letty, "I nearly died wi' fright!"

"Water's mighty icy this time o' year," said Nathaniel, "but when I was yoong an' foolish I dinna seem t' mind."

"Are ye goin' t' give us a demonstration today?" asked Alec with a grin.

Nathaniel laughed heartily. "No, no. I hae na jumped into the Lindow fer years. How 'bout yerself, Alec?"

"Not today! But, Nathaniel, isn't that a part o' the Dormin on the other side, there?"

"Aye. A side o' it few people see—another part o' the charm o' this little meadow o' oor's."

The Dormin to which Alec referred was the thick and verdant Dormin Forest, a small but unusually dense little wood measuring approximately a mile across and no more than two miles in length. Since its discovery centuries earlier the Dormin had been under special royal protection, though it remained unfenced and rather loosely enforced. It was teeming with dozens of species of trees and shrubs, moss and grasses, ferns and wildlife. No hunting, cutting, collecting, or gathering of any kind was allowed; during the warm months of late autumn a stream of biologists and botanists from Scotland's universities made their way to the Dormin to study its spectacular array of flora and fauna.

But today the picnickers only gazed at the Dormin from across its bordering river, content with the splendor of their own grassy meadow. Letty and Joanna spread out the blanket beneath a large elm and set out the lunch from the basket.

"Ah, ye've seen t' everything, Letty," said Nathaniel.

"Joanna did most o' it," said his wife.

"So ye think we ought t' keep her, then?" asked Nathaniel, flashing a grin toward Joanna. "Mighty fine yoong woman she be t' have aroun'."

Joanna blushed at Nathaniel's tease, then laughed.

"I thought she already was oor own," said Letty. "I'd already forgotten she was but oor guest."

"Weel, the Lord be thanked fer sendin' her to us, that's fer sure," said Nathaniel.

A leisurely meal followed, to the drone of inquisitive bumble bees overhead and the sound of gently flowing water.

Joanna felt light with a joy she had never known.

Thoughts of Alec stole into the edges of Joanna's consciousness quite by accident and wholly unnoticed by her. There remained an unspoken nervousness within her stemming from their first quarrelsome encounter on the beach. He had never mentioned it. But she felt she should apologize for her rudeness, though she was too embarrassed to bring it up.

Alec, for his part, however, showed not the slightest hint of a corresponding tenseness. He talked and laughed easily. But was there more to this rugged young Scotsman than could quickly be discerned by the superficial gaze of a near-stranger like Joanna? Casting him a sidelong glance, she found him silent and thoughtful, gazing into the Dormin, seemingly mesmerized by the slow flow of the Lindow, as if his gaze might be able to penetrate the rich, tangled forest.

How Joanna would like to have screwed up her courage to ask him about his thoughts! But she could never have intruded so. Besides, that was the one area where she had already discovered that his tongue did not flow freely—when talking of himself.

Lunch completed and the conversation dying to a peaceful silence, Alec stood and stretched his long limbs.

"I'm fer a bit o' exercise," he said. "Nathaniel, why don't we take oor guest t' the top o' the Marbrae?"

"Alec, ye forget my age! I hae na climbed the Marbrae fer five years an' dinna think my auld bones are up t' that hike today. Not that I dinna intend t' do it again one day. But today . . . I think I'll jist leave that t' the two o' ye youngsters."

Alec turned toward Joanna with a questioning look.

"I'm agreeable," she said. "But what's the Marbrae?"

"A great hill on the other side o' the road from where we left the wagon," said Nathaniel. "A great hill, but not quite a mountain. Rises steeply from the valley here an' ye can climb t' the very top in only an hour—an easy enough walk . . . that is, when ye're yoong."

"We'll meet ye back at the wagon in two hours, Nathaniel," said Alec.

He then led the way, and for the next hour Joanna found herself desperately trying to keep pace with her long-legged companion. The trail was narrow, necessitating walking in single file. Conversation was therefore infrequent as Alec seemed intent on their destination. By the time they gained the summit, she was out of breath, perspiring, and ready to drop.

Turning around and first perceiving her state, he said, "I'm sorry I've gone too fast fer ye."

"Oh no," said Joanna, a bit breathlessly. "I'm tired, but . . . well, I made it."

"Whenever I come here I can't seem t' keep from walkin' fast. I always get caught up in the adventure o' it. I guess I forget I've been here before an' am a bit used t' it."

It took a few moments sitting on a rock regaining her wind for Joanna to begin to take in the view that spread out before her. Then she saw why Alec had wanted to make the climb, and why—even though he had apparently been here many times—he termed the hike an adventure.

Below them, on the side opposite the more gradual eastern slope up which they had ascended, the Marbrae dropped off abruptly. Joanna gasped as she peered carefully over the precipitous edge and quickly retreated a step or two to the safety of Alec's side.

"Oh my!" she exclaimed. "That's quite a cliff!"

"But jist look at the view, Miss Matheson. Doesn't it jist make ye forget every care ye ever had?"

The Lindow River, winding its way through forests and fields on its slow trek toward the sea, floated on noiselessly below them on the west, widening considerably at its mouth, or firth.

"Yes," she answered, "I suppose you're right. I wonder where Nathaniel and Letty are right now?"

"That's easy," said Alec. "I'll show ye."

He walked confidently toward the cliff, reached it, then looked back. Joanna stood stock-still, not moving a step.

"Don't be afraid," he said. "No harm'll come t' ye. Here, take my hand."

He turned toward her with outstretched arm and offered his right hand.

Gingerly Joanna approached a few steps and reached toward him. His large, rough hand closed firmly around hers, tiny and weak inside his powerful grasp. But she sensed that it was a good hand which now held her tight, a hand of strength and safety. She continued toward the edge until she stood close by his side, clasping his hand like a vise, terrified yet feeling secure at the same time.

"If ye look down there," said Alec pointing with his left hand, "where the river seems t' disappear fer a moment, ye'll see that the forest an' trees appear a bit darker. That's the Dormin. Few o' the folks that come visitin' it know about this place an' what a view o' things ye can get from here. Weel, that's where they are, jist on the other side o' the river from the Dormin. Ye can almost make out the lush green o' the meadow, but I canna tell if it might jist be my eyes playin' tricks on me."

"I think I see it!" said Joanna excitedly.

Further north, the sea spread out in all directions in a vast expanse of deep blue, splotched with green and occasional patches of gray. Under the day's clear skies the thin line of the horizon was sharp and clearly defined. Toward their right some six or seven miles distant lay the small buildings of Port Strathy, brown brick and white-washed walls discernible against the backdrop of the green fields and blue sea. Further beyond, Ramsey Head rose mightily out of the sea, huge even from this great distance. To the east was Strathy Summit, with the low-lying fields, pastures, and wooded areas of Strathy valley between it and the place where they stood.

"It's . . . it's breathtaking!" said Joanna, retreating a step or two.

Alec released her hand and sat down on a large rock several steps away from the cliff.

"Why," Joanna went on, unable to contain her expressions of delight at the scene, "you can see everything from here."

"Aye, 'tis a gran' place," he said. "Nathaniel an' Letty have their meadow. But this has always been my special spot."

"You come here often?"

"When I need t' think, or get away from my cares. I sit an' look oot t' sea an' sometimes imagine I can see oor Viking ancestors sailin' their great ships across the sea."

"You're a descendant of the Vikings?"

"Aye, but that was hundreds o' years ago."

"I suppose I've never made the connection in my mind," said Joanna. "The Vikings were so fierce and barbaric, and after meeting Nathaniel, I've grown to think of Scotland as a gentle land."

"Ah, but yer typical Scotsman's a rough-hewn character. We're a tough breed. Remember the man who attacked ye? Scotland's history is a violent an' bloody one. Surely ye've heard o' the battle o' Culloden an' Glencoe an' the feuds between the rival clans like the MacDonalds an' the Campbells? No, 'tis no gentle place, this Scotland o' oor's.'

Alec fell silent, and when Joanna glanced over toward him, his eyes seemed to be staring at the view but his thoughts seemed far away.

Alec was pondering his own words.

He had almost said too much, revealed more of himself than he wanted to. Why he should have done so he didn't know. Perhaps it was the spell of Marbrae, or was it feeling at ease with Joanna? Only Nathaniel knew just why he had left his home to set up practice in Port Strathy—best it stay that way.

He looked down at his hands and the hint of a shudder stirred his frame. Yes, he knew of violence . . . only too well.

"What's that?" asked Joanna pointing to a ridge about a mile off which stood out from the green valley which stretched out below them toward the sea.

Alec pulled himself out of his reverie. "That's Braenock Ridge. 'Tis a stretch o' rocky moorland, full o' little but brown shrubbery, an' is not good fer much. But there, can ye see . . ."

He pointed and Joanna followed the direction of his arm.

"Jist look, aboot in the middle o' it, ye can jist barely make it oot. 'Tis the last bits o' the ruin o' an ancient Pict village," he said. There was little to be seen other than some piles of rock covered with creeping ivy and surrounded by a few scraggly looking shrubs.

"History says one night a Viking ship landed in oor harbor an' the Viking warriors made their way inland an' fell upon the village, slaughterin' every man, woman, an' child in the place."

His voice caught on the words. But he determined to go on with the grisly tale. "'Twas so sudden," he resumed, "that they had no chance t' defend themselves wi' as much as a single blow."

"How awful!" Joanna breathed with a slight tremble.

"An' all jist because they wanted somethin' t' eat. So the story goes, but I expect there was more t' it than that."

"They could have just taken it. They didn't have to kill everyone."

"But that's how it was. I expect the Picts would hae done the same if the tables had been turned. An' that same blood is mingled wi' the inhabitants o' the land today. An' many a Scotsman takes pride in that fierce, savage past. No, Miss

Matheson, yer new friend Nathaniel . . . he's the exception. An' even he has that same blood flowin' through his veins."

"Why then is he such a gentle, compassionate man?"

"It's not bein' a Scotsman that sets him apart. It's his faith. Surely ye've noticed the way he talks aboot God an' the Scriptures?"

"Well . . . I guess I hadn't thought of it. But, yes, now that you mention it I do recall him referring to God. But he's not a churchy sort of man."

"Exactly my point. He's different. He neither fits the pattern o' bein' a rough Scotsman or a religious clergyman sort. He's jist . . . Nathaniel."

"Well then, what's so different about him?"

"Don't ye see? It's because he lives his faith. He doesn't spend all day talkin' aboot it or preachin' at ye or puttin' on airs. He jist rolls up his sleeves an' gets on wi' livin'. His faith is jist reflected in the kind o' person he is."

"It sounds like he's had quite an impact on you."

"Aye," said Alec slowly after a moment's reflection. "I suppose ye're right. I met him soon after I came to Strathy. He an' Letty sort o' took me in, ye might say. Kind o' like they have yersel'. An' I soon found I'd never met anyone like the man before. I couldn't help wantin' to be like him. He's honest, forthright, not afraid t' speak his mind, not afraid t' jump into the fray if he thinks somethin' isn't right. He doesn't care what the townspeople say aboot 'im, always wantin' the truth t' come oot more than anythin'."

Joanna looked at Alec, not sure if he had finished speaking.

He was gazing into the distance, absorbed in his own thoughts. The face intrigued her. Just now she noticed something she hadn't seen in it before. Little of the savage was evident. There was, in fact, a gentle flow to his features that reminded her of the very words he had been speaking about Nathaniel. Yet burning in his eyes Joanna could detect a remnant of a certain untamed, forceful energy, perhaps a fierceness not unlike the rugged coastline or the green mystery called Dormin.

"And what about you, Alec?" Joanna asked, surprised with her own boldness.

He did not answer immediately.

When the words finally came, they were slow and measured. Joanna could feel the deep sense of personal introspection in his tone—as if he was confronting an old dilemma which had already been round and round through his brain dozens of times but for which he had not yet discovered a satisfactory solution.

"The Bible says t' turn the other cheek," he began. "It says many such things. An' I believe the words. An' I see the fruit o' doin' them in Nathaniel's life. An' that's how I try t' live my life. But . . ."

He paused.

His eyes bore into the distant sea, as if the elusive answer might lie there. "I suppose tryin' isn't always enough. The words o' Paul the apostle aboot sums it up fer me—'the good that I would do I don't do, but the evil I would not do, that I do.' It's some comfort t' know that Paul struggled wi' what lay at the very bottom o' his bein'."

"I don't understand," said Joanna.

"It's jist that evil lies at the core o' us all, though not all hae had it come t' the surface an' . . . an' . . . weel, 'tis hard t' put into words." *Maybe someday*, he thought. *But not just yet.*

"I'm sorry . . . I didn't mean to pry."

"There's one thing else Paul says aboot it, though, that there's hope through Christ. I have t' remin' myself' o' that."

A heavy brooding silence followed Alec's words.

When he spoke again his voice was an obvious attempt to lift the mood and divert the course of the conversation away from himself.

"But ye haven't seen everything," he said, rising and offering his hand once more as he helped Joanna up from the rock where she sat.

"Look over in that direction, Miss Matheson," he said, turning for the first time toward the south, where the Lindow shrank in size as it disappeared from their sight in the distant hills of its origin. "Beyond all we can see, away t' the south and west, lie the Scottish Highlands."

Joanna quietly drank in everything. Then it became her turn to grow introspective. This whole land seemed like another world, from another time, another age. Yet suddenly, more than ever, Joanna found she wanted to be a part of it.

She wondered if she ever could.

18

Flame Dance

ALEC MACNEIL HAD lived on Scotland's rugged northern coast for twenty-three of his twenty-seven years, the four-year break a result of his veterinary training in Edinburgh. He had been raised just west of Ramsey Head.

Alec's father had been a highly esteemed fisherman in his community and had died in a storm at sea when Alec was fifteen. The young boy had always intended to follow his father to the sea, and even during his teen years had already become a fisherman of no small skill. But soon after his father's death, the local veterinarian had needed an assistant and had taken young Alec under his wing. Realizing his mother and sister would require support from a safer and more dependable source than the sea, Alec decided to follow his new line of work. The old vet took a liking to Alec and offered to finance him through veterinary school.

By age twenty-two, Alec had everything he wanted—a profession he loved and a promising future. Most of all, he would be able to support his family. Things could not have been better for Alec and would have continued thus except for that night . . . that night which would always burn in his memory.

It had been a busy week. As he rode home from his final call of the day, he was nearly asleep in the saddle. His house was around the next corner and he was thinking of hot soup and biscuits when he jerked to attention, startled. He thought he'd heard muffled cries down the darkened side street as he passed. His vet's instinct forced him to stop and investigate. Some animal in trouble, no doubt.

But it was no animal!

In the dim light of the late fall evening, he could just make out the form of a man's arm raised to strike a helpless victim.

"Hey!" he yelled to distract the man as he ran down the alley toward them. On reaching them, Alec tore the man from his victim and in that moment, he saw a woman lying on the ground, dress torn, face bruised and a trickle of blood oozing down her cheek where the man had struck her.

It was his sister!

In unrestrained wrath, Alec spun around, viciously grabbed the man and threw him bodily against the side of the brick building. He raised his arm to strike him but the man slumped into a heap on the ground. He lay motionless for some time, and upon closer inspection Alec realized the man's head had smashed against the wall. He would never move again.

When the whole sordid incident came to public light, Alec was lauded as a hero. The dead man turned out to be an unsavory character from Aberdeen who was wanted there for numerous crimes. But none of this mattered to Alec.

He had killed a man.

In rage and violence, his own two hands had taken a life. It tormented him day and night. He lived in fear should his wrath rise again against another—perhaps next time, his victim would not be so culpable. And, too, there seemed a vague change in the attitude of his friends and neighbors toward him, an effort on their part to avoid arousing his anger.

Perhaps it was all in his mind. But when the position in Port Strathy opened up, Alec wasted no time in applying.

Jacob Greely, the vet in Port Strathy, needed an assistant; Alec fit the bill perfectly. The two struck up an immediate friendship and the older man hardly blinked an eye when Alec revealed his past. Jacob respected the lad all the more, not only for his forthright honesty, but also because his deed had so clearly disturbed the lad.

Then within a year, Jacob died, leaving his practice to Alec.

Alec loved his work, even on mornings like this when Billy, the stable boy at Stonewycke, pounded unmercifully on his door at 6:30 a.m. The lad had no way of knowing Alec had only moments before (or so it seemed) crawled back into bed after spending several strenuous hours with Hootons' sick Galloway.

"What can it be, lad?" Alec asked as he pulled on his overalls.

"Mr. Innes sent me, sir," Billy replied. "'Tis Flame Dance. He's some sore ailin'. We never seen 'im like this. Mr. Innes says fer ye t' come right away."

Alec disappeared inside the house to pack the few items he thought he might need and then hurried to the stable to saddle his own smoke-gray gelding. He wondered what could be wrong with the great roan stallion, the late laird's favorite horse. He remembered when the stallion had been born four years earlier. Jacob had been alive then, but he let Alec officiate at the difficult delivery. The moment the newborn colt heaved its already massive bulk up on willowy legs, Alec knew the horse would be special.

And he had not been wrong. Flame Dance soon proved himself the fastest horse in the county, and that with little or no training. The laird developed something of an obsession, working tirelessly to prepare Flame Dance for national competition. But the horse's racing career ended almost before it had begun when he began to reveal himself as a one-man horse. The laird brought in the best jockeys his position could buy, but all efforts at racing on the circuit ended in futility. Yet the laird so loved the horse that even the loss of potential glory could hardly quell the thrill of riding him.

A year ago Flame Dance had cut his leg, and from that time on Alec began to develop a special bond with the stallion. Just prior to the laird's death, Alec had actually ridden the great horse. Since that time he visited the estate at every possible opportunity, hoping to relieve at least a portion of the loss an animal must feel upon the death of a loved master. Inside, Alec harbored the secret hope that in time the magnificent animal might give to him the same affection he had previously given the laird.

Now what could be the matter? he thought as he galloped through the open gates of the estate, Billy already a quarter of a mile behind on his own horse. Alec slowed his horse to a trot and directed it past the house and around to the back where the stable was located.

The moment he walked into the horse's stall, his stomach lurched. He stopped, face deathly pale, and closed his eyes momentarily as he sighed a long, bitter sigh. Flame Dance stumbled about, his twitching flesh lathered with sweat from the agony he was in. His eyes were glazed over, staring blankly ahead, and he showed no signs of recognizing Alec.

"Dear Lord!" Alec groaned, "not this . . . please, not this." Then, aware of the factor's presence seemingly for the first time, he turned sharply toward Walter Innes standing near the stable door. "Innes," he snapped, "why didn't ye call me sooner?"

"I—I thought 'twas but a bit o' colic, Alec," said the factor, directing his eyes helplessly toward the ground. "I been drenchin' him but nothin' seemed t' help the poor beast."

"Probably nothin' can," sighed Alec. "But get me some soap an' water, will ye?"

Alec opened his bag and took out a thermometer. He knew, however, he was only going through the motions. Still, he thought within himself, maybe—just maybe—Walter's diagnosis, not his own, might be right.

Innes returned with a bucket of soapy water and Alec began his examination. Flame Dance offered not a flutter of resistance, giving still another confirmation to Alec's initial fears. The examination took barely five minutes. At last Alec rose slowly. Now it was time for his eyes to avoid the factor's fearful and probing face. But there was no reason to put the horse through any further torment.

"He's got a badly twisted bowel," Alec said in his blunt and professional manner.

"What can ye do?" Innes asked desperately.

Alec swallowed hard. His throat had gone dry.

"Walter," he began, "ye know yersel' there's nothin—"

"Alec," cried the factor, "ye can't be tellin' me there's not a thing ye can do fer him! Surely ye can—"

"Walter!" said Alec with the raised voice of helpless agony. "The bowel's twisted. It'll just get worse till it kills him from the inside. An' it's an awful death. Ye know that, Walter."

"But," insisted Innes, "couldn't we jist—"

"Don't ye understand, man?" Alec interrupted again, this time with a finality in his tone. "I have t' put him doon."

A mournful wail followed from the lips of the factor. "Not him! There's got t' be some . . . first the laird . . . now his poor horse. Oh, I've ruined it all—"

"Listen, Walter. I'm sorry I spoke rough wi' ye before. There was nothin' anyone could have done." Alec tried to make himself believe his own words as if they might answer for his own inadequacies.

"No, 'tis all my fault," Innes persisted. "At first, I blamed the horse for the laird's fall, but 'twas me. I should have checked that saddle. I should have—"

"Stop it, Walter! The laird was too old and sick t' be oot riding. Ye canna blame yersel'."

"No. I'm guilty. He trusted me."

"Weel, ye're wrong," said Alec, "but I'm not goin' t' argue wi' ye. Hardly matters now, anyway. An' right now I have to take care o' the horse."

"Ye'll do it, then?" Innes asked. "I couldn't."

"Don't worry," Alec replied. "Leave if ye must."

The two men walked out of the stable silently. Alec went to his horse where he drew out his rifle from its pouch alongside the saddle. Innes disappeared somewhere behind the stables.

This is my occupation, Alec thought.

Every job had its moments of distastefulness, but what could compare with this? His stomach nearly failed him at the mere thought of what he was about to do. It never became easy, never failed to make him physically sick. But it was a necessary evil all vets had to cope with however they could. He had done it before. And he would have to do it again.

But it would never be easy.

This time he almost failed altogether. His sweaty fingers trembled as he tried to squeeze the trigger. All he could see was Flame Dance, that magnificent horse, in his glory—proud and mighty, full of fire and vigor. A vision rose in his mind's eye of the day he had first ridden him. A frosty morning, just cold enough so that the horse's every breath hung in the air, his throbbing nostrils sending great hot puffs of smoke-like energy into the chilly morning, while Alec laughed aloud on his back, urging him through the knee-high grass of the meadow.

Slowly the vision faded and the cruel chill of reality swept through Alec, sending a shiver up his spine.

Now the once mighty horse was . . .

Oh, Lord!

Alec groaned deep within. Perhaps he would never have been able to pull that trigger had Flame Dance, at the final moment, not glanced up at Alec through his final agony, with a glassy look of pain in his eyes. Was the poor animal begging for the mercy of death?

Finally, with tears stinging his eyes, Alec did what had to be done. It was his job.

An hour later, Alec reclined on a grassy dune a quarter mile from town. He had left the house as quickly as possible. He and Walter would bury Flame Dance later, after the emotions were settled somewhat. But for the moment, he had to get away. No doubt Walter, too, would need time to himself.

Often when he sought the solace of nature, Alec rode to Marbrae. Something about the awesome power of being so high above the landscape filled him with fresh vitality and peace. But today, there was no time for the long ride. He had an appointment in town and hardly needed a strenuous ride to tax him still further after the morning's events.

He sat, gazing blankly at the steadily rising tide, only vaguely conscious of the repetitive crashing of the waves on the sandy shore. A white and black pelican with an injured wing limped sadly by, yet he hardly noticed. His usually compassionate veterinarian's heart could hardly be moved today; it had already been stretched to the limit of its endurance.

He tried to pray.

"God . . ." he began, but the words fell silent even before they began.

Was it right to brood over the death of a horse? His emotions were nearly as taxed as if it had been a man. Was that the proper response, the spiritual response, what Jesus would have done had it been His horse?

But even as that question rose in his mind, another followed in its wake. Was it not said two sparrows are worth but a farthing? Yet not a single one falls to the ground without the Father's knowing . . . and caring.

So God, too, was grieved.

Alec found some comfort in that thought.

Yet it consoled him little, for he was the one by whose hand Flame Dance's life had come to an end. Once more he saw the great beast slump motionless to the ground where he lay as the fatal bullet found its mark. Again, the memory brought tears flooding to his eyes. He tried to remind himself what had been ingrained into him at Edinburgh's College of Veterinary Medicine—these were but poor dumb beasts. They did not understand or respond to pain in human fashion. Under the circumstances it could only be a mercy to be given relief . . . only a mercy. . . .

Alec had not intended to fall asleep, but it is difficult to solve life's pressing dilemmas on two hours of sleep. When he began to come to himself, he wasn't certain whether the rustling of the breeze in the gray shoreline grasses had awakened him or if he had just slept his fill. The sun had risen high in the sky, but it was not yet noon.

Alec rolled quietly onto his side, expecting to see a rabbit in the grass. They were everywhere, it seemed, especially in the clusters of thick, high grasses that covered the dunes fifty feet inland from the water's edge. If it hadn't been the breeze that had startled him awake, surely some jackrabbit was making for cover. Instead as he turned he perceived the form of a woman, partially hidden by the low-lying hill of sand she was ascending. The sun pierced his eyes, and he could make out her silhouette against the blue sky, but none of her features. She had apparently not seen him.

Alec watched her slow movements through the soft sand, realizing at last that it was Joanna. His natural inclination in his present frame of mind was to remain silent. But then remembering their first awkward meeting not far from this very spot, he decided to speak.

"Ho . . . Miss Matheson!"

Joanna looked up, mildly startled.

"Hello . . . Mr. MacNeil, is that you?"

"Aye," he replied.

"I didn't know anyone was here. I haven't disturbed you, have I?" She too remembered that first meeting.

"No, not really."

"I was just out for a little walk," she said. "I came into town this morning with Nathaniel, hoping to have received some word from home."

"It must be hard fer ye not knowin'."

"Yes. I was certain Dr. Blakely would have had something here for me by now. I guess it would ease my mind even if he only could tell me things were the same."

"Weel, ye shouldn't let it bother ye that there's no news. The wireless is still new around here and poor Olive hasn't ironed out all the kinks in it yet. We dinna get many wires, but most of those that do come usually take forever t' get here . . . if they get here at all."

"Oh," Joanna said, her countenance noticeably wilted. "You mean I may not hear anything at all?"

Alec immediately saw his blunder. "Oh no, mem! Yer're sure t' hear . . . I mean, it doesna always foul up. Ye need not worry." His speech ended awkwardly and he fell silent.

Joanna continued to stand and they both felt more awkward than ever.

Finally Alec spoke again, attempting to alter the direction of the conversation. "Ye like the shore an' the beach then?"

"Oh yes, I love it. There was nothing like this where I was raised."

"There's nothin' like it t' encourage the Lord's peace when the mind gets muddled . . ." He looked out at the crashing waves and for a moment forgot to finish his sentence. His thoughts were still full of the awful events of the day.

"But . . . I've intruded. I'd better be going," said Joanna, moving away.

"Weel," said Alec, "ye might have intruded . . . but 'tis a welcome intrusion, I assure ye. When I came here I thought I needed t' be alone. But maybe I need some company after all. Wrestlin' wi' the paradoxes o' life is gettin' me nowhere."

"I doubt I can be of any help, Mr. MacNeil," she said, then smiled.

"Weel, the first thing ye can do, Miss Matheson, is t' leave off callin' me Mr. MacNeil. I've never been much comfortable wi' such formality. I'd be pleased if ye'd jist call me by my given name, Alec."

"And you'll return the favor?"

"Aye, that I will . . . Joanna," he said with a smile.

He took a moment to study her as she stood framed in the sunlight. Her auburn hair was piled atop her head with a few strands falling to either side of her face; her skin was creamy, in contrast to the rough-hewn toughness of the farm women he had grown accustomed to. She had already become used to her new surroundings and was no longer the insecure stranger she had been less than a week earlier.

"Weel," he said after a moment, ". . . sit ye doon, then, Miss . . . ah, Joanna."

They laughed together at his error. Then she sat on the sand near him, spreading her blue and white cotton dress about her feet. Still she found she could not read his face, the flicker of introspection that had momentarily settled there. He was not one to reveal too much of himself at a time.

A long silence ensued.

Joanna looked down at her folded hands. Alec had retreated into the privacy of his own thoughts, and again she felt awkward about having stumbled into his time of retreat. He looked past her toward the open sea. It had always been hard for him to speak his feelings, to share with another his innermost thoughts. He did not know why he should want so desperately to do so just now—except that his heart was too heavy to enable him to bear the burden alone.

"I had t' kill a horse today," he said at length, still gazing into the distance.

"I'm sorry," she said, tilting her face up toward him. "It must be difficult for you."

"He was a grand animal, Flame Dance. I helped deliver him four years ago. His name spoke o' much more than his colorin'. From the moment o' his birth, there was a spark in his eyes—a vigor . . . he was so alive! Ah, 'twas more life in that horse than his flesh could contain and he was so fast! Like a fire ragin' through dry grass."

"Perhaps he's finally free now," ventured Joanna, groping for words. Alec did not respond for some time and she wondered if the statement had upset him.

Finally he spoke, continuing to stare straight ahead: ". . . they shall mount up with wings as eagles; they shall run and not be weary. . . ."

He paused briefly, then went on.

"I know that wasn't intended fer horses, but can ye imagine what it would be like fer him—if indeed there be an afterlife fer beasts—t' run with wings? Even the wind would seem slow!"

"Remember him like that," Joanna said softly, with gentle encouragement in her voice.

He sighed, then turned his blue eyes toward her in gratitude.

"I will," he said. "Thank ye."

"You have a great love for animals, don't you?" said Joanna. "It's more than just a living for you."

"Aye, ye're right. 'Tis my way o' servin' God. I've always been better aroun' animals than people."

"Your religion is important to you, isn't it?" she asked.

"In a manner o' speakin'. But I dinna like t' think o' mysel' as a religious man."

"I don't understand."

"People can be religious aboot many things," he replied. "But I would hardly be doin' my faith justice to jist say I was religious an' leave it at that. An' I'm not so sure I am, anyway. I love God, an' I want t' serve Him and His creation, but not because I'm religious. I suppose it's because havin' once seen His love, what else could I do?"

"What do you mean, 'having seen His love'?"

"It's different for everyone, but mostly I think it's when ye come face-to-face wi' Him and ye realize He still loves and forgives ye no matter who ye are . . . or what ye have done . . ." His voice died away reflectively.

"My grandmother used to say such things, but . . ." She hesitated a moment before continuing. "But there are some things even God wouldn't forgive."

"I've never yet found that t' be so," Alec said softly, noting the momentary flicker of pain that had revealed itself in Joanna's eyes.

"I know I should feel differently," Joanna continued. "Both my grandmother and mother shared that kind of faith. My mother died when I was born. She was . . . very good. I would have wanted to be like her. But I never got the chance. It was because of me—"

She stopped abruptly and a flush crept into her cheeks. "I don't know why I'm saying all this."

"I'm sorry about yer mother," said Alec. "An' ye blame yersel', do ye?"

"No!" she almost shouted. "How could I?" she went on quickly. "I was only a baby."

"Then God?" His eyes seemed to penetrate her very soul.

"Of course not!" There was an unmistakable edge of defensiveness to her tone, but even that did not prevent a tear rising to her eye.

"Perhaps I *do* blame myself . . . I don't know," she went on after a moment's pause. "You seem to have something very special, Alec. Maybe . . . maybe someday I will come face-to-face, as you put it, with God."

"Maybe," he said, knowing this must have been her way of saying she had not yet chosen to follow God. Instinctively he felt enough had been said. He certainly felt no compulsion to preach to her. No one—least of all himself—could be talked into seeing God's love. She would have to meet Him for herself, however and whenever that moment came. Then and only then would she be able to deal with the inner turmoil of the guilt she felt. For him the encounter had come late one summer night alone on the sea. For Joanna it would come soon enough, when the time was ripe.

As if by mutual consent, they fell silent, each content to enjoy the tranquillity of allowing the other time for inner reflections. No word was spoken for perhaps five minutes.

With reluctance, Alec finally stood.

"Weel, I've got several more rounds t' make today," he said as he stretched his long limbs. "Do ye need a ride anywhere?"

"Thanks," said Joanna. "But I'll be meeting Nathaniel in a while. I think I'll stay here for a few more moments." She smiled.

"I'm glad ye happened along, Joanna. Maybe sometime ye'd like t' come wi' me on a round or two. They're not all so intense as a cow birthin' or a horse killin'. Sometimes it's right fun."

"I'd like that."

As Alec strode away down the beach toward town, he wondered to himself why he didn't ask her along now. But, then, it seemed she wanted to be alone.

There would come another time.

19

A Sinister Plot

"I DON'T CARE what it takes . . . you get those papers!"

"But," answered one of the others, noticeably cowed by the lawyer's tone, "how far do ye want us t' go? I mean . . . ye don't want us t'—"

"Whatever it takes! Do you understand me?"

Palmer Sercombe stopped pacing around his inner office and glared at his two reluctant accomplices. The dimly lit china lamp cast but a shadowy light and only vaguely illuminated Sercombe's companions.

"'Tis more than we expected, sir."

"Are you asking for more money?" Sercombe snapped.

"If I be understandin' ye aright, weel . . . we'll be takin' a greater risk, an—"

"Don't talk to me about risk!" the lawyer said, almost to himself. Then he turned his attention once more toward the other. "Twenty quid—and that's all!"

"Twenty apiece?"

Sercombe nodded. The other two exchanged silent glances of agreement.

"You'll get half now," the lawyer went on, "and half when the job is successfully completed."

He handed each of the men their share of the money which he had retrieved from his desk drawer, then escorted them out the rear entrance. "Don't come back here," he added. "I'll meet you tomorrow night behind the inn; nine o'clock. Have the papers! You'll not get a farthing more until the job is done."

Sercombe closed the door and bolted it.

What a seedy lot! he thought with disgust. But it was exactly what he had been looking for on his recent trip to Fenwick Harbor. It had been much too risky to use a local person; he should never have resorted to it. But he'd panicked the moment he'd laid eyes on Joanna Matheson's papers.

Perhaps there was good reason to panic.

But he was too smart for that sort of thing. From now on he'd make no more such mistakes. He couldn't afford to.

He sat down at his desk. Even alone in his office he did not slouch or lean back. He picked up a pencil and began to jot a few ideas down on a pad. There was still, after all, other work to be done. Soon, however, the brisk movement of the pencil slowed and then finally stopped. With elbows propped up on his desk, he held the ends of the pencil in both hands, thinking.

Everything had been going so well. What kind of despicable coincidence could have brought that confounded girl all the way from America!

And where in God's name had she gotten hold of those documents?

If only she had delayed a month, or stopped on the way to visit London.

Of course, her claim could be a ruse. Who could have put her up to it? Perhaps the deed was a forgery. Yet, the documents looked too authentic.

He had to get his hands on those papers!

But even with the Matheson girl's meddling interference, all was not lost. He merely had to speed things up. If he could get done in the next week what should have taken two or three, then he could relax. Even if she had suspicions, there would be too little time for her to do anything. The fact that she had gone to the Cuttahays' played into his hand. She must, for the moment, see no reason to press the issue. She had not been back to see him and he had heard nothing about any further attempts to get into the house. The attack by his hired ruffians would certainly alarm her. But even if she were able to make the connection and trace it back to him, by then he would hold the documents and she could persist all she wanted—it would be to no avail.

Those two vagabonds had to be successful—there was no room for failure.

He had to have those documents. Everything hinged on that single fact—everything!

Suddenly the pencil snapped between the pressure of his fingers.

20
Attack!

※

JOANNA COULD HARDLY believe she had come all this distance only to find the lawyer away. Gordon Ogilvie had been called out of town on business and was not expected back for two days. She so hoped this old friend of the Cuttahays' might have been able to shed additional light on her grandmother's papers. Now she would have to wait; it seemed she had already been waiting a lifetime.

The inland village of Culden should have offered a tourist from America a pleasant day, with its unusual inn, ancient brick and granite cathedral, and hospitable Scottish residents. But for Joanna it proved symbolic of one more disappointing dead end.

Perhaps she should not have left without Alec.

After all, he had been kind enough to escort her to Culden. But she had no idea how long his calls in the area would take and had no desire to sit alone waiting all day in a strange town. Therefore, she opted to begin the two- or three-hour return journey alone.

She directed her bay mare at a leisurely pace. There was no real hurry to get back, although the thought had occurred to her to try once again to get into Stonewycke Castle. Perhaps this afternoon would prove a better time. Still, she was in no rush and only held a tenuous control of her horse's reins.

The road between Culden and the bridge over the Lindow was a lovely one—thickly forested on her left, and on the right, heather-covered meadows which sloped gradually upward toward distant snow-covered peaks.

The mare's gentle clip-clop on the hard-packed dirt surface of the road lulled Joanna's mind into aimless reflection. The events of these past weeks jumped into her mind in disconnected bits and pieces; try as she might, she could create no order out of the chaos that had happened. Jason . . . MacDuff . . . Sercombe . . . her grandmother.

Would she ever learn anything about her grandmother's past? Would she ever see Jason again?

All at once the image of Alec sprang into her mind. He was certainly not a man of the world like Jason Channing. Yet he had stirred an introspection she had not known before. That was a quality—perhaps even a gift—not every man possessed.

Preoccupied, she paid little heed to the two approaching riders. She would have ridden right by, except that as they drew near they hailed her to stop.

She reined in her horse.

"Mornin', mem," said one of the riders, lifting his wide-brimmed hat politely, revealing coal black eyes underneath, deep-set above a bushy brown beard. The man who spoke sat tall in his saddle; his companion—a shorter, stockier man—remained silent.

"Uh . . . good morning," Joanna returned reticently. Glancing nervously toward the one who had not yet spoken, an involuntary shudder tingled through her spine. A beard would no doubt have been a vast improvement to his scarred and pock-marked face.

"Ye headin' fer Strathy, mem?" asked the bearded rider.

"Yes."

"Not safe fer a leddy like yersel' t' be oot on the roads alone."

Joanna said nothing.

"We'd be mor'n happy t' ride along wi' ye—fer yer protection, mem."

"No need," said Joanna, afraid her uneasiness was showing. It occurred to her that this could become awkward if they continued to press her.

She gently reined her mare to the left and urged her gradually forward, trying to circumvent the riders, but as she did so the scarred man moved to block her path.

"We'd feel sorely guilty, mem, if anythin' was t' happen t' ye," the bearded rider said. A cold chill shot through Joanna as she noticed his hand slowly move to rest on the butt of a carbine strapped to his saddle.

When thinking about it later, Joanna was not sure whether it was good sense or sheer panic that prompted her to do what she did next. In any case, fear had by now nearly overpowered her, and she knew she must act quickly or face some terrible danger.

In a desperate instant of decision, she dug her heels unmercifully into the flanks of her horse.

The mare shot between the horses of the two men, leaving them momentarily stunned by the suddenness of Joanna's daring maneuver. Her heels kicked frantically, prodding the horse on. She lashed the reins across its neck. Daring to cast a hasty glance behind confirmed the worst of her fears—the two riders had already gained a full gallop and were matching her speed stride for stride.

Still she lashed with the reins, digging into the mare's heaving sides with her heels. But that she could hope to reach the Cuttahay farm seemed a slim—if not altogether impossible—prospect.

Joanna never rode so fast; she felt as if she were flying. But she was an inexperienced horsewoman and only sheer terror kept her grip tight and forestalled inevitable disaster.

She rode on, not turning again. She knew the two men were near; the thundering of their horses' hooves reverberated in her ears.

Suddenly a sharp blast pierced the air.

The carbine!

She had forgotten about it. The first shot had probably been intended as a warning. Wouldn't the wisest thing to do be to stop? Maybe she could reason with them.

Yet something drove her on.

In the distance, perhaps two hundred yards away, Joanna saw the narrow wooden bridge across the river. If she could just reach it first and then somehow lengthen her lead on the other side, maybe . . .

Sheer tenacity, however, bolstered with hope, could not have prevented the mare's tiring legs from stumbling over the large rock which lay in the middle of the road. At the speed she was moving it was impossible to recover in time. The horse crumpled to her knees and Joanna was thrown over her head. Springy shrubs at the side of the road broke Joanna's fall but she was momentarily stunned, bruised and cut.

The two riders, having drawn almost alongside to her right, galloped past, unable to rein in their horses, moving at full stride, for some distance. It allowed time for Joanna to scramble to her feet. Every muscle in her body ached, but she managed to plant her feet firmly beneath her and run for the brush at the side of the road. Half stumbling, half running, she made her way through the bushes and farther from the road. The farther she went the denser and taller the growth became.

Soon trees surrounded her and the forest thickened with tightly bunched trees and undergrowth. Shrubs, bushes, brambles, and ferns inhibited every step she tried to take.

She glanced back in haste, seeing nothing, but voices were not far behind. A branch across her way tangled her feet and sent her sprawling on her face. She struggled, groaning, back to her feet.

The voices came closer!

Joanna scrambled over a fallen log, sweating, moist dirt from the forest floor smeared on her riding breeches and face, unconsciously crying out in her desperation, yet afraid of uttering a single sound. Tears streamed down her smudged face as she struggled forward, heart pounding, each breath accompanied by a sharp pain in her chest.

Finally she had to stop . . . if only for a moment. She had to catch her breath.

Silently heaving deep draughts of oxygen into her aching lungs, Joanna listened intently.

Except for her own labored gasps there was silence all about. The light was dim; only occasionally patches of sunlight penetrated the thick, leafy foliage overhead.

"There she is!" a deep, angry voice shouted.

Alas, the short stop had given Joanna's position away. She saw him now—the tall one—some fifty feet away, directing his accomplice around her flank, trying to cut her off in two directions.

She turned and flew, to the limited extent speed was possible in the tangled underbrush, forcing herself to run as swiftly, yet silently, as she could. After a few minutes she paused once more. She heard nothing. Could she have at last eluded pursuit?

Then she heard the two men shouting. They seemed, for the moment to have lost track of her position. She crept forward, away from their sounds, now forcing herself to move as slowly and with as much stealth as possible.

A twig snapped beneath her foot.

Joanna froze in place, kneeling down instinctively.

Suddenly a shot rang through the silent forest, but it was far from its target.

Then Joanna first realized her extreme danger. If they caught her now, so far from the road, neither would have qualms about killing her and leaving her body where it would never be found.

She had to get back to the road!

Joanna resumed her snail's pace escape, bending low to avoid being seen. She feared she was lost, but tried to move in a wide arc and thus return to the road and to her horse.

It was her only chance.

A great fallen tree forced her to the left. She had lost all sense of direction. Now she could only plunge onward and hope she was headed toward the road and not deeper into this tangled maze.

Over the tree she climbed, then again toward her right . . .

All at once, no more than an arm's length in front of her, loomed the scarred face of her pursuer. His yellowed teeth gleamed as his lips parted in an evil grin. The scream that forced itself out of Joanna's mouth was hardly more than a cry choked down by terror.

"Now, mem, where's them papers?" he rasped in a cruel voice as he brandished a large knife in his left hand, its cold steel hovering dangerously inches from Joanna's throat.

"I . . . I don't have them," said Joanna, "they're . . . they're not here."

"Weel, where is they? Come now, ye don't want t' rile me, does ye?"

"I . . . don't have . . . they're not here." But Joanna knew he didn't believe her lie.

"Ye's angerin' me, mem!" he said. "I can get 'em my own way, ye know," he added in a tone which made her shudder.

He lunged toward her.

Instinct made Joanna duck to the right. As he recovered from his misplaced blow, she turned and flew, giving no heed to caution.

If he caught her now—she was dead!

With her life at stake, panic drove her with no thought of the noise she made or the desperate cries for help escaping her frantic lips.

Her sleeve caught on a branch.

She gave it a frantic yank, tearing the once-beautiful cotton fabric and leaving a large chunk behind. The hideous enemy was only a few paces behind. She expected at any moment to encounter his bearded partner or to feel the sharp, cold steel in her back.

Glancing back for a quick look she did not see the figure of a large man step into the path of her flight. With a sickening thud she crashed against him with her full weight and felt his strong arms enclose about her.

A familiar voice was calling her name but it was faint and distant. Her vision blurred by perspiration and exhaustion, mingled with loose strands of wild hair. Her mind grew fuzzy and her head faint. Where had she heard that voice?

Her knees buckled beneath her, and she knew no more.

Alec had scarcely a moment with Joanna before the attacker was upon him. He set Joanna's limp body down as quickly as he could—she would have to recover from her faint on her own. Standing, he spun about to face the scarred face of his antagonist. Alec grabbed the hand still holding the gleaming knife, attempting to twist the assailant's arm and wrest it from him. The battle was fierce, for though the enemy was a small man his strength proved almost equal to Alec's. However, in the end a groaning cry signaled his weakening and a moment later the knife fell on the forest floor.

Alec loosened his grip, but his compassion was unwise; the other broke away and sent a gnarled fist squarely into his jaw. He lunged at Alec, bringing him to the ground. But his advantage was short-lived. All the gathered centuries of Scottish temper rose in Alec's blood. He rallied and pounded his fist into the man on top of him, sending him backward.

Alec jumped to his feet and lurched forward, grabbing the man as he staggered backward and slammed his body into a nearby tree. His fist was raised to strike what would have been the decisive blow when he faltered. His heart pounded in his temples. His mind lingered between rage and fear.

Hesitating, he began to lower his fist.

Suddenly a shot ripped through the air, shattering the bark of the tree. The slug missed Alec's head by three inches.

Joanna began to come to herself only moments after Alec set her down. Even while struggling to regain her feet she remained in a daze. Then she saw the approach of the bearded man, rifle in hand, too late to scream a warning to Alec.

She lunged toward him just as the shot rang out, grabbing the villain's legs with her hands. He was knocked off balance and the gun flew from his hands. Alec quickly let his first attacker loose and turned his attentions in the other direction. The tall, bearded man was more nearly Alec's size and his muscular frame appeared as strong as his intent was evil. He quickly regained his feet, swore a vile imprecation at Joanna, and—now angered—strode toward his adversary and in an instant had delivered two powerful blows to Alec's midsection.

"Ye'll see what comes o' meddlin' where ye're na welcome!" he cursed with a growling voice. "We'll leave the two o' ye i' the forest fer rat's meal!"

In another moment Alec was fighting off both men. The shorter of the two located his knife where it had fallen and poised himself to send its razorsharp steel point into Alec's back the moment his friend had him sufficiently occupied.

Perceiving his intent, Alec backtracked keeping both men in front of him. The tall man sent a blow to Alec's head, dazing him momentarily. Almost at the same instant a stinging stab of pain pierced his right shoulder and he felt his warm blood flowing from the gash of the knife.

He kicked at the short man, trying to hit his knife hand with his boot while guarding his other side against his companion.

Another piercing shot brought the melee to an abrupt halt.

The three men fell apart and immediately Alec looked in Joanna's direction, where, pale and trembling, she clutched the carbine with quivering fingers.

The two attackers backed off, eyeing Joanna intently, and fled into the woods without a word.

Joanna dropped the gun, her body shaking as she at last let the pent-up sobs loose. Alec hastened to her side.

"'Tis over, noo," he said, trying to soothe her as he gathered her into his arms. "'Tis over . . . everythin's all right," he whispered over and over. But even as he did so he kept a wary eye peeled for any hint of recurring trouble. He stooped to retrieve the gun, just in the event its use should again become necessary. Holding it with his left hand, he clutched Joanna's quivering body with his weakened right arm. He brushed a strand of hair from her face and gently kissed her forehead. Gradually Alec felt Joanna's trembling tears ebb as she regained her strength.

He tried not to think of the sickness in the pit of his own stomach. The rage surging through him had been more overpowering than he would have believed possible. He shuddered to think what he might have done to the first man had not the gunshot from his partner interceded. He had lived in fear of a moment like this for years.

Could he have killed again?

The uncertainty was almost as horrifying as the act itself.

Almost without thought he took Joanna's hand and led her from the depths of the forest.

21

Plans

※

LETTY WRUNG WARM water from the clean cloth.

Nursing a wound was something she could do, but understanding why such a wound would be inflicted was too much for her gentle mind. The moment she had seen Joanna and Alec, tears welled up in her eyes, not only for their obvious pain, but that two persons she dearly loved should have been so victimized.

It was past dinnertime when the two rode in together on Alec's horse; Joanna's had wandered off after its fall and they were too exhausted to attempt a search. They hoped the mare would find her way back. If not, they would return to the Dormin to find her. In the meantime, the Cuttahays rushed them into the house and immediately tended to their wounds—superficial cuts and bruises, but nonetheless painful.

Alec bore a deep knife gash in his right arm.

"We can be thankful 'twas no worse," said Letty after Joanna gave a brief account of the incident.

"'Tis a shame the scoundrels got away again!" said Nathaniel in an outrage.

"Not *again*," Joanna corrected. "Neither of these men was the one you scared off in town the other day."

"But ye say they were still after the papers, lass?"

Joanna nodded. "They told me to give them the papers, just like that."

"'Tis a good thing the lad came along. How did ye come t' be in Dormin right then, Alec?"

Alec had been silent since they entered the cottage.

"I left Culden just after Joanna and was tryin' t' overtake her when she was accosted," he replied in a sober tone.

"Weel," fumed Nathaniel, "I'd like t' get me hands on Tom Forbes."

"But Joanna said it wasna him," cautioned his wife.

"I'll warrant he knows somethin'! I should hae turned him o'er t' the Ballie soon's I saw that bandage."

Nathaniel paced the floor in silence for a moment. Then he stopped abruptly and faced the others.

"It's always back t' them papers," he said. "Someone's willin' t' kill fer them. Which makes me think mor'n more that what we all been thinkin' aboot Joanna bein' one o' *the* Duncans 'tis true."

"If only I could get *into* the house and talk to some of the people," Joanna sighed. "I feel certain someone would tell me something."

"Maybe they *could*, lass," Letty interjected. "But the question is, *would* they? Walter's already shown himsel' t' be tight-lipped, an' though he's a good man, he can be stiff-necked when he wants. Comes o' that Highland blood o' his, I suppose. An' Mrs. Bonner . . . well, if she's under orders from Mr. Sercombe too, I expect she'll be bound t' obey. The only other body there is auld Dorey."

"I doobt ye'd get a straight word from him," Nathaniel put in. "But I expect he'd have a mite t' say aboot the Duncans—he's been there near as long as I can recollect."

"What's wrong with him?" Joanna asked. "The way people talk, you'd think he was crazy."

"Na, na. He's harmless, t' be sure," Letty answered. "Keeps t' himsel' an' tends his flowers. Stays in the castle or on the grounds mostly. I only recall seein' him in toon once—oh, must be years noo. Come right int' the Crearys' yard, he did. That was when Doug Creary's mama was still livin'. Weel, auld Mistress Creary stood on the porch an' watched as he began diggin' up the earth aroun' the front o' the hoose—guess she was jist too surprised t' say anythin'. Then he took some plants he had in his knapsack an' laid them int' the groun' an' planted some seeds. All this, mind ye, wi' oot a word spoken. He watered the plants an' then wi' a smile an' a tip o' his hat he strolled away leavin' Mistress Creary wi' her mouth hangin' open. In a few months the plants was a-bloomin' an' before ye knew it the Crearys' yard—what used t' be the poorest in the valley—was nearly as pretty as Stonewycke's own. The other folk decided they liked the idea an' soon every yard aroun' was bright wi' flowers!"

Letty smiled joyfully and for a moment forgot the terrible events of the day. "If that be crazy, then it couldna harm us all t' have a bit more o' it."

"If I could just have even a few minutes to talk with him," Joanna said.

"If he can talk at all," added Nathaniel.

"He spoke to me when I was there the other day," Joanna said hopefully.

"Did he?"

"Well, only one word. He seemed frightened. Then Mr. Innes drove up and he ran away."

"Alec," said Nathaniel, turning toward the younger man. "Ye're oot t' the hoose now an' then. What do ye think?"

Until then, Alec had remained detached from the group. The muscles of his jaw rippled with inward tension.

Perhaps it was the pain in his shoulder, thought Nathaniel. But his quiet seemed to come from more than physical pain. Nathaniel had a suspicion, but he knew he could not offer a word of comfort to the lad without revealing his secret—which even Letty did not know. When the time came for Alec to tell, the decision would have to be his alone.

"Are ye all right?" Nathaniel asked slowly.

Alec lurched to his feet. "I jist need some fresh air," he said, and stalked from the room.

The cool, sharp evening air felt good. But it could not clear his muddled thoughts. Since that dreaded night in his hometown he had desperately avoided even the hint of conflict. And now he seemed caught up into the middle of a conflict more dangerous than he dared even consider. When he saw Joanna so battered and desolate, he had wanted to protect her, to come to her aid. For those few brief moments . . . he had wanted to kill! He still trembled at the thought.

And he knew that if he found her threatened or in danger, he would have to jump into the battle on her behalf again.

What was he to do?

What is expected of me? he wondered. *What does God require? What would have happened to Joanna if I had not been there?* He closed his eyes and clenched his teeth as the agony in his mind increased.

He heard the cottage door open and a soft footstep approached behind him. But he could not turn to meet it.

"I'm sorry," Joanna whispered. "I'm so sorry to have brought all this on you. I . . . I've been so thoughtless. You people have been so kind to me, and look how I've repaid you."

"No!" said Alec, spinning around to face her. "Ye must not say that . . . or think it, even. It's not ye! It's me. Ye've asked nothin' o' us. Ye had a need and we—I helped ye . . . an' I would do it again. I would hae to."

"I don't understand."

"Ye've brought nothin' on me. I brought it on mysel' . . . or maybe God has brought it on me. I've been runnin', an' what if I'd turned my back on ye too? I can't do that . . . I don't think that's what the Lord would want. An' yet . . ."

"Alec," said Joanna, "please, what's troubling you so?"

"Ye're probably thinkin' maybe I am a babbling idiot t' be speakin' like this. I thought I had it all worked oot in my mind. But—"

He stopped abruptly.

"Alec. What is it?"

"Four years ago somethin' happened—my sister was attacked. When I saw the man, I grabbed him an' . . ."

He stopped again and covered his face with his large hands, hiding the tears that had begun to flow.

"I . . . I," he stammered, "I *killed* him!"

"Oh, Alec!"

"They called me a hero, but I felt like the very devil. With my bare hands . . . I took a life."

He held his hands up toward her.

"These hands . . . hands that are supposed t' give an' protect life—these very hands . . ."

Again he covered his face in shame.

Joanna gently reached out, clasped his hands in hers, and said: "Alec, these are good hands. All I see in them are the tender, loving hands that gently placed that baby calf before its mother."

"But today . . . I think I could have killed again. I . . . I was so full of anger when I saw what they had done that—"

"But, Alec," she interrupted, squeezing his hands more tightly in hers, "you had no choice! Those men were trying to kill me. And they would have."

He shook his head in confusion, unable to speak.

"Alec," Joanna went on, "I saw what happened. You did what you had to do, and no more. When you had that man against the tree, you could have struck him again. But you didn't. Your anger didn't control you. You subdued it."

A long silence followed.

At length Alec calmed and raised his eyes to look at Joanna.

"Alec, thank you for what you did. You saved my life today. And after what you've told me, it means even more. But I'll not ask anything more of you or Nathaniel or Letty. I cannot involve innocent people any further in—"

"Innocent!" Alec said, laughing for the first time. "Lass, ye hae no say in the matter. We are boun' t' help ye."

"I'm afraid I couldn't ask you to help me with what I plan to do next."

"An' jist what would that be?"

As she had listened earlier to the discussion about Dorey, Joanna had found herself thinking once again about her initial reason for coming to Port

Strathy—her grandmother's plea to find her family. That remained the one thing she still had to resolve. And to that end she knew one thing that had to be done. She would have to try again.

"I'm going back to Stonewycke tomorrow." Her words were flat and unyielding, braced against argument. Something was happening inside her. She felt a change. The old, timid, quiet Joanna was slowly giving way to a new, more confident Joanna. And she could not help but think the change a good one. Perhaps this decision was her way of helping the change along by asserting herself in a direction she felt she had to go. "I want to see this Dorey. Somehow I think he can tell me something."

"It could be dangerous. Ye know what's been happenin'. These men won't give up."

"It's something I have to do," she insisted. "My mind's made up."

"Then I'll be goin' wi' ye," said Alec.

She opened her mouth to protest, but before she could, he said, ". . . an' I've made up *my* mind."

She smiled.

"I'll be most happy for that," she consented.

22
Dorey

WALTER INNES HAD no reason to suspect the Cuttahays' luncheon invitation.

A widower, he was often the glad recipient of the generous hospitality of the neighborhood. This morning seemed no different, though it had been quite some time since he had socialized with anyone. Since the laird's death, he found he preferred to remain on the property, either at his own little cottage or at Stonewycke itself. But more than once he remarked to himself that "it was like closin' the byre door after the cow got oot." Still, there was Dorey and Mrs. Bonner, the housekeeper; and the house itself *was* in his care.

When Nathaniel had stopped by that morning, Walter suddenly found himself longing for company, especially the company of these friends who never failed to lift his spirits. And there was no doubt his spirits could use some help right now. It crossed his mind every now and then that maybe he was going as daft as

Dorey himself. It would do him good to get out for a while; Mr. Sercombe was sure to understand.

He closed the gate and locked it—another new policy handed down by Sercombe, this one only yesterday. *A lot o' useless effort if ye ask me*, thought the factor to himself. The ancient cast iron gate was a mere formality as protection from intruders, for the surrounding portions of the iron fence had fallen into disrepair years ago, now supplemented in part by the thick, ten-foot hedge.

Walter turned left, and his lanky figure paralleled the hedge as he turned down the steep path into the rocky gorge along the side of the road. The footpath did not lead toward the town but offered a shortcut west to the valley in which the Cuttahay farm lay.

Yes, this was just what he needed.

The laird's death could not help but change the character of life at Stonewycke, but of late it had become almost like a prison. Not that it had ever been a cheery place, even during the laird's lifetime. But at least then everyone was free to come and go as they pleased. Now, however, no one came to the House—not even for deliveries. The lawyer's security precautions had turned it into a mausoleum. Walter had even considered giving up his post—he'd no doubt be losing his job soon enough anyway, once the property was sold. Yet he could not neglect the deep loyalty he felt toward the great estate.

Deep in thought, Walter walked across the grassy meadow on the other side of the gorge. He took no notice of the two furtive figures behind him, approaching the gate he had just locked. He did not see them test the lock, then, finding it secure, creep around the fence eastward to the breach just where the hedge began.

Joanna argued against the subterfuge.

But she trusted Alec; and when the Cuttahays went along with his suggestion, she consented, knowing they were doing it for her benefit. As she and Alec crawled through an opening in the hedge, seeing Stonewycke with all the potential secrets it might reveal so close, she forgot her earlier hesitation.

The house loomed before her in its ancient gray splendor. Stone laced with ivy, towers, parapets, and ramparts—possibly the very home of her grandmother. Buffeted by conflicting emotions, she walked slowly toward the door. If nothing else succeeded on her trip to Scotland, she could at least know she had touched a portion of the past she had come seeking.

"Do we try the front door?" Joanna asked.

"There still might be a few o' the servants aroun'," replied Alec.

He paused, then suddenly turned the opposite direction. "Come on," he said, "I hae an idea."

He led her around the house the way she had gone before, past the little rose garden, still farther to the stables and beyond, and through a tree-lined courtyard. When Joanna's eye caught a glint of the sun reflecting off the roof of a glass greenhouse, she knew their destination.

She had hardly had leisure to frame any definite opinions about the man she had assumed was the gardener. On her previous visit he had departed so hastily.

And from what she had gathered from hearing others talk about him, she expected the man known as Dorey to be frail and rather simple-minded, with an empty stare in his eyes. But as she walked into the greenhouse, she instantly realized her presentiment could not have been more inaccurate. His trim broad-shouldered frame was bent now, but it hinted of past glory, as did his thick mass of snow-white hair. But his face! At a glance Joanna saw that it bore the mark of the aristocracy of the family he served; even his simple, homely work clothes could not hide the noble look of his aging face.

He looked up slowly as they entered.

Joanna saw that she had been correct, however, about the far-off gaze in his eye; it was so different from the look of alarm which had greeted her when they met briefly before. He turned toward them, stared directly forward, but appeared to take no notice of their presence.

"*Primula Scotica,*" he said, as if continuing an ongoing conversation with himself that they had interrupted. "Lovely, isn't it?"

Joanna looked toward the tiny, purple-red blooms in the wooden planter where the man's deft fingers gently loosened the soil.

"Yes . . . it is," she answered, feeling suddenly awkward.

He looked at his visitors again, glancing back and forth, finally resting his eyes on Joanna. Forcing his vision into focus, a brief questioning frown crossed his brow, then just as quickly disappeared. The distant, glazed look reappeared.

"Do you know flowers?" he asked.

Joanna shook her head.

"The Scottish primrose—not many in this area, but mine are doing well. The ones you see in the valley are a different variety. But this strain is very rare." His voice lacked the heavy brogue she had already grown accustomed to; if she knew anything about accents, she would have identified an Oxford ring in his. "I suppose I shall have to try them outside the nursery eventually, but . . ."

His soft voice trailed away in a few mumbled words and he returned his attentions to the plant he was cultivating.

"Even the most delicate o' flowers can be hardier than they look," Alec ventured. Dorey looked hard at him for a moment.

"Yes . . . perhaps," said Dorey, then paused. "I . . . I know you, don't I?" he added in an uncertain tone.

"I'm Alec MacNeil—I've tended some o' the laird's animals."

"Ah, yes. You're the young vet."

Just as quickly as the promise of dialogue had begun, Dorey lowered his eyes and began to putter about with some of the other plants on his workbench, offering not another word. He sprinkled a handful of fertilizer into the pot of a brilliant orange azalea, worked it deftly into the soil, gave it a swash of water, and stood back to admire his work. Then he turned his attention elsewhere, picked up several small pots containing leafy plants Joanna did not recognize, and carried them to his worktable. Gently he loosened the velvet-like green foliage and commenced the operation of transferring them to larger pots.

Joanna and Alec watched with fascination, neither feeling an inclination to disturb the serenity, content for the moment to observe Dorey's skillful ministrations. So complete was his absorption in his work, Joanna was certain he had forgotten they were present. Joanna was wondering how she might reinstate the conversation when Dorey broke the silence.

"Was there something you were wanting?" he asked, not looking up from his work.

"We—we hoped just to have a visit with you," answered Joanna cautiously.

"I have no visitors." His voice sounded almost apologetic.

"We didn't mean to intrude," said Joanna, "but I've wanted to meet you, and the last time I was here—"

"Then . . . I don't know you?" he said, glancing up and eyeing her intently. "But I thought . . ." He paused and a cloud of perplexity crossed his face; then he looked back down and never completed the sentence.

"My name is Joanna. I've come from America."

"America?"

"Yes . . . I arrived only a few days ago."

"But surely . . . it's Alastair you'd be wanting to see. He's gone now . . . dead, you understand. He was the laird, you know . . . I am his houseguest. I'm afraid the place is just not the same without Alastair. You will be disappointed, I'm certain—but of course you are welcome. It's too bad, though. Alastair always loved visitors."

"What will you do now that the laird is gone?" Joanna asked.

"Do? Well . . . tend my flowers just like I've always done. They will always need tending, you know."

"Will you stay here?"

"I have no place else to go. It's been so long—"

"I mean will you stay here, at Stonewycke?"

"Oh, the house. Yes, of course. Palmer has arranged everything for me. A very generous man. I don't deserve it, but he knows I could never leave. I know I'm only a guest, but this is my home."

He stopped and looked hard at Joanna, as if trying to remember something.

"Yes, I shall stay. Nothing will change. It won't be the same, but still nothing will change. That's the way it is here—always the same, always . . ."

His voice trailed away again as he plucked off one of the delicate primrose blossoms and held it up toward the light in admiration. "There is none lovelier, don't you think?"

"Yes," agreed Joanna, trying not to allow her voice to betray her disappointment that the conversation had turned so abruptly back to the flowers.

"Yours are especially lovely," she added.

"Thank you. I work with my flowers . . . and I love them."

Neither Joanna nor Alec said a word. Dorey continued, however, taking no notice of them.

"Sometimes it takes such an effort to think. Maybe that's why it's so peaceful here. I don't have to think. I can just visit my flowers and work in the nursery. I suppose it's odd that I would find peace here, you know . . . after . . ."

He paused, wiped one eye with the back of his sleeve, then looked down at his hands. "Oh no!" he exclaimed, seeing the delicate blossom crushed between his fingers which had steadily tightened as he spoke, "I've ruined it!—I was going to give it to you . . . I know how you love them . . ." The confusion once more passed over his face and halted his words. Then a look of frustration grew out of it and he said, "But why have you come here?"

"I hoped we could be friends," she said.

"Friends . . . why me? I don't understand?"

"I came to Scotland all alone. I hoped to find my grandmother's family here."

"Family is important," he said, seemingly recovered. "I have no family either. There are some relations in London, but they hardly count."

"Were you related to the laird?" asked Joanna tentatively. She debated within herself how far to push the discussion.

"Related? I'm his houseguest—the laird's. He's dead, you know. Quite a scholar was Alastair—ancient Greece . . . loved history. But it's quiet here now. Even the servants are gone—except the housekeeper, and Innes. Palmer says this is best—too much activity isn't good for me, he says. And I have my flowers. Alastair had this nursery built for me."

"That was kind of him," said Joanna.

Dorey returned to his repotting with vigor. After a lengthy silence, Joanna swallowed, took a deep breath, and prepared to ask her next question.

With her heart thudding in her chest, she said: "Did he have a sister?"

"Sister . . . who? Alastair?"

"Yes. Did Alastair have a sister?"

"Sister . . . ?" he repeated.

Joanna waited but soon realized either his mind had wandered off again or he did not intend to answer her question. He bent over his workbench, to all appearances oblivious to her words. Joanna proceeded:

"I didn't want to bother you, but . . . well, since you have lived here so long, I thought you might be able to tell me something. You see, my grandmother's name is Margaret Duncan—"

Joanna did not finish her sentence.

As he stood straight up the look on Dorey's face stopped Joanna short. With the words he winced and a momentary frown wrinkled his brow. Then, just as abruptly, his countenance went blank. His attentions returned to his table and his hands accelerated their activity, moving frantically at their work.

"*Sinningia,*" he said. "They'll have a lovely red and white blossom. Need plenty of light and humidity. You wouldn't think a tropical plant like this could grow here, would you? But of course, it must stay in the nursery. And I must watch over it—"

"Please . . ." Joanna implored.

"Joanna," Alec gently interrupted. "Perhaps we could come another time t' visit."

"Another time," said Dorey. "Yes . . . another time. That would be nice, young man."

He looked at Joanna again. A trace of knowing passed through his eyes and his lips formed a faint smile—the first she had seen. "Yes . . . you are always welcome here," he went on. "I'm glad you've come back. You must come again—we'll have tea. But now I must go . . . yes, I really must go . . ." and with those parting words, he hurried past them out of the greenhouse.

23

News from America

OLIVE SIGHED HEAVILY as she lifted her hand to knock on the Cuttahays' door. She didn't like telegrams—they never brought good news. She hadn't been at all thrilled when the laird installed the telegraph machine in Port Strathy and even less when the duty of tending it fell to her. It had been a plague ever since; the only good thing about it was that precious few messages ever came over it.

Now she bore a message for Joanna and she knew the contents would further burden the already troubled girl.

Letty answered the door.

Joanna sat by the fire still pondering her visit with old Dorey. She had had such high hopes for the encounter but like everything else, it had ended in disappointment. The old man was probably crazy just like everyone said and would not or simply *could* not tell her anything. Whatever her grandmother had sent her here to find seemed bent on eluding her—first, through the death of Alastair, her only link with the past; now, through the disorientation of an old man.

Yet her grandmother had passionately urged her to come here, with good reason—though Margaret Duncan could not have guessed at these recent developments. Something terrible was happening, but what it was and how it involved her grandmother, Joanna did not know. If Margaret was truly Alastair's older sister, then she should have been the heir. But still . . .

Her thoughts drifted off unfinished as she became aware of Olive's presence.

"Joanna, dear," she said. "This came for you today." Her voice sounded grave.

Reluctantly, Joanna reached for the paper Olive offered. She opened it and saw Olive's precise printing:

JOANNA
YOUR GRANDMOTHER HAS GONE HOME STOP HAVE MADE ALL
THE ARRANGEMENTS STOP NO NEED TO CUT YOUR TRIP SHORT
STOP

DR. BLAKELY

"It's so cold and impersonal!" Joanna said. Olive had thought so, too, but she
had excused it as a typically medical approach to a crisis.

For a moment Joanna could think of nothing else, her mind seeming to have
frozen. She looked up at Olive, her face blank. Then slowly her countenance
contorted in grief as the reality of the message dawned upon her. Olive put her
strong arm around Joanna, and Letty rushed up to offer what comfort she could.

"I'm sorry, lass," Olive said.

"Is it her grandmother?" Letty asked Olive. The storekeeper nodded. "Oh, dear
child!" Then when Letty read the printed words, she squeezed Joanna's hand. "I
ken 'tis hard fer ye right now, Joanna, but like these words say, she's with her
Lord now. Try to take comfort from that."

"I should never have left," Joanna cried.

"You only did what she wanted," Olive said.

"She shouldn't have died all alone . . ." Joanna answered. "And what good
have I done here, anyway!"

Joanna walked to the fire and stared into the flickering flames. She shivered
despite the warmth. *It's over*, she thought. *My grandmother had one last hope,
and I failed her. She died knowing her home would never be restored to her.* Now
Joanna realized that must surely have been what her plea had been all about. Her
grandmother was dying when Joanna left; the doctor had as much said there was
no hope. Yet Joanna had maintained in her heart the smallest of hopes that she
might find something in Scotland that would bring healing to her grandmother.

That would never happen now. This message rang with an awful finality. What
did anything else matter? From the beginning all her efforts seemed destined to
end in futility. She should never have made that promise and thus raised the
woman's hopes. Maybe she never realized what a failure her granddaughter was.
Perhaps I can go home and forget all my failures, Joanna thought miserably.

Home! At the thought Joanna cried anew. Her grandmother was the only home
she had ever known; with her gone . . . she had no home. She had begun to feel
attached to this place, these people, but she had no reason to stay now—besides,
she would only bring trouble on them too.

She turned around to face the two women who had become her friends. As she
looked on their kind, sympathetic faces, she knew she had grown to love them.
How could she leave this place?

"I'm so thankful you two are with me now," she said, trying to form her
quivering lips into a smile. "It's going to be so hard to leave . . ."

"Leave, child?" Letty interrupted, sounding almost as dejected as Joanna.

"I came here at my grandmother's request," Joanna replied. "Now that she's
gone I don't see the purpose of staying."

"Do you think her death makes your promise any less binding?" Olive asked, her natural gruffness making her words sound sterner than she perhaps intended.

"I was doing this for her . . ." Joanna began, but suddenly she recalled that part of it had been for herself also. Still, she had already been too selfish.

"If your grandmother was Lady Margaret Duncan," Olive went on, "and I think we can be pretty certain she was, then there is more to this than simply fulfilling a dying woman's last wish. This land meant so much to her that she spent her last words on it. And now something wrong is happening here. Stonewycke needs you, Joanna, now, more than ever before."

"What can I do against all the violence and threats?" was Joanna's anguished response.

It was Letty who gently replied, recalling the dear memory of her own mother's stories of times long past. "Ye can do what anyone wi' Ramsey blood in her veins would do," she said. "Ye can do what Lady Margaret herself would hae done if she had seen her people threatened. Joanna, hae ye considered that it's not mere chance that ye hae come jist when ye have?"

"I don't want to fail her," Joanna replied.

"Ye willna, lass. I ken ye willna."

"I suppose I don't have much choice." Joanna blinked back a fresh rush of tears. "And I truly don't want to leave this place just yet. I'm growing to love it so."

Then the three women embraced one another and wept together. There were tears even in Olive's shrewd old eyes.

24

Overheard Words

THE FIRE FLARED with a noisy spattering of sparks.

Sandy Cobden tossed another log into the hearth. The conversation was lively that evening among the small gathering of locals in the Bluster 'N Blow's common room, and the ale had begun to flow freely.

"If I hadna seen't wi' my own eyes I wouldna believed't!" boomed Rob Peters as if he were still shouting orders aboard his herring boat.

"'Tis no more'n Mr. Sercombe promised," said Sandy from behind his counter.

"Aye. But I always say, 'Don't count yer chickens afore they be hatched.'"

"Weel, it sounds t' me as though they be startin' t' hatch. So maybe we can start countin' noo," put in Doug Creary. "One thing's aye fer certain, those men were excavatin' the new harbor, sure's day."

"Things'll be changin' here noo!" added Sandy, and he poured another round of ale as if to celebrate.

"Aye . . . change fer sure," MacDuff's voice drawled with uncertainty. "Maybe more'n we're wantin'."

Nathaniel had listened in silence. His chief purpose in coming that night was not to socialize with his neighbors but to gather information. After his chat with Walter Innes and Joanna's visit with Dorey, he felt the time had come for him to put his shoulder to it, as he said, and find out whatever he could. The news of the arrival of workmen from Aberdeen had certainly been unexpected and had thrown the whole town into an agitation of excitement and speculation.

"Ye never know," he finally interjected into the discussion. "It may be that MacDuff's right. Not all change be fer the best."

"That's easy fer ye t' say, Nathaniel," said Rob. "Ye havena had t' risk life an' limb comin' in an' oot o' that harbor every day. I say 'tis high time somethin' was finally done aboot it." As if to seal his words with a stamp of authority, he lifted his mug to his lips and took a long draught of ale, then set it down on the thick oak table with a resounding thud.

"'Tis jist a shame the poor laird had t' die fer it t' happen," added Creary.

"Aye, but it shows who cares fer us, after all," said Rob.

"Sercombe?" Nathaniel said with a dubious scowl.

"Don't bite the hand that's feedin' ye, Nathaniel," returned Rob.

"Weel," said Nathaniel, "'tis true enough that one hand may be feedin' me, but 'tis the other hand I'll be worrin' aboot."

"Are ye tryin' t' malign the word o' Sercombe?" snapped the innkeeper.

"Not a bit o' it, Sandy," Nathaniel answered, realizing he'd been foolish to make an empty accusation. "I'm jist sayin' the land's not sold yet, so let's hold back oor celebration till then."

The conversation continued on, filled with speculations—some founded, others groundless—on the extent and specific form of the anticipated improvements. Each carried his own set of notions, based more on his personal needs and wishes than on any foundation in fact. On one thing, however, they were all agreed—a great day was coming to Port Strathy. Before long, one of their number stood and toasted the health and long life of the lawyer they had been fortunate enough to have take an interest in their town—Palmer Sercombe. He took his seat to the resounding cheers from his companions, and they continued thus, long into the evening through several more pitchers of Sandy's finest dark ale.

Nathaniel had chosen to hold his peace and had just decided to take his leave when the door of the inn opened and Tom Forbes walked in, wearing mud-splattered riding boots and breeches and a heavy, dark-brown leather coat.

"Hey, Tom," called Rob Peters, "come on over an' join yer friends fer a drink or two!"

Forbes said not a word, waved off the invitation with a tired look, and slunk toward a corner table where he sat down alone. His wide-rimmed hat cast a dark shadow over his face. Nathaniel eyed him intently, but Forbes seemed to pay him no attention, possibly never having realized it was Nathaniel who had driven him away that night in the alley.

Deciding to remain a while longer, Nathaniel turned his attention to Rob Peters' outline of how the new harbor ought to be constructed, while MacDuff— farmer that he was—proceeded to refute every point. There were several suggestions as to the best possible location for the new fish processing plant and then the discussion digressed so far afield as trying to decide who the foreman should be. Peters thought he might give up fishing altogether and operate his own schooner service to Aberdeen. MacDuff suggested that if any improvements were made, they ought to first make the roads fit to use.

Just then, two men entered the common room, glanced around, then walked toward Forbes's table and sat down. The talk at Nathaniel's table grew immediately hushed in the presence of the two strangers.

"Couple o' workmen, I'll warrant," said Rob in a muted tone.

"That tall un's a rum 'un, he is," whispered MacDuff, glancing over his shoulder at Forbes's companions.

But Nathaniel scarcely heard a word. The moment they had appeared his heart gave a leap. No shadows could hide the bushy black beard of the one or the scarred face of the other. They were speaking in whispers; Nathaniel strained his every nerve to make out their voices, but he could only make out periodic snatches of the conversation.

". . . hardly my fault," Forbes was saying, ". . . ye jist bungled the job, that's all . . ."

"Ah! we had the lass," the bearded man replied, "till that meddlin' big fella . . . if he hadna . . ." By now, the conversation at Nathaniel's own table had again risen to an excited pitch and drowned out the remainder of the man's speech.

"Do ye understan' what ye're t' do this time?" Forbes was saying when again Nathaniel was able to discern their voices.

"Mr. Sercombe—"

"Quiet, ye fool!" snapped Tom, loud enough for anyone to hear. But no one took much notice.

"Ye can count on us, man."

"I hope ye're right. If ye blunder't again, there'll be the devil fer us all t' pay . . . likes no mistakes . . . kind o' man he is. Now—get out."

"How 'bout a glass o' ale first?" suggested the short, scarred man who hadn't spoken till now.

"Get out, ye idiot!" Tom nearly shouted.

The two men rose and skulked from the inn.

After a few moments, trying to appear oblivious to the recent proceedings at the corner table, Nathaniel rose, bade his farewells to his tipsy friends, paid

Sandy his tab, and slowly exited the Bluster 'N Blow by the back door, where, he said, he had tethered his horse.

The cold night air rushed against his warm face. Hurriedly, he crept around the edge of the inn to a point where he could keep an eye on the front door. In another five minutes, out walked Tom Forbes, who turned up the street toward the few shops.

Once he judged himself a safe distance behind, Nathaniel set out behind, keeping a sharp eye on his quarry and a careful mind on his feet so he made no unnecessary noise. Past the chandlery and Miss Sinclair's store Tom walked. It came as no surprise when he halted in front of the lawyer's office, looked quickly about, rapped three quick times on the door, and then entered the darkened room noiselessly.

Hesitating only a moment, Nathaniel stepped out from the shed he had crept behind, hastened to the buildings, skirted the outside wall of Miss Sinclair's store, and at length arrived at the back alley which ran past the row of buildings. In a moment, he arrived at Sercombe's back door. The shade was drawn and there could have been at most a single candle inside illuminating two larger-than-life figures against the window. He leaned his ear up to the edge of the window and listened.

". . . it may be our only recourse," came a voice Nathaniel quickly identified as Sercombe's.

"I know they're bunglers, but I say let's at least give the two Fenwick boys another chance." That voice was Forbes's. "No one knows them here . . . an' ye canna be implicated yersel'."

"It hardly matters now that the Cuttahays and that cursed vet have seen those documents."

"But ye said yersel' they couldna do a thing wit'oot the papers in hand. If we can jist get 'em—"

"They might still find a way."

There followed a long silence.

"All the same," he continued, "if she's out of the way, those papers would be meaningless."

"Gettin' the papers is one thing. Murder's another. I'll have no part o' that. I told ye that in the beginnin'."

The lawyer made a hollow attempt at a laugh.

"Come now, my friend. You had no trouble with the laird."

"That was different," Forbes said. "He was old . . . his time had come. An' besides, the old fool deserved what he got. An' I didn't kill him—if he'd been a better horseman—"

"A moot point, I'm sure," Sercombe laughed. But he instantly sobered. "Remember, my friend. We all—including yourself—stand to lose a great deal if this thing is delayed. Our buyer will be here soon—in a matter of a few days. I want no loose ends muddling up our end of the deal. And from now on, don't use the front door. In fact—we had better not be seen together again. I see no need for further interviews—*if we each hold up our end!*"

Suddenly, Nathaniel heard the latch of the rear exit rattle. He scrambled for a place to hide and crouched behind a garbage bin just as the door opened. Had Forbes gone toward the left instead of the right he would have nearly stumbled over Nathaniel's bent body. For the time, however, Nathaniel remained hidden and whispered a silent prayer of thanks.

He waited until the footfall of Forbes's retreating steps could no longer be heard. In another minute, the candle in the lawyer's office was extinguished and he heard Sercombe exit through the front of the building, locking the door behind him. Nathaniel waited another few moments, then rose, straightened his stiff back, and carefully crept around the building the way he had come.

The street was deserted. In the distance, the voices of his friends at the Bluster 'N Blow could still be heard. He hastened back to the inn, retraced his steps around back, untied his horse and led it away. Once out of earshot of the inn, he mounted, dug his heels into the horse's flanks, and raced home as fast as his horse could carry him.

He had to take immediate precautions against another attack. He only hoped he wasn't too late and admonished himself for delaying so long following Forbes. What if the two men were at his home this very moment!

Nathaniel could have spared his horse the frantic gallop. But he had no idea that even as he led his horse away from the inn, the two men had doubled back and were enjoying another round or two of ale.

Whatever their intentions, they would not accomplish them until their thirst was well quenched.

25

A Second Legal Appraisal

NATHANIEL GALLOPED UP to the house, dismounted in a thick cloud of dust, and rushed inside.

Joanna sat in Letty's cozy kitchen sipping tea, still feeling numb from Olive's recent news. Letty busied herself over the breadboard, despite the hour, uneasy over Nathaniel's long absence and unable to retire until her anxiety had been stilled.

As Nathaniel burst through the door he glanced to the right and left, taking in the peaceful setting, and simply uttered, "Thank God!" He took off his hat and collapsed in a chair. Alarmed by his obvious apprehension, the two women plied him with questions. But try as they might, neither was able to draw a word out of him as to what had happened in town to cause such concern.

"It's time we was all in bed," he said at length, and they finally consented.

As Nathaniel lay quietly down beside his wife a few minutes later, his eyes remained wide open. The moment he heard the deep steady rhythm of Letty's breathing—the signal she was finally asleep—Nathaniel eased himself out of bed. He dressed, tiptoed back out into the living room, placed another log on the dying fire, and took his rifle down from over the mantle. He checked to make certain it was loaded, then sat down in his favorite rocker—the gun lying across his lap in readiness—with his back to the fire and his face toward the door.

Nathaniel rocked back and forth and waited. Gradually his eyelids began to droop. A man of great energy and superb health, the strenuous day had finally caught up with him.

All at once Nathaniel started forward.

He hadn't meant to drift off. How long he had been asleep he had no idea. It was the dead of night and the eerie silence hung heavy. But there could be no doubt—the soft thud of a footstep on the porch had awakened him.

He clutched the handle of the rifle.

The front door opened with a creak, and through the opening the light of the moon streamed into the cottage. In its glow Nathaniel could make out the silhouette of a tall, bearded man . . . a figure he had seen only once before—tonight at the inn. Almost immediately he could smell the stale scent of ale about him.

The moment for action had come.

Leaning forward, poising himself in preparation for battle, and saying to himself, "In the name of the Father, Son, and Holy Ghost, Amen," Nathaniel sprang from his chair with a bound and rushed toward the enemy screaming, "A diabhuil mhoir, tha thu ag deanamh breug!"

Before the terrified burglar could recover his dazed wits, dimmed by alcohol and further sedated by the conviction that the entire house was asleep, he received a punishing blow from the butt of the rifle squarely in his chest.

Stunned, he staggered backward and, mistaking Nathaniel for Alec—whom he already had reason enough to fear—turned and fled the house, knocking down his bewildered partner as he scrambled back through the door.

Shouting a torrent of whatever Gaelic he could recall from his childhood, Nathaniel bolted after him and discharged two deafening shots over their heads. Their imaginations heightened from the liquor (of which they had had considerably more than two rounds), the suddenness of the attack, and the alien sound of Nathaniel's high-blooded Gaelic shrieks, the two hoodlums sprinted down the road. In mortal terror that a demoniacal madman was pursuing at their heels, they did not stop until they dropped, exhausted, half a mile from town.

And ever after—though not around Port Strathy—when recounting the incident, they swore the maniac had fired a minimum of ten shots directly toward them and they had only escaped with their lives as a result of their shrewd maneuvers and the speed of their retreat.

It took over an hour to settle down Joanna, Letty, and assorted clamoring farm animals after the chaos of shouts and gunshots. Reiver scampered about the precincts of the farm barking encouragement to the other animals and warning to any and all future trespassers. But there was no further activity that night.

In the morning Joanna refused to heed Nathaniel's warning to remain in the house. The memory of events during the night, supplemented by Nathaniel's graphic recounting of his evening in town, sent a cold shiver down her spine, but it only hardened her resolve. No longer could she play a disinterested role in this drama which seemed determined to envelop her. She had grown attached to this town and its people and she would not shrink from her duty.

In the meantime, she had to get the documents to safety. No one—Nathaniel, Letty, Alec, or herself—would be safe until they were out of the house and secure.

"We must see Ogilvie," said Nathaniel the next day. "He's a good man. He'll know jist what's t' be done."

"I'll have t' get t' Culden in secret," said Alec. "They may be watchin' the hoose."

"*You?*" exclaimed Joanna. "I'm not going to put you in any more danger on my account. I'll go see Ogilvie."

"No, no, lass, the lad's right," replied Nathaniel. "'Tis best that he does it."

"Maybe I'm being foolhardy," insisted Joanna, "but I'm going. If Alec wants to go too, that's fine. But I'll not stay here while he goes alone."

The Cuttahays looked at one another. Alec sighed, knowing her mind was made up.

"And besides," added Joanna, "I want to hear for myself what he has to say. They are my own grandmother's papers."

"If ye must hae it that way," said Nathaniel at length, "ye must go at night. That's yer best chance t' slip away wi' oot bein' seen."

After an early evening slumber, they arose shortly after midnight, had a cup of tea and some oatcakes, and set out for Culden. Alec led by the most circuitous route possible, avoiding all main roads until they reached the river. After crossing the Lindow bridge, they rode past Dormin, and Joanna could not shed the eerie chill that assailed her at the memory of her last time along this very road.

It was some time before dawn when they finally rode slowly into Culden and through its main street. All was still and every door was yet barred against the night. The clip-clop of their horses' hooves echoed through the vacant streets.

They rode past Ogilvie's store-front office, knowing he would never be there at such an hour. Alec led the way to the lawyer's residence, a substantial stone house several streets off the main thoroughfare. They dismounted, tied their horses, and walked to the front door, feeling for the first time a bit sheepish about what they were compelled to do. But the harsh reality of the truth finally enabled Alec to raise his hand and give a sharp rap to the solid wood door. Several moments passed and Alec knocked again. Finally they heard the soft shuffling sound of slippered feet approaching the door.

Gordon Ogilvie opened the door, bleary-eyed, clad in woolen robe and carpet-shoes, and scrutinized the two before him with mingled puzzlement and annoyance. A slight middle-aged man with sparse salt-and-pepper hair, he was wearing wire-rimmed spectacles well down on his nose.

"What in the name of—"

His voice creaked over the words and he paused to clear his throat.

"Do you realize it's the middle of the night!"

"More near t' mornin' than ye'd think, sir," Alec replied.

"Alec MacNeil?" Ogilvie said, still puzzled. "I have no animals, as you know. Not that I'm unfond of them, but the little beasts always set me sneezing."

"Fish make fine pets," Alec suggested.

"Oh, do they?" Ogilvie hinted at a smile. "But not overly affectionate, I'd imagine."

Alec laughed outright.

"Well, young man," Ogilvie went on. "I trust you haven't awakened me at this ungodly hour to discuss the merits of piscatorial housepets."

"No, sir, that I haven't," Alec said. "And we're truly sorry t' intrude on ye like this—but ye'll see 'tis important when we tell ye why we've come."

"Well . . . come in, come in."

The lawyer ushered them through a tall-ceiled room, down a carpeted hallway toward the back of the house, and into the kitchen.

"Come, sit here at the table," he said. "I think I can get a fire going in the hearth—see, it's still quite hot." He worked on the fire with a poker and a few chunks of dry wood while Alec and Joanna seated themselves at a large, round oak dining table.

By the time he again turned to his guests, he was out of breath. "Now," he said, "what seems to be the problem?"

With that, Alec introduced Joanna and between them they provided the lawyer as complete an account as they could of the events leading to Joanna's coming to Scotland and all that had happened since her arrival.

"My, my, my," was all he said once they had finished. "This must be an extremely difficult time for you, Miss Matheson. Please accept my sincerest sympathies over your grandmother's parting."

"Thank you, Mr. Ogilvie," Joanna replied. "It has been hard, but I suppose it's helped knowing there might still be something I can do for her."

"Yes, that is the best way to look at it." He rubbed his chin thoughtfully for a while, then he added, "I daresay, I could use a cup of tea—will you join me?"

Ogilvie busied himself filling a kettle with water, muttering something about his housekeeper being away, then set the kettle on the stove.

"It is a shame all this other business has come up to interfere with your original plans." He took cups from the cupboard and poured cream into a small pitcher. "Mr. Sercombe is a colleague of mine. Of course, I hardly know the man, and can't say he's been a favorite with me. But then, that wouldn't help much in a court of law, now would it?" He chuckled lightly. "And as I said, he's an associate of the bar. I would hesitate to interfere where there wasn't some rather solid evidence. Do you see what I mean? The best thing for you to do, and this would be my recommendation, Miss Matheson, is to forget trying to prove anything against Sercombe and concentrate on affirming your own position."

"My . . . er, my . . . position?"

"Yes. Isn't that what this is all about, your descent from James and Atlanta Duncan?" asked Ogilvie.

"I . . . suppose I really haven't had a chance to think of that."

"Yes, of course—you've only just heard of your grandmother's passing. But, my dear, as difficult as such considerations might be at this time, you must understand that if you hope to stop Sercombe, you need to think in these terms." He paused as the hissing kettle occupied his attention. After a moment, he continued, setting cups before his guests. "In other words, Miss Matheson, if you are the great-granddaughter of James and Atlanta Duncan, then the implications are abundantly clear."

"You don't mean . . ." Joanna began, but found she was unable to say it.

"I mean, young lady, that you are in the direct line of descent. You mentioned some documents you possess concerning the property; there are no other claimants that I'm aware of. It's all very straightforward and direct," he concluded, dumping three teaspoons of sugar into his tea.

"Are you saying," Joanna stammered, "that I . . . I could be the heir to the estate?" At last the unspoken question had been voiced.

"Certainly. That's what this early-morning meeting is for, is it not, to talk about proving your claim?"

"Yes, Mr. Ogilvie," put in Alec. "But ye see, 'tis still so new to Joanna."

"I know," replied Ogilvie. "And you must forgive me if I sound rather heartless and cold. But my dear Miss Matheson, it appears as if time were rather crucial here. And as difficult as it may be, you might well be called upon to lay aside your grief in favor of some, shall we say, affirmative action. Your grandmother knew she was dying when she issued her request, yet she felt nothing could stand in its way."

Joanna sat dumbfounded, allowing the full weight of the conversation to sink in.

"I didn't come here seeking the property," she said at length.

"That is all well and good, my dear, but it may be your only way to stop these—well, what you seem to consider dubious schemes. Sercombe is a most cunning man. He's never careless. If what you imply is true, I'm certain he's taken every detail into account—everything, that is, except an unknown heir turning up out of the blue. And that will be the only edge you possess."

"And if I'm not the heir at all . . . if this deed isn't authentic—"

"Nothing is certain. And there's no use speculating." He lifted his cup and took several sips before continuing. "Perhaps we ought to have a look at those documents before we make any more wild conjectures."

Joanna brought out the ancient papers she had carefully folded in her purse. They seemed even more frail now than when she had first discovered them. She handed them across the table to Ogilvie who spread them out before him.

The lawyer scrutinized the papers for some time without saying a word. He tapped his finger against his mouth, and an occasional *hmmm* escaped his lips. Periodically an eyebrow cocked as he continued to peruse them in silence.

At length he looked up and drew a deep breath.

"It's little wonder someone is after these papers," he said. "If you had not appeared here just now, with these papers, Sercombe would have been able to go ahead with his plans with little to impede him. He is, after all, the family lawyer; he has power of appointment; there has been no heir. It is, I must confess, all rather convenient for him. But now, with these documents, that's another story."

"Is it simply the possibility of my being the heir?" asked Joanna.

"That's only part of it. You see, a deed is . . . well, it is after all a *deed*. And this one appears to be . . ." Here he paused and once more tapped his lips thoughtfully with his finger. "This quite appears to be the original deed drawn up by King George himself when the Ramsey lands were reinstated to them following the Jacobite Rebellion. You see, the Ramseys were among those staunchly loyal to Bonnie Prince Charles who, as punishment for their partici-pation in the rebellion, had their lands confiscated. Then some forty years later as a conciliatory gesture, George reinstated the lands to the heirs of the rebels. You will note the date here—1784."

"Can we stop the sale with this deed, then?" Joanna asked.

"If the deed was left with your grandmother fifty years ago, no doubt no one even knew of its existence. And it is likely another was since drawn up, perhaps by Sercombe himself using the authority of his power of appointment. I imagine such a document is already in his hands if the transfer to the new buyer is to take place as imminently as you say."

Ogilvie paused to refill their cups with tea.

"Do you know anything about the new buyer of the land?" he asked.

Joanna shook her head.

He glanced toward Alec.

"Nothing, sir," he said. "We've all heard rumors, ye know."

"Ummm . . . I see," said the lawyer slowly.

"So where does that leave us, Mr. Ogilvie?" asked Joanna.

"I would say it leaves our friend Palmer Sercombe in a rather precarious position," he answered, with the faintest gleam in his eye. "Your possession of this deed, and if you can prove your position in the Duncan family—which, of course, you must be able to do to verify that these papers aren't merely a fraud—well, it quite puts Mr. Sercombe out in the street, so to speak. It may well even nullify his power of appointment."

"It's all coming so fast," said Joanna, "I . . . I just can't understand it all."

"My dear, your grandmother was Margaret Duncan, is not that what you told me?"

"Yes."

"As the eldest child of James Duncan, she should have inherited the estate—surely you have realized that?"

"Yes," answered Joanna tentatively. "But I thought she was disinherited or relinquished it by going to America."

"Do you know that for certain?"

"I don't know anything for certain."

"The fact that she held the deed, you see, that's the crucial point. By being the natural heir in the blood line of the family—as her birth had made her—the property was hers. And the fact that she held the deed, well, that authenticates her right beyond the shadow of a doubt."

"But it hardly matters," interjected Alec. "Even if Alastair was the legal heir . . . even if his sister had let go any claim on it, Joanna would still inherit. He had no children. She still stands next in line."

"Ah, yes, but then you would have Sercombe's power of appointment to contend with. If Alastair, as the true heir, had turned over power of appointment to him, then he does have legal right to do what he chooses. But if Alastair wasn't the rightful heir, then a power of appointment issued by him would not be binding, at least with regard to the disposition of the estate.

"There is one other odd thing about this deed," the lawyer went on, perusing the document once more, a finger held thoughtfully to pursed lips. ". . . yes, quite odd."

"What is it?" asked Joanna.

"No doubt it escaped your notice, but there is a signature here at the bottom—*Anson Ramsey.*"

He paused and Alec and Joanna waited for him to continue.

"This deed was drawn up in 1784, probably because at that time lands were reinstated to certain rebellious factions of which the Ramseys were a part—namely, the Jacobite Rebellion. The names are faded now, but you can make out the signatures of Robert Ramsey and the King. But below them is Anson Ramsey's signature."

"Who was he?" asked Alec.

But Joanna remained silent. She knew the name only too well. She had gazed over and over at it on her grandmother's family-tree embroidery.

"Anson Ramsey was Robert's son and heir," Ogilvie replied. "Still, I see no reason for his name to appear on a deed, unless . . ." His finger found its way once again to his pursed lips.

"What was he like?" Joanna asked when Ogilvie's sentence trailed away unfinished.

"His whole tenure as laird was rather peculiar. He was extremely beloved of his people. Of all the lairds, since the Ramseys came to Strathy, he was one of the few who actually made this area his home. He was a good man, most benevolent toward his subjects. There was great prosperity here during his life, largely due to his influence. The one flaw in his life proved to be his two sons. They were both said to be scoundrels. Then when he was still in his prime, Anson died a rather sudden and untimely death."

"Was he . . . murdered?"

"It was a hunting accident. But there was considerable speculation as to whether it was truly an accident. It happened between Dormin and Culden. He and his sons were alone. Nobody really knows what occurred. There were rumors he had threatened to disinherit his sons if they did not begin to act worthy of their station. But I wonder about his signature here. And under his name are the words: '*In accordance with the 'title transfer' to be presented forthwith.*'"

"Was the land transferred to someone else?"

"Yes, it does rather sound that way, doesn't it?" said Ogilvie. "But if that were the case, knowledge of it must have been lost. Because the land remained with the Ramseys. His son, Talmud, inherited the land in due course, after his father's death. No, I just can't say what this means."

"Sounds t' me as if he was plannin' t' transfer it," said Alec. "Maybe he jist never got aroun' t' it."

"You may be right," said Ogilvie thoughtfully. "If there was a 'title transfer' document, that would certainly tell us more. But I doubt such a paper even exists. Possessing this deed with other necessary proofs, Joanna is most certainly the heir. But if the property was later transferred, well . . . that might change everything."

"What if Sercombe has it?" suggested Joanna. "He has been the family lawyer for years."

"Yes," said Ogilvie slowly, "that could certainly change your position dramatically. And that might, after all, be Palmer Sercombe's ace in the hole, as it were."

26
Nathaniel and Letty

THE RETURN RIDE to Port Strathy was long.

A solemn silence hung over the two as they plodded along. Perhaps the need for sleep had overtaken them after their stealthy midnight journey. Perhaps the threatening overcast sky cast a pallor over their spirits. Or even more, perhaps the thoughts of each were occupied with Ogilvie's assertion as to Joanna's position in Port Strathy's affairs. Joanna herself was not sure whether the visit with the lawyer was cause for celebration or sackcloth. She had learned a great deal, to be sure. Yet she still had no specific direction to follow. In the meantime, the lawyer had promised to look into a few details on his end—discreetly of course.

It was shortly before noon when they reached the Cuttahay cottage.

The clouds had amassed thick and menacing, and the two narrowly escaped a sound drenching. With weary bodies they approached the door. What a relief it would be to sit down in front of the fire with a warm cup of tea!

Unexpectedly Olive Sinclair met them at the door. Whatever greeting she uttered was lost to their ears as they saw beyond her the tidy little cottage in complete disarray.

"What happened!" Alec groaned, brushing past Miss Sinclair. "Nathaniel . . . Letty!" he called, seeing neither of his old friends, his voice trembling with fear.

Quickly he spun back around and faced Miss Sinclair. "Where are they?"

"They're all right," she answered. "They're resting in bed."

Alec turned again and started toward their bedroom.

"Wait, Alec," Olive called after him. "Just calm yourself, lad, and let's sit down and I'll explain everything to you—at least as far as I can."

"Hoo can I sit when I ken somethin' dreadful must o' happened?"

"Well, stand then! But you'll not be disturbing Nate and Letty after my just getting the two of them to sleep." Her rising voice peaked until it threatened to wake the sleeping couple with none of Alec's help.

Apprehending her firm resolve, Alec yielded and slumped into Nathaniel's rocking chair. Joanna, who had been standing in the doorway during the exchange, moved into the room, trembling, and stood silently before the fire, horrified at this latest outbreak of violence.

The table in the kitchen was overturned, as were most of the pieces of humble furniture in the living room. An overstuffed couch, the one item of luxury that the Cuttahays owned, had apparently been slashed with a knife, its cotton and feathers scattered about the floor. One of the room's large windows was broken, but no glass was to be seen; Olive explained that a stool had been thrown through it, sending the breakage to the ground outside. The single indoor plant, an ancient green and yellow sansevieria, lay in three pieces on the floor, its pot shattered, dirt scattered about the room.

"I came here two hours ago," Miss Sinclair began. "I found the place much as you see it now, except that Nathaniel, poor soul, was in here bent over Letty—weeping."

Alec jumped from his seat, but Olive reached out a hand and grabbed his arm.

"Don't worry, lad," she said, "she'll be all right. But Nathaniel was afraid to leave her alone to get help. 'Twas only by chance I happened along. I fetched the doctor. Letty's arm was broken, and he set it. Nathaniel had a mild concussion; he had been unconscious for a time."

"How?" said Joanna, finally finding her voice.

"Nathaniel says they broke in just after breakfast. He said they were after the two of you, but once they realized you weren't here they seemed bent on destruction. He said one of the men yelled, 'See what comes of meddlin' where you're not wanted, old man!' Something like that."

"Did he know who they were?" asked Alec anxiously.

"They had scarves over their faces. He wondered if one might have been Tom—you know, Tom Forbes. Wasn't sure of the other. But then, it could have been the two men he feared off the night before. He just wasn't sure; they burst in so fast and started beating on the two of them—the poor dears!"

"Oh no!" Joanna moaned, covering her face with her hands. "What have I done? What have I done? None of this would have happened if I hadn't—"

Alec was at her side in a moment. "Now ye can't go blamin' yersel', lass," he said.

"Then who else?" Joanna replied. "I should have known—"

"We both should hae known," said Alec.

"Only the Lord himself knows what's going to happen," said Miss Sinclair. " 'Tis no use crying about it now. Letty and Nathaniel will both be fine, and praise the Lord for that! And that's mostly what matters. What's happened has happened. We just need to look forward now. Come and sit down: we need to have a little talk."

Alec led Joanna to the rocking chair where she sat down. Alec gathered his long legs beneath him and sat on the floor. Miss Sinclair laid another log on the fire, where it crackled into flame, then pulled a three-legged stool in front of Alec and Joanna and lowered herself stiffly onto it.

"Am I to take it, lass, that the two men were after you or your documents?" she asked.

Joanna nodded. "It's a nightmare."

"It can't go on," said Alec angrily. "I've got t' do somethin' t' stop those men."

"But, Alec," insisted Joanna, "it's not your fight. It's *me* they're after."

"It's bigger than just yourself," said Miss Sinclair. "There's something afoot here that involves us all. That's why I came out here this morning. Sercombe left town at dawn today. I hate rumors, but in my business I can hardly escape them. And folks are saying he's off in Aberdeen to fetch the bloke who's buying all the land. Most likely they'll be back in four days and everything will be about over then. The transfer of the title is supposed to be taking place just a few days after that. I heard something about a public gathering when the signing'll take place and the money'll be delivered and all that."

"I just don't know what to do," sighed Joanna. "We saw a lawyer in Culden today, a Mr. Ogilvie."

"Good man, he is," Olive assured her. "Yes, a fine man. You can trust him."

In deep thought Alec finally burst out, "Joanna, I know ye're reluctant, an' ye're a woman, an' ye think folk won't accept ye 'cause ye're new here, but the time's goin' t' come when ye're goin' t' have t' make public who ye are. The people have t' know."

"I . . . I don't know," said Joanna.

"No!" Alec nearly shouted. "This has gone too far. It must be stopped."

He jumped to his feet and stalked across the room. "I know I've had t' wrestle wi' my own stormy nature an' my desire t' be like the Lord. An' ye've helped me t' get it worked oot within mysel'. But there's a time fer doin' what's right an' fightin' wrong, e'en if ye hae t' set aside yer meekness fer a time. An' if I hae t' go t' Sercombe an' Tom Forbes an' the other bla'gards an' wring their necks t' find oot what's afoot, then so be it! I jist can't sit by—"

Suddenly he stopped, sighed deeply, and turned toward Joanna. "I'm sorry. Maybe I'm bein' a bit hasty. I jist can't stand t' see people I love hurt, but I'll wait fer ye, Joanna. We'll do what ye think best."

"Oh!" moaned Joanna. "I just don't know what to do!"

"You have to do what's right, that's all," said Olive. "Stand your ground."

"But how do I know what's right?"

"Trust in the Lord to show you." Olive laid her coarse hand on Joanna's arm.

"But I don't even know what that means," replied Joanna with a frustrated voice. "Don't you realize? I'm not like you or Nathaniel or Letty. I don't know *how* to trust your Lord. I thought I was doing the right thing by going to Culden with Alec. But just look at what came of it. It's all my fault that this happened to Nathaniel and Letty."

"Joanna—"

"But it is my fault! It wouldn't have happened if I hadn't come here."

"The Lord's hand was in your coming. You can't blame yourself."

"I should never have come! I'm just causing trouble. That's all I've ever done all my life."

"Don't talk like that, Joanna," said Olive tenderly. "The Lord loves you. He just wants you to trust Him to do the work He has for you. You can't do that until you accept His forgiveness. And then you must forgive yourself, child. That's what life with our God is all about—forgiveness. We're all sinners before Him, you know. But He can wash the past all clean."

"But I told you . . . I don't know how. I haven't had any practice. I don't even know what it means to trust Him."

"Have you never given your heart to the Lord, child?"

"No—I suppose I haven't," replied Joanna.

"You can't live by trusting Him till you've given yourself to Him," said Olive.

"But I don't know how to do that."

"Oh, 'tis simple, child. You just have to open your heart and tell Him you need Him and invite Him to come in and live with you."

Joanna turned thoughtful for a moment, then burst out. "Maybe I could do that if I didn't feel so guilty about what happened to Nathaniel and Letty!"

And with the words she ran from the house.

Alec started toward the door after her, but Olive placed a restraining hand on his arm.

"She needs to be alone, Alec."

"But I can't let her oot alone after all that's happened."

Just then they heard the creaking of the byre door as it opened, followed by the wooden thud of its closing.

"She'll be nearby, lad," Olive replied, looking steadily at Alec.

After a few moments, Alec turned back inside, and together the two began to set about restoring order to the ransacked cottage.

27

If Anyone Knocks

❧

GUILTY!

The word rang through Joanna's mind as she ran from the house, tears streaming down her face. It had fallen from her lips so carelessly. Yet now that she had spoken it she realized that the same feeling which had haunted her all her life was at the root of her present troubles. She had never been able to conquer the guilt she felt about her mother. And now there were more lives being ruined because of her!

She was weeping by the time she reached the barn, but she had to get away, to escape . . . from everyone, to hide from the world so they couldn't see the shame and stains of guilt which blackened her soul. Sobbing as she ran, the warm tears stung her eyes and blurred her vision. The homey warmth of the barn with the rich aroma of friendly animals and honest work should have been comforting, but she was hardly conscious of her surroundings. If only she could run, and run, and run and never come back, never see anyone again. Then no one else would be hurt by the curse of injury and pain which she seemed to carry with her wherever she went.

Oh, God! she thought. *How can they talk of trusting God, of doing right, of standing up for truth when life is so cruel? Oh, if only I hadn't come here! I do nothing but cause pain wherever I go!*

What had she gotten herself into? She never meant to cause trouble. She had only wanted to fulfill her promise to her grandmother. Now it seemed everything was crashing in upon her. Because of her, violence and pain had come to the once sleepy little village of Port Strathy. Some curse was upon her; it followed her and touched all those whom she contacted. She alone was guilty; some unknown evil was part of her very being!

Suddenly Olive's words rang through her mind: "The Lord loves you. You can't do the work He has for you until you accept His forgiveness. You can't learn to trust Him till you've given Him your heart."

Joanna stopped and threw herself down on a mound of straw.

"Oh, God!" she wept. "I want to know you like they do. I want to learn to trust you. God—help me!"

She could not go on, but hid her face in her hands and wept in bitter sorrow. How alone she was! How far from home! She had no mother, no father, no grandmother. Not even a home!

All at once a small voice—was it just a thought in her mind, or was someone speaking to her?—seemed to say: *"You are not alone, child. I love you."*

Joanna looked up and swept a sleeve hurriedly across her eyes. She was alone. She glanced about, as if not believing the words she had heard in her mind. Then she recalled something her grandmother read to her so very long ago: *Yea though I walk through the valley of the shadow of death, I will fear no evil: for thou art with me . . .*

Joanna strained to hear more as if all the words she had ignored as a child would suddenly come back to her. "I don't deserve such promises!" she sobbed.

Then other words tumbled into her brain; she had heard them more recently: *He loves and forgives ye no matter who ye are . . . or what ye have done.* She thought for a moment of Alec and what he had experienced to bring him to that place.

No matter what ye have done . . .

"Did Alec mean I don't have to deserve you, God?" she found herself asking.

And that same voice within her seemed to resound, *"Yes!"*

"Oh, God," Joanna wailed. "I want to be clean! I want to know you! Help me know how."

But even as she uttered the words she realized she already knew. Hadn't Olive said it was simple? Hadn't she told her how?

"If only it could be true!"

At last the years of pent-up self-condemnation was released and Joanna wept with bitter remorse. When the deep and agonizing wells of guilt and sorrow had spent themselves, she sat up, glanced around, and—though her eyes were red-rimmed and her voice still quivered with sobs—she felt strangely steady. Then she folded her hands in prayer, following the habit her grandmother had taught her as a child, breathed deeply, and said: "Lord, I need you so desperately! Won't you please come into my heart and stay with me, and show me how to live?"

An hour later the kitchen door opened.

As Olive turned toward her she knew immediately a change had come upon Joanna. Her eyes were still puffy and red, but her face glowed with the release from the bondage of her past.

"You were right, Olive," she said softly. "He has forgiven me."

"Aye!" replied Olive with a smile. "And has He shown you what you're to do?"

"No. Not yet. But I'm sure He will. He has forgiven me, and for the moment that is enough."

28
Aberdeen

❖

THE SLEEK BLACK motor car wound its way cautiously through the narrow city streets.

The few automobiles found this far north were scarcely larger than the buggies and carriages the streets had been designed for, and maneuvering a full-sized Rolls Royce through horse-carts and staring crowds proved no easy task. An unrelenting rain pelted the auto, and the chauffeur gritted his teeth as he peered through the smeared window, wondering if he had missed his turn.

The two men in the backseat sat oblivious to the driver's misery. With higher things on their minds, they were accustomed to leaving such trivial worries as the weather to their lessers.

Palmer Sercombe stroked the rich leather seat with his palm.

He enjoyed this, he had to admit. And the convenient portable bar from which his companion served their drinks was impressive indeed. It was the finest Scotch he had ever had the pleasure of drinking.

Sercombe had long been associated with wealthy, powerful men. Yet somehow it had never been enough only to rub shoulders with wealth. As he scanned the luxury all about him, he felt a tingle of satisfaction knowing that soon—yes, very soon—he would possess the means to command his *own* power—wield his *own* wealth. He had waited many years for this moment.

It would be his finest hour!

His face broke into a grim smile of triumph.

But first things first, he thought as he returned his attentions to his companion, a businessman in a gray three-piece suit.

"Am I to understand," he was saying, "that there is danger the deal may fall through?"

"Not at all," the lawyer replied.

"Your wire sounded urgent."

"I only felt we should take steps to move along more quickly. I have drawn up all the necessary papers—they will become finalized in a week."

"Why the haste? I didn't expect to be called away from London for several weeks more."

"A small problem has cropped up. Nothing but an annoyance. It's being dealt with—in fact, by this time it should have already been taken care of."

"A problem?"

"Some papers I need. Actually, we don't need them to continue; it would just be more, shall we say, expeditious if I held them firmly in my possession prior to the close of our escrow. And those papers should be in my office even as we speak. Two of my local colleagues were sent to retrieve them the morning I left."

"What makes these papers so vital? I thought we had everything necessary before us when we met last time in London."

"Yes, of course. But a woman has shown up."

"Don't they always?"

"I'm afraid this one may try to lay claim to the inheritance."

"You assured me there were no heirs . . . no sticky difficulties that would come back to haunt us."

"I'm sure she will prove nothing but a fraud. We will see to that. But she has certain documents—"

"You've seen them?"

"Yes."

"And you let them slip away? I thought you had more backbone than that."

"Don't worry. She will have been eliminated before we arrive."

"You'd not be fool enough to kill her!" The man seemed more shocked at Sercombe's stupidity than at the prospect of murder.

"We both stand to lose a great deal here. I plan to do what must be done."

"Well, do what you want. But just remember—I didn't hear a thing."

They nursed their drinks in silence for a few moments.

At length Sercombe said, "I thought we might have a bit of a public show with the signing of the papers. A town meeting, banners, couple of speeches—that sort of thing."

"Is that really necessary?" asked his companion with the tone of a parent humoring the whims of a child.

"We must make a show of good faith—I don't want to be hounded the rest of my life by disgruntled tenants. I plan to make some token improvements. They are simple-minded people. They have no concept of the true value of the land. We'll repair their harbor, as we've discussed, hand out some cash indulgences—"

"What does all that matter? The whole place will be under water within three years."

"And remember," said Sercombe with a smirk, "I never heard a thing."

"I don't care what you hear or don't hear."

"It won't all be under water, only the low-lying inland areas. Port Strathy will still be there, and so will its people. We have to make attempts to mollify them."

"Everything I plan to do is all legal and aboveboard; which is more than I can say for you. Actually, what I'm doing will benefit them more than your farcical little harbor."

"Unfortunately, two-thirds of the population won't be around to reap those benefits." Sercombe chuckled wryly.

"A minor point!" The man's white teeth gleamed through a cunning smile. "A stint in Glasgow or Edinburgh will do the poor devils some good."

The car swerved and skidded on the slippery road. Sercombe's companion rapped sharply on the window separating the driver from the rear seat.

"These provincials can't even drive properly!" he muttered with disgust.

29

Doug Creary's Sow

❊

FOR THE NEXT three days things settled into as much of their old routine as could be expected. Alec saw to a number of chores he had neglected and resumed his rounds throughout the neighborhood—keeping, however, as close an eye on the cottage as he could manage.

With a relieved sense of quiet joy, Joanna filled her days ministering to Nathaniel and Letty. When the following morning dawned, Letty was much improved and insisted on rising to fix breakfast. A good part of Joanna's energies had to be expended to convince her to remain in bed. Her next most difficult task was to prevent Nathaniel—notwithstanding the headache which lingered from the blows he had received—from going out to perform his usual chores.

In the end he agreed to rest for one day. But no more.

This provided Alec the opportunity to lead an exhuberantly enthusiastic Joanna through all the morning rounds of cow-milking, stable-cleaning, and pig-feeding. As she tromped through the stalls in Letty's knee-high rubber boots, not even the pungent smell of manure sloshing beneath her feet could dampen the eagerness she felt to be on the giving rather than the receiving end of the Cuttahays' goodwill.

A cheerful smile remained on her lips and a song in her heart throughout the day, and the next, taking the old couple tea, sweeping out the house, restoring order, and maintaining a warm fire glowing on the hearth. Her freedom from the burden of self-blame allowed Joanna to receive the benefit in her spirit of such ministry of love and caring. Truly the healing of her deep emotional scars had already begun. Alec repaired the broken window and Joanna prepared a huge pot of stew, not without a good deal of verbal assistance from Letty in the bedroom. By then Nathaniel, who could not be confined a moment longer, was up and about in tolerably good spirits.

Had she been able, Joanna would have instantly traded all possible claim to any inheritance for a future with this simple couple.

Four days after the attack on Nathaniel and Letty, Alec stopped by to help Nathaniel with his livestock. However, the work was prematurely interrupted as Douglas Creary's son came running up, out of breath, calling for Alec. There was an emergency with their pig.

"Take the lass with ye, son," suggested Nathaniel. "We'll be fine here."

Alec eyed him for a moment, then ran inside to ask her.

She declined on the Cuttahays' behalf. She must stay, she said; they needed her.

But the two older people protested so vehemently Joanna realized they might feel worse if she remained behind. At length, therefore, she consented.

"There's little time t' lose," said Alec. "My horse is ready t' go, an' 'tisn't far. We'll ride together. Letty'll want the boy t' rest awhile before he follows."

They rushed outside, and Alec took Joanna's hand and helped her onto the horse's back; then he swung up into the saddle behind her, took the reins firmly, and off they galloped.

In the high delight her spirits had enjoyed the last few days, the ride into town on horseback was exhilarating. The wind blowing in her face, the surging power of the horse's muscles flexing beneath her—all intoxicated her still further. And Alec's proximity as he urged the horse on contributed as well to the mood of joy and abandonment she felt welling up within her. She leaned back until she felt her back against his great strong chest. His forearms tightened around her waist. With her hair blowing back in Alec's face, Joanna let out a spirited laugh from the sheer ecstasy of the moment. *He may be what my schoolfriends in Chicago would term a "country bumpkin,"* she thought. *But underneath that crude, homespun exterior lies a tender and compassionate man, with just enough humor and impulsiveness to make him interesting. What girl in her right mind wouldn't be proud to—*

Her thoughts were interrupted by shouts from the house in front of them.

A poor cottage with thatched roof and chipped paint confronted Joanna. She took special note of Dorey's garden situated bravely in front in full color with another spring. Doug Creary and his youngest son stood on the ramshackle porch and extended a friendly greeting. Creary was a tall, lean man in his mid-thirties. His skin was coarse and deeply tanned from years of exposure to the elements, but there was a welcoming sparkle in his eyes. It reminded Joanna of the warmth she had seen in his wife's greeting the first day she had arrived in Port Strathy.

He said very little as he led them around back to the pen where his sow was confined.

The animal lay on her side, howling in obvious misery. Alec immediately began his examination amid her ear-piercing cries.

"I canna tell ye what's wrong wi' her," said Doug. "She's been bellerin' like that since early this mornin'."

Alec examined the animal's body and when he touched its right forefoot, the shrieks rose to such a crescendo Alec feared she would disturb the inhabitants in faraway Aberdeen.

"There . . . that's it!" he cried.

But when he gingerly lifted the foot, the pig showed her strength was by no means yet spent.

"Hold her, Doug!" he said, struggling to keep her from throwing him off and escaping.

Alec probed further while the racket continued. Finally he withdrew a thorn the size of a small nail.

"All right, Molly . . . the show's over," Alec said, dumping some powder into the wound. "Ye'll be feelin' yer old self now."

"Glad ye saw fit t' come, Alec," said Doug. "She's a braw sow, she is."

"I'm sure ye canna afford t' lose her, then."

"Aye, ye speak the truth there. But things look t' improve aroun' here real soon. Why, Rob Peters be thinkin' o' settin' up a schooner service, an' ye know what that'll mean."

"I'm not sure I do," Alec replied.

"Why, his troller's goin' t' be up fer sale an' I'll jist ha' enough t' buy her." Doug's face beamed as if the troller were already in his possession.

"Sounds like ye've come into some good fortune," said Alec. "Congratulations!"

"Thank ye, Alec. But ye must o' heard aboot the money?"

"I heard talk o' a new harbor."

"But that's not all!" exclaimed Doug. "Each o' the tenants are set t' get fifty poun's. Fifty poun's, man, did ye hear me! All o' us!"

"That's a lot o' siller, no doobt, Doug."

"Port Strathy's finally goin' t' take her place amoong the great fishin' ports, an' that's the truth. We're goin t' make oor mark. We all could stand t' do right well, an' fer a long time."

Alec glanced at Joanna. They exchanged an unspoken sign their host did not notice.

As Alec and Joanna made ready to depart, Rose Creary came out of the house, with her little smudge-faced daughter clinging to her apron. Rose held a tiny bouquet of nasturtiums and daisies bound together with a faded red ribbon. She held them out to Joanna with a look of bashful admiration on her face.

"'Tisn't much," she said. "But we're right honored t' hae ye visit oor home."

"How sweet of you!" exclaimed Joanna.

To her surprise, Joanna felt a tear rising in her eye. "They're lovely," she said. "Thank you so much."

As they rode away from the Creary home, Joanna's mood was peaceful and subdued. There would be no need to hurry now and they could enjoy a leisurely ride back out into the country. She could just sit, with Alec's arms around her, and drink in the serenity of being with him and no one else.

"Why don't we swing by Olive's?" suggested Alec. "I'm sure she'd want t' know Letty an' Nathaniel are doin' jist fine."

"Ummm," purred Joanna, turning and casting him a satisfied smile, "whatever you say. I'm yours for the rest of the day!"

Alec laughed and turned the horse toward the center of the village.

Arriving at the store, Alec swung down off the horse, took Joanna's hand and eased her to the ground, unaware of two piercing eyes taking in the entire scene from inside the building. He tethered the horse at the rail and led the way to the store's front door.

Just as they were about to enter, the door swung open and an elegantly dressed stranger stepped onto the walk. Taking no notice, Alec continued on into the building, not realizing Joanna had stopped dead in her tracks as the stranger had flashed his coal-black eyes full upon her.

"Good Lord!" he breathed, "it *is* you!"

Joanna was dumbstruck, her face suddenly grown deathly white.

30

Jason Channing

IN SILENCE JOANNA allowed Jason Channing to lead her by the hand away from the store.

"I thought I would never be able to get you alone," he said.

"Don't you think you were a bit rude to Alec?" said Joanna haltingly, finding her voice for the first time since seeing Channing.

"Rude! My dear, you have to be direct with these simple folks; I'm sure he hardly noticed."

They walked toward the harbor, past the Bluster 'N Blow, and to the water's edge. There Channing turned and led Joanna away from town along the seafront.

"Regardless," he went on, "do you realize how long it's been since I saw you last? It seems like years! I've thought of nothing else. So at least allow me to be excused on that basis."

"Really . . . Jason," said Joanna, recalling immediately the discomfort of his flattery. *Oh, why did I let him take me away from Alec?* she thought.

"Joanna, you are so beautiful." He paused and turned toward her, lifting his hands to cup her cheeks between his palms. "How could I erase the lovely vision of you from my mind?" He sighed. "Oh . . . how I've missed you!"

"How did you find me?" asked Joanna, squirming to back away. Why were this man's attentions so disquieting? *Please, God, don't leave me now!*

"What does it matter?" he replied. "What is important is that I have found you. Fate has led me to you. How can there be any doubt we belong together?"

"I . . . I don't know, Jason. A lot has happened to me since I came here."

"That's what you wanted, wasn't it? Adventure . . . that sort of thing?"

"No, it's more than that. I'm not the same person I was when I came."

"Nonsense. You're still my shy, little Joanna—just like the day I found you."

"No, Jason, I've changed. I've grown. There are things I care about, people I have grown to—"

"Don't tell me you're in love with that yokel I saw you with!"

"What? Oh, Alec . . . in love—no, of course not," replied Joanna, notably flustered.

"Then what can possibly stand in our way? Joanna, I love you . . . I want you. I have longed for this moment when we would be together again."

He pulled her toward him, wrapped his insistent arms around her waist, and kissed her. His lips were warm and vibrant. Momentarily she relaxed and returned his embrace, but then eased herself gently away.

"Oh, come now, Joanna. Surely by now you've had enough of those little games you were playing on the ship. You've had time to think, to grow up. I was patient with you then because I knew all this was new to you. But you're a big girl. It's time you learned about the real world."

He kissed her again, and again. This time she did not pull away.

"And you know you love me too," he said at length.

Joanna did not reply. Maybe he was right. Did she even know what love was? *Oh, Lord*, she thought, *what am I to do?*

"Why did you come to Port Strathy?" she asked softly, making conversation.

"Ah, Joanna," he replied. "Let's reserve all the talk for another time. Come with me." He turned, took her hand, and led her back the way they had come.

"Where are we going?"

"To my room at the inn."

Something about his evasive tone put Joanna on her guard.

"But you still haven't told me why you came," she said.

"Is that a note of suspicion I detect in your lovely voice?" he said, his smile full of merriment. "Come to my room. Let's celebrate our reunion. Then we can talk about it. You can ask all the questions you like. Besides, you should know I came to see you. I told you before—I make a habit of going after things I like."

Sensing a reluctance in her spirit toward this man whose vows of love tempted her, Joanna stopped. Something clicked in her mind.

"You're here about the estate, aren't you?"

"What does it matter?"

"It matters to me," she persisted. "You are the man we've been hearing about!"

"You know I hate to mix business with pleasure," he said, pulling her toward him once more. But this time she stiffened, not yielding to his embrace.

Affronted, he added, "What simpleton here cares anyway!"

"I care, Jason. This place is special to me."

"Yes, I can see where it would be," he replied, his hidden motives gaining the upper hand over the oily blandishments of his charm, "if you can get your greedy little hands on it." Derision marked his tone.

"It's not like that at all. How could you suggest such a thing?"

"I knew there was some claim to the inheritance. Before this moment I only had the vaguest suspicions, though I should have put two and two together."

His lips cracked into a wry smile. Joanna was silent.

"It seems as though we've become competitors. But I'd much prefer to think of us as business associates—beautiful partners."

"What do you mean?"

"I could pull some strings—make sure that inheritance was in the bag for you. Then I wouldn't have to shell out a dime to Sercombe—or should I say shilling? No matter. Anything we'd make after that would be clear profit. We could make a bundle, you and I, Joanna."

"What are your plans? What are you going to do with the estate?" The man's words suddenly sounded foreign, distant from the simplicity of the new life she had discovered.

"Technically, nothing. It's the water rights that interest me—the river will do the rest."

"The river?" asked Joanna, confused.

"The Lindow. It's a sweet little deal. I've been wanting to expand my operations into Europe. All I have to do is create some hydroelectric power up here—and you name it, I can do it. Labor's cheap . . . no nasty unions to contend with—"

"Electricity? But there is no electricity here."

"Not yet. But it's coming. Haven't you heard—this is the industrial age, Joanna. I'll make electricity here, and industry won't be far behind. And I'll be sitting right—"

"Do I understand you?" interrupted Joanna with rising emotion. "You're going to build a dam on the Lindow?"

"For openers."

"And the valley, the farms?"

"Are you kidding? You know how dams work. Don't be naive, Joanna! It's going to be one big lake—Loch Channing . . . how does that sound?"

He burst into a laugh.

Joanna barely heard him, for a vision suddenly sprang into her mind. It momentarily confused her, for there in her mind's eye were Jason and Alec standing side by side. Could there be two more divergent personalities? Jason, with his polished glamor, flashy smile, and smooth-talking assertiveness—a man who nearly eclipsed Alec's simple countenance. Yet what were these compared to Alec's forthright honesty? He was a man who had only his obscure little cottage and horse to call his own, a simple vet with mud and manure on his boots, whose days were spent giving of himself to the neighbors who depended on him. But did he not have more than money, prestige, or power could ever hope to gain? She suddenly realized that her newfound faith was causing her to reshape her priorities—to really see what was most important in life.

Joanna's thoughts were interrupted as the sound of Channing's laughter brought her mind back to the present.

"Listen, sweetheart," he was saying, "if you work with me on this, I can guarantee you'll be on easy street for as long as you like. But if you work against me," and here his voice lowered to a whisper which could hardly be distinguished from a growl, "you'll have nothing. And I mean nothing—at all."

For a moment Joanna's lips moved silently, unable to form the words stuck in her throat. Her head was spinning. How could she ever hope to resist such a powerful man? How could she ignore the vacillating emotions that threatened to overwhelm her?

"Why did you choose Port Strathy?" she asked in a voice that sounded so small, trying to maintain her composure.

"I met Sercombe in London last year. I happened to mention I was interested in foreign investments. One thing led to another . . . you know the routine."

"And what does he plan to do with the money?"

"I don't care if he plans to buy a yak farm in Madagascar."

"But he's going to keep the money, is that it?"

"You don't think he's a complete idiot! But why all the questions? Is this an inquisition or something? It's hardly your concern if you join forces with me. I'll take care of all the details."

Joanna opened her mouth, then closed it and was silent.

She had to get away to think!

". . . why all the questions?" Channing had asked, and the phrase rang in Joanna's mind.

Finally the words she had sought surfaced and she spoke.

"Because, Jason, you don't expect me to make a decision without all the facts?"

"There's really no decision for you to make, you know."

He paused, as if thinking what tactic to use, then continued. "Oh, come now, Joanna—you know how right we are together. Let's stop arguing and go to my room. We'll have a drink or two, relax, and see what happens. All this can wait till later. What happened on the ship was a long time ago. You can't refuse me again."

"Oh, can't I?" she said with a marked edge to her tone.

"You're turning into quite a woman, Joanna. I like that! Come."

He took her hand to lead her into the inn.

All at once Joanna visioned all the people she had met since arriving in Port Strathy—the Cuttahays, Olive, the Cobdens, the Crearys. In a flash she saw their cottages, their flower beds, their struggling gardens. Dorey's face came into view, then a picture of Doug Creary's pig and the look on his son's face while watching Alec work. If Channing had his way, all this would be gone—the simple life, the valley, the awful, beautiful forest called Dormin, the barns, the fields, the flowers.

Was this her land?

Were these her people?

Was she indeed one of them? Had she been led here to fight on their behalf? To preserve a way of life which gave meaning and purpose and joy? Did God truly have a hand in leading her here, to these people, to somehow fulfill a destiny among them?

A resolve began rising within her. If this were her chosen path . . . if God had indeed led her to this place, to this moment, for a purpose, then there could be no doubt that He would also give her the strength to do what He was calling her to do.

Silently Joanna sent forth a prayer: "Oh, Lord, now more than ever I need your guidance! Give me strength. Help me do what you want me to."

Then she turned and faced Jason Channing with a boldness she had never before known.

"Jason," she said, "I can get the inheritance, with or without you. If you want to work with me, you would have to make major changes in your plans."

"I don't make concessions," he replied flatly.

"It seems we agree on one thing," she answered. "But I have no intention of letting you get your hands on the land. Sercombe may be a swindler. But what you intend would destroy these people's lives, homes, history—their whole meaning."

"So we're feeling rather noble about it all I see," he said. "No one's going to be left homeless in the streets. So they have to relocate—it won't kill them. That's progress. It happens all the time."

"You don't have any concept of what this land means to them. Some of these families have been here for generations."

"These are new times, Joanna. This is the modern age. Times are changing."

"Well, these people have something here—something far more valuable than your progress, your industry, your wealth. And I won't let you take it from them, Jason!"

She moved away from him and turned to walk back toward the store.

"Joanna," Channing called after her, stunned and angered at her rebuff. "Joanna! I believe I told you once, but I'll tell you again—I *always* get what I want!"

She stopped and turned to face him.

"Not this time, Jason," she said steadily, then continued down the path.

"You're making a big mistake!" he called after her. But she did not look back again.

31

Communion

JOANNA RODE AS fast as the horse would carry her.

The slope of the grassy hill was hardly steep and the mare was able to keep moving at a full gallop all the way to the top. Still Joanna urged her on. Her hair streamed out behind her. She could feel the perspiration from the horse's back.

All at once she reeled in, jumped to the ground, and ran on foot, still higher up the slope, till her lungs cried out for rest and the sweat gathered on her forehead, back, and arms. Exhausted, she threw herself on the grass laughing. Within moments, however, the sounds had turned to sobs. Inexplicably and uncontrollably she wept aloud, unable to stem the confused array of emotions pouring out of her.

Her mare approached cautiously, nuzzling its moist nose into Joanna's tear-streamed face.

"Watching a grown girl cry?" she asked, sniffing, then wiped her eyes with her sleeve.

A low, rumbling whinny was the horse's only reply.

"Come here," she said, rolling over and giving the huge horsey head a hug.

She sighed deeply. The tears had done their work and swept away the black clouds of doubt and uncertainty.

Leaving Channing, Joanna had found Alec waiting for her at Olive's store. They rode back to the farm in silence. She knew it was cruel to give him no explanation. But at the moment there were simply no words she had to offer. She would tell him all in time.

"I have to be alone for a while, Alec," she had said when they reached the cottage. "I have to think."

In silence he saddled Nathaniel's mare and watched her ride off over the meadow and up the hill on the other side. Alec was too strong to be hurt, but he was too human not to feel the chill of her silence as he stood viewing her retreat.

On the top of the little peak, Joanna stared at the valley beneath her. The Cuttahay farm stood a mile away. To her right she could barely make out the outline of Stonewycke Castle. Port Strathy lay at the ocean's edge two miles distant between the two.

It all comes down to this, she thought.

This valley . . . this land.

She had come here on a vague quest with nothing but an old woman's words and a few antique relics—no friends, no prospects, hardly even a future. Now it seemed she had more than she bargained for, more than she was prepared to handle.

She sighed again.

What was she to do?

Lord, she thought, *how am I to know what to do? Help me hear your voice . . . make everything work out right for these people.*

Then as she silently sat reflecting on the scene spread out before her, the memory of Olive's words came flooding back into her mind: *The Lord loves you. He just wants you to trust Him to do the work He has for you. You can't do that until you accept His forgiveness.*

I've done that, Joanna thought. *I've accepted His forgiveness and He has cleansed away the guilt which has clung to my soul since before I can remember.* But now it seemed something more was required of her before she would be able to hear His voice telling her what she was to do next.

All at once the rest of Olive's words came back; she had forgotten them until now:

And then you must forgive yourself, child. That's what life with the Lord is all about.

How could Olive have known? It was only now just becoming clear to Joanna herself what had been at the core of her trouble all along, what had kept her shut tight to any intrusion by her father, her grandmother, even God. The blame she had placed upon herself for her mother's death, and even her father's had steeled her heart against the acceptance of forgiveness. For at the bottom of her deepest self, she knew she wasn't worthy.

That night in the Cuttahays' barn she had at last been able to unlock her heart and open it to receive God's forgiveness. Not because of any worthiness on her part—she knew now that didn't matter—but because God forgave her without conditions.

Yet she had still not released herself. How could she serve God until she realized He was in control of *everything*? Even her father and mother had been in God's hands, as were all these folk in Port Strathy. What had happened had not been *her* doing.

Is that it, Lord? thought Joanna. *Have I accepted your forgiveness, but still haven't forgiven myself?*

The only answer was the gentle breeze flowing through the grassy field. Yet even as Joanna framed the question, she knew that Olive's words reflected the truth she needed to hear. Why should the Lord speak again, when the answer had already been given through the words of her friend?

"Help me, Lord," she sighed. "Help me do what I must do."

In reply the thought came, *For this you do not need my help. I have washed you clean. Now you must accept it.*

Drawing in a deep breath, Joanna rose to her knees, and then at length said, "If you find me worth forgiving, Lord, then it is faithless of me to do anything less. Dear Lord, I do—"

She paused, hardly able to force the words out.

"—I do . . . *forgive myself!*"

The tears which followed were quiet tears—tears not of joy or elation, but of release, of letting go of a lifetime of condemnation and guilt. In her deepest heart, Joanna knew that the Lord's healing of her past had now begun in earnest. For the first time in her life she felt whole.

And for the first time since arriving in Scotland, she felt ready to do what had to be done for these people. God had led her here not only to work His healing in her soul, but so that she might do what had to be done on behalf of these people she had grown to love. And though she had no way of knowing it, God had led her here in answer to her grandmother's prayer for one she loved. For though the generations come and go, God's work of reconciliation goes on unceasingly, and the prayers of His children do not go unheard.

Out of the midst of her thoughts, suddenly Joanna recalled words she had heard long ago. She wondered that it had taken so long for them to have meaning for her: ". . . and lo I am with you always, even unto the end of the world."

She sat upright.

"Was that your word, Lord?" she asked herself. "Will you be with me no matter what?"

I am with you . . . I will lead you.

The phrase resounded in her brain like a cymbal.

"There could be no other way I would be able to face this crisis," Joanna murmured aloud.

I will lead you! came the same small voice within.

Joanna rose, took hold of the mare's rein, and began walking down the hill, feeling a welling surge of courage, optimism, and strength. *I will lead you.* The promise spun through her thoughts . . . *I will lead you!*

She turned her gaze out to the sea and thought of the Vikings Alec had so graphically portrayed—a strong people, men of courage and stout hearts. Brutal sometimes, yes—but nevertheless men of might and valor. She thought of the ancient Highland chieftains she had heard about—men whose loyalty to clan and principle knew no bounds.

Were these stalwart men her own ancestors as well? Did she have their heroic blood flowing through her veins?

Yes!

She was certain of that now.

This was her homeland. These were the roots from which she had sprung. She took pride in these people and their simple virtues and their robust characters because she was one of them!

A resolute determination arose within her.

She *would* see this fight through to the end! If her lot in life was to lay claim to her destiny as the last of the Duncan line, then so be it. She had not come here by accident. The Lord's hand had been on her all along, since her earliest days, since before she was born, preparing her for this moment.

She jumped onto the mare's back, dug in her heels, and galloped down the hill toward the farm, with the words "*I will lead you*" ringing in her mind.

32

Dorey's Disclosure

THE FOLLOWING MORNING the rain clouds, which had only produced intermittent showers for two days, at last released their pent-up floods. It poured all through Nathaniel's chores, and when he finally burst into the house shortly after 10 a.m. he was drenched to the skin.

"Aye, ye're finally gettin' t' see a full-scale northern storm," he said to Joanna. "An' jist wait till the dead o' winter! Then ye'll really see a sight o' weather!"

"But it makes the cottage so cozy," replied Joanna.

"I'm grateful Alec was able t' get that window fixed in time," added Letty. "This storm would hae been a mean one wi' a hole in the wall!"

Letty was still reduced to performing only the simplest of tasks on account of her arm, so Joanna busied herself in the kitchen. She still had no clear picture of what she was to do next. But after yesterday's experience on the hillside, her confidence remained high and her spirits buoyant. She had faith the next step would be revealed at the proper time.

Shortly before 2:30 came a sharp knock on the door.

Amazed anyone would be out on such a day, Nathaniel rose and went to the door. There stood Walter Innes, water dripping from his wide-brimmed hat.

"Walter, whatever brings ye oot i' such a squall?" exclaimed Nathaniel. "Weel, come in, man, come in!"

"I'm deliverin' a message," said the factor, running a wet hand across his equally wet face.

"Weel, at least ye can dry off afore ye give it t' us," insisted Letty. "Come over an' stan' by the fire."

Innes complied, although he was too wet for the fire to accomplish much in the way of drying his clothes.

"Weel, what's yer message, Walter?" asked Nathaniel at length.

"'Tis not fer yersel', man," the factor replied. "My message is fer Miss Matheson."

"Me!" exclaimed Joanna.

"Aye, mem. It's from Dorey. He wishes ye t' join him fer high tea this afternoon—that is, if ye're not mindin' the weather."

The rain notwithstanding, the words were scarcely out of the factor's mouth before Joanna had disappeared, only to return a moment later with coat and hat. This was her opportunity, and she didn't need to be asked twice! The chance to visit again with the strange old man—gardener or houseguest, or whatever he was—was too exciting to let pass. Surely he must know a great many of Stonewycke's secrets. Joanna only hoped this time they might be able to speak more freely.

She hardly felt the rain.

And it would have made no difference, besides. Walter Innes' message had come as a sweet breath of wind from the high places. Joanna tingled with anticipation to see what would come next.

This time she entered the property by the front gate, as a guest rather than a housebreaker. She felt a shiver of awe as she approached the great carved door, knowing that somehow the mysteries of her personal history were held within its walls. The factor clanged the bell announcing his entry, and it sent sharp peals of command reverberating inside. Without waiting for an answer, he lifted the latch, swung the massive door forward with a creak, and led the way inside. Hastening toward them was a dumpy little woman with graying hair. Arrested in mid-flight, she stopped, motioned to the factor with a nod of the head, which he returned. Neither spoke a word. Innes went no farther, but the housekeeper proceeded to lead Joanna through one massive hall after another, all draped in dark brocades and velvets and filled with austere furnishings that looked to be from another age altogether.

Finally they came to a halt before two matching doors. The housekeeper slowly opened both, revealing a spacious banquet hall. The long table in the center was bedecked with candelabra, bowls of flowers, and settings of fine china and glassware. It was clearly large enough to seat fifty, but today only one lone banqueter sat at the far end of the table. The man known as Dorey appeared forlorn as he looked up at his guest with a wan smile.

Dressed in formal attire, with the house and its servants apparently at his command, he can be no mere gardener, Joanna thought. The mystery of his strange presence deepened as she entered, for his bearing and carriage were altogether different than the two previous times when she had seen him in his rough work clothes. The noble look she had caught in his eyes once or twice now returned full force. But even more than that, a change had come over him. Although he was more than sixty-five years of age, a light seemed to be burning in his eye, as if he had just awakened from a long sleep.

"How good of you to come," he said. He rose and went to her.

"Thank you for the invitation," replied Joanna, smiling as he took her hand.

"What else could I have done? I'm afraid I may have been rather rude when you last came," he said. "Not one of my better days."

"Not at all," said Joanna. "We barged in on you uninvited; you were perfectly—"

"No matter," he interrupted. "Come and sit down . . . please."

He led her to a seat near his. "Wasn't it good of Mrs. Bonner to prepare this for us? We're not much accustomed to guests here anymore. There was a time, though, when this great house boasted grand banquets and parties. But I'm afraid those days are past . . . gone . . ."

He spoke in a detached tone, as if it were a great effort to speak at all.

Mrs. Bonner began to serve their meal. Fresh baked salmon, piping hot wheat bread with creamy butter churned only that very morning, barley soup, and fresh garden vegetables. Joanna was hardly hungry enough to do such a feast justice; she had still not fully adjusted to the unusual eating schedules she found in Scotland. In addition she found difficulty in calming her inner excitement in wondering if there was more on Dorey's mind than a simple social visit. But her host seemed neither to notice nor to mind her scanty appetite.

The main course was followed by a tray of delicate pastries and sweetcakes. Dorey chatted about the house; but his talk focused mainly on trivial memorabilia— occasionally fading in and out of the present, but for the most part remaining considerably lucid.

"That chandelier there, you see, above our heads. It was shipped from Italy over seventy-five years ago. Every piece was broken and had to be replaced. It took over two years to finally get it in place."

"You seem very familiar with the history of Stonewycke?" Joanna ventured.

"Ah, yes, I suppose I am," he returned.

"More so than a mere houseguest would be, I should think," she ventured still further. "How long have you been here?"

Dorey's face seemed to go blank for a moment, then he said, "How long . . . ? I don't know. Most of my life, I suppose. It was all so long ago. I lose track of time. The mind forgets, you know."

Joanna nodded. Before she could decide what to say next, Dorey resumed in a new track. He told of past lairds and ancient battles that took place when the great house was more than simply a residence, but rather the chief line of defense for the surrounding valley.

"Of course that was long before our—I mean before my family . . . I should say the laird's family, came to possess the property. It was given by the king, you know."

Joanna gave a half nod, unsure if she had heard him aright.

"Then you are related to the laird's family?" she said.

But Dorey went on as if he hadn't heard, "Ah, if this old house were a living organism, it could stand proud. Would that such could be said of us human beings. I suppose it's only fitting that a majestic house like this can survive hundreds of years, while mortal life spans only . . . a fleeting . . ." but his voice trailed off as he rose and turned away from the table.

Motioning Joanna to follow, he led to a much smaller room adjacent to the great hall, warmer and more homelike than any she had yet seen. A fire crackled cheerfully in the hearth. They took chairs on either side of the fire, and sat down.

"I once thought," Dorey continued, "that survival was the cruelest form of punishment. Perhaps that is why, in the end, I allowed myself to survive. This great house here," he paused to sweep his arm around in a great gesture, "this place became to me like my nursery is to my flowers."

He stopped and rose, and restless, walked to the room's large picture window and stood mesmerized by the huge drops pounding against the pane of glass. *This is certainly no madman,* Joanna thought to herself. Whatever notions the townspeople had, this was surely a man who had been misunderstood.

The silence was long.

At length Joanna gathered her newfound courage.

"Mr.—"

"Do call me Dorey; everyone does, you know."

"But, Dorey," she began again, "I don't even know your real name."

"It's unimportant," he replied. "No one has used that name for years. I even begin to forget it myself."

"But you know that Mr. Sercombe plans to sell the land . . . this house? . . . the whole estate of Stonewycke?"

She held her breath, but Dorey's response did not indicate shock at her words.

"Yes . . . these things happen. Time marches on . . . generations pass. Besides, there is no heir; something must be done, I suppose."

"No heir?" Joanna repeated, at last approaching the question she had been wanting to ask since her first day at Port Strathy. "But surely there are other Duncans—"

"I am not in the line," he interrupted. "I am but a distant cousin."

Joanna sat upright, masking her shock at his words as best she could. "But . . . but . . ." she stammered, "what about the others? Was the laird— was Alastair left without anyone else?"

"I told you, there is no heir," he repeated.

"I . . . I believe my grandmother was born in Port Strathy," said Joanna. "She died recently and her last words were of her girlhood home. That's why I came, hoping to find others of the Duncan name. Relatives."

"There are no more Duncans."

"But I thought you just said—?"

"Only a second cousin . . . it's a distant family tie—from all the way down in London. I don't even deserve the name."

"Then you *are* a Duncan?" said Joanna, trying desperately to hide the emotions mounting inside.

"From a distant branch of the family," he repeated.

"But if there is no one else, it seems the descent would ultimately fall to you?"

"I could not—"

"Is it because people say you're unfit?" said Joanna gently.

"I would not take the land, even if I were fit," said Dorey, speaking with a firmness Joanna had never heard from him. "James Duncan would turn over in his grave." He gave a dry chuckle. "Now that would be the bitter irony, wouldn't it, for me to inherit the old rascal's estate?"

He laughed again, this time more loudly, thoroughly enjoying the idea which had apparently struck him for the first time.

Then he stopped abruptly, turned and stared into the hot embers of the dying fire, as if he were fading again into a distant memory of the past.

"No, better it go to strangers . . ."

His voice trailed off.

When he spoke again, his tone had returned to the soft, far-off sound. He seemed to have forgotten the estate altogether and the look on his face spoke of remembered pain.

"He had no right to do what he did, you know."

Glancing up, Joanna realized he was crying softly. She was afraid to speak. He was now clearly floating in and out between the present and the past.

". . . then she was gone. It was too late. I fell apart. The man had played a cruel trick on me. But he must have told you all about it—"

"No," he said suddenly, glancing up at Joanna; ". . . there, I've gotten it all wrong again, haven't I?"

He stopped short, staring at Joanna for a few moments, and then his face seemed to come back to reality.

Hardly knowing what to say, Joanna tried to pick up the previous threads of the conversation. "But if the estate is sold to strangers, what if they let it run down?"

Dorey turned toward her, confused again. He had an agitated look in his eyes, and his mouth was contorted in confused questioning.

"But . . . but you," he stammered in bewilderment, ". . . that couldn't—I mean, you would never let . . . you love the land, don't you, Maggie?"

The response poised on the tip of Joanna's tongue died the moment she heard the name.

"I . . . I—" Joanna faltered, but no more sounds would come.

The final word Dorey had spoken dashed against her ears like a brick, a blow that pierced directly to her heart.

"You love this land," Dorey went on, now wandering in the private world of his own rekindled memory, suddenly awakened after being blanked out for over forty years. "How you must have suffered when you left. Your mother suffered too, you know. She knew neither James nor Alastair cared for the land. They only sought the power of it. She longed for you to return . . . never stopped hoping. That was why she gave you the deed. She was certain it would bring you home in the end. She came to care about me, I think, for your sake. That was why she invited me here. She and Dermott tried to make life comfortable for me, after— you know—after my mind closed to everything that had happened. It could have worked out . . . in time . . . I could have followed . . . could have found you . . . if that father of yours hadn't driven you away so that you died before I could come—"

He paused, his voice rising in anger.

Longing to hear more, Joanna squirmed from the intrusion into a private conversation of which she was not a part.

"—he had no right," the old man went on. "I never told you this, but when he found out that—"

"Dorey," Joanna said, interrupting him.

Startled, he glanced toward her.

"Dorey," she repeated, "I'm not Margaret."

He stared deep into her eyes, blinked, then scanned her face, as if seeing her for the first time.

"No . . . no, of course you're not," he said. "My mind . . . it's filled with cobwebs, you see. Things seem so confused. No, you aren't. But . . ." His voice drifted off once more.

"I would like to hear more about my grandmother," said Joanna softly after a moment. "That is, if you'd like to talk about her."

"Your grandmother?"

"Yes. My grandmother was Margaret Duncan. She died recently. That's why I'm here."

"Died . . . recently? But I thought . . ." He stopped for a moment, then went on. "But there's so much I don't understand. Was I confused about that too?"

He glanced around the room, then rested his eyes once more on Joanna. They were full of tears.

"I haven't spoken of Maggie, even thought of her, in years," he began, once more rational and clear-eyed. "Seeing you, I suppose, triggered some deep memories—you look so much like her, you know. What would you like to know about her?"

"Whatever you want to tell me."

"Oh, she was a joy—so young and vibrant . . . sweet, like the very land she loved."

"You and she were . . . close?" Joanna asked tentatively.

"Oh yes. Atlanta hoped the promise of the inheritance would make her return. Atlanta always expected her to come to her senses and return to claim it. She was certain the thought of her brother being the laird would send her home."

"Why did she leave Scotland?"

He winced and glanced away momentarily.

"Oh Lord . . ." he began, then swallowed and groaned softly. "I made her leave! I—whom she trusted and loved. I forced her from home . . ."

He paused, then seeing the puzzled expression on Joanna's face, summoned the effort to continue.

". . . I thought it was for the noblest of reasons, but it all turned on me like a wild animal."

He buried his face in his hands.

"In the end, she believed I had deserted her . . . for that I shall never be able to forgive myself."

He slumped back into his chair; his shoulders shook in silent sobs.

Joanna could not speak. Every thought that came to her lips melted away, hollow and useless.

"I hated James for a while," Dorey went on, as if now that the gate was open the tide of his words could not be stopped. "But mostly . . . I hated myself. It is a coward who hides behind words like safety and honor and wisdom. She was the brave one! And I even grew to hate God. I could not forgive Him for the loss of the only precious being I had ever known . . . oh, Maggie!"

His voice caught in a sob.

Joanna rose and walked slowly toward him, then laid a gentle hand on his shoulder.

"She loved you in the end," she said softly, the meaning of her grandmother's last words suddenly becoming clear to Joanna. "She spoke of you before I left her."

"I didn't deserve it," he replied. "What kind of man sends his wife—"

"Wife!" Joanna interrupted, "I thought she was married in America."

"Our time together as husband and wife was brief . . . too, too brief. James was in a rage when he found out. He hated my family . . . disdained me. And in many ways I was deserving of it. He had higher hopes for his daughter— George Falkirk, the son of the Earl of Kairn. I . . . should never have intervened. But then the rascal was no better than I . . . poor Maggie. She deserved better than either of us."

"But she loved you—" said Joanna, trying to comfort him. He cut her off. "Love is not always enough."

Were they talking about the same Margaret Duncan?

This love of Theodore Duncan's youth seemed so different from the woman Joanna had known and grown too late to love. Yet here they were, knit together in a bond of love for the same woman. For Joanna knew that Dorey loved her still.

He shook his head bitterly.

"How my sins have hounded me!" he went on, clearly in agony at the memory. "I tried to hide from them, but they caught up with me. No . . . love is never enough . . . Oh, God, why?" he shouted in an agony of anger and remorse.

"Dorey," said Joanna, not sure how to express the thoughts that were so new to her, "if your sins have followed you, perhaps . . . it is because God could not let go of you . . . because He loves you and wants you to find forgiveness."

"I deserve none," replied Dorey, who began weeping anew.

"Then maybe it is you who need to forgive. God cannot give you the forgiveness He has for you until you stop blaming Him for what happened. None of us deserve forgiveness. But God loves us enough to give it anyway."

Joanna was surprised at her own words, but they seemed to flow of their own volition.

"Would that it were true . . ." His voice trailed off in despair.

"Dorey . . ." Joanna said, and as she spoke she reached up to her neck and loosened her grandmother's locket which she had worn constantly since arriving in Scotland. She unfastened the catch and held the open locket to him.

"This is you, isn't it'?"

The old man nodded.

"She wore it until her last days," Joanna said.

"Oh, dear God . . ." The man sobbed as he tenderly wrapped his fingers around the precious reminder of his youthful love.

He lifted his head to face her. "At least there's one thing," he said. "There's you. Perhaps it is true that God is merciful. I thought she was dead. That is what they told me. She, along with the child . . ."

His voice trailed away as he gazed steadily at Joanna.

"The child!" Joanna could barely form the words.

"The child . . . who was forever lost to me . . . the child I would never see."

"Whose child, Dorey? I don't understand . . . whose child? I have to know."

"Why, Maggie's, of course. When she left she was carrying our child. But I would never see the baby . . . our baby."

"Dorey," said Joanna, the tears flowing from her eyes, "*my* grandmother had only one child—my mother."

"I . . . I should have known . . . the first day you came . . . the moment I laid eyes on you."

Weeping, Joanna fell to her knees at Dorey's side, laying her head on his lap with her arms around his bent frame. He patted her hair tenderly with his gnarled hand and gently stroked her tear-stained cheeks. A single tear made a lonely track down his face, but his heart beat with joy at the loving reunion that had come after more than forty years of waiting.

This was more than Joanna had dared hope for when she set foot on that ship in New York harbor as an innocent young girl cast adrift into the world. Even now she was afraid to believe what she knew in her heart was true, that here—thousands of miles from what had once been her home—she had found her grandfather!

33

Joanna's Resolve

THE SWEET SMELL of hay filled Joanna's nostrils.

Nathaniel had finished his morning's chores and his cows had been led out to pasture for the day. The barn stood silent as the late morning's rays of sun filtered through the cracks in the siding. Joanna sat high atop a stack of baled hay reflecting on the events of the previous day. Nathaniel and Letty had been understandably overjoyed as she had recounted her talk with Dorey. And that evening they had enjoyed a festive time of celebration, welcoming Joanna into her Scottish heritage as full-blooded kin to Port Strathy's leading family.

Indeed, as that family's heir apparent.

But this morning, after the excitement had settled, Joanna discovered a streak of melancholy running through her she couldn't explain. Was it the letdown after reaching a cherished goal? Or was it the weight of responsibility she now felt resting on her shoulders?

Now, as she sat in the empty barn collecting her thoughts, tears came to her eyes. Were they tears of joy—or tears of fear?

She didn't know.

Yes, she was happy. But at the same time, the awe she felt sometimes overpowered her—an awe that occasionally took the form of apprehension over the future, and at other times as thankfulness to the God she was only beginning to know.

He had led. She knew He would continue to do so. As she looked back over her entire life she could see vividly that He had been with her all the way. Even through all those years of pain and loneliness. She had never really been alone. He had been preparing her for this moment.

Joanna heard the rusty latch of the barn door lift and the door swing open. Without glancing up she instinctively knew who was there.

"I thought I might find ye here," Alec said when he spotted her where she sat. "Letty told me everythin'. I'm happy fer ye."

"Thank you, Alec," replied Joanna softly with a smile.

"I haven't seen ye since . . . since we came back from town together two days ago. Ye was pretty silent on the ride here. Is . . . is everythin' all right?"

Joanna did not answer for a moment.

"Yes," she said at length, "yes, I'm fine. There have been so many things on my mind."

"I didn't mean t' pry. I jist sometimes . . . it's jist hard to tell what ye lasses are thinkin'."

"If you try to worry about what a woman is thinking, Alec, you will always be confused! Don't you know—that's how we of the fairer sex keep you men on your toes."

Alec's face spread into a broad grin. "It is good t' see ye laugh again. Ye was so somber before."

"The man you saw me leave Olive's with . . . he has caused me no small amount of emotional uncertainty."

"I could see," said Alec, shifting uneasily on his feet, "that he was some taken wi' ye."

Joanna sighed. "Yes, I suppose you're right," she said.

"And yersel'?" said Alec.

"Me?"

"It seemed the two o' ye knew each other right well."

"He was on the ship I sailed on from New York. His attentions swept me off my feet for a while—I thought I was in love with him."

"And were ye?" asked Alec stiffly.

"I don't know. Maybe I was . . . for a while. But that was before—"

She stopped and glanced quickly down to where Alec stood. She hadn't intended to say anything, but out it had come.

Though showing nothing on his face, a pang of hope shot through Alec's heart at her words. "Before what?" he wanted to shout; but he kept silent.

"Oh, Alec," Joanna hastened on, diverting the conversation. The time would come to explore her present feelings. But that time would have to wait. "Alec . . . what will happen to Dorey if I lose the estate? Jason will surely destroy the place if he gets his hands on it."

"The Lord will take care o' old Dorey," said Alec in measured tone. "But don't ye worry. Ye'll not lose the estate."

"How can you be so sure?"

His eyes seemed to pierce her as he said, "I've come t' know a little about ye, Joanna, in the short time we've been together. Ye're not the same uncertain girl that first came here. An' I know this—ye won't allow it t' happen."

"If only I had more say in the matter! But what if I turn out to be completely powerless? If only—"

She looked away from Alec for a moment, then back.

"You don't know how stupid I've been. I'm afraid I've incurred the wrath of a very powerful man—a man who isn't accustomed to losing."

"The man ye was with the other day?"

"His name's Jason Channing. He's the man who's buying the estate—a friend of Sercombe's."

"But what could this land mean t' the likes o' him?" asked Alec.

"The land means nothing to him—nothing except a way to make money. But what matters even more to him is winning. And he'll fight this to the bitter end because I did something to him no one else has done—I turned him down. I said *no.*"

Noticeably relieved Alec said, "There, ye see. Ye're turnin' into a mighty strong Scots woman, ye are, Joanna Matheson. Ye'll do what ye need t' do. An' I'd put my money on ye t' win this one!"

"Thank you, Alec," said Joanna. "But don't forget. Whatever victories we may gain in this before it's over are half yours. You've been with me from the start."

The sound of urgent approaching hoofbeats halted their conversation. Alec turned and ran to the door of the barn. Joanna scrambled down from her perch and followed close behind.

It was Walter Innes.

"Innes!" shouted Alec, hurrying out to meet him, "ye've got yer poor horse in a heat o' lather."

"I know," the factor apologized. "But I figured it'd be quicker t' ride o'er the shortcut than t' take the motor car, an' I thought ye'd want t' know immediately." He swung down, removed his dusty hat, and wiped his brow with a broad sweep of his forearm.

"Know what?" asked Joanna stepping forward.

Walter approached the two, then with an awkward bow addressed Joanna: "My Leddy," he said, "I had a talk wi' Mr. Dorey an' he told me who ye are. This is a great day fer Port Strathy—'tis all I can say, an' I'm prood t' be the factor o' yer house. But—"

He paused.

"I'm afraid you're assuming quite a lot, Mr. Innes," said Joanna. "It's hardly my house. But nevertheless, I thank you for your kind words and your support."

"But," Innes went on, "weel, My Leddy . . . I only hope . . . that is, weel, I'm afraid somethin's wrong."

"What is it, man!" Alec exclaimed.

"Mr. Sercombe was at the house this mornin'. I was oot—chores, ye know. But Mrs. Bonner, she says they had a bit o' a row, they did."

"Who?"

"The lawyer an' Mr. Dorey. Mr. Dorey said he wasn't happy aboot the sale an' wanted t' hold up the proceedin's. Especially, she said he told Mr. Sercombe,

seein' as there was now an heir. Then Mr. Dorey said he could prove beyond
doobt that Miss Matheson," here he paused and nodded toward Joanna, "that she
was the heiress o' the estate. Weel then Mr. Sercombe jist laughed in his
face—laughed right in his face! Mr. Dorey kept insistin' an' finally Sercombe
stopped his laughin'. Mrs. Bonner says he became downright surly. Then
he—Mr. Sercombe that is—shoved poor Dorey aside and went runnin' all
through the house, lookin' fer somethin'. He searched high an' low, gettin'
angrier an' angrier the whole time. Mrs. Bonner, she says she was afraid t' say a
word. He threw rooms an' doors an' wardrobes open and rummaged through
drawers, but whatever he was lookin' fer he must not o' found it 'cause then
finally he grabbed Dorey by the arm and led him from the house. She says Dorey
seemed calm enough, as if he wasn't afraid o' the man. But Mrs. Bonner, she
didn't know what t' do an' as they was leavin' she said, 'Where are ye takin' oor
Mr. Dorey?' Sercombe jist smiled one o' his cunnin' smiles an' said, 'Don't ye
worry about a thing, Mrs. Bonner. We're jist goin' t' my office so Dorey an' I can
discuss the matter further,' an' then they was gone."

"But you don't believe Sercombe?" Joanna asked.

"I hardly know what t' believe, My Leddy. Mr. Sercombe has always been
most kind t' me, an' t' Mr. Dorey too. But up till noo he's always been firm about
keepin' Mr. Dorey at the house—any business was always taken care o' there."

"Dorey is in danger," said Joanna with growing alarm. "I know that man
means no good to him."

"Nothin's goin' t' happen t' Mr. Dorey, My Leddy," Innes replied. "Ye can
thrash me good if it does. But one thing I can tell ye fer certain. Nobody—not
Mr. Sercombe or anybody—will be talkin' Dorey into anythin' against his will.
Why, mem, since ye was there yesterday he's been a new man. I think he's but
lapsed back into his old self only once."

"How was that?" asked Joanna.

"'Twasn't nothin' t' worry about. He jist says t' me—it was last night, a bit
late—he says, 'Baxter'—that was the factor before me—'Baxter,' he says,
'where does the Lady Atlanta keep her private papers? I know it's none o' my
business, but . . .' Then he must o' realized I wasn't Baxter at all, an' he
stopped. Then said he had t' tell ye somethin', Miss Matheson. That was all there
was t' it."

A moment's silence followed. Joanna glanced at Alec.

"First thing we must do," said Alec, "is t' make sure Dorey's safe. I'm ridin'
into town t' see if he's at the lawyer's office. Walter, ye stay here with Joanna an'
the folks."

Walter nodded his approval.

Alec mounted his horse.

"There's one more thing," added Walter. "I dinna ken if the one thing has t' do
wi' the other. But jist aboot the time when Sercombe was at the house, I was
headin' into the stables t' do some work. At the time I didna know the lawyer was
wi' Dorey. Weel, who should I find but that good fer nothin' Tom Forbes,

snoopin' around in the stables—diggin' through the hay an' muck like a scavenger. Soon as he saw me he lit off like a hare. Anyway, I don't know if it means anythin'."

"Oh, it means somethin'," said Alec with a knowing look. "I only wish I knew what."

"Alec," said Joanna, grasping his arm, "be careful."

"Don't ye be worryin', lass, I will be." He smiled, laid his hand gently on hers, then quickly swung his gray gelding around, dug his heels in and galloped away.

Joanna spent the remainder of the morning and the early afternoon wandering idly about the cottage, roaming about fields close by, with now and again another peek inside the barn. But she could not keep her mind on any task. Her instincts told her Dorey was in trouble, and she couldn't still the anxiety in her heart. At every sound she glanced up and ran to look down the road, thinking it might be Alec returning with news.

About two o'clock Joanna walked aimlessly into her room to gather up some laundry, when her eyes fell upon her grandmother's music box sitting on her dresser. She hadn't listened to it, even noticed it, in days. She ran her hand along the finely carved walnut top, then opened it and wound the key. The delicate strains of Brahms' lullaby floated to her ears like a balm of peace.

The images the nostalgic melody raised in her mind were now clear and well defined. They had names, personalities, histories. There were mental pictures of actual landscapes. There were real faces.

"Oh, Grandma," Joanna whispered, reaching for a handkerchief to wipe the moisture from her eyes.

Her mind had been obsessed with Maggie Duncan, yet that young girl was far removed from the woman Joanna had known. Even now, when the word *grandmother* came to her lips, she could only visualize the nearly unconscious woman lying on her deathbed.

Margaret Duncan's frail voice and cryptic words drifted back to Joanna's mind, as clear as if she were still alive: ". . . don't let them take it, Joanna—it's yours!"

What else had she said?

Joanna remembered she had spoken of someone. She had paid so little attention then, because the words meant nothing. Now she realized her grandmother had been talking about Dorey. But what else . . . hadn't she also spoken of her mother?

". . . before I left . . . my mother . . ."

Desperately Joanna tried to recall the exact words.

"Find it . . . the treasure . . . in the nursery . . ."

Joanna snapped the music-box lid shut. A heavy fog lifted from her brain. Why hadn't she thought of it sooner?

"Of course!" she said to herself. "Something is at the house! Something so important it was all my grandmother could think about as she slipped into a coma."

Joanna jumped up from where she sat on the bed. She knew what she had to do. She didn't know what it might be. But whatever her grandmother had been speaking of—she had to find it . . . before it was too late!

She opened the drawer and set the music box inside. Her eyes fell on the folded embroidery she had also brought with her from her grandmother's locked bureau drawer. The sight sent a shiver up her spine. For this was not *Margaret's*, it was *Maggie's*—a sweet young teenager, in love and heartbroken. She tenderly unfolded the linen and now saw—as if for the first time—names that had come to mean something to her. From the hand-stitched family tree stood out the names of Robert, Anson, Talmud, Atlanta, and others.

And the blank spot where the name had been neatly torn away—where the name *Margaret Duncan* should have been, directly beneath the names Atlanta and James—had Margaret herself ripped out her own name? Was it another impulsive act of this youngster, feeling perhaps the sting of her father's rejection?

Grandma, thought Joanna. *You do deserve a place there. I will personally embroider your name in the proper place where it should have always been. You shall take your rightful stand in this family.*

Refolding the linen, she caught up her coat and tucked it inside. She then slipped from her room unnoticed, outside, and into the barn. Perhaps it was foolhardy to go off alone. If Nathaniel or Walter saw her go, they would insist on accompanying her.

But she had come to Scotland alone, perhaps to find meaning in her life. And notwithstanding the deep and loving friendships she had made, she now had to stand and carry out this final part of her mission alone as well. Her very being as a woman demanded it. Come what may, her mind was set; she had to learn to stand on her own two feet.

Besides, she consoled herself, *no doubt by this time Alec and Dorey would already be back at the estate.* So she would not be alone in her search after all.

Saddling the mare she reflected on how she had hated her riding lessons in Chicago. Now she was thankful she didn't have to worry about not being able to ride a horse. She led the mare out the barn's back door, walked her about half a mile to the east away from the road before she mounted. Then she mounted, doubled back, and rode toward the town, paralleling the road about a quarter mile to its east so as not to be seen. Reaching Port Strathy, she wound through the southernmost back streets and alleys, arriving finally at the road out of town toward Strathy summit. Because of the steep, rugged incline, she was forced to stay on the road by which she had first entered the village. But she saw no one, rode on, turned south toward Stonewycke, and rode the entire way without meeting a soul.

34
The Search

❄

ONCE AGAIN THE great iron gate towered before her.

Joanna tested the lock; it was open.

She swung the gate wide and walked in.

"The nursery . . ." The words resounded in her mind as she made her way up the cobblestone path. What did her grandmother mean? There was the greenhouse of which Dorey was so proud. But hadn't that been built by Alastair? Was there perhaps an older greenhouse, even a garden then called the nursery?

If only Dorey were here to guide her!

The full implication of searching such an immense place suddenly struck her. It could take days, even weeks! Especially as she had no idea what she was even looking for! What did the words mean?—"*You mustn't let them take it; it's yours . . .*"

Entering the courtyard, Joanna instantly saw that Alec's horse was nowhere to be seen. Dorey was undoubtedly not here, either.

She walked boldly up to the door, clanged the bell, and waited.

There was no response.

She rang again, but silence was the only reply. The place was utterly deserted.

What if Sercombe had spirited Dorey off, hidden him away, and then returned to the house to continue his search at his leisure? That would explain the open latch at the gate and the forlorn emptiness. Certainly he would not have allowed Mrs. Bonner to remain while he did his dirty work.

A churning formed in the pit of Joanna's stomach. No doubt, Sercombe was either in the house at this very moment, or he was planning to return. Why else would he have taken Dorey away?

She gingerly tried the door's latch.

The door swung open and she stepped inside.

"Well, here I come. Mr. Sercombe," she murmured aloud. "You'd better be ready for me because I'm not turning back now!"

The door shut with a bang and Joanna stood motionless till the echo resounding through the vast, cold hallways died away. She cocked her ear and listened. No sound was to be heard.

At first, she walked aimlessly about, gathering courage. The high ceilings, the walls draped with rich tapestries portraying ancient events, the ornately carved chairs and hall-trees and sideboards, the tiled floors, above all, the awesome silence, combined to create an atmosphere more like that of a cathedral than a home. What a contrast this was to the Cuttahays' warm, cozy little cottage! Here it would be sacrilege to lay a finger on a single piece of china. It was hard to imagine people actually living here.

Dorey's comment came back to her about banquets and gay parties. The sounds of a string quartet drifted into her consciousness. The room was filled with brightly dressed women and men in tails and top hats. Carriages were pulling up outside in a steady stream. The sounds of laughter could be heard. Now the host escorted the hostess to the dance where they led the company in a Haydn minuet.

What a gay ball it was!

Just then the bell sounded and the butler announced: "Ladies and gentlemen, the Lady Joanna Matheson . . ." She stepped forward, in shimmering ball gown and jeweled tiara, to take the hand of . . .

Joanna's vision faded. All that remained were the solitary footsteps of a young child racing through the long hallway. "I wonder what it was like to grow up here?" Joanna wondered.

Then all fell silent once more, and Joanna was left alone with reality. Forward she walked, approaching the great wooden staircase. Up it she climbed, then proceeded down the hallway in which she found herself. Turning into room after room, sometimes only for a moment, occasionally for a more thorough look, she began to explore the house of her ancestors. Not knowing where she was going or what she was seeking, she allowed impulse and instinct to guide her. On she went, through more rooms—some small, others huge, many empty—through a magnificently stocked library, and up another flight of stairs to the third floor, down several long hallways. At length she came to a narrow backstair. Following it she found that it led to a large, empty tower room. Descending the backstairs the way she had come, she came out again on the second floor.

For the first time Joanna felt a sense of bewilderment. She had turned in so many directions she was no longer certain of her bearings. She had come back down to the second floor but hadn't seen this hallway before. It must lead toward the main staircase up which she had ascended earlier. As she made her way along, Joanna continued to scrutinize the rooms on her way. She paused a moment in one of these. The afternoon sunlight streaming in drew her to the window which was toward the southwest corner of the mansion. Gazing out she was met with a curious sight. She found herself looking out toward the rear of the house and from her high vantagepoint she could see what appeared to be a walled garden. But it was wild and tangled and unkempt. She wondered at the sight, for the rest of the grounds were so meticulously groomed by Dorey. How odd that this particular spot should have been overlooked! The first chance she had she would explore it, but for now she had to return her attentions to the inside of the great house.

Leaving the room she proceeded on, but there was something so solemn about the place that she had not yet been able to bring herself to touch anything.

All at once the hallway ended abruptly. Issuing from its end, in both directions were two smaller passageways. By this time she was so disoriented that she had not a notion of which would be the more likely to return her to the house's main staircase. About to follow the one to the left, she became aware for the first time of two massive oak-paneled doors which stood directly in front of her. How could she have missed them as she approached down the wide hallway?

She tested the doors, found them unlocked, and stepped inside.

The room in which Joanna found herself was decidedly different than any she had yet encountered. It was a large room, but the lowered ceiling gave it a warmer feel. The furnishings possessed a distinct Mediterranean air—spindly and delicate compared to the massive wood furnishings found in the rest of the house. At the opposite end, French doors opened onto a veranda, from which descended a narrow, circular stair to a little courtyard full of an assortment of nicely trimmed shrubs and small trees. Dorey's care had clearly kept it lovely, though probably none but his own eyes had seen it for years.

Joanna wondered whose hand had chosen this unique decor. Could it have been Atlanta Duncan herself? It was not difficult to envision her great-grandmother on a shopping trip in Italy.

Atlanta . . .

All of a sudden, Joanna was aware she was trembling. Could *this* be Atlanta's room? If so . . . what secrets might it contain?

She walked about with a feeling of awe and reverence.

Then the words flooded back upon her memory:

". . . my mother . . . the day I left . . . gave me . . ."

All at once Joanna could not content herself simply to gaze with wonder at all these ancient possessions. She had to stir up the settled dust of the past and unravel whatever mysteries this house contained.

Her eyes fell upon a small French provencial secretary to the left of the French doors. It held only three drawers. Joanna had to force each one open; she must have been the first in decades to attempt such an exploration. At least she had beat Sercombe to this room!

The first drawer contained envelopes and blank sheets of stationery embossed with a family crest; there was nothing else save a few dried-up pens.

The next drawer held more promise.

It was stuffed with several stacks of letters with strange names—an M. Browne of London, Clara Seaton of Suffolk, and a Richard Bosley of Glasgow. Most of the dates on the letters ranged between 1860 and 1870, but Joanna soon realized they contained nothing but the typical chit-chat exchanged by friends. The correspondence from Bosley proved the sole exception. It was a bill for certain remodeling done at the house, dated June 5, 1870. The rest of the letters told Joanna little. But they left one thing certain—every one was addressed to Atlanta Duncan, and one, much older than the rest, to Atlanta Ramsey.

Joanna had indeed penetrated the old matriarch's personal desk—her own great-grandmother.

The third drawer was empty.

Joanna closed the secretary and wandered slowly about the room. Undoubtedly because of the remarkable collection of works in the library, Joanna all at once realized she had not seen a single book in any of the rooms she had been in thus far. But here, a tiny but impressive set of leather-bound editions was enclosed in a fine walnut bookcase. On the top shelf sat a complete set of the works of William Shakespeare—bound in red morrocco with gold lettering and gilt edges. Below sat several glass and porcelain trinkets and a large black family Bible.

Joanna walked toward the case, stared for a few moments at the beautiful set of books, and absently began pulling down the volumes and flipping through them one by one while her mind was occupied elsewhere. She withdrew *A Midsummer Night's Dream* and *Macbeth* and *Romeo and Juliet.*

Replacing them, she lifted the family Bible and opened its leatherbound board covers. Her first instinct was to find the page showing the family tree. A hasty glance told her she would have to return for a closer inspection later. Then she flipped quickly through the remainder of the book. It gave the appearance of being new and scarcely used. However, toward the middle of the book, the pages fell open naturally to the twenty-third Psalm where several folded pieces of paper dropped out and to the floor. Joanna stooped down to pick them up. She gently unfolded the pages, yellowed with age, and immediately recognized the crest she had seen on the stationery in the secretary. The letter was written in a beautiful feminine script and began:

My dear daughter Margaret . . .

Joanna swallowed, took a deep breath, and tried to still her racing heart before continuing.

". . . how I regret the events which led to your untimely estrangement from your home and family. I wish with every fibre of my being that we could turn back the clock to those joyful days before our unhappy tragedy. You must remember how glad those days were, even if you care to remember nothing else. How you delighted in our rides over the grassy hillsides and our picnics on Ramsey Head! Ah, listen to the rambling of a sentimental old mother—but those are the memories I cherish in the depths of my heart. And I know we could recapture those days if you would but return.

There, I have said it!

You may think it cruel of me to ask you to return to the bosom of your sorrow, but ask I must. This is where you belong, my dear Margaret.

Your father is gone, dear. I do not ask you to grieve for him, but rather to think that now you could find happiness here once again. Especially in that I also bring you the joyous news (which perhaps Mr. Connell has already done) that your Ian is alive! Oh, Maggie, please return! For this is your home.

But perhaps even more than these things, dear Margaret, you cannot allow the land to pass to Alastair. The land is yours, daughter, it has always been and always will be. I have made sure of that. You need only to claim it. Alastair is an alien to the land, as was his father; but I know that for you, the land is your very soul—as it has always been for me.

Margaret, I am at my wits' end with fear of what will happen to my beloved Stonewycke. I have pledged to myself never to reveal a secret that has been for generations hidden, indeed, thought lost forever. I feel more closely akin to my grandfather Anson than I ever thought possible. I know now what drove him to do what he did, for often I was nearly driven to the same extreme and I used my knowledge of Anson's intention to work my will over your father many times. But now he is gone and I have hidden it, and I look only to you to carry on the legacy of the Ramsey name, if only you will return to claim your heritage, and the love both Ian and I share for you . . .

There the letter ended.

Joanna turned it over, vainly hoping to discover more. But there was nothing else. Atlanta Duncan's poignant pleading with her daughter apparently progressed no further than an ancient burial in the depths of her daughter's favorite psalm. How could Joanna have known that before completing the letter, Atlanta had received word that her daughter was dead?

Joanna read the words of the twenty-third Psalm of David with renewed insight: "He maketh me to lie down in green pastures: He leadeth me beside the still waters. He restoreth my soul . . ."

Joanna sat on the elegant, dusty divan. She reread the letter. What might have happened had Margaret received this letter? How differently things might have turned out!

And there was that name Anson again . . . what could it all mean? Once more her thoughts drifted toward her grandmother's cryptic words, and now, here, her own mother added still further to the mystery.

Joanna rose and leisurely returned to the secretary. Perhaps she had overlooked something. There had to be at least one clue—it was Atlanta's desk, after all.

Tiring of the seeming hopelessness of her quest, Joanna sifted aimlessly through the stacks of envelopes, bills, letters and miscellaneous old papers. There was a letter *from* Atlanta to the same Bosley. She was about to pass it by when it suddenly struck her—wasn't it a bit odd that the services of a carpenter from Glasgow would be enlisted for minor remodeling? Glasgow was a great distance from Strathy.

He could have been a family friend, Joanna thought. *Or simply the best in his particular field of work.*

The letter from Atlanta to Bosley revealed nothing, simply a settling of accounts. But it was followed by one from the Glasgow carpenter dated 1846, over twenty years before the bill she had first seen. She withdrew the single sheet from its envelope and read, in the most businesslike format:

"We are happy to report that we can commence work on your new nursery in two weeks—"

Joanna gasped with growing excitement as she continued:

"We feel certain we will have the job in question complete well before the blessed event. In our estimation only one wall will have to be removed and the window you requested—"

The letter fell from Joanna's hand.

Of course!

She had been so preoccupied with Dorey and plants and greenhouses that a child's nursery had never occurred to her. How could she have been so stupid? It was so clear!

Margaret had no doubt been speaking of her own childhood room; she had been born in August of 1846.

"That's it . . . that's it!" Joanna shouted jumping up from the divan. "It's in the *nursery!*"

Hastily she scanned the remaining contents of the drawer, hoping to find a drawing or some plans for the work or something which would give her an idea of where to look. But there was none.

She ran from the room and looked left and right, down the narrow passageways, and then straight ahead along the wide corridor down which she had walked from the back staircase. If she had been in Atlanta's room, no doubt the nursery would be close by.

Joanna hastened to the room directly next to it, apparently another bedchamber. It contained a heavy four-poster bed, wardrobe, and bureau. A brief glance at the contents revealed nothing of promise.

She ran down the hall to the room on the other side of Atlanta's. At first glance it appeared nearly as uninteresting, although considerably smaller.

It was little more than an alcove containing a settee, a velvet-covered high-backed chair, and low round table in front of the settee. Joanna shook her head in dismay and turned to leave. Whatever made her think a nursery would have been kept all these years? Even if Atlanta had kept it intact from sentimental reasons, surely Alastair would long since have dismantled its memories. Any secret that lay hidden within the nursery had no doubt been carried off with the rest of the furnishings long ago.

Glancing behind her for one final sidelong sweep of her eyes, the room's only window arrested her attention.

That's odd, she thought. The window was not only twice as high as it was wide, but also the glass appeared to run right up against the wall at the corner. "They certainly didn't plan that window very well."

She turned back into the room, walked toward the window, and pressed her face against it. The glass appeared to continue on, through the wall which ran perpendicular to the exterior surface, and into the next room.

Well, the adjoining room that shares this odd window bears looking into, she thought.

Back out into the hall she hurried, turned to her right, and found she had to walk some twenty feet before coming to another door. When she looked inside, to her surprise, she discovered no window butting up against the righthand wall at all but a single large window centered exactly in the middle of the wall. In addition, there was no conceivable way—at least according to her first judgment—that this room could have filled all the space between the rooms she had traversed in the hall.

Joanna stepped back out into the hallway, puzzled, and was about to return to the smaller room from which she had just come when a paralyzing sound seized her attention.

She strained to listen. It was unmistakable—the pounding of approaching hoofbeats!

Sercombe!

Panic gripped her. She would have no chance alone, especially if he found her here, searching the house. And what if those other two men were with him?

Joanna crept down the hall as noiselessly as possible. The hoofbeats soon eased. Somehow Joanna reached the back staircase. Should she go down and seek a hasty escape from the house? If Sercombe was not alone they might have all the doors blocked. They certainly would have seen her horse by now.

Below, she heard the tramping of heavy feet upon the tiled floors.

She quickly made for the third floor and the tower room.

35

Alec and Channing

A LEC RODE HARD.

Leaving Joanna and Walter Innes at the Cuttahays', he made for Port Strathy in a full gallop, his indignation rising with each bend of the muddy road. He reached the town's outlying cottages in ten minutes but did not slow until he rounded the corner of the main street. In a flurry of earth and a clatter of hoofs, he reined in his mount directly in front of Sercombe's office. With a single motion, he swung down and covered the distance to the office door.

It was locked.

He shook it, but the door did not even give a hint of submitting to his strength. He kicked at it. Then he wiped away a layer of dust from the window and peered inside, but all appeared dark and lifeless.

Alec hurried next door to inquire of Miss Sinclair anything she might have seen of Sercombe's movements. She had not seen him all day.

In frustration, Alec heaved his tired frame upon his horse. He thought for a moment, then dug in his heels and sped eastward out of town toward Stonewycke. Perhaps Dorey had been taken back during Walter's absence. Near the top of the hill on the main road, he slowed his pace. He could almost feel the fatigue rippling through the gray gelding's muscles—the animal had to rest. Alec plodded on up the hill, slower but undaunted.

At Stonewycke nothing stirred. No horses were in sight; Mrs. Bonner was gone; and a ride around the entire grounds revealed nothing. Dejected, Alec returned to town where he cantered up and down the streets, asking those he encountered if they had seen Sercombe or Dorey. After two hours of fruitless search and inquiry, he guided his tired horse back to the Cuttahay farm.

When he arrived, however, he discovered that now not only was Dorey missing, but Joanna as well, with neither Walter nor Nathaniel able to offer so much as a clue about when she had left or where she had gone.

"What if they've captured the lass, too?" he said more in frustration than anger. "How could the two o' ye let her oot o' yer sights?"

Alec spurred his beleaguered horse back toward town.

Once again he rushed straight to Sercombe's door; this time he was not disappointed. A light was visible inside.

Alec stormed the door and threw it open without pausing to knock. "Sercombe, ye bla'guard!" he shouted, "ye've gone too far, an' now ye'll have t' answer—"

"Who do you think you are!" came a voice from the opposite side of the room, where Jason was reclining easily on the velvet settee.

He stood to face the intruder.

"You!" exclaimed Alec. "Ye're no better than that scoundrel lawyer friend o' yers. But ye're through here, the both o' ye!"

"My, my," Channing said in a measured tone. "I thought you country bumpkins were supposed to know your place. But it appears I'll have to put you there myself."

Alec bristled, but he resisted the urge to throw himself at this gentleman whose exterior appeared so refined.

Instead, he simply said, "Where's Sercombe?"

"I can hardly think it to be any concern of yours."

"I'm makin' it my concern, an' ye better too, if ye know what's good fer ye," came Alec's fervent reply.

"Is that a threat?" Channing's calm voice was betrayed only by a dark glint in his eyes.

"'Tis but the second time I've laid eyes on ye, Mr. Channing, but I'm likin' ye less an' less with each passin' minute. Even so, I don't figure I have a battle with ye—jist yet, at least. But ye're pushin' me t' my limit."

Channing threw his head back in laughter.

"I thought you hillbillies had no limits," he said, then laughed again, amused at his own clever wit.

"If ye know anythin' concernin' the whereabouts o' Dorey or Miss Joanna, ye better tell me or it'll go the worse fer ye," said Alec.

"So that's it!" exclaimed Channing in mock delight. "It's jealousy for the pretty young hussy that makes you—"

At last the dam of Alec's patience gave way.

With an explosive burst, all the fury of his Viking blood surged within him. He took the distance between them in two strides and with his powerful hand grabbed the adversary by his immaculate white shirt and lifted his feet off the ground.

Undaunted, but struggling to control his trepidation, Channing growled, "You scum! You will pay for this foolish attack!"

He thrust his hands into Alec's face, freed himself momentarily, and sent a well-planted fist smashing directly into Alec's nose.

Stunned, Alec reached up to feel the blood starting to flow. A second punishing blow fell on his right ear. Heartened by his apparent success, Channing charged with redoubled effort. Alec retreated, trembling at his outburst but still finding strength within to form a silent prayer for restraint.

"'Tis Sercombe I'm wantin'," he said in forced tones.

"Stand and fight, you coward!" yelled Channing.

"I tell ye, my fight's not wi' ye, much as I would relish givin' ye the thrashin' ye deserve," fumed Alec.

"You yellowbelly," taunted Channing, "it's I who am thrashing you!" Channing delivered another blow to Alec's midsection.

Alec clenched his fists trying to control the passions within him. "I'll not be fightin' ye, Mr. Channing—ye're not worth it."

"You coward!" raged Channing and he prepared to strike again.

But at that moment, the door swung open and Palmer Sercombe entered. Alec whirled about and faced him squarely.

"What is the meaning of all this!" Sercombe exclaimed.

"Mr. Sercombe," said Alec, trying his best to calm the hot rush of his anger, "I want no more o' fightin' today. I dinna want t' do anythin' we'll both regret. But what have ye done wi' Dorey? An' where's Joanna Matheson?"

"None of this is any of your concern, MacNeil."

"I've made it my concern. Now where are they?" said Alec advancing, "Or I'll measure yer length on the floor there!"

"Mr. Duncan is in my charge. I hardly need to inform you of the arrangement set up legally by the laird himself before he died. And I shall therefore do with him what I deem in his best interests. And any attempts on your part—"

"Yer legal arrangements mean nothin' t' me! Ye're a scoundrel, Sercombe, an' I'll see ye hanged if—"

"Tut, tut, my friend," said the lawyer coolly. "Don't threaten me. I have the law on my side. You interfere with the proceedings of justice in this matter and I'll bring in the constable to have you arrested. Then we'll see who hangs!"

"I tell ye, ye bloody charlatan, if ye hurt either o' the two o' them, ye'll hae t' answer t' me an' these bare hands o' mine! After that they can hang me if they will. But ye'll not be watchin' me swing, for my body'll be followin' yers t' the churchyard!"

Sercombe laughed a low, cutting laugh. "Don't worry, my friend," he said, "old Dorey is fine. I wouldn't harm a hair on his old gray head. I've simply withdrawn him from the house, for his own protection, to keep him away from hotheads like you."

"And Miss Matheson?" said Alec, retreating a step.

"As for your pretty American filly, I haven't laid eyes on her. For all I know she's taken up residence in the house on the hill she seems so bent on calling her own. Why don't you look for her there? But it will be her only chance to see the place. Before long, it will belong to Mr. Channing, and this foolish little charade she insists on playing will all be over!"

Realizing Sercombe would tell him nothing more, Alec took one final look of disdain at the lawyer then strode from the office, mounted his horse, and galloped up the street, directing the gelding east and up the hill.

Sercombe walked to his companion, who was rubbing a bruised and swollen fist.

"I've just had a most enlightening discussion with our friend Theodore Duncan," he said. "He revealed some rather interesting prospects. We have to get up to that house and conduct a more thorough search than I was able to this morning with people about. Seems this Matheson girl may be more of a threat than we'd thought."

36

The Nursery

JOANNA FLEW UP the back staircase two steps at a time.

At the top, she stopped, crumpled to the floor and tried to still her heaving chest and pounding heart. She listened once more.

The footsteps drew closer.

Was it her imagination, or did she hear someone calling her name? The distant voice sounded alien to her terror-stricken senses. But there it came again—it was her name, muffled by the walls and corridors and rooms and ceilings of the great house.

"Joanna . . . Joanna . . . !"

She stood and crept silently down the stairs, straining to hear better.

"Joanna . . . Joanna! Where are ye, lass!"

"Alec!" she cried, hardly able to contain her relief. "Alec, I'm here!"

Joanna ran down the stairs again to the second floor, turned and raced through the maze of corridors, finally reaching Alec just as he reached the landing of the main staircase on the second floor.

"Alec," she said breathlessly, running into his arms, "it *is* you. I was so afraid . . . I thought—"

"'Tis all right," he soothed. "I'm jist relieved ye're all right."

"Is Dorey . . . with you?" she asked.

He shook his head. "No, I haven't found him yet. But Sercombe says he's fine and I think he's tellin' the truth. But what do ye mean goin' off alone like that?" He continued without waiting for an answer, "Poor Letty is nearly beside herself . . . not t' mention the rest o' us."

"I'm sorry," Joanna replied. "It was something I had to do and I saw no reason to involve anyone else. But, Alec," she continued excitedly, "I think I've found the nursery!"

"Ye have! Weel, where is it?" he said beginning to forget his own anxiety as he was swept up in her excitement.

"Here . . . in the house. Upstairs. It's a baby's room. And I think I've found it!"

"Let's have a look."

She ran back up the stairs with Alec at her heels. After a confused moment or two they reached their destination. "I'm not positive this is it," she said. "And it's walled off, so I haven't actually been inside. But it has to be."

Alec gave her a puzzled look.

"Come on," said Joanna, taking his hand. "I'll show you!"

She led back down the corridor and to the alcove next to Atlanta's room.

"You see this wall. Fix its position in your mind. Now come next door."

Joanna half ran to the adjoining room. "Look, no window. If this was the back of the same wall we just left, we would see the remainder of the window coming out from this side."

"Very unusual," Alec admitted.

He paced off the distance between the two doors, did some additional measuring in each of the rooms, and finally announced, "There's twelve feet unaccounted for . . . must be that much space between these two walls unseen and hidden, with no door—"

"The nursery!" exclaimed Joanna. "I just know it, Alec!" Her eyes shone with excitement.

"But why would it be blocked off?"

"Who knows? Maybe Atlanta kept it up for a while in hopes her grandchildren would occupy it. Maybe after Margaret left she wanted to preserve it as a reminder of happier times. Maybe she purposely wanted to seal some secret there. Perhaps her husband sealed it up out of spite. But I know that whatever my grandmother was telling me has something to do with that room. We *have* to get inside!"

"It's walled up. What would ye hae me do, knock down the wall? Hoots!"

"Why not, Alec? Why not!" she implored.

"But . . . but, Joanna. It's a *wall.* If anyone was t' find us here—"

"I have to get in there. Don't you see? And besides . . . it may be my house, after all."

A hint of a smile lit her eyes as she spoke.

"Weel, Dorey would certainly raise no objection," said Alec, a grin gradually creeping over his face. "I'll run down an' get some implements from the tool shed—My Leddy!"

"Please, Alec," said Joanna with a laugh. "I can take that from Mr. Innes, but not from you. And I'm not 'the leddy o' the house' jist yet, ye know!"

Alec laughed, delighted at her attempt at her mother-tongue, and raced off.

Joanna seated herself on the velvet chair in the alcove. Her thoughts drifted back to her grandmother's final days and hours. Was she at last poised on the threshold of fulfilling the woman's final wish? What would they discover behind that fateful wall?

It hardly seemed two minutes before she heard Alec's footsteps clumping back up the stairs, accompanied by the clanging of two picks and a heavy, iron crowbar. Joanna moved the chair to the opposite side of the room. Together they lifted the settee and carried it away.

At last, Alec lifted the pick, stood before the wall a bit hesitantly, looked at Joanna with a final questioning gaze as if to ask, "Are ye sure?"

Understanding his doubt, she simply nodded.

Raising the pick high in the air above his shoulder, and warning Joanna to stand well back, Alec swung down the handle with all his might. The pick's tip crashed into the wall with a resounding thud, but penetrated much deeper than Alec had anticipated.

"'Tis not stone an' mortar at all!" he shouted. "'Tis only some framin' boards an' a couple coats o' thin plaster. They must not o' intended it t' be a permanent change. I'll be through this in no time!"

Alec struck the wall three more times with powerful swinging blows, then paused. Already he had enlarged the hole to about a foot in diameter.

"Can you see anything?" asked Joanna, coming forward.

"Not yet. The dust o' the crumblin' plaster'll have t' settle before we can see inside."

"Pound out some more," insisted Joanna. "I want to go inside."

"Then turn yer back. I want no chips flyin' off an' strikin' ye in the face," said Alec, and once more raised the instrument high overhead.

This time he did not stop until he had demolished a two-foot-wide by four-foot-long hole through to the other side. He set down the pick and chipped away the rough edges by hand.

"That's enough . . . that's enough!" cried Joanna. "Let's go through!"

Joanna bent low and poked the upper portion of her body into the hidden area between the two rooms. That they had indeed discovered a walled-up nursery there could no longer be any doubt. But it was nearly black inside, the only light coming from the hole they had made, and that, with their bodies before it and in it, provided too little to see a great deal.

"We'll need a candle," she called back to Alec. "They've walled up the window on this side too."

"I'll run an' fetch one," said Alec. "I jist happen t' know where Mrs. Bonner keeps a few."

He disappeared but was back before Joanna had the chance to miss him. Carefully he lit the wick, handed it through the hole to Joanna, then crouched down to follow her through it.

At last they stood in the small darkened chamber. An eerie silence fell upon them as they looked about in the semidarkness. Several child-sized chests and dressers lined the walls, a sideboard with two faded stuffed toys lying on top of it. There was a single bed at the far end, opposite what would have been the window. It had clearly been used by a young child—probably a girl, judging from the decorative frills on the lace canopy above it. A certain mournful nostalgia seemed to pervade the place, covered with the undisturbed cobwebs of decades of disuse. A thin layer of dust lay over every inch of the room, like a freshly fallen sheet of fine November snow.

Neither Joanna nor Alec spoke a word.

As they reverently made their way around the neglected nursery, the shadows from the flickering candle in Joanna's hand cast up ghostly phantasms of the past. A number of pictures adorned the walls: an exquisite copy of Raphael's *Sistine Madonna*, a large framed linen tapestry displaying a family crest and genealogical record, a copy of Gainsborough's *Blue Boy* with *Pinky* beside it and a number of other prints and stitcheries. Joanna was immediately drawn to an oil original portrait, still displaying vivid colors, of a mother and daughter. It hung above the head of the bed and she immediately knew it must be a painting of Atlanta and Margaret when the latter was about nine.

Joanna held the candle up close to the painting, studying the two faces, with a growing sense of fulfilled belonging stealing over her quiet spirit. With moist eyes, she turned to Alec.

"This could be a painting of me. It's remarkably similar to what I looked like as a young girl."

They walked throughout the room a second time, taking time to absorb what was contained in it. The most striking feature remained merely the atmosphere of hushed antiquity, an unearthed Egyptian tomb which had been preserved as lifelike as possible.

"There's something here, Alec, something we're meant to find. I know it . . . I can *feel* it."

"Do ye hae any idea what we're lookin' fer?"

"No. But it's almost like I can feel my grandmother reaching out to me and saying, as she did before I went away, 'It's there, Joanna . . . it's there. You have to find it!' "

"If only we had some idea—"

"We'll find it. I know we will." There was a certainty in her voice that came from something more than wishful thinking.

Silence fell again, but another ten minutes of exploration yielded nothing. At last Joanna sat down on the floor next to the doorway they had broken through the wall.

From this vantagepoint, Joanna's eye fell on *Blue Boy*. It had always been one of her favorites. Her eyes moved to the right to take in the huge, brightly flowered tapestry. Something about it suddenly struck Joanna; she had overlooked its familiarity the whole time they had been in the room. She could never have seen it before. Yet she was sure, impossible as it seemed, that she was not laying eyes on it for the first time.

She stared directly at it for several long moments. Around the outside edges were ornately woven leaves and flowers, of a multitude of hues and colors. The top third exhibited the family crest with the single word Ramsey beneath it in the most intricate Old English script imaginable. Underneath was a line-drawn family tree.

Then Joanna snapped to attention.

She jumped from the floor and hastened to the tapestry, held the candle aloft and close, and squinted to read the tiny names woven with thin black thread into the fine linen fabric.

"That's it! Of course. Alec, this must be it! This is the *original* of the family tree. Margaret must have copied this in making the smaller one. This *had* to have been Margaret's room!"

"But what's the secret?" asked Alec.

"I still don't know!" said Joanna excitedly. "Wait a minute . . ." She reached into her coat pocket. There lay Margaret's embroidery where Joanna had placed it before leaving the Cuttahays'.

She handed the candle to Alec, then held up the sampler.

"It's just the same," she breathed.

"Could that hae anything t' do wi' yer grandmother's secret?"

"I don't know. Let's take the big one down and take it out into the light. If it has something to tell us, we'll be more likely to see it there."

Back in the alcove, they scrutinized the tapestry for a moment.

Then Joanna saw it. Something was wedged in front between the tapestry and its frame. She tried to pry it out with her fingernail, but succeeded only in breaking the nail. Alec was more successful with his pocket knife. It was an old, rusty key.

Slowly Alec shook his head. "If that's yer grandmother's secret, lass . . . in a place like this it might take forever t' find where it fits."

"There's got to be something else!" Joanna said. She looked behind the tapestry which Alec had braced against the settee. Its back was covered with thick, old paper. Smoothing her hand over it, the paper gave slightly under the pressure of her touch. She stood in silence for a moment as if resolving a dilemma in her mind. Satisfied at length with her decision, she set to work.

She ran her fingers along the edges of the paper where it was attached to the frame. Suddenly she stopped where the paper seemed more loosely adhered than in other places.

Doubtful, she looked at Alec.

"Go on, lass," he encouraged. "It can easily be fixed. 'Tis too late t' stop noo."

Joanna began to pry away the paper, with the feeling that she was desecrating something precious. But she reminded herself of her grandmother's words. Only half of the paper was lifted away from the frame when the envelope fell out onto the floor. With trembling fingers, Joanna picked it up and opened it. An aging parchment document was inside.

Together, she and Alec hastily read the document. After a moment Joanna looked up to Alec. Their eyes met, but no words were necessary. The document said it all.

"We have to get this to Ogilvie," was all Joanna could say. "This changes everything!"

"If Sercombe knew about this—" Alec began, then stopped abruptly.

"What is it?" asked Joanna.

"I heard something."

They listened. Now Joanna heard it too—the unmistakable sounds of horses riding across the cobblestones. There were at least two, perhaps more.

"That's not Dorey," Alec said, "not ridin' so fast."

"Sercombe?" asked Joanna in alarm.

Alec nodded. "He's searched this house once. An' now wi' Dorey an' Mrs. Bonner gone, he intends t' try it again."

"He couldn't possibly know about this?"

"I dinna ken what the rascal knows. But he's a clever one, an' covers all the angles. I wouldn't trust the likes o' him as far as I could throw him. We've got t' get oot o' here."

"But my horse is in front. They've already seen it! How can we possibly get away?"

"Mine's oot back," replied Alec. "I think I can find the back way oot. Come on!"

Joanna slipped the key and the document into her pocket, then they sped from the room, carefully closing all the outer doors to conceal their activity, and stole down the corridor to the back stairway.

The sounds of horses had stopped; below and behind them they could hear the footsteps climbing the main staircase. Down the backstairs Alec and Joanna crept, as quickly as they dared. Reaching the ground floor, Alec grabbed Joanna's hand, led her through several narrow corridors, turning first to the right and then to the left in regions of the house she had never seen, and at last to a small service door which opened behind the house near the stables.

"Come," said Alec still leading, "my horse is in there."

In a minute he was in the saddle, swung Joanna up behind him, and then prodded the horse carefully forward. As they rounded the back of the great house, Alec said, "Now hang on, I don't want t' lose ye!"

He grasped the reins tightly and dug in his heels. The horse reared slightly, then exploded around the front of the house and out the gate, with Joanna behind, clinging tightly to Alec.

"Mr. Sercombe . . . Mr. Sercombe!" shouted an alarmed Tom Forbes as they shot past his lookout post at the front door, "they're here! They're gettin' away!"

He rushed through the door, still shouting.

Scarcely slackening his speed, Alec turned his horse from the main road, down the path through the ravine, up the other side, and then away across the open pastures like the wind, toward the Cuttahays' cottage. There he hastily saddled two fresh mounts for himself and Joanna, and told Walter Innes to stay until they should return. They remounted and were off once more with Alec shouting over his shoulder, "We'll be back as soon's we can . . . an' Walter, ye'd better make sure ye hae a gun."

37

Culden Again

TWO HOURS LATER, Alec and Joanna sat across from Gordon Ogilvie in the sitting room of his home after their hot and tiring ride.

"Are you sure you want to be riding back this late?" the lawyer asked as he replaced his cup in its saucer and dabbed the corners of his mouth with a napkin.

"'Tis best we stay where we can keep an eye on Sercombe," Alec replied.

"Ah, yes," said Ogilvie with a glint of knowing in his eyes. "He'll bear some extra watching now."

"I'm afraid for Nathaniel and Letty," added Joanna. "We have to get back as soon as possible."

"I can hardly believe what you've found," Ogilvie went on, "though I'm sitting here staring at it with my own eyes. Who would have thought—why, I've scarcely ever heard of—well, if it doesn't stop Sercombe, it should certainly slow him up a mite."

"Let's hope so," said Joanna, "but are you certain we're not too late?"

"Almost a hundred years too late, judging from this document," Ogilvie reflected. "But I shouldn't think that makes it any less binding. I'll have to send off a wire or two, confirm legal precedents and all that sort of thing, maybe even a trip to the county seat if I can't do it by wire."

"Is there time?" asked Alec anxiously.

"I don't know. It would be best if I could go to Aberdeen, but there certainly isn't time for that. I should be able to have confirmation in time for the meeting—two days from now. Didn't you say that's when the signing is to take place?"

Joanna nodded. "But don't you think," she said, "that what you've discovered about Channing's plans would be enough to stop the proceedings?"

"No doubt that would make the townspeople turn on Sercombe. But their displeasure, no matter how scathing, won't have any legal effect on the sale, short of causing a riot."

He leaned back and took a sip of tea. His fingers unconsciously sought his spectacles and adjusted them on his nose, as if the ritual would somehow uncover something he hadn't yet seen.

"I opposed Sercombe once," he said, turning his gaze out the window for a moment's brief retrospection. "It involved a questionable boundary between the Duncan property and one of my clients—a minor dispute, really. But I think he's been resentful of me ever since."

"Why . . . what happened?"

"The court sided with me. He directed some very caustic remarks toward me afterwards."

He leaned forward, fiddled once more with his spectacles, and returned his attention to the paper on the table before him.

"No," he went on with a weary sigh, a rare momentary glimpse into the lawyer's age, "there has to be a legal way to block him. Otherwise, believe me, he'll make mincemeat of us all."

"And is this legally binding?" asked Joanna.

"Your birth certificate and other proper documentation would be best, of course. But by the time we had those the sale would be over and we could do nothing. This is the only chance we have. You can only be thankful you found it first."

"We best be goin'," said Alec, rising.

"I'll do what I can," stated Ogilvie, who did not sound as though he looked forward to the work but whose latent spirit of competition was slowly being roused against his former adversary.

"Thank you, Mr. Ogilvie," said Joanna.

"We'd best meet at the Cuttahay farm the mornin' o' the meetin'," said Alec.

"Very well," returned Ogilvie, showing them to the door. "I shall be there bright and early two mornings hence."

As his two visitors mounted their horses and rode off, Gordon Ogilvie shook his head and tapped his fingers thoughtfully against his tightened lips which already seemed to be ruminating on the possibilities. "My, my, my . . ." he breathed.

The excitement of the day had brought with it a certain exhilaration which sustained Alec's and Joanna's stamina during the hasty ride to Culden. But conversing with Gordon Ogilvie had slowed the flow of blood in their veins and by now their reserve of energy had been nearly spent.

It was evening when they rode out of Culden, the shadows had begun to lengthen, and the gloaming bathed the landscape in its pink and orange shades. To their left the Dormin already lay thickly shadowed. As they rode past Joanna resolved that once all this was settled she would explore the forest under more pleasant circumstances.

They crossed the narrow wooden bridge over the Lindow and now their eyes were drawn to the Marbrae's summit to their right. They rode some distance on when Alec reined in his horse and stopped.

"Let's ride up the Marbrae," he said, turning to face Joanna. "The view at this time o' the day is one ye hae t' see!"

"I'm so tired," replied Joanna.

"It'll take but a few minutes each way," insisted Alec.

Nodding her consent, Joanna followed as Alec turned off the road and led them up the path they had walked together once before. Up the steep terrain and over the rocky ground their sure-footed horses took them until at last they stood on the peak. Dismounting, they tied their horses to a scraggly bush and walked slowly about, gazing downward in all directions.

Everything appeared so different in the evening light. The harbor and town lay beneath the fog which was inching its way inland. The farms of the valley were silent from this distance. The Dormin was by now but a dim blob below them and far off in the east the sun's last reflections of the day bounced irregularly off the geometric walls and windows of Stonewycke.

"What will ye do," asked Alec softly, at last breaking the silence, "if things don't work out?"

"What do you mean, at the meeting?"

"Aye, if Sercombe should win after all?"

"I don't know. I've tried not to think about it."

"I know ye hae said ye no longer hae a home in America. But that's still yer home."

"Not anymore, Alec."

"But if this town, this valley, should go t' Channing . . . what would there be fer ye here then? Unless ye . . ."

He floundered over the words but somehow they weren't coming out the way he had intended.

Joanna looked at Alec for a long moment. Then she turned toward the setting sun. She hadn't wanted to face these decisions. What if she had no home here after all?

"There's my grandfather," she said at last.

Why couldn't she say what was really on her heart?

"Aye, Dorey'll be needin' ye, an' that's a fact," Alec replied. He felt ready to burst with the swelling emotions within him. *Speak what ye feel, man!* he shouted inwardly.

But there remained one uncertainty still gnawing at him. He had to know.

"An' Mr. Channing might be seein' fit t' stay," he blurted out. He regretted the words almost before they were said.

"Mr. Channing!"

Joanna spun around, her face a distorted picture of mingled surprise and anger.

"He's a gentleman o' some means," Alec stammered. "Many women'd be glad t'—"

"Alec MacNeil! How dare you!" interrupted Joanna. Her anger now flashed unvented. "That you would even think I'd have anything to do with that— that . . ."

She exhaled a sharp breath.

"I don't even want to talk about it!"

She swept past him down the hill toward the horses. Hastily untying hers, she swung up into the saddle and trotted off down the path.

Alec stood stock-still for several moments, forlorn and bewildered. He could not have felt more the bumbling fool. This wasn't at all why he had suggested the little side-excursion to Marbrae. Why did he bring it up?

Now he wondered if he would ever have another chance.

Slowly he walked toward his horse, climbed into the saddle, and followed her down the mountain and toward Port Strathy.

38

Decisions

JOANNA RODE INTO the Cuttahay farm still ahead of Alec but considerably cooled down from her outburst on Marbrae. She walked toward the house, and a look of surprise stirred her tired features when she was greeted by Olive Sinclair who sat inside with Letty and Nathaniel.

In answer to her questioning gaze, Olive was the first to speak.

"Oh, lass," she said, "I'm afraid it's not good news I'm bringing."

"Something's happened to Dorey!" said Joanna in alarm.

"No. He's still missing, to be sure. But no harm's come to him that anyone knows of."

Just then Alec walked through the door but said nothing.

"Olive rode oot," said Nathaniel, "t' tell us Sercombe's moved up the meetin' by a day—tomorrow at noon!"

"Oh no!" exclaimed Alec. "'Tis not enough time! We only jist left Ogilvie tellin' him not t' come till the day after."

"We should have expected the scoun'rel t' do somethin' underhanded," said Nathaniel.

"'Tis a miracle we heard about it at all," said Olive. "He tried to keep it from us, and that's for sure. You know I'm usually the first to hear of any bit of gossip that happens in the town. But this morning 'twas nary a soul entered my store. Then after lunch, Rose Creary comes in. She looked around for a while and picked up a few things. Then she comes up to the counter—she was real tight-lipped she was, all this time. But then just as she was about to leave, she blurts out, 'Miss Sinclair, ye have as much right to know as anyone!'

"'Know what?' I asked.

"'Aboot the meetin'. It's been changed t' tomorrow an' Mr. Sercombe said that if that girl from America was t' come she would try t' spoil everythin' fer the toon.'

"'But why shouldn't I be told?' I asked—and a perfectly logical question it was, if you ask me.

"'He said that if ye or the Cuttahays or the vet knew they would tell her—an' then she would make trouble fer all o' us. He was spreadin' the word aroun' the toon fer everyone t' come but t' keep quiet aboot it t' ye all. Weel, I dinna ken the girl mysel'. Though I did see her once or twice an' she seemed nice enough.'

"'And why did you decide to go ahead and tell me, Rose?' I asked.

"''Tis jist that, weel, if the lass has somethin' t' say it seems we ought t' have a chance t' hear it—that's what I'm thinkin'.' So some of our thanks should go to Rose," Olive concluded with a long sigh.

"Weel, there's one positive side t' yer account," said Alec. The others cast questioning glances his way. "The Crearys dinna appear t' hae gone completely over t' Sercombe's way o' thinkin' in this—an' that makes me think there jist might be others who'll listen t' Joanna."

"'Tis true, lad," said Nathaniel. "But ye'll be forgettin'—'tis evidence that's wanted jist noo, not talk."

"And Mr. Ogilvie has it," said Joanna dejectedly. "And he's not coming back for two days."

"I'll have t' ride back an' fetch him," said Alec.

"Lad, ye must be exhausted," Nathaniel said.

"There's no choice," replied Alec. "I can rest a wee here first, an' then be off. Ogilvie an' that paper hae t' be at the meeting or else all is lost, whether he has time t' send his wires or not. But we'll do what we can no matter how many judges or lawyers we hae t' wake up between now an' then."

"I'll fix ye some bread an' broth," said Letty rising. "An' then make a bed fer ye."

"Maybe ye can get the motor car from Innes," suggested Nathaniel.

"O'er these roads, I'm afraid it wouldn't be as fast as usin' my horse an' takin' a short-cut or two," Alec replied. "If the meetin's at noon, I should be able t' get back in time. The rest o' ye go an' don't wait fer me if I'm not back. Stall Sercombe however ye can."

"But what aboot poor Dorey?" asked Letty.

"He's the only person who can verify who I am," said Joanna.

"I'll go fetch Walter with mornin's first light an' he an' I will go an' find him," said Nathaniel. "Somebody must o' seen him."

"In the meantime," said Letty, "ye must get some warm food in yer stomach, Alec, an' then lay yersel' down fer a rest, poor lad."

Alec laughed. "Ye forget, Letty, that young men like me are built rugged, like oor Scottish coast!"

"Na, maybe so. But I'd still have ye rested an' wi' food in ye before startin' oot."

"I concede t' yer motherin' instincts, Letty," replied Alec with another laugh. "I'll jist see t' my horse an' then ye can hae yer way with me."

Alec turned and left the house. Olive rose to help Letty with the bed and supper. Nathaniel poked at the fire and threw in another log. Trying to slip out unnoticed, Joanna followed Alec outside. He had removed the saddle and now stood by his horse rubbing him down and talking softly in his ear.

He heard the soft footfall of Joanna's approaching step but did not turn around.

"Alec," she said, "you will be back for the meeting, won't you?"

"The way I figure't," he replied with his back turned, "I hae t' be."

An awkward silence followed.

"Alec . . . I'm sorry."

"No need, mem."

"Yes . . . yes, there is. I shouldn't have snapped at you. Forgive me . . . please."

Alec turned and faced her. "Ye should know ye was already forgiven, even before ye asked," he said, hesitated a moment, then added, "It's jist sometimes hard fer a man like me not t' be a bit envious o' a man like that Channing o' yers, who—"

"Alec," Joanna interrupted, "believe me, you have nothing to be envious about—especially of him."

Alec did not reply but continued stroking his horse's back.

"Do you think there's time for Ogilvie to do anything?" Joanna asked, returning the conversation to the predicament at hand.

"We'll jist hae t' do oor best."

"Alec . . ." said Joanna, then hesitated and looked away.

"What is it?"

"I just don't know if, well . . . I don't think I could face the meeting and everything that might happen if—"

"If what?"

"—if you weren't there with me, Alec."

Alec turned toward her and looked into her eyes. "I'll be there," he said. "But . . . Joanna," he went on, and as he said her name his voice revealed a slight quiver, "ye be careful, do ye hear?"

He reached out cautiously and took her hand in his. "If fer some reason I should not make it back, ye watch yersel'."

"I will, Alec."

"I couldn't live wi' mysel' if somethin' was t' happen t' ye while I was away."

"Don't worry. Nothing will happen."

"Those men hae no scruples. They may try t' harm ye."

"You just hurry back as fast as you can. And, Alec . . . you be careful, too."

"I'll ride like the wind."

39

The Old Man and His Past

NEAR THE POINT where Ramsey Head's rocky bulk shot into the northern Scottish sea sat a cluster of remote sea caves. Most remained under water except during extremely low tides. Two or three, however, managed to remain snug and dry no matter what the watermark. They provided frequent shelter for the many wild goats roaming the grassy heights of the Head when they came down the leeward side of the promontory during the fiercest of the wind's wintry blasts. But today the voice of other occupants kept the goats from drawing too close.

Two men crouched in the dark depths of the cave farthest to the east of Strathy. One reclined against the rock wall with a rifle resting across his knees. He was just bringing a flask of whiskey to his lips with shaky hand.

It was Tom Forbes.

"Consider yersel' lucky, yer lairdship," he said with a slurred voice, then took a swallow from his bottle. "It could hae gone worse fer ye if I hadna stepped in fer ye."

"Thank you, Tom," replied the other man with a tone of genuine gratitude. Dorey Duncan sat opposite his captor, pale and bedraggled, his hands and feet rather sloppily bound with a length of rotting hemp.

"None o' yer 'thank ye, Tom,' nonsense, yer lairdship," Tom shot back. "I know yer kind, as if I weren't even good enough fer ye t' git angry wi'."

Forbes took another long swallow from his flask.

"Weel, the shoe's on the other foot, noo. Ye ain't got nothin'—an' it'll be me as gits called yer lairdship—me who folks'll look up t'. That's why I telled them not t' harm ye—I want a Duncan"—he spat the name out with revulsion—"t' see someone else struttin' aroun' their gran' estate!"

"I'm sorry you feel the way you do, and I can understand, Tom. But believe me—"

"Pah!" Tom spit at the ground. "An' ye're jist an innocent bairn, aren't ye?"

"I doubt I'm innocent of anything—though I don't know what your grievance is." Even as the words were out of his mouth Dorey wondered if this wasn't one more sin to lay to his account, a sin of omission, remaining silent far too long. Yes, he had seen Alastair's carelessness toward his tenants. But he had said nothing. What could he have done?

But finally—now that it appeared too late—Dorey was beginning to realize that he loved Stonewycke and Port Strathy and these people. Yet all his life he had never shown compassion to them, to people like Tom Forbes. Even the gardens had been tended for his own pleasure.

"Maybe ye was jist a crazy loon all these years," Forbes broke into Dorey's thoughts with a sneer. "But it doesna matter—it should hae been ye yersel' what hanged."

"What . . . I . . . I don't . . ." Dorey stammered. But he did not know what to say.

Lately things had been growing clearer to him, yet there was still such a fog at times—a terrible fog. It reminded him of—

But before he could lay hold of the half-formed image seeking to shape itself in his mind, Tom Forbes's voice cut through the air again.

"My daddy only did yer dirty work. I was jist a child, but I heard him tell my mither what happened—he was driven t' kill the laird Falkirk. But ye . . . ye . . ." Forbes's voice blabbered to silence, his alcohol-dimmed brain unable to choose between accusations. He lifted his flask once more to his lips. Dorey rubbed his hands across his face. "Oh, God," he moaned. "How could I have let his happen . . . ?"

It had been raining. Such a storm poured down from the heavens that it could cleanse the earth with the sheer force of its power. When Ian had stumbled from the stables at Stonewycke after James's violent outburst, he thought he would never return there again. But somehow he made his way back, vaguely sensing he must have the horse Maukin, for in his muddled thoughts he saw only one solution to his problems—he had to finish what he had begun at the inn earlier that evening. He had to find George Falkirk, the man who stood between him and his love.

Yet even as Ian led the chestnut mare from the stable he felt a reluctance in his step. He wanted desperately to see his Maggie, to feel her closeness, to hear her gentle voice. "Oh, Maggie . . ."

But he was afraid.

There was the fear of what James would do if he tried to come back. But there was something else as well—a nebulous ache in his heart, a fear he could not even name, that Maggie would not—could not—choose him over her father. And Ian Duncan—who had run away from his fears all his young life—could not face this above all fears. And so he crept from the estate, and when he was far enough away, he mounted the mare and galloped into the lash of the storm. All his fears and frustrations galvanized into one awful goal: Falkirk would pay for what he had done!

At Kairn Ian had the dubious fortune of discovering his adversary alone in the stable. Whatever he was up to saddling his golden stallion at that late hour, Ian could not guess. But it made things easier for him.

"Falkirk!" Ian shouted.

And when the handsome, arrogant face of the gentleman turned toward Ian, there might have been something of a smirk on it. For at that moment, Ian—drenched to the skin with pale face and wild eyes—did not appear an enemy to be taken seriously. Still, Falkirk had misjudged Ian once that day, and had received a thorough thrashing as his reward. He would not be so foolish again.

"You have your nerve!" Falkirk shouted in return. "I've had it with the likes of you. If it's another fight you want, then let's get on with it." And with the words he charged Ian, knocking him to the strawcovered dirt floor of the stable.

The events of the evening had drained much of Ian's strength. He was not nearly the foe he had been in the Bluster 'N Blow earlier. But strength was not so necessary when anger and fear dominated his very soul. For some moments the two men grappled in the dirt until at last Ian thrust Falkirk's powerful form away from him.

Regaining their feet, they stood glowering at one another. Then Falkirk's eye strayed to a nearby table where lay a knife used for cutting leather. He grabbed it quickly and lunged toward Ian.

"I'll be in my rights to kill you!" Falkirk cried. "You're a maniac!"

"No!" Ian rejoined, dodging his thrust. "It is I who would be right—!"

The knife shot toward Ian once more. In vain he tried to grab Falkirk's wrist to deflect the blade, but he misjudged and hit the blade instead, slashing his hand across its palm. Blood gushed down Ian's arm and onto the floor.

Ian froze. Likewise shocked into momentary inactivity, Falkirk made no move toward him.

In that brief flicker of suspended time, suddenly Ian realized that one of them was going to kill the other. He had come thinking of killing. But in the blind rage which was driving him, actual killing had been far from real. All at once he knew it could *really* happen. Either he or Falkirk would die. It could end in no other way.

His mind suddenly filled with abhorrence at the thought.

But Ian was never to know whether he would then have turned away. For in the next instant Falkirk sprang to life and lunged at Ian with the bloodied knife. This time Ian caught Falkirk's arm and thrust him forcefully away. Falkirk stumbled backwards, tripped, and fell—crashing his head against the corner of the table where the knife had lain. The young lord's body sprawled out on the hard, packed dirt, a trickle of blood oozing down his temple. Slowly Ian approached, but Falkirk did not move again.

"I've killed him!" The words rasped soundlessly from Ian's lips. He waited only long enough to see that the proud figure still did not move, then he clutched his injured hand to his body and flew, in an agony of self-incriminating despair. The storm swallowed him up, and the first of many fogs settled over his brain. He would not know until almost fifty years later that George Falkirk had stirred once more that night, had risen to argue once more, only to be brought down again and for the last time by the hand of a greedy cohort of the hapless heir of Kairn.

Dorey looked down at his hand and rubbed the scar on his palm as if its old wound still lay gaping open and bleeding. For so many years he had fled from pain—from the pain of remembering. But even now as it finally flooded over him, he realized that his ability to feel the old pain again indicated the beginning of healing.

Suddenly he saw the events of that terrible night as if they had just happened. His hands now trembled as they had then when he fled the scene of the crime he feared he had committed. Yet pain was not all he could now recall, for there were also visions of sweet moments with Maggie; riding the spirited chestnut Maukin and the graceful black mare Raven, discovering the beauty of the land, and no less the beauty of Maggie Duncan herself. There had been pain—yes. But there had been wonderful times also. And perhaps Dorey regretted most that as his mind had obliterated the pain, it had also denied him the treasured memories, the memories that would have been a comfort to his old age. If only . . . if only . . .

"Oh, God . . ."

Ian Duncan had cursed God that day many years ago. Was it possible for Dorey to call upon Him now?

How could he?

For now he saw so plainly what he had done. He had heaped the blame for all that had happened upon God because . . . because he was too much a coward to place the blame where it rightly belonged—on himself. And if that was so, was not God merciful indeed to have protected him all these years from the agony of self-recrimination and from the constant threat of self-destruction which had assailed young Ian Duncan?

"But why, God? Why have you done this for me? Why have you watched over me all this time until I was ready to see things as they really were?"

Then Joanna's words came into his mind. *If your sins have followed you, perhaps it is because God could not let go of you . . . because He loves you and wants you to find forgiveness.*

You never meant ill, did you, God?

All those years you were reaching out to me, protecting me, caring for me, waiting for me to open my eyes. Oh, how little I deserved it!

Dear God, can you ever forgive me for what I have done . . . for what I have done to you by accusing you for the result of my own sin?

"Oh, God . . . *please forgive me!*"

Yet even as he softly spoke the words, Dorey knew he was forgiven. At last he knew the cleansing balm he had kept at a distance for so long. For the enmity he had nurtured in his heart against God was finally sundered—broken like the chains of his guilt and the fog of his past. At long last he knew not only peace but a purity that comes only from utter emptiness and humility. In accepting God's forgiveness, he had himself forgiven God for imagined wrongs . . . and he had forgiven himself.

He was free!

Yet the present turmoils still surrounded him. Tom Forbes, clutching a half-empty flask of liquor, continued to gape at Dorey accusingly. He was completely unaware of the silent reawakening of Dorey's mind, and the rebirth of his spirit.

"Go ahead, sleep, old man," Tom scoffed. "Git guid an' used t' the hard earth—it might be the only bed ye'll ken from noo on!" He erupted into a roar of laughter which echoed through the rocky cave.

Dorey wondered how many others in Port Strathy shared Tom's bitter feelings against the Duncan family, supposedly their protectors. It was hardly any wonder that the townspeople were in favor of a sale of the land which would profit them and signal the departure of the Duncan name from the land forever. The change would not be grieved. Indeed, it would be welcomed.

If only Joanna had come sooner, thought Dorey.

If only . . .

What good did it do to bemoan past mistakes and things that might have been? Yet perhaps that would be his greatest heartbreak—knowing that at the bottom of it all, he had been the cause of the rent in the land. He had torn the family apart, had divided the once proud name of Stonewycke, and had driven the one person away who would have cared for the land and its people as a rightful landowner should.

Joanna might have cared the way Maggie did. But now it seemed it would be too late for her also.

"Make yersel' comfortable, crazy auld Dorey," said Tom at length. "'Tis boun' t' be a long night fer ye. I'm goin' t' get some wood fer the fire an' a crust o' bread fer ye. By noon tomorrow, it'll all be o'er an' ye'll be free again."

Tom rose and staggered out of the cave. Dorey tested the ropes that bound him but was unable to make them yield. Then he settled back into further thoughts of days gone by.

Dorey was free, it was true; a peace he had never known before surged through him. The prayer his own dear Maggie had prayed for him—thinking him already dead—that day so long ago on the American prairie had at last been answered. He had found his peace with God, as had Maggie, through the miracle of forgiveness. And in God's wisdom the miracle had come to him through the grandchild of their brief yet far-reaching love. They were three lives—Maggie, Ian, and Joanna, their granddaughter, the new Lady of Stonewycke—brought together in love, torn apart in pain, and brought together again. Yet all three were sealed together for eternity by the everlasting bonds of God's forgiveness. All that now remained in Dorey's heart as necessary to complete his repentance was his public vindication—to restore some of what he felt he had robbed Maggie of so long ago. Slowly the darkness of evening descended around Dorey, and the only sounds he heard were the lapping of waves on the cave's mouth and the shrill call of sea gulls in the lengthening shadows.

40

The Town Meeting

"I WAS SURE he'd be back by now," said Joanna half to herself.

She continued to pace back and forth in the small cottage, glancing out the window every couple of minutes.

Notwithstanding her fatigue from the previous day, she had arisen before seven o'clock and her uneasiness had been growing steadily ever since. Of course Alec would have already been in Culden while she slept. By ten o'clock, she had begun anticipating his return in earnest. Her rational side reminded herself that Ogilvie would have to do in a few mere hours what should take several days; and that for him and Alec to reach Strathy by noon would be no small miracle in itself. But her emotional side started with every sound, and she scanned the road for the cloud of dust which would signal approaching horses.

But no horses came.

Olive had returned to open her store as usual. In town, children were playing and yelling in the street in anticipation of the great holiday. The mood was festive. The sounds of workmen hammering and sawing in the distance blended with the nearby shouts of energetic youngsters and the steadily increasing buzz of conversing townspeople beginning to gather in the shops and on the streets.

This was a long-awaited day!

By eleven o'clock, small clusters of people began making their way to the grassy meadow to the west of the harbor where a makeshift podium was nearing completion. Jason Channing sat comfortably in Palmer Sercombe's office and lifted a glass of cognac toward his friend, toasting their success.

But at the Cuttahay cottage Joanna could concentrate on nothing but the anticipated sound of a rider galloping toward them. Then her heart skipped and she ran to the door. The clop-clop of horse's hoofs and the jingling of harness could be heard outside. She threw open the door.

At any other time she would have been delighted to see Olive's friendly countenance. But today, her face fell. Yet the normally austere woman was grinning broadly. She threw aside the reins and nearly bounded from the wagon.

"Joanna!" she exclaimed. "We've made a terrible mistake. This explains everything. Look!" She was waving a piece of paper.

Puzzled, Joanna stepped forward. A hundred ideas reeled through her mind, but none came near to guessing what had caused such excitement in the storekeeper.

"I told you that machine's been a plague," Olive said. "I'd tear it out myself, except for once it brought good news and we didn't even know it!"

"I don't understand."

"We've had telegrams go astray and get delayed in Glasgow before, but none this important. It's certainly not fair what it put you through—"

"Olive! Please, what are you talking about?"

"I'm sorry, lass. I just got so excited I got ahead of myself. Look for yourself. We should have received this telegram *first!*" She handed the paper to Joanna.

Joanna scanned the few lines of the telegram. She looked up at Olive, her brow wrinkled in bewilderment, then she reread the wire. Perhaps she had had too many disillusionments lately to accept this message with the outright ecstasy that Olive had. Perhaps she was afraid to believe that such a wonderful thing could have happened. But her newfound faith had already taught her that God could do anything, that miracles do indeed happen. Whatever the case, she knew God was in control and that she need not fear, she need not even fear disappointment. He was there to support her in all things.

So for the third time she read the wire, scrutinizing it with both wisdom and hope:

JOANNA STOP HAVE WONDERFUL NEWS STOP MARGARET HAS WAKENED FROM COMA AND IS ON ROAD TO RECOVERY STOP SHE IS ENCOURAGED YOU HAVE GONE TO SCOTLAND STOP THIS NEWS HAS BEEN BEST HEALER OF ALL SAVE FOR THE GREAT HEALER STOP WILL KEEP YOU INFORMED OF PROGRESS STOP PRAYER IS THE MIGHTIEST MEDICINE STOP DR. BLAKELY

According to the date on the wire, it had arrived in Scotland the day after Joanna stepped foot in Port Strathy. She looked at the date again and again. It had been sent *before* the one she had thought brought tidings of her grandmother's death. This explained why the other had lacked any personal note or words of comfort. Suddenly it was clear: the previous telegram—sent after this one—had merely been a progress report—her grandmother was well and home in the old house on Claymor Street.

As the news settled over Joanna and she was able to fully accept it for the miracle it was, a smile gradually stole over her face.

Olive gave her a hug; by that time Letty had come out and the three shared the joyous news together as they had also shared the grief.

"It must not have been too long after I left that she came out of the coma," Joanna said. "If only I had waited a few more days."

"Aye, lass, but if ye had waited," Letty remarked, "ye would not hae been here in time t' stop Mr. Sercombe."

Joanna nodded, but a shadow began to creep across her face. "I haven't stopped him yet," she said. "I'm beginning to wonder if I can."

"The Lord has done some mighty things," Olive started. "We can leave it in His hands without fear."

"Yes, I know that now," said Joanna. "But now more than ever, it means so much more. This is my grandmother's land. I can't lose it now when she is so close to finally having it after so long. And then there's Dorey . . ." her voice trailed away in a heavy sigh as she began to feel the heavy responsibility now upon her.

"Dinna worry aboot Dorey," Letty replied, her voice full of faith in her heart. "Nathaniel and Walter are lookin' fer him. He'll be found."

"Oh, he *has* to be," Joanna said. "He must be told that his Maggie is alive!"

At length Olive climbed back into her wagon; she had to finish up a few things at the store before the meeting, but she would meet them there, she said. Letty and Joanna went back into the house to continue the interminable waiting.

The time of the meeting drew nearer and there was still no sign of Alec.

At about eleven-thirty, Nathaniel came riding up on his plow horse. Walter, he explained, was still out looking for Dorey.

Despite her prayers for faith and strength, there still remained a gnawing anxiety within Joanna.

"Come now," said Nathaniel. "Dorey or no Dorey, we've got t' get t' toon fer the meetin'. Who can tell what we might be called on t' do there?"

"What about Alec?" Joanna framed the question reluctantly.

"We canna be waitin' fer him. If he isn't there, we must do what the Lord puts in oor path t' do. If Alec an' Ogilvie are na the means t' stop Sercombe, the Lord'll show us somethin' else. Now come, lass, ready yerself. I'll bring the wagon aroun' an' we'll be off."

Thirty minutes later Nathaniel and Letty Cuttahay entered the outskirts of the town which had been home to them all their lives, bringing with them their "adopted" daughter from America. What the future held for this town, none of the three could tell. But they would know in less than an hour.

"Where can Walter be?" said Nathaniel. "As if it's not enough that Alec's not back yet. Walter's one o' the few allies we have."

"Dinna ye be too sure o' that," said Letty with the confidence that sprang from her deep faith. "I'm thinkin' we may find more people side wi' oor Joanna than we think, after they've heard her story."

"Perhaps Walter's not coming back means he's found Dorey," said Joanna hopefully.

"I'm hopin' ye may be right there, lass," Nathaniel replied. "But we'll not hae t' wait long fer an answer. Here comes Innes now!"

The two women looked up to see the factor driving up in Alastair's motor car. The engine sputtered to a stop and Innes climbed out with a look of desperation on his face.

"What news do ye bring, Walter?" asked Nathaniel, clearly distressed when he saw the look on Walter's face.

"None too good, I'm afraid," returned Innes. "I've searched the town high an' low . . . but no Dorey. I asked everyone I dared. No one's seen a thing."

"Weel," said Nathaniel thoughtfully, "the meetin's aboot t' begin, an' we're no good wantin' him."

"I'm goin' back t' try the hoose once more," said Walter, "an' I'll do my best t' be back in twenty or thirty minutes. It's oor last chance."

The automobile coughed and hissed away in the direction from which it had come.

"God go wi' ye, man!" shouted Nathaniel after him.

As Nathaniel led the team toward the meadow, it was obvious that nearly the whole town had already arrived and was waiting in readiness. Random noises of anticipation rippled through the crowd, then fell sharply as the wagon neared. Heads turned, many showing surprise at the sight of Joanna, then gradually they returned to their previous conversations as Nathaniel parked the wagon and secured the horses. They found their way to the rear of the crowd and sat down on the green grass.

Olive approached and took a seat next to Letty.

"Don't mind them," she said to Joanna, gesturing toward the crowd with her arm. "They're just a little surprised to see you, that's all. They'll get used to the idea of your presence in time."

A hastily built wooden dais stood at the head of the open area. It was covered with a huge canopy that flapped a monotonous cadence in the gentle sea breezes. In addition to the men, women, and children seated on the ground, some twenty or thirty men—fisherfolk and farmers and several shopkeepers—clustered about the platform, no doubt discussing the events soon to commence. Two or three out-of-towners in fine suits were also on hand to witness the event.

Joanna, Olive Sinclair, and the Cuttahays were soon swallowed up by the enlarging crowd. Joanna could not help noticing an occasional unfriendly glance her way. A few moments before 12 o'clock, Rose Creary slipped silently into place next to Miss Sinclair but seemed to avoid Joanna's gaze.

"Rose," said Joanna, facing her squarely, "I hear I owe you a debt of thanks."

"Hoot, mem!" said Rose finally looking her way. "I did nothin' more than what should o' been done."

"It took perhaps more courage than you are aware of," said Joanna, "and I want you to know that I appreciate it."

"I'm honored t' be counted one o' yer people," said Rose. "An' I know Mr. Creary'll stan' by ye, too."

Rose beckoned her husband, who now joined the small group with their children in tow. Doug offered no word, but lifted his cap and smiled a bit of a nervous smile toward Joanna.

Any further conversation was interrupted by a stirring of activity in the front of the crowd. There were scattered shouts and applause as a handsome new automobile drove up and stopped directly in front of the platform. With a flourish Palmer Sercombe stepped out, flashed a broad grin, and waved to the assembly. Following him was Jason Channing and two other men in dark suits carrying briefcases and looking sufficiently important for their task. Joanna could see a distinct look of triumph in Sercombe's otherwise impassive countenance. She sighed, knowing his triumph might indeed be well-founded.

Oh, Alec, she thought, *why aren't you here?*

Climbing the steps of the podium behind the lawyer, Channing maintained a detached look of smug indifference.

"How could I have loved him?" Joanna wondered in disbelief.

Across the crowd his piercing eyes looked for hers. She refused to look away and set her jaw, her eyes hanging on to their grip with determination in silent combat. *I'm not beat yet, Jason Channing*, she thought. Yet even as she did so, her heart pulsed with a fear of the power he represented. She turned away at last, shot a quick glance over her shoulder, but no Alec was yet to be seen.

The vicar, William P. Donaldson, approached the podium, took a deep breath, and spoke with a deep and melodious voice.

"A most cordial afternoon, my good people," he began. "Let us open this auspicious occasion with a word of prayer."

He paused while the crowd spread out below him settled into silence like a bird settling its wings. He was a thickset man with round face, pink cheeks, and squinty eyes. Spectacles would have greatly improved his vision, but they remained safely tucked into his pocket only to show themselves in times of dire emergency.

"Oh, Lord God Almighty, we thank Thee for looking down upon Thy humble servants with pleasure, and we beseech Thee this day to bestow Thy blessings on the proceedings which are to follow. And, Lord God, we thank Thee for the kindness and generosity of the men who are making possible this step forward for Port Strathy and its people. Amen."

Joanna struggled to keep her eyes closed, trying to focus her mind on the words of the vicar. When she opened them she saw Nathaniel was missing. Her eyes scanned the crowd and finally she spotted him at the edge of the meadow, near a clump of trees. Walter Innes stood with him and they appeared deep in conversation. But her attention was immediately diverted back to the dais when she heard the vicar say, "And now I give you our very own . . . Palmer Sercombe!"

Cheers and applause rose from the crowd.

The lawyer stood, walked to the podium, shook the vicar's hand, and turned toward the assembly as a smile formed on his lips.

"My dear people of Port Strathy," he began. Each word was precisely measured and carefully chosen. "This is indeed a momentous occasion for *our* town, one which will go down in history as the moment when prosperity began to shine her light upon us, and when each one of you here began to walk down her golden path—"

He was interrupted by further cheers.

"I am glad," he went on, "—indeed, I am honored, to have a small part in it. It is with sadness, however, that I recall it has come on the wings of sorrow. But you can be certain our dear Alastair Duncan is even now looking down on these proceedings with his approval . . ."

Joanna glanced about, wishing Nathaniel were beside her telling her what to do. She could discern nothing from looking in his direction, although his countenance seemed serious as he and Innes spoke.

". . . and now without further ado," Sercombe was saying, "I would like to introduce the man who is making all this possible, for you and for our town"—the lawyer waved his hand in his companion's direction—"Mr. Jason Channing! Please, Mr. Channing, would you offer a word to our people?"

"Thank you," said Channing, rising. "I certainly appreciate your kind reception and I look forward to many enchanting times in your fair town, for which I have such great expectations."

The cheers grew louder and louder.

Sercombe held up his hands, beckoning for quiet.

"Now, I see no reason to delay any further. Let us get on with the purpose of this gathering." The lawyer's words were met with the roaring assent of the crowd. "You have all been called here, not only to witness, but thereby to actually participate in a historic signing of legal documents . . ."

Joanna's heart pounded within her chest and she could feel the blood rushing from her extremities. Sercombe's words faded into a blur and she could hardly make out what he was saying. Several officials around the table behind the podium busied themselves in readiness.

She knew the dreaded moment had at last arrived. It was up to her, stranger though she was to most, to stop the proceedings. Terrified, she exhaled a long sigh and looked quickly about her one last time. The eyes of Letty, Olive and Rose were all upon her. She felt a pressure on her arm and reached over to return Olive's squeeze of encouragement.

One last glance at the Creary family sitting so close instantly brought into focus whom all this was for.

It was not for her!

It was for them, and all these people like them, who possessed precious little and were being given empty promises. It was all she needed to strengthen her resolve to the decision point.

Joanna licked her dry lips, tried to swallow, and wished desperately for a glass of water.

41
Maggie's Legacy Fulfilled

WALTER INNES HAD raced back up the hill to the great house. After another futile search of the grounds, he saddled the only remaining horse and began to scour the countryside, looking into every deserted shed and barn of the outlying parts of the estate. Again he returned to the house, hoping that perhaps Dorey might somehow have escaped and found his way home. But another quick look around told Walter that the house was still deserted.

Dejectedly he walked toward the stables, thinking—trying to remember something, anything which might provide a clue to Dorey's whereabouts.

Suddenly he remembered the day he had seen Tom Forbes rummaging around in there.

"What could've he been about?" mumbled the factor to himself, hurrying to the place where he had accosted Forbes in the middle of what appeared to be a search.

Ten minutes later, Walter Innes was back in the car tearing down the road toward the town meeting with renewed energy. Maybe they didn't know where Dorey was, but at least now they held one further bit of evidence of who was involved.

When he reached the meadow, he did not even wait for the vicar to finish his prayer before walking hastily toward Nathaniel. He fairly dragged the man away from his place in the crowd.

"Nathaniel," he said with urgency in his voice. "Ye was right all along—but 'tis a sorry pass!"

"What did ye find?"

Innes pulled a shiny object from the pocket of his trousers, looked hurriedly about him to make sure no other eyes were near, opened his hand to show Nathaniel, then after an instant closed his fingers over it once more and dropped it back into hiding from whence it had come.

"Do ye think it's Forbes's?" Nathaniel asked.

"He was lookin' in the stables that day fer somethin'. An' besides this, Flame Dance's harness is missin'—the one the laird was usin' the day o' his fall. I remember wonderin' if I should bury it wi' the poor horse, after—weel . . . ye know. But I decided not to, an' then laid it in a chest wi' the laird's other ridin' things. But now—it's gone."

"Not much we can say wi'oot the harness," said Nathaniel. "Would jist be their word again' oor's. An' Forbes would have any number o' reasons why his knife was in the stable."

"But if they—"

"I know. 'Tis a serious thing; they'll be havin' t' face the Lord, at least. But we mustn't make accusations wi'oot proof, ye know."

"'Tis worse than I imagined them capable o' doing," said Walter in dismay.

"If we're t' do anythin' wi' it, somethin' will turn up oor way."

His words were cut short by a tremor radiating through the crowd. At first Nathaniel could not discern what had caused the people to stir. Then he saw Joanna making her way slowly forward toward the dais.

"By golly!" he exclaimed proudly, "the lass is goin' t' do it!"

Joanna walked straight ahead, looking neither to the right nor left. At this moment, she had no desire to see the looks of disapproval and hostility on any of the faces which were now straining in her direction. What she would say she couldn't imagine. But the impulse inside her had compelled her to rise. Alec had said to stall them however possible.

Sercombe's mouth hung open in mid-sentence. Channing leaned forward in his chair, neither annoyed nor angry. He appeared almost eager for the inevitable confrontation.

"What may I ask . . . what is all this about?" asked Sercombe, struggling to maintain his cool composure.

"Mr. Sercombe," said Joanna. Her voice sounded small, and all at once she was aware of the utter silence of the crowd, every eye riveted on her.

"Mr. Sercombe," she repeated, gathering strength, "I . . . I cannot allow these proceedings to continue."

Rediscovering his momentarily lost sense of composure, and sensing the sympathies of the crowd behind him, Sercombe said, "What seems to be the problem, Miss Matheson?" His tone had shifted; now he attempted to patronize her, as if his best strategy was not to take her seriously.

"You know very well what the problem is." Joanna took a breath to still her pounding heart.

She had drawn the battle-line in the dirt now.

"I think maybe it's time the townsfolk here," she continued, "learned the whole story about this sale . . . and about why I'm here."

"They know all there is to know," he replied with a caustic edge to his tone. "Unfortunately, why you're here is a matter for speculation. Although I must say your greedy scheme to dash the only hope this town will ever have to rise above its poverty is—"

"There is nothing I want more for Port Strathy," interrupted Joanna with rising voice, "than prosperity! But the cost is too high, Mr. Sercombe, and when the price is paid there will be no prosperity at all, only heartache. Why don't you tell them of your own greedy scheme to—"

"Miss Matheson! You are out of order! If you do not return to your seat this moment, I'll have no choice but to have you bodily removed."

"Let the leddy talk, Sercombe!" yelled a voice from the back of the crowd. It was Doug Creary.

"Shut up, Creary!" hollered another. "She's none o' yer concern!"

"Please . . . please, my dear people," puffed the vicar, rising. "Peace, please. This can all be settled in an orderly fashion, I'm sure."

"Give her a chance t' have her say," came MacDuff's craggy voice.

"She is only trying to cause trouble for you all," said Sercombe.

"That's right," murmured numerous voices throughout the assembly. "We know how this sale will help the town! She's jist tryin' t' spoil it all!"

"Sit down, ye foreigner!"

"Go back where ye came from. We don't need the likes o' ye here!"

Losing her composure amid the shouts and catcalls, Joanna felt a rush of blood to her cheeks. She couldn't get flustered now!

"Sit doon, lady! We wants none o' yer troublemakin' here!"

Suddenly a deep, smooth voice rose over the tumult: "I'd like to hear what the lady has to say."

The words had come from behind Joanna. She swung around and saw the speaker to be Channing. His eyes glinted with merry confidence and the slight upturned corners of his mouth were the only hint that he viewed this challenge as a highstakes game. He nodded at her with an imperceptible motion of his cocked head and invited her to play the game.

"Thank you, Mr. Channing," said Joanna, coolly returning his nod. She then turned toward the quieted crowd and began, "I came to this town a stranger. But even before I set foot in Scotland, half my heart was here. For this very town is the home of my ancestors—people like Robert, Anson, Talmud Ramsey and Atlanta Duncan. And my grandmother, Margaret Duncan, told me—"

"Now we know yer game!" yelled a surly voice, as the rest of the crowd began to buzz as it registered its astonishment.

"So ye come to get yer clutches on the inheritance?" shouted one. "Weel, it won't work, lassie. That ploy's been tried too many times."

"Hey, I'm a Duncan too!" shouted another, who had already drunk more than was good for him. His jeers were accompanied by laughter which drowned out any hope Joanna might have had to continue.

Behind her she could feel the black eyes of Jason Channing reveling over her discomposure.

"I never even knew about the inheritance when I came," Joanna said more loudly, trying in vain to make herself heard. "I don't even care about it—"

"A likely story!" came a shout followed by an uproarious guffaw. "Did ye hear that . . . she never knew a thing about the inheritance? Ha . . . ha . . . ha!"

". . . but if the inheritance is rightfully mine," she continued, "I will lay claim to it in order to prevent these two men from carrying out their intended villany. Mr. Channing, you have been gracious enough to allow me to speak—I should like to return the favor. Perhaps you would like to tell these folk just what your plans for Port Strathy and the surrounding area involve."

The crowd quieted.

Channing stood. If her maneuver caught him the least bit off guard, he did not show it.

"Port Strathy shall remain untouched, unchanged—except for the better, and strengthened with a new harbor and various other improvements I have in mind for the homes and land. I intend to bring Port Strathy forward into the twentieth century. The people shall receive everything they expect, I assure you, and much more."

Once again there were cheers amid the spectators. This was what they had come for.

Joanna blanched. Dare she, in front of all these people, call him a liar to his face? And without proof?

"Miss Matheson," said Sercombe, at length coming to himself after being caught off guard by Channing's move, "unless you have something beyond these groundless statements regarding your own dubious ancestry, I think it best that you leave the proceedings of this assemblage in hands more capable than your own."

He turned toward Joanna as the final words left his lips, but the look on her face startled even him. Joanna had not even heard the lawyer's last little speech, for she was staring with wonder over the heads of the crowd toward the edge of the meadow. At first, those seated near the front only wondered what had suddenly come over this strange girl, but gradually heads began to turn to follow her stare.

Her trance at once broken, Joanna descended the steps from the platform, and began making her way through the crowd toward the object of her gaze.

A lone figure shuffled forward, as if his strength had all been used up long ago. But, though slow and tired, his step was far from feeble as straight on he came.

Joanna reached the old man, threw her arms around him. "Grandfather!" she said, "what have they done to you!" Tears filled her eyes.

At the word a general murmuring began near the front of the crowd, but it was soon stilled by the continuation of events before them.

"I'm fine, my dear," he said, but she could sense he was weak. Dorey continued toward the platform. Every eye was upon him.

A flustered Sercombe tried to regather the momentum but it was of no use. A great curiosity concerning this man who had so long been an anomaly among them kept every eye riveted on him as he advanced toward his goal.

"You must rest, Dorey dear," Joanna said. "I have something to tell you."

"No, Joanna, there is something I must do."

"It can wait. I must talk to you, Dorey. There is news of—"

"It has waited too long already, do you understand . . . too long."

She nodded. It was the only response she could give, for tears were streaming down her cheeks at the mere thought of what she had to tell him.

Nathaniel had risen from his place and approached to assist Dorey.

"Dorey," he said, "it was Tom Forbes that had ye?"

"Yes, poor soul—he had been wronged so terribly. He was all confused."

"Where is he?"

"Out in the caves at Ramsey Head—in a drunken stupor. Nathaniel, have mercy on him. There is hope even for the most wretched of us."

While Dorey mounted the dais, Nathaniel spoke a few words to Innes, who then made a hasty departure from the meadow for the shoreline to the east of town.

The silent townspeople readily observed the change in Dorey. For with all his disheveled appearance from two days in a cave, there was in him a certain grim lucidity. He appeared more than ever the laird he perhaps should have been.

The crowd spread apart before him. The heckling had ceased. For whatever reason—either his look of helplessness or the gentle spirit that seemed to have overtaken him—they were all now willing to listen with respect. Even Sercombe could find no words to swing the tide of events back in his direction.

With Joanna standing beside him, Dorey addressed his fellow villagers:

"I have lived among you these many years known only as Dorey—a name conferred upon me because I could not bear the sound of my true name. Palmer Sercombe and Alastair were among the very few who knew I was a Duncan. I could not face who I was or what I had done, and they showed mercy to me by allowing me the comfort of anonymity.

"But I must now face many things, even if I bear a name that may not be worthy of your respect. Indeed, in my own right I have lived beneath the station that was mine. I have seen how the roots of bitterness have grown deep through the years and no mere apology from me will suffice to heal your wounded hearts. You have been tenants and servants of a house and a family that has, in recent years, not done for you all it could have, or should have. For my own part in this, I am now truly sorrowful. Most of you knew me only as a sick old man residing under the care of the laird. In reality I was more a part of this family than you know. For just before her voyage to America, Alastair's older sister—the true heir to Stonewycke—Margaret Duncan and I were married. And this young woman who stands before you today is the daughter of the child we bore."

A renewed ripple of astonishment passed through the crowd.

"It was my intention to join my beloved Maggie in America, but then—events overtook me, and—" He paused, wiped his sweating brow, then attempted to continue.

But before he could speak, Joanna leaned toward him and whispered something no one else heard into his ear. In his intense joy, he closed his eyes and breathed: "Dear Lord . . . !" He could find no other words. For what could he say? The dream of a lifetime had been fulfilled.

His Maggie was alive! Could he believe his ears?

Yet there still remained the terrible fate of Maggie's dear land to deal with. He had walked out of the cave on Ramsey Head with a purpose, and with Joanna's whispered words it became even more imperative that he somehow continue.

He took a deep breath and with a new timbre of excitement, began again. "Today, however, is a day of new beginnings. Today, I ask you to listen and make a choice. This land is not yours—but in every way, each of you *is* the land. By your sweat and toil and tears the estate and land known as Stonewycke has become the sweet and fertile valley that it is. Can you now stand by and watch this valley we all love so dearly pass on to strangers bent on destroying it for their own gain so that you may have a few farthings today which will be quickly gone tomorrow? Can you allow this to happen when . . ." He paused and looked back to where Joanna sat. The radiance of her face told him it *had* to be true!

". . . *when there is still one alive*," he continued, "whose love for the land, though it has been from afar, is nevertheless more binding in that her devotion goes as deep as blood."

He stopped, looked at Joanna again, smiled, and then went on, gathering strength as he spoke.

"My good people, it is for this very love of the land that this legacy passed down from one generation to another to finally rest on the shoulders of the granddaughter of the true heiress of Stonewycke—Lady Margaret Duncan, who has entrusted it into the hands of this young woman now standing before you. She came here a stranger, but she saw immediately the most precious quality of this place—the folk like the Crearys, and MacDuffs and Cuttahays, and she was not afraid to take a stand against some very dangerous men. Not because she cares for her own gain, but because she sees the richness of the life you now enjoy, a life that is filled with simple peace and beauty. And neither she nor I want to see you lose—"

Dorey coughed and he wavered on his feet. Joanna moved quickly to his side, took his arm, and led him to the chair which had been vacated by the vicar. She had by now lost all interest in the meeting. She was beginning to realize that what was happening here today went beyond land ownership and inheritances. Lives had been miraculously healed, hearts had been made whole. God had been at work and He would not cease until that work was done.

She took Dorey's hand and for the moment it seemed enough to be near the man she had unknowingly come to Scotland to find.

But Palmer Sercombe was not touched by the display of emotion. He walked aloofly to the podium.

"Mr. Duncan," he said, "you have made some rather strong claims—I might even be induced to listen to them. But still . . . I see no evidence or proof. And thus, given that the *legal* right to conclude this business was given me by the late laird, it is now time to move ahead with—"

"Proof, ye say!" came a creaky voice from midway through the crowd. It was old Stevie Mackinaw who had broken his habit of reclusiveness to attend this historic meeting. "I hae ben i' this toon longer den efen Mr. Doorey Dooncan— an' anyone wi' eyes t' see't can see that the leddy up tere is the image o' Mawgret Dooncan."

Sercombe chuckled. "Now we have evidence from a lunatic and a senile old man!" he jeered. "Come now. I think we have heard enough."

With a flourish Sercombe produced a folded sheaf of papers from his breast pocket. "I have here the document which will finalize the transfer of the Duncan estate to Mr. Jason Channing," he said. "As you know, it provides for a cash settlement to every tenant family under the Duncan domain, money which you will all receive within the week."

He turned toward the table behind him, picked up a fountain pen which was prominently located on it, and affixed his signature to the paper.

"And now, Mr. Channing . . . if you will?"

Channing stood, and with only a fleeting look at Joanna where she still sat at Dorey's side, he took the pen and signed his name. Then he drew a check from his own pocket, handed it to Sercombe, and the two men shook hands to the sound of scattered applause and a few cheers from the townspeople.

Interrupting the momentary celebration, however, all heads began to turn toward the road from the south, where a new sound came thundering toward them.

42

Sercombe Unmasked

A S JOANNA'S HEART sank within her, the galloping sound of an approaching horse arrested her attention.

Its hoofs slashed at the grass as it tore between the last of the trees and into the meadow. The gray gelding's flanks were foaming, but the rider continued to dig his heels unmercifully into its sides. He reined in the horse as it pranced sideways, drew near the gathering, jumped down, threw the reins aside, and hastened toward the platform.

"Alec!" said Joanna, springing up and running toward him.

"What is the meaning of this intrusion, MacNeil?" demanded Sercombe with a sneer.

"I've got information that may alter yer proceedin's a mite, Mr. Sercombe."

"Now I've seen everything," muttered Channing with a laugh. "What with castles in the background, I'm almost reminded of—"

"Ye better keep that mouth o' yers shut, Mr. Channing," snapped Alec in return, "an' think twice before ye open it unwisely again. I'm in no mood fer the likes o' yer comments."

"Another threat, country boy?" replied Channing.

Alec bristled but any would-be response was cut off by Sercombe.

"I'm afraid you're too late, MacNeil," said Sercombe. "This meeting is all but over. The papers are signed and the transactions are complete."

"I think we'll all be stayin' fer jist a wee bit longer," said Alec. "Mr. Gordon Ogilvie will be here in a moment. His horse is a bit slower than mine. But whatever ye may have done already, he has some interestin' things he'll be wantin' t' discuss wi' ye."

"Any discussions can be carried on with the new owner of the land," said Sercombe. Then turning to address the crowd, he said, "Thank you all for coming. This meeting is adjourned. You will be receiving notification of what will be coming to you within ten days."

"All o' ye stay where ye are!" shouted Alec. "An' that goes fer ye too, Mr. Sercombe," he added as an aside. Then he said again to the crowd in a loud, commanding voice, "These proceedin's aren't done wi' yet, an' ye all will be wantin' t' hear what remains t' be said!"

"MacNeil . . . if you don't—" Sercombe began, the wrath clearly visible on his face. But before he could complete the sentence a second horse broke clear into the meadow and Ogilvie rode up. He dismounted in front of the platform, puffing profusely and mopping great beads of sweat from his brow.

"My, my," he wheezed. "I do hope there won't be much more of this."

"What is the meaning of this interruption?" Sercombe snarled, his temper at last rising to the surface.

Ogilvie cleared his throat.

"Pardon the intrusion," he began, "but I had small choice. I daresay you will humor me a moment while I get some papers from my satchel."

"Ogilvie, you always were a buffoon and an idiot. I'll humor no one," said Sercombe. "We have all the legal counsel we need for the present. Now you can just turn around and go back the way you—"

"No need to become abusive, Mr. Sercombe. But with or without your permission . . ."

He paused and took out a single paper from the leather case he had been carrying.

". . . with or without your permission, I'm afraid you will have to heed this. I have here an injunction blocking the sale of the Duncan estate."

Sercombe snatched the paper from his hands, looked hastily at it, and tore it into several pieces.

"It's too late," he said with scorn. "The transaction is consummated."

"Hardly, sir," returned Ogilvie. "The sale was never binding in the first place."

"Bah! That's a lie!"

"It is impossible to sell what was never yours, Mr. Sercombe. You are an attorney. You know the laws of the land. Miss Matheson is the legal heir to the estate since she is the laird's closest living relative. I believe I am correct when I state that the terms of the laird's will specify that your Power of Appointment is to take a subordinate position with respect to the establishment of the proper heir. And certainly you cannot be ignorant of the steps required in such a case. But you never so much as attempted a proper search."

"This . . . this woman has no credentials!" Sercombe spat out the words. "She has given me no reason to believe her story, save for some ancient-looking deed which any charleton could steal or forge."

"That is the purpose of this injunction. I have sent inquiries to America. Miss Matheson's 'credentials' shall arrive forthwith. Until which time there shall be no sale or any transactions regarding the Duncan estate. But from what I have seen I will go on record as saying that I believe Miss Matheson's claim is well-founded. And the two magistrates with whom I spoke this morning—none too pleased at being aroused so early, I must say—agreed with me that there is at least sufficient evidence to block what you have tried to do today. And now, Mr. Sercombe, I believe you will find this in order."

The crowd, straining to hear every word, reacted to the conversation between the two lawyers with a mingling of whispers, questions, and puzzled glances. They knew Alec, but most had never seen Ogilvie in their lives.

"Does this mean we don't git oor harbor?" yelled one.

"What aboot oor money?" called out another.

"My dear people," began Sercombe, still trying to patch together his scheme with his oily-smooth voice, "I can assure you this is little more than a well-orchestrated hoax. We will fight this woman and her cohorts—in the courts if need be. You will get what you so rightly deserve. I will not allow this greedy little strumpet to swindle you."

Alec stepped forward. "Ye're lucky I'm a man o' great restraint," he said through clenched teeth. "I'll let yer words go fer now, because Mr. Ogilvie has somethin' more t' say. But one more word o' that kind aboot Joanna Matheson, my friend, an' I'll not be responsible fer what'll follow. An' that's no threat; that's a solemn promise!"

"Just a bit of information I procured by wire from Aberdeen," Ogilvie said. "I have a friend on the License and Planning Council who was able to inform me that an American industrialist was recently granted a Writ of Variance which would enable him to build a dam on the River Lindow. By the time of completion in 1917, the entire Strathy valley would be a reservoir for the hydroelectric station of his design."

"Mr. Channing," said Joanna, standing again and breaking her long silence, "would you care to comment on your plans once more to the people?"

"Business is business," he replied icily.

Gradually the townspeople pieced together bits of conversation. Most were by now more than a little confused and a general buzz of anxious questions filled the air.

"The *whole* valley? . . . electricity . . . Mr. Sercombe, did ye know all aboot this? . . . what aboot the harbor?"

One by one they began to recall Dorey's words which reminded them how greatly they did love the land. Their strong Scottish hearts began speaking more loudly than their hopes of newfound prosperity.

As the tumult began to become disruptive, Nathaniel walked up with Tom Forbes firmly in tow. His drunken night in the dank and dirty cave told on his appearance.

"You drunken fool!" said Sercombe under his breath. "Don't say anything!"

But Tom scarcely heard. By now there was a crowd about Nathaniel who was attempting to lead Tom's staggering form up onto the platform where he could be heard.

"Tell them what ye told me, Tom," he said.

"He were dyin' onywa'—I jist helpt speed't along a wee. 'Twas merciful, it wa'." The slurred words tumbled unrestrained past his swollen tongue. "But killin's na fer me. I wouldn't kill 'at girl when he askt—nor ol' Dorey neither. We was all goin' t' get somethin' oot o' it—'at's what he said. But the laird wa' dyin' . . . he wa' dyin' onywa', so 'twasn't the same. I'm no killer."

"How did ye do it, Tom?" asked Nathaniel.

"Jist took a litt'l slit o' the harness. He'd fa' evenshuly . . . didn't haf t' cut clean thru. But I can't fin' m' knife . . . haf ye seen m' knife, Nathaniel?"

"Who was ye workin' wi', Tom?" asked Nathaniel. "Who made ye cut the old laird's harness so he'd fall?"

"Why . . . Sercommy, who else? Ye know that, Nathaniel."

The crowd gasped and glanced around for the lawyer whose fortunes had shifted so abruptly.

But he was gone.

By the time Tom's drunken admission was completed, Sercombe was behind several trees making for his office as fast as his legs would carry him. No sense hanging around arguing with these fools any longer. Let them have their bloody land; it was worthless anyway. Let them have their wretched, smelly fish and their pale flowers. There were better things in life than this cursed place.

"He's gone!" Nathaniel exclaimed.

"He'll not git far," said Walter Innes. "I'll be after him."

"Don't trouble yourself," said Ogilvie. "Before Alec and I left Culden we instructed the magistrate to take the necessary measures if our suspicions proved correct. I believe someone is already on the way to see our friend, Mr. Sercombe."

As Joanna listened to these proceedings her mind seemed to whirl. Suddenly she felt detached, as if she were watching some nightmarish drama from an audience in a theater. How could any of this be real, arguing and swindling and kidnapping—and even murder? And yet here were these real people acting out this drama . . . and, regardless of how detached and horrified she felt, she was one of them. Then she remembered something she had till now forgotten:

". . . *if only the land had belonged to the people instead of our corrupt family . . .*"

Her grandmother's words, though they had been lost in the confusion of so much else. Now they seemed the most important of all. In Margaret Duncan's time the struggles over this rich land called Stonewycke had caused nothing but strife and pain, and who knew what the strifes in earlier centuries had been? They still had not ceased. And to that legacy of deception and greed could now be added murder. It had to stop. The words re-echoed in Joanna's mind—*It had to stop!*

Perhaps Sercombe was right. Perhaps it was time for a change. Joanna thought of the aging document she had found in Maggie's nursery.

But Channing's voice jarred her thoughts back to discord around her.

"I think it's time for me to take my leave," he said, standing.

Joanna turned and faced him squarely. "Just how much did you know about all this?" she asked.

"If I was involved in any of Sercombe's ruthless schemes, not to mention murder, do you think I would be hanging around? I'm as innocent as a newborn babe."

"I suppose we could never prove anything beyond the fact that you are a heartless opportunist."

"And you can't go to jail for that, baby." He stopped and shot Joanna a broad smile. "But I'm ready to write out another check, sweetheart . . . this time pay to the order of Joanna Matheson. Just say the word and we can share in all this, together!"

Joanna stared with piercing gaze into the black eyes which had once so swept her off her feet.

"Jason Channing, I renounce you to your face. Now, as you said, it is time for you to take your leave. Go, and never return to Port Strathy again!"

Channing's smile became ashen. He turned slowly, almost in disbelief that she had rejected his offer, and slunk away through the crowd.

"Now, Mr. Ogilvie," said Joanna, forming her resolve in words that had only until this moment been in her thoughts, "will you be so kind as to share with the good people of Port Strathy about the other document we discovered?"

"With pleasure, My Lady," returned Ogilvie. Then he turned toward the crowd, many of whom had settled back into their places, and began:

"Let me first congratulate both you, My Lady, and you good people of Port

Strathy. I am confident you will find yourselves far more fortunate to have Lady Joanna heir to the Duncan estate than you could imagine. When Lady Joanna came to me with the deed to the land she had in her possession—given to her by her grandmother Margaret Duncan prior to her death—we were at first puzzled by a veiled reference to some other deed which had been drawn up generations ago by the laird at that time, Anson Ramsey. It was only yesterday when the 'Transfer Document' came to light, found in the house by Lady Joanna and Alec MacNeil. They brought it to me and I saw at once that it was a portentous discovery."

He paused to take a breath. Joanna seized the opportunity to finish for him.

"My grandmother, Margaret Duncan, is *not* dead, Mr. Ogilvie," she said. "We just learned the wonderful news today." Then turning to the crowd she went on.

"Thinking she was dying, my grandmother sent me to Port Strathy to make right the injustices that had been done to this land. When I came, I had no idea what I might be called upon to do. For a time I thought the only way to stop the destruction that would take place would be to claim the inheritance. But I realize now that it was not the *property* my grandmother was concerned about—it was *you*! I have seen that from the time she was a girl here. She was intensely concerned with the well-being of the tenants and fisherfolk of Stonewycke.

"She was not unlike her great-great-grandfather, Anson Ramsey. His love for Stonewycke also went far deeper than just mere acreage. He could see what Dorey said to us all just a short time ago—you folk *are* the land. It is you who have built it up, tilled it, worked it. Yet, you were always at the mercy of lairds and ladies who alternately abused or ignored you. Anson couldn't bear the thought of his sons, whose motives he didn't trust, misusing the land and its people. So he had a document drawn up which transferred the ownership of the vast majority of the Stonewycke lands to each of its individual tenants. Each person was to own outright his particular house and plot of land, the Ramsey family retaining the house on the hill with a surrounding area of 1,000 acres."

"Unfortunately," broke in Ogilvie again, "Anson's life was cut tragically short; he never had a chance to implement his desire, and the Transfer Document was lost. Somehow, we assume, it found its way into Atlanta Duncan's hands, and then yesterday, Miss Matheson found it where it had lain hidden all these years."

"I have struggled greatly," Joanna said, "over what should become of Stonewycke. I know now that I should do what should have been done a century ago. And I know that the true Lady of Stonewycke will give her affirmation to this. As soon as all the legalities are settled, the Duncan family will refile Anson's Transfer Document, and the land shall belong to you!"

A great cheer broke from the astounded crowd.

Joanna stood by, tears running unchecked down her cheeks, with a great smile of joy on her face. Slowly Dorey rose, walked to her side and placed his arm about her.

"'Tis a wonderful thing you've done," he said. "After all these years, at last the strife will be ended. Maggie can come home in peace. How could we ever have known that our love for each other and the land would find its fulfillment through our own granddaughter."

"All I wanted when I came I have found, which is wealth enough. And that is you, my dear grandfather!"

"Ah, you know how to bring joy to an old man's heart!"

"As for the estate," said Joanna as loudly as she could above the commotion, "there can be only two persons who should rightfully have dominion over it and its adjoining lands. That is my grandfather, Mr. Theodore Ian Duncan, and his beloved wife, Margaret Duncan. He will be laird and she will be the Lady of the property—as soon as we can bring her here—for as long as they live."

Another roar went up from the townspeople who by this time had left their places and clustered toward the front to shake Dorey's bony hand and offer their best wishes to her who from that day forward was known simply as Lady Joanna. And as they came, all former hostilities aside, behind the two stood Nathaniel and Letty, Olive and Alec—each of whom beamed with pride at the Lady their lass had become. Off to one side, suddenly shyly reticent because of the great tears which had formed in his eyes, stood old Stevie Mackinaw who had known Maggie longer than anyone in the town. It would be many months before he would again sleep an entire night through in the anticipation of once again laying eyes upon his beloved Lady of Stonewycke.

43
Alec and Joanna

※

FOAM-TIPPED WAVES WASHED up around Joanna's bare feet.

The morning's sun shone bright against the vivid blue sky, and the cold water splashing freely about her ankles sent little shivers of refreshment up her spine.

In every way it was a perfect day.

Channing had set sail yesterday for London. Sercombe had not been seen since the meeting, but Mr. Ogilvie remained confident that he would be rounded up to face justice before the week's end. Tomorrow, Joanna would leave for America to bring her grandmother back home to Scotland. But for now she basked in a few moments of rest, feeling peaceful and free to enjoy the beauty about her.

Alec walked along the sandy beach at her side. How different this day was from the first time they met here! But he was thinking neither about the sunshine nor the beach nor the events of the past several days. His eyes, and his heart, were focused entirely on the young woman at his side.

"Ye look every bit the fishergirl, lass," he said smiling. "Only there never was one so bonny!"

"That's the nicest compliment I could ask for, Alec."

"Weel, ye are bonny. Any man would be proud—"

"I mean calling me a fishergirl," she said.

"How's that such an honor, My Leddy?"

"Don't you see, Alec! It's the farmers and fishermen and plain folk around here that make the land what it is. I want to be a part of that. When I think of my grandmother's life up on the hill—in the grim old house—all the subterfuge and mistrust and scheming. Give me the simple life under a homely roof with oatcakes and boiled potatoes!"

"But it's what's in their hearts that matters," he said. "Tom Forbes's simple life as a fisherman didn't help him."

"Yes," Joanna replied. "And I think Letty and Nathaniel would always be their humble selves even if they lived in a palace."

Alec stopped a moment. He picked up a stone and tossed it out into the lapping waves. There was something he had to say, and he hadn't realized until now how difficult it would be to say it.

At length he spoke, gazing not at Joanna, but at the sparkling green water.

"I suppose yer own home'll be callin' ye noo?"

"Oh, Alec! I could never go back there to live. This is my home now."

"Will ye go live at the big hoose, wi' yer grandmother an' Dorey?"

"I don't know. I don't want to lose the life Nathaniel and Letty have shown me. They've taught me so much about life's true values."

"Ah, but ye're a gran' leddy now."

"I don't want to leave the simplicity of life I've found here."

"But ye'll be happy wherever ye are. An' ye'll bring yer light even t' the big stone hoose on the hill."

"I think I would be happier in a cottage. Let my grandmother manage the house and the estate. For me . . . I want to live and love and raise my children under a humble Scottish peasant roof."

"Ye will one day be the heiress o' Stonewycke an' its title."

"Do you think that matters to me? That doesn't change who I am. I don't want people—people I love--to feel differently toward me now."

"But ye are a highborn lady."

"Oh, Alec, don't do this to me!"

"It's jist that I know my place, an' I'm feared o'—"

"But you also know me. Your station, or mine, makes no difference to me. I feel the same toward you. Please, Alec, feel the same toward me."

She turned, and added quietly, ". . . that is, if you do have feelings for me."

"Joanna," Alec stammered, "I . . . I couldn't presume t'—"

"Please, presume!" she pleaded.

"Are ye sayin' . . . ?"

"Yes. Haven't you known?"

Alec could not lift his eyes to meet hers. It seemed as if the whole sky was pressing down its silent weight upon him. Her words had raised a storm in his heart. Could she possibly mean what his throbbing soul had heard?

Almost trembling he spoke, although the voice that came was scarcely more than a whisper: "But . . . I'm nothin' but a poor vet . . . nothin' t' offer ye but a simple cottage."

"And love?" Joanna added.

"Ye . . . ye're not sayin' ye would consider marryin' one so far beneath ye?"

"I don't need to consider anything," Joanna replied. "I belong with you, Alec."

"Lass," he breathed with intense quiet, "I love ye."

He could say no more, although the pulsating joy in his heart seemed ready to explode. A quiet, contented joy filled Joanna's heart. For the first time in her life she knew she belonged. In the simple love of this strong man she had at last found her true home.

All at once Alec threw his hat into the sky, leapt into the air with his hands extended high above him, and shouted aloud—a yell of childlike animated delight.

Joanna walked close to his side and slipped her hand tenderly through his arm, laid her head against his shoulder, and silently they continued on down the strip of sand—together and in love on the little Scottish beach on a lovely summer's morning.

Epilogue:
The Lady of Stonewycke

⁂

I T SEEMED THE heather was especially vibrant this year.

Of course, the scraggly bush with its magenta flame could not have known how special this particular moment of this particular year would be. But it almost seemed to have prolonged its season just to give a returning child of Scotland an extra measure of intense joy and delight.

In nearly fifty years, Maggie Duncan had all but stopped thinking of her homeland. But she could never stop dreaming of it. If it was not the brilliant heather, then her dreams were filled with wild waves crashing against a jagged coastline, or the eerie breeze whistling across the surface of a lonesome and barren moor. True, the dreams had often turned into nightmares from which she would awaken drenched with perspiration. Yet in the end she had determined to put the past behind her and to give her new life the chance it deserved—the chance her daughter deserved also.

But always her homeland tugged at her in the depths of her being.

God had worked wondrously in Maggie's life. She had learned to forgive, and to accept His life within her as the mainstay of her existence. But He did not, nor would He perhaps want to erase the memories of her beloved land.

She did not speak much of it at first. The hurts were too deep. And later—by then it did not seem of much use. But when death had reached out and had nearly closed in upon her, she could not prevent her weakened mind from speaking of what still lay so near to her heart. Had God's hand not been upon her all her life? This accident could have been no mere chance.

Indeed, the eye of the Almighty had never lost sight of her heart's desire and only, as the years passed, was waiting for His perfect timing to fulfill the legacy He had begun in her heart so many years ago.

Today Maggie looked the very picture of that young Scottish lass who had climbed this very hill so many years ago. But this day's rendezvous was even more special. Her gray hair was pulled back into a neat bun, but the autumn breeze blew several errant strands about her face. Her step was slower and more cautious, especially one leg, than it had been in the old days. But the glow on her face was nonetheless evident.

It looks just the same, thought Maggie, *except perhaps that our two patient friends, Raven and Maukin, are missing.*

She smiled. *Imagine me upon that spirited black mare now!* The thought brought a laugh to her lips. She could not contain the merriment which threatened to burst her heart in very gladness; certainly mere age could not keep it back.

Such had not been the case as she had lain on that hospital bed in Denver, however. There was a moment she had nearly given up. God had been good to her. Perhaps too good. But she was tired. Her weary bones told her it was time to rest. She had fought the good fight. She had learned to depend on God, though it had required the most painful of circumstances to bring her to the point of relinquishing her self. But now it was time to go home . . . home to be with her beloved Ian at last.

Yet Maggie's spirit ran too deep to succumb easily to temporal yearnings. Even though the death which reached out for her was near and real, her truest self could not yield to its compelling lure. The God who had guided her through life stretched out His hand to bridge the gap in her personal strength.

She awoke one sunshiny morning, and her soul immediately told her that all this had not been for nothing. Some unknown sense of anticipation gradually stole over her, though she had no idea what to expect.

Then Joanna's telegram had come.

How could she even fathom the words which shouted out to her from the page? *Her Ian—alive!* . . . still waiting for her after all these years!

The very thing she had dreamed of for nearly fifty years, the thing even her deep faith could not believe, was true!

How quickly the remaining days of recovery had passed after that. "Miraculous!" had been Dr. Blakely's conclusion. But it was no more a miracle than life itself, than the Creator of life bringing about His marvelous will. Two people of His choosing, brought together in His perfect time: it was worth any wait! By the time Joanna had arrived, Margaret was already back on her feet. Dr. Blakely's colleagues were confounded at her progress, but the doctor himself had learned long ago never to be surprised; he, too, served a higher Master.

When she had at last seen him in Aberdeen, Maggie realized all over again that any period of waiting, no matter how long, will, when it is over, seem but a passing moment in the memory. Suddenly it had not been years at all, but only days since they had parted. The waterfront of the gray city brought back ancient memories, mingled with the unpleasantness and sting of parting. Yet when her eyes first saw his face, all that melted away. She looked beyond the signs of the years—the white hair, the deep crows' feet, the stooped shoulders—and knew he had not changed.

But when he smiled, then she knew he *had* changed. There was a new look in his eyes, a look deeper than mere age could account for. She had not time to ponder upon it, however, for he gently took her in his arms, then bent over and kissed her tenderly on the forehead, a kiss warm and real.

"Ian!" she said, speaking the name to the one she had not once addressed since that day on this very dock when they had parted forty-seven years before. He struggled to speak her name, but could not. She looked up into his face, wet with tears, smiled the smile he had remembered so often in his dreams, and was content.

Maggie's thoughts returned from Aberdeen to the present. There was so much to remember again. Like when Joanna had shown her the key found in the back of the tapestry, she had looked at it dully for a moment. Then suddenly she recalled what she had thus far only revealed in her delirium—"it's in the nursery." She had forgotten having hidden the key that fateful night, and now took Joanna to the overgrown, walled garden, and, after some effort, had managed to fit the key into the rusted lock. But search as they might, the treasure she had dug up that stormy night was never to be found. There were *some* things she could not remember, it seemed. Either she had forgotten where they had buried it, or else Digory had later carried it off to forever free the family of the poison of the greed it was sure to create. Dying a poor man as he had, Maggie was certain the faithful servant had put the treasure someplace where it would never tempt the heart of man again. And after all, the treasure had never meant anything to her; unearthing it had only been a way to thwart Falkirk and her father. Inside, a part of her rejoiced that it was not be be found.

Now the only memory she need concern herself with was the love she and Ian had shared then, and could now share again. This climb up the hill bordering Strathy's fair valley was richer by far than any earthly treasure. But the slope had become steeper and she was a little out of breath. She was aware of her weak leg, but at least there was no pain. The doctor had agreed that the trip to Scotland would be the best thing for her, but had admonished her to "take it easy." She had not been strictly obedient in that, but how could she when the heather was in bloom and when this "muckle land" made her feel so young again!

Soon a figure came into sight at the top of the heather-covered hill. Tall and lean, with head held high, Ian Duncan bore himself with a dignity "auld Dorey" had never had the will or the courage to assume. All life had drastically changed for him that day in the damp cave on Ramsey Head. At last he had ceased his flight from the One whose love had been pursuing him, and finally bowed in acknowledgment of the God who had never once forsaken him. Maggie's own prayer for him, resounding through the ages and across the miles, found its fulfillment at the hand of the master Potter who had fashioned them both—the One who had created them to love Him first, and who now willed that they spend the rest of their lives loving each other. And in that healing in the cave, Dorey was for the first time able to face himself, and was thus given the courage Ian Duncan had always been meant to have.

As Maggie drew closer to the object of her morning walk, he smiled and held out his hand. It brought to her mind the undefined change she had noticed at the moment of their first reunion in Aberdeen. His smile had lost its haunted, troubled quality. In his youth, though he had been an expert at masking it, there was always the vague impression that his smiles and laughter had been bought with a price.

All that was now gone. No shadows hovered about his smile. His face at last reflected the contentment the Creator intended—overspread with joy, not only having his Maggie by his side, but also in the peace, pure and undefiled, which dwelt in his heart.

She returned his smile, then laughed in unashamed delight.

She reached for his hand, and their fingers touched and intertwined. If they held each other tighter than necessary upon occasion, they could not be blamed; they had so many years to make up for. They had learned how precious was every moment in life; not a single second was to be looked upon lightly.

This morning was no less special than that first one in Aberdeen as the breeze now wafting over them did its best to bend the purple heads of the thick wild bushes. It was all so reminiscent of the days of their youth. Yet suddenly Maggie realized it was even better. They were now *one* as they might never have had a chance to be in their rebellious youth—one for the first time in the love of their common Lord.

"It is as if time has waited for us," Ian murmured into the wind.

"Yes," Maggie answered peacefully. "So little has changed . . . and yet so much."

"One thing has not changed," he said gazing into her eyes, "and will never change. And that is my love for you, my dear Maggie."

"Nor mine for you, my husband."

Together they turned and walked slowly down the hillside, with the morning sun at their backs and the sea of heather at their feet.

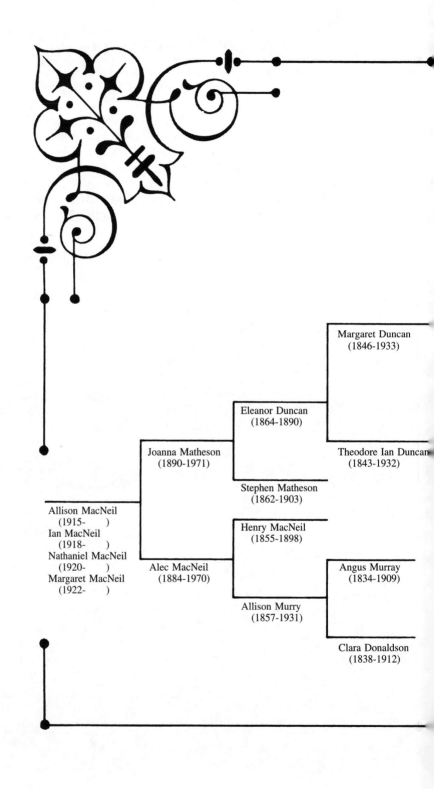

Margaret Duncan
(1846-1933)

Eleanor Duncan
(1864-1890)

Theodore Ian Duncan
(1843-1932)

Joanna Matheson
(1890-1971)

Stephen Matheson
(1862-1903)

Allison MacNeil
(1915-   )
Ian MacNeil
(1918-   )
Nathaniel MacNeil
(1920-   )
Margaret MacNeil
(1922-   )

Henry MacNeil
(1855-1898)

Angus Murray
(1834-1909)

Alec MacNeil
(1884-1970)

Allison Murry
(1857-1931)

Clara Donaldson
(1838-1912)

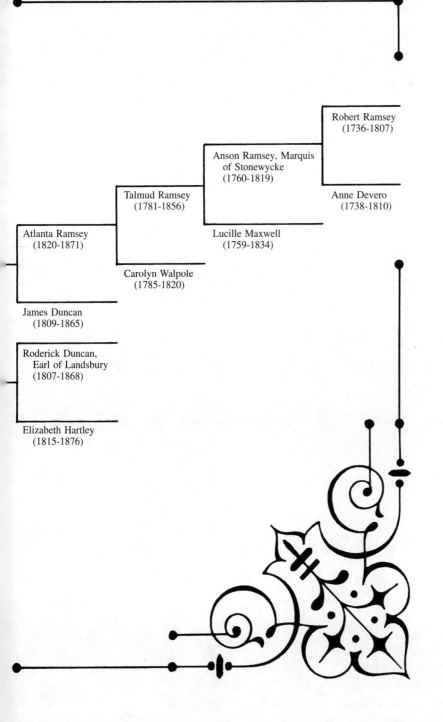

Robert Ramsey
(1736-1807)

Anson Ramsey, Marquis
of Stonewycke
(1760-1819)

Talmud Ramsey
(1781-1856)

Anne Devero
(1738-1810)

Lucille Maxwell
(1759-1834)

Atlanta Ramsey
(1820-1871)

Carolyn Walpole
(1785-1820)

James Duncan
(1809-1865)

Roderick Duncan,
 Earl of Landsbury
(1807-1868)

Elizabeth Hartley
(1815-1876)